KING'S BLOOD

The Kinsman Chronicles

King's Folly

Darkness Reigns: Part One

The Heir War: Part Two

The End of All Things: Part Three

King's Blood

Kingdom at Sea: Part Four

Maelstrom: Part Five

Voices of Blood: Part Six

THE KINSMAN CHRONICLES + BOOK TWO

King's Blood

JILL WILLIAMSON

BETHANYHOUSE

a division of Baker Publishing Group
Minneapolis, Minnesota

© 2017 by Jill Williamson

Published by Bethany House Publishers
11400 Hampshire Avenue South
Bloomington, Minnesota 55438
www.bethanyhouse.com

Bethany House Publishers is a division of
Baker Publishing Group, Grand Rapids, Michigan

Printed in the United States of America

ISBN: 978-0-7642-1831-6

Library of Congress Control Number: 2016942746

This is a work of fiction. Names, characters, incidents, and dialogues are products of the author's imagination and are not to be construed as real. Any resemblance to actual events or persons, living or dead, is entirely coincidental.

Cover design by LOOK Design Studio

Author is represented by MacGregor Literary, Inc.

17 18 19 20 21 22 23   7 6 5 4 3 2 1

To Brad Williamson, my hero

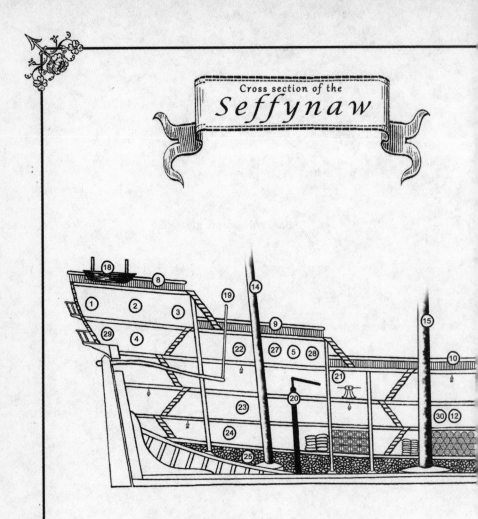

Cross section of the
Seffynaw

1. King's cabin/office
2. Admiral's cabin
3. Dining room
4. Royal cabins
5. Masters' cabins
6. Officers' cabins
7. Foredeck
8. Stern deck

9. Quarterdeck
10. Main deck
11. Middle deck
12. Lower deck
13. Hold
14. Mizzenmast
15. Mainmast
16. Foremast

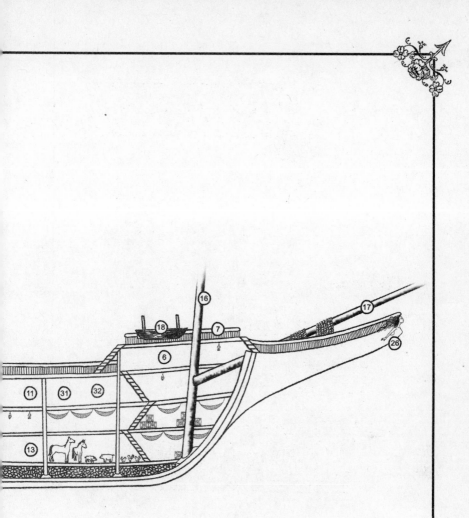

KEY PLAYERS

ARMANIA

House Hadar

Echad [EE-kad]-**Rosâr Hadar**, king of Armania

+ **Schwyl**, Echad's onesent

+ **Captain Lebbe Alpress**, captain of the King's Guard

+ **Zenobia**, Echad's concubine

+ **Lilou Caridod**, Echad's mistress

Brelenah-Rosârah, Echad's first wife, Wilek and Inolah's mother

+ **Captain Rayim Veralla**, captain of the Queen's Guard

+ **Hawley**, Brelenah's onesent

Wilek [WILL-ek]-**Sâr Hadar**, son of Echad and Brelenah

+ **Sir Kalenek Veroth**, Wilek's High Shield

  ○ **Novan**, Kalenek's backman

+ **Agmado Harton**, Wilek's backman

+ **Dendrick**, Wilek's onesent

Laviel-Rosârah, Echad's second wife, Janek's mother

Janek-Sâr Hadar, son of Echad and Laviel

+ **Sir Jayron**, Janek's High Shield

+ **Hinckdan Faluk**, Earl of Dacre, Janek's backman

+ **Timmons**, Janek's onesent

+ **Mattenelle**, Janek's concubine

+ **Pia**, Janek's concubine

+ **Sir Kamran DanSâr**, son of Echad and Zenobia

+ **Fonu Edekk**, friend to Janek

Thallah-Rosârah Orsona, Echad's third wife, Trevn's mother, Ulrik's great-aunt

Trevn-Sâr Hadar, son of Echad and Thallah

+ **Sir Cadoc Wyser**, Trevn's High Shield

+ **Ottee** [Ot-EE], Trevn's onesent

Valena-Rosârah, Echad's fourth wife

  ○ **Enetta**, Hrettah and Rashah's nurse

+ **Hrettah-Sârah Hadar**, daughter of Echad and Valena

  ○ **Sir Kenard Taldun**, Hrettah's High Shield

    ○ **Ulmer Gelsly**, Kenard's backman

+ **Rashah-Sârah Hadar**, daughter of Echad and Valena

  ○ **Sir Zeric Meray**, Rashah's High Shield

    ○ **Rey Kael**, Zeric's backman

Other Armanians

Onika [ON-ik-ah], the True Prophet, a blind woman

+ **Tulay** [TOO-lay], honor maiden to Onika

+ **Yoana** [Yo-AHNA], honor maiden to Onika

+ **Kempe** [KEM-pay], Onika's personal maid

+ **Rustian**, Onika's dune cat

Mielle, Kalenek's ward, honor maiden to Lady Zeroah

Amala, Kalenek's ward, Mielle's little sister

+ **Darlow**, Mielle and Amala's nurse

Inolah-Sârah Orsona-Hadar, daughter of Echad and Brelenah, mother of Emperor Ulrik

+ **Princess Vallah Orsona**, Inolah's daughter, Emperor Ulrik's sister

Sârah Jemesha, Echad's sister, Oli and Eudora's mother

Oli Agoros, Duke of Canden

Eudora Agoros, Oli's sister

Admiral Hanray Vendal, admiral of the king's fleet

Captain Aldair Livina [Liv-EE-nuh], captain of the *Seffynaw*

+ **Quen** [Kwen], first mate

+ **Norgam Bussie** [BUHS-ee], second mate

+ **Nietz** [Neets], master's mate

+ **Shinn**, master's mate

+ **Zaki**, sailor

+ **Bonds**, sailor

+ **Rzasa** [RAW-zuh], sailor

Hara, the king's cook

Shemme, Hara's daughter, a maid

Father Burl Mathal, medial priest of the Rôb church

Jhorn, a retired soldier and amputee

Grayson, a boy with a gray rash

The Omatta Clan

Rand, leader of the Omatta

Meelo, Rand's son

Zahara, Rand's daughter

Teaka, Rand's mother

Errp, Teaka's newt

Traitors to Armania

Barthel Rogedoth (also known as **Prince Mergest III**), former Pontiff of Armania, uncle to Loran of Sarikar

Dendron, a great shadir, bonded to Barthel Rogedoth

Filkin Yohthehreth, Rôb prophet

Zithel Lau, Rôb priest

SARIKAR

House Pitney

King Jorger Pitney, king of Sarikar, the God's King

Prince Loran Pitney, Jorger's son and heir

+ **Princess Saria**, Loran's daughter

+ **Prince Thorvald**, Loran's son

Zeroah Barta, Loran's niece, betrothed to Wilek Hadar

+ **Doth**, Zeroah's guard

+ **Ephec**, Zeroah's guard

Rystan Barta, Duke of Tal, Zeroah's little brother

Prince Rosbert, Jorger's son, Loran's brother

+ **Lady Riyah**, Rosbert's daughter

+ **Lady Tesslia**, Rosbert's daughter

+ **Lord Kanzer**, Rosbert's son

RUREKAU

House Orsona

Emperor Ulrik Orsona, emperor of Rurekau

+ **Sir Iamot** [EE-uh-moht], Ulrik's High Shield

+ **Taleeb**, Ulrik's onesent

Prince Ferro Orsona, Ulrik's younger brother

General Balat, head of the Igote guard

Kakeeo, Rurekan sheriff

Burk, a Rurekan passenger

MAGONIA

Ruling Clan

Mreegan, Magonian Chieftess

+ **Kateen**, First of Mreegan's Five Maidens

+ **Astaa**, Second of Mreegan's Five Maidens

+ **Roya**, Third of Mreegan's Five Maidens

+ **Rone**, number One of Mreegan's Five Men

+ **Nuel**, number Two of Mreegan's Five Men

+ **Vald**, number Three of Mreegan's Five Men

+ **Torol**, number Four of Mreegan's Five Men

+ **Gullik** [GUHL-ik], number Five of Mreegan's Five Men

Charlon, Mother of the Deliverer

Magon, a great shadir, bonded to Mreegan and Charlon

Krola, captain of the *Vespara*

TENMA

Priestess Jazlyn, High Queen of Tenma

+ **Qoatch** [KO-ach], Jazlyn's eunuch slav, a seer

Gozan, a great shadir, bonded to Jazlyn

MAIN SHIPS OF THE FLEET

Seffynaw [SEF-EE-naw], Rosâr Echad's ship, flagship of Armania and the fleet

Rafayah [Raf-AHY-uh], the vice flagship of Armania

Berith [BAIR-ith], advance guard ship of Armania

Baretam [BAIR-IT-am], Emperor Ulrik's ship, flagship of Rurekau

Gillsmore [GILS-mohr], the vice flagship of Rurekau

Kaloday [KAL-UH-dey], Loran's ship, flagship of Sarikar

Vespara [Ves-PAR-uh], Chieftess Mreegan's ship, stolen from Sarikar

Amarnath [EY-mahr-nath], Barthel Rogedoth's ship

The Wanderer, Grayson's first ship

Malbraid, Rand's ship

Taradok [TARE-uh-dok], Zahara's ship

THE GODS OF THE FIVE REALMS

Arman, the father god

Athos, god of justice and law

Avenis/Avennia, god/goddess of beauty

Barthos, god of the earth/soil

Cethra/Cetheria, god/goddess of protection

Dendron, god of nature

Gâzar, ruler of the Lowerworld, bringer of death

Iamos, god/goddess of healing

Lâhat, god of fire

Magon, goddess of magic

Mikreh, god of fate and fortune

Nivanreh, god of travel

Rurek, god of war

Sarik, god of wisdom

Tenma, the mother god

Thalassa, virgin goddess of the sea

Yobat/Yobatha, god/goddess of pleasure and celebration

Zitheos, god of animals

The Prophetess urged the people to hurry and leave the land. "For otherwise," said The Prophetess, "you will all die!" So the people set out from the Five Realms, traveling by sea into the unknown, trusting Arman to do as He promised and lead them to a new land, a good and spacious land of plenty.

—*The History of the Armanites*, Hinckdan Faluk,
Castle Armanguard 27

Part Four

Kingdom at Sea

PROLOGUE

Gozan flew through the Veil, just out of reach of the ocean's spray. Behind him his swarm followed, a cloudy mass of colors and shrieking sounds. He wished for silence but hadn't the energy to rebuke them just now.

If things didn't change, he might never have the energy again.

In the distance the Armanian king's flagship *Seffynaw* sat low in the water, a fat tub stuffed with treasure and humans whose greed had nearly killed off their race. The shadir had played their part as well. Gozan hadn't realized the effects of his dependence on human bonding. None of the shadir had. They had always taken for the sake of taking, for pleasure and power and to please their master Gâzar. They had not ever considered consequences.

But now they must, for their way of life was at risk.

Gozan reached the *Seffynaw* from its starboard side and circled the hull. He soared above the railing and onto the stern deck. Slights and commons filled the area, invisible to the humans seated at a table there. Magon stood at the back of the ship, leaning against the taffrail. For centuries she had preferred to take form as a human female. Gozan never understood why she wanted to look like her slaves.

His shadir swarm met Magon's, and the cacophony of the two groups intermingling grated on Gozan's nerves. "Silence!" he yelled.

To their credit all obeyed, even those shadir loyal to Magon.

Gozan folded his arms and let the soles of his feet rest on the deck so that he stood before Magon, looming over her frail, human form.

She smirked at his posture. "Greetings, Rurek."

The name sent fire through his limbs. "I am Gozan now."

"Still hiding, are you?"

"Waiting." He had never been hiding.

"Well, I have waited long enough," she said, which brought cheers from her votaries. "We must act before all is lost."

"You have a plan, then? How to survive this setback?"

"I'm bored with no access to my mantic," said one of Magon's slights. "It's no fun merely whispering in ears. I want the humans to see me and be swayed by my influence."

"Mine hasn't seen me since we left the land," said another.

"Mine either," said a third.

"They are completely out of evenroot on my human's ship," said one of Gozan's brood.

"Mine too!" echoed the first of Magon's slights.

"Stop fretting, all of you," Magon said. "We simply must lead these ships to land. Once the humans plant and harvest new evenroot crops, our power over them will return."

"But it takes at least three months to reap a harvest," a slight said.

"And harvesting that early, the roots will be small," said another.

"Patience," Magon said. "We must remain calm and focus on leading the ships to land."

"But, master," Masi said to Gozan, "with so little evenroot, we have no control over the captains of these vessels."

"We only need control the one who leads," Gozan replied.

Snickers broke out among the slights, and a common behind Magon said, "Humans will never agree on the same leader."

"They will follow Armania," Magon said. "They always do, despite my efforts."

"Then we must work together to lead the Armanians to land," Gozan said.

"I have no power in Armania yet," Magon said. "I am close. But my mantics are divided at present as to how to proceed."

Typical. Magon bored too easily. "You never could stay loyal to one human."

"Where is the fun in that? It's much more entertaining to bait them against each other. Better than hiding for decades in a lowly position."

"Jazlyn is loyal to me," Gozan said, "and now that she is High Queen of Tenma, I am in a place to use my power to advance her realm."

"The real problem is that I am uncertain where land is," Magon said. "The humans are headed to an island now, but if they are to plant a substantial amount of evenroot without interference from religious zealots, we must lead them to a great expanse."

"Are you certain another exists?" Gozan asked. "Perhaps only this mysterious island remains."

"This world is vast, Gozan," Magon said. "If there is a great stretch of land out there, my swarm will find it."

This sent Magon's votaries into a flurry of color and objections.

"Go without you?"

"We mustn't leave you, Great One. We would be lost apart from you."

"Lost without your guidance."

"I refuse to leave your side," a purple slight said. "I will die before I do."

"Die, then!" A wave of Magon's hand obliterated the purple slight into a wisp of smoke. Her votaries scattered briefly, then cowered at her feet, trembling.

"Are you ready to listen?" she asked.

Her swarm stared at her, eyes wide and contrite. Some nodded. Not one made a sound.

"I have no need of you here at present," she said. "You will be of better use to me seeking out land. Remember, as your great shadir, I can summon you all at a word. And no matter how far you drift from me, call on my name and you can always return."

It would pain them, though, to be parted from her, and it would weaken her to be without their energy. Gozan hesitated to join her risky plan, knowing it would cost him as well, yet he couldn't afford to be left in the dark. "My shadir will go with yours," he said.

A heavy silence fell over their group. The two swarms appraised one another as if trying to decide whether or not such a joining was in their best interest.

"We might as well get started," Magon said, and she set about dividing her followers into four groups with a common at the head of each.

Gozan did the same with his swarm.

"Do not return until you have found a fair amount of land or until I summon you," Magon told her shadir. "Now fly!"

As her swarm flitted away, Gozan lowered his voice to his own. "Return to me when summoned, when you find land, or if you sense a betrayal from Magon's swarm. I want them tracked at all times. Understood?"

His shadir throbbed and spun their agreement.

"After them!" he yelled.

They shot away like streaks of smoke on the tails of fire arrows. He watched them, pride welling inside. They would not fail him.

"You are vulnerable without your swarm," Magon said. "As is your mantic."

"And you are not?"

She smiled. "My mantics still have stores of evenroot."

"If it's a fight you seek, you will not win. Alone, I am stronger than you."

She cackled. "I have no wish to fight you, Rurek. My fight is with Dendron. It always has been. I cannot defeat him alone, but we might do so together."

She did not tempt him in the least. He hadn't even seen Dendron since The Great Parting. "I have no quarrel with Dendron."

"Not now," Magon said, "but Dendron has a hold on Armania. The realm is his. And once the humans find land and set up their seats of power, Armania will rule. It will not be long thereafter that we will all come to odds with Dendron. I have a plan to protect myself. You should too."

"Perhaps, but I will not seek out trouble now."

"Be ready, then, for trouble will find you."

Gozan flew away from the *Seffynaw* without answering. Halfway back to the *Baretam*, he risked a little of Jazlyn's power to enter the Solid. He instantly felt the wind shift the hair on his body. He breathed in the ocean's smell, heard the sea foam sizzle, admired his reflection rippling over the thick waves. Without his swarm around him, he appeared small. He reached his hands down into the water and basked in the cool moisture.

Even at this distance, he could feel Jazlyn's strength draining. Disheartened, he shifted back into the Veil and his senses instantly dulled. Unless Jazlyn could find Emperor Ulrik's evenroot, before long she would lose sight of him completely.

The thought birthed a well of terror within him. If he could never again enter the Solid, he would go mad. Life in the Veil was but a haze of the Solid. He cursed the sunbird, Nesher, for keeping his kind from it. It resolidified his vow to Lord Gâzar. He would continue to help the humans destroy each other. The more souls won to Lord Gâzar's domain, the greater loss Nesher would suffer and the longer Gozan could enjoy the Solid realm that the sunbird had created for his pathetic humans.

TREVN

Prince Trevn exited his cabin and ran down the dark corridor, enthused by the movement of the ship around him. By the time he reached the first crossway, however, he was so winded he had to stop and steady himself.

His second chance at life had brought an eagerness to make each moment count, but perhaps moving ahead slowly would be wise. It would not do to have his appearance frighten Miss Mielle Allard.

Cadoc, his High Shield, pounded to a halt behind him. Brawny, with keen eyes and a dozen braids bound in a warrior's tail, the man was determined not to let his charge get the best of him. He had five years on Trevn yet stood a hand shorter. "Your Highness? Is something wrong?"

"No, Cadoc." A few deep breaths calmed Trevn's heart well enough. He moved forward at a walk, hands on the bulkheads on either side. He felt better. Truly. His head no longer burned with fever, and the gash Hinck had accidentally stabbed into his abdomen had mended to a pucker of light pink skin. A vast improvement over the wound brimming with pus that had left him delirious with fever. His mind spun at all he might have missed. "Are we nearing Odarka yet?" he asked.

"Left the port yesterday," Cadoc said.

"Already?" Trevn stopped and faced his shield. "How many days did I sleep?"

"Three, Your Highness. We only stayed one night at the Port of Odarka. It's been five days total at sea so far."

Disappointment flashed over Trevn to have missed such a historic moment. "How many ships were waiting to meet us?"

21

"We added ninety-five from Armania and another seventeen from Rurekau. Lost about a hundred reamskiffs between us all. Last I heard, total ships in the fleet numbered six hundred twenty-nine, and we've accounted for just shy of one hundred seventy-nine thousand people."

Almost triple the number that had left Everton five days ago. "What happened to the reamskiffs?"

"Too small to handle the rough seas. People kept falling overboard. King Echad held council in the Port of Odarka with Prince Loran and Emperor Ulrik. They ordered all reamskiffs abandoned or tied for tow and the passengers dispersed among the rest of the fleet."

That seemed wise. Reamskiffs were little more than rafts. "Is King Jorger ill?" Trevn had learned of his cousin Ulrik's ascension to the throne of Rurekau from Sir Kalenek, but what had become of King Jorger?

"Missing. Princess Nabelle as well. Prince Loran had hoped they were together, but Lady Zeroah saw her mother taken by angry commoners when they were driving through the Sink."

How awful.

Cadoc went on. "Prince Loran is holding out hope that his father took refuge on another ship and will make his way to the *Kaloday* soon enough."

In light of the time that had passed, such a thing seemed unlikely. Trevn continued down the corridor, wondering what else he'd missed. "How did Odarka fare in the Woes?"

"Little of the island remained, but the duke had managed to evacuate all who lived there."

All. A pang of guilt seized Trevn for the thousands who had perished in Everton. Though he supposed it would have been less complicated to evacuate a sparsely populated island over a city of forty thousand souls—closer to seventy thousand considering the rural populations.

This remnant from the Five Realms had survived a harrowing ordeal, yet the mood on board the *Seffynaw* had been optimistic—before Trevn's fever had put him in bed, anyway. The fleet had left death and destruction behind and was sailing toward Captain Livina's new island, eager to start over and build a bright future. A thrill ran through Trevn at the excitement of it all. Once the people settled on the new island, Trevn would go out with the explorers and look for more land. He was finally getting a chance to travel beyond the bowl. His dreams had come true, though the cost had been far too high.

Trevn reached the next crossway and paused, suddenly uncertain where he was. The ship descended a large swell, knocking him against the bulkhead. He stayed put and jerked his head for Cadoc to go ahead. "Lead the way, Cadoc. I'm completely turned around."

Cadoc moved past, and Trevn followed, his thoughts drifting to how Ottee had made him so late. Because of the boy he would hardly have any time to spend with Mielle before Wilek's meeting.

"For a moment there, I feared I might have to punish young Ottee for disobedience," Trevn said of his new—temporary, he hoped—onesent.

"It was clever of you to ask him to choose your clothing for the morrow after he finished his chores," Cadoc said.

Desperate was more like it. "He is overly obsessed with my wardrobe. It seemed to be my biggest hold over him."

Cadoc reached a crossway and turned right. "He is quite eager to please."

"No, he is eager to tag along." Trevn followed Cadoc around the corner. The crossway stretched out ahead. In the distance Trevn could see the indentations of two more lengthways. His cabin was on the starboard side of the ship, he reminded himself. "I fear Ottee is too wild to make a good servant. A onesent should make his master's life easier, not more trying."

"He's a boy," Cadoc said, as if this excused Ottee's insubordinate tendencies. "I suspect he will try your patience a great deal, but he's young enough to train well. And Captain Livina assures me that it is against Ottee's nature to lie."

"So he might be disobedient and trying, but at least he will be true? Is that to be my consolation?"

"After Beal's betrayal, I should think such a trait would be most welcome." Cadoc turned right at the center lengthway.

Ah, Trevn had his bearings now. King's galley behind them, main deck straight ahead. They swept into the narrow companionway and started up to the quarterdeck, which was the quickest route to the stern deck, where Ottee had said Miss Mielle Allard might be. "I would rather have Hinck," he said.

"Hinck was your backman, not a onesent."

"He did both for me," Trevn said, knowing that wasn't the full truth. But Hinck couldn't serve even as Trevn's backman at the moment since Trevn's brother Wilek had given Hinck over to Janek, Trevn's other—possibly false— brother, to continue spying on the traitor.

Everyone sought to make Trevn miserable, it seemed, but today was a new start. First and foremost, Trevn was healthy again. This enabled him to start his apprenticeship with Admiral Vendal, in which he would not only be learning to captain a ship, he would better understand the kingdom's dilemma at sea. Right now he was on his way to see Mielle, who always brought him joy. And, perhaps most important of all, Wilek and his cobbled-together Wisean Council were going to question Janek this midday. Should the man be as treasonous as they all believed him to be, he would remain in his prison in the hold and Hinck would return to Trevn's side where he belonged. Let Hinck train Ottee for onesent duties and leave Trevn out of it. He'd much rather spend time with Mielle.

Trevn and Cadoc exited onto the *Seffynaw's* quarterdeck. Daylight seemed overly bright after spending so many days inside. He took a deep breath of salty air. Commoners crowded the quarterdeck, most of them sitting in circles on blankets as if enjoying a picnic. Trevn followed his shield up a simple stairway, which now marked the division between classes topside.

He did not see Mielle among the scattered nobles on the stern deck. Trevn kept to the rail and nodded in reply to bows and greetings from those who recognized him. One of his half sister's maids suggested Mielle might be serving food on the main deck, so Trevn and Cadoc went back down to the quarterdeck, this time crossing its length. They approached the mizzenmast and helm, the latter of which had been fenced in by a makeshift rail that hadn't been there when they'd left the Port of Everton. The sailor at the whipstaff wore the blue half-cape of an officer. His sharp golden eyes followed them, so Trevn stopped and asked, "Your name is?"

"Norgam Bussie, Your Highness. Second mate."

Trevn nodded. "You have a light hand on the whip, Master Bussie."

"Every able man can 'hand, reef, and steer,'" Bussie said.

Trevn had heard the sailors' phrase before. Very soon he hoped to *hand*le lines, *reef* sails, and *steer* the *Seffynaw*. Steering was the only thing he'd done before, so he knew enough about that to sound wise. "Very true, Master Bussie, but there's a knack to steering a beast this vast. She takes time to change directions. My guess is that one doesn't become second mate by leaving a twisting trail in the ship's wake."

This earned Trevn a grin and a nod of respect.

"What is the purpose of this fence?" Trevn asked of the rail around the helm.

"Captain Livina ordered it built to keep people from sitting here," Bussie said. "Dangerous enough having so many on deck. We need 'em outta the way so we can work."

Indeed. Trevn gazed beyond the mizzenmast, over the front rail of the quarterdeck and down the length of the ship. People covered the main and forecastle decks like pebbles on a road. Should a storm come . . . "There is no more space below deck?"

"Just as many people below and no more hammocks, or we'd hang 'em triple," Bussie said. "They're already doubled up most everywhere."

"I see." And Trevn would go down and see with his eyes when he got the chance.

"The Heir's mother, Rosârah Brelenah, has organized a troop of women to tie rope into new hammocks," Cadoc said. "Perhaps that'll help."

"Some," Bussie said, "but we can't use all our spare rope for hammocks either. Gotta keep some for sails."

Trevn nodded. No matter what, such a crowded ship was a pending disaster. At least they weren't going far. Captain Livina had discovered his new island an eleven-night from Everton. The fleet was likely moving much slower in order to stay together, but even if the journey took twice that time, as long as the weather remained in their favor, they should survive easily. The *Seffynaw* had enough water to last three months, food to last even longer. But were all the ships in the fleet as well prepared?

Trevn and Cadoc continued on. When they reached the main deck, the stench choked him. He pieced together a combination of unwashed bodies, feces, urine, livestock, and what passed for a slaughterhouse. Trevn had sailed dozens of times before and had never smelled anything so wretched. Some people sat in clusters. Some alone. All were refugees, fully reliant on the *Seffynaw* and her crew to keep them afloat. They each lived on the small piece of deck they occupied. No more, no less.

Trevn would never again complain over the smallness of his cabin.

With so many seated on the deck, it was difficult to traverse. Trevn and Cadoc kept to a narrow path someone had chalked out on the wooden deck. When people recognized Trevn, most stood and bowed. He stopped to talk with some, wanting to know their thoughts. The chalk path, he learned, had been Captain Livina's idea. An attempt to provide a clear way for his sailors to move about the ship.

Trevn spotted Mielle on the forecastle near the starboard rail. She stood nearly as tall as his own six feet, had ginger skin, eyes a man could swim in, and long brown hair braided into a hundred fine plaits. She wore her light blue dress and held a basket over her arm, passing its contents—rounds of bread—to the people around her.

"May I have some?" Trevn asked.

She looked up, and her face broke into a smile. "Trevn!" She threw her free arm around his neck, and he hugged her close. "Oh, I was so worried."

"About me? Just taking a long nap."

The commoners around them cheered. Over Mielle's shoulder Trevn found nearly every face on the foreside of the mainmast fixed upon them.

"Are you fully healed?" she asked, letting go.

"Nearly so."

"I've missed you. Kiss me."

Trevn glanced around. "In front of all these people?"

"Yes! I want them all to know I am yours. Few believe it now that Lady Zeroah has cast me aside."

So Trevn kissed her well and good, drawing another cheer from the crowd, which made him laugh and put an end to the fun. He took hold of her hand. "Tell me, what have you been doing?"

Mielle nodded to a young noblewoman, who looked near her age. The girl was shorter, strikingly pretty with soft brown skin, long black coils of hair, and a figure accentuated by a fitted green-and-gold dress that bordered on teasing.

"You remember my sister," Mielle said.

"Miss Amala?" Trevn quickly tried to hide his surprise. But this couldn't be. Mielle's younger sister was only weeks past thirteen. Trevn had last seen her in a child's dress that bared her knobby knees.

The girl curtsied, glanced up through long eyelashes, and smiled slowly. "I am so pleased to see you fully mended, Your Highness. We were all desperately concerned about your welfare." Her silky voice gave Trevn a chill. Was she talking that way on purpose? Mielle did not seem at all bothered, so Trevn assured himself he must be imagining Amala's forward behavior.

"We have been helping Rosârah Brelenah distribute food above deck," Mielle said. "There are ever so many people and no good way to reach everyone but to take it directly to them. Amala helps me. As do the sârahs Hrettah and Rashah and their mother when they have the time."

"Some of the guardsmen help as well," Miss Amala added.

"Because they are ordered to, not because they care," Mielle mumbled.

"Master Gelsly cares," Miss Amala said. "His contingent was stationed in the Sink before the Woes. Every day he gave a portion of his midday repast to beggars. I feel much safer when one of the soldiers accompanies us, Sâr

Trevn. They are all so strong, and with all the attacks, some of these common men frighten me."

"Tuhsh, Amala! Hold your tongue," Mielle said, before Trevn could ask. "Take your basket and hand out the bread to those people there." She pointed Miss Amala down the rail toward the stern. "Sâr Trevn and I will finish here."

"Very well." Miss Amala curtsied to Trevn. "Pleasure and joy to you until we meet again, Your Highness."

Trevn nodded politely. "Good midday, Miss Amala."

Once the girl was out of earshot, Mielle growled and stomped toward the closest group of people.

"What's wrong?" Trevn asked.

"Would you like some bread?" she asked, passing a roll to each who held out a hand. "When we finish," she told Trevn in a low voice, "I'll tell you exactly what's wrong if you take me someplace private."

Trevn needed no more motivation that that. He helped Mielle distribute the remainder of the bread, then spirited her away to the stern deck, where they might talk, Cadoc following all the while like a distant shadow.

"Now, tell me what is bothering you," Trevn said when they stopped to stand at the taffrail.

"Too much! You were ill, and I feared you would die. I had nightmares that you did. I have nightmares of the Woes too. I feel guilty all the time, just for being alive. So many died. So many I couldn't save. I still see them in my memory. I fear they will haunt me forever."

They haunted him as well. "You saved so many, Mielle. You did the best you could."

"And Sâr Wilek came and took the Book of Arman from me. He said the prophetess told him to read it. I didn't think you would mind, but I've been feeling so guilty about not asking you first."

"I can relieve you there," Trevn said. "The book is meant to go to Wilek, so you did right in giving it to him."

"Rosârah Brelenah says we're sailing to an island. She says there is plenty of food, yet I am to give only one roll a day to each person. One! In my heart I sense she is lying to me and we have little food. What if we run out? What if we never find this island? It's what the people fear. I tell them what the rosârah says, but they don't believe her. And I'm not sure I do either!"

"Believe it," Trevn said, squeezing her hand. "Captain Livina's island is only an eleven-night from Everton. It might take us a few days extra to find it since the fleet is moving so slowly, but trust me. We will reach it."

Her brow furrowed. "Then why ration the food so sparingly?"

"With this many people a little caution never hurts," Trevn guessed. "Besides, the almshouse back in Everton gave one roll a day. How could the people possibly expect more on board an isolated ship?"

"And then there's Amala!" Mielle said. "She has decided to dress like a woman and flirt with men. Kal scolds her, but the young sârahs have taken a liking to her and made her over. Kal didn't dare refuse them. So Darlow and I can do nothing but nag and fret, knowing it will all come to ruin. Then there's Lady Zeroah . . ." Mielle stifled a sob.

Mielle did seem to be carrying a thousand burdens. Trevn put his arm around her. "Lady Zeroah has not apologized for her ill treatment toward you?"

"She denies it ever took place! Yet she refuses me as her honor maiden, claiming she is too grieved by the loss of her mother to endure companionship."

That, at least, made sense to Trevn. "Well, I am mended, so one of your wrongs has been righted. Perhaps the others will improve in time?"

She rewarded his words with a small smile. "I hope you are right."

"I feel sure of it. Now, come. I have an hour or so before the council meeting and want to explore the ship. Will you accompany me?"

"Anywhere," she said.

✦　✦　✦

Later that midday, Cadoc opened the door to the captain's private dining room and Trevn stepped inside. Spots danced before his eyes as they adjusted to the lantern light in this windowless chamber, which seemed glaring after the dark corridors and stairs. A woman was speaking. Rosârah Brelenah's voice, though Trevn did not yet see her.

People had gathered around the long table in the room's center; a few guards stood around its perimeter. Trevn blinked and counted twelve in the room. Not as many as he had first thought. Everything seemed more crowded aboard a ship. As faces came into focus, they were instantly recognizable. Wilek, Father's Heir, sat in the king's place at the end of the table. Behind him stood his shield, Sir Kalenek Veroth, underneath the severed head of Barthos, which now hung mounted on the wall above. Seated on Wilek's left along one side of the table was Teaka, Wilek's mantic advisor he had appropriated from Randmuir Khal of the Omatta; beside her the Duke of Canden, Oli Agoros, newly appointed to the council, wearing a wooden arm to replace the one eaten by Barthos; then Kamran DanSâr, a stray the king had fathered on his concubine years before even Wilek was born, also a new council member; and Miss Onika, the True Prophet, who had saved them all with the God Arman's warnings.

Onika was a pale woman, blind, with eyes the color of water. Every time Trevn saw her, he tried desperately not to stare and failed. In a world where everyone had dark skin, her mere appearance fascinated him. He longed to speak with her, to find out what land she had come from, if all her people had skin and eyes like hers, and what language they spoke.

On the other side of the table sat two original members of the Wisean Five—brothers Danek and Canbek Faluk—and standing in her place to the Heir's right, Wilek's mother, Rosârah Brelenah. Trevn wondered what had become of Barek Hadar, the fifth member of the council. On his own ship, perhaps?

The rosârah's eyes blazed as she spoke. "We have not been at sea a week and already there have been three reported attacks. I insist the women and girls be divided from the men."

"With all due respect, Your Highness," Canbek said, "there is no room for any such division."

"This ship is only so big," Danek said. "We are going to have to make compromises to accommodate the needs that arise."

"A compromise will do nicely," the rosârah said. "There must be some small section of the deck that could be tented aside for women."

"Why on deck, Your Highness?" Canbek asked.

"Because pregnant women need fresh air, and I will not ask them to fight for a length of rail each time they try to come aloft or wait hours in line to use the heads. Nor will I abide any more attacks upon these innocents. I demand all rapists be executed as a warning to all."

"I will speak with the captain about a private place for the women," Wilek said to his mother, "and ask the king's advice regarding sentences for those who attack women and girls."

"Thank you, my son." Rosârah Brelenah took her seat.

A bugle made Trevn jump. Shrill in his ears, he quickly recognized his own tune and glared at the herald. Had he seen the man when he entered, he would have insisted on silence.

"His Royal Highness, Trevn-Sâr Hadar, the Second Arm, the Curious," the herald said.

Everyone stood and accorded Trevn with the bows due his station. Trevn wasn't sure he liked being the Second Arm of Armania, but if Janek was not the king's son, he would have to get used to it.

"Trevn!" Wilek turned to his shield. "Kal, send word to Father that we are about to begin. And have the guards escort Janek to the anteroom." Wilek skirted the table and came to stand before Trevn, looked him up and down, and smiled wide. His shorn hair still looked strange to Trevn. "When I got word from Sir Cadoc that you were awake, I praised Arman. You are truly mended? Master Uhley cleared you?"

"I have not seen the physician," Trevn confessed. "But I bathed, dressed, and ate a full meal."

His brother frowned. "I want you to see Master Uhley as soon as possible."

"As you wish," Trevn said. "Will you question my mother today as well?" Rosârah Thallah had been confined to her cabin on charges of duplicity, and Trevn longed to know whether they were true.

"Not today, I'm afraid," Wilek said. "I've had to delay Janek's trial twice now, as Father insists on being present yet has been too ill to be out of bed. I had hoped that distance from Rogedoth and his mantics would bring back Father's health. I fear it has only made things worse. He has been increasingly confused and forgetful."

"Perhaps their magic was keeping a sick man well rather than inflicting disease."

Wilek's thoughtful gaze fixed on Trevn's. "I had not considered that, brother. Could be that they were keeping him alive until he declared Janek Heir. Then they would have let his illness take its natural course."

"A valid theory," Trevn said, though the set of Wilek's jaw proved he had already accepted it as fact.

Rosârah Brelenah approached them and curtsied, a single dog cradled in one arm. "Sâr Trevn, it does my heart good to see you here, healthy and strong. The sârahs and Miss Mielle will be relieved as well. Arman is not yet finished with you, it seems, and we are all glad of it."

"As am I, rosârah."

A door opened on the bulkhead behind Oli's and Kamran's seats. Two attendants pushed King Echad into the room and steered the rollchair to the end of the table, where someone had already moved away Wilek's seat.

Most stood and bowed, but for Rosârah Brelenah, who curtsied, and Miss Onika, who remained seated.

"I will leave you, my son," Rosârah Brelenah said softly to Wilek. "May the God be with you. And, Sâr Trevn, I bid you good midday."

Trevn nodded to the first queen, then turned his attention to his father. One of the king's attendants had tucked blocks under the wheels to keep the chair from rolling with the waves. Lebbe Alpress, captain of the King's Guard, stood behind the king, in the position Sir Kalenek had vacated. Sir Kalenek now stood beside Miss Onika.

King Echad of Armania sat in his throne poorly, a husk of humanity. He had lost a vast amount of weight. His brown skin was dotted with sweat and hung loose from his cheeks, chin, and throat; it had a bluish tint, especially under his eyes, which dug deep in their sockets, the whites veined in blood. Lesions marred his face, the biggest of which had cut his left eyebrow in two. Since the king had no eyebrows left, someone had penciled them in. He wore his usual wig of warrior's braids, which looked pristine and completely out of place on such a sickly body.

Wilek elbowed Trevn and jerked his head toward the king. "Greet our father. And remember he is ill. I pray he keeps his head for this trial. I need him."

Trevn snapped out of his shock and went to bow before the king.

"It is good to see you well, my son," Father rasped in a voice that sounded far too weak for what once had been such a forbidding man. "Perhaps I will follow your lead, eh?"

Trevn doubted it, but he said, "I hope so, Father."

"Prophetess," the king yelled to Miss Onika, "will I live?"

"You are yet breathing, Your Highness," the pale woman said.

"Bah!" Father scowled. "She is a terrible seer. Knows nothing of why Janek betrayed us all," the king said to Trevn, spittle flying from his thin, cracked lips. "All this time, Janek was not even of my blood. He lied to me, as did his mother and father. Deceivers all, and I the victim of their games."

"You will see them brought to justice, Father," Trevn said, hoping to appease the man.

"True, my son." Father coughed, which jiggled the skin under his chin. "Trust that to be my own prophecy, pale one," he yelled to Miss Onika. "Just you see if it isn't." He turned his attention to the guards on the opposite end of the table. "Bring in Janek at once! I want this over and done with before tonight's full moon."

WILEK

Wilek cringed at Father's mention of the full moon. He had talked with the king about this! The man had agreed to cease all sacrifices to Barthos, whom Wilek had proved was nothing more than the trophy on the wall above. He hoped that Father didn't plan to make an offering of Janek.

Since Mother had departed, Wilek took her seat to the right of the king. Trevn sat on Wilek's right and Danek's left. Wilek's high collar itched, and he fought the urge to scratch, not wanting to bring attention to the rune he was hiding or his short hair. He had aggravated the king by refusing a wig, but—Godslayer or not—he couldn't stomach wearing warrior's braids another man had earned.

He had barely finished the thought when the door opened and Janek was brought forth, hands tied behind his back.

The once vigorous and commanding sâr was hardly recognizable. He had been in captivity since before they'd left Canden, only a few days shy of a fortnight ago, yet his gaunt body, large black eyes, and sullen mouth gave him the appearance of a man native to the Sink. His time in the hold had sullied his fine red-and-blue ensemble to a dingy maroon and charcoal. Wispy black hair coated his cheeks and chin. His cornrows had frizzed near out of their braids. Oddly he wore no shoes, and one of his toes was bloody.

Wilek did not envy his half brother's time spent in the hold.

The guards sat Janek in a chair at the opposite end of the table and stood on either side, as if to keep him from escaping. Where they feared the man might run off to on a ship as crowded as the *Seffynaw*, Wilek couldn't guess.

All this he noticed in a glance, but what gave him pause was the hunger in Janek's eyes. Was it desperation? Injured pride? Determination? Wilek should have sent Hinckdan to visit Janek's cell to see if he could learn anything. He needed to prove that Janek was in league with Rogedoth in trying to kill Father and usurp the throne.

Wilek broke the silence. "Janek Pitney, you have been charged with treason against the crown of Armania. How do you plead?"

"I don't understand the charge," Janek said.

Wilek's ire spiked and he raised his voice. "How can I be more clear?"

Janek cocked his head to one side. "Well . . . if I am Janek *Pitney*, I am of Sarikar and I cannot very well commit treason against Armania. And if I am Janek *Hadar*, which I am, then Janek Pitney does not exist."

"Do not allow him to confuse you, my son," Father said. "Proceed to the questioning."

Wilek set his jaw and looked down to the scroll anchored on the table before him. "This council wishes to know: What is the purpose of the sect Lahavôtesh?"

"I know not," Janek said in an agreeable voice that belied the fierceness in his eyes.

"Do not lie," Wilek said. "I have several witnesses who count you a part of that sect."

"Ask *them* for the sect's purpose, then," Janek said, "for I know nothing of it. Why not instead ask me about my mother and father, for you have that incorrect too, and I have longed to set you straight and claim Justness for the wrongs you have done me."

He dared make accusations of his own? Wilek should have known that Janek would be difficult. "We will get to Rogedoth in a moment," Wilek said, his voice tight. "Traces of evenroot powder were found in your chamber in Canden. Can you explain that?"

"I cannot. Drugs dull the senses. I would never use them. Have you questioned my concubines? They might have taken some. Pia, perhaps. The woman keeps things from me."

"Have you ever seen your concubines using evenroot?" Wilek asked.

"No."

"Have you—"

"I want to hear about Pontiff Rogedoth," Father said, interrupting Wilek. "How long have you known he was Prince Mergest III of Sarikar?"

"My mother told me on my fifteenth ageday," Janek said.

"And she convinced you to continue with the deception that I was your father?"

Wilek sighed and sat back in his chair as Father took the reins of the interrogation out of his hands. At least he was of sound mind.

Janek beamed at the king. "Barthel Rogedoth, or Prince Mergest III of Sarikar, if you prefer—for that part you do have correct—is not my father. He is—"

"Do not lie!" Wilek said. "We have already established that he is your father."

"Will I be allowed to speak or not?" Janek asked the king.

Father waved his hand at Wilek. "Let him have his say."

Janek smiled. "Thank you, Father."

This hardened the king's expression, but he said nothing.

Janek steepled his fingers and crossed one ankle over his knee. "In the Armanian year of 834, King Ormarr of Sarikar disinherited his eldest son, Prince Mergest III, for his cultish practices. He was a mantic and had founded the Lahavôtesh." Janek paused, expression smug, as his audience sat spellbound. "In his exile Prince Mergest moved to Armania with his wife and two young daughters. He took on a new name, Barthel Rogedoth, and joined the Rôb church, where he worked his way up the ranks. Wanting more for his daughters than a lowly priest's life could offer, he devised for them to be adopted into the well-born Nafni family."

Father coughed. Canbek whispered to Danek. Wilek, too, felt unease at the direction this story had taken. Could he have been mistaken? *Let it not be so!*

"Silence," Wilek said to the council, and "Please continue" to Janek, failing to control the waver in his voice.

Janek took his time before speaking again. "As we all know, Laviel Nafni was married to Rosâr Echad in the Armanian year 848. She bore him a son named Morek a year later, and I came along the following year. So you see, the Pontiff is not my mother's husband or my father, as you accuse. He is instead my mother's father and my *grandfather*." Janek stood, chin high, shoulders back. "I *am* Rosâr Echad's son, and I demand Justness for how I have been mistreated in this matter."

No. Wilek turned in his chair to Teaka. The old mantic woman had convinced him that Janek was Rogedoth's son—all based on the testimony of her shadir. Now her eyes were wide, remorseful. She bowed her head, acknowledging her mistake.

Had her shadir been mistaken or had it purposely tricked them? Either way, he should not be surprised. Trevn had warned him against trusting black spirits—had been right to. Wilek never should have taken the word of a mantic's black spirit as truth. Janek's explanation made much more sense than what Teaka had surmised from her shadir. A queen might risk unfaithfulness to her king, but to bear another man's child and claim such a child as the king's own . . . Such audacity would be beyond foolish.

And Rosârah Laviel was no fool.

"How it relieves me to hear this truth, my son," Father said to Janek. "I knew in my heart that you were mine."

"I have not enjoyed being parted from my family, Father," Janek said.

Wilek needed to grasp control of this interrogation before he lost everything. "We will discuss Sâr Janek's request for Justness in a moment," he said, "but first we must take into account his collusion with his . . . grandfather to kill the king and put himself on the throne."

"Yes," Father said, nodding gravely. "What say you against this charge, my son?"

Janek gazed penitently at the king. "If that was truly my grandfather's plan, I had no knowledge of it," he replied. "It was my mother's desire to see me declared Heir. That much I know. I can produce two letters on the subject between her and Rosârah Thallah."

This news stunned Wilek. "What is the nature of these letters?"

"In their plotting to make me Heir, the two women arranged my marriage to Princess Vallah of Rurekau. When they first presented the idea to me, I believed Wilek had been killed. So I agreed, wanting to do all I could to keep Armania stable."

Wilek doubted that very much.

"Only when I discovered the letters in my mother's chambers in Canden did I realize that she and Rosârah Thallah had been conspiring with one another long before then."

Wilek glanced at Trevn and saw that his brother looked as unconvinced as Wilek felt. The king, however, to Wilek's alarm, looked completely persuaded.

"Why would the rosârahs Thallah and Laviel conspire together?" Wilek asked Janek. "It is no secret that the two have never gotten along."

"My mother wanted me declared Heir. To coerce the support of Rosârah Thallah, she promised that if I someday became king, Sâr Trevn would have the title of Heir until I produced a son of my own."

This Wilek didn't doubt for a moment. The third queen had always been ambitious for Trevn. Why couldn't she let things alone?

"So you see," Janek said, "none of that was my doing. Father, I ask Justness for the wrongs done me. Will you, in your great mercy and wisdom, grant me that much?"

Too soon, Wilek thought, fighting a smile. Janek should have waited a bit longer before pressing for Justness. Rushing the topic made him look eager, and Wilek could tell from the king's stiff posture and squinted eyes that the man was not yet appeased.

Father scowled at Janek. "What do you ask for Justness?"

The council fell silent, waiting to hear what Janek would say. His eyes shifted to Wilek and he cocked one eyebrow in confidence. "That my Heir ring be returned to me."

Everyone watched the king, who stared at Janek as if weighing the situation in his mind. If Wilek were to lose his position as Heir . . . Janek could not lead this expedition! He knew nothing of sailing. Nothing of starting a new colony. Nothing of politics. It would bring disaster.

"That I cannot give," Father said finally. Wilek released a relieved breath and felt those around the table relax. "Justness amends must be equal to the wrongdoing."

"But Wilek stole my place as Heir with his false accusations of my birth," Janek said. "I did nothing wrong."

"Not so," Father said, as lucid as Wilek had seen him recently. "You knew Rogedoth's true identity and kept it from me. We may never prove whether or not you were working with him in his quest to murder me and take my throne. We might never know whether or not you have taken evenroot or tried your hand as a mantic. And we have no way of confirming that you did not order your servants to help your mother and grandfather escape their transport to the *Seffynaw*, but—"

"I did no such thing!" Janek yelled.

Father raised his hand. "My decision is final. The only Justness you will receive from me is keeping your life and your title as sâr. You must decide where your loyalties lie, my son. With me or with your grandfather."

"Is not my presence here answer enough? If I were loyal to my grandfather and his ambitions, I would be with him, wherever he is. But I support *you*, Father. On that you can count."

"We shall see," the king said.

The questioning went on. Wilek asked about evenroot, the Lahavôtesh, Lady Lebetta's death, and the identities of Armanian mantics. If Janek knew the answers, he gave nothing away. Wilek's frustration mounted with each dead end.

"I grow tired," Father said. "Janek, you are dismissed. The rest of you I will see on the stern deck tonight for the sacrifice."

Wilek closed his eyes, wilting. He had hoped the man had forgotten tonight was a full moon.

Everyone stood for their sovereign's departure. "Find a convict to sacrifice to Thalassa," he added, and his attendants paused his chair before the exit.

Wilek looked up, frowning. "Thalassa?"

"Barthos betrayed my loyalty," Father said, scowling up at the cheyvah head mounted on the wall. "But Thalassa has so far given us safe passage. She will take Barthos's place in my five. You would all be wise to join me in paying tribute to the goddess of the sea."

"You are wise to say so, Your Highness," Canbek said.

No one else spoke until the door closed behind Janek and the king. Sir Kalenek moved Wilek's chair to the end of the table. Wilek sat down and rubbed his hands over his face as the rest of the council took their seats.

"I, for one, am glad Sâr Janek is not false," Kamran said. "I've always liked him."

"Liking him is different from trusting him," Oli said. "We'd be wise never to do that."

"Will the rosâr really sacrifice at sea?" Danek Faluk, Duke of Highcliff, asked.

"Oh yes," Wilek said. *Of course he will.*

"Father has never consulted logic before," Trevn said. "No reason he should start now."

Maybe so, but Wilek must try. He dismissed the council and set off to talk with his father. He strongly believed Miss Onika's claim that Arman had allowed the Woes to destroy the Five Realms because of the people's wicked ways. Resuming human sacrifice would not set the fleet on a better path. With overcrowded ships and too many inexperienced captains, they were vulnerable at sea. Best not to tempt He Who Made the World.

✦   ✦   ✦

"Father refused to listen to reason," Wilek said as he exited his cabin for the sacrifice, his High Shield, Sir Kalenek Veroth, in front and Agmado Harton behind as his backman. "With Janek's reinstatement as a prince of Armania, I dared not push too hard."

"At least the sacrifice will go swifter on the ship," Kal said. "Without the long ride to Canden and back."

"I preferred the distance," Wilek said. "It always forced me to think long and hard about the life being wasted."

"Not wasted, really," Harton said. "Sacrificed to a goddess. Thalassa's probably the first face the poor soul sees when arriving in Shamayim. She will put him in a place of utmost honor."

Wilek used to believe that, but not anymore. He paused at the crossway and glanced back, taking in Harton's lazy eyes and easy smile. "After everything we've been through with the Woes . . . Miss Onika . . . killing Barthos . . . Do you really believe that, Hart?"

His backman shrugged. "I can't explain everything, but I do know that we killed a cheyvah, not a god."

Kal had stopped as well, and Wilek took in the stark contrast between his grim and scarred High Shield and his handsome, skirt-chasing backman.

"Just you keep your opinions on that to yourself," Kal said. "Rosâr Echad believes our sâr killed Barthos—formally adding Godslayer to his title. We will give him no reason to doubt his choice, you hear?"

"Yes, sir," Harton said.

They continued down the corridor. Wilek didn't care what people thought about the past. It was the future that bothered him. Human sacrifice was wrong—forbidden by Arman. Yet until Wilek became king, he was powerless to stop it. And if he pushed his father too far, he might lose his place as Heir. "According to the Book of Arman, life is valued above all else. Arman does not wish us to pour out our own lifeblood for offerings, be they love or guilt offerings."

Since Wilek had been reading Trevn's Book of Arman, he had discovered just how many ancient Armanite traditions the Rôb church had changed. The biggest had been the worship of several dozen new gods in addition to Arman. It was because of this that Armanite believers had started referring to Arman as "the God" or the "One God." Wilek had always admired Arman but had never once believed him to be the only god. All that had changed now, and Wilek wondered how he had ever believed anything else.

Kal turned up the companionway, and they met a young woman coming down. A young woman of twelve years who should have been in bed.

"Hrettah!" Wilek said, wondering what the princess was doing out alone at this hour. She reached them, and Wilek grabbed hold of her shoulder, noticing she was holding a bronze canister in her arms. "What are you doing?"

"Couldn't sleep," she whispered.

"Well, go back to bed and try," he commanded. "Where is your shield?"

She merely shook her head and sprinted away, her bare feet slapping the wood floor of the corridor.

"What is she up to?" His mother's concerns about the attacks on women and girls came to mind. He would have to speak with Rosârah Valena in the morning. It was far too dangerous for Hrettah to be out at night alone. Wilek could not protect those who did not follow the rules.

✦　✦　✦

"You have been convicted of wrongdoing and sentenced to die," Father Burl Mathal said. "Tonight you atone for yourself and all Armania."

This line usually belonged to the king, but halfway through the ceremony he'd had a spell and forgotten what to say. His aides had taken him back to his chamber, and the Rôb priest went on alone.

Without a tongue the convict merely rasped. He had killed a man in a knife fight and had taken on substantial wounds of his own, including the loss of his tongue. Master Uhley said he wouldn't last more than a day or two, which was why Wilek had chosen him.

Mathal looked up to the recently remodeled Thalassa pole. It had once held a bronze of Barthos's likeness at the top, but Father had ordered it changed for tonight.

"Here is our exchange, goddess!" Mathal said. "Here is our substitute. Here is our atonement. This man goes to death so that we might earn your favor and proceed to peace and long life." The priest nodded to the guards, who tipped up the plank until the convict slid off and over the side.

The man's tongueless scream sounded like a raven's caw. A splash followed.

A gasp turned Wilek's head. A young woman ducked behind the mizzenmast. Miss Amala Allard, if Wilek wasn't mistaken.

For sand's sake! Were all the young ladies exploring this evening? "Did you see her, Kal?" Wilek whispered, though he knew the answer already from the grim expression on his shield's face.

Kal grunted. "I will see that Miss Amala makes it safely back to her cabin where she belongs and that she knows how inappropriate it is for a young lady to be out alone at night."

Wilek nodded, and Kal slipped away to deal with his youngest ward.

Wilek had once thought Miss Mielle a handful, but Miss Amala had turned out to be twice as bold with no common sense whatsoever. He did not envy Kal's responsibility in raising the girls.

With Kal off scolding his ward, Harton escorted Wilek to his chambers. As per routine, Harton entered first to clear the room, then Wilek followed.

Before Harton could step out, a guard knocked and pushed open the door. "Forgive the interruption, Your Highness. You are needed in Rosârah Valena's chambers right away. Sârah Hrettah has been attacked."

Hrettah! Wilek scurried from the room, knowing this had been his fault. When he'd found Hrettah wandering before the sacrifice, he should have sent Harton to escort her back to her cabin. Why had he been so careless with her safety? There was no way to keep security on board a ship so overcrowded. How many more would be attacked before they reached the island?

If they ever found the island.

Aldair Livina had assured them all that the place existed, but almost seven months before that, the king had demanded the former admiral's early retirement for insanity in the wake of his wife's affair and later death. On the word of Trevn and Duke Odarka that it had all been a mistake, Wilek had convinced the king to reinstate Livina as captain of the *Seffynaw* with the charge of leading the fleet to the island he had discovered.

But Wilek had been wrong about trusting Teaka and her shadir in regards to Janek's parentage. What if he had been wrong to trust Captain Livina as well?

Wilek and Harton followed the guard down the lengthway. The ship surged beneath him and he steadied himself against the bulkheads just outside Rosârah Valena's cabin. Once he regained his footing, he entered and found Princess Hrettah reclining on a longchair.

"Wil!" The princess jumped up and clutched him. "She took my face! She took it and put it on her own!"

"What happened?" Wilek asked the fourth queen. He could not fathom why anyone would dare attack one of the princesses.

"A sailor found her bound and gagged, roaming the foredeck," Rosârah Valena said. "She cannot recall what happened except that she saw a woman's face change into hers."

"She took my face, Wil, and walked away looking like me."

Wilek's stomach churned. Charlon on the *Seffynaw*? The mantic woman had impersonated Lebetta after she'd been killed. Could a mantic take the form of the living?

He glanced at Harton but couldn't ask questions about mantics in front of an audience without giving away the secret of his backman's mantic past. "Fetch me Teaka," Wilek told a guard, who raced out the door to obey. Wilek settled onto the longchair. "Hrettah, sit with me."

She did so instantly, her wide brown eyes staring helplessly up into his.

"What did this woman look like?" he asked.

"She was no taller than me. She had lighter brown skin and gray eyes. Her hair was short, done up in side braids and knots. And she spoke in a foreign tongue."

It sure sounded like Charlon. Wilek fought the shiver that stood his arm hair on end. He would not let anyone see his fear, especially not Hrettah.

"Did she say anything to you? Do anything?" he asked.

"She cut off some of my hair. I tried to scream, but my voice wouldn't work."

A mantic for certain, but why take Hrettah's likeness? He suddenly thought of seeing Hrettah earlier, when they'd gone up for the sacrifice. "Hrettah, did you see me tonight? In the crossway just before the stairs to the stern deck?"

Her frown answered his question before her words. "Did I see you where?"

"My daughter knows better than to go traipsing about the ship alone, Your Highness," Rosârah Valena said.

"I'm sure she does." Wilek hugged the girl to his side and stroked her hair. "You're a good girl, aren't you?"

"Wilek." She leveled a glance at him. "I am not a child."

"Will you be all right?"

"If you will catch that woman."

"I promise to do so."

The door opened. The guard he had sent for Teaka had returned without her. Kal was with him, though.

"Well?" Wilek asked.

"A, uh, private word, Your Highness?" the guard said.

"Very well." Wilek followed the guard into the corridor, Kal and Harton with him.

"The old woman is dead," the guard said when the door was closed. "Found her lying in her bed. Looks to have died from old age, yet her cabin has been ransacked."

Wilek heaved a sigh. Randmuir Khal of the Omatta's mother, dead? The man had never liked that Wilek had persuaded her to act as his advisor. Now he would be furious.

"There's more, Your Highness," Kal said, nudging the guard.

"The first mate and ship's boy both saw Sârah Hrettah enter the old woman's cabin just after dark," the man said.

"Ah." Charlon had killed Teaka. It made perfect sense. Teaka had betrayed Charlon by breaking the compulsion over Wilek and helping him escape the Magonians. If Charlon was on board, she must have decided to enact revenge.

Wilek shuddered. "Charlon of Magonia is on board the *Seffynaw*."

CHARLON

"You have failed," Mreegan said.

The Chieftess of Magonia sat on a chair beside the window in Lady Zeroah's cabin. A cabin aboard the Armanian flagship *Seffynaw*. Mreegan and Charlon both had reddish-brown skin and the gray eyes of a mantic. But Mreegan's beauty outshined all. Tall where Charlon was short. Shapely where Charlon was formless. Graceful where Charlon was awkward. Though Charlon did not look like herself at present. She wore the mask of Lady Zeroah Barta.

Charlon stood across the small room. Back to the door. Arms crossed. Defensive. "I have not failed yet."

"I grow tired of sharing the goddess with you," the Chieftess added. "A great shadir deserves better than your dismal efforts, don't you think?"

Such words! "Magon would disagree," Charlon said. "The Great Goddess believes in me."

"You should have succeeded in this assignment long before we became stuck on boats in the Eversea," Mreegan snapped. "You are weak, even after compelling yourself with magic. These people would hang you if they found out who you really are, yet you still harbor compassion for them."

Not all. For a girl in a trunk, always. Such a thing was wrong. No matter who the girl was. Or that she had twice spat in Charlon's eye. "What would you have me do?"

"Give up your quest and release Magon to serve me alone. We will return to the *Vespara*, where I can devise a new plan. We must find land. Once we have a home, then we can worry about the prophecy of the Deliverer."

43

To the *Vespara*. A place Mreegan would rule over Charlon as Chieftess. The role the Great Goddess had promised. Promised Charlon would have. Once she became Mother. "I will *not* go. Not until I conceive the Deliverer. The *Seffynaw* carries all the Hadar men."

"You have had more than enough time to catch one of these princes, yet you continue to wait on Prince Wilek."

"He is the natural choice."

"We are out of time!" Mreegan yelled. "I have no more ahvenrood. We must return to the *Vespara* before our masks wear off. I leave at nightfall. With or without you."

Ah, here was proof! That the goddess trusted Charlon. Better than Chieftess Mreegan. For the great shadir had taken Charlon to the old woman Teaka. A simple spell and stores of ahvenrood came to Charlon. She eyed the bronze canister on the sideboard and smiled. She did not need Mreegan's root now. Nor would she tell Mreegan so.

Because Mreegan would take it. For herself.

Charlon lifted her chin. Stood tall. "I will not abandon Magon's call. I do not fear the future. Of failing masks or living at sea. Magon is with me. Always. She will protect me."

Mreegan stood, strode toward Charlon, shaking her finger while she spoke. "You are a weak fool. I misread your anger as strength, but it has never been anything more than self-pity. I was mistaken to declare you Mother."

Charlon stood firm. "I *am* the Mother. You will see."

Mreegan shook her head. "The day of the Mother will come, but I no longer believe she is you."

"Magon has told me. I am the Mother. I will not fail her."

"Yes, well, you cannot succeed without ahvenrood, and I have no desire to be executed alongside you when our masks wear off and Prince Wilek sees who we really are." Mreegan walked past Charlon. Toward the door.

"Magon will provide," Charlon said to her back. "Your lack of faith shames the goddess. That you would walk away. Away from her decree . . . You are not worthy to lead Magonia."

Mreegan turned, her face a veil of thunder. "You dare insult me after all I have done for you? You are a fool. Your mask is failing and your token host is dying. Can you not smell her death approaching? You have failed."

"Not yet."

"Nightfall, if you wish to return with me." Mreegan opened the door and left.

"You will regret abandoning me!" Charlon yelled after her.

The door fell closed on her words. Charlon flipped the lock. Sank onto the bed. Gritted her teeth to fight off tears that threatened.

Alone again. But for the captive. Hidden in the trunk under the bed.

The cabin *did* reek. Of death. Charlon could not disagree. But the smell was not Zeroah. King Jorger had died. The first day of the voyage. Heart forever silent. Mreegan had used magic to push his body out the cabin window. And once Mreegan knew her ahvenrood was nearly gone, she had magicked the struggling Flara out the window as well. Splashing water. Drowning maid.

Zeroah might have died too, if not for Charlon. She would not allow Mreegan near the girl. Charlon let her out once a day. To eat. To drink. To use the privy bucket. Mreegan had mocked Charlon for it. But Charlon knew. Knew what it was like to be captive.

Charlon wanted it to end. For Zeroah's sake. For her own too. But she would not let Mreegan decide when.

She stood. Paced across the room to the mirrorglass. Studied the reflection of Lady Zeroah. Tired of wearing this face. Even more weary of the black mourning dress. To honor the death of Princess Nabelle. The color did not make the skinny girl more attractive. Perhaps she was simply too plain. Too plain to tempt Prince Wilek. His concubine had been provocative. Now that Charlon had more ahvenrood, she might risk a small spell to enhance the girl's figure.

It would not help. Mreegan was right. Charlon had no hope. No hope of seducing Prince Wilek. Lady Zeroah was too demure. To behave differently would call unwanted attention. Besides, the prince had little time for his betrothed. His father was ill. Too ill to pressure him to marry. With Princess Nabelle gone and Prince Wilek preoccupied with his duties as Heir, the contracted wedding seemed forgotten. That his people came first did not surprise Charlon. Not in the least.

"Go to Prince Janek instead," the Chieftess had said. *"I imagine he would delight in claiming his brother's betrothed for his own."*

No doubt he would. Such a task might prove easier. It mattered not which prince fathered Charlon's child. So long as he was a Hadar. Yet she abhorred Prince Janek. He was everything she hated in a man.

The Chieftess had also suggested Charlon wear Mielle's mask. Approach Prince Trevn. In his youth he might not so easily recognize a trap. And while Charlon would enjoy putting Mielle in a trunk—for a day or two, at least—she was not yet ready to give up on Prince Wilek.

Lies, her heart said. Charlon simply did not like Chieftess Mreegan telling her what to do.

The Chieftess was wrong. She would see. Now that Charlon had plenty of ahvenrood. And Magon's help to use it. Success would come. And once Magon declared Charlon Chieftess of Magonia, Mreegan would be sorry.

✦　✦　✦

Charlon woke the next morning to the reek from the trunk under her bed. Too strong to ignore another day. A spell would mask the stench for Charlon. But she could not so easily cast such a spell over everyone on board.

Lady Zeroah must have a bath.

Charlon moved the trunk out from under her bed. Then she opened it.

Zeroah lay curled inside. Flinched at the light. Groaned. She was skinnier than ever. Skeletal. Had sores on her face. Two flies crawled over her greasy tangle of hair. Charlon's heart leapt within. How had flies gotten inside? *Help the girl!* her heart said. *This is wrong.*

Charlon knew it. But not how to stop it. She hastened to free the captive from her prison. Tipped the trunk on its side. Pulled the girl out and removed her gag.

Now lying on the floor, Zeroah groaned and writhed. Did not stretch her legs. Did not try to stand, just cried for water.

Charlon poured a cup from the sideboard. Helped the girl sit and drink. Charlon poured a second. Put some cheese and figs on a plate. Carried the trunk out into the corridor. Compelled the nearest maid to clean it without question.

Went back inside and waited while Zeroah nibbled at the food.

The girl had fought hard the first two weeks. Lost her fire after. Charlon's heart ached to look upon her. Charlon had done this. Become the monster she'd always hated.

"Do not look so sad," Zeroah rasped. "I have forgiven you."

The words shocked. More than a strike to the face.

The girl kept talking, as if to herself. "He Who Made the World has forgiven me for my selfishness. He answers my prayers even though I deserve no such devotion. Arman is good to me. I want to be good also."

"Arman?" This was the name of the father god. Torol believed him a great shadir. Magon said he was nothing but myth.

A knock at the door. The maid returning with the trunk.

"Silence," she whispered to Zeroah, then said through the door. "Leave the trunk there and bring a tub filled with warm water. And tools to clean my hair and nails." It would be a saltwater bath, unfortunately. But it would greatly reduce Zeroah's stench.

"Yes, lady."

Charlon waited until the maid's footsteps padded away. Opened the door and pulled the trunk inside. The wood was moist from cleaning. Smelled fresh. "This is how your god is good?" she asked Zeroah. "By allowing you to be kept? Inside this?"

Zeroah eyed the trunk warily. "It is his love for you that allows my captivity."

A deity love a human? Charlon doubted even Magon loved her. And they were bonded. In shared purpose. "Explain your meaning."

"The One God does not control his people. He gives us freedom to live how we wish. Sometimes our choices hurt others. You might not count yourself among his faithful, but Arman loves you, even though you deny him."

A strange accusation. "I have never denied this name."

"You have never called upon it either."

"Why should I? He has never shown himself to me." Like Magon had.

"Did you not see him unleash his wrath upon the Five Realms for ignoring his decrees? How he saved a remnant of followers loyal to him? Have you not noticed how he has saved his servant Sâr Wilek time and again from your plotting?"

"Enough!" Charlon compelled Zeroah to silence. Yet her mind raced with echoes of their conversation. There was more she wanted to ask. But she did not want Zeroah to think her interested in her god. Magon was all Charlon needed. She would save her questions for Magon.

The bath came. Charlon compelled the maid to enter, bathe Zeroah. The woman's shock over seeing two Zeroahs, one appearing frail and mute, did not worry Charlon. She would forget everything. The moment she left the cabin.

The maid coddled Zeroah. Fussed over every sore. Scrubbed the girl's hair thoroughly. Then lifted her out, wrapped her in a robe, and clipped her fingernails and toenails to perfection. All the while crooning or humming. As if Zeroah were a wounded bird.

Such kindness made Charlon long to be treated so. She had been too afraid. To allow anyone to groom or bathe her. Such touching seemed wrong somehow. Unnecessary. Yet this woman's actions and joy as she served Zeroah contradicted any wrongness.

When the maid finished, Charlon told her to put Zeroah back. Into the trunk. The maid balked, refused. But Charlon could not do it. So she compelled the maid to obey.

Finally Zeroah was back inside. Hidden away. Weeping silently. Waves of guilt overcame. Charlon placed a sleeping spell on the girl. To relieve them both.

The maid stowed the trunk discreetly beneath the bed. Charlon erased the maid's memory. Sent her, stupidly, on her way. All forgotten.

But not Charlon. She remembered all. The mere knowledge of Zeroah inside the trunk made Charlon want to leave. She purged out the ahvenrood poison. Once she was well, she took a sip of root juice and locked the door behind her. Set out for the stern deck.

The sun had not been up for long. Charlon looked into the Veil. Shadir were rare on board the *Seffynaw*. But she found one slight. Watched it swirl around the legs of a sailor. A sailor hauling ropes across the deck.

Magon, I need your help. I do not wish to fail you.

Magon appeared beside her then. Looked identical to Mreegan. Had given her likeness to the Chieftess.

Why is my servant sad? the great shadir asked.

As the pair circled the deck, Charlon told her all that had happened. Of Zeroah's praises for her god. Of Chieftess Mreegan's assertion that Charlon had failed.

They walked as if they were two friends taking a stroll. Charlon took care not to trod upon anyone. Magon, transparent and invisible to all eyes but Charlon's, simply floated through anyone in her path.

Do not fear, Magon told her. *My plans are certain and will not fail.*

Relief washed over Charlon. All things were possible with Magon at her side.

İᴨᴏʟᴀʜ

As always, Empress Inolah of Rurekau found Master Jhorn on the *Baretam*'s foredeck. The legless man had fashioned a red cushion with straps that he slung over his back, except when he wanted to sit down. He was seated on the cushion now, looking out through the rail's rungs at the surrounding ships of the fleet. His beard hid his mouth from view, but the expression of his eyes and the slant of his brows gave voice to the pain he would not speak of. She knew he missed his charges, Miss Onika and the boy Grayson.

"May I join you, Master Jhorn?" Inolah asked.

The man looked up in surprise. "Of course, Empress. You are very welcome, though the deck is wet here, so I do not recommend you stand too close to the rail."

"I have brought a stool." Inolah motioned to the guardsman behind her, who stepped forward and set the stool beside Jhorn and his cushion. Inolah settled down, instantly relieved to be off her feet. "I do not go anywhere these days without a place to sit."

"I cannot blame you for that," Jhorn said. "Will the child come soon?"

"Another two months or so, I suspect. Are you well, Master Jhorn? Do you need anything?"

"Only more patience, I'm afraid."

"I am sorry Ulrik has not included you in his meetings."

Master Jhorn waved his hand as if scaring off a fly. "I am no one to him.

49

I am no one to anybody, which is how I like it. Onika and Grayson are safer that way. I only wish I were with them, but I must trust them to Arman now."

Inolah liked this strange man. After having lived so long in a realm where men made themselves gods, to hear the God's name spoken from the lips of any man . . . She felt peaceful in his presence, which was strange considering he had lost his legs by such violent means. But peace came from knowing Arman—such peace had helped her survive years of an abusive marriage and great loneliness.

"I fear I am losing my children," Inolah said. "Ulrik has chosen advisors too like his father. And he keeps Ferro with him always, even when inappropriate for one so young."

"You must give him space and time to make his own mistakes," Jhorn said. "Only in hindsight will he see how true you have been."

Perhaps. "Unless he remains blinded."

"Trust him to Arman, lady. You taught him well."

She wanted to trust Ulrik to Arman. She really did. "I fear he has turned his back on the God. His father taught him the opposite of all my training. It is no surprise that he is confused."

"Confusion is a natural part of life," Jhorn said. "Now that he is grown, you can teach more by your silent example than by use of your voice."

Inolah sighed. "Stop telling him what to do? Is that what you mean?"

Jhorn winked. "Your words, lady, not mine."

She supposed he was right. How hard, though, for a mother to stand by in silence and watch her son destroy himself and his nation.

Enough sorrow. She needed a change in topic. "How is Master Burk?" she asked, remembering how much Kal mistrusted the headstrong young man. "I hope he has stayed out of mischief."

"Young Burk has shaved his head and joined the Igote."

"Has he? I would think the obedience required of a military man would disagree with his pride."

"As did I," Jhorn said, "but it seems to be a fair price to pay for the power it gives him over everyone else. The Igote uniform demands respect, whether or not the man wearing it is worthy. Young Burk has found a way to have respect without having to earn it."

Now that did sound like him. A Rurekan male, through and through.

A page approached and bowed deeply.

"What is it?" Inolah asked.

"Emperor Ulrik requests your presence at a council meeting in his private dining hall."

"Now?" Council meetings were usually held in the mornings.

"Yes, lady. I am to bid you to come at once."

Inolah nodded and turned back to face Jhorn. "I apologize that our visit was cut short today. I will think more about being a silent example."

Jhorn pushed himself up onto his stumps and bowed. "I am honored, Empress."

✦　✦　✦

Inolah stifled a groan as she sat down to dinner in Ulrik's private dining room. These days she felt hungry and full at all times, her ankles were as thick as her knees, and her back ached constantly. She had not been so uncomfortable this early in her previous pregnancies. The older she got, the harder childbearing became. Thankfully she would never be pregnant again.

From her place at the foot of the long, narrow table, she could see everyone well. Two musicians seated in the corner of the room played soft music on lyre and harp. *How odd.* At the head of the table, Inolah's eldest son, Ulrik, the recently appointed Emperor of Rurekau, sat upon his throne. He had taken to dressing as his father had: no shirt, bare chest inked in henna tracings, tan trousers embroidered in gold thread, black boots, and a floor-length cape of gold velvet. As per Rurekan tradition, his head was shaved and the tracing that covered his scalp dripped down around both eyes like a mask of tattoos. Unlike his father, Ulrik never took off the heavy ceremonial crown—despite there being lighter ones for everyday use. He also wore a single gold chain around his neck as the symbol of his office.

She could not believe he was just shy of seventeen.

His little brother, Ferro, sat on his right. Recently turned nine years old, Ferro was a smaller mirror image of Ulrik, right down to the velvet cape, except he wore a gold circlet and a sleeveless white shirt. On Ferro's right sat General Balat in his brown-and-gold Igote uniform, beside him Sheriff Kakeeo. Across from those two men, Ulrik's High Shield, Sir Iamot, and Ulrik's onesent, Taleeb, occupied the other side of the table. All of them, including Ferro, had shaved heads and henna tracings, but none so elaborate as Ulrik's.

The only empty chair at the table was the one on Ulrik's left, across from Ferro. This Ulrik had set aside for Priestess Jazlyn, High Queen of Tenma.

The priestess had been High Queen for as many days as Ulrik had been emperor, and the woman had taken to her new authority with as much—or more—vigor as Ulrik had his. Inolah should have listened when Kal had warned her about Ulrik's unhealthy interest in the priestess. With so many women to fawn over him, Inolah had been certain he would forget the Great Lady once he was crowned. But he had not. Quite the opposite, in fact. During the many weeks they had traveled aboard the ship from Jeruka to Everton, her son had become completely obsessed with the Tennish queen. She, of course, had spurned all his advances, whether he invited her to dine, dance, or simply walk the ship in his company. Her answer had always been no.

Tennish women didn't marry and viewed romance as a weakness. Men were slaves in Tenma, so it was no surprise that the woman had no interest in Ulrik. But the young emperor thought so highly of himself that Tennish customs were no barrier to his desires. He pursued the priestess as relentlessly as she denied him. Inolah worried that when his patience finally wore thin, he would respond in anger and the mantic woman would destroy him with her magic as she had his father.

The musicians ended one song and began another—a slow love song, Inolah realized in a sudden rush. While the High Queen wanted nothing to do with Ulrik romantically, she insisted upon attending his council meetings and having her say where her people were concerned—no matter that they were no more than twenty of the five hundred sixty-three souls on board the *Baretam*. Apparently this dinner "meeting" was yet another step in Ulrik's continuing plan to woo the woman. Inolah had to admit her son was persistent.

The door opened, and Qoatch, Jazlyn's handsome eunuch, held it open as his Great Lady entered the room. The High Queen was dressed as always in an elaborate white gown and pearl-studded gold diadem. She looked no more than twenty, had a perfect figure, flawless dark brown skin, wide gray eyes, full lips, and coils of jet-black hair that fell past her waist. Inolah felt herself dim in comparison and glanced at her own thick wrists, bulging stomach, fat arms . . . *Stop it, Nolah*, she chastised herself. Mantics could look however they liked, and Inolah had no doubt that magic had enhanced a face and body *that* perfect.

The High Queen stopped just behind Ulrik and her shrewd gray eyes took in the arrangements. "What's this?" she asked.

Ulrik pushed back his chair and stood, bowed deeply to her. "High Queen, welcome. I have been so busy of late that I must combine business with dinner. I do apologize if this inconveniences you. If you have not yet eaten, you are most welcome to partake of our meal."

"I am not hungry."

Disappointment that only a mother could see flashed in his eyes, yet he masked it well as he sat down and drank from his goblet. "Do sit, Great Lady. We were just about to begin."

Jazlyn eyed him warily, then jerked her chin at the eunuch, who jumped to pull out her chair. Servants entered, carrying covered trays and pitchers. The aroma made Inolah's stomach growl, yet she did not think she could eat one bite.

Once everything had been laid out on the table and all the wine poured, Ulrik began the meeting. "Lead us in our discussion, General Balat," he said, picking up a wedge of melon that was long past ripe. "What grievous problems faced us this day?"

"I'm afraid there are pirates among the fleet, Your Eminence," Balat said.

"Pirates!" Ulrik seemed offended by the very idea. "What makes you say such a thing?"

"A ship was taken," Balat said. "The *Noohrez*. It was a midsize fishing vessel carrying one hundred thirteen souls. The pirates came at dusk, just after the crew had pulled in the nets, catching them off guard."

"Did they kill the crew?" the shield, Iamot, asked.

"Seven fighting men were killed," Balat said. "Another twenty-one were thrown overboard and are suspected to have drowned. The pirates made the men choose whether to sail as crew or work as fishermen. Any able-bodied man who refused was put overboard. The *Noohrez*'s own crew sailed her away, directed by a few dozen pirates left behind to oversee things. A few hours later the pirates lowered a dinghy with a handful of women and children."

"Why?" Ulrik asked. "Were they causing trouble?"

"They say not. There were other women and children left aboard, and I've spoken to each of the survivors. The women weren't ugly or diseased, so I cannot discern why they were put out of the ship."

"The pirates want us to know they are here," Inolah said.

Ulrik scoffed at this. "Why would a pirate want that? They pride themselves on being stealthy."

"Which they were, I gather, if no other ship witnessed this crime," Inolah said. "General Balat, did the survivors see the name of the pirate ship or know what type of vessel it was and if it was part of our fleet or someone else's?"

"The *Taradok*, Empress. She was a two-masted, lateen-rigged cog. Relatively small, but highly maneuverable. I do not know where she came from."

"I see no reason why they would give themselves away on purpose," Ulrik said. "It's ludicrous."

"Not really," Jazlyn said. "How much more terrifying is a story of invisible pirates moving through the fleet? I agree with the empress. The pirates let these women and children go free so that they could tell the story to the rest of us. Now that we know there are pirates out there, willing to steal ships and kill, fear will spread among an already vulnerable population."

Ulrik took a long drink—a trick he learned from his father that meant he was giving himself time to think. He set down his goblet and leaned back in his chair. "A fair point, Great Lady," he said. "We must be on the lookout for these pirates—beat them at their game. Sheriff, the task goes to you."

"How will I hunt down a ship that small?" Kakeeo asked.

"Figure it out," Ulrik said. "What else is there, General?"

"Our supplies are running low," Balat said. "We were unable to restock our stores in Everton or Odarka since the Woes kept us from docking or even sending dinghies to shore. We last replenished in Highcliff, over two weeks ago."

"The new Armanian island is close, is it not?" Ulrik asked.

"Yes, Your Eminence," Balat said, "or so they claim. I would like to put together a landing party to be ready to go ashore immediately when we arrive."

"I will be part of that," Jazlyn said.

"No," Ulrik said. "No landing party. Not until we know what we're dealing with. It could be this island suffered the Woes as well. We would be wise to go slowly."

"I ask only to prepare a landing party, Your Eminence," Balat said. "It would not set out until you gave word to do so."

"Very well, General," Ulrik said. "Choose your party, but I will approve every member."

"It is right that you should do so, Emperor Ulrik," Jazlyn said slowly. "But do not forget that I am not yours to command, nor are my people. It is my wish to explore this new island and determine whether or not it is right for Tenma. Do not stand in my way."

Silence passed as everyone awaited Ulrik's reply.

Concern etched his face. "I would never, Great Lady. I only fear for your safety."

Priestess Jazlyn inclined her head, which was the closest she ever came to bowing to Ulrik. She stood then and smoothed out the creases in her white gown. "If there is nothing else, *Emperor*, my people await my return."

Ulrik stood, and everyone else at the table mirrored him. "Good evening, Great Lady."

She left without a farewell, Qoatch trailing behind.

The moment the door closed, Ulrik fell into his chair, slouching low like a lazy boy. "She will never respect me. She hates me!"

"The priestess takes offense at all of us," General Balat said. "She does not wish to be aboard the *Baretam*. She and her people talk of leaving the first chance they get."

Ulrik leaned forward and banged his fist on the table. "That is exactly my concern! If I give the priestess a chance to leave this ship, she will never return. So I will not permit her to leave."

Silence fell over the table. Inolah could resist no longer. "You seek her respect, yet you would keep her prisoner? To what end?"

He lifted his goblet, noticed it was empty, and set it back down, frowning. "I seek to make her my bride, Mother. I thought that was plain."

Somehow the following silence seemed greater than the one before. Inolah looked around the table and saw that none of Ulrik's craven advisors would look him in the eye and call him a fool. Again she must do the ugly work.

"You cannot force a woman to love you, Ulrik, and certainly not by keeping her prisoner."

"Going to accuse me of being my father again, I suppose?" he asked.

"Quite the opposite. Your father would have had her arrested, maybe even whipped, for defying a direct order, but you respected her when you granted her wish to rule her own people. And she bowed her head in thanks. That is the type of behavior you should continue if you wish to win her heart."

His dark eyes flashed. "Why do you always do that? Compare me to him? He is dead, and I don't care to hear about what he would have done."

"I only said that to praise how you—"

"I don't want your praise!" Somehow Inolah had become the focus of Ulrik's crushed pride. "You think me too young to be a competent ruler. You think me a fool where the High Queen is concerned. You think Sir Kalenek is smarter than me. You went behind my back and released the prophetess Onika on his order." He gestured around the table. "I have plenty of wise men to advise me. I am no foolish lamb. I am a ram with horns of fire, and it is well past time you left the hard work of ruling Rurekau to the men. Good night, Mother. You may go."

Tears choked her throat, flooded, and overflowed her eyes before she could try to fight them back. The pregnancy had long ago taken control of her emotions, but this time she could not blame them alone. She picked up her handkerchief from the table and dabbed her cheeks, stood, and walked down the length of the table toward the door.

"Come, Ferro," she said to her youngest son. "I shall get you put to bed."

"No," Ulrik said. "I am his guardian now. Ferro is old enough to sit up with the men."

Inolah swayed and had to grip the back of a chair to keep from stumbling. General Balat jumped up and grabbed her arm. "Easy, Empress. Are you well?"

I am heartbroken. Ulrik, in all his overwhelming insecurities, had lashed out at her. She knew that Jazlyn's continual rejection was toying with his self-worth. And his mother's presence and contributions had emasculated him in a place where he sought to have ultimate wisdom. She did not wish to abandon him, but as Master Jhorn had suggested, perhaps that was exactly what she must do.

"Your wish, my son, is granted," she said. "I bid you good night. And when we arrive at the new island, I will leave you and Ferro to your very wise council." She swept from the room before allowing Ulrik a chance to reply, though Ferro's cries of *"Mama!"* made it very hard to keep going.

Grayson

Grayson sat on his knees, scratching the heavy stone over the main deck, rubbing off brackish grime until the creamy wood beneath shone through. If he missed a spot, Nuel would tell that Roya woman, and she liked to punish anyone who made mistakes.

As Grayson worked, he daydreamed. Over and over, he relived his past. This usually made him feel good, especially when he pretended things had gone differently. His favorite was to imagine that he had gotten out of the dinghy before the thieves had cut the lines. Now he was living on the *Seffynaw* with Onika, Sir Kalenek, Prince Wilek, and the king of Armania, whose name he could never remember.

Other times he dreamed he had taken the first thief's knife, pushed both thieves overboard, and saved the boat. In that dream Sir Kalenek had been so impressed with Grayson's bravery that he told the prince, who knightened Grayson for his heroism.

But neither of those things had happened. Instead Grayson had first been taken to *The Wanderer*, a dirty, fat ship that normally carried grain—so said one of the young sailors. Grayson didn't like being on *The Wanderer*. It had been very crowded, and no one shared their food with him, so he'd sneaked around eating crumbs and crusts and fruit cores, and sometimes stealing food and water.

Jhorn wouldn't have liked that, which made Grayson feel guilty. So when the ship anchored with the fleet at a place called Odarka, and a man called Nuel came aboard offering jobs on a great ship called the *Vespara*, Grayson had happily volunteered. A great ship must have better food. Plus he felt it might even provide a way back to the *Seffynaw* or even Emperor Ulrik's *Baretam*.

He had been wrong.

The man Nuel had lied about the jobs. Those in power on the *Vespara* were Magonian. And the Magonians had wanted slaves, not workers. The new men and boys had been forced to empty and clean chamber pots and slop buckets, to scrub blood and entrails from the deck after animal sacrifices, to do whatever they were told. Any who moved too slowly would be struck. Any who made mistakes or disobeyed had to face Roya, who tattooed a rune on their necks that forced them to obey by magic.

Grayson had managed to avoid this so far by using his abilities. Jhorn had always told him not to, but Grayson figured this was an emergency. He had obscured the color of his dappled skin so that his masters would think him filthy rather than special. And he sometimes walked in the Veil where no one could see him. At first he'd been scared to, knowing that a Magonian ship would have lots of shadir on board. But when he finally gave in and tried it, he saw only one black spirit. This confused him. Where were all the shadir? Even though he didn't see them, he took care to only enter the Veil when he had no other choice. He did not want these people or the black spirits to know what he could do.

These worries brought Grayson to his daydreams of getting off the *Vespara*. He had hoped Sir Kalenek might come rescue him. But day after day passed, and the *Vespara* sailed so far back from the rest of the fleet that no one would ever pay attention to them.

No one came for Grayson. He had been forgotten.

So he set his mind on escape. He had been brought aboard on the boat fall and figured he might be able to use it to get away. There were two problems with this plan. First, he couldn't lower the dinghy by himself. That took at least two men. Second, the ship traveled too far from the rest of the fleet. So even if Grayson did manage to launch the dinghy, he wasn't certain he could ever row as far as he would need to.

Yelling near the boat fall caused him to look up from his work. Some men were hoisting a dinghy. One man shouted at another, who hollered at a group of sailors. All of them sprinted away but came right back with more men. Nuel arrived, ordering them all to carry things like a big chair made of woven branches, a rolled red rug, and lots of dried palm leafs. The rug got rolled out beside the boat fall. The chair put on top. Men lined up on both sides, each holding a palm leaf.

Grayson thought all this very strange. He went back to scrubbing but kept an eye on all those men, wondering who was coming and why this person had sparked such a fuss. When the dinghy reached the top, a woman sat inside all by herself. She wore a green dress that made her look like a rich man's housemaid. Grayson thought she was about twenty or so years old.

"Help me out, you oaf!" The woman all but threw herself into the arms of the men, who dropped their palms to lift her out of the boat and sit her in the chair of branches. Then all the men kneeled in a hurry and bowed with their heads touching the deck.

Bowing to a servant? That was strange.

Sir Kalenek had once dubbed Grayson a spy. In that moment, that was what Grayson decided to be. Surely Sir Kalenek would want to know about what was happening here. He set aside the sandstone and pushed into the Veil to conceal himself. Then he got up and walked toward the people crowded around the strange woman.

"Oh!" she cried, pressing her hands against her cheeks. "It's happening already. I thought I had more time."

Grayson gaped as her skin began to bubble and stretch. Her straight black hair turned copper brown and curled into wispy strands.

As her body changed, she continued barking orders. "Two, see that my room is prepared. I'll need a bath. Where is my First? I must petition Magon for cleansing."

"Here, Chieftess." A woman holding a mat shoved between the men.

This was the Chieftess? What happened next reminded Grayson of what Priestess Jazlyn did to purge evenroot poison from her body. Grayson bet it did the same thing. The Chieftess prayed to the shadir she had bonded with, asking it to heal her of the poison she had taken to do her magic spells.

Grayson knew her shadir would be coming now, but he still couldn't see it. The group of people around the Chieftess remained still, watching her pray. Suddenly a young woman stepped out from the crowd. She had reddish-brown skin, gray eyes, and long coils of copper-brown hair. Was she another mantic? Or maybe another one of the women with numbers for names?

She reached down to the Chieftess, who looked up and took hold of her hand.

"I have healed you," the young woman said.

A chill ran over Grayson at the spiritual sound of that voice. That was no woman. It was the shadir! The other people seemed not to see or hear it. Only the Chieftess responded. Grayson watched, shocked. He had never seen a shadir pretend to look human before. They usually looked like monsters or two animals squished together.

The Chieftess's body continued to change, stretching as colors faded from one into another, all while she held the hand of her shadir.

When the change ended, Grayson gasped. Couldn't help it. The Chieftess now looked exactly like her shadir, as if they were twins.

The shadir vanished, and the Chieftess stood and walked away from her throne, stepping over the kneeling people. "Is my bath ready?" she said to no one in particular.

"Yes, Chieftess," a man said, jumping up and chasing after her.

"Chieftess?" asked another man who stood up from the crowd. "What happened to Charlon? Is she dead?"

The Chieftess glanced back at the man. "Not yet. But she will be soon enough. She is a fool and a failure. Oh . . ." She chuckled, frowning at the man. "Don't look so glum, Torol. I know you liked her company. But trust in me and you will forget her soon enough."

The man bowed his head. "Yes, Chieftess."

Once the Chieftess and her cluster of followers had moved out of earshot, Grayson slipped away to the bow and gazed out at the other ships on the horizon. The *Vespara* followed the fleet at a distance—never came close to any other ship. Grayson could not tell which, if any, of the tiny specks out there might be the *Seffynaw*.

Why hadn't Sir Kalenek come to rescue him?

Grayson did not want to be on this ship. He wanted to be with Onika and Jhorn. Missed them very much. He did not like Magonians. Shadir frightened him. Mantics frightened him too. That a powerful bonded pair had come aboard the *Vespara* terrified him. If one of them were to notice his skin, to really look at it, or if they saw him in the Veil, they might learn what he was. And then, just as Jhorn had always warned, they would use Grayson for their evil purposes.

He had no idea what that meant, but it sounded bad. Now more than ever, Grayson needed a way to escape. But how?

KALENEK

K al stood behind Wilek's chair, watching a sailor move in the rigging above. The king had ordered a midday meal served at his round table on the stern deck. His rollchair had been secured, facing the back of the ship and the fleet. Wilek said this gave his father pride to see so many ships at their back, following his lead.

Though it was truly Admiral Vendal's lead.

Wilek sat on the king's right, sârahs Hrettah and Rashah on his left, and Miss Onika, as the king's new prophet, sat directly opposite. Sârs Janek and Trevn had been summoned, but neither had shown up.

Kal risked a glance at Onika then, stunned afresh by her beauty. She had, again, removed her straw hat, which was sitting on the table before her. The sun made her hair and skin look white and soft like freshly picked cotton, though the burns she had suffered from the sun over the past month had darkened her skin some and brought out several freckles on the bridge of her nose. The only one not eating, she sat with her hands in her lap, her glassy gaze focused on the center of the table. A bowl of pino melons sat there, but Kal knew she did not see them.

Her dune cat Rustian lay under her chair. Every so often his tail reached up, touched Onika's arm, then curled back down around his feet.

A shadow shifted, catching Kal's attention. The sailor had moved back to the mizzenmast and was climbing down. Good. Kal relaxed a bit until Harton's bark of laughter pulled his gaze to where he and the guards were blocking the stairs from the quarterdeck, talking with Onika's newly appointed honor

61

maidens, Tulay and Yoana. Kal glared at the group. No one took their jobs as seriously as he did his.

Yet few had failed so horribly, inspiring such hypervigilance.

Kal had only ever wanted to do his job well, but good intentions had never been enough. He had lost his men back in the Centenary War. He had lost his wife and child. And now he had lost young Grayson. His frantic search of *The Wanderer*, where he'd hoped to find the boy, had led only to the knowledge that Grayson had taken a job aboard another ship. Apparently several employers had come looking for able-bodied sailors. And while Grayson was truly only eight or nine years old, his being a root child had given him the body of a young man.

Six subsequent ships had been thoroughly searched, and three claimed never to have hired workers from *The Wanderer*. Wilek believed the captain of *The Wanderer* had lied about the ships he'd done business with, and further questioning of the crew and passengers revealed as much. Several remembered Grayson's dappled skin, but not one person could recall the name of the mystery ship, as if someone had erased it from their memories.

This convinced Wilek that the Magonians were to blame. While anchored in the Port of Odarka, they had learned from Prince Loran that Magonians had stolen the Sarikarian flagship *Vespara* and likely kidnapped King Jorger as well. But no sign of the *Vespara* had been found among the fleet. Wilek surmised they were somehow hiding themselves with magic. After all that Kal had seen of mantics in his day, he had no doubt it was possible.

"Come now, True Prophet," the king said, his voice winded and raspy. "Tell me what will be served for dessert."

"Miss Onika does not prophesy on demand, Father," Wilek said. Rosâr Echad had been told this over and over, yet he continued to ask Onika to perform parlor tricks like a jester.

"A child should obey her elders," the king said, rapping his ringed knuckles on the tabletop. "Should obey her king. Tell her so, Wilek. Tell her to obey me!"

When Rosâr Echad became angry these days, his sunken eyes reminded Kal of a shadir he'd seen during the war. He concentrated to keep his mind from drifting to that place as it was wont to do.

Onika chuckled. "Prophecy is a gift from Arman, Your Highness, not a way of fortune-telling."

The king growled. "Arman, Arman. He is all you talk about!"

"Where is Janek?" Wilek asked. "You did invite him, did you not?"

"Indeed I did," the king said. "He had better not spurn my goodwill after I pardoned him. I can understand his anger. Having been locked up for more than a fortnight would make anyone upset, but he has yet to meet Miss Onika. Normally an exotic woman like her would bring him running to have a look. Perhaps he isn't feeling well. Tell me something about Janek, prophetess. Why isn't he here? Is he ill?"

"Father, she does not prophesy on command."

"Yes, yes, so you've told me," the king said. "And where is Trevn?"

"Perhaps the messenger could not find him," Wilek said. "He does tend to wander."

"Always exploring." The king slammed his palms on the table. "Everyone rejects me. Even you, prophetess, ignored my summons last night."

"Arman allowed you to bring destruction upon yourselves once," Onika said. "Yet you test his patience a second time by sacrificing to other gods?"

The king's brow furrowed. "Test Arman? How have I done this?"

She turned her crystal gaze toward the king. "You killed a man in the name of Thalassa. This displeases Arman, who made all in his image. Never will I stand witness to such idolatry. Do not expect it of me."

Kal looked from face to face around the table, taking in each shocked reaction. All seemed to be waiting to see how the king would respond to such words.

He laughed, though it was not a joyful sound. "You are too outspoken for a woman of common blood. You set a poor example for my daughters. Had you not saved the lives of my people with your premonition of the Five Woes, I would have *you* sacrificed to Thalassa this very moment."

"Arman would never allow it," Onika said, looking back toward the bowl of melon. "He is my protector and has a plan for my life that does not end in death by your hand. You fool yourself in thinking you are the most powerful being in this world, but you are no more important than any other man, woman, or child."

The king slapped the table. "I am Rosâr Echad, ruler of Armania!"

"Yet still a human," she said. "Just like me."

"Enough abuse!" The king grasped the wheels of his rollchair, tried and failed to move himself, then gestured wildly to his attendants. "To my cabin. I have had my fill of this company. Summon Lady Zenobia and tell her to be ready to sing."

No one spoke as the attendants wheeled the king toward the hoist that had been assembled beside the stairs on the starboard side of the stern deck. Once the king was far enough away, Wilek broke the silence.

"Miss Onika, do take care in how you speak to my father. He is a dangerous man. To bait him is unwise."

"I spoke the truth and will always do so, Your Highness," Onika said. "I apologize if I brought offense, but I fear no man."

Kal marveled at how every time Onika spoke, she left people either speechless or furious.

"Kal," Wilek said, "I would like to walk the main deck with my sisters. Would you remain with Miss Onika and escort her to her cabin when she is finished here?"

"Of course, Your Highness," Kal said.

He stood silent as Wilek and the sârahs departed with Harton and the other guards. The servants cleared the dishes from the table. When they had gone, Kal spoke.

"Would you like to return to your cabin, Miss Onika?"

"If you don't mind, Sir Kalenek, I would like to sit here in the sun a while longer. I cannot see it, but the warmth helps me remember what it looks like. Does that sound strange?"

He moved around the table until he was standing beside her. "Not strange but sad."

Pink lips curved into a gentle smile. "Do not be sad for me. My life is filled with joy."

"But for Jhorn," Kal said, despair welling as he spoke the next name. "And Grayson."

A cruel rush of silence stretched between them. Gone went the gentle smile as Onika's expression became very serious.

"I promise you, Sir Kalenek Veroth, that you and I are not destined to have the same conversation over and over for as long as we shall be friends. It was Arman's plan that Grayson be parted from us. I have always known it. Jhorn had hoped to avoid it by keeping him with me, but one does not thwart Arman's will. Grayson and I shall be reunited again when the timing is perfect."

Her words did not remove Kal's guilt. "It's my fault he's gone."

She reached out to him. "Take my hand."

Kal took hold. Her hands were soft and a little clammy, but her gentle touch pleased him. He so rarely touched anyone without force.

"When it is time, Sir Kalenek, you will find Grayson and set him free. You will fulfill your calling as rescuer."

Warmth throbbed in his chest at the mesmeric sound of her voice. That had been a real prophecy, not just words of wisdom or warning. Still, the helplessness he felt at having lost Grayson warred with the knowledge of what her words implied. It couldn't be that easy. Nothing in life was that easy.

"Tell me a story, Sir Kalenek." She pulled their joined hands down to her lap, making Kal hunch awkwardly. He supposed she, as a blind woman, had no idea how bent over he was. He pulled close the chair on her right and carefully sat on its edge.

"What kind of story?"

"About you. Your first love."

He suddenly felt cornered and pulled his hand away. Why would she ask such a thing? Did she really expect him to answer? "I'd rather not."

Rustian came out from under the chair and rubbed his head against Onika's leg, purring. Onika sank her pale fingers into the dune cat's thick, golden fur. "I know the story of your marriage did not end happily, but I imagine that was not how it began."

Kal did not wish to discuss Livy with anyone, especially Onika. "Liviana was not my first love, Miss Onika." Frustrated, he added, "I am surprised you don't know that already."

She gave him a scolding frown. "I am not omniscient. I only know what Arman gives me when it is needed. And I am only seeking to know you better, Sir Kalenek. To talk as friends. Who was your first love, then, if not Miss Liviana?"

He sighed.

He shouldn't talk to Onika of such things, but with no one else around and that pretty face not looking away from his scars in horror, he supposed he could humor her some. Besides, he didn't have to name names. "She and I were children together in the castle. I trained in the practice yard with her brother—and her on occasion. She was older than me, and the mischief we found with each other was honestly her idea before it was mine."

"How much older?"

"A year and a half in age, but several in experience." He grinned at the memory. "I was not her first admirer. She had cultivated a reputation for her young self that was well on the way to being scandalous had her father not stepped in when he did and ordered her properly married."

"She was married off, but not to you," Onika said.

"I hated her father for it." And he'd hated the king even more so when, in the wake of Inolah's marriage, he had forced Kal to train as an assassin. The man had taken away all the light in Kal's life and cast him into darkness.

"How long after that sorrowful end did you meet your Liviana?" Onika asked.

"Eight years until I met her. We married a year later. And a year after that, I was sent to the war."

Onika reached out, feeling the air until her hand found his elbow. She ran her fingers up his arm and stopped on his shoulder, leaned close, and squeezed. "Thank you for sharing, Sir Kalenek. I suspect there are many more powerful stories in your past."

"That is likely true of everyone," Kal said, inhaling her sweet smell and hating himself for such an indulgence. He should not allow her to touch him. It would only make keeping his distance from her that much harder.

"Kalenek," a woman said from behind him.

Kal leaped from his chair and spun around, drawing his sword. Darlow—Mielle and Amala's nurse—stood there, arms folded, expression bent in fury. Kal's heart sank, despite its pounding. This had to be about Amala. He pushed his blade back into its sheath. "What has she done now?"

"She has not only modified another gown to have a lower neckline after I forbade her to do so, she accepted an invitation from a young man to explore the ship and has slipped away with him, unchaperoned. I cannot abide this! She will be ruined, and I refuse to take the blame."

"We all fall sometimes," Onika said. "Miss Amala will learn, in time, that every fall is an opportunity to stand."

Kal closed his eyes. Why couldn't Livy's sisters have been anything like her? Both Mielle and Amala were wild and determined to ignore his sound counsel. He opened his eyes and shouldered past Darlow, annoyed that Amala's disobedience had cost him time alone with Onika. "I will find her, Darlow. But first I must secure a guard for Miss Onika." He looked over the railing to the quarterdeck and spotted Novan Heln and two other guards talking with the pilot. "Heln!" he yelled, and the young man looked up. "Come and guard Miss Onika."

"Yes, sir."

Satisfied, Kal turned back to the women. "I am sorry to abandon you, Miss Onika. Master Heln is coming to take my place."

"How delightful! I look forward to speaking with him."

Kal bristled, remembering how well Onika and Novan had gotten along on their trip through Magonia. He headed for the stairs.

"We will talk again soon, Sir Kalenek," Onika called after him.

He twisted to look back. Onika was standing and had put on her straw hat. Her honor maidens joined her now, and Rustian, who wound his way between her feet and wrapped himself against her leg.

"I look forward to it, Miss Onika."

She smiled then, showing her teeth. The sun glinted in her eyes and he thought her the most beautiful creature to ever exist.

The thought sent him down the stairs in a hurry. *Livy* had been the most beautiful creature to ever exist. His wife. His precious wife who had died. And besides, none of this mattered. Onika was the True Prophet. She could not be courted like an average woman. Two such as them did not belong together, and Kal would not pretend the possibility existed when he knew better.

He bumped into someone. A man standing by the rail. "Excuse me." He stepped around the man and realized he had walked the entire quarterdeck without even realizing it. Time to find Amala, and quickly.

He combed the main deck, then up to the forecastle. He found them by the anchor. His face burned at the sight of his younger ward. The gods had blessed the girl with a woman's body at far too young an age. Her gown was too tight and low-cut for a young woman, let alone a girl of thirteen. Kal recognized the young soldier she was with as some minor noble's son. Gedry, Gefrey? Something like that. He served as a backman to the shield of one of the young princesses.

"Amala, there you are," Kal said. "I've been looking for you."

She smiled at him, but he caught the flash of annoyance in her eyes. She grabbed Gebly's arm and leaned against him. "Ulmer, have you met Sir Kalenek Veroth, my warden?"

Sands, she was calling the boy by his first name already?

The backman had the decency to straighten his posture and bow his head in respect. "Not officially, no. Good midday to you, sir. It's an honor."

"Your name?" Kal said.

"Ulmer Gelsly, sir. Miss Amala talks about you constantly."

"I doubt that very much."

"Kal, don't be rude. He's like that sometimes," she told Gelsly. "It's because of his scars. People stare so much it's made him a perpetual grouch."

Rage gripped Kal in such a familiar fury he had to fight to keep himself from flashing back to the war. Gelsly had the decency to look away from his face.

Kal gritted his teeth until he had found enough control to keep his voice even. "Forgive us, Master Gelsly, but we are needed elsewhere at present." Kal extended his arm to Amala. "Shall we?"

"I want to stay here with Ulmer."

"You will go when you are told, young lady, or suffer consequences you will not enjoy."

Amala took hold of Kal's arm, squeezing until her fingernails bit through his sleeve and into his skin. "Good midday, Ulmer."

The boy inclined his head. "Good midday, Miss Amala, Sir Kalenek."

Kal dragged her away. They'd barely made it down to the main deck before she started in.

"I have never been so humiliated!"

"Then you should wear a dress that covers your charms rather than flaunts them."

She gasped. "Now you insult me? Do you really hate me so much?"

"Just enough to save your reputation."

"My reputation was not in danger."

"Your reputation—" People were looking at them. He aimed toward the doors inside and lowered his voice. "Keep this up and your reputation will be ruined. You are thirteen. You are not supposed to be dressed like a woman for another year and a half. Nor are you supposed to go on unchaperoned outings with young men, ever. Not even grown, responsible young ladies do that."

"Mielle does. She goes wherever she likes with the sâr. And he will marry her and make her a princess and what will I be?"

He pulled her inside and the darkness blinded him. He stopped, on high alert as he waited for his eyes to adjust.

Amala jerked away from him, folded her arms. "I hate you," she muttered.

If she kept this up, it wouldn't be long before the feeling became mutual. He took hold of her arm again and pulled her with him down the lengthway.

"You don't understand how I feel and you don't care," she said, her voice quiet.

He breathed in deeply through his nose. "I have always cared about you."

"Mielle has the sâr. You have the prophetess. I want someone to love me too."

Kal stopped walking and stared at the girl, shocked. "I do not have a romantic attachment to Miss Onika."

A roll of the eyes. "I'm not as stupid as you think I am. I see how you stare at her. Everyone knows you love her."

Kal growled, anger climbing within him. He wanted to deny it, to shake Amala and tell her to stop such rumors now, but he simply gripped the girl's arm, his hand trembling as his pride crumbled, leaving him exposed and far too vulnerable.

Amala's countenance softened. "Kal, I saw people dying in the streets in Everton. Drowning in the sea. Killing each other. And now we ride on boats to some mysterious island that likely doesn't even exist. I know we are all going to die. So I intend to enjoy what time I have left. I intend to be happy. And I won't let you make me a prisoner."

His memory flashed to Livy, dead in their bed. He had ordered her to stay home when she'd wanted to go to Everton and wait out the rest of her pregnancy with friends. He'd thought it too dangerous for her to travel during a war. He had made his wife a prisoner, and it had killed her and their child. "Very well, Amala," he said, defeated. "But we do this my way."

TREVN

Trevn sat with Admiral Hanray Vendal on the man's balcony, watching the ships follow in the *Seffynaw*'s wake. Over the past few days the admiral had lectured on many important subjects: inter-ship communications, diplomacy between realms, negotiation tactics, and potential hazards at sea. The organization of the fleet would be Trevn's final lesson from the admiral for a while, as today—at Trevn's request—he would be put on a watch to work as a sailor.

"Convoys fall into two categories," the admiral said. "Those created for military missions and those that routinely escort merchant vessels. Our convoy consists of three columns with two squadrons of warships on each side, running a zigzag course."

"Similar to a flank guard?" Trevn asked.

"Exactly like that. Though I set the course, the *Berith* galley warship sails ahead of the *Seffynaw*."

"Like a scout?"

"More like an advance guard. She's there to protect us from surprise and to give aid should we be attacked. I also have three armed merchant ships following in back of the fleet as bait for any who might attack from the rear. And before you ask, yes, they act as a rearguard."

"Because of the pirates?"

"That's part of it," the admiral said. "But it's always best to prepare for the worst. Pontiff Rogedoth might be a real threat to our fleet, as might the Magonians who commandeered the *Vespara*. And even with all our precautions, a small ship could easily slip between the flank warships and overpower some of the smaller vessels. We push for the island and, if need be, will chart our next course from there."

"Vendal? You in here?" a man's voice called.

"Ah, here is Captain Livina," the admiral said, standing. "I was nearly finished anyway. If you have no further questions, Your Highness, let's get you set on a watch. If you're certain that's what you want?"

"I am." Trevn rose and followed the admiral inside.

Captain Aldair Livina had bent over the admiral's table, examining the charts that had been anchored there with pins. The thin man of average height with a graying, mossy beard glanced up, bowed quickly to Trevn, and resumed his investigation of the chart. "You think this a faster route than the one I gave you, Hanray?"

The admiral stopped beside the captain. He was taller and thicker than Livina, which made the older man look almost frail. "From what I know of northern currents, yes," the admiral said. "If you remembered your coordinates correctly, I believe we can reach the island in ten days, even at our slower speed."

Livina grunted, pacified it seemed, since he stepped away from the chart table and regarded Trevn. "Sâr Trevn, how goes the apprenticeship?"

"Very well. I have learned much from Admiral Vendal."

"But you'd like a chance to climb the mast, is that it?"

Trevn chuckled. "I admit, I am looking forward to it."

"Forgive my bluntness, Highness," Livina said. "You've been sailing plenty in your life. You know what kind of ship this is. You know the names for everything and most of the maneuvers. You've even steered by tiller and whipstaff. So why play the hard role of seaman when you can sit here with the admiral each day in this fine cabin and learn navigation?"

Everyone expected a sâr to care only for his own pleasure, but the Five Woes and Trevn's own brush with death had shown him that living for himself would not help the realm of Armania survive this catastrophe.

"Captain Livina, while lectures and reading are an invaluable tool in educating a man, I have found hands-on experience enhances comprehension. I want to understand every part of this ship, from your duties all the way down to that of ship's boy. Once we reach Bakurah Island, Sâr Wilek will send explorers to look for more land. I intend to be on that expedition."

"Then you shall, of course," the admiral said. "It is our duty to serve the throne in any way we can, isn't that right, Captain?"

Livina shrugged. "Suit yourself, Highness. But it's terrible hard work. You might not like it."

Trevn's face burned, but he reminded himself that he had earned his reputation as the firebrand of Castle Everton. "If I fail, I will find some other way to aid my brother in his role as Heir. But I assure you, Captain, I will not fail."

Another grunt. "You'll join the Starboard Watch under Norgam Bussie, my second mate, and report to his master's mate, Nietz. Start by shadowing Rzasa, one of the apprentice sailors. And since Sâr Wilek took young Ottee to be your servant, the boy can apprise you of his former duties as ship's boy."

It would do to start, but Trevn would not be satisfied with so limited a view. "I will also require the opportunity to learn from the carpenter, the caulker, the cooper, the scrivener, the steward, the cook, the physician, the diver, the navigator, the pilot, and the mates. Admiral Vendal, I'm sure, will have more to teach me in the future, as will you, Captain. I don't mind starting at the bottom, so long as nothing is omitted from my training. I also bring Sir Cadoc, my shield, with me, which adds another man to the Starboard Watch."

Captain Livina folded his arms. "If it's work you want, it's work I'll give you, but understand this: As apprentices under my command, you and your man work for me. That means giving up your authority over me where matters of sailing are concerned. You're part of my crew. What I say goes. There'll be no talking back. Understand that?"

"Yes, sir," Trevn said, bristling under the man's authoritative tone.

The captain grunted. "Sailors are working men. Coarse, rude, and rough. Some'll shock you, and they'll do it more if they see they can get a rise out of you. They'll call you names, to your face and behind your back. They'll hate your soft hands, which won't stay soft for long if you truly work hard. You face a hard battle of them accepting you, prince that you are. And I advise against you letting your father or brother or shield fight your battles for you. That will only make the men hate you more."

"He's a sâr, Captain Livina," the admiral said. "No one would dare hurt him."

"I am not afraid of any man," Trevn said, then grinned. "You assume they will all hate me, Captain. I intend to prove you wrong."

✦   ✦   ✦

And that was how Trevn found himself with Rzasa, the young apprentice assigned to the Starboard Watch. A brown-skinned Blackpool boy with a thick accent, Rzasa wore a faded jacket the color of green olives, tattered gray trousers rolled up to his knee, and red socks pulled up just as high. He wore no boots. Just the socks on his feet. When Trevn asked why, Rzasa shrugged and said his feet chilled easily. He was no older than Trevn, but the wistful deepness of his dark brown eyes gave the impression that he had seen enough trials to last a hundred years.

"Apprentices are just young sailors without much experience," Rzasa said, limping on his right leg as they made their way across the main deck. "We do what most sailors do. Wash and sand the decks, paint, make repairs, check ropes and sails, replace or mend bad ones. We also move sails, furl or unfurl 'em. Man the pumps. Lower and raise anchor. And if we're boarded, we pick up a sword and fight to defend the ship."

"I can do that much," Cadoc said, glowering. He had worked hard to obtain his honorable position as High Shield and disliked being forced to apprentice as a sailor.

"Rzasa!" Nietz called down over the quarterdeck rail. The master's mate was short, exceedingly strong, wore bronze rings in both ears, and had a blue scarf tied over his head that matched his master's half-cloak. His nose had once been split down the middle and now twisted a bit to one side. "That hawser is dry. The three of you coil it and store it in the locker." He turned his back on them, and Trevn couldn't help but think it was as broad as a shield.

Rzasa led Trevn and Cadoc single file toward the foredeck along the chalk path. "Only ship's boys are ranked lower than apprentices," he said, "so everyone else can give us orders. But we're not slaves. So don't let the other sailors trick you into personal services. Most of the officers are fair, but watch out for Shinn. He's master's mate on the Port Watch and a mean one. If he comes after you, grit your teeth and take it. The less you say, the less you'll get from him. Usually."

"What about Nietz?" Trevn asked.

"His bark is fierce, but he's a good-natured fellow. Likes to sing songs about wave women when he drinks too much."

The three worked together to coil the thick rope into the hawser locker. They'd barely stored half the line when Trevn's breath started to heave. His trousers pinched his thighs when he crouched and his sleeves did the same to his arms when he bent them. He shouldn't be surprised that fine clothing was ill suited for work as a sailor.

A distant voice from above pulled Trevn's gaze skyward. A man in the crosstrees quickly vanished behind the fore topsail. "When do we climb the masts?" he asked.

"We have to climb up there?" Cadoc asked, squinting into the sails.

"Soon as you can," Rzasa said. "Climbing the mainmast is what terrifies most first-timers, but you're not really one of us till you do."

Trevn couldn't wait.

"Sâr Trevn? What in the Eversea are you doing?"

Trevn straightened at the familiar voice. Fonu Edekk, his brother Janek's close friend, walked toward him with Trevn's half brother Kamran DanSâr and some grizzled commoner.

"Learning to sail," Trevn said, continuing to feed the line to Rzasa. The sun cast the three newcomers' shadows over the hawser as they stopped behind Trevn. "I plan to join the expedition for new land."

"Honestly, Trevn, you'll catch sun sickness if you keep this up," said Kamran. "It's madness for a sâr to work so hard."

"Thank you for your concern, but I disagree."

"It's the sâr's choice," the commoner said, lumbering toward them with an assertive bearing. He had skin the green-gray color of rotten spinach and wore a blue thick wool hat with a rolling brim. He squinted one tawny eye at Rzasa while the other looked crookedly away. "Some passengers are complaining of a stench on the starboard side of the aft hold, Rzasa," the man said. "No doubt they've helped themselves to the cargo and made a mess of it. Leave the hawser to the shield and take Princey to the hold. Find the broken barrel, and clean it up."

"Yes, Master Shinn," Rzasa said.

Master? It was then that Trevn noticed the blue master's half-cloak thrown back over the man's shoulders like a scarf. So this was the foreboding Shinn.

"Look alive, sailors!" The man glared at Trevn and strode away.

"You heard the man," Kamran said to Trevn. "Look alive, Princey." And he and Fonu followed Shinn, chuckling.

"I don't like being separated from you," Cadoc said.

"We talked about this," Trevn reminded Cadoc. "I'll be fine. You keep an eye on those two. Find out why they're so friendly with Master Shinn." Trevn walked with Rzasa toward the companionway.

When they reached the cargo hold, the putrid stench reminded Trevn of the Blackwater Canal in Everton, which had carried wastewater through the city. "Stinks like Gâzar's garden."

"You would know," Rzasa said, grinning as he entered the cargo hold. "Shinn haunts my dreams. Everyone's afraid of him. Even the cap'n. They say he lost both his eyes to pirates and his good one come from a sand cat."

Trevn laughed at this, but Rzasa's somber demeanor sucked away all the fun. "Is he sick? His skin looked strange."

"Scablands Blight, he says." Rzasa turned back and whispered, "Watch out for his brother Zaki. He's without a tongue and half a wit—crazier than Shinn. Wears a red handkerchief tied round his arm to keep him from killing."

"Killing who?"

"Everyone. He's a murderer. Killed hundreds. Only the red handkerchief keeps him tame."

Trevn doubted very much that his father's ship would employ murderers.

They had just located the broken barrel when Ottee, Trevn's new onesent, found them. The slight boy had black skin, brown eyes, a head full of soft, curly hair, and a missing pinky finger on his left hand.

"I've finished every task you gave me, Sâr Trevn," he said, panting as if he'd done every task while running. "What stinks?"

"Broken barrel," Rzasa said. "Grab those buckets and help us clean it up."

The barrel, which had been filled with salted whitefish, had toppled off the end and cracked. Most of the fish were now spoiled. They scooped up the mess with the buckets and hauled it to the main deck, where they dumped it into the sea.

Halfway through the job, the bells tolled for the start of the evening one watch, but Rzasa said they must finish. Once they did, they went up to the deck to report. As it was a new watch, they found the first mate, Quen, manning the whip, Cadoc loitering beside him. Rzasa gave Quen his report of the spill, and Quen dismissed them.

"Just like that we're off duty?" Trevn asked as they walked away.

"Unless you want to climb the mainmast," Rzasa said.

"No thank you," Cadoc said.

But Trevn did, even with his entire body sore from work. "It's got to be the mainmast?"

"Yep," Rzasa said. "Best if you go it alone your first time. You can take the mast or the ratlines."

Trevn peered up to the mainmast. There wasn't much to hold on to but some stays that ran up the sides and a yard at the top of each section. He glanced to the ratlines, which began at the outer railings. "How far up?"

"All the way to the masthead," Ottee said. "There's something written there, and you gotta tell the cap'n what it says to prove you done the climb. If you're going to climb the rigging, always go on the windward side so you don't get blown off into the water."

"That's good sense," Trevn said.

"Which way you going?" Rzasa asked.

"Ratlines." Trevn took the stairs to the main deck and wove through the pockets of people clogging up his path to the ratlines on the windward side of the ship. A sailor coiling rope saw him coming and paused to watch. The dull buzz of conversation from the commoners eased off as they too fixed their gazes on the Third Arm of Armania.

The rigging rose in sets, each reaching to a different height on the mainmast. Trevn stepped toward the middle set, which stretched all the way to the top. He grabbed the shroud just above the deadeye and leapt up on the rail, swinging himself around and placing one foot on the ratlines. Instantly he could feel the tilt of the ship and how the wind pushed his weight into the rigging. Always climb on the windward side. *Thanks, Ottee.*

The ratlines gave surprisingly little slack as he pulled himself up from one to the next. He moved quickly, knowing he had an audience to impress. He climbed through the lubber's hole at the maintop platform and up, up, up until the ratlines ended at the topsail yard. There he took hold of the rigging farthest out so he could keep his body close to the mast, then climbed up to the crosstrees. The roll of the ship felt even more pronounced now. How much harder might this be in a storm?

Still he climbed, hand over hand. There was no longer any purchase for his boots, and he realized now why sailors went barefoot in the rigging. Tomorrow he'd leave his boots in his cabin.

He scrambled easily onto the lookout platform. The raven cage was attached to the side, and one of the birds watched him. The wind this high up chilled the sweat on his arms, making him shiver. The ship dipped and rose in the slow pitch of the sea, a constant rolling. At this height Trevn felt like a bee perched on a swaying flower.

He had only a little ways to go, so he wrapped his hands in the rigging and climbed to the top, where he hooked one arm around the masthead so he wouldn't slip, and took in the view. He could see for leagues on all sides. He marveled at the size of the fleet. Hundreds of ships carrying the survivors of the Five Realms. Beyond, the vastness of the Eversea made this ship seem small, even after so great a climb.

He glanced down to the tiny faces below. Ottee whooped and waved, jumping up and down as if Trevn had been his champion on the tournament field. Rzasa and Cadoc stood with him. Master Quen was still at the helm, Nietz beside him.

At the quarterdeck rail overlooking the main deck, Trevn caught sight of a woman in a familiar red-and-yellow dress on the arm of a man. He squinted, his pulse suddenly throbbing in his chest. It was Mielle. She was looking up at him, holding on to the arm of Kamran DanSâr!

That Miss Amala held Kamran's other arm did not faze Trevn. The memory of Mielle dancing with Kamran at Rosârah Brelenah's court back in Everton obliterated all caution. He needed to be on the deck, as soon as possible.

Trevn shimmied back down to the lookout platform. He had spent years watching sailors slide down the backstays. He not only felt he could do it, he was sure that doing so would impress Mielle and the watch. He wasn't wearing gloves, so he removed the handkerchief from his pocket and tied it around his palm. He grabbed hold of the stay through the handkerchief and hooked his opposite knee around it as well, then jumped off.

He shot down the slick rope, realizing too late that the backstay had been recently coated in tar. He wrapped his other arm around the stay at his elbow and hooked both ankles as well. He was already gaining speed. He squeezed with his hand, hoping to slow himself, but the heat burned right through the handkerchief. Two-thirds of the way down, when he conceded that his firebrand ways had finally killed him, he set his boots against one another at an angle and felt himself slow as his soles scraped back the tar. This helped, and he slammed feet-first against the quarterdeck, just managing to stick the landing in a low squat.

Ottee raced toward him, cheering. "Down the backstays, whoopee!"

"Well, ain't you the skylark?" Rzasa said.

Nietz grunted. "The sâr has a death wish the gods almost granted."

"Indeed," Master Quen said.

"Trevn!" From his left a creature clad in red-and-yellow silk tackled him. Mielle felt solid in his arms and smelled like flowers. She squeezed from him what little breath remained, then let go and punched his arm. "What were you thinking jumping off the lookout tower?"

Trevn caught sight of Kamran and Miss Amala still standing by the inner rail. "I saw you with Kamran."

"Oh tuhsh, Trevn." She rolled her eyes, but he could tell from the twist of her lips that she was pleased. "You saw me chaperoning my foolish sister with a man twice her age, a pair that, unfortunately, I must return to immediately." She kissed Trevn's cheek and strode away.

"A fine show of bravery, Sâr Trevn, and a decent first climb. You see the mark at the top of the masthead?"

At the sound of Captain Livina's voice, Trevn regarded the man, who was standing at the port rail. He gaped, abashed. He'd been so taken by the view, then jealous seeing Mielle with Kamran . . . "No, sir. I forgot to look."

"It's a mighty nice view up there, sailor," the captain said, "but when I send a man into the rigging with a job to do, he'd better not forget to do it. You could have killed yourself wearing boots in the rigging, and you scraped half the tar off that stay coming down, so you'll be the one to re-tar it next watch. Ottee, show the *skylark* where the tar is kept."

"Yes, sir," Ottee said, dragging Trevn away by the arm.

Rzasa limped up to join them. "There's to be dancing on the lower deck tonight," he said. "You could come during the first watch. There'll be women there. You probably got better things to do, though, being a prince and all."

See there, Captain? Rzasa had accepted him already. "I thank you for the invitation, Rzasa. I shall come, and bring a woman of my own."

Rzasa grinned broadly. "You mean Miss Mielle, don't you? Everybody says you're going to marry her."

Such a comment startled Trevn. "Do they?"

"I've heard that too," Ottee said.

Trevn didn't know what to make of this revelation, so he dodged the serious topic with a joke. "Master Mielle Allard . . . I suppose it has a nice sound to it."

✦ ✦ ✦

That evening, Mielle on his arm, Trevn arrived in the sailors' berth on the lower deck charged with excitement. Lanterns hung swinging from the deck head on the perimeter walls. In the middle a group was dancing, the taller men hunched slightly to keep from hitting their heads. Trevn led Mielle to dance straightaway, and they quickly became the center of attention. The crowd cheered them on, and they danced until they could no longer stand. Rzasa found them and led the way to the opposite end of the berth and to a circle of sea chests.

"Sit on my trunk," he said. "There's room for both."

So Trevn and Mielle sat. Cadoc stood beside them, surveying the crowd with narrowed eyes.

The sailors were playing a dice game that Rzasa called Throw. Trevn took advantage of their diverted states to examine them fully. They were all of them greasy-haired, rough-skinned, and scarred. Of those he had met, Nietz had two crooked fingers to match his crooked nose. Skooley had a thick scar from nose to jaw that formed a hairless part in his beard. Bonds had the familiar kink of a broken nose as well as a gouge of pale skin along one temple. Rzasa had the limp, of course, and Ottee the missing finger. Shinn the glass eye and blight. And his brother Zaki added a once-broken nose to his severed tongue. Sailing, it seemed, was a dangerous job.

Trevn soon caught on to the game of Throw and asked to play.

"It's a betting game, Princey," Shinn said, "but only for what you have on you or can fetch this moment from your trunk. We don't take pay-you-laters on the lower deck."

Nothing in the pile on the floor in the center of the circle tempted Trevn in the least. Shabby coats, worn boots, dull knives, an assortment of bronze or ivory buttons, and a handful of coins. Yet these were treasures to these men. All that most of them had in the world.

"You shouldn't gamble, Trevn," Mielle said. "It's against Captain's rules, or so Kal told me."

"Captain don't bother us with any of that, lady," Shinn said. "He trusts his mates to keep order. Besides, I wouldn't mind the chance to win myself a night with you if Princey here is willing to play."

Mielle squeezed Trevn's arm, and an instant of despair flashed through him. "The lady is not mine to gamble, Master Shinn. And I'll thank you to watch your manners where she is—"

"If she's not yours, I claim her," Shinn said, leering at Mielle.

She stood, hands on her hips and glaring at the man, which only made his grin broaden. "No one lays claim to me, Master Shinn. To the rest of you, good night. I have had enough of such company. Until tomorrow, Sâr Trevn." She stamped through the center of their circle and left.

"Cadoc," Trevn said, nodding toward Mielle. "See that she makes it safely to her cabin."

"I should not leave you here alone," Cadoc said.

"I'll be fine. Quickly, now. Miss Mielle is more important at present."

His shield growled but trudged after Mielle.

Trevn went back to the negotiations. "The lady is gone, Master Shinn, thanks to your rudeness. But I'm in." He pushed his hands into his pockets and withdrew his grow lens, a charcoal pencil, and a square of folded blank parchment. He leaned forward and dropped his items into the center pile.

Bonds snatched up the grow lens and held it to his eye. "This is a fine piece."

"It's all right," Trevn said. "I have another one."

"Princey has plenty to share," Shinn said. "So let's play."

"New man throws first," said Nietz, passing Trevn the dice.

"Pick your main number, Princey," Shinn said.

"Seven," Trevn said, knowing it was the most common. He rolled, and the dice clattered on the wood deck. Two threes. "Six," he said.

"That's your chance number," Nietz said. "Now roll again."

Rzasa caught up the dice and passed them to Trevn, who this time rolled a nine.

"Roll till you get your chance number and win," Nietz said, "or till you get your main number and lose."

One *lost* on the main? Trevn shouldn't have chosen a seven, then. Despite that fact, three more rolls produced an eight, ten, and finally a six.

"You win," Rzasa said. "Take something back from the pot. It don't have to be yours."

Trevn reached out to Bonds, who was still holding his grow lens. "I'll take that, thanks."

Bonds handed it over, and the roll passed to Nietz.

Trying to purposely lose a game of chance might prove difficult. Since Trevn had chosen poorly with a seven as his main and won, he feigned a gullible superstition and stuck with the number each round. Eventually he began to lose. Whenever someone lost, Shinn, as "the house," claimed one of the loser's items from the pot. When the dice next came to Trevn, Shinn had claimed all his things.

"So I'm out, yes?" Trevn asked, looking from face to face.

"Can be," said Nietz. "Or if you want to keep playing, you can put in something else or take a loan from the house."

Trevn noted Shinn's crooked grin. He would be a fool to put himself in this man's debt. "But you don't take pay-you-laters."

"A loan is different," Shinn said. "You borrow from me, and I give you the goods to pay in now. Then you owe me interest."

"Which is what?" Trevn asked.

He nodded to Trevn's right hand. "That's a fine ring."

Trevn scoffed. "I will not gamble my signet ring."

"Your clothes, then," the man said. "We're about the same size."

"The sâr is two hands taller than you," Nietz said.

"I can hem sleeves and trousers," Shinn said. "It's the width that matters, and there we're akin."

"If I put my clothes in the pot, I'll have nothing to wear," Trevn said. "I see no other players here wearing only a smile."

The men chuckled.

"Keep your clothes for now," Shinn said. "If you win back your belongings twice, you can give *them* to me as interest and keep your clothes. But if you lose, it's all mine."

"You don't have to," Rzasa whispered, with a furtive glance at Shinn.

"I know." But Shinn had irritated him from the start with his rudeness to Mielle. Trevn wanted to make the man regret it. "I'll take your loan, Master Shinn."

And this time Trevn played to win, choosing mains that were less probable. He won four passes in a row, then lost two. Won three, lost three. Every time the dice came his way, the eagerness grew. Anxious to beat Shinn, Trevn craved the chance to get ahead again and again, to win six rounds.

Until he lost six.

Zaki chortled and put his arm around his brother, hugging him to his side.

"I'll take my interest now," Shinn said.

Trevn's face tingled. It had happened so fast. He couldn't believe how quickly he'd gone from being ahead to losing it all, but he made an effort to stand and keep his posture strait, his chin high, and compose an expression of manly dignity.

He undressed as fast as he could without trying to look like he was hurrying. He removed his belt, tunic, and undershirt, tossing them into the pile, then kicked off his boots.

Shinn rushed forward and began picking up his discarded clothes. The moment he lifted a boot, Trevn stopped him.

"Not my boots. Our agreement was for my clothes."

Shinn's evil eye fixed upon Trevn. "I meant your boots too."

"You did not mention them in your initial request."

"That's true, Shinn," Nietz said.

Shinn glared, his gaze sweeping over the circle of men. He finally shrugged. "Keep your boots, then, Princey, but I'll take the rest."

Of course he would. Trevn took off his trousers, and while he was crouched, pulled back on his boots. Then he stood and pitched the wadded trousers at Shinn, who scrambled to catch them.

"This was fun," Trevn said cheerily as he walked out of the circle toward the stern bulkhead. "But I think it's time for me to go. Ottee, find Sir Cadoc and tell him I retired to my cabin for the night."

✦ ✦ ✦

"Gambling away your clothing, Trevn?" Wilek said the next morning. "I am not your mother, but I am tempted to scold you soundly for such foolishness."

"I as well," Cadoc said.

"Scold me if you must. But I tell you I suffered enough on the walk to my cabin."

At this Wilek cracked a smile, inducing one from Cadoc.

"It was incredible!" Ottee said from Trevn's side. "He stripped down like he cared naught what anyone saw of him and marched off as if we'd all bored him to tears."

Trevn glanced down at his onesent. "I am glad you found the situation entertaining, boy, but I was humiliated. I heard them laughing."

"Sounds like you deserved it," Wilek said.

"Oh, it was funny, to be sure," Ottee told Wilek, "but it was ever more grand to see him treat Shinn's great triumph over him as if it was nothing." He turned his eager expression on Trevn. "He'll hate you forever, I suspect, but the men will think it the greatest joke."

Distant ringing sent Trevn to the door. "That's the change of the watch, Wil. We've got to go."

"You've yet to tell me anything you've learned!" Wilek said.

"Very well. Most of the sailors don't believe Bakurah Island is real. They think we're sailing into the unknown. That rumor, Mielle tells me, has spread among the commoners, as has word of the pirates. The people are afraid."

"The island is real, but so are the pirates," Wilek said. "We've received word of two more stolen fishing vessels with witnesses left behind to implicate a ship called the *Taradok*. The Duke of Highcliff believes she belongs to Zahara Khal."

"Any relation to Randmuir Khal of the Omatta?" Trevn asked.

Wilek grimaced. "His daughter."

Thoughts spun in Trevn's mind as he sought out a connection. "Perhaps she got word of what happened to her grandmother?" Ottee peeked in the doorway, reminding Trevn of the hour. "That is all the talk I've heard, brother. Now I really must go."

"Do try and behave yourself," Wilek said. "Your reputation has no place to go but up."

Trevn and Ottee made their way to the quarterdeck as quickly as possible and found Nietz waiting. And grinning.

"Perfect timing, Ottee!" Nietz said. "Someone got sick on the main deck. You and Boots go clean it up."

The nickname drew Trevn's gaze to Nietz, who was smirking at him. "Get to it, then!"

"Told you," Ottee said to Trevn as they fetched empty buckets. "Good nicknames only come to sailors who are liked."

Trevn couldn't argue with that.

✦ ✦ ✦

Over the next week Trevn became Boots as he worked as a sailor. He much preferred tasks on deck, especially in the rigging, though when Shinn was around—always wearing the clothes he'd won off Trevn—the man seemed determined to keep Trevn below deck.

As Ottee's shadow Trevn learned to clean the massive stew pots in the sailors' galley, empty the privy buckets in the officers' cabins, scrub the decks, feed the chickens and pigs kept in pens on the quarterdeck, splice line, pick oakum, sew canvas, tie a host of knots, ring the bell at the watch change, trap and kill rats, and fetch things for the sailors.

Some of the chores overlapped in Rzasa's position as apprentice, but here Trevn got to climb in the rigging and work the sails. His favorite role was acting as lookout. He'd always loved climbing, and the top of the mainmast had supplanted the red-and-brown striped roof of Thalassa's Temple as Trevn's favorite place to think. The word carved atop it was *Wansea*, the name of Captain Livina's first wife.

In both roles Trevn learned to call his superiors *sir*, which might have been the most difficult lesson of all.

One dawn watch Trevn sat on the quarterdeck with Rzasa and Ottee, picking oakum. This involved meticulously pulling apart fragments of old, discarded rope. The oakum would eventually be mixed with tar and used to seal planks in the ship. The work was so monotonous Trevn's eyes had started to cross.

The sharp fibers of hemp sliced, pricked, and slivered into his hands, which were dry already from so much salt water.

"Hey, Boots," Nietz called. "Get aloft to the main topgallant yard and check the reef lines. All the pull is going straight back when it should aim up diagonally into the body of the sail."

"Yes, sir!" Trevn tossed his chunk of rope back into the pile, eager to climb.

The sun had risen by now, and the sky was bright and clear. He scurried up the windward side of the ratlines to the maintop, through the lubber's hole in the platform, and up even higher to the main topgallant yard. There he saw that someone had tied the clew reef line wrong. He fixed it, then continued up to the lookout, staring out across the wide expanse of blue. A bird, white as snow, soared overhead, and as he turned to follow its flight his gaze caught a crest of green and brown in the distance.

"Land." It really was. "Land!" he yelled down. "Land to port beam!" He wasn't the only one to have seen it. Signal flags were waving high on three of the nearest ships.

They had reached Bakurah Island. A few days before schedule, as the admiral had predicted. Trevn pulled out his grow lens and studied the shoreline. It didn't seem to have much more than a sloping elevation. There were no cliffs or cracks that he could see, no river holes, no distant mountains. The strangeness of that and the multitude of trees set him on guard. From what he knew of land, this didn't look large enough to support the passengers of some six hundred boats. Trevn squinted into the distance but saw no other islands from this vantage point. Beneath the ship, the water was so clear that he could see a massive coral reef with colorful fish darting about.

No reason to stay up here now. He shimmied back down the lines, wanting to find Mielle and tell her the news, eager to find a way to shore and explore.

WILEK

Wilek sat at the desk in his father's office, the Book of Arman before him. Kal and Harton were the only other people in the room. Harton stood beside the door, Kal beside the desk. Wilek pushed the tome to the end of the desk and tapped the stack of pages with his finger. "According to the words of this book, I, my brothers, our father . . . we should not be surprised that the Five Realms fell apart. We poisoned it with our blasphemy of He Who Made the World."

Kal glared down on the stack of parchment as if it might bite him. "How can you be certain anything written by men is true?"

"This book was written by prophets of Arman," Wilek said.

Kal scoffed. "So they claimed to be. Are their accounts backed by witnesses?"

Wilek didn't know or care. "The words feel true, Kal." He nudged the pages closer to his shield. "Read it for yourself."

Kal folded his arms. "Is that an order, Your Highness?"

The man's hostile reluctance surprised Wilek. "Of course not."

"Then I have no desire for deeper knowledge about any of the gods. They have forsaken me time and again."

Kal had experienced great losses. "You must wonder over the point of life."

"I wonder more over the point of death and suffering. What answers did this tome have in regard to that?"

Wilek knew, but he doubted the answer would appease Kal. "Rurek turned his back on Arman's protection when he left the Father's realm to see for himself what the world held. In doing so, he entered Gâzar's realm, where death and suffering abound."

"Rurek had good reason to leave," Kal said. "If Arman would have given him more answers, his son would have known what dangers lay outside his realm. By keeping his secrets, he forced his son to become a killer."

"The god of war didn't do too badly for himself," Harton said, closing in from the door. "Became a deity and got a whole realm named after him."

"So the story says," Kal said. "It's only a story. You both know that, right?"

"Rurek is one of my five," Harton said, referring to the five gods a Rôb believer chose to worship. The young man was Rurekan, so his allegiance wasn't surprising.

Wilek, however . . . his entire belief system had been shaken. "I used to think so, Kal, but now I'm not so certain."

Kal growled in frustration. "You killed Barthos. You know the gods are false."

"I know Barthos is false," Wilek said. "Arman has proved otherwise to me."

"Coincidences," Kal said, turning away to look out the window. "So will you worship Rurek too? And what of his brother Sarik and their mother Tenma? Why not the whole family?"

Wilek shook his head. "This book says nothing of the others being deities. Only Arman. We humans have twisted the truth of this book into wild stories."

Kal merely scowled, and his scars made him look much older than his thirty-one years.

Wilek wanted to talk to Kal alone. "Harton, run and ask Captain Veralla if he has received any new reports on the pirates this morning. Also ask if he has located Teaka's newt. That Teaka's killer could use the creature to find even more evenroot disturbs me."

"Yes, sir." Harton shuffled to the door. "I wouldn't believe that account of Rurek, Your Highness. He is a powerful god."

Not according to the Book of Arman, but Wilek had no desire to debate his backman at present. He bound the book with twine and waited until the door shut behind Harton, then asked Kal, "Does Miss Onika know of this book, I wonder?"

The man still stood looking out the window. "I know not."

"Well, you must ask her. Perhaps she can shine greater meaning on the words of this text." He laid his hand on the pages, smiling at Trevn's squarish handwriting, amazed that his brother had copied this entire tome.

"When word spreads that Miss Onika is a true prophet, people will try to use her," Kal said.

"I didn't mean to use her," Wilek said. "I simply respect her wisdom in regards to Arman's teachings."

Kal turned around and fixed his dark eyes on Wilek. "I know that, Your Highness. It's others who will not respect her. They will see her as a tool, if not a toy."

Wilek could read Kal too well. "Others like my father, you mean?"

Kal's expression remained passive. "Your words, not mine."

The man was entirely too overprotective of the prophetess. It occurred to Wilek then that his shield might have feelings for this woman that stretched beyond that of a guardsman. They had spent many weeks together in their journey to Everton. A simple test should reveal all.

"She is an unusually beautiful woman," Wilek said, staring at the Book of Arman as if deep in thought. "My father thinks I should marry her." He glanced at Kal and saw the man's jaw clench. Oh yes. His shield admired more than Miss Onika's prophetic ability. "Have you any objections to such an idea?"

Kal would not meet Wilek's eyes. "It would be cruel to reject Lady Zeroah after all this time."

"True." Wilek paused as if carefully weighing Kal's comment. "But why couldn't I marry both?"

Kal looked away, his face wrenched in agony, brow pinched, eyes fierce.

Perhaps Wilek had taken his game too far. "Kal," he said, voice low. "You know me better than this. I have never wanted more than one wife. Besides, Arman's book forbids it."

Kal fixed hopeful eyes on Wilek. "It does?"

"Yes. I was only teasing you. I know you dote on Miss Onika."

Kal stepped back as if he'd been struck. "Why would you say that?"

How could a High Shield be so naïve? "Because I have eyes. Whenever she is in the room, you are watching her. One might think you are her shield rather than mine."

Kal shook his head. "Jhorn asked me to keep an eye on her."

"One eye, Kal, not both."

Kal squirmed then, like a boy tired of sitting still for his portrait to be painted. Wilek couldn't help it, and he laughed out loud.

Kal started for the door.

"You are leaving me now?" Wilek asked. "Who will protect me?"

"Ask Arman, if he is truly so powerful." Kal opened the door, but before he could leave, Harton ran inside. He set both hands down on the glossy wood surface of Wilek's desk. "Land." He drew in a deep breath. "Land has been sighted!"

✦   ✦   ✦

Wilek stood on the quarterdeck with Kal, Harton, and Dendrick in the crisp morning air, watching through his grow lens as the scouting party set up camp in grass that reached well past the waist. He'd never seen so much green. The island was covered in spindly trees swathed in thick green leaves and more grass than Rurekau had once had sand. But no cliffs or high elevation. Did that mean no reamways of freshwater? He'd hoped this place would have land and water enough to support them all.

Rayim Veralla approached, dressed in his Queen's Guard captain's uniform. "Are they there yet?"

"Yes," Wilek said. "They're just now setting up the tents."

Captain Livina had anchored the *Seffynaw* well out from the reefs. Even then, the first dinghy launched had run up against one and sprung a leak. The oarsmen had rowed her back for repairs and launched a second boat, that time making their way more carefully.

"What do you think?" Rayim whispered. "Is there room enough?"

"I don't yet know." Wilek peered through his grow lens again. "I have asked the signalmen to send messages to the Rurekan and Sarikarian flagships. I've called a meeting of the Wisean Council tomorrow midday and hope their ambassadors will join us. I know it will take many more days to fully explore, but by tomorrow our men should have a grasp of this island's size and whether or not it is habitable. Together we must determine if this land can support us all."

"I'm not sure it can." Trevn's voice. He'd appeared at the rail. "From the masthead I could see no elevation. No cliffs or cracks or river holes. Might not be any freshwater."

Wilek examined his brother, who wore a sailor's outfit right down to his bare feet. "Do you mean to tell me you climbed the rigging? And where are your boots?"

Trevn grinned. "Sailors don't wear boots."

"You are not a sailor."

Trevn folded his arms. "The only way to learn everything is to start at the bottom."

Wilek studied his brother. He supposed it might be better to let him spend his time climbing the rigging and swabbing the decks than dallying away every free moment in Miss Mielle's company. "Is that a bruise on your face?"

Trevn rubbed his palm over it. "Dirt, more like."

"Father will foam at the mouth. And your mother . . ." Wilek stopped himself, recalling that Trevn's mother was confined to her cabin until her trial. He should really get that taken care of. Tomorrow, perhaps. "Where is Sir Cadoc?"

"Wil, please," Trevn whispered. "Trust me?"

Wilek looked deep into his brother's eyes and saw a combination of determination and desperation there. He knew enough of Trevn to doubt that any command could stop such a grand experiment. He'd likely grow bored and move on to something else soon enough. "Just don't let Father see you like this. Ever. Now clean yourself up and come ashore. I plan to question your mother while we are here, though that likely won't happen until tomorrow."

"I'll come tomorrow, then," Trevn said reluctantly. "And you'll have to clear my leave with the second mate. I don't want to be accused of abandoning my watch. We're assigned to cargo and are expecting a lot of work."

"What cargo?" Wilek asked.

"We helped load all those tents this morning. Any moment now we expect the order to haul up the empty barrels and load them so the shore crew can refill them with water and send them back."

"There is no need to move water barrels until we get word that this island has freshwater," Wilek said. "Besides, we might remain on this island for good."

Trevn looked away, lips pursed. Was he unwilling to publicly contradict the Heir a second time? Despair nagged at Wilek's mind that Trevn's concerns about the lack of freshwater had mirrored his own. By Captain Livina's initial assertion, this island should be near the size of Odarka, and while small compared to the former vastness of the Five Realms, such a place could support two hundred thousand people, at least for a time.

If there was freshwater, some sort of food source, and land to cultivate.

Wilek pushed doubt aside. He would go ashore and let his trained team of explorers make a full assessment. Then they'd all know for certain.

"Dendrick." Wilek waved his onesent over. "Inform the second mate that Sâr Trevn has been summoned by the Heir to attend the Wisean Council meeting on shore tomorrow. Make it clear that this is my command. He is not in any way abandoning his watch. The very moment the council excuses him, he will return to the ship. That could be tomorrow evening. It could be in three days. It is my decision and not his, is that understood?"

"Yes, Your Highness." Dendrick strode away.

"Thank you, Wil! It about killed me when Master Bussie said I couldn't go right over to explore." And with that he sprinted away.

Wilek fought to contain his exasperation. "Was I this trying in my youth, Rayim?"

"Not at all," Rayim said. "You were born with a maturity that many men never reach."

It was kind of Rayim to say so, but Wilek knew better. It was not maturity that had kept him above reproach but fear that any misstep might be reason to be sacrificed to Barthos.

As that depressing memory filled his chest with regret, it heartened Wilek to know that Trevn had lived his life free from that kind of terror.

"Harton, ready the boat fall for my retinue. We shall leave for shore within the hour."

✦   ✦   ✦

The rest of the day erupted into chaos.

Before Wilek even had the chance to reach the island, the beach was stormed by a fleet of dinghies and cutters from other ships. Rayim's men sent everyone back until the island could be evaluated, but many made landfall on a different beach. These desperate people were going to overtake this haven before Wilek could make certain it was safe.

When he finally waded through the foamy surf on the long, sandy beach, it was after lunchtime. He pushed aside thoughts of his growling stomach, eager to find a member of his scouting party, hear their report, and perhaps explore a little himself.

This island was unlike anything he'd ever seen. So much greenery and flowers. Not even Sarikar had been so lush. The air was warm now and smelled of salt, kelp, and something sweet. The air buzzed with gnats, and in the distance, some type of bird trilled its call.

He waded through grass that reached his waist as he approached the growing settlement of tents. His scouting party had only gotten a two-hour start on the rest of the fleet, so they didn't know all that much. They had discovered one freshwater creek—above ground—which instantly set Wilek's mind at ease. There were also fat ground-dwelling birds with gray-and-white feathers, and a type of furry pig. Some of each had been killed and butchered for Hara to see what she could make of them.

By the time Wilek entered his tent, he felt confident. The sand in his boots and the gusts of salty wind that tangled his short hair filled him with nostalgia. He dared hope. Could they be home?

For the next few hours Wilek entertained meeting after meeting with advisors, officers, council members, and staff, all the while wondering what his explorers would say.

Dendrick brought the answer well into late midday in the form of a disheveled young man named Lanton Jahday, who bowed when the onesent introduced him. He looked to be about Wilek's age. He had a flat face, golden eyes, and wore his hair in finger-sized braids that reached his shoulders. Water dripped off the ends of his braids, and his clothing—wet and covered in soil and bits of broken grass—clung to his skin.

Wilek noted how the man's hands trembled. He caught Wilek's gaze and moved his hands behind his back. "Forgive me for making a mess in your tent, Your Highness."

Wilek wasn't concerned. "I was told Master Keppel is head of the exploration."

"He is, ah . . . He sent me."

Wilek cared more for the news than which person delivered it. "Your report, then, Master Jahday? You have good news, I hope."

"I'm afraid not, sir, uh, Your Highness."

At those words several emotions came upon Wilek at once. His blood ran cold, his skin flashed with heat, panic flared in his chest, and his mind screamed a hundred fears.

He fought to show none of this on his face, however. "Explain."

"The island *is* habitable," the man said. "We found the creek not far from here and followed it inland. It led to a freshwater spring about three leagues away."

Excellent news. "Then what is the problem?"

"The size of the island, sir. It *appears* much larger than it really is. We traveled no more than ten leagues before reaching the other side, where we could easily see the illusion. The island is surrounded by a reef barrier, though it's unlike any we have ever seen."

"How so?"

"It has sand. And trees and plants that are growing somehow, on coral. I suspect that with the closeness to the island, seeds have carried on the wind, by birds, or even the currents."

"You suspect."

"There is nothing like this in the Five Realms, sir. We had coral reefs, to be sure, but not like this. We suspect that the island is, perhaps, the remains of an extinct volcano, and that it is surrounded by a lagoon and reef. And while it will take weeks to explore every bit of the habitable land and months to determine whether we could plow, plant, and grow food in this soil, quick math gives us a sound estimation that this island could support no more than fifteen thousand people in the long term, maybe twice that if the settlement focused less on agriculture and more on fishing."

Jahday stopped then, seemingly at the end of his report. The silence ran deeper with each breath. Wilek should say something. Be a leader, despite his shock and disappointment.

"Thank you, Master Jahday," he managed, and those four words gave him courage to say more. "Tell Master Keppel to continue his exploration. The Wisean Council will convene tomorrow at midday with the ambassadors from Sarikar, Rurekau, and Tenma. Find out as much as you can by then about the habitable size of the island, whether or not fields could be planted here, and if our livestock might graze." There certainly appeared to be plenty of grass for sheep and goats.

Jahday nodded. "We will have a report ready, Your Highness."

"Dismissed."

Lanton Jahday all but ran from Wilek's tent. When the door flap fell closed behind him, Wilek looked to Dendrick and the two shared looks of condolences.

"What can I do, Your Highness?" Dendrick asked.

"Give that report to my father for me."

Dendrick's eyes widened. "Of course, Your Highness."

Wilek laughed. "I'm only jesting, Dendrick. I will go to Father and see what he says. But first, could you bring Miss Onika here? I would like to speak with her before I talk with the king."

Dendrick bowed. "Right away, Your Highness."

"If I do not return from my father's tent by sunset, send Rayim to check on me. After delivering such news, Janek could yet become Heir of Armania."

✦ ✦ ✦

Wilek left Kal and Harton outside his father's tent and found the king inside, dressed for dinner and sitting in his rollchair. One of his attendants rubbed oil over his bald head.

"My Heir, what news? How do you find the landscape? Can we build right away?"

"I'm afraid the initial report is that the island is too small to accommodate the entire fleet."

The man's sunken eyes glared at Wilek. "I don't care about the entire fleet. I care about Armania. This is our land. Livina found the place months ago. The other realms can shove off and find their own island."

"I fear it is even too small for Armania, Father. Initial estimates state that the island might be able to support between fifteen to thirty thousand people."

The attendant set the wig on Father's head, but the king pushed it off and shooed the man away. "Later!" Then to Wilek, "So which is it? Fifteen thousand or thirty?"

And so the discussion went on, Wilek having very little information to appease his father, who seemed convinced that he could bully the facts to his liking. Wilek finally decided that only Miss Onika's word might sway things.

"We could leave enough people here to set up a colony. Perhaps King Jorger or Emperor Ulrik might like to do the same. But as the island is too small to support even the people of Armania, we must look for a larger landmass. Miss Onika believes we are to sail northwest and—"

"Onika, Onika. That woman unnerves me! She speaks and everyone jumps to obey. Why should she rule us? I see no royal heritage in her blood. I see no proof, even, that she prophesies truth."

"Surely you must have felt the warmth burn within your chest when she prophesies."

"Mantics." Father massaged the flab of skin at his neck. "She tricks us with her powers."

This again. The man's memory was slipping. "We have investigated this already, Father. You asked me to assign her two honor maidens, so she is never alone. I have questioned them and her personal maid. She does not take evenroot."

"She does, I tell you! She takes it in plain sight, then magics us all to forget."

Nonsense. "And here I thought you wanted me to marry her." His father had said Wilek shouldn't pass up an opportunity to sire an heir on a prophetess and get some of her magic in the Hadar bloodline.

"Not I! You know what I always say about women, my son. The darker the skin, the richer the soil. Your Lady Zeroah is the perfect bride. But the prophetess? Whoever saw a woman with skin like a hairless cat? It's not natural. It's not."

So said the sickly bald man. "Father, I—"

"Never you mind, son. I will catch her in the act, then you will see. Now, if you aren't here to tell me you've arrested Miss Onika, what do you want? You never come to my royal apartment without reason."

✦   ✦   ✦

Wilek left the king and walked with Kal and Harton toward the meeting tent. There dinner would be served in fashion to whichever royals or nobles had chosen to come ashore tonight. Along the way they met a squadron of Igote guards from Rurekau. Had his nephew the emperor accepted his invitation? Wilek searched the bald heads for a circlet of gold. Seeing none, he wondered if Ulrik had instead sent an ambassador.

"Kal!" A woman dressed in green peeled away from the Igote and traipsed through the tall grass, headed toward Wilek.

Recognition set in and a smile claimed his face. "Nolah!" Wilek yelled. It was his sister, Emperor Ulrik's mother. The thought crossed his mind that she had grown very fat, until he remembered Kal telling him she was expecting a child.

She averted her gaze from Kal to Wilek. "Wil?" She grabbed up her skirts and ran to him, throwing herself into his arms. The hardness of her belly surprised him. He would have imagined a child's first home to be a soft place like the bodies of the women who carried them.

"Brother of mine, I didn't recognize you with short hair!" She squeezed him tightly. "I so wanted to come to you at Odarka, but Ulrik would not part with me. Though now I am all but banished."

Concern filled Wilek. "Whatever for?"

She released him. "I will tell all later. You have my Vallah?"

"She is aboard the *Seffynaw* with our mother. I will have her brought ashore tomorrow morning."

"Praise Arman. She is well?"

"Very, and enjoying young Rashah's company. Let us not stand out here where the gnats swarm. Come to dinner where we can eat and catch up."

Kal led them, along with Inolah's guards and maids, to the meeting tent, where a herald announced both Wilek and Inolah to the small crowd already seated.

"His Royal Highness, Wilek-Sâr Hadar, the First Arm, the Dutiful, the God-slayer, Heir to Armania. And Her Eminence, Empress Inolah Orsona-Hadar, the Determined, Mother of the Emperor of Rurekau."

The people stood and genuflected as Wilek and Inolah made their way to the head table.

"The Godslayer?" Inolah asked. "How did that become part of your title?"

"A long story," Wilek said.

Soon they were seated at the high table, where servants brought out platters of meat. Inolah's maids sat with Harton at a table on the floor. Kal and Inolah's shield stood behind their seats.

"Did Ulrik and Ferro come with you?" Wilek asked.

"They did not. Ulrik sent two ambassadors. He has anchored the ship and is waiting to hear a pronouncement on the suitability of the island."

"That is wise, I suppose," Wilek said. "It will keep Rurekau, at least, contained."

"His reasons are nothing more than folly. He worries the High Queen might escape his grasp. And Ferro. Ulrik insists on keeping the boy at his side constantly. He is training him as his Heir—until he marries and has a son. Then perhaps Ferro will be banished too."

"What do you mean banished?"

"I'm afraid I have lost both my boys to Ulrik's ambition. Too many times I interfered with his plans. Letting Kal and the pale prophetess go free used up the last of his forgiveness. But I do not wish to talk of my problems just now. What of our brothers? I have never once laid eyes on Trevn and so look forward to meeting him."

"You will do so tomorrow," Wilek said. "He will be at the council meeting."

"Excellent! And Janek, who had the audacity to marry my Vallah? Since I have heard nothing to the contrary, I take it we must still claim that soulless tyrant as our own?"

"Indeed we must," he said and told her of the trial. "I am still puzzling out his involvement in this mantic treachery. Father forbade him come to the island until after the meeting. I feel they are both nursing their pride. No doubt a little more time will return their egos in full force."

Everyone stood when the king arrived, and Inolah went to greet their father. Many had remained on board the *Seffynaw*. Besides King Echad, Wilek and Inolah were the only others seated at the high table tonight.

The mood in the meeting tent was somber, as most had heard the initial report on the size of the island. Wilek was thankful for Inolah's presence, as it had greatly lifted his spirits.

The sound of the herald's horn jolted them from their conversation. Not expecting Janek or Trevn, Wilek looked up in surprise. Prince Loran of Sarikar stood in the doorway with his daughter, Saria, who was Trevn's age; his son, Thorvald, who Wilek thought to be eleven but looked closer to eight or nine; and his brother Prince Rosbert. Ywan, King Jorger's middle-aged onesent, was also present, along with four Sarikarian guardsmen.

"His Royal Highness, Loran Pitney, King of Sarikar, the God's king," the herald announced.

"Since when is Loran king of Sarikar?" Inolah whispered.

"King Jorger went missing during the Woes," Wilek said. "It could be they declared him dead." Lady Zeroah would be devastated to hear of yet another loss to her family.

Loran came to stand below Father's seat at the head table. He bowed politely. Since Father could not, Wilek stood and returned the bow.

"Where is Jorger?" Father barked.

"Dead, I'm afraid," Loran said. "I was crowned aboard the *Kaloday* just two days ago."

"Who said Jorger was dead?" Father asked.

"I received a messenger bird from my uncle Mergest—known to you as Barthel Rogedoth. He claimed my father died at the hand of Magonians."

The tent erupted into noise.

Wilek sank to his chair, staggered by the news. King Jorger murdered, and Rogedoth the betrayer, alive? Wilek had been searching for Rogedoth's houseboat these past two weeks to no avail. He had been hoping the man had perished in Everton during the Woes.

"Is Rogedoth allied with Magonia?" Wilek asked.

"I know not," Loran said. "But my uncle also informed me that he has wed Lady Eudora Agoros and claimed rule of Sarikar, which he says is rightfully his."

"Married to Eudora!" This outburst from Oli Agoros, who sat with Hinckdan Faluk at a table on the floor. The duke had feared his sister might be allied with their enemies, but to marry a man more than three times her senior?

"His actions put Sâr Janek in position to be declared Heir of both Sarikar and Armania," Loran said, "should you and your father meet an early death, which my uncle's missive suggested you would."

"He threatens the life of me and my son?" Father yelled.

"He hints at a plot." Loran motioned to Ywan, who passed a scroll up to Father.

"A plot he no doubt devised," Wilek said, moving to read the scroll over

Father's shoulder. It said nothing more than Loran had claimed, but he recognized Rogedoth's narrow handwriting and seethed inside. They must bring this man to justice!

"I bet my mother had a hand in this," Oli said. "My sister would never have married otherwise."

"But why would Lady Eudora go along with it?" Hinckdan asked. "She swore to me she did not wish to be queen."

"They might not have given her a choice," Inolah said. "No one gave my daughter a choice when she was married to Sâr Janek."

"They are both of them traitors!" Father said.

"More to me than you," Loran said. "It is my throne he has claimed as his own."

"And my second wife who helped him do it," Father said. "She will be executed for this. Sacrificed to Thalassa."

"We have to catch them first," Wilek said. "And we have no idea where their ship is. How did his messenger bird know to find you?"

"My uncle stole a Sarikarian warship called the *Amarnath*," Loran said. "Our birds are trained to find other ships. Plus I am near certain he is using mantics."

Father bellowed a cry of rage. "Double the guard around me and my Heir. And send five ships to scour the fleet. They must not return until they've found the *Amarnath* and *Vespara*."

"Even if we found the ships," Wilek said, "I would be hesitant to approach knowing they have one or more mantics on board."

"Does not your son have a mantic on board, Empress?" Father asked Inolah.

"The High Queen of Tenma, yes," Inolah said. "She is not in his service, though, but a passenger. He does not trust her, and for good reason."

"No mantic can be trusted," Father said.

Wilek knew better. It wasn't so much the mantic that was untrustworthy, but the shadir.

✦   ✦   ✦

Wilek slept poorly that night. All hope of a future on Bakurah Island had been shattered. And now this news of Rogedoth the betrayer still plotting against House Hadar. Did he plan to take Armania for himself or his grandson Janek?

To fight such enemies, Wilek needed help. Trusted allies. He had Hinckdan, at least, who had managed to infiltrate Janek's retinue—though as a newcomer, Janek likely didn't include him in everything. If only Wilek had someone even closer to Janek. A woman, perhaps.

Lady Pia.

He clapped his hands in the darkness of his tent, giddy to have remembered his grandmother's final gift before the Five Woes had claimed her life in the fall of Everton.

"Janek's concubine Pia," she had said. *"The girl is my spy. A good one too. She will help you keep an eye on your brother. Tell her I gave you the word* weed, *and she will serve you the same."*

Wilek climbed out of bed, lit a candle, and quickly penned the single word on a slip of parchment. He rang for Dendrick, apologized for the hour and the odd request, then went back to bed, feeling hopeful for the first time all day.

✦ ✦ ✦

The next morning, before the Wisean Council convened, Wilek pulled Hinckdan aside. "What have Janek and his friends been up to? Are they plotting against my father or me?"

"Not that I'm aware of," Hinckdan answered. "Janek longs to rule, but he is lost without Pontiff Rogedoth and Rosârah Laviel to give him direction, and he is not cunning enough on his own to match you politically. He is bored senseless and still suffering the lack of evenroot, which makes him ill and moody. So he toys with his retinue, asking us to entertain him in all number of ridiculous ways." Hinckdan held up his hands, the palms of which were stained reddish brown. "His latest demand was that Fonu and I paint his portrait. And when he hated it—which, why wouldn't he? We're not artists—he made us recite the whole of *The Consort of King Barthek* and pelted us with slices of melon each time we faltered a line. Do tell me I can quit him finally?" He looked at Wilek with such a beseeching expression, it was almost difficult to say what he must.

"I need you to remain with him a while longer," Wilek said. "This news of Rogedoth's marriage might change Janek's motivations. I want to know his opinion on the matter. His real opinion."

The spark in Hinckdan's eyes faded. "Very well."

"I know that it is not an easy task, Hinckdan, but you are doing Armania a great service."

Hinckdan released a heavy sigh. "As a royal cousin, what else would I do but serve?"

Trevn

Trevn admired Bakurah Island as four of Wilek's King's Guards rowed him to shore in a dinghy just after sunrise. The many shades of green not only surprised him, they beckoned. Grass as high as a man's waist and a thick forest of slender trees swayed in the salty sea breeze. The trees looked too wispy to climb, but that wouldn't stop Trevn from trying. Some sort of bird cawed in the distance, another tittered a song. And the flowers . . . Red and white ruffles, bulbous purple trumpets, tiny golden discs, and pink bells. Trevn doubted Janek had yet bothered to look at the land, for if he had seen the lush vegetation, he would have been on the first boat over.

The dinghy reached the shore, and Wilek's guards escorted Trevn—carrying a map tube loaded with plenty of paper and charcoal—across the hard-packed sand and through a maze of paths in the tall grass. They approached the meeting tent where over two dozen guards stood posted outside. In fact, now that Trevn saw them, he noticed even more guards milling about.

"What does the king fear with his overuse of guardsmen?" Trevn asked the nearest guard.

"A threat was made against him and Sâr Wilek, so the rosâr doubled security."

More like quadrupled. "What kind of threat?"

"Don't know for certain, but word is it came from one of Sâr Janek's supporters, though the Second Arm claims to have no knowledge of any such plot."

Janek *would* claim that. Trevn knew not what to make of his wayward brother. Never once had Janek seemed interested in duty or ruling until Wilek had gone missing a few months back. Then Janek had sprung forward and shown a different side of himself.

Trevn would never underestimate his brother's ambition again.

He arrived in the meeting tent and found Oli, Duke of Canden, who filled him in on all he had missed yesterday. That Cousin Eudora had married Pontiff Rogedoth of her own volition, Trevn found absurd. The girl had never made an ambitious decision in her life, and marriage to a betrayer like Barthel Rogedoth was extremely enterprising.

It did not surprise him that the former Pontiff had declared himself king of Sarikar, though it seemed a strange time to declare war, which was exactly what he'd done with his missive to King Loran. He'd also foolishly united Sarikar and Armania against a common enemy.

The inadequacies of Bakurah Island and its unique reef barrier came as Oli's second piece of news, and while Trevn understood the magnitude of this situation on the fleet, it fascinated him. He hoped to sneak away to explore between his mother's trial and the council meeting.

The meeting tent had been set up like the great hall back in Castle Everton. A long table had been elevated at the far end. Ten audience tables sat in two rows of five. Between the rows, directly opposite Father's rollchair, a single chair sat empty. Trevn's mother would sit there shortly and be questioned. He hadn't spoken to her in almost two weeks. It shamed him that he hadn't thought of her at all except to wonder over her guilt. How sad that he didn't even miss his own mother. What did it mean?

Trevn took his chair on Father's left. The king was speaking to Lebbe Alpress, captain of the King's Guard. Four of the five members of the Wisean Council had already arrived.

"Trevn." Wilek appeared behind his chair. "You look much better."

"A man can wear many things," Trevn said. "It does not change who he is inside."

"Perhaps not," Wilek said. "But where we royals are concerned, perception is everything. If we look like we don't care, our people will believe it."

"You and I have different opinions on what it looks like to care about our people," Trevn said. "Janek dresses like a king and cares only for himself. I dress like a sailor and learn how our people live and work. My actions prove I care more than any silk doublet could ever say."

Wilek sighed. "This is not the time to debate such a subject. We will question your mother first, then proceed with the rest of our meeting, which is to discuss next steps in regard to this island. We will eat a short repast, then reconvene with the representatives from the other realms to attempt a joint decision."

Trevn nodded and Wilek returned to his seat.

"What is that smell?" Father asked.

"Ropes and tar," Danek said from two seats down on Trevn's left. Hinckdan's father looked like an older version of his son, right down to the huge dimpled smile. "I daresay we will not escape the stench until we leave these ships behind for good."

Trevn no longer noticed the smell, but he was likely the culprit. He glanced at his hands in his lap and the rough calluses the ropes had left on his palms. No doubt the stench had already buried itself in his skin.

A woman sank onto a cushioned seat on Trevn's left. She was great with child and dressed like a queen. Her hair was two shades of bronze and black, done up in small coils that reached her elbows.

Trevn gathered in his mind the only name he felt appropriate. "Empress Inolah?"

She turned, posture straight, eyes deep brown. "Correct. And you are . . . ?"

"Sâr Trevn."

She lit up in a smile. "Little brother, I am pleased to finally meet you." Her eyes shifted as she studied his face. "How much you remind me of my Ulrik. He is but one year your senior."

"And now an emperor." *The unlucky man.* "I look forward to meeting him."

Father called the council to order, and all fell silent. Trevn turned away from his elder sister to regard the king, and in the process saw that his mother had been brought in. She had more than filled the lone chair, hands bound before her. Her eyes were fixed on his. He held her stare and raised one eyebrow to challenge her to redeem herself, then focused his attention on Wilek, glad he did not have to lead these proceedings himself.

"Rosârah Thallah," Wilek began. "You come before this council on charges of duplicity. What say you?"

"A reliable witness tells the truth," Mother said. "And I swear to do so upon the life of my only son, Sâr Trevn Hadar."

Trevn could see her turn toward him, but he kept his gaze on Wilek.

Father nodded to Wilek. "I accept her oath as valid. Continue, my Heir."

Wilek cleared his throat and looked to a sheet of parchment on the table before him. "Explain to this council how you came to be involved with the cult Lahavôtesh."

Mother wrung her huge hands. "I overheard Rosârah Laviel speaking of Havôt to her ladies. I asked her about it, and she said it was not for me. This only made me more eager to be a part of it. It was common knowledge that Rosârah Laviel was the rosâr's favorite wife, and I wanted to experience anything she found worthwhile.

"Shortly thereafter I was approached by several different women. I do not know who they were. They always were cloaked in black and came to me at night. They told me that I was being watched, measured. And finally that I was found worthy."

Exactly what Hinck had experienced before he had been brought into the Lahavôtesh. Wilek asked Trevn's mother for names. She gave only Rosârah Laviel, Sâr Janek, and Beal, who had been Trevn's onesent until he had tried to kill Trevn and take the Book of Arman.

"Was Beal a member before or after you?" Trevn asked, steeling himself when all heads turned in one motion to look at him.

"Before," Mother said. "Rosârah Laviel encouraged me to hire him as your onesent upon your arrival in Everton. She said he was good at his job and well respected. I wanted her to like me, so I took her advice."

Considering this led Trevn to another question. "Did Beal kill Father Tomek?" he asked.

"Yes," Mother said, hanging her head.

"On your order?"

Her head snapped up. "No! Beal is Moon Fang's hand. Was, anyway."

"Who is Moon Fang?" Wilek asked.

"The high priest of the Lahavôtesh faith. He ordered Beal to kill Father Tomek for being an Armanite," she said.

"Then you sent your personal guards after me?" Trevn asked.

"Not after you. After the book. It's all that wretched book's fault! That's all he wanted."

"Moon Fang?" Wilek clarified.

"Yes. He said it must be destroyed at all costs. I never understood he meant to risk even the life of my only son."

All that time, Trevn's mother and Beal had been the ones tracking him for the book. And the book had been hidden in the secret room in Mother's apartment. He would laugh, if it wasn't so sad.

"Why did Moon Fang want the book destroyed?" Wilek asked.

"He said it was heresy."

"Is Moon Fang Pontiff Rogedoth?"

Her eyes went wide. "I don't know. Perhaps. That would make sense."

Wilek went on to ask several questions about Lady Lebetta, his concubine who had been murdered. Mother said Moon Fang had ordered her death when she refused to kill Wilek.

"So Beal killed her?" Wilek asked.

She shook her head. "One called Red Ream. I don't know his real identity, but he is a friend of Sâr Janek's."

Wilek rubbed the bridge of his nose and asked why she had suggested to Rosârah Laviel that Janek wed Princess Vallah of Rurekau.

She wiped tears off her cheeks. "Because he was going to rule! Everyone knew it. Laviel was most favored. The king was ill. And you . . ." She nodded to Wilek.

"What about me?" Wilek asked.

"They said you would not be chosen by your father. They said Janek was stronger."

"Who is *they*?" Wilek asked.

"Rosârah Laviel and Pontiff Rogedoth."

"I have heard enough," Father said. "Thallah Orsona, I hereby banish you from the realm of Armania. I will have my guards transport you to Emperor Ulrik's ship at once."

Mother staggered to her feet. "You can't banish me!"

"Guards!" Father yelled.

Trevn stood up at his seat. "Are you certain this is necessary?"

"A woman you cannot trust deserves no place in your household, boy," Father said.

Trevn knew the man spoke wisely, yet that hardly mattered. "But she is my mother."

"You will do better to be weaned from her," Father said. "Sit down."

Trevn's face burned as he lowered himself to the chair and watched the guards wrestle his mother from the tent. Father had mistaken his meaning. Trevn did not need to be weaned from his mother. He had been desperate to cut the binds between them for several years now. But that did not mean he never wanted to see her again.

He forced himself to watch as the guards dragged her away. She fought and screamed long after she had gone out of the tent.

Inolah squeezed Trevn's shoulder. "Ulrik will see that she is well cared for."

Trevn supposed that was true. But how would the young emperor handle his great-aunt's interference in his rule of Rurekau? The thought made Trevn smile.

Servants brought in trays of cold fowl, pork, and local fruit, all native to Bakurah Island. The meats were excellent, but Trevn didn't think the fruit was meant for human consumption. It was yellow, the size of grapes, but had the texture of a green melon and very little flavor.

Before long the representatives from Sarikar and Rurekau arrived, but none from Tenma or Magonia.

After the meal everything shifted. The representatives took seats at the high table. From Rurekau: General Balat and Sheriff Kakeeo. From Armania: Father and Wilek. And from Sarikar: King Loran and his brother Prince Rosbert. The tables on the floor were filled with observers from all three realms. Trevn sat with Oli and Hinck. It was the first time since escaping Everton that Trevn had gotten to speak to Hinck as a friend.

"Why are *you* here?" Trevn asked. "Shouldn't you be back on the ship at Janek's beck and call?"

"The king forbade him to come ashore until the meetings were over," Hinck said. "So Janek sent me here to be his ears."

"He keeping you busier than I did?" Trevn asked.

"Ever so much more," Hinck whispered, "and at the most ridiculous of tasks. I would much rather chase the firebrand of Castle Everton over rooftops than play human candelabra."

"What?" Oli asked.

"Janek made Fonu, Jayron, and me each hold a lit candle in each hand," Hinck said. "The last one holding both won a night with Lady Mattenelle." Hinck held up his hand, baring streaks of long burn scars. "I did *not* win."

Oli's chuckle ended on a happy sigh. "Ah, I miss the things he comes up with . . . but not being the one to suffer through it. It was always great fun unless you were his pawn."

"I am always his pawn," Hinck said. "Janek sent me here yesterday to investigate the island and bring back a report. And when I went back with a basket of cuttings of island ferns and flowers, he went mad with fervor and made me row back to the island to dig up one of each and put them in pots in his tent so he could examine them when he arrived later today. I was here all night digging up plants."

Hinck's misery relieved Trevn. He had worried his friend might actually be enjoying himself with Janek and wouldn't want to return to Trevn's service when all his spying finally came to an end. Apparently not.

Wilek called for attention and opened the session with a summary of the history of Bakurah Island, with its discovery by Captain Livina just over six months ago. As Armanian men had been the first to step foot on the island, Wilek had permitted head explorer Rost Keppel to name an Armanian settlement, which he called Khamesh in honor of the lost Five Realms.

Wilek called forward Master Keppel, a short, stout man with a bush of gray hair atop his head. The explorer explained all that Oli had told Trevn of the land, but in more scientific terms, which Trevn greatly appreciated. Upon further exploration yesterday and well into the dawn hours this morning, Keppel had determined that Bakurah Island could support no more than twenty thousand people.

This statement did not produce much reaction. It seemed that word had already spread throughout those present.

"Thank you, Master Keppel," Wilek said. "The Wisean Council of Armania has discussed this matter fully. Our survivors far outnumber what this island can support. Therefore it is our recommendation that each realm leave its own settlement here while the rest of the fleet searches for more land."

"Searches where?" Prince Rosbert asked.

"That is something we must discuss," Wilek said.

"Why not let Rurekau have the island?" General Balat asked. "We have under twenty thousand people."

Wilek sifted through some scrolls on the table before him. "It's my understanding, General Balat, that Rurekau has over twenty-three thousand when the Tennish refugees are included. Do you plan to shift the refugees to another realm's ships?"

"No," Sheriff Kakeeo said. "We cannot do that."

"If we each leave a settlement here," Wilek said, "we each have reason to return."

And what no one seemed willing to say aloud was that, should the rest of them perish, each realm would have survivors to carry on the ways of their people.

"Whom would we leave behind in this settlement?" General Balat asked.

"That would be up to each realm to determine," Wilek said. "Armania has found a volunteer to lead our settlement should this council choose that option. Lord Faxon and his family, formerly of Fogstone, would stay here, along with as many families that wish to join them, the number of which is dependent upon the decisions of the other two realms here today."

"Sarikar is prepared to leave a settlement here," King Loran said. "My cousin Prince Naten has volunteered to remain, along with his extended family."

Prince Naten was the younger brother of Rosârah Brelenah, Father's first wife and Wilek's mother. Prince Naten and his wife had three grown children, each married with children of their own. They were a much more noble offering to Bakurah Island than Armania had made.

The discussion went on, and it was finally agreed upon that General Balat would return to the *Baretam* and inquire as to whether or not Emperor Ulrik wished to leave a settlement. His answer would determine the number of people each realm could leave behind.

Then came the discussion of which direction to sail next.

"We must sail north," Father said, "with Nivanreh's Eye at our backs. The god of travel will guide us to land."

"Your god of travel is no more than the Southern Star to us," King Loran said. "Our priests feel we should travel northwest."

"The prophetess Onika agrees," Wilek said.

"Who says we must remain together?" General Balat asked. "Perhaps we should all go our separate ways."

"To what end?" King Loran asked. "We have contracted our children in marriage for centuries. Rosâr Echad's Heir and my niece are to marry soon. Would I never see Zeroah again?"

"We now have Bakurah Island as a base," General Balat said. "We could cover more sea if we split up."

This debate went on another hour. No one could agree on what to do. Father was set on traveling north by the southern pole star Nivanreh's Eye. King Loran wished to stay close to Armania, but he wanted to sail northwest as his priests felt the God was leading them. General Balat and Sheriff Kakeeo were divided. The general wanted to go their own way, but Kakeeo insisted the Emperor would want to stay with the group.

In the end King Loran submitted to following Armania north for a time, and the Rurekans planned to return to the *Baretam* to ascertain Emperor Ulrik's will in the matter.

The meeting began to disperse. Oli took off without a word. Hinck had to return to the *Seffynaw* and let Janek know he could now come to the island. Trevn lingered, undecided what to do with himself. He desperately wanted to do a little exploring and mapping but felt he needed Wilek's permission to stay since he had brought no tent or staff of his own. Up ahead his brother moved slowly toward the exit with Inolah, Sir Kalenek, and Harton, so Trevn started after them.

Outside, as the line of people moved through a narrow path in the grass, the wind carried the smell of flowers and something sharp and bitter. Trevn imagined some sort of leafy plant or cactus, though this island seemed void of cacti. It was much greener than any place he'd been. The trees grew close, their narrow trunks limber and bobbing in the wind, leaves rustling.

A shout drew his gaze back to his surroundings. Up ahead bronze clashed. Trevn could not see past Harton. From behind him guards charged by, cutting new paths through the tall grass and drawing their blades as they circled Wilek. Servants and commoners scattered, some screaming as they fled whatever confrontation lay ahead.

"Not me!" Wilek yelled. "To the king!" And all but two of the guards scampered away, allowing Trevn a clear look at his brother.

He saw nothing suspicious. What was all the fuss about?

"Ho, up!" Sir Kalenek yelled, his dark eyes scowling through the press of bodies. "Protect the Heir!"

Battle cries rose, a trilling sound that made Trevn want to climb a tree to get a better view.

Suddenly part of the crowd was moving back toward them, men with leather masks and swords in hand. Trevn backed up a step, uncertain what to do. His arm brushed against someone, and he sprang to the side. It was only Empress Inolah.

"They seek to kill Wilek," she said.

Trevn looked back and saw the truth of that. The attackers ran toward the men protecting Wilek. Beyond, another group had swarmed the guards around the king.

Sir Kalenek, Harton, and the two remaining guards had drawn their weapons and put their backs to Wilek. Inside their circle of protection, Wilek drew his own blade. Trevn had not worn his sword—didn't even know where it was. He'd last seen it on the floor of his royal cabin.

Harton turned to face Trevn, blade raised. He scowled and waved Trevn back.

"Get the woman out of here," Harton said as the first attacker engaged Sir Kalenek. "Find a place to hide!"

Trevn turned toward Inolah. "We must go," he told his sister, thinking they might run through the grass as the servants had or return to the meeting tent and perhaps sit under one of the tables. Behind them blades clashed, men grunted, leather armor creaked.

"No," Inolah said. "We stay back and wait for a weapon."

What? Trevn glanced back to the melee in time to see Sir Kalenek finish off the first attacker. The man fell into the grass with a mournful scream. Sir Kalenek yelled and passed his sword to his left hand, anguish twisting his scars further. Had he been struck?

Inolah swooped down upon the dying man and pulled the sword from his hand. He fought her, his other hand holding his entrails, which were spilling out from a slash in his side.

Inolah won the tug-of-war and swung the sword across the calves of one of Sir Kalenek's attackers. The man fell. One of his comrades turned to face Inolah, and the empress leapt forward to meet the attack, sword trimming a wedge in the tall grass as she swung.

Trevn pushed aside his awe and ran toward Inolah's first victim. He pried the man's stiff fingers off his sword and claimed it as his own. Tentatively he inched toward the fray, quickly determined that there were too many attackers, and realized he didn't know how to help.

Sir Kalenek cradled his right arm to his side as he fought. "Ho, up! Squad! To me!" he cried. "Where is everyone?"

A blade arced toward Trevn's head. He ducked but lost his footing and fell onto a blanket of trampled grass. Cadoc's words from his arms lessons screamed in his head: *"Stay on your feet!"*

A blade stabbed down toward Trevn and he rolled just before it plunged into the grassy soil. Trevn kicked the man in the gut. His attacker stumbled back, losing his hold on his sword. Trevn grabbed the grip of the pinned sword and used it as leverage to jump back to his feet. His attacker pulled a dagger from his belt, but before he could use it, Trevn rammed his blade into the man's stomach, screaming as he did.

The sword went in more easily than he would have expected. The man's dark eyes stared out of his mask, wide with shock. Then they both turned their gazes to the sword in his belly.

Trevn should pull it out. Right?

He tried, finding it harder than expected. The man collapsed before Trevn could finish the task. With him on the ground, it took both hands to remove the sword. Trevn stood holding it, dazed, eyes fixed on the bloody tang.

He had killed a man.

The fight hemmed him in on all sides. Inolah called Trevn's name, snapping him out of his stupor just before another man engaged him in battle. Trevn fought on, plagued by the clash within him—elation at having defended himself and the horror that a man was dead because of him. Too much happening at once. Shouts tore out around him. Blades clanked. More yelling drifted from afar.

Then someone called a retreat and Trevn's attacker turned and fled. They were giving up! Reinforcements must have arrived.

That quickly, the battle was over. Wilek, Sir Kalenek, Harton, and the two guards stood alone. A few paces away Trevn crouched back to back with Inolah. He released a pent-up breath, thankful they had all survived.

Wilek walked out from the center of his guards to the man Trevn had killed. He crouched and used his bloodied sword to slice off one of the man's hair twists that stuck out from under his mask.

Wilek held it out to Trevn. "This kill was yours, my brother."

It was an ancient Armanian tradition for a warrior to take a lock of hair from every kill. Some still did, and threaded them into their own hair twists like trophies. More often these days the practice was done only in ritual, and only for a man's first kill.

Trevn had always felt the tradition barbaric, but having lived through such an attack . . . having survived it . . . He reached out slowly and took the hair twist from Wilek, chilled and conflicted by the feel of the coarse hair between his fingers and thumb. He met Wilek's eyes, then saw movement behind his brother. A man had risen from the dead, dagger in his fist. Trevn extended his hand and yelled, "Look out!"

Sir Kalenek pushed Wilek aside and twisted to meet the assailant, shoulder first. The impact of their bodies knocking together pushed them both to the ground. The other guards converged on the assailant, giving him no chance at a second attempt.

Trevn was relieved to see Wilek unharmed. Sir Kalenek lay moaning in the bloody, trampled grass. He lifted his head to look at his wound. Trevn extended his hand.

Sir Kalenek grabbed it awkwardly with his left. "Help me sit."

Trevn pulled the man upright. "He got you?"

"Under my arm." Sir Kalenek used his left hand to lift his right elbow up under his chin. He grimaced. "Pull something off one of the dead men . . ." He swayed. "To stop the blood flow." His eyes lost focus, and he collapsed.

CHARLON

Charlon stood at the railing on the foredeck, studying the island. Still stunned the Chieftess had abandoned her. Left her to deal with this alone. Magon had wanted them to work together. But Mreegan had become impatient. Such behavior was shameful. That Mreegan would walk away from the great shadir's plans.

She was not worthy to lead Magonia.

But perhaps this division was necessary. A step that brought Charlon closer to becoming Chieftess. When Charlon succeeded, Mreegan would be sorry. Would regret having doubted Charlon.

Wilek had gone ashore. Without a word to his betrothed. Charlon knew the land was important to everyone's survival. She still found his devotion to his betrothed pathetic. He hadn't spoken to Charlon in three days.

What to do? Magon had been cryptic of late. Answered all of Charlon's questions with proverbs and encouragements. *Keep trying*, Magon had said. *Have faith in me.* But Charlon didn't want to try anymore. Didn't want to have faith. Didn't know what she wanted.

To sit inside her tent with Torol. Yes, that would do.

Only she had no tent now that they were at sea. And Torol was on the Magonian ship. With Mreegan. Jealousy surged within, but she calmed herself. She must focus.

But why? What if Mreegan and Magon were wrong about the Deliverer? Maybe the prophecy no longer applied now that there was no land to subdue. What would be the point? Of ruling a fleet of ships with no harbor?

Still. She needed the title of Chieftess. Then no one could hurt her again. And all would respect her. She would be powerful. Yet rule with wisdom and compassion.

But not until she succeeded in her quest.

Perhaps on the island Prince Wilek would be more relaxed. Now that they'd found land, there might be a celebration. With dancing and drink. She couldn't risk being absent. The one night he went looking for a woman's company.

Charlon started back to her cabin. She would pack her second black dress. Go ashore. The distance from ship to land was much closer than Fairsight Manor had been to Castle Everton. She should have no trouble maintaining Lady Zeroah's mask. She would have to leave the girl in the trunk for a few days, though. She pushed the guilt aside. She had no choice.

She prepared quickly. Instructed some servants to carry her things to the boat fall. Bid they erect her tent beside Prince Wilek's. Once they'd gone, she hid the bronze canister of ahvenrood in a cupboard and set a spell over the corridor outside her door.

Anyone who came looking for this cabin would forget why.

✦ ✦ ✦

The boat ride to the island was tedious, as was trudging through the sand and tall grass to reach her tent, which, when she arrived, was not yet assembled. A valid enough reason to visit Prince Wilek. Then she discovered the distance. Her tent was being set up far from his. In an entirely separate clearing.

She fought to pull her skirts through the long grass. Dreamed of wearing a kasah again. Had made it halfway down the narrow path when someone called Lady Zeroah's name. Charlon looked up. Found an adolescent boy coming her way. She had never seen him before. But the size of his smile was proof: They were more than acquaintances.

"It has been so long," he said, his voice still a child's. He was well built for his age. Wore a sword and fine clothing.

Charlon curtsied, curious as to the boy's identity.

He laughed. "So formal. Surely an embrace is appropriate for a brother, yes?"

Ah. This wiry youth must be the mysterious Lord Rystan. "Weren't you on another ship?"

"I was. Sâr Wilek summoned me aboard the *Seffynaw*. I'm to take Mother's place on the Wisean Council."

Heat flashed over Charlon. "You? Why not me? I'm older."

He looked confused. "I didn't ask for the position. I assumed you, as the sâr's wife, would have conflicting interests."

Charlon relaxed. "That must have been the reasoning."

This realm had too many rules. Especially for women. No surprise they accomplished little. Hope surged, though, to hear someone refer to her as the sâr's wife. Perhaps Prince Wilek was planning the wedding. Maybe she would awake one day to a summons to the altar.

She sought a polite dismissal. "It was nice to see you again, brother. Sâr Wilek awaits my arrival in his tent. I don't want to keep him waiting."

"We shall have plenty of time to talk now that I will be on the *Seffynaw*." Lord Rystan did not move out of her way. Opened his arms wide and grinned. Dashing little monster. She leaned forward. Allowed him to grab her waist. Stiffened at the fierceness of his embrace. Patted two fingers against his shoulder. The compulsion she had placed on herself to remove her fear of human touch did its job well enough. But her mind always reminded her that touch was dangerous.

Lord Rystan finally let go. Walked off, waving joyfully. "Until dinner, dear sister."

Charlon tramped on through the grass. Lamenting yet another complication to her role as Lady Zeroah. She needed to finish her mission, and soon.

She finally reached the clearing. Beheld the royal tents of King Echad, Prince Wilek, Prince Janek. A large meeting tent in the distance. She nodded at the guards outside and entered Wilek's tent. Found him in a meeting with his brother Janek. Also present were Sir Jayron, Lord Dacre, and Wilek's backman.

Charlon stiffened at the sight of Harton. *Run*, her heart said.

But her mind said, *No*. She had to stay. Had to take her place at Prince Wilek's side, despite her hatred for his backman.

The tent looked similar to Wilek's cabin aboard the *Seffynaw*. His father's large desk had been brought over. As had Wilek's bed, two longchairs, several stools, a sideboard table, and a changing screen. The princes were standing a great deal apart from the others. She focused on their conversation. They were discussing traitors. Again.

"Yes, I know many of them," Janek said, perusing a scroll.

"But you didn't know they planned to attack Father and me?"

"Of course not! I have had more than enough trouble from the mutinous behavior of my acquaintances. I cannot help it if they are zealous on my behalf and choose to break the law. I want nothing to do with their treason. And I have never encouraged it."

"Why do they persist? We have no land to rule. No Castle Everton or Seacrest to fight over. We have nothing but ships."

Janek shrugged. "I have no idea what goes on in their deranged minds."

"They shall all of them be executed before we leave the islan—" Wilek noticed her. "Lady Zeroah, good midday. I did not know you had come to the island. Why aren't you enjoying first sleep?"

She curtsied. "I was eager to have solid ground under my feet. And my tent is not yet assembled. Would you mind if I waited here?"

"Not at all. Your brother Lord Rystan is on the island. I will call him."

"I have already seen him."

"Oh, good. You, uh . . . have none of your maids with you?"

"I left them at the tent. To see it properly set up." She winced inside, hoping that sounded noble.

"Surely you lovers don't want me about," Janek said, walking toward her and the exit. "We will give you some privacy." He stopped before Charlon. She curtsied to him. "What a pretty dress, lady." A glance to Wilek over his shoulder. "My brother is a lucky man."

"Janek, we are not through yet," Wilek said.

"I've told you I know nothing of this situation. Kill them all, if you feel you must. They've brought it upon themselves." Janek inclined his head to Charlon. "Lady Zeroah."

She curtsied again. "Good midday, Sâr Janek," she said, regarding him thoughtfully as he quitted the tent. Sir Jayron and Lord Dacre followed him. Perhaps Mreegan was right. She had likely put her efforts into snaring the wrong man.

To Charlon's great relief, Harton slipped out with the other men. Wilek did not notice this until the door curtain fell closed. He sighed heavily. Walked toward his desk, which was laden with scrolls. He pushed them aside. Looking for something. "Allow me to ring Harton back, lady. It isn't proper for us to be unchaperoned."

Charlon spied the bell on her side of the table and snatched it up. It betrayed her with a soft clink that caught Wilek's attention. He reached out. She tucked the bell behind her back.

"Sâr Wilek, please. We are both adults. We are betrothed. If not for the Five

Woes, we would have been wed these past few weeks. Let us not stand on ceremony. I simply want to sit with you. Talk without the awkwardness of a chaperone. Especially your backman."

"I don't see why Harton bothers you, lady. He has always served me loyally, and was a great help in this midday's attack."

"An attack? Who would dare?"

"We think they were a part of Rogedoth's mantic cult."

Oh, the dreaded cult again. Prince Wilek was obsessed with it. Charlon decided to press more against Harton. "Are you so certain Master Harton is not part of this cult?"

"I am positive."

"But you said he lied to you. Lying to a prince is treason."

"Everyone deserves a second chance, lady."

Not Harton. "Perhaps, but some things are unforgivable."

"Did Harton interfere with you in some way?"

Oh, if he only knew. But perhaps this was how she might be rid of him. She asked Magon to help her produce tears. "He has never done anything obvious, Your Highness. It's the way he looks at me."

Wilek stepped toward her, brow pinched. "How?"

She leaned against his arm. Rested her head on his shoulder. "Let us talk of something else. Choose a date to marry. I want to bear you a son. So that no man will ever be tempted to raise a sword against you."

"I have told you that we will marry once we reach land."

"But we are on land this moment!"

"True, but I'm afraid we cannot stay here. It is too small. We plan to leave a colony and continue north. Our hope is that this island is the first of many. We might find our new home any day. And I promise you that I will put our—"

And then *he* came back inside. Charlon stiffened. *Get away,* her heart said. *Protect within.*

"Forgive me, Your Highness," Harton said, glancing briefly at Charlon. Not recognizing her of course. "The king is asking to see you."

"I must go." Wilek took Charlon's hands. Looked into her eyes. "Lady, we will marry within a week of finding our new home. That is all I can promise for now." He kissed both of her hands and released them. Walked away with *him.*

And Charlon was left alone. Again.

114

What kind of a man refused the pleasures of the flesh? If Charlon had not felt the passion in Prince Wilek's kiss back when she wore Lady Lebetta's mask, she might believe that he preferred men.

But no. He preferred his memories. Charlon doubted he would ever get over that Lebetta woman.

Enough. Charlon was finished. Finished wasting time. Finished waiting. She would visit Prince Janek. Tonight.

Hinck

J ust look at it!" Janek cried. "My biggest sandvine. Dead."

Hinck jolted awake, pulse pounding, disoriented. He was reclining on a longchair in Janek's tent. Ah, he'd dozed off again. If he wasn't careful, he'd end up a pawn in a nasty prank.

He sat up and swung his legs off the side, hoping such a position would keep him alert. Janek's tent felt empty with only six people inside. In the past, when Janek held court on a journey, his tent had been filled with dozens of jubilant carousers. Now, besides Hinck, Janek had only his concubines, the Honored Ladies Pia and Mattenelle, who sat on mats by his feet in their traditional two-piece gowns; his Rurekan shield, Sir Jayron, who paced behind Janek, foreboding with his henna-tattooed head and sculpted beard; and Kamran DanSâr, the king's stray son, who lay on another longchair, smoking a poured-stone pipe.

All faced Janek, who sat on a wicker throne, holding a potted plant on one knee. The Second Arm of Armania had lost much in the past three weeks, the dearest of which was the desertion of his closest friend, Oli Agoros, who now did nothing but drink wine and moan about the loss of his arm. But Hinck could hardly blame him for that.

"I had hoped freshwater from the island stream would revive it," Janek continued, "but I fear it's too late. I now have only one sandvine left on board the ship. One."

"What if you planted this one here on the island, lord?" Lady Pia suggested.

116

He frowned at her. "And leave it behind?"

"With time and rain and rich soil for its roots to grow deep, it might yet live, eventually go to seed, and populate the island with sandvines."

Lady Pia never ceased to impress Hinck with her quick thinking. She always seemed to know just what to say to appease Janek.

Lady Mattenelle was the opposite, always moaning and fawning over which-ever male was closest, and using her beauty to get whatever she wanted. "I think it's an omen," she said, adding a new blade of grass to the mat she was weaving. "We are going to die, and these ships are but massive death boats carrying us all to Shamayim."

"None of that," Janek snapped. "I am sick of such talk. If I hear another word of dying, I shall send you to the pole."

"There is no pole at present," Kamran said. "If you must punish her, send her to me."

Janek ignored him. He'd never sent his concubines to the pole, though he had done so to his friends, who shockingly always returned to his company afterward, reticent and as loyal as ever.

"I itch for root," Janek said. "It is not as bad as it once was, but the craving lingers."

"Wine helps," Kamran said, taking a swig from the goblet in his hand.

"Shall I fetch you more?" Lady Pia asked.

"Yes, do," Janek said.

"Is there no root to be had on the entire ship?" Hinck asked as Lady Pia rose and refilled Janek's goblet with wine.

"Oli always had a vial," Lady Mattenelle said.

"Do not speak his name!" Janek yelled.

The tent fell quiet. Lady Mattenelle set her full attention on weaving her mat, as if someone else had mentioned the deserter's name.

Sir Jayron bravely broke the silence. "Sâr Wilek's mantic advisor had a vast amount of evenroot, but no one has been able to find it since the woman was killed."

Janek began his performing laugh, the one that rose slowly in volume until he made enough noise to be practically yelling. This always meant he was about to reveal some grand secret. Oftentimes these were completely ridiculous. But every once in a while, he really did shock.

All eyes watched the prince, who was nursing a confident smile. He got up, set his dying sandvine on the floor beside his throne, and walked to his bed. "Sir Jayron told me how Wilek brought the old woman to Canden, how she used her little creature to search for evenroot."

"That was how he caught the Pontiff and your mother with root," Kamran said. "Lau and Yohthehreth as well."

Janek crouched at the head of his feather mattress that lay on the floor. He picked up a lidded straw basket, stood, and started back to his chair. Hinck had seen him with that basket many times in the last week. Figured it held seeds or something related to gardening.

"Fortunate that the old woman didn't start in my chambers in Canden," Janek said. "Fortunate that you warned me, Sir Jayron. Fortunate that when I heard of the woman's death, I went to her chamber with my empty root vial and waited until Errp came to me." He lifted the lid, and a pale lizard scampered onto Janek's wrist. Its tongue darted out, tasting Janek's skin, and then it crawled up his arm and stopped on his shoulder.

"*You* have that thing?" Sir Jayron grinned. "Sâr Wilek still has guards looking for it."

"How did you know its name?" Lady Pia asked.

"Did you kill her?" This from Kamran.

"I cannot reveal my sources, Lady Pia," Janek said. "And *no*, Kamran. I am not a murderer, like you. But someone on board the *Seffynaw* has the old woman's evenroot. And I want it. Errp will help me find it. Perhaps even find her killer and appease my brother. But I need a reason to search."

"You're a sâr," Sir Jayron said. "You don't need a reason to do what you want."

"Please," Janek said. "These days I must walk on glass around the Heir and break nothing. He nearly arrested me again today because of Fonu and his idiotic plans. Attacking when my father had doubled the guard. What a fool."

"We're all good with swords," Kamran said. "Form us into a squadron to seek out those dastardly supporters you claim to know nothing about."

Janek grinned. "And which of you will I execute first?"

"Fonu, who else?" Kamran said, blowing out a stream of smoke from his pipe.

"You won't ever catch anyone truly guilty," Sir Jayron said. "But it would give you permission to search cabins, and in doing so, you're sure to find someone hiding something."

"You must call yourself Master of the Order," Lady Pia said.

"Master of the Order of the Sandvine," Hinck said. "Lady Pia could sew us all silk sandvine blossoms to pin upon our breasts, medals of honor to wear as we seek to instill peace on board the *Seffynaw*, support Sâr Wilek as Heir, and stamp out any traitors to his name."

A spark lit in Janek's eyes. "All while I am gathering evenroot to myself. And when I have it, I will have power over them all. Oh, I like this very much."

"But will Sâr Wilek allow it?" Kamran asked.

A slow smile spread across Janek's face. "He will if I first gain permission from our Father. I will think more on this. Right now you must all help me plant my dying sandvine. Perhaps, as Lady Pia has suggested, it will take root or go to seed and next spring bring about a fresh crop on Bakurah Island for its colonists."

"Good evening." Fonu Edekk entered the tent, his presence bringing a curious silence over the group. He was a short, muscular man with black skin, full lips, and a big nose.

"What are you doing here?" Janek demanded.

Fonu strode over to Janek's chair, hands behind his back. "I came to speak to you."

"Most involved in today's attack were captured," Janek said, "though your name was not on Wilek's list of rebels. Where have you been hiding yourself?"

"In the forest. I've had a message from Moon Fang."

Janek drained the rest of his goblet of wine. "Of course you have. What does he want now?"

"He is sending a boat to fetch us. To take us to his ship."

"Ridiculous!" Janek said. "I am not going anywhere."

"Why not?"

"Why shouldn't I turn traitor on my father and side with his enemy? You really need ask?"

"He has made himself king of Sarikar," Fonu said. "You are his Heir."

"To rule what nation? Armania is on the *Seffynaw*, not on whatever ship my grandfather stole. How can he even ask this of me? After he took Timmons from me and left me to rot in prison. I must appease my father, not anger him further. Had you succeeded in your endeavor, we might be having a very different discussion at present. But you failed. So away from me. I want nothing to do with your mutinous plots."

"After all we've done to forward your claim, you would abandon us?" Fonu asked.

Janek picked up his potted sandvine from the floor. "No one consulted me on this foolish plan. Yet you expect me to stick out my neck to help you clean it up? Impossible. Your last effort to put me on the throne left me in a holding cell for three weeks. I won't risk myself again for your reckless ambitions. You may leave. You're no longer welcome here."

"Yet Kamran gets to stay?" Fonu asked. "He is one of us. And Nellie and Jay—"

"Kamran was wise enough to fix his own problems without groveling to me. Get up, all of you. We must put my sandvine in the ground." Janek carried the plant past Fonu and out of the tent.

✦ ✦ ✦

After returning to Janek's tent, everyone resumed their former positions except for Janek, who fell back on his bed and stretched out.

"I'm hungry," he said, patting his stomach. "Kamran, go find me something to eat. Pia, rub my feet. They're sore from all that walking."

Lady Pia walked to his bedside, knelt, and removed Janek's boots. Hinck couldn't imagine how the lady managed it so often with a smile on her face.

Kamran returned and Janek demanded that he, Hinckdan, and Lady Mattenelle act out a play. Lady Mattenelle hated playacting because she was terrible at it. Kamran had been acting out plays for years in the court of the king. Hinck was new to the sport, but he'd fared well enough at spying so far. Acting was just more of the same. Plus he enjoyed embellishing his lines to make them more dramatic. Janek seemed to like it too because he always gave Hinck the heroic roles and made Kamran the villain.

Hinck caught Lady Pia staring as he waxed poetic in the role of Athos, god of justice. She often watched him closely when he was acting, and it made him nervous. Of the two concubines, most men fawned over Lady Mattenelle, a goddess of a woman, to be sure, with her voluptuous body, huge amber eyes, long coils of black-and-gold hair, pouty lips, diamond nose ring, and a helpless way of talking that made men want to open doors and canisters for her.

Lady Pia, on the other hand, had an athletic body with just enough muscle to make her intimidating. She had dark brown eyes, a black onyx nose ring, and wore her hair straight and cut at a circular angle, starting at her left shoulder and tapering around to her right elbow. Everything about her seemed strong and fierce, yet she served Janek with the utmost humility and her alto voice sounded like music.

A guard pulled aside the tent flap for a maid carrying a platter of food. It was Shemme, Cook Hara's daughter. She wore a black dress under her apron, still mourning the loss of Kell, her betrothed, who had died in the Woes.

"Put it here on the end of my bed," Janek said, his devious gaze locked on the girl. "What is your name, maid?"

Shemme kept her gaze on the dish. "I am Shemme, Your Highness."

She grasped the lid, but Janek set his hand over hers. Hinck's stomach lurched. Surely Janek wouldn't pursue Shemme? She was pretty in a gangly, young sort of way. Hinck's age and terribly shy.

"Your skin has a red tint. Have you Magonian blood in your veins?"

Her eyes flashed wide and her bottom lip trembled. "I don't know what you mean."

Janek gave her that slow, confident smile. "You're not in trouble, Miss Shemme. I find Magonians delightfully mysterious."

Before Shemme could reply, Sir Jayron let in a page boy. He handed a roll of parchment to Sir Jayron, who read it, narrowed his eyes, and carried the message to Janek.

"What is it?" Janek asked with a hint of exasperation. He took the message and read it. Whatever words were scratched upon the parchment changed all his plans. "Leave," he told Shemme.

The relief on the maid's face as she scurried from the tent matched that in Hinck's heart.

Once she was gone, Janek told the page, "My answer is yes. Deliver it instantly."

The boy nodded and ran off.

"What is it?" Kamran asked.

Janek handed him the scroll. "Do take note that I have done nothing to instigate this visit. She comes of her own accord. So you see, it is obvious that I am the favorite of every woman."

This type of comment usually produced a snorting laugh or snide comment from Kamran, but the look on the stray prince's face after he read the scroll could only be described as stunned.

A breath later Hinck saw why. The drape pulled aside, and Lady Zeroah Barta entered. Alone.

Was she insane? What did she mean by coming here by herself?

"Sâr Janek." Lady Zeroah took hold of her black skirt and curtsied. "I hoped to get to know Sâr Wilek's brothers better and thought I would visit you first. I did not realize you had company."

"They were just going," Janek said. When no one moved, he clapped his hands. "Get out!"

Everyone jumped to their feet. Hinckdan moved toward the exit, staring at Lady Zeroah in a daze. What madness had come over her?

All five exited the tent. Sir Jayron took his post outside the doorway with the other guards. Lady Mattenelle wandered off toward the soldier's tents. Kamran mumbled something about getting some food and chased after her.

Hinck stumbled down the path to the main tent, his thoughts a fog of confusion. Where was he going? He stopped to rub his eyes, frustrated that he did not know his own mind. Lady Pia passed him by, and suddenly he remembered. Janek had sent them away. *Why*, he could not recall. A new woman, likely.

Lady Pia set off down the trail toward the ocean. Hinckdan followed, wanting to sit on the sand and think. He willed Lady Pia to take the next path to Lady Zenobia's tent. Instead she slowed, turned her head, and met his gaze.

He stopped in his tracks.

"Sorry." She stepped off the path and into the waist-high grass. "Am I blocking your way?"

"No," he said, nervous to be speaking to her alone, to be so close. They were nearly the same height, and Hinck suddenly longed to be tall like Trevn.

"Where are you going?" she asked.

"I'm not sure," he said.

"Me either. Was Kamran smoking his pipe tonight?"

Hinck tried to remember. "I think so."

"Perhaps he was smoking something other than tobacco."

That would explain why Hinck felt so strange. He grinned, relieved not to be losing his mind. "I bet you're right."

Lady Pia's dark gaze seemed to cut through his, as if she had the power to read his thoughts. The moonlight glinted in her eyes and off the black onyx jewel in her nose.

She blinked and the spell was broken. Women should not have such power over a man. Hinck didn't like the way it made him feel completely helpless.

He thought of Lady Eudora and how she had used him. "Lady Pia, do you think love and fidelity possible? I mean, have you ever known it to be true?"

"You ask such a question of a concubine? What would I know of love and fidelity?"

A fair point. "Forgive me . . . my thoughts are scattered. It's only . . . Why do so many women say they want loyalty, then allow themselves to be used?"

"I cannot speak for *so many* women. Can you be more specific?"

"Well, yes. Lady Eudora told me she never wanted to be queen. So why marry Pontiff Rogedoth?"

"You have more experience with Lady Eudora than I do. Did she say something different before allowing you to use her?"

Hinck sucked in an injured breath and stalked off through the grass toward the ocean, annoyed at himself for bringing up the subject in the first place.

He reached the beach and dropped onto the soft, dry sand, leaning back on his arms. The night sky was clear, the waning moon still plump and bright. Out on the glassy water the fleet sat like floating candles, lighting the sea as if reflecting the stars above. The waves rushed in and out, splashing against a cluster of rocks off to his right and sizzling up the hard-packed sand toward his feet before sliding away again. Distant music and laughter trickled from the camp on his left. The peacefulness set his mind at ease.

Footsteps scuffed through the sand behind him. He glanced over his shoulder. Lady Pia. She walked straight toward him, her silky skirt swishing with each step. She stopped on his right. "Something bothering you?" she asked.

He squinted out to the dark sea. "I realize it is no secret how much I once admired Lady Eudora."

"Once?" Lady Pia asked. "Don't you admire her still?"

He shook his head. "She used me to anger Janek. She never truly cared for me."

"You sound like a jilted female."

He looked up to her, saw her fight back a smile, which made him desperate to defend himself. "I am not so bad, you know, as young men go. I have a fortune and land—well, I did. Sâr Wilek assures me I still have my title, so unless we all drown, I will likely own land again someday. I am not cruel. A woman could do far worse than to marry me."

Her eyebrows rose. "You want to marry."

He rubbed the back of his neck, flustered. "Sit down if you insist on talking to me. Looking up at you is giving my neck a crick."

In one sweeping motion she sank crosslegged beside him, her skirt fanned out like a seashell over her legs and feet. He leaned forward, lifting his hands from behind him and setting his elbows over his bent knees.

"There was a time when you and Sâr Trevn were inseparable," Lady Pia said. "Do you miss his company?"

"Sometimes." Trevn could be trying, but Hinck missed his friend a great deal.

She sighed, staring up at the night sky. "If only we had a minstrel to employ," she said, mercifully changing the subject. "This evening is too beautiful not to be cast into memory by words."

"Are not concubines learned in such things?" Hinck asked.

"We are trained to entertain, but that does not make us gifted."

The waves rushed toward them and fizzled out but two paces from where they sat. Hinck watched them glide back out to sea.

"I can't imagine your occupation would be easy," Hinck said.

"It isn't, even with a kind master. Lady Lebetta was an exception. Sâr Wilek treated her almost like a wife. The rest of us are not so well off. Our *occupation*, as you put it, often leads to an early death."

Her words shocked him. "Sâr Janek hurts you?"

She chuckled. "Nothing so dramatic as that. It is stress that kills so many concubines and mistresses. The stress of having to constantly be flawless. Beyond the physical demands of our relationship, we have one duty we cannot fail."

"Obedience?"

She winked at him. "Not if we are clever. We must learn our charge well. Know his needs before he asks. Listen to his woes. Comfort him in the way that best fits his personality. We must be unfailingly charming, devoted, amusing, and beautiful yet never detract attention from our lord, lest we outshine his glory."

"That sounds near impossible."

"Perfection is impossible, but that is our role."

They sat in silence and stared into the night. Lady Pia began to fidget, threading her fingers together and apart. He wondered what she was thinking. Why she was here. What could possibly be making her nervous. While Hinck's memory was still foggy, he was nearly certain that Janek had not commanded her to give Hinck any special attention. So what did she want?

A minstrel, she'd said. Someone to cast the beautiful night into words.

Hinck looked up at the starry sky and made his best attempt at poetry. "In a boundless expanse are we, two, where grains of sand are the multitude. In a black field is the moon, one, abounding in stars . . . thieving . . . its solitude." He winced inside, hoping that would do.

124

From the edge of his vision, he saw Lady Pia's head turn to look at him. His cheeks burned at her scrutiny and he shrugged one shoulder. "Not very good."

"You made that up?" she asked. "Just now?"

Another shrug. "I like words."

"You are very good with them, Lord Dacre. *You* without any training at all as a concubine."

Hinck chuckled, pleased by her praise and teasing. And in that moment everything changed. He saw Lady Pia, not just as someone Janek owned, but as a human being. And he liked her very much.

KALEΠEK

S tay in the line!" Kal's commander yelled.

Kal stood with the other soldiers, side by side, forming a shield wall, waiting for the impact of obsidian pikes. Hundreds of hooves tore into the earth, charging them.

Any moment now.

"Brace yourselves!"

Pikes splintered against the shield wall. Kal flew onto his back. He quickly rolled to his feet, moving his hand just as a hoof stabbed the ground. He thrust his sword up under the horse, nearly gutting the poor animal. It reared back and Kal tripped over a broken sword, this time falling on his face.

"Now! Now!" his commander yelled. "Kill the horses! Kill the camels! Kill the men! No prisoners! Strike them down! Go!"

The horse's limp legs fell over Kal, and for a moment he played dead, watching its rider through slitted eyes. The man found his feet and engaged one of Kal's comrades. Kal wriggled out from under the animal. Something thudded beside him. A head. Derson's. A young man from his squad.

Kal woke with a jolt and found himself lying on a cot in his tent, the light of day brightening the blue canvas overhead.

He had been wounded in an attack against Wilek. He recognized the bitter taste of a soporific on his tongue and wondered how long they'd kept him asleep. The wound on his side stung terribly. He lifted his arm and took a moment to inspect the damage. It wasn't as bad as it had first seemed. The knife had pierced through Kal's shirt and sliced off a swath of skin and muscle.

126

This left the wounded area quite large but not all that deep. Kal would have to change the bandages often to keep away infection, but it had stopped bleeding and wasn't painful enough to keep him laid up.

He climbed out of bed and put on his shirt, sober as he reflected on all that had transpired. The members of the royal family had done a better job of protecting themselves against their attackers than Kal had done as High Shield. His debility left him feeling impotent and ineffective. Wilek could have died. It was unfair to the realm that he continue in his position. The Heir of Armania was simply too important—worth far more to the welfare of the realm than Kal's pride.

The secret had gone on long enough. It was time to confess.

He left the tent and made his way along the scythed grass path to Wilek's tent. The guards nodded to him, let him pass without question.

Would this be the last time Kal entered Wilek's domain so freely? His chest tightened at the thought. He made no sound as he entered. Wilek was, thankfully, alone, poring over scrolls at his desk. Kal cleared his throat. "Good morning, Your Highness."

Wilek looked up, his face brightening as he stood. "Kal! It's good to see you. Should you be out of bed so soon?"

"A flesh wound. It will scar like the rest."

"You saved my life."

"You would have fared better on your own, Your Highness."

"I doubt that very much."

Kal removed his shield ring and set it on Wilek's desk. "I must resign as your shield."

Wilek frowned, face pinched in confusion. "You cannot be serious."

"I am very serious, Wil. Please allow me to say all that I must before you object."

Wilek sat down, somber. "Go on."

Kal pushed emotion aside and forged ahead. "You know of my occasional bad dreams."

"Night terrors. About the war."

Kal hated calling them night terrors. It sounded so weak. But he *was* weak. And it was time to admit the truth of it. "It is more than that. They come nearly every time I sleep. Also when I engage in battle."

"Dreams of battle?"

"No, Your Highness. This is while I'm awake and fighting. The clash of swords, the screams, any sign or smell of blood . . . it takes me captive, and suddenly I am in the war again. In Magonia. I see my old enemies. And I lose myself in the haze. I am able to fight only with part of my senses. And worse . . . my hand." He lifted his right hand and formed a fist. "The moment I strike out, it begins to lose feeling. Eventually my entire arm goes numb and I—"

"You drop your blade."

Kal hung his head. "You have seen it?"

"I've heard rumors. I thought I might have seen it once, but I assured myself it was merely coincidence. How long has this been happening?"

"Close to two years now."

"Two years!"

"At first I thought it would go away. Then I believed I could will it away." Kal shook his head. "Truth is, I'm a broken man, Wil, unfit to serve you even as a guardsman."

"Have you spoken to the physician?"

"I spoke to one in Highcliff when I was there last year. He was perplexed. Said many men who fought in the war still suffered mystifying ailments. Suggested I find a new trade and choose a life of peace."

Wilek sat back in his chair. "Kal, I just can't believe it. Is this in any way connected to your financial problems?"

Kal had not expected Wilek to ask that. Did he know Kal had lost Liviana's family house on Cape Waldemar? Did he know that Mielle had applied as Lady Zeroah's honor maiden to help cover expenses? "That's not important."

"Explain," Wilek said.

"I would rather not, Your Highness."

"Kal, you are my friend. What could be worse than what you've already shared?"

Kal sighed deeply. "Very well." Though when he tried to say the words, he found it more difficult than he had ever imagined. "Captain Alpress is a friend of the physician I saw in Highcliff. He heard of my visit—my problems, my diagnosis. He threatened to tell you everything if I did not pay for his silence each month."

"*That* is how you lost the house on Cape Waldemar?"

So he knew. "It is, sir."

"I thought maybe you gambled, though I had never seen anything to hint at it. That the captain of the King's Guard would blackmail anyone is unacceptable. You should have told me. I would have found you a position elsewhere. Did you truly fear otherwise?"

"It was my pride that refused to let me confess. I have always wielded a sword. I still can't imagine life without one at my waist. I know no other trade. And I feared the disgrace such a confession might bring upon Mielle and Amala."

"You fear too much," Wilek said. "I will not let you go from my service, Kal. I have told you before: You are my friend. I do not make friends easily. I cannot do without you."

"I'm afraid you must."

Wilek stood. "Hush and let me think!" He paced behind his desk, arms crossed.

Kal watched, pained that he had done this to such a worthy man. He did not wish to abandon Wilek. Life would be bleak without his friendship.

"I would make you my advisor if that would not be so suspicious. I do not wish to make your secret known."

"Thank you, Your Highness."

"You have heard the talk that I should wed Miss Onika?" Wilek asked.

Kal winced. "Yes."

"Calm, Kal. I have no intention of doing so. But her unmarried status makes her a mark to many men. I wish to honor her above myself and set her apart, if that is at all possible. Therefore I will do two things. I will make Inolah her companion. Between the two of them they can choose their retinue of women and maidens. That will do to protect her honor. You will be her High Shield."

"Wil, I cannot shield anyone!"

"This is in name and reputation only. In this position you may assign a squadron of guards to you both. Let those men protect her life while you act as her eyes."

Kal tried to imagine such a thing. "I'm not sure I understand."

"Miss Onika has her honor maidens, and now she will have plenty of guards. But she also needs someone to watch her back. To listen and be vigilant. Who seeks to befriend her? Who despises her? Who fears her? I want to know everything. And you will tell me."

Hope surged within Kal. That he would be able to remain close to both Wilek *and* Onika . . . "So I am really more of a onesent."

"Yes, and my spy. But to the world, I shall call you High Shield of Arman, a new office created for the protection of the True Prophet. I want everyone to know that Miss Onika is revered and special to our realm. She is the reason we lived through the Five Woes! She deserves the very best we have to offer, even my own man—my best man. As High Shield of Arman, no one would dare cross you."

Kal doubted that very much, but he cared deeply about Wilek and Onika, and dared not refuse. "What about you? An attack was just made on your life. You will need a proper shield."

Wilek sighed. "I must give Harton the chance."

Kal had misgivings about Harton. "Can you trust him?"

"I believe so. He acted as my shield in your absence and did as well as anybody could. He saved my life against Barthos, as I've told you. It would be wrong to pass him up."

"His morals are questionable," Kal said. "And being Rurekan doesn't help."

"That's why I intend to make Novan Heln my backman. At your word, he is as moral as a Sarikarian."

Kal chuckled. "I know that to be true. Heln is a fine man. I feel better already knowing he will be Harton's shadow." And conscience. "But if I sense that I am at all putting Miss Onika at risk, you must promise to replace me."

"Fair enough," Wilek said. "Let me know if you become concerned. And I will talk with Captain Alpress. He will not bother you again."

✦ ✦ ✦

Kal returned to his tent and found Miss Onika and Rustian waiting outside with Jhorn.

At first glance most people assumed that Jhorn was a dwarf, but the man had lost his lower legs in the war. They now ended just above the knee, where his pantlegs were sewn shut over the stumps. Jhorn had a dozen or so hair twists that hung down to his shoulders and a beard he had braided into one long plait that coiled like a pig's tail. He was sitting on a red cushion on the ground outside Kal's tent, holding a set of glossy carved canes across his lap. These were used to vault himself around.

The sight of the legless man slowed Kal's steps, instantly reminding him of the war and worse—filling him with guilt and fear. He wanted to leave, hide from anything that forced him to face his own failures, but today was a day for confessions. And he owed Jhorn a big one. Had Onika told the man already? How Kal had lost Grayson the day the Woes hit?

"Sir Kalenek!" Jhorn said, smiling. "I am glad to see you on your feet. Onika has been concerned for your well-being."

"Only Onika?" Jhorn must want to kill Kal for having lost the boy.

Jhorn waved a hand. "Oh, I didn't want you to die either."

"Sir Kalenek." Onika reached out, feeling the air. "Are you well?"

Kal took her hand and squeezed it. "I am here, Miss Onika. I was only grazed. You felt the scars on my face and will know what I mean when I say the wounds there were far greater."

"I wish you had not been wounded at all."

"It was my fault, but I have rectified it as best I could. Come inside, both of you, and I will explain fully." Kal did not want the entire camp to hear his news.

They entered Kal's tent. Jhorn leapt through the small space with ease and settled onto his red cushion on the floor beside the fire. Rustian led Onika to the cot, and Kal helped her sit. Kal remained standing between them. In Onika's presence, his nose suddenly acquired an increased sensitivity to the rank smell of his lodgings. Perhaps he should have remained outdoors in the fresh air. Best get on with it so that Miss Onika could leave as soon as possible.

"I have resigned as Sâr Wilek's shield," he said. "My affliction, as you once called it, Miss Onika, is a danger that nearly cost him his life."

"I am sorry, Sir Kalenek," Onika said. "I know how much you care for Sâr Wilek. But you did what you had to, and that is admirable. Honesty is the first step to freedom."

"So you agree with the physician, then, that a life of peace is all that's left for me?"

"Why would any man seek a life of violence?" she asked.

Rustian stalked over to Kal, rubbed against his leg, and purred. Kal stroked the dune cat's back. "Violence is the only life I've ever known."

"I don't know what Arman has planned for you, Sir Kalenek," Jhorn said. "But he wants to help you heal from your pain. There is no reason to suffer the way you do. I can help you, if you'd only let me."

"Another time," Kal said, not in the mood for Jhorn's mystic theories on reliving his past. Certainly not when he had one more confession to go.

Jhorn shrugged as if Kal were only bringing misery upon himself. Perhaps he was.

"What will you do now?" Onika asked.

"Assist you, if you will allow it," Kal said. "Sâr Wilek has asked me to be your onesent. I am to choose a squadron of guards to protect you while I act as your eyes."

"It's about time," Jhorn said. "That brother of his has me most concerned. He'd like nothing better than to make Onika his mistress."

"*Jhorn*," Onika said.

Jhorn folded his arms. "I'm not afraid to say what must be said."

"I promise that Sâr Janek will cause her no problems," Kal said, realizing his promise would mean very little after his next confession. "Now I must say something to you, Master Jhorn. I don't know whether or not Miss Onika has told you, but I have searched far and wide and have found no trace of Grayson. I take full responsibility for having lost him."

Jhorn's expression stiffened, like chiseled marble, and his words seemed forced. "Onika says this was Arman's will, so I am determined to trust the God, though it tears me up inside."

"You raised the boy," Kal said. "He is like a son to you."

"No, Sir Kalenek. It's more than that. He *is* my son."

"But you said . . . How?" Kal asked.

"Years ago I worked as one of Rosârah Laviel's guards. She and Rogedoth made me an offer, paid me handsomely to carry on an intimate relationship with her sister Darlis—no questions asked. Weren't no chore to me—the woman was a beauty and I was a foolish young soldier. Thought myself blessed by the gods to have drawn such an assignment. I had no understanding of what they were trying to do."

"And what was that?" Kal asked.

"Rogedoth had heard the legend of the root child. He used his younger daughter as an experimental subject, made her take evenroot while she and I carried on. And when she got pregnant, he made her take root then too. And that's where the real damage is done, turns out. Root affects the child in the womb, making it grow faster. And, as Rogedoth hoped, gives the babe special abilities."

"So when you took Grayson from the sick ward . . ." Kal said, recalling Jhorn's story of abducting the boy from Rosârah Laviel.

"I was rescuing my own son. I knew by then how they meant to use him. I couldn't let them. Which is why I didn't want to come with you to the *Seffynaw*. I was worried Rogedoth and Laviel would recognize me and guess who Grayson really was. But Empress Inolah told me they were gone, so I came."

And found Grayson gone. "Are you certain the boy has powers?" Kal asked.

"Oh yes, though I'm not sure they're as impressive as Rogedoth had hoped they'd be. You saw how the water didn't affect him," Jhorn said of the time Grayson had fallen into the poisoned red lake. "Also, he can speak any language—whether or not he's ever heard it before. He can see into the Veil, actually enter it. I've trained him to pretend he can't so that mantics and shadir won't notice him, but sometimes the creatures there take him by surprise. Shadir are beyond ugly, in their natural form."

Kal knew that much. "So the whole time we traveled with Priestess Jazlyn, he could see her great shadir?"

"Yes," Jhorn said. "And that beast was by far the most powerful shadir Grayson had ever seen—that he remembered, anyhow. Rogedoth had a great shadir. I saw it years ago when I'd taken evenroot with Darlis. Grayson might have seen it as a baby."

The news floored Kal. When he'd heard that Rogedoth was a mantic, he reasoned that the man must have had a shadir. But he'd never considered the Pontiff had bonded with a great.

Kal would have to make sure Wilek knew this right away.

"Sâr Wilek thinks Grayson might be aboard the *Vespara*," Kal said. "He has sent out several ships to find both the *Vespara* and Pontiff Rogedoth's *Amarnath*. If Grayson is aboard either, we will find him eventually."

Jhorn met Kal's gaze, his expression grave. "If Grayson is aboard any ship with mantics, Sir Kalenek, it might be too late."

WILEK

I am honored, Your Highness." Novan bowed and departed the tent.

Wilek took a deep breath. He could scarcely believe all that had happened since coming to the island. Losing Kal that morning had been a terrible blow, but it had all gone much smoother than he would have thought possible. Harton had eagerly accepted the promotion to High Shield, and Novan Heln seemed just as enthusiastic about serving as Wilek's backman. Wilek was glad of it, but still sore over the situation. Why would Arman let this happen? Why not heal Kal? The man deserved healing ten times over, in Wilek's opinion.

Dendrick poked his head into the doorway of Wilek's tent. "The empress is still waiting, Your Highness," he said.

Sands alive, he'd forgotten he'd summoned Inolah. There were simply too many issues demanding his attention. "Send her in." Once he dealt with this final thread, the entire ordeal involving Kal's resignation would be patched up.

A moment later Inolah arrived, looking completely exhausted. Her pregnant belly seemed bigger than ever, and Wilek wondered if he might be assuming too much in asking her here now.

"Are you certain you have time to see me?" she asked.

Her teasing tone brought a smile to Wilek's face. "Forgive me, sister. Just when I start to think I am clearing away parts of the workload, a host of new problems falls into their place."

Inolah eased herself onto the chair across from his. "If you are so busy, I can't imagine why you would waste time talking with me."

"It is purely selfish. I have news and a proposition."

"For me?"

"Yes, but first the news. In order to make it clear to everyone how much I regard and trust the prophetess Onika, I have given her my High Shield. Sir Kalenek Veroth will serve her now and take charge of her personal guard."

"You feel she needs such protection?"

"I do. There has been grumbling about her already. If we do not find land soon after we depart, I will trust her word above any other. Many will think that foolish and will panic. I fear she might become a target for those wishing to send me a message."

"But why Kal? There are dozens of other decorated soldiers you could have chosen."

"Well, now. This next part stays between us." And he told her about Kal's malady and how this "promotion" and change of duties was Wilek's way of keeping him close. "He is too wise to force into retirement, and I cannot do without his friendship and counsel."

"Poor Kal," Inolah said. "I knew that he had suffered losses from the war and that he'd been hurt, but I had no idea it ran so deep."

"He cannot abide our sympathy, Nolah, as I'm sure you can imagine. Now, whether that fool son of yours knows it or not, you also are far too valuable an asset to ignore. I would like you to be Miss Onika's companion."

"That's all? Seems little for so *valuable an asset.*"

"It's very important. She is the True Prophet who has been foretold for centuries. She is young and beautiful and very outspoken, and I must protect her in every way I can."

"How can I refuse? With a new baby coming, I will likely be too busy for anything more taxing."

He hoped he wasn't taking advantage of her. The pool of people he could trust was small, indeed. "I have one more request, though I don't think it will tax you."

She narrowed her eyes. "What else could there be?"

"Our young cousin, the Duke of Canden, Oli Agoros. He may not look it, but I suspect he is suffering greatly." Wilek told her about the night their father had sacrificed them to Barthos, who had turned out to be a cheyvah beast. "Oli lost an arm in the fray, yet I am unscathed. He is aimless and morose. He has no purpose, even though I put him on the Wisean Council. His family turned traitor to the crown, he has abandoned his friends—claiming to despise them—and he thinks shadir are haunting him with the intention of feasting on his soul."

"Shadir?"

"He was part of the mantic cult I told you about. This was another reason he sought to end his life by volunteering as a sacrifice to Barthos. But, Inolah, he is a clever man, funny. I really like him. He could be an asset to the realm if we can pull him back from the abyss, so to speak."

"So you want me to fix him."

"His mother has abandoned him. Your son has cast you aside. I thought . . ." He shrugged.

"Oh, I see," Inolah said. "You thought we might fix each other. Well, for you, brother, I shall try. But in my experience, young men don't much appreciate strange old women butting into their business, even if they are distant relations."

"Which is why I intend to place him under Kal on Miss Onika's staff. Kal will find some official use for him. You make sure he shows up each day."

"Between Kal and me, the young man doesn't stand a chance," Inolah said.

Another problem potentially solved. "Thank you, Inolah."

"I do not look forward to more sailing."

"It is a great disappointment," Wilek confessed.

"How long will we remain on the island?"

"Another night, at least, though likely two. I must wait for your son's answer before determining which Armanian people will remain here. For now, we are refilling all the freshwater casks and gathering as much fruit and game as this island has to offer. Some of the commoners have requested grass for weaving baskets and mats, so I've let groups come ashore to cut it."

"I hesitate to add more to your list," Inolah said, "but I feel you should be aware of the growing problems between Rurekau and Tenma. It is rather juvenile, I'm afraid, but will explain why Ulrik refuses to leave his ship."

"Do not apologize. Understanding his position would help me a great deal."

"It began innocently enough," Inolah said. "A couple of Rurekan sailors requested that, Tennish or Rurekan, the young boys help out around the ship to keep them busy and out of mischief. Ulrik found this a reasonable request and commanded that it happen. High Queen Jazlyn heard about it and reversed his order for her people—though there were only three Tennish boys involved. She claimed that her people were passengers, invited by the emperor, and need not work."

"Seems petty," Wilek said.

"Ulrik was angry, but admirably let the matter go. This left the three Tennish boys bored with nothing to do, so they began helping around the ship anyway, in spite of the High Queen's command. It seemed for a while as if the priestess would let this pass. Then Tennish women began seducing Rurekan sailors. Before anyone realized what was going on, nearly half the members of the crew had been tattooed as slavs under the control of the High Queen."

Wilek shivered and massaged the back of his neck, where he still bore the tattoo of a Magonian slav. "How awful."

"This left Ulrik's crew divided against itself—half loyal to their emperor, the other half at the mercy of the Tennish queen. Ulrik did nothing for over a week. When Tenma's founders' day came along, he hosted a banquet in the High Queen's honor. While he entertained her and her people and lavished them with praise, he had also ordered a search of the ship. His men seized every bit of evenroot they could find in the High Queen's cabin and added it to his own stash of powder, tubers, and plants he has hidden in a secret place."

The hairs on Wilek's arms stood on end. "Grounds for war, from a Tennish perspective, especially considering how rare evenroot is now." The hallucinogen had been valuable to mantics before, but now that they were at sea and could grow no more, it was priceless.

"The High Queen declared war on Rurekau, only now she claims she does not have enough evenroot to do any serious magic. Ulrik is too paranoid to leave his ship for fear she will find the evenroot in his absence, nor will he permit her to come ashore."

"Wouldn't he be better off with her gone?"

"*I* think so, but he is smitten with her. She claims that Rurekau is abusing her people and threatening their way of life, but she cannot be trusted. Her shadir is a great. The power it can wield . . ." Inolah shook her head. "Together they caused Mount Lâhat's eruption. They killed Nazer. They destroyed Lâhaten and all who could not flee fast enough. She and her creature are ruthless. I am not sorry that Ulrik has taken her evenroot. I wish he would destroy it all."

"The High Queen will find no sympathy from me," Wilek said. "A mantic abducted me and kept me prisoner—"

A commotion outside his tent brought him to his feet just as Harton ducked inside.

"You must come right away, Your Highness," he said. "Randmuir Khal of the Omatta is here asking to see you."

A chill settled over Wilek. He had known he would have to face Rand someday. The man would not have taken Teaka's death easily. "Send him in."

"I think it's better if you come out, Your Highness," Harton said. "He brought an army, and our men are holding them back."

✦ ✦ ✦

Wilek wove his way behind Harton through several dozen onlookers and three layers of guardsmen, finally stepping onto the packed sand of the beach where two half circles had formed: one of Armanian guards wearing blue and brown, one of Omatta nomads clad in shades of black and gray. A middle-aged man with twisted locks of brown hair and a wispy beard and mustache stood at the center of the visitors. Randmuir Khal. His son, Meelo, stood beside him, lips still melted away by the spell Charlon had cast.

"Rand," Wilek said, nodding politely. "It's good to see you."

But Rand's eyes were on Inolah. "Expecting a child, I see? Congratulations."

"This is my sister Inolah, Empress of Rurekau," Wilek said.

Rand snorted. "Well, don't you all give yourselves a lot of fancy titles? Claimed this island for Armania, have you?"

"All of the Five Realms will share this land," Wilek said, "but there is not enough room for everyone in the fleet. We are setting up a colony of twenty thousand people. The rest of us will sail on in search of more land."

"Any reason the Omatta can't come ashore?" Rand asked. "We're most of us Armanian."

Wilek was more concerned about them being mercenaries and outlaws than he was by their mixed nationalities. "That depends on what you want," he said. "You and your armed men don't look very friendly."

"Came to talk to you. Where is my mother, Wil?"

Every face in the crowd turned toward Wilek. "I sent a message by bird that—"

"I got your message," Rand snapped. "What did you do with her body?"

"To leave her on board was impossible," Wilek said, feeling terrible. "I had no way of knowing whether you had received my message, if you had even joined the fleet."

Meelo growled and Rand put his arm around the man. "Just tell us what was done."

"We had a last rites ceremony for her on the *Seffynaw*," Wilek said. "We wrapped her body for shipping and set her out in a death boat."

"My mother in a death boat?" Rand yelled. "I thought royal spawn were educated about the world. Magonians must be burned on an altar to their goddess, Wil. You have doomed my mother to the Lowerworld."

A hundred accusing stares locked onto Wilek. "Forgive me, Rand. You are Armanian. I assumed your mother was as well."

"I carried your pathetic soul-bound body out of captivity, and this is how you repay me? Tell me you found her killer, at least."

"It was a mantic," Wilek said. "But we have not yet apprehended the culprit."

"And all these people are following *your* ship? Letting you lead them? You who can't even find one woman's killer?"

Such taunting made Wilek remember how helpless he had felt when he had been seeking out Lebetta's killer. He whispered to Rayim, "Maybe we should bring him inside my tent."

Rayim shook his head. "I'll not let him anywhere near you, not in his state. Perhaps a change of subject will help." He raised his voice. "Tell me, old friend. You wouldn't know anything about pirates harassing this fleet, would you?"

"It's not us, if that's what you think," Rand said. "Not yet, anyway."

"And if I think it's your daughter?" Rayim asked. "What did you tell me Zahara's ship was called again? *Taradok*, right?"

A grin. "I never told you what her ship was called, and for good reason. You want to know her business, you'll have to ask her." Rand pushed through his men, walking back toward the sea. "Come on, men. It's clear we're not welcome here."

"I am sorry about your mother," Wilek called after him. "She was a hero to us all."

Rand turned back, his eyes a narrow glare. He pointed at Wilek. "Don't. You used her like you royals use everyone else."

"To do what was necessary to save the realm," Wilek said.

"Maybe. Or maybe it was only to save yourself."

✦ ✦ ✦

A noise woke Wilek. Panic seized him that Rand had returned to take revenge for the death of his mother, until a bird squawked and lighted on the roof of his tent, shaking the canvas. Wilek watched the bird's shadow for several deep breaths, then sat up and faced the darkness of night, frustration flooding him. Ever since Charlon had abducted him, he slept far too lightly. Now he would be wide awake for hours. Perhaps he should ring for a sleeping drought.

"Your Highness," a woman said in a low voice.

Wilek jumped, reached under his pillow for the dagger he had kept there since the abduction. It was missing. He glanced at the bell hanging above his bed. Should he reach for it? Or yell for the guards?

"Don't call the guards. I am not here to harm you." The black silhouette of a woman stepped into the orange glow from his fire pit, holding up his dagger. She laid it gently on the foot of his bed. "It is Lady Pia, answering your summons."

Oh. Janek's concubine, dressed all in black. Relief engulfed him. Two nights ago he had sent the woman a message with Gran's password. How had she gotten past the guards? "Shall I light a candle?" he asked.

"No," she said. "It is imperative that no one ever see us together. I will never stay long. First, you should know that I have, for four years now, served your father as a Knife. The king has not made use of me in almost a year, but should he call upon me, I will come to you for direction."

Wilek stared at the slight woman, shocked. She was a royal assassin?

"Second, Sâr Janek still wants to be Heir of Armania and someday rule, but he is not currently working directly against you. He seeks evenroot more than anything and has found Teaka's newt Errp. He plans to use it to search the ship for Teaka's supply of evenroot, hoping, in the process, to catch Teaka's killer and impress you and your father."

Janek actually wanted to do something useful? "How did he get the newt?"

"That matters not. The rosâr will likely grant him permission to search, and when you learn of it, I urge you to let him take this path. It will keep him occupied from more destructive mischief. I shall keep you informed of everything he finds."

"Thank you," Wilek said, awed by Gran's gift.

"I have one more item," Lady Pia said. "It is grave."

"Continue."

"There is a rumor spreading that Lady Zeroah visited Sâr Janek's tent late last night. Alone."

Heat filled Wilek. "What!" He threw off his blanket and jumped out of bed.

Lady Pia backed up a step. "Please keep your voice down, Your Highness. And remember, this is only a rumor."

Wilek stopped, put his hands on his hips, and tried to calm himself. "What are the details of this rumor?"

"It is most strange. No one seems to have any memory of seeing her, but I did overhear Sâr Janek tell Sir Jayron that Lady Zeroah had come to him and that they had been intimate."

Betrayed again? Why? "Did Janek say he summoned her?"

"Not that he told Sir Jayron. He seemed surprised by her visit, yet boastful, as always."

Wilek stood in place, keenly aware of his bare feet, cool against the woven mats on the floor. His trousers had twisted slightly at the waist and around his knees. On his finger, his signet ring felt heavy. Here he stood in the dark of night and heard in his mind a herald blow his tune on the trumpet and call out his name: *Wilek-Sâr Hadar, the First Arm, the Dutiful, the Godslayer, Heir to Armania.*

In the face of such blatant rejection, nothing mattered. Not his rank, not his hard work this past month, nor his fighting against traitors to save his realm. The lady simply wanted Janek instead of him. He wasn't enough for her. He had never been enough for anyone.

Lady Pia merely watched him. He could see her now, a dark shadow with two pinpricks of reflected light from the dying fire to mark her eyes. "I will try to learn more," she said, "and come to you at once should I hear further rumors or see her anywhere near him."

What would he do? he suddenly wondered. Would he expose her to all? Could he marry her, knowing of this? He didn't think he could. But if it offered stability to the realm, he might have to.

Or perhaps nothing had happened and it was only a rumor Janek had started for fun.

"Do you have any tasks for me?" Lady Pia asked.

Wilek's mind was completely distracted. "I don't know at the moment. I shall have to think on it. How will I summon you?"

"Place a rug in front of your door, whether you sleep in a tent, ship's cabin, or a bedchamber. I will be watching, always, and will come to you at night."

"That will do," Wilek said, not knowing how to end the conversation.

Lady Pia nodded and walked away, not toward the door, but to the back of the tent. Somewhere in the darkness, she vanished. Wilek walked the way she'd gone but could see no sign of her. She must have slipped under the tent's edge, but not one ripple marred the canvas wall.

He went back to bed but could not sleep. He relived Pia's visit over and over, repeating her words in his memory.

"A rumor . . . Lady Zeroah visited Sâr Janek's tent late last night. . . . I did overhear Sâr Janek tell Sir Jayron that Lady Zeroah had come to him . . . they had been intimate."

First Lebetta had betrayed him. Now Lady Zeroah. Wilek was far from perfect. He had been too busy to court the girl properly. Had put her off too long. But a delayed marriage was no excuse for such treachery. If she had done this, it could not be undone.

What had come over her? The loss of her mother and now her grandfather must have ruined her mind. Regardless, it was unacceptable.

All of it.

Trevn

Trevn had managed to spend two full days on Bakurah Island before Wilek remembered his pledge to Master Bussie and sent him back to the *Seffynaw*. But whether Trevn had been climbing limber trees, examining coral reefs, drawing maps of the island, or loading cargo onto the ship, his mind was consumed by the life he had taken. He kept seeing it over and over in his mind, the moment his sword had entered his attacker.

He had killed a man.

He hadn't told Mielle yet—had barely seen her. Rosârah Brelenah kept her as busy as Captain Livina kept the sailors. Everyone had work to do if they were to sail into the Northsea in search of land. After leaving Everton, once they'd forgiven themselves for living while so many had died, they'd felt hopeful with the destination of Bakurah Island in mind. But now that had fallen through, and while a small portion of people had stayed behind to start the colony, the majority could not. That left those on board keenly aware that they must sail on, even to their deaths—which many felt was exactly what would happen.

Word finally came that they would leave the next morning at dawn, intensifying their final hours into a frenzy of last-minute demands. Butchered pigs and birds were to be taken to Hara; sacks of feathers, pelts of pig fur, and bushels of cut grass for weaving were delivered to Rosârah Brelenah; and freshly carved water jugs full of drinking water were hauled down to Master Bylar, the steward, to be stowed in the hold.

Trevn was on dawn watch. The captains Livina, Alpress, and Veralla met to determine that all who were leaving with the ship were accounted for. Then

Captain Livina called the watch to raise anchor, and Trevn manned one arm of the capstan, pushing with the other sailors to lift that which kept them within reach of hope. Once the anchors were up, Bussie ordered Rzasa and Trevn to climb the foremast and stand ready to unfurl the sails.

"May Thalassa give us a safe voyage," Captain Livina said, "and may Mikreh lead us through the Northsea to a land more bountiful than this."

Or bigger, anyway.

"Ease the rope on the foresail," Bussie called up to Rzasa and Trevn, who set to work.

Moving from forecastle to quarterdeck was much easier now for the sailors. While Trevn had been on the island, Captain Livina had employed the men in building a suspended platform of rope harpings over the heads of the passengers clogging up the main deck. The sailors could now scurry about unhindered, loosening or fastening lines and sheets, hoisting sails, and tightening the rigging.

They would go slowly this first day back at sea, as it would take time for all the ships to assume the order of the fleet. Once the *Seffynaw* was northbound and had found favorable winds, Bussie called Trevn and Rzasa to join Cadoc on the quarterdeck to patch holes in a spare mainsail. Trevn had never used a needle and thread before, but his fingers had always been adept with small details, and though his stitches were fat and crooked, he fared much better than Cadoc, who had yet to even thread his needle.

"Captain Veralla used to help us mend our things when we were traveling," Cadoc said. "He said we were all used to women doing our work and that none of us knew which end of the needle was which."

"What woman did *your* mending?" Trevn asked.

"My mother." Cadoc glanced over the port rail to the vice flagship. "She and my father are aboard the *Rafayah*."

"I am glad to hear it," Trevn said, realizing that he knew nothing of Cadoc's family and not liking how self-absorbed that made him feel. "I should like to meet them when we land."

"They would like that," Cadoc said. "Mother especially was relieved to have me working as a shield. She thinks I'm safer in this position."

Trevn dropped his section of the sail into his lap. "After Beal tried to kill us in my mother's apartment?"

"I have no intention of ever telling her about that event," Cadoc said.

"Ottee said you killed a man on the island," Rzasa said to Trevn.

"What?" Cadoc roared, staring at Trevn as if scolding a child.

Trevn ignored his shield's reaction and met Rzasa's dark eyes, wondering who had told Ottee. "Some rebels attacked Wilek and I got drawn into the fray. It was him or me. I saw that quickly enough." He probably would have died, standing there stupidly, if it had not been for Inolah's quick action. His sister, great with child, had killed three men. A woman worth knowing better, he decided.

"I don't like how killing makes me feel," Rzasa said.

"You've killed before?" Cadoc asked, incredulous.

"Twice," Rzasa said. "I served aboard a merchant ship my first three years. We were attacked by pirates a half dozen times. In those situations it's kill or be killed."

"I keep dreaming about it," Trevn said. "Reliving the moment, I mean."

"That's normal," Cadoc said.

It was? "How long until it stops?"

His shield shrugged. "Impossible to know. Every man is different."

The bells rang for the watch change. Trevn wouldn't be meeting Mielle until after the midday watch, so he, Cadoc, and Ottee joined Rzasa and the sailors for breakfast.

Breakfast for the average sailor turned out to be a rock-hard roll, a slice of whitefish, and mush. Rzasa poured tea over his roll to soften it. Trevn did the same but found it all quite bland, especially since there was no salt or spices to be had for sailors.

Nietz entered the galley, copper mug in hand. "Eating with us now, are you, Boots?"

"Sir Cadoc and I thought we'd give your fare a try," Trevn said.

Nietz chuckled. "So we'll never be seeing you in here again, is that right?"

Trevn lifted his mug in mock toast. "I drink to your foresight, Master Nietz." And he choked down a glob of lukewarm mush.

Nietz sat with them. "Heard you got into a scrape on the island."

"Wasn't my idea," Trevn said.

"Rarely is. I know Sir Cadoc has trained you to fight with a sword, but if you ever want to learn how to stop a man with your bare hands, I'd be willing to show you."

The offer surprised Trevn. "I would like to learn."

"Next watch," Nietz said. "You and I will have some fun."

After breakfast Trevn went to bed, hoping to catch a few hours' sleep before the midday watch. But as he lay in his hanging cot, he kept seeing his sword stab that man, hearing the soldier's gasp, smelling the blood, seeing it on the ground, his blade, his hands.

He hadn't strung the dead man's braid in his hair like a soldier. Instead he'd hidden it in the bottom drawer of his desk. He saw no reason to brag about having killed anyone. And that was the only reason he could see to wear the braid. He didn't understand why so many soldiers did it. To look threatening, perhaps? In that regard Trevn supposed it worked.

He wanted to find Mielle, to tell her about it, so she could comfort him. But as he couldn't see her until after the midday watch, he would have to suffer until then.

✦   ✦   ✦

Mielle's consolation over Trevn's ordeal on the island was everything he had hoped it would be. They'd met in the cabin she shared with her sister and nurse, both of whom were on deck as Miss Darlow chaperoned Miss Amala's outing with the sârahs and their guards. This left no one to chaperone Trevn and Mielle but Cadoc, who took his usual place out in the hall. An ineffective chaperone, which suited Trevn just fine.

Mielle sat on the bed, leaning against the wall. Trevn lay on his back with his head in her lap, looking up into her face as he told his tale. She exclaimed over the danger he'd encountered, praised his bravery in standing by Wilek and the king, and lauded his skill in protecting himself and his pregnant sister—which wasn't at all how it had happened, but Trevn did not correct her assumption. Mielle cherished his remorse at having killed but reminded him that villains brought such consequences upon themselves. All these things were said while petting his hair or face, holding his hand, or rubbing his shoulders. None of these ministrations changed what he had done or washed the memory from his mind, but her words and actions mollified his conscience in a way that no other person had been able to.

"You are too good to me," Trevn told her when finally she fell silent. "Is there something I can do for you?"

She grinned down on him. "My friendship requires no compensation."

"There must be something? We could talk of Miss Amala or Lady Zeroah?" Mielle had lately sworn not to talk of either, claiming she would only annoy herself.

"Actually . . ." She touched her throat. "I would like my shard necklace. I had packed it in Zeroah's trunk before she cast me out."

Well, that wasn't right. "If she has something of yours, she should return it to you."

"I doubt she knows she has it," Mielle said.

Trevn sat up. "Then let's ask her."

"Oh, no, Trevn. I don't want to speak with her."

He pushed himself off the bed and reached back for her hands. "You don't have to. I will." He pulled her up until she was standing in front of him. "Let me try, please?"

"Thank you, Trevn." And she kissed him.

✦　✦　✦

Trevn, Mielle, and Cadoc found the door to Lady Zeroah's cabin locked. No one answered when they knocked, so Trevn decided to find another way in. "Wait here with Miss Mielle, Sir Cadoc."

"What are you going to do?" Cadoc asked.

Trevn grinned. "You'll see."

"Why is this so important, Your Highness?" Cadoc asked.

"Because we must find Miss Mielle's . . ." But Trevn could not remember what she had lost. "What was it, Mielle?"

She shook her head. "I don't recall. It must not be very important."

But it was. He just knew it. Why couldn't he remember? "Stay here. I'll be right back."

"Hurry," Mielle called after him. "I don't like being here when I can't remember why."

Trevn ran up to the stern deck, found a length of rope, and tied it on the rail above where he thought Lady Zeroah's cabin to be. It was then that he remembered they had been looking for Mielle's shard necklace. How strange that they'd forgotten before.

Trevn swung his legs over the rail and lowered himself quickly, winking at two boys who were staring. Hand over hand he let himself down past the port windows of his father's cabin. Another level down brought him to the square window of Lady Zeroah's cabin. He pushed the curtains aside and kicked his legs through the opening. He waved up at the boys, who were now watching him from over the stern rail, then slid into the cabin.

The room smelled dank and slightly of decay. He pushed open the curtains to give himself enough light to see his way to the door and wondered how Lady Zeroah had locked it from the inside when she was not here. He unlatched it, opened it, and Mielle, whose back was to him as she faced Cadoc, yelped and spun around.

"You madperson!" She swatted his arm. "How did you get in there?"

He pulled her inside and shut the door in Cadoc's face. "Where's your sense of adventure?"

"I still don't remember why we're here."

"To find your shard necklace," Trevn said.

"Oh, that's right!" Mielle tugged at his sleeve. "But she will catch us. Then she will hate me even more."

"She is horrible for hating you in the least." He scrutinized the cabin and found two trunks under the desk. He set upon them like a treasure hunter but found nothing but dresses upon dresses. Mielle searched a small box on top of the sideboard that contained jewelry.

"It's not here," Mielle said. "Perhaps she discarded it."

"Knowing what it meant to you?"

Mielle shrugged and sat down on the bed. "I refuse to believe I was so deceived by her. She is not an evil person. I must have done something to wrong her, but I can't think what."

Trevn opened a cupboard on the sideboard and caught sight of a bronze canister embossed with a prickly leaf design. He reached for it but stopped when Mielle called to him.

"There is a trunk under here. Can you help me?"

Trevn joined Mielle at the bed built against the bulkhead. He got down on his knees and pulled out an ornate wooden trunk, which took far more effort than expected. "This is heavy."

Mielle crouched beside him and reached for the latch. "And locked."

Trevn grinned. "I can pick locks."

"Who would teach a sâr such a thing?"

"I taught myself." He reached into her hair and pulled out a hairpin. "This should work."

A curl fell loose, dangling down past her chin. Trevn resisted the urge to tug it and started working on the lock. With Mielle watching so eagerly, it took much longer to open than he would have liked. When finally the latch sprung, he sat back and let Mielle do the honors.

She lifted the lid and screamed.

"What?" Trevn lunged forward to see inside.

Lady Zeroah's gaunt face looked up at him, eyes frantic, lips cracked and bleeding. An awful smell wafted from her emaciated body, which had been forced into a fetal position, her feet curled in on one another.

"Oh, Zeroah! What has happened?" Mielle lifted the lady's limp hand in both of hers.

Trevn stared at Lady Zeroah, thoughts clicking into place. He recalled Wilek's story of what had happened to Hrettah. "Wilek said the mantic who kidnapped him had once looked like Lady Lebetta. What if the same woman took Lady Zeroah's likeness?"

"Yes." Mielle stared at him, face lit with a certainty that brought both relief and fear. "That would explain everything. Oh, Zeroah! You didn't abandon me after all!"

"We must trap the impostor before she realizes we know," Trevn said.

"First we must free Zeroah from this trunk. Help her, Trevn. Then call Master Uhley."

Trevn stood, grabbed Lady Zeroah under the arms, and lifted. She did not come easily, but once he managed to budge her, she rose with effort. Her knees remained tight against her chest, her feet tucked beneath her. Trevn carried her to the bed and laid her there. She rolled to her side, still curled into a ball.

They stood over her, staring, when suddenly she whispered, "Have they wed?"

Mielle sat on the bed and took hold of Lady Zeroah's hand. "What, dearest?"

"Sâr Wilek," she croaked. "Married?"

"No! Oh, Zeroah, he isn't. The wedding was postponed. She has not taken your place."

"Arman be praised." Zeroah began to cry.

Mielle stroked her hand and tried to calm her.

Horrified, Trevn turned away. It all made sense now. Wilek's story about the mantic who had abducted him. She must have followed him and captured Lady Zeroah, still trying to achieve her goal of conceiving a Deliverer for Magonia.

Trevn went out into the crossway where Cadoc was still waiting. "Find Lady Zeroah and see that she is detained. Do not frighten her. Tell her Wilek wants to speak with her about the wedding and to wait for him in the captain's dining room. Post a half dozen guards outside and order them to keep her there on threat of their lives. She is a mantic and might be dangerous. Then find Wilek and bring him here. Tell him that Lady Zeroah has suffered a grievous mishap."

"I don't understand," Cadoc said. "Lady Zeroah has suffered an accident here, yet I am to find her elsewhere?"

Trevn didn't want to risk sending the full truth to Wilek by message. He would explain everything once his brother arrived. "Do not ask questions," Trevn said. "Simply do your part. All will be explained in time. Now go!"

WILEK

Wilek raced through the crossways and lengthways, Harton and Novan keeping pace behind him. Sir Cadoc's message had left Wilek wildly frantic and confused. Not only had the shield known nothing of what had befallen Lady Zeroah, he had looked utterly shamefaced, as if he were keeping a secret. Wilek hoped that Janek had in no way been involved. He reached the appropriate door and found Trevn standing outside.

"Lady Zeroah is a mantic in disguise!" Trevn spat out. "Sir Cadoc is detaining her in the captain's dining room on the pretense that you wish to discuss plans for your wedding. We found the real Lady Zeroah in here. She is alive but quite weak."

Understanding instantly gave way to mortification, and Wilek clenched his jaw to keep from screaming. No wonder Lady Zeroah had gone to Janek, had dismissed Mielle, had been desperate to marry. He should have seen this. Of course Charlon would have chosen his intended as a mask. How had this not occurred to him the moment she first had spoken after his return from Canden? Had she been so good an actress? That his oversight might have brought harm upon the real Lady Zeroah . . .

Trevn tugged on Wilek's arm. "Brother, are you listening?"

"Lady Zeroah . . . the real one. She has been here all this time?"

"In a trunk under the bed," Trevn said softly. "I called your mother and the physician. They are with her now."

Alarm rang through Wilek, and he barged past Trevn and into the cabin. Even with the curtains tied open to let in the chilled sea air, the cabin stank of body odor and urine. One of his mother's little dogs yipped at his ankles. He stepped over it, located the physician standing at the bedside, and found his mother and Miss Mielle sitting on the foot of the bed, a frail woman between them.

Lady Zeroah. She sat hunched over, staring down at the floor in that familiar way of hers. It had been too long since he'd seen her bashfulness.

"What has happened here?" he demanded.

All faces turned toward him. Lady Zeroah cried out and hid her face in the crook of Miss Mielle's arm.

"Wilek." His mother stood, blocking his view of Lady Zeroah. "Ask Sâr Trevn your questions while you calm down."

"Forgive me," Wilek said, embarrassed by the entire ordeal. "I am only concerned for the lady's welfare." He twisted around, found Trevn standing by the door and holding the dog. "Tell me how you came to discover this great evil."

"We came here looking for Miss Mielle's necklace," Trevn said, scratching the dog's ear. "She had last seen it packed in Lady Zeroah's trunk, but since their falling out . . . The cabin was locked—I mean, empty, so I . . ." He shifted the dog into his other arm. "We came inside to have a quick look."

Wilek walked to the window, saw the rope swinging outside, and stifled a sigh.

"It was a good thing too," Trevn said in his defense. "We found Lady Zeroah in that trunk. She looked near death."

"Dehydrated," Master Uhley said. "Malnourished as well."

Wilek eyed the trunk Trevn had indicated. It seemed so very small to house a person. "How long has she been a prisoner?"

"Since a week past the day I received the letter renewing your pledge," Lady Zeroah said, her voice but a whisper. "Twenty-nine days total if my marks are to be trusted." She pointed to crude hash marks along the inner rim of the open trunk.

Horror rose up inside Wilek as he stared at the marks. *Arman, why?* He forced his gaze away, walked toward the end of the bed, past where his mother stood screening the victim from view. His gaze found Lady Zeroah's, her golden eyes sunken and dim. "So very long?"

She looked away.

"Arman kept her safe," Mother said, stroking the girl's hair.

But why had the God let her get captured at all? Wilek turned back to Trevn. "You said Sir Cadoc has detained the impostor in the captain's dining cabin?"

"That's right," Trevn said. "He told her you wish to discuss your wedding."

Lady Zeroah whimpered, drawing Wilek's attention back to her frailness. "Does the name Charlon mean anything to you, lady?" he asked.

Golden eyes peeked around Mother's arm and met his gaze. Lady Zeroah nodded, loosing a tear down one cheek. "Charlon took my place. The woman called Mreegan used the face of my grandfather." Tears welled thickly in her eyes. "Grandfather's heart gave out, so Mreegan became Flara instead. But Charlon said Flara is dead now too."

So solved the mystery of King Jorger's whereabouts. "I am deeply sorry, lady. Your losses have been great." And what about Princess Nabelle? Did Lady Zeroah know that her mother had died in the Five Woes? "Is Chieftess Mreegan aboard the *Seffynaw* too?" he asked. "And what of their men and the other maidens?"

"The men sail aboard the *Vespara*, a ship they stole from my grandfather. Mreegan returned there weeks ago. She had run out of evenroot powder and wanted Charlon to leave with her. But Charlon refused. She had found a new supply of evenroot."

Because she had killed Teaka. "Where does she keep the evenroot?"

"I know not. She does not take it in front of me."

Wilek reached toward Lady Zeroah, who shied back from his hand. He paused, wondering if he shouldn't touch her. He decided he must and set his hand on her shoulder, which felt bony beneath her filthy gown. She flinched but this time did not draw back. "I will avenge you, lady." He gave her shoulder a soft squeeze, bowed to her, then told his mother, "See that her every wish is granted. I must deal with the impostor." He turned and quitted the room. Novan and Harton were waiting outside, and the three set off for the stairwell.

"Wilek!" Trevn called after him. "Do you need help?"

Wilek glanced back. Trevn stood just outside the door, still holding the dog. "Stay with her, Trevn. Make sure she is taken care of. I must not lose her again."

"Of course," Trevn said. "You can count on me."

Wilek, Harton, and Novan made their way to the captain's dining room. They found Sir Cadoc and a squadron of King's Guards in front of the door. Wilek stopped, suddenly hesitant to enter.

"This woman is capable of great magic, Harton. Am I foolish to confront her?" He glanced back to get his shield's reaction, but only Novan stood behind him. "Where is Harton?"

Novan spun around. "He was right behind me."

"The one person who can advise me on such matters." Wilek rubbed his chin, frustrated. "Perhaps we should simply kill her."

Novan frowned. "Kill an unarmed woman?"

"She is armed, Novan. With magic."

Novan's brows sank. "I am yours to command, Your Highness," he said, drawing his sword.

Wilek set his hand on Novan's arm. "No swords yet. Let me talk to her first. I want her to know she has been discovered. I want to see what she will do." He waved the guards back from the door. "Stay here, all of you." He knocked twice, then let himself in. Novan followed and shut the door behind them.

Lady Zeroah—Charlon—sat at one end of the table, in the king's place, Wilek couldn't help but notice. She stood, curtsied, and smoothed out her skirt as she stepped away from the chair. "You wanted to speak to me, Your Highness?" she asked.

Wilek approached slowly, marveling at how well her spell was cast. "Lady, do you think it appropriate to have a human sacrifice at a wedding?"

Her eyes lit up. "Would you like one?"

"My father's idea," Wilek said. "I told him it was finally time to plan my wedding to Lady Zeroah, and he went on with all kinds of nonsense about pleasing the gods. I am against human sacrifice on principle, but if you insist on attending the celebration, that is the only way I shall accept your presence there."

A wrinkle on her forehead deepened. "If *I* insist, Your Highness?"

"Novan, with me." Wilek strode toward her, grabbed her shoulders, and pushed her against the bulkhead. Novan was at his side in a breath, sword drawn.

Charlon grabbed his arms and dug with her fingernails. "What are you doing? Release me!"

"I underestimated you, Charlon," Wilek said.

Her eyes swelled and her lips stretched into a smile. "You know. How?"

"We found Lady Zeroah in a trunk."

Her brow pinched. "I regret the pain I caused her." She glanced at Novan, then over Wilek's shoulder. "Where is my brother?"

Wilek nearly let go. "Your *brother*?"

"I recognized Harton Sonber at once, though he did not know me through my mask," Charlon said.

154

That couldn't be. Wilek glanced at Novan, whose confusion matched his own. "Harton never mentioned having a sister." Was this why the man had slipped away?

"He would never have told you. That he sold his sister. Who was thirteen. To a brothel. Took the money to become a soldier. A soldier in Armania."

No wonder Lady Zeroah had so disliked Harton. Because Charlon disliked him. "You are Charlon Sonber?"

She spoke a foreign word and began to change, slowly. Height shrank, figure swelled, skin lightened to a reddish brown, eyes turned from gold to icy gray. Her hair lightened as well, now brown and curly and a great deal shorter that Lady Zeroah's jet-black lengths. Several hair pins dropped to the floor, followed by a coil of braided hair.

"Twice you've come for me, and twice you've failed," Wilek said. "I will not give you a third opportunity."

Her nostrils flared. "I don't need one. Your brother Janek did what you would not. I carry his child. A child who will deliver Magonia from the tyranny of men."

Janek! "You have maligned the reputation of a kind and innocent lady. You have helped kill a housemaid. Murdered my advisor. No doubt caused the death of the King of Sarikar. I wouldn't be surprised to discover you have committed more than twice that list of crimes. And now you will die. Novan, make it count."

The backman lifted the point of his sword to her breast, but before he could strike, an explosion threw Wilek to the floor. He rolled all the way across the room. The door opened against his leg, and Rayim and several guards rushed inside, exclaiming over the damage.

Rayim crouched and helped Wilek sit. "Are you all right?"

Wilek pushed Rayim aside so he could see. A hole had been ripped right through the bulkhead. Wilek crawled toward it, scrambling to his feet as he went. He passed by two guards helping Novan stand and reached the hole where a third guard grabbed his arm.

"Careful, Your Highness. It's a long ways down."

Below, the Northsea surged, carrying the ship along. He saw no sign of anyone in the water. He lifted his gaze, scanning the water farther out and eventually the horizon and dusky sky. Night was falling. *Please let her be gone, Arman. Forever.*

Novan appeared at his side, brushing splintered wood from his uniform. "Where did she go?"

"If she values her life, off this ship," Wilek said, loud enough that anyone who might be invisible would hear. "Find me Agmado Harton. Now!"

✦ ✦ ✦

"You do not deny this charge?" Wilek asked.

Harton stood before the desk in the king's office, a guardsman on either side. He shrugged. "Selling a girl in Rurekau is no crime."

"That doesn't make it any less despicable in Armania," Wilek said. "You are my High Shield, yet when you heard the name Charlon, you abandoned me."

"If she *was* my sister, I didn't want to risk running into her, knowing how powerful a mantic she'd become. You've talked about *Charlon* for weeks now. It is not so common a name in Rurekau, and I wondered if it might be her."

Of all the insolent . . . "All this time you wondered if your sister was on my ship and might be a powerful mantic seeking to do me harm and you said nothing?"

"I was wrong. But what is done is done. I cannot undo it. You want me to give up my salary to make up for it? Justness? Is that what you want?"

Wilek wished it were that simple. "I want to see a conscience in you, but I'm afraid you have none."

"I do not have *your* conscience. And I never will. But I am not without standards."

"Rurekan standards."

"Those standards saved your life once," Harton said.

"Your job is to protect my life every moment!" Wilek fought to keep his temper in check. "Your sister made her accusation in public, Hart."

"You will punish me for something I did years ago?"

"I will punish you for abandoning your post and keeping valuable information from me!" Had he known Harton had sold his thirteen-year-old sister, he never would have hired him in the first place.

"You will regret this," Harton said.

Wilek's neck tingled. "Is that a threat?"

"No. A warning. With a mantic seeking to harm you, I am the best man to keep you safe. My knowledge of mantics gives me insight none of your other soldiers have."

That was the main reason Wilek had decided to keep Harton on board the *Seffynaw*. "I am not dismissing you from the guard, Harton. Should I have need of your mantic expertise, I will call on you." He held out his hand. "The ring, please?"

Harton pulled off the shield ring and tossed it on the desk, where it clunked and rolled to a stop. "What happens now?"

"I am reassigning you to the Queen's Guard under Captain Veralla."

"But that's a demotion!"

"It cannot be helped." Wilek wasn't certain he should keep Harton aboard at all and trusted him to no one but Rayim. "Report to Captain Veralla for your new assignment. And thank you, Harton. You have been a friend to me, and I will not forget that."

Harton looked as if he doubted the veracity of Wilek's words. He bowed curtly, spun on his heel, and marched away.

Wilek dismissed the guards and sat staring at the ring. What did it say about a sâr who could find no shield to protect him?

Sands! He needed to appoint a new High Shield. He wished he could have Oli, but that wouldn't do. Promoting Novan made the most sense. The young man had only been with Wilek for a week, but he had been true bringing Kal's message of Miss Onika across the crumbling Five Realms. Wilek would need a backman from a family he could trust, though. No more promoting outsiders. Lady Zeroah's brother, Lord Rystan, came to mind.

A knock and Dendrick's voice drew his attention. "Your Highness?"

Wilek looked up. "What is it?"

"Sâr Janek's Order of the Sandvine has discovered that the first mate Quen has been using his cabin as a brothel. He is paying women to entertain men there and keeping a cut of the profits."

Wilek groaned and rubbed his eyes. "Arrest him and put it on the agenda for the next council meeting."

"Yes, Your Highness."

"If there's nothing else, Dendrick, I need an hour's peace. Can you see that I get it?"

"I will stand outside the door myself, Your Highness."

✦   ✦   ✦

By the time Janek arrived, all of the anger inside Wilek had cooled to numbness. He studied his brother as Janek slouched in the chair before the king's desk. The ridged brow that he'd inherited from his grandfather. Sleepy eyes as if he had reveled long into the night. A short beard in the Rurekan style, inspired, no doubt, by Sir Jayron. The small scar on the end of his nose that Randmuir Khal's daughter had given in answer to his affections. Janek wore his hair braided in five warrior locks, a tradition common to humble warriors who did not wish to flaunt their killings. But Janek had never been in battle, and this one choice exemplified all that he truly was: a vain, selfish deceiver.

"You summoned me, oh important Heir?" he asked.

"I did," Wilek said, confident in his authority over his brother. "It is my understanding that you have a confession for me."

"Really? And what am I confessing?"

"Bakurah Island. Think hard."

"Ah." Janek had the decency to lower his head. "Wil, listen, I didn't go after her. I swear. I never would have. But she came to me."

"And if your wife came to me? You'd be fine with that?"

He chuckled. "Be reasonable, brother. My wife is only six."

He would turn this into a joke. Every muscle strained against vaulting over the desk to strangle Janek. But Wilek calmed himself. Violence would make him feel better, but the truth would hurt Janek far more. He put his hands on the desk and leaned toward his brother, took a calming breath. "Lady Zeroah has been kept prisoner, locked in a trunk these past four weeks."

Janek's face creased in confusion. "That's not possible."

"Oh, I know it sounds like the tale of a bard, but it is possible. Trevn and Miss Mielle found her just this midday. She was put there by a Magonian mantic seeking to conceive a child with Hadar blood."

Janek's expression fell away slowly and his eyes grew large as comprehension dawned. "She was not Lady Zeroah."

"No, she was not," Wilek said, greatly satisfied to see that Janek could experience mortification. "Dear Lady Zeroah has been greatly abused, and now, thanks to you, she has been freed from her prison to a tarnished reputation. But that, though beyond despicable, pales at the notion that your vainglory might have given the Magonians a weapon to use against Armania."

Janek swallowed, speechless for the first time ever, Wilek surmised.

"You see my side of things now, do you?" Wilek asked.

Janek winced. "I cannot imagine she conceived a child."

"Do not dare brush this off!" Wilek yelled. "That is all. Get out."

Janek stared at his hands, contrite, perhaps, for now. Wilek doubted it would last. After a moment Janek stood, walked in silence to the door, then turned back.

"I have been useless. I see that now. Beyond useless. I have risked the safety of Armania, and for that I am deeply grieved. I will make this up, Wil. I'll find a way to help you with the ruling of the realm. I am the Second Arm, after all. And I can begin by weeding out any who stand against you and setting them on the right path."

Wilek had expected indolent mockery of the severity of his behavior. So while Janek's remorseful attitude surprised him, he did not trust it.

"I should like to see that," Wilek said, knowing he would ask Lady Pia to keep him apprised of Janek's every move to help *"with the ruling of the realm."*

CHARLON

Magon carried Charlon from the *Seffynaw*. Together they flew like birds. Through the twilight sky. Over the blackish Northsea. Skimmed raucous waves. The splashing heights of water drenched Charlon. Fully herself again. Her small feet had lost Lady Zeroah's silk shoes over the ocean. The black gown was too tight and too long. Now hung wet and heavy.

Charlon did not care. She marveled at Magon's power. Wondered what would become of her. But she did not ask. The goddess did not seem in a mood to talk.

Charlon felt her ahvenrood stores draining. She had taken a full dose this morning. Magon must have used it. To save them. To fly. And all Charlon's ahvenrood had been left behind in Lady Zeroah's sideboard. She had only her flask left.

They approached the nearest ship. It could not be the *Vespara*. Mreegan kept it far from the fleet. Magon soared toward the stern deck, and the ship's name became visible.

Rafayah.

Magon set Charlon on the wood planks of the stern deck. Lady Zeroah's gown pooled at her feet. Charlon felt weak. People were scattered about, but none seemed to notice them. Magon had made them invisible. It would not last long. Charlon needed to purge.

She fell to her knees. Lady Zeroah's soppy black gown bunched underneath her. "I have failed you," she said aloud. "Failed the task you set before me."

"Yes," Magon said. "You disappoint me."

Fear of losing Magon welled within. *Make her stay*, her heart said. Charlon wanted to. Desperately. "Do not abandon me," she said.

"Why should I remain? You have lost your power over Armania."

"I could be with child," Charlon said, hopeful that her time with Prince Janek had not been for nothing.

"You are not," Magon said.

Despair fell heavy. Charlon wept. "Will you heal me, at least? Of the ahvenrood?"

"Why should I?"

"Because I love you. Take me back to the Chieftess and I will serve you loyally forever."

"You don't have enough strength in you to power such a spell."

"I have more!" Charlon sat down. Pulled up her skirt to her leg sheath. Removed the flask. It was full. Enough root juice for a week of major spells.

Magon narrowed her eyes. "Your ways are not my ways. And my ways are not yet complete."

Hope surged within. Charlon dared not speak. For fear the goddess would abandon her.

"I will not cast you out," Magon said. "Not yet. But you must be punished."

Dread pinched her heart. Charlon had been punished many times. *Run*, her heart said. But Charlon must stay. If she was to please Magon.

"You will remain here. Do not try to use your ahvenrood, for I will not answer to heal you until your exile is complete."

"How long will it last?"

"Until I say it is over. Find the women's tent. Volunteer to serve as a midwife. There you will be safe from harm."

"But I know nothing of midwifery," Charlon said.

"You may cast one last spell to give yourself this knowledge," Magon said. "Purge afterwards, and I will heal you before I go."

Charlon fell to her knees on the stern deck. "Your mercy is great, goddess. I am forever in your debt."

"Indeed you are. But I believe you are worthy of it."

Charlon cast her spell. Depleted every bit of ahvenrood within. Then she purged the poison to the Great Goddess. Tears spilled down her cheeks. She did not know. Would Magon come back for her? She had no choice but to obey.

"Trust me, and prove your allegiance by remaining faithful," Magon said as Charlon came back from the haze. "If you do this, I will return for you when the time is right."

Magon vanished.

Charlon became visible then and nearly upset a sailor carrying a length of rope looped over one arm.

"Get out the way, woman!" he spat. "What you doing on the deck? You hurt?"

Charlon stood, gathered up her long skirt, and set off in search of the midwives.

Hinck

inck sat in the corner of Janek's cabin, fingering the silk sandvine Lady Pia had given him. He had never expected Janek to like his ridiculous idea, though it was good that he had been included. At least he could keep Wilek informed if Janek took things too far as Master of the Order of the Sandvine, which he was certain to do.

Already today the Second Arm of Armania had bypassed common decency by inviting Agmado Harton into his circle. Wilek's former shield and backman had been released from the Heir's employ, yet Janek welcomed the man warmly, bidding Lady Pia to give him a goblet of wine and pin a white silk sandvine to his uniform.

"So she only looked like Lady Zeroah?" Kamran asked Janek. "But she was really a mantic?" He looked to Harton. "And *your* sister?"

"That's right," Harton said.

"So I didn't lose our bet," Kamran said to Janek, "because that woman was not the real Lady Zeroah."

Janek sighed. "Yes, yes. But I might back out of this bet altogether. I saw Lady Zeroah just this morning. She is skeletal." He shuddered.

Of all the . . . Hinck asked a question before he said something he would regret. "What did the mantic impostor want?"

Janek took a long drink from his cup. "To get with child, Wilek says."

"That was why the Magonians abducted him before," Harton added. "They want a child of Hadar blood to fulfill some ancient prophecy."

"And it didn't matter which Hadar sired this child," Janek said. "My father

163

or even Trevn would have sufficed. Apparently Wilek, ever loyal to tradition, would not lie with his intended until they were married, so she came to me."

"I'm sure your reputation gave her hope," Kamran said.

"I tell you, she was nothing special," Janek said. "Of all the things I've heard about Magonian women, I had expected more."

Hinck got up and carried his goblet of wine to the sideboard, where an array of food had been laid out. He wanted none of it. He'd just needed some space from Janek and those like him.

Lady Pia approached with the bottle of wine. "Can I fill your cup, Lord Dacre?"

His goblet was still half full, but he held it out to her, admiring the way her long earrings dangled against the curve of her neck and shoulder. She filled his goblet, then set down the bottle and reached for him.

His hand trembled as she opened the folds of silk on the sandvine she'd pinned to his breast. "Yours is different," she said softly. "If you open the petals like this, it forms the exact shape of the moon we saw on Bakurah Island that night."

She let go. And as the petals folded back in place, she picked up the wine bottle and went to fill Sir Jayron's cup.

Hinck noticed his hand was wet. He'd been shaking so badly he sloshed wine over the side of his cup. Why was he always such a feather heart around beautiful women? He drained enough of the wine that it couldn't spill, cleaned his hand, then returned to his seat in the corner.

"The rest of you should know that it was Master Harton who thought to look for Errp when that old Teaka woman was killed," Janek was saying. "And this morning he told me his sister left a large store of evenroot behind when she fled the ship."

"In Lady Zeroah's cabin?" Lady Pia asked.

"I believe so," Harton said. "But since I no longer work for the Heir, I have no reason to search her cabin."

"Indeed," Janek said. "So the Order of the Sandvine must find a reason, and soon. I want that evenroot, Master Harton. And I will rely on your expertise in searches to aid my cause."

İNOLAH

I nolah received word that breakfast would be served on the stern deck of the *Seffynaw*. She arrived with Vallah and found only three ladies eating: Miss Onika, Sârah Hrettah, and Miss Amala. Around the table, four times as many male guardsmen stood sentry, Kal among them. No sign of her cousin, Oli Agoros, who had promised to meet her here. How vexing.

"Hrettah, how fares Rosârah Valena?" Inolah asked.

"My mother is unchanged," Hrettah said. "She fears the hard little fruits from the island made her sick."

"I ate the fruit and do not feel ill," Miss Onika said.

"Nor I," Inolah said.

"Janek believes some of the commoners brought several illnesses aboard," Hrettah said. "He and his Order are investigating the matter."

"What qualifications does Sâr Janek have to make such inquiries?" Kal asked. "He is not a physician."

This comment steered the conversation toward another concern with the Order of the Sandvine, Sâr Janek's supposed contribution to maintaining safety on board the ship. Apparently they had searched Miss Onika's cabin for evenroot, much to Kal's displeasure. Miss Amala further annoyed Kal by praising Sâr Janek's new order. Inolah would have enjoyed the debate between Kal and his ward if she weren't growing ever more concerned about the Duke of Canden's absence. The moment breakfast ended, she left Vallah with Rashah in Rosârah Valena's cabin, then set out with her guardsmen to find her cousin.

Oli Agoros had a master's cabin on the main deck. She knocked on his door. When no answer came, she tried the handle and found it unlocked.

"Please wait here," she told her guards, then went inside and closed the door behind her. The room was dark and smelled of dirty laundry, tobacco, and wine. Discarded clothing covered the floor—all male, thankfully. It only now occurred to her that her cousin might not have been alone.

But alone he was. She found him sitting on the floor under his hanging cot, leaning back against the bulkhead. The cot swung just over his head with the rocking of the ship. He was asleep, shirtless, gripped a sword in his left hand, and held a bronze canister pinched between his side and what remained of his right arm.

What in all the Northsea had he been doing?

Though she felt like an ogler, she studied his severed arm. Oli was a fit young man. His chest, shoulders, abdomen, and left arm were muscular. But what remained of his right arm was much thinner than the left. Surprisingly she saw no evidence of stitches or even scarring. The entire nub was smooth skin, as if he'd been born that way. A brand had been burned onto the upper arm in the shape of a rune. *Strange.* As was the way he'd fallen asleep holding the canister.

His wooden arm lay on the floor by his legs. She picked it up, intrigued. Someone had carved a hand and arm of dark brown wood. It turned at the elbow, permanently bent, and ended where a muslin sleeve had been glued to the wood. This Oli normally wore on what remained of his arm. There were ties at the top to secure it around the upper arm and neck. These were sweat-stained and creased from heavy use.

Inolah set the arm on the sideboard, then turned back to her charge. She found two full bottles of wine on his desk and a third on his sideboard, all unopened. She saw no signs that he had been drinking, nor did she find a pipe or any tobacco, despite its lingering smell.

Though she hated to wake him, she decided she must. No grown man should be sleeping well into the morning like this. But with that sword in his hand, she must be careful.

"Oh, Duke? Oli? Wake up, please." When he didn't move, she gripped the wall for balance and squatted slowly, which was becoming harder to do with each passing day of her pregnancy. She picked up two tunics and threw them at his face, one at a time, while slapping her palm on the wall and yelling, "Wake up, Oli. Right now!"

He gasped, his eyes flashed open, and he lifted his sword. It wobbled in his hand, and she pressed back against the door, uncertain whether he lacked the strength, stamina, or skill with his left hand to use it well. His eyes rolled in his head as if he were trying to see her but couldn't. The whites were red and his pupils very large. Her heart sank. He'd consumed something. But what?

Time to disarm him. She slipped past his legs and easily took the sword right out of his hand.

"Hey!" he yelled. "Give that back!" Yet he did no more to retrieve it but move his eyes.

She dropped the sword into his hanging cot, then stepped over his legs to his right side and took the canister.

This made him howl. "Nooo! That's mine! I need it. Give it back." He reached with his good arm and looked for her with eyes that could not seem to find her, though she stood but three paces away.

She fought back a groan. She had seen this before. Not the whining, but the rolling eyes and the lethargy.

A knock on the door and one of her guardsmen called out, "Are you well, lady?"

"I am fine," she said, setting the bronze canister on the sideboard. She prised up the lid and sighed again. As she suspected, it was over half full of white powder.

Evenroot.

Where had Oli gotten this root powder? How much had he taken to put himself into such a haze? And had he purged the poison to a shadir or was he dying?

Since she could do nothing about that, she replaced the lid on the canister and sent one of her guardsmen for a servant. Then she kept busy by gathering all his clothing into a pile beside the door, which she opened to get some air circulation.

The servant arrived. Inolah bade the man take the duke's clothing to be washed, then return with a tub and water for a bath. By the time he had gone, Oli's eyes had cleared some.

"What are you doing here?" he asked.

That he could see her eased her fear for his life. "You ignored my summons to breakfast."

He stretched his good arm. "I was not in a mental state to attend a public meal."

"I realized as much when I found you."

He sat forward and hit his head on the bottom of his hanging cot. Wincing, he rubbed his forehead, then crawled out. "What did you do to my cabin?"

"Tidied up a little." She walked to the sideboard and picked up the canister.

He pushed to standing. "Put that down."

Inolah's guards stepped into the doorway. She shook her head at them. "First you must confess where you got it and why you ingest what's inside."

He glared at her. "Why are you here? You don't even know me."

"My brother does. And he cares about you. Asked me to check on you."

"If he cared, he'd check on me himself."

"You think no one cares about you? Is that why you tried to kill yourself?"

"Kill myself?" His stump moved toward his face. He scowled at it, then rubbed his face with his left hand. "Fine," he said. "If you must know, I have an addiction that wine will not satisfy."

"To evenroot."

He nodded. "When I heard about the mantic and that she had fled, it occurred to me that she might have left behind her supply. I went instantly to Lady Zeroah's cabin. Rosârah Brelenah had just moved the girl so that servants could clean and air the room. I volunteered to supervise the refurbishment, and once the rosârah and her staff had gone, I searched until I found what I was looking for."

"You are a duke and a royal cousin. You should know better than to search someone's room without permission or take what is not yours."

Oli hung his head, ashamed, it seemed, by her words.

Interesting. Praise and disapproval had an immediate effect. "You are a fine young man," she added, wanting to balance her words. "Well respected and greatly admired by my brother the Heir. He tells me you saved his life. He has not forgotten your sacrifice."

A shrug. "Anyone would have done the same."

"You were training to be a general in the King's Guard. I suspect you know more of men than to believe that a true statement. There are too many cowards in the world. Too many idlers. Too many egoists who think themselves better than everyone else. You are none of those things. You are a fighter, Oli Agoros, and there is no reason you should stop fighting now."

The servant returned with a washtub and two more servants, each carrying a bucket of water.

"Your bath has arrived. You will clean yourself up, shave—unless you've decided to grow a beard—get dressed, then come to my cabin. This," she patted the bronze canister, "comes with me. We will discuss it over lunch. Is that clear?"

"Yes, ma'am."

Oh, Inolah did like the sound of that. Obedience from a young man such as Oli Agoros exuded potential. He was a soldier who obeyed commands, unlike her own son who'd been trained to have everyone fall at his feet. Inolah felt certain that, in time, she could help Oli Agoros overcome his enslavement to evenroot to become an asset to himself and Armania.

GOZAN

Gozan floated in the corner of the High Queen's cabin aboard the *Baretam*, listening to his human slave plot uselessly with two of her acolytes. Gozan had told Jazlyn the only way to get what she wanted, but she resisted. And so they remained captives of the cocky young emperor. Gozan's energy had dwindled from the loss of evenroot and his swarm not having returned from their search for land. If he lost Jazlyn completely, he felt he would survive. He had lasted centuries before without a human bond. He would wait until another human made itself available. The wait might be long, but it would surely happen at some point. Unless evenroot became extinct.

"Forgive me, High Queen," said the acolyte called Niklee, "but I still don't understand why you can't take the evenroot back."

Jazlyn stood at the small round window of the cabin, looking out at the sea. The two acolytes sat behind her on cushions on the floor. Qoatch, the eunuch, had posted himself as sentry beside the door. Gozan was invisible to all but the High Queen and her eunuch, whom she had made a seer years ago.

"Because I do not know where the emperor has hidden it," Jazlyn said. "It is too great a risk to use what little power I have to search the cargo hold. And even if I found the root, I would be too weak to both steal it and fight the emperor's men."

"But if you found the evenroot," Niklee said, "you could take more and make yourself strong enough to defeat them."

"There would not be time to purge," Jazlyn said. "I would collapse, and they would take me prisoner and reclaim the evenroot I had just found. No, it will not do."

"But you did so much with one vial when you were imprisoned in Lâhaten," Niklee said. "You destroyed the city, killed the emperor, and escaped in time to purge. You are so powerful, Great Lady. You could find the root, carry it to another ship, and purge there, where they could not follow."

Jazlyn shook her head. "It is too risky. If I knew where the root was hidden, then I might attempt it."

Gozan was annoyed not to have been able to find it yet. A shame they had no letaha aboard.

"Let *me* search, Great Lady," said the one called Zinetha, rising up onto her knees. "I would need but a taste of root to make myself invisible. And I would not leave the cargo hold until I found it for you."

"I do not have any root to give," Jazlyn said, turning to face the women. "I have taken the last of it. I don't even have enough to make *myself* invisible."

The acolytes gasped, shocked by this news.

Lies. Gozan smirked at the High Queen. She had one vial left, but without it her true age would be revealed, and the vain priestess wanted to keep that a secret above all else.

"What if the emperor starts taking the root?" Niklee said. "Would he be able to steal your shadir?"

Yes, he would, Gozan said, knowing only Jazlyn and the eunuch could hear.

"No," she countered, glaring at Gozan. "Ulrik is afraid to even try the root. After what he saw it do to his father, he dares not risk his sanity or his throne."

The priestess knew the young man well. Gozan had tried convincing him to take the smallest taste, to no avail. And without his tasting the root, Gozan could not gain power over him.

"We need our own ship, Great Lady," Zinetha said.

"That has been my goal from the start," Jazlyn said, "but I am afraid it is impossible."

Nothing is impossible, Gozan said.

Jazlyn and her eunuch looked his way.

"If you have something useful to add, Gozan, say it," Jazlyn said. "Otherwise do not speak."

I have given you the answer, but you refuse me, he said.

"Because I know better."

*Only fear and superstitions hold you back from having ultimate power,
Great Lady.*

"You forget I am not some fool to fall for your lies," she snapped. "Do not
mention Dominion to me ever again. If you want to help, find the evenroot."

A hush passed over the room. The acolytes, unable to see or hear Gozan,
glanced about, wide-eyed and fearful, knowing that their High Queen conversed with her shadir.

Their fear pleased Gozan.

"Our queen is wise to resist such temptations," the eunuch told the acolytes.
His words set them both at ease.

Gozan glared at the eunuch, who often dared disagree with him. Qoatch's
faithful service to Jazlyn was unprecedented, so Gozan tolerated the man for
her sake alone, but there were days he wanted to kill him.

Gozan longed to convince Jazlyn of Dominion. In the absence of evenroot,
it was the only way to create a bond between human and shadir. But too many
shadir had taken advantage, and the Tennish priestesses had been warned
against the practice. Giving a shadir full access to one's body and soul was
not easily reversed, gave the shadir more power than the human, and almost
always lasted until the human's death.

A knock captured everyone's attention. The eunuch opened the door, and
Rosârah Thallah waddled inside. The third queen of Armania was all rolls of
flesh with stubby arms and legs. If she had a third eye, she would look very
much like Gozan's common shadir Masi.

"Good evening to you, High Queen Jazlyn," the woman said, her voice
high-pitched and nauseating. "How do you and your companions fare in
this cozy cabin?"

"As well as any prisoner of war," Jazlyn said.

"Come now, don't be dramatic. A crushed spirit dries the bones. Now hear
my excellent news. My great-nephew, the emperor, requests your presence
in his private dining room at the end of first sleep."

This was the location the emperor had been holding his council meetings of late, but Jazlyn had refused to attend since the emperor had seized
her evenroot.

"The Great Lady has no interest in a council that does not recognize her
authority," Qoatch said.

Rosârah Thallah turned her rotund face toward the eunuch and frowned.
"Surely this eunuch does not answer for a queen."

"My answer is the same," Jazlyn said. "Unless the emperor is giving me back my evenroot, I no longer wish to attend his council meetings."

"I see. Well, many curry favor with a ruler, Your Highness, as I'm sure you know. And she who answers before listening, that is folly, indeed. How much more might you gain by hearing his proposal?"

Jazlyn walked toward the woman and stared for a long moment before finally speaking.

"I will come," she told the queen. "But you tell him that this is the last time I will hear his proposals if all he has to offer is the pleasure of his company."

"A violent tone entices anger, Great Lady." The queen wobbled to the open door and glanced back. "While peace brings wisdom." She chuckled and walked away.

Only when Qoatch shut the door did Jazlyn growl her frustration. "That woman entices anger. Qoatch, help me dress. And, Gozan, you will come with me and watch for any trickery. I do not trust the tadpole or his toad-like aunt."

Gozan said nothing. Jazlyn, he knew, trusted no one but herself.

✦ ✦ ✦

As the High Queen's protector, Qoatch led the way into the emperor's private dining room. Gozan followed with Jazlyn. The room was dark, lit only with a candelabrum holding five white tapers in the center of the long table. Emperor Ulrik stood waiting at one end, hands behind his back. He wore white silk embroidered in gold. The large crown atop his shaved head hid all of the henna tracings except those around his eyes, which made him look sinister in the low light. Five Igote guards stood along the bulkhead behind him, silent and still as statues.

"This does not look like a council meeting," Jazlyn snapped.

"I never said it would be," Ulrik said. "I apologize if my aunt misled you."

"I misunderstood." Jazlyn walked around Qoatch, deeper into the room. "Is this yet another ploy to force my company or do you truly have a proposal that will restore my authority over my own people?"

"The proposal is even better than that, Great Lady, if you will sit and join me." He pulled out the chair to his right.

"I will *not* sit and join you," Jazlyn said. "I have wasted enough time on your games. Tell me now what you propose so that I may answer and return to my cabin."

The emperor chuckled. "Your obstinance becomes you, Great Lady. But since you wish it, I will come to my point. It would do our people good if you and I could find a way to work together."

Jazlyn narrowed her eyes. "To what end?"

"Peace, of course. If our people see the two of us getting along, they will follow suit."

"You are naïve to think so. Only a ship of my own and the return of my evenroot will end my fury."

"First remove the compulsions you placed on my men."

"I cannot do that without my evenroot."

Ulrik sighed. "Let me prove to you that I am not my father. I propose a marriage. Between you and me."

She barked out a laugh. "You are insane! You know full well that Tennish women do not marry. I find such an offer greatly insulting."

He frowned. "Am I so repugnant?"

"You are a fool to even ask such a question. It shows how little you know about my people and the mother realms in general. You respect only your ways, not ours."

"I mean no disrespect, Great Lady, but times have changed. If we were safe in the Five Realms with no threat of extinction, I would agree with you. But our land is gone, and you have no ships. The Tennish refugees are scattered."

"That was your doing!" Jazlyn yelled, and Gozan knew that if she had been filled with evenroot, she would have crippled the emperor with her magic. "You scattered my people. You forced your rule upon us, and when we defended ourselves, you stole our evenroot and made us prisoners. In that, you yourself declared war upon Tenma."

"Think back, Great Lady," Ulrik said. "It was you who declared war upon Rurekau and my father when you came to Lâhaten. You who told my mother I would be easily defeated. Dividing your people from you was a caution I took to protect my realm. You cannot expect that I would have placed your interests above my own. To endanger Rurekans at the expense of pleasing you?"

She continued to glare, but her eyes softened. The young man might be arrogant and rash, but he was no fool. "I thought you divided us to provoke me."

Ulrik's brow pinched. "I confess I enjoy teasing you, but it would have been cruel to provoke anyone as the world fell apart. Forgive me if my decision upset you."

Jazlyn said nothing.

"I must marry and produce heirs to strengthen my rule. I have not hidden my affection from you. I find you to be the most intelligent, beautiful, and intriguing woman I have ever known. You fascinate me, Great Lady, and that is my motivation to marry you. In exchange I would make you my empress. There is power in that. Not the magic you greatly desire, but power to protect your people from starvation and abuse."

She studied him, as if considering his argument. Gozan knew better. Jazlyn would give up all her people if it meant obtaining that store of evenroot.

"I want the freedom to protect my people my way, not yours," she said.

"I cannot return your magic," Ulrik said. "To do so would put a noose around my neck and expose my realm to attack. You and I could be blissfully married for fifty years and still I would not trust you with a speck of root."

Jazlyn smiled then, but it did not reach her eyes, and Gozan knew they finally understood each other. "Emperor Ulrik, you honor me and my people with your proposal, but I must refuse. As I said, Tennish women do not marry and bear children for men. What you ask of me is to renounce all that I am, and I am not yet so desperate. I will await your solution to our problems that does not end in a marital bond between us. Good evening." She strode from the room. Qoatch followed.

Gozan remained with the emperor.

The young man watched Jazlyn until the hem of her white gown vanished beyond the doorframe. Then he fell back into his chair and took a drink from the goblet before him. "I will win you, Priestess," he murmured to himself.

Pathetic, the way humans fixated upon each other. Gozan crouched beside him and spoke into his ear. *Evenroot will help you win her. Try it. You will see. It is the only way to make her yours.*

The emperor swatted at his ear as if a fly had buzzed near, then he growled and stood. "Fetch General Balat," he told one of the guards. "It is time I disposed of some troublesome cargo."

WILEK

Wilek entered the sitting room of his father's royal cabin. There were six people present: two guards, three servants doing various tasks, and Schwyl, father's onesent.

"I need to see him," Wilek told Schwyl. "How is he today?"

"We accomplished some tasks this morning, Your Highness, but he lost his way after about an hour. Then he was . . . um . . . He was resting when I left him. Let me see if he is awake."

Tense, Wilek waited in the empty circle of chairs where his father liked to sit with his favorite friends. Lady Zeroah had encouraged Wilek to pray to Arman for his father's healing, but that only brought on guilt. Arman must know that Wilek wasn't sincere about such a prayer. His father's illness complicated the business of running the kingdom, but if he were well, his morals would do the same, perhaps worse. The only things Wilek felt true praying for were finding land, catching the pirates, and stopping Rogedoth from whatever insurrection he was plotting. When Wilek thought of everything mounted against him, it seemed too much to bear. But if he focused only on one item at a time, he could manage. One step. Then another. And another.

So many things awaited the king's approval. Wilek needed to act, and to do so, he needed the king not only awake but coherent.

Schwyl returned, Lady Zenobia and two other concubines in his wake. "He is expecting you, Your Highness. I have made sure you have the privacy you need. I fear he is a bit lost at present, however."

Dread fell over Wilek, yet he caught himself before he fell into despair.

One step at a time. He would go in. Perhaps talking with the man would bring him back.

"Thank you," Wilek told Schwyl, then entered his father's bedchamber. The rosâr was sitting up in bed, a thin blanket tucked around his shrunken form.

"Wilek! You must come to my aid." Father waved him over with both hands.

Wilek approached slowly. "What is it, Father?"

"Schwyl will not bring my grandson to see me."

"What grandson, Father?"

The man sputtered. "Echad." At Wilek's blank stare he added, "Echad II? Janek named him after me?"

"You allowed a stray to take your name?" That did not sound like Rosâr Echad Hadar. The first. Wilek fought back a smile, glad he could find humor here.

"What stray?" Father asked. "I speak of my only grandson, born to Janek and his wife."

Wilek could not follow. "Janek's first wife?"

"You know very well he has but one wife—unless you count your niece Vallah. But I'm sure you know I permitted the child an annulment, in light of the pairing having been orchestrated by traitors."

"That was very fair of you."

"I am a fair man. But I am old and have earned the right to see my grandson."

"Perhaps he is with his mother," Wilek said.

"Yes, that could be. Sârah Onika teaches him, you know. Normally I would not permit a boy of eight to spend so much time with his mother, but since she is a prophetess, well, he must learn her ways."

Janek and Miss Onika? "When did they marry?"

"It's been years now. I wasn't certain about the woman, but Janek was so set on it, I gave permission."

Hopelessness crept upon Wilek, but he held tight to the scrap of parchment in his hand and tried a new tactic. "I will ask Schwyl to bring the boy to you right away. But first I need your approval to change directions. We have sailed into serpent-infested waters. Captain Livina and his navigators would like to alter the course to the northwest so that we may pass safely by."

Father looked stricken. "Leave Nivanreh's Eye?"

"Only until we are safely around the serpents. The navigators will keep Nivanreh's Eye in their sights the entire time so that we will not lose our way."

"These serpents are dangerous?"

"Oh, yes, Father. The bard's tales are factual. They can crush a ship with their tail alone." Wilek had no idea if that were true, but he'd rather not find out the hard way. He picked up Schwyl's quill and ledger from the table near the bed, set his parchment on the ledger for a hard surface, and handed it and the quill to his father. "Sign at the bottom, Father, and we will be able to keep our distance from the creatures."

Father took the items and scratched his name in the appropriate place. "We should double the sacrifices to Thalassa, as well."

"Next full moon," Wilek said, taking back the parchment. "I will tell Schwyl about it at once. And that you wish to see your grandson." He walked toward the door, giddy that he had gotten what he needed. The fleet could change direction both to avoid the serpents and travel the way that Miss Onika and the Sarikarian priests felt they should go.

"Don't forget I want to see my grandson," the king called after him.

"Yes, Father," Wilek said, leaving the room.

✦ ✦ ✦

That night, since Captain Livina was on watch, Wilek borrowed his cabin to have a private dinner with Lady Zeroah. They ate at the captain's desk while Novan and Rystan played dice with Miss Mielle and Hrettah at the larger table. Wilek found Lady Zeroah more tongue-tied than ever. The young woman kept looking around at the bulkheads and deck heads as if they might close in on her at any moment. She ate quietly, so Wilek filled the silence with the story of getting his father to sign for the change in direction. He was pleased that when he stopped to sip his wine, Lady Zeroah spoke.

"I am glad you found a way to get what you needed from your father."

There now. That wasn't so hard. Perhaps Lady Zeroah needed to move ahead one step at a time as well. "Yes, but I'm not the only one. After I saw my father, I spoke with Schwyl about Father's demand to see his imaginary grandson. He told me that several days ago Janek asked for permission to marry Miss Onika, and my father consented!"

"Oh dear. I hadn't heard about that."

"Neither had I. So I asked Miss Onika. Janek has not yet spoken to her."

"I am glad of it," Lady Zeroah said.

"As am I. But I couldn't let it stand, so I wrote a decree declaring Miss Onika an alien citizen with her own rights so that she could legally refuse Janek if she wished to. To do so I had to tell my father this was so that we could begin trade with her nation."

"And he signed the decree?"

"He did. I tell you, with the right story anyone could get him to sign anything. He is dangerous. I must put a stop to it, yet at the same time, I am finally able to do what needs to be done. I am torn."

"You are under a terrible burden. One hand does the work and the other holds a weapon to protect against threats. But living like this every day would exhaust anyone. Let those you trust take some of the work so that you do not carry it all."

"I am trying," Wilek said, "but there are few on this ship I fully trust."

"My grandfather used to say, *'Tread carefully, weigh each decision, then act. A life of indecision is a life not lived.'*"

"King Jorger was a wise man."

She smiled sadly. "He was. I will miss him." She sighed. "There is too much sadness around us at present. I want to laugh."

"Let it be at Sâr Janek's foiled marriage, then," he said, lifting his goblet.

They both chuckled as they drank to laughing at Janek, but the bleakness of such humor quickly dried up and they sat again in awkward silence.

"I fear I am poor company, Your Highness," Lady Zeroah whispered. "No matter where I go on this ship, it all seems so small, like the trunk. Even on the deck, where the air has a chance at freshness, it is still so crowded."

Wilek's heart wrenched at the idea that she suffered still, simply from being aboard a ship, something he could not change no matter how much she wished it. An idea came to him. "You have not seen the balcony, lady. May I show it to you?" He stood and offered his arm.

It was not an overly large space, but it was situated on the stern and looked out over the sea and the ships behind them. To the west the sun sat low on the horizon, making its way into the sea for the night. A longchair occupied the space. Wilek helped Lady Zeroah sit, then settled beside her.

"Is this better?" he asked.

"I did not know there was such a place on this ship. The air truly smells fresh."

"It doesn't always," Wilek said. "The wind is in our favor tonight."

Silence followed. They had begun their relationship with niceties, and now they were right back where they had started.

"Lady, I must beg your forgiveness. I once had the opportunity to execute

Charlon Sonber and did not. And later my brother Trevn warned me that you and your grandfather were not well when he saw you both in Sarikar. Miss Mielle noticed it even before Trevn, yet none of us heeded her concerns or understood what they might have meant."

"Do not blame yourself, Sâr Wilek. There is nothing to forgive. Who could have expected such a deception?"

Wilek should have. For ten weeks he had been Charlon's prisoner. He knew her. Agmado Harton had broken the soul-binding between them, but that was no excuse to grow careless. So much of Lady Zeroah's behavior had been suspect in the last days of Armania. The way she had behaved during the final quake, demanding her trunks, abandoning Miss Mielle. He had simply been too preoccupied with the evacuation to give the matter proper thought.

"I am ashamed, lady, that I almost married her. Had the earthquake not come when it did, I would have." He forced himself to look into her eyes. "If you wish to withdraw from our betrothal, I understand and will release you with no penalty."

She suddenly looked frightened. "Do *you* wish to withdraw?"

"Not at all, lady. I would marry you this moment if I could."

This brought forth a radiant smile. "I imagine that looking at me might remind you of things she did while resembling me. Did she cause you much embarrassment?"

Should he tell her? "I may as well be perfectly honest, lady. If you have not heard already, you will soon. The only harmful development is that she—well, it seems she carried on an affair with my brother Janek in your name and likeness."

Lady Zeroah's eyes watered. "Oh dear."

"Her entire motive in abducting me was to produce a child of Hadar blood. Apparently she did not care how that came to be and lost patience when I would not . . . I did not lie with her. I felt we should wait until we were properly wed."

Lady Zeroah began to cry.

Wilek did not know what to do, so he kept talking, hoping to at least comfort her if he could. "I have informed Sâr Janek of the truth. He knows you never came to him and that his selfishness might have given the Magonians a weapon against us. I have no doubt that, in time, your reputation will be mended entirely."

The tears ended as abruptly as they had begun. Lady Zeroah wiped them away and looked Wilek squarely in the eyes. "Sâr Wilek, had she succeeded in her efforts to win you . . . I could never have married you. I am so grateful for your discretion. It is a trait I admire in any circumstance, but that it saved our marriage, I admire it even more so."

"Thank you, lady. I am pleased that there is still hope for our betrothal." And, because there was little time to waste, he added, "How would you like to proceed? I wish to know your will."

"I have but one concern, Your Highness," she said. "I am an Armanite by birth and belief. You are not. Traditionally children are reared in the faith of their father, but the fulfilment of prophecy in the Five Woes and the Root of Arman, coupled with the suffering I experienced in the mantic's trunk, have inspired me to live out my faith boldly."

"I find that surprising," Wilek said. "I would think you bitter at the God for not protecting you."

"I was so angry at first. I fought hard against Charlon, scratched her face and tore at her hair. But the magic gave me no way to escape. I knew Charlon had done this, not Arman. I felt like he was telling me not to struggle but to rest. That if I would be still and trust him, he would fight for me, make use of my pain somehow. So I tried to do that, and I comforted myself with words and songs from the Book of Arman."

"Like what?" Wilek asked, wondering if he might recognize them.

As she recited, she closed her eyes and smiled. "*'He will cover you with his feathers, armored and protected in the shelter of his wings.'*" She glanced at Wilek. "That was my favorite. And also, *'He is my hiding place. In his arms he protects me from the attacks of my enemies.'* Whenever I lost hope, I would picture myself in his arms or under his wing, and peace always came."

Gone was her timidity when she spoke of her god. Her passion surprised and fascinated Wilek. He craved such peace for himself. "You know the God well."

"I have always known him. I was raised to. But in the solace of that trunk, I came to know him so much deeper. He sustained me in the darkness. I live today because he willed it. He is generous in affliction, patient with failure, and worthy of complete devotion. I want my children to know Arman as I do. Sâr Wilek, I cannot abide idol worship in my family. I will not teach it to my children. I cannot."

Her voice had risen with each word, and though her eyes shone with moisture, she did not cry. She was fierce and determined, and Wilek found her courage beautiful. He reached out and stroked her cheek, wanting to ease her concern. "I understand you perfectly, lady. Rest assured that my heart on the matter of idol worship is in line with yours. I must confess, I have been reading Trevn's copy of the Book of Arman and have found answers to so much that I have always questioned. I have never been devout in worship to any god, so this is all very new and different. But I believe Arman is the One God and that he sent his prophet to save this remnant. For what? I can only guess to start again, and this time to honor He Who Made the World."

"You . . . Truly? You will convert?"

He had shocked her. She had expected him to refuse. "Not publicly. Not yet." Wilek felt a coward to say so aloud, but there was too much at stake. "At this precarious time with the king so unpredictable, I dare not risk the fleet or my position as Heir by blatantly defying his convictions. All I can promise is that upon my father's death, I will openly declare Arman as my One God and set about reforming Armania to the Armanite faith. Until then I must, as your grandfather said, tread carefully."

"Oh, thank you!" She threw her arms around his neck in an emotional embrace. "Your answer has given me more joy than any woman deserves."

"You deserve every happiness, lady," Wilek said, pulling her back so he could look into her eyes, "but I do not do this for you. I do it because I have come to see that Arman is true and holy and all-knowing. I could never serve any other god. I owe him everything—my very life."

"Then your faith is real," she said, still sounding surprised.

"It is." Though not yet as bold as hers. "You will marry me, then?"

"Yes, I will, Your Highness. But . . . I am not fully recovered from being so long in the trunk. I am frightened of small spaces—of being trapped. My legs feel much better now that I've been walking, but they cramp easily. Perhaps I should ask the physician if he thinks I should wait to marry."

"I will speak with him," Wilek said. "Know that I will do all I can to help you recover fully. And if you would rather wait to marry, we shall wait."

She shook her head. "I do not wish to wait, Your Highness."

He took hold of her hand and squeezed it gently. "Then let us plan a wedding at sea."

GRAYSON

We are back on course, at least?" Chieftess Mreegan asked as she walked across the main deck.

"Yes, Chieftess," Kateen said, scurrying along beside her. "My shadir found the fleet and led us to them."

Chieftess Mreegan sneered. "I am glad to hear that *some* shadir are loyal."

Grayson peeked under the edge of the dinghy he was hiding beneath. It was one of three that sat upside down on the main deck, and he liked the view it gave him when he wanted to spy. When the fleet had sailed away from the Armanian island, the *Vespara*, which had been hiding on the other side of the lagoon, had gotten left behind. Grayson knew from eavesdropping that the *Seffynaw* was leading the fleet, and it relieved him to know they had caught up again.

"How is our water?" Chieftess Mreegan asked.

"We are on our last four barrels. Torol's water makers take three days to fill half a barrel, so they are not helping quickly enough to make a difference."

The Chieftess grunted. "And how much food is left?"

"Two crates. But some of the workers have been fishing and—"

"Two?" the Chieftess shrieked. "Have you been feasting without me?"

"I swear I have not, Chieftess. None of us have."

"Lies!" Chieftess Mreegan said. "Everyone lies to me. Even my own shadir. She tells me Charlon still lives when I know she must have been hanged by now. Yet Magon stays away. Why is she disloyal to me after so many years together?"

No one dared answer. Grayson couldn't blame them. The Chieftess's

183

swinging moods scared him. The longer they were at sea, the crazier she became. No answer would make the woman feel better. Nothing ever did.

Grayson had done plenty of snooping since he had dubbed himself spy and had learned a lot about this ship. The Magonians had stolen it from Sarikar, but they hadn't loaded many supplies. They also hadn't stocked up at the island. Chieftess Mreegan had been too afraid to get close, worried they might be seen by a powerful mantic who could attack. Grayson didn't think there were any other mantics besides Priestess Jazlyn. He wondered who was more powerful: Chieftess Mreegan or Priestess Jazlyn?

He also wondered why the fleet hadn't decided to live on the island. From the sounds of things, that had been the original plan. So what was the plan now? Chieftess Mreegan didn't know, and it was making her crazier than usual.

The Magonians had no real captain aboard. Besides the crew Nuel had bought from *The Wanderer*, the original crew had been stolen off the docks in Brixmead and compelled to obey. A man called Krola had been put in charge, and while he pretended to be the captain, he knew none of the right things to say about sails and ways to turn the whipstaff.

The Magonians didn't have very many people on board. Grayson had counted just over two hundred one day when Chieftess Mreegan had held a ceremony on the main deck. And from his time on the *Baretam*, he knew this ship could carry three times that many.

"Chieftess!" Roya ran across the deck from the helm. She was the meanest of all the women and terrified Grayson. "My shadir brings news of Charlon."

"Speak," the Chieftess said.

"As you predicted, she was discovered aboard the *Seffynaw*. Magon helped her escape to a nearby ship."

Chieftess Mreegan's brow sank over her icy gray eyes. "Which ship?"

"My shadir did not know," Roya said. "That was all Magon told him."

Chieftess Mreegan screamed as if someone had poured hot coals down the back of her kasah. She started yelling the mantic language. A wave of her hand and Roya was thrown through the air, right over the side of the ship. Grayson heard her scream, heard the splash. The Magonians scattered. It was their best defense when the Chieftess threw a tantrum, which lately she did almost daily.

Kateen ran toward Grayson's hiding place under the dinghy. He scooted back from the edge. Footsteps pounded to a halt outside, and the woman dropped to her knees.

She was coming in!

The first maiden fell onto her stomach and rolled under the dinghy. She sat up and scrambled into the middle between the two benches, breathing hard and muttering. Her eyes met Grayson's. For a moment the two simply stared at each other. Grayson thought about pushing into the Veil to hide, but then she would know he had magic. He was more afraid of anyone knowing about that than he was of getting caught.

Kateen drew her finger across her lips, and he nodded, relieved that she had not chosen to send him out to face the Chieftess.

A silent moment passed where they both watched each other and listened. No more screaming came from the deck. Perhaps the madness had ended.

Suddenly the dinghy flew up into the air like a straw hat lifted by a gust of wind. Grayson crouched down. Kateen screamed. The dinghy spun through the air and crashed in the center of the main deck, behind where Chieftess Mreegan stood over them, glaring down. The dinghy continued to tumble, sides splintering with each rotation. It came to rest right side up, rocking on its keel.

The wind blew Chieftess Mreegan's hair back from her face: terrible and fierce with eyes cold and burning. Behind Grayson, Kateen stood, lifted her hands as if to defend herself, but she could not do magic like the Chieftess. The maidens required mats and bowls to cast their spells. The Chieftess only need speak.

Stuck in the middle, Grayson panicked. Without meaning to, he used his power and pushed into the Veil.

He saw the exact moment when their hate-filled eyes softened in surprise, looked away from each other, and focused on him.

Grayson wished he were underneath one of the other dinghies on the main deck.

Then, suddenly, he was.

He panted over his fear, wondering how he'd done it, wondering if the women had seen him move. He fell to his belly and peeked out from under the dinghy. The women were standing a few paces away, twisting around in confusion.

"Did you see that?" Chieftess Mreegan asked.

Kateen nodded. "The boy is a mantic."

They knew.

"Who would have taught a boy such things?" Chieftess Mreegan asked.

A racket across the deck turned their heads. Grappling hooks sailed over the side of the ship, hooked tight to the railing. Men clambered up and over the sides, swords in their hands and leering grins on their faces.

"Pirates!" Torol yelled from the quarterdeck.

Chieftess Mreegan and Kateen ran toward the invaders, who were dressed in black and carried swords. Grayson should get out from under the dinghy, run to the foredeck. Instead, like he had moments ago, he wished he were there.

And he somehow traveled to the foredeck instantly.

He laughed out loud, tickled by this new discovery. He had not known he had such an ability. He wanted to try it again, but shouts on the main deck reminded him of the invaders. He looked back to the fray, able to watch from the foredeck and stay out of danger.

A short battle ensued. The pirates were not prepared to fight against magic. Probably had no idea what kind of people were on this ship. The women used their magic to disarm the pirates and throw them overboard one by one. Once the deck was clear, Chieftess Mreegan turned things around.

"Form a crew to board that ship, Kateen. I want all of their food."

As the Chieftess turned to pirating, Grayson stayed on the foredeck, out of the way. From this distance he saw the name of the pirate ship: *Dartsea*. It was a midsize boat with a small crew for its size. How many ships had the *Dartsea* pirates attacked? Was this their first time losing?

In the end the Magonians left the *Dartsea* behind with the remaining pirates bound together on the main deck. Chieftess Mreegan let them live, hoping they would tell their pirate friends to beware of the *Vespara*.

Alone for hours on the foredeck Grayson practiced his new ability of popping from one place to another by way of the Veil. The more he did it, the more he wondered how far he might be able to go. Could he go from the *Vespara* to the *Seffynaw*? Dare he risk it?

He decided he should first try to pop from one end of the ship to the other. He concentrated his thoughts on the upside-down dinghy stored on the port side of the stern deck, then moved. But when he exited the Veil, he wasn't under a dinghy. He was standing in one that was hanging from the boat fall! The craft rocked under his movement. He sat down, hoping that would make the boat still.

Why had he come out here? Was this the same boat that was usually on the deck? He stood carefully and saw that the deck was empty where the dinghy usually lay upside down.

He must have gone to the dinghy he knew, not the place it had been. Did that mean he couldn't pop to places he'd never been?

On a hunch he concentrated on Torol's cabin and moved again.

He exited the Veil in the dark corridor outside Torol's cabin. Grayson had never been inside, so apparently this was the closest he could come.

He sighed. He had never been aboard the *Seffynaw*. Had only seen it from the outside. He dare not try and pop there, for he might end up in the sea outside the great ship. He would have to be careful with this new ability. Perhaps more practice would reveal a way to escape.

Grayson popped back up to the foredeck, but the smell of food lured him to the underside of a table on the main deck.

The mantics had purged their poison and were healthy again. All of the Chieftess's important servants were present. Even Roya had somehow gotten out of the sea and back on board. Grayson pushed out of the Veil long enough to reach up and grab a piece of flatbread.

"Pirating is the answer," Chieftess Mreegan told her followers. "It's the best way to survive this journey. We will take what we need when we need it. And we will follow the Armanian flagship. They will lead us to land. There we will set up camp and make a new plan to subdue them. Then I will find Charlon and make her pay for deserting me."

"You are wise, Chieftess," Kateen said.

"For now, let us find that mantic boy. Pass around a bottle of root juice, Roya, and set your shadirs searching."

Grayson popped back through the Veil to the foredeck to hide.

TREVn

The days went by in snatches of work and sleep. One week passed in relative ease. A second brought nothing but downpours of rain, so much that people complained. Trevn knew better. He insisted every empty barrel be brought above deck to catch the water. After leaving Bakurah Island, they'd had enough water for twelve weeks. Now they still had enough for twelve. Despite Wilek's confidence at having changed course to the northwest, they could never afford to grow lax while their destination remained unknown.

The farther north they traveled, the cooler the temperature. Today the sky had been gray and murky. It had not yet rained, but the fog was thick. The sails were shortened and the sea anchor was dropped—a precaution to reduce speed and keep from running into the other ships.

The strangest sounds came out from the fog. Trickles of water, a glub, a sigh, gushing water followed by a splash, and the occasional moaning of some sea creature. When on watch, Trevn liked to sit perfectly still—or stand in the rigging—and ponder the source of each noise.

His demanding schedule left little time to see Mielle, as she was often preoccupied with feeding passengers or helping plan Lady Zeroah's wedding. Trevn had grown thinner from so much physical activity. He gloried over his callused hands and muscled arms, which to him were the greatest proof of his learning to sail. His daredevil ways made hanging from the rigging a joy on a sunny day, and a thrill when he clung to it in the dark or when rain made everything slippery and the wind threatened to blow him away like seed.

And now Nietz was teaching him to fight—not with swords like a noble prince, but with fists and feet and teeth. Incapacitation was the key to survival in such nasty brawls, so Nietz said. It was all rather vulgar, though extremely effective at quickly ending a confrontation. It also shed some light on how so many sailors had broken noses and fingers.

As the midday passed and evening came, the fog and clouds had cleared. Captain Livina sent Trevn to apprentice with Master Granlee, the navigator. This was one of Trevn's favorite things to learn. The navigator was a thin man in his fifties with a stately posture and narrow fingers, which he used to operate the cross-staff, a tool that measured angles formed by the sun, moon, or stars over the horizon and helped fix the ship's position on the vast expanse of the uncharted Northsea. Master Granlee had spent their first few hours of each session teaching Trevn how to use the cross-staff and giving him time to practice. Once Trevn had the basic idea, the man had spent the next nights explaining how a navigator might use guiding stars to keep a ship on course at night.

"Guiding stars are those that have just risen or are about to set, depending on whether your course be an easterly or westerly one," Granlee said as they stood together on the stern deck that night. "Most guiding stars can only be used to steer by for a certain time. When the star rises too high or moves too far to either side, the next star to rise at the same point is used in its stead."

"How many stars does it usually take to get through the night?" Trevn asked.

"It's rare to need more than ten guiding stars for a night's sailing," Master Granlee said, "but since we are sailing north, we have no need of guiding stars." He sighed. "The farther north we travel, the longer the nights. I don't know the star path here like I do back home. In fact, some of these constellations puzzle me."

"How so?"

"I've never seen them before," he admitted. "A navigator should know the sky well enough that a mere glance at the stars suffices to give him his bearings. Now, I can chart courses and calculate latitude as well as any man alive, but I do not know these waters. Or these new stars." He gestured at the northern horizon. "Do you know the first trick of navigation?"

"I don't," Trevn admitted.

The man grinned. "Follow the coast."

Trevn chuckled politely and studied the stars, his gaze traveling back to

Nivanreh's Eye. What he saw made him uneasy. "Master Granlee, it seems that the Southern Star is directly behind us."

"Well done, Sâr Trevn. You are a quick learner. The king believes the god of travel will lead us to land, and so we sail before him and pray he guides us well."

"But that order was changed two weeks ago," Trevn said. "We should be sailing northwest."

"Oh, we did for a time, but last night the admiral bid we sail north again on the path set by Nivanreh's Eye."

"Excuse me," Trevn said, walking away. "I must speak with the captain at once."

✦   ✦   ✦

"Admiral Vendal," Wilek said. "Schwyl says you visited the king yesterday."

On a hunch Trevn had gone first to Captain Livina, who took one look at the night sky and cursed Admiral Vendal and Rosâr Echad for their foolish superstitions. Trevn had awakened Wilek and told him everything. Now the two brothers stood in the admiral's cabin with a bleary-eyed Vendal.

"I did," the admiral said, "but why is that cause to wake me in the middle of the night?"

"You superseded an order from the king," Wilek said.

"No, I asked him to change his order back, to trust his instincts. *You* superseded his order, Your Highness."

Wilek's jaw tightened, so Trevn jumped in. "Why do you care which direction we sail? Why do you feel north is best?"

"When in doubt, I have always sailed by Nivanreh's Eye," the admiral said. "That is a much safer decision than taking the word of an aberration."

King Loran, does he mean? But Wilek's guess made better sense.

"You are referring to Miss Onika?"

"She is no prophetess," the admiral said. "She is a witch. Feed her to the sea and we will find land, I guarantee it. There is a curse upon this voyage."

Such open hostility shocked Trevn, who looked again to Wilek to respond.

"We are all alive today because of Miss Onika's warnings," Wilek said. "Have you forgotten so soon?"

"Athos warned of apocalypse long before the aberration came alone. Justice came from the hand of Athos and always will."

"You're Athosian?" Trevn couldn't believe it. An Athosian fanatic leading the fleet.

Admiral Vendal straightened his posture. "I am."

"Athosians reject my father's sovereignty," Wilek said. "They wish me and my brothers dead."

"I don't deny that many Athosians do," the admiral said. "But I simply wish us to find land, and I know that Athos will lead us there if we are true to him."

"This fleet needs an admiral who is true to the king," Wilek said. "I can see that you are not. Novan," he called, waving the man over from where he stood just inside the door. "Arrest the admiral. He is relieved of his duties. Rystan, fetch Captain Livina and bring him here."

"You would give rule of the fleet to a madman?" Vendal asked.

"Better a loyal madman than a disloyal mastermind," Wilek said.

The admiral was taken into custody, ranting as he went that Athos would bring judgment upon them all.

"Captain Livina is not crazy," Trevn told Wilek as they sat on a longchair in the admiral's cabin and waited for the captain to arrive.

"Do you honestly think I would reinstate him as admiral if I thought he was?" Wilek asked.

"Then what of Father?" Trevn asked. He had always joked of his father's insanity, but their current reality was not at all humorous.

"I would like to call a council meeting and move for a regency period, until his health improves."

"That seems best," Trevn said.

"Yes, but will the rest of the council think so? I doubt Kamran or Canbek would vote me into power."

"Danek, Oli, and Rystan," Trevn said. "That is three of five in your favor, brother. That's all you need."

Before Wilek could answer, shouts on the deck outside brought him and Trevn to their feet.

"Serpents!" a voice called out.

Wilek started toward the door. "In all this drama with the admiral, we forgot to give the order to change the heading."

Trevn and Wilek ran from the admiral's cabin and out onto the quarterdeck, where they found Bussie at the whip. The deck was pale with predawn light.

"Where are they?" Trevn asked.

"Just one so far," Bussie said. "It's attacking the *Berith*. Dead ahead."

Trevn left Wilek and ran across the platform of rope harpings that passed over the main deck. He continued all the way to the forecastle, not stopping until he reached the bow. The waves were high and Trevn gripped the rail to hold himself steady. They were a safe distance back from the *Berith*. Close enough to read the words on the stern, but far enough back to turn about. He saw no serpent. The galley ship was heeling slightly to port and taking on water through its port oar piercings. Half the oars on that side were missing.

Then the sea swelled until the surface broke. A glossy gray head rose out of the waves. Trevn was looking at its back, so he could see only that its neck was so long it looked like a giant snake. A steamy breath puffed out from its head just before it rammed the port quarter, snapping the remaining oars in half. The ship jerked, the hull cracked, and a hole splintered just above the waterline.

"They're hit!" a lookout yelled down. "The *Berith* is breeched on the port side!"

The galley was listing now. And the more water it took on, the slower it went. The *Seffynaw* would have to move or the two ships would collide.

Trevn ran back across the harpings to the quarterdeck. Captain Livina was on deck now. He had taken command, though Bussie still manned the whip.

The captain yelled, "Clew up the mains'l! Stand by to heave to!"

The crew on watch raced to their stations.

"I don't want to be anywhere near that beast when it's roused up like that," he told Trevn. "I'd come about if I didn't have a fleet at my back." Then he yelled out, "Square the main!"

On the harping platform the crew hauled the starboard braces to square up the main top. This reduced the ship's speed almost instantly.

"Hard to starboard, Master Bussie."

The second mate obeyed, and the ship turned into the wind. The royals on the fore and mizzen tops lifted, and the ship came to a stop, drifting to port.

"Hold her steady!" the captain yelled, and the crew kept her in position by hauling and slacking on the foresheets.

Once they had drifted a good distance west of the wreck, the captain gave the orders to make the ship fall off and sail forward again. The foresheets were hauled to, the spanker was eased out to port, and the helm put hard a-port. Once the sails filled, the ship started making headway again. The main sail was set, all sails trimmed, and the ship quickly picked up speed.

While all this had been happening, bowmen soldiers had flooded the main deck and lined the port rail. Captain Alpress paced behind the King's Guard, shouting orders to ready their bows.

"Take command, Master Bussie," Captain Livina said, walking toward the stairs to the main deck.

"I've got the deck," Bussie said.

Trevn chased after the captain, following him to the main deck and the line of soldiers.

"Captain Alpress!" Livina yelled. "Order your men to lower their weapons at once."

"Why would I do that, Captain?"

"Because I command it, and the safety of this ship outranks your desire to hunt."

"That beast is killing people, or can't you see that?"

"Fire one arrow at the serpent and you lure it to us. I have experience with these beasts and know their minds. Trying to kill one is suicide. Now order your men to stand down!"

Alpress set his jaw and glared at the captain.

"Stand down, Captain Alpress!" Wilek had joined them, and he did not look happy. "Any man who fires at the serpent will face the pole."

Captain Alpress gave the order for the soldiers to lower their bows. The *Seffynaw* closed on the *Berith*, listing slightly as nearly everyone on deck lined the starboard rail for a view. Shouts, screams, and splashing rang clear across the water, accompanied by low moans from the serpent. Soldiers on the *Berith* had already engaged in war against the creature. A shower of arrows rained down almost continually, but most of them glanced off the creature's thick skin. Perhaps one in fifty stuck, and when this happened, the creature howled and thrashed, knocking into the sinking ship and breaking her further.

The serpent suddenly rose out of the sea, its neck like that of a giant eel. It slithered onto the *Berith*'s main deck and curled around the mainmast, knocking people aside as it went. Its front legs appeared—no, those were tentacles. They clutched the starboard rail just as its head turned back for the water. Its weight and its hold on the mast pulled the ship down. Men dove into the water moments before the *Berith* went under completely.

The *Seffynaw* passed by all this in relative silence, broken by a few whispers and murmurs of horror. Trevn couldn't believe how quickly the *Berith* had gone under. He imagined the creature dragging the entire ship all the way down to the sandy ocean floor where—

Something shot out of the ocean, spraying a salty gush of water over the starboard side of the *Seffynaw*. The cold water drenched Trevn, but he ignored it, shocked to see that the *Berith* had bobbed to the surface. It still lay on its side. Water ran off its hull. Trevn heard a man sputtering and coughing somewhere but could not see him.

A chorus of screams rang out from the *Seffynaw*, pulling Trevn's gaze to the front of the ship. The serpent was again moving toward the *Berith*, gliding on the top of the water like an arrow, sending hundreds of ripples spiraling like ribbons in its wake. This time Trevn could see its face. It had three deep-set black eyes and a maw of tangled, needlelike teeth. Instead of ramming the *Berith*, it dove over the top, rolling the ship with its movement. Trevn stared in awe as its full body curled out of the ocean. Slimy and scaled like a giant fish, yet its back end was made of five tentacles. The first tentacle grabbed hold of the *Berith's* bow. The second coiled around the mast. But the other three tentacles inadvertently lashed out at the *Seffynaw*.

One struck the hull below the waterline, jolting the entire ship. Another raked the freeboard, tearing a jagged line through the bulkhead of the main foredeck. When it reached the open waist, it got caught in the platform of rope harpings. This triggered the beast to pull away, which ripped the harpings off the entire front of the starboard side. Its third tentacle shot up to help, scraping along the main deck and knocking onlookers into the water like a giant hand wiping crumbs from a table. People screamed. The *Seffynaw* lurched to starboard under the serpent's weight. The creature was still occupied with its attack on the *Berith* and seemed only mildly annoyed that one of its tentacles was caught.

"Cut the harpings!" Captain Livina screamed.

Trevn sprinted toward the steps and pushed his way through the crowd, pulling his boot knife as he went. He arrived at the same time as Nietz, Bonds, Zaki, and a half dozen men he recognized from the Port Watch. He sawed at one of the harpings that had pinched itself into the slimy flesh of the serpent's tentacle. His blade suddenly seemed quite small when set against the task of cutting so many ropes.

"We need swords!" Bonds yelled.

"You need only cut the ropes around the tentacle," Nietz said firmly. "One by one, men, and keep your heads."

The *Seffynaw* had already begun to twist in the water, caught as they were with the creature in light of their previous momentum. Captain Livina shouted orders at the men in the rigging to change the sails to compensate.

There must have been two hundred ropes tangled around that tentacle, and the beast shook the *Seffynaw* a few more times as it tried to pull away. Trevn sawed ropes until his hand felt numb, then all of a sudden the ship jolted upright and the tentacle slithered away.

The men cheered. Someone clapped Trevn on the back. The *Seffynaw* glided slowly onward. And Trevn looked over the broken rail at the people in the water.

"Lower a dinghy!" he yelled, shoving his way through the crowd back to the quarterdeck. The main boat fall was at the forecastle, but there was a lesser-used one at the stern. Trevn ran up to the quarterdeck and all the way to the stern. Dozens of people came along, nearly trampling one another in their attempt to keep the wreckage of the *Berith* in sight.

Trevn found Captain Livina at the stern rail, watching a dinghy row to pick up survivors. There were two soldiers in the craft and they had already rescued three people. But a second serpent had arrived and was picking off swimmers. Each time the creature struck, several women around Trevn screamed. He felt helpless to do anything but pray that Arman would spare as many as possible.

He and Livina stood together, looking back on the carnage and the sinking *Berith*, which was now difficult to see since the *Rafayah* had followed the *Seffynaw* around it. The last Trevn saw before the *Berith* sank beneath the water was a serpent swallowing a man who'd been swimming toward a broken yard.

The *Idez*, which trailed the *Rafayah*, fired upon the first serpent. The creature turned away from the scattered swimmers and rammed a hole into the ship's side. The *Idez*'s mast heeled critically to starboard.

"Can the *Idez* recover?" Trevn asked the captain.

"It *could*, but only if they stop attacking. Not every captain knows better than to engage a sea serpent. Opening fire might seem like the right thing to do, but it's usually a fatal move. I am thankful Sâr Wilek backed up my order."

"Are serpents impossible to kill?" Trevn asked.

"Not impossible. But you see how one took down a ship, attacked a second, and doesn't look all that wounded. If we let them, the pair will do much more damage to the fleet before they die. I will have the signalmen send a message through the flags to warn the other captains not to attack."

"We will need to find a new warship to sail before us," Trevn said, thinking back on his lesson with the admiral.

"Hopefully not a galley," the captain said. "Oar piercings are a hazard so far from the coast. Did you see why?"

"They let in water and the freeboard went under," Trevn said. "Closer to land the men could probably swim to shore, and if the ship doesn't sink too quickly, there might be time to beach it for repairs."

"But not out in the deep," the captain said, finishing Trevn's thought. "Let us hope the admiral chooses a sailing ship to lead us from now on, and that this is the last we will see of any serpents."

"Did the Duke of Tal find you, Captain?" Trevn asked, remembering the admiral's arrest.

"He said Sâr Wilek wished to speak with me, but the lookouts spotted the serpents before I could report. Is something wrong?"

"Admiral Vendal has been relieved of his duties," Trevn said. "I believe you are about to be promoted."

HINCK

Hinck made his way to the stern, wondering if this was the best idea. All day long the brand on his shoulder had itched, and though he tried his best to ignore it, he knew the likely cause. Oli had confirmed his worst fears.

"It's a summons from Moon Fang. There will be a meeting tonight," Oli had said, *"And you shouldn't go."*

Hinck didn't want to go. It was the last thing he wanted to do . . . but it was also his best hope of learning what the cult had planned. Not appearing could be just as dangerous. So with Oli's help they fashioned a rough mask and sent Hinck on his way.

Oli's final words resounded in Hinck's mind. *"Whatever happens, don't take evenroot. Once you get addicted, it's near impossible to stop, plus you'd have to give your soul to a shadir to be healed."*

As if he needed the reminder.

Hinck descended to the hold, wandering the crossways and lengthways until he spotted a lone guard wearing a helmet and sitting on a crate before a compartment door. "Who comes this way?"

Hinck wasn't sure how to answer. Was this a normal guard, seeking a place of solitude? Or was this one of the Lahavôtesh? "I seek the Sanctum of Mysteries," he tried.

The guard stood and opened the door. "You have found it."

Simple enough so far. He only hoped his hunch that there was no evenroot was true. Because if he were wrong, he did not know how he would manage to refuse the milk of Gâzar in such small company.

He stepped past the guard and inside the compartment. At first he saw nothing but a lone oil lamp sitting on the floor. By the time the guard closed the door behind him, the compartment had come into focus. Hunched over as he was, he could not have expected anything as foreboding or grand as the chamber underneath Canden House. Yet there was no altar here at all. Nothing but a circle of masked folk sitting on crates and barrels around the lantern. He quickly counted eight in the room besides himself. Three were women. As was the custom, all wore black.

"Come in and join the boredom!" a man said. His voice, while somewhat mad, was slightly familiar. He wore a red mask that was painted to look like drops of water.

Hinck perched on the end of a vacant crate. The group sat in near silence for far too long. Hinck grew fidgety and stiff but forced himself to remain still, not wanting all those masked faces fixated on him again. Since he had been the newest initiate at their last gathering, everyone probably knew exactly who he was.

"He is not coming," said a woman in a white mask with golden leaves.

"He might still." This from another woman, whose mask was covered in swirls of blue and yellow paint.

"I told you he wouldn't," said the man in red. Fonu, Hinck realized with a jolt. Now that he was speaking without yelling, the voice was unmistakable. "He has abandoned us. After all we've done for him. Cast aside like dull blades."

"Dull blades can be sharpened, Red Ream," a man said. His mask was dark blue with a jagged lightning bolt cutting across it.

Fonu glared at Hinck. "Why bother sharpening when you can pick new blades whenever you please. What kind of a mask is that, anyway, Hinckdan?"

"No names!" said the woman with the white-and-gold mask.

"What does it matter?" Fonu reached to the man beside him—whose mask was a yellow sun—and ripped it off. It was Sir Garn, the emissary from Rurekau. The henna tracings on the sides of his neck looked like dirt in the low light.

"How dare you!" he cried.

Fonu pulled off his own mask. "There is no longer a point in secrecy," he said, his face shining with sweat. "We must know who we are if we are to know whom to trust."

"And we should trust *you*?" said the third woman, whose mask had pink and white flowers on a green background.

"Janek has abandoned us," Fonu said. "He would let each and every one of us hang if it meant saving himself. We must decide what to do apart from him."

The woman with a blue-and-yellow mask removed it. It was Lady Mattenelle! "Fonu is right. Sâr Janek does not serve the King of Magic. He serves only himself."

"I too have witnessed this." And the man with a black-and-gold mask took it off. Kamran DanSâr.

A dune cat mask went down to reveal Canbek Faluk, Hinck's uncle. Hinck knew the man had always been corrupt, but to see him here, a part of this group, it shocked him.

"Moon Fang has made himself king of Sarikar," Uncle Canbek said.

"Everyone knows that already." The woman in the white-and-gold mask removed it. The Honored Lady Zenobia, longtime concubine of Rosâr Echad, mother to Kamran.

With the removal of her mask, the last two in the room took off theirs. The lightning-bolt mask had belonged to Janek's shield, Sir Jayron, and the pink and white flowers on green had masked Rosâr Echad's newest mistress, the actress Lilou Caridod.

Hinck saw no reason to keep his mask on. He loosed the ties and pulled it into his lap, keeping his gaze on the lantern.

"Because of Sâr Janek's unpredictability, Moon Fang married Lady Eudora so he himself could lay claim to the Armanian throne," Lady Zenobia said.

Hinck still couldn't understand why Eudora would have married the old man. It seemed so unlike her. He reminded himself he didn't care for Eudora anymore. She was not nearly as mysterious as Lady Pia, not that Hinck would allow himself to develop feelings for the concubine either, since she belonged to Janek.

Fonu voiced the very question Hinck wanted to know. "Why would Eudora have married an old man? It was no secret she never wanted to be queen. Never wanted to marry at all."

"I imagine she changed her mind when she realized it was the only way to overthrow the rosâr and his Heir," Zenobia said.

"More like her mother forced her," Fonu mumbled.

"There is more," Zenobia said. "My shadir tells me that Moon Fang has commanded us to sink this boat."

"Sink the boat?" Canbek cried.

"The serpent nearly did that yesterday," Kamran said. "They're still patching up the bulkheads on the main deck."

"He asks us to drown ourselves?" Sir Garn asked. "Is he mad?"

"He wants us to escape first, of course," Zenobia said. "But with everyone else dead, succession of the Armanian throne would pass through Eudora to her firstborn son. As her consort and the child's father, Moon Fang could then claim rule of both Sarikar and Armania."

Hinck couldn't help it this time. "Lady Eudora is expecting a child?"

"Not yet," Zenobia said. "But soon."

Hinck fought back a shiver of revulsion. Rogedoth was old enough to be Eudora's grandfather! What was she thinking? Could Fonu be right? Had Eudora been forced into this?

"What about Janek?" Fonu asked. "We can't let Janek drown."

"Moon Fang says if he is not for us, he is against," Zenobia said.

Everyone began talking at once.

"I didn't agree to any of this," Fonu said. "The man would truly kill his own grandson? He's insane."

"Rosârah Laviel would never approve of her son's death," Mattenelle said. "And I agree with Fonu that Eudora would not marry Moon Fang of her own free will. He must have used his powers against her. Maybe against Rosârah Laviel and Sârah Jemesha, as well."

Sârah Jemesha was King Echad's sister and Oli and Eudora's mother. Apparently she was on whatever ship Rogedoth, Laviel, and Eudora were on.

"How much root did he have stored on that boat of his?" Kamran asked.

"Plenty," Zenobia said.

"Then why won't he share some with us?" Kamran asked.

"Who cares about that?" Lilou Caridod asked. "What shall we do?"

"I just don't see how any of this matters right now," Fonu said. "We should focus on finding land first, then worry about who will rule."

This was one of the smartest things Hinck had ever heard Fonu say.

"It would be easier if Sâr Janek had not abandoned us," Lilou said. "We could use his counsel."

"The dungeon scared him pretty badly," Mattenelle said. "He doesn't want to do anything to endanger himself until he is on solid ground with a force of soldiers loyal to him."

Hinck decided to speak up. "I don't understand Roge—Moon Fang's plan. Even if we sank the boat, and even if we reverted to right of first blood, succession wouldn't pass to Eudora. Emperor Ulrik ranks under Trevn. And Prince Ferro after him. Then Oli. *Then* Eudora." Then Hinck.

"If Rosâr Echad and half his family are dead, no one will care about right of first blood," Uncle Canbek said. "Whoever takes power will rule this weak nation, and if Sâr Wilek and Sâr Trevn are dead, Moon Fang can do whatever he wants."

"He is working a separate plot to take control of the Rurekan flagship," Lady Zenobia said to Hinck. "And the Duke of Canden would go down with the *Seffynaw*. That would leave Eudora next in line."

"Oli too?" Fonu said. "You realize he is asking me to murder my two closest friends?"

"They both abandoned you, Fonu," Kamran said. "You have no friends but us."

"How does one sink a great ship, anyway?" Uncle Canbek asked.

"Compel a serpent," Fonu said.

"Does anyone have any evenroot?" Sir Garn asked.

"I don't," Uncle Canbek said.

The others echoed him.

"What about the Magonian's root Sâr Janek was looking for?" Sir Garn asked.

"Gone," Kamran said. "The Order of the Sandvine has yet to locate any root, despite that being our true purpose."

"How can we sink the ship without magic?" Lady Mattenelle asked.

"We can't," Uncle Canbek said. "The hull is too thick."

"Sure we can," Fonu said. "We just need to run it into a reef."

"We've left the reefs behind us," Sir Jayron said.

"Chop a hole in the hold with a boarding axe?" Fonu suggested.

"You'd get caught before you breached the hull," Sir Jayron said.

"She might go down if we rammed another ship," Kamran said.

"Or if one rammed us," Uncle Canbek said.

"Who would steer us into another ship?" Lady Zenobia asked. "None of us have any business manning the helm."

"Master Shinn might do it," Kamran said. "Fonu and I have made a friend of the man. He tells us things, but I'm not certain he'd be willing to destroy the ship, even if we promised to take him with us."

"Ask your shadir to help convince him," Lady Zenobia said. "We must obey Moon Fang's order and soon. You work on a plan to crash the ship. I will find a way to get us off the ship before you do."

This was agreed upon and the group departed. Hinck walked the corridors in a daze, shocked that he had just taken part in a casual discussion of treason and the premeditated murder of over six hundred souls.

Worry besieged him. If he did not warn Wilek right away and something happened, Hinck would never survive the guilt. So he went up to the main deck and set off toward the royal cabins. As he passed the doors to the king's galley, someone darted out, grabbed his arm, and dragged him inside.

Hinck struggled with his attacker in the darkness until the prick of steel at his throat stopped all movement. Oh gods. This was it. He was going to die.

A breathy voice whispered in his ear. "Where are you going, Lord Dacre?"

"Lady Pia?" Dumbfounded, he didn't know whether or not to relax. "What are you—?"

"Silence!"

The intensity of her whisper did the trick. Hinck dared not breathe. Out in the corridor footsteps approached. Passed by.

Once the steps had completely faded, Lady Pia gripped his tunic in her fist and slammed him against the wall. "You are getting careless, lord. If Sir Jayron had found you outside Sâr Wilek's rooms tonight, he would have killed you."

Hinck understood that much completely. The rest, however . . . "But why did you—?"

She pressed the knife point deeper. It pricked his skin. He gasped, terrified. Was she trying to help him or kill him? Should he try to fight her off? To get away? Was she alone? He wished he could see anything at all.

He felt her breath on his face a moment before she pressed her lips against his. Stricken again by her erratic behavior, he remained still. So much confusion enveloped his mind. He noticed, then, the spicy incense that clung to her. It mixed with the strong smell of bread from the galley. Delight reeled through him at the feel of her kiss, but he fought against it, certain she would cut his throat next and drink his blood as a sacrifice to whichever god of the Lowerworld she served.

When she finally broke away and stepped back from him, she said, "You were hungry. Take a tray back to your cabin. Obey me and it will save your life. And be more careful in the future. I will warn Sâr Wilek of their plans." She opened the door, and the light from the lantern outside lit her profile as she exited.

When the door swung shut, enclosing Hinck in darkness again, he sank down the wall to the floor, knees bent. He swallowed, astounded by the actions of this mysterious woman.

Then he remembered the danger still awaiting them. Sink the ship. They were trying to sink the ship.

And if Wilek didn't find out and stop them, it might be the end of House Hadar.

PART FIVE

MAELSTROM

WILEK

Upon the toll of the midday bells, a company consisting of fifty people assembled for a royal wedding on the foredeck. Some sat on stools, benches, or trunks they'd brought up from their cabins, but most stood. The wedding tent had been dug out from the hold and half erected along the port rail, as there wasn't room enough to set up the full circle.

Wilek had put aside all other cares for this moment. The search for new land and the rebels plotting to sink the ship would have to wait. Today he would be married.

The ceremony between Sâr-Regent Wilek Hadar and Lady Zeroah Barta began with prayers in ancient Armanian, which were chanted by Father Burl Mathal, the only priest Wilek trusted after the Heir War conspiracies. This was the priest's second attempt at performing this ceremony, and Wilek had instructed that it should go much swifter than the original had been scheduled to. A small altar stood on the priest's left; a brazier burned coal on his right. Wilek dared not risk an open fire any larger or it might catch the rigging, so the sacrifice would be small. Wilek hoped that Arman, understanding their predicament, would grant mercy.

When the prayers ended, Father Mathal called Wilek forward with his five witnesses—Rayim, Kal, Janek, Trevn, and Dendrick. Wilek read from a scroll a list of gifts he had offered Lady Zeroah as a bride-price. Rystan, the Duke of Tal, accepted them on his sister's behalf, as he, despite being only thirteen, was now the head of the Barta family, and Lady Zeroah's welfare fell to him until she was married.

Wilek's five men erected a canopy of blue silk and cloth of gold in the small open space between Father Mathal and the assembly. The canopy had five poles, and each man held one.

"Who wishes to marry this day?" Father Mathal asked.

"I wish to marry Lady Zeroah Barta," Wilek said. "And she has accepted my suit."

"Come under the holy canopy," Father Mathal told them both.

Lady Zeroah stood with her five witnesses—Miss Mielle, Wilek's mother, Hrettah, Rashah, and Inolah, since Rosârah Valena was still too ill. Zeroah's deep blue and bronze dress had rendered her a most lovely object for the delighted assembly to gaze upon. A thick veil covered her face and fell to her waist.

Miss Mielle and Wilek's mother each took hold of one of Lady Zeroah's arms and led her under the canopy. The two sârahs carried the long train. Wilek stepped in through the back of the canopy and positioned himself opposite his bride. The female witnesses formed a line behind Zeroah, while Wilek's men continued to hold up the canopy.

"Kneel in this holy place," Father Mathal said.

They knelt, and Wilek, without being asked, took hold of Lady Zeroah's hands. It was strange not to be able to see her face, as the thick veil hid it from view. He imagined her looking down, shy as always.

Father Mathal began another ancient Armanian prayer. Since they had no doves on board, he sacrificed a bird from the crow's nest and drained the blood into a consecrated bowl. This he placed on the altar to his left, dipped a feather into it, and sprinkled the blood over Wilek's and Zeroah's heads as he chanted a petition of blessing to Arman—as Wilek had requested. When he finished, he butchered the crow, cut out its breast, and set it and the whole bird on the coals. "Arman, accept this fragrant offering."

As the bird cooked, Wilek prayed thanks to Arman for protecting Lady Zeroah when Charlon might have killed her.

Father Mathal removed the cooked meat and tore it in three. He handed a piece to Wilek and one to Lady Zeroah, keeping the last piece for himself. "With your own hands, wave this breast before Arman, a token of your regard to the God you serve."

Wilek held the small piece of warm meat with both sets of fingers and lifted his arms above his head, bowing in prayer as he did. Lady Zeroah and Father Mathal did the same.

"Now feast upon this wave offering and rejoice in Arman's blessings."

Wilek ate the meat, which had already cooled in the brisk sea air. Lady Zeroah's hand threaded up under her veil as she too ate.

"In the sight of these witnesses," Father Mathal said, "we ask the gods to bless this union. Drink now from the cup of life, that you may live long in the land the gods will give you."

He handed the goblet to Wilek, who drank and passed it to Lady Zeroah. She lifted the cup under her veil to drink, then handed it back to Wilek, who passed it to the priest.

"I charge you now to consummate this marriage in the wedding tent and return with the bridal cloth as evidence of the bride's purity," Father Mathal said.

Wilek's men removed the canopy and set it aside, then formed a line that stretched between the bridal tent and where Wilek and Lady Zeroah knelt. The female witnesses lined up facing the men, together forming a path for Wilek and Zeroah to walk through.

Wilek, suddenly nervous, stood and helped Lady Zeroah to her feet. He offered his arm, she took hold, and they walked down the makeshift aisle toward the tent, where Hinckdan and Oli stood holding open the door flap.

It was but ten steps at the most, but with so many eyes upon them, and considering their destination and objective, the journey seemed an eternity. Somehow they made it without cursing, crying, or fainting dead away. They passed inside and the curtain fell closed, shrouding them in what at first appeared to be darkness. Wilek's eyes adjusted. They stood alone in the blue tent, which glowed orange overhead from the sun's rays. There was nothing inside but a bed made up of a neatly dressed feather mattress with a white linen cloth spread across the center, a small table holding an amphora of wine, a lit lantern, and two bronze goblets.

Outside, the crowd cheered, then someone started a wedding song—Hinckdan, by the sound of the voice. The majority of the assembly joined in.

> "Together they walked into the wedding tent
> To close on the vow of this blessed event.
> Outside did come, a sweetly sung song
> Intoned of witnesses from the throng.
> 'Most lovely maid,' said the noble bridegroom,
> 'Be not thou afraid, instead presume
> My troth shall endure, long as life in me lasts,
> Rest you secure, long after youth is past . . .'"

Wilek and Zeroah were alone for the first time all day, though the singing outside did not offer the peace he had hoped for.

"The singing is quite distracting," Lady Zeroah said softly.

"Agreed." Wilek took hold of the hem of Lady Zeroah's veil and lifted it over her head. He briefly met her golden eyes until the veil tangled with a comb in her hair. Distracted, he set about extricating the fabric from the tongs of the comb and accidentally pulled the comb out completely. Zeroah's coil of hair unwound, falling in large twists down around her shoulders. Studying her, he rather liked the outcome of his clumsiness.

"You are very pretty, Zeroah," he said.

He caught sight of a small smile before she lowered her gaze to her hands, which were fidgeting before her. "Thank you, Your Highness."

"Wilek," he said. "I am Wilek to you now."

"Very well, Wilek."

Outside, the song ended. Someone shook the tent supports and trilled like a skylark, which brought a wave of laughter.

Zeroah clasped both hands over her mouth, holding back laughter of her own. Thankfully another song began—a slower song, which suited much better.

Wilek took Zeroah's hands from her mouth and held them captive. He leaned in to kiss her, but she pulled back. "It's a lovely day outside, isn't it?"

"It is. I'm glad it didn't rain."

She nodded. "That would have been a shame."

Wilek leaned in to kiss her again. This time their lips touched, and then—

"Will you take a second wife?"

He released a silent breath, understanding she must be nervous, and wanting to be patient. "I do not plan to. Sometimes a king must, for political reasons. Alliances and such. But as Arman forbids it, if ever I find myself needing to make alliances, I will strive to find another way."

This made her smile, and he managed to kiss her and keep her silent.

✦   ✦   ✦

Wilek and Zeroah took their time helping each other re-dress, and when they were ready, they exited the tent to much exultation. Wilek handed the bridal cloth to Kal, who took it to Father Mathal to be verified. Wilek watched as the priest passed the cloth to Rystan, who fairly blushed to be the keeper of proof of his sister's virginity.

Father Mathal announced the couple properly wed, and a general shout of joy rose up. The festivities continued while the fifty witnesses came forward to sign the marriage contract. Once everything was legal, Wilek and Zeroah started a procession from foredeck to stern, accompanied by a piper playing a jovial tune as they greeted the long line of well-wishers. Wilek's stomach twisted each time he clasped hands with one of the traitors Hinckdan had identified. Fonu Edekk, Canbek Faluk, Lady Zenobia, Sir Jayron, and all the others. How could these people smile and wish him well when they were plotting ways to kill him? He would have arrested them all by now but had been waiting until they formed an actual plan, hopefully involving Janek, so that Wilek could wipe out the whole nest of vipers at once.

Zeroah, sârah of Armania, would not hear of a feast given only to the fifty official witnesses. Not when the ship would fill with the smell of food, taunting hungry commoners. So all were invited to celebrate—despite Trevn's concern that they should start rationing food more strictly. Wilek understood but knew that the people were restless, worried, and grieved. He felt a celebration would do them all some good.

Tables had been set up for the wedding guests on the stern deck, but on the main deck, a row of tables filled with food lined each outer rail. This way people could pass down the line, filling their hands, their own dishes or baskets, and even in some cases their shirts held out like sacks. They took their meal back to their places on the middle deck and feasted in small groups.

Between the two galleys' cooks, their staff, and an additional twenty assigned to help, the team had prepared four large hogs, three goats, six massive whitefish, and dozens of pinkfish. There were garnishes of pepper sauce, a cinnamon wine gravy, a pear compote, thirty bowls of barley pudding, three platters of honey-glazed turnips, twenty loaves of nettle bread, and—for dessert—raisin twists, scones with spiced jelly, baked apples, currant custard tarts, and fig fritters.

Nobility alone received wine, but Wilek did order two casks of ale be opened on the main deck for the rest and heard no complaints.

As a precaution, Wilek ordered Rystan and Dendrick to fill a tray for the head table to be certain the food had not been tampered with. Wilek sat on his father's right during the feast, and the man, who was in his right mind at the moment, bestowed his congratulations.

"A fine ceremony, my son. I only wish you would have thought to sacrifice to Thalassa."

"Arman is important to Sârah Zeroah," he said, smiling at his bride.

"Yes, yes, but you are the sâr and the future king of Armania. Give your wives too much and they will expect it always."

"Yes, Father. I shall take care," he said. Zeroah looked away, which inspired Wilek to risk a little more for his newfound faith. "I have finished reading Trevn's Book of Arman. Father, it seems we have greatly offended He Who Made the World. You should consider reading Arman's laws and instituting them."

"Who is Arman that I should obey him? Rôb gives us plenty of gods to worship. I dare not force my people to follow only one. And who is to say that Trevn even transcribed the tome correctly? No, the Rôb text has never steered us wrong."

"Except that it led us to our near destruction."

"Superstitious nonsense, my son. Armanites would have us counting the hairs on our heads to please their One God. Life should not be so difficult. We have always been a nation of plenty. We should not apologize for that."

"If you would but read the book—"

"Look at me, my son. I am old and sick. I will not waste what little time I have left poring over the erroneous ramblings of the ancients. I want to enjoy my final days. Take Arman in your five if you must, but leave my choice to me."

"Yes, Father." Wilek examined the platter of meat before him, thinking he was a poor messenger to carry Arman's book to a man such as his father. He glanced at Zeroah, found her watching him. She smiled and kissed his cheek.

"I should have married again," the king said, staring wistfully at them. "To have only four wives must displease the gods. No wonder we wander the sea, lost. I should send word to the other ships in search of a suitable mate."

"Why not marry one of your concubines?" Wilek asked.

"Perhaps I could," Father murmured, contemplating. "A fine idea, my son. I will think on it." He took a shaky gulp of wine, which left a drop trickling down his chin. "I would have liked to bestow gifts upon you this day."

The showering of gifts had been postponed until they reached land and could build a new castle to keep such things. His father's offer provided the perfect opportunity for Wilek to help Trevn. "There is a favor I would like, though it is a bit unconventional."

"What is your request, my heir? Even up to half the realm, it will be given to you."

Wilek fought back a smile, pleased that his father had walked so eagerly into his trap. "I would like you to grant permission for Trevn to court Miss Mielle Allard."

It was a request not only from Wilek but from Kal as well, who'd recently caught Trevn and Mielle alone, kissing, and forced Wilek to promise to do something lest Kal hurt the young sâr in his attempt to protect Mielle's honor. Wilek knew the king's likely response and was not surprised.

"Outrageous!" Father said. "A prince cannot wed a commoner."

"The Five Realms are gone," Wilek said. "Once noble and wealthy women are now no richer than the commoners who cover our decks, nor are there any more scores of princesses for him to consider."

"He need not have scores. Only one. To start. If he wants to wed commoners after that, I might allow it. But his first wife must be chosen carefully. She cannot be just anyone."

"Is there even one worthy candidate, Father?" Wilek asked, knowing full well there were several. "He must marry someone. The people adore Miss Mielle. She is their champion. Just you see how they would rejoice to see her made a sârah of Armania."

Father growled. "The ages are wrong. It will upset the gods."

Wilek felt the door closing and switched to another path. "Should they actually marry, it very well could. But . . . things might never get that far. Trevn has always enjoyed flouting authority. If you refuse his request to court Miss Mielle, I fear he might do something rash. But if he were granted permission to court her . . ." He turned to Zeroah and gave her a quick wink. "He will likely grow bored."

Father smiled slowly. "You mean to trick him."

It might happen the way Wilek suggested, though he knew enough of his youngest brother to doubt it. Trevn had a disposition much more like his own than Janek's. While they were all of them spoiled, Trevn's upbringing in Sarikar had done for him what Chadek's sacrificial death had done for Wilek. They both had seen the corruption in Armania and disdained it, rather than embraced it.

"If that's what it takes," Wilek said.

Father chuckled, delighted by the deception he thought he understood. "Very well. If that is the wedding gift you wish for yourself, give them my permission to court. But if you sense he is not tiring of the girl, let me know at once and we will come up with a plan to separate them."

Wilek kept his expression plain. "Thank you, Father. You are very wise."

The king gave a sad smile in return. "I am dying, Wilek. You know that, don't you?"

Wilek stared at the king. His father. It was the first time he'd heard the man admit weakness. "The physician fears as much."

"It is my dying wish that Rogedoth be thwarted in his attempt to rule anywhere. I mean to write a will passing over Janek as my second."

"Are you certain, Father?"

"I was wrong to doubt Janek's loyalty, but I cannot risk Rogedoth using his grandson against us if he gets the chance. We must never give him that chance."

"I fear Magonia more than Rogedoth," Wilek said, surprising himself. Rarely did he share so honestly with his father. Still, he did not say he feared never finding land most of all.

"Don't. Those women are trouble, make no mistake, but Rogedoth has invested his life in taking the Armanian throne. He may have claimed Sarikar for now, but it's Armania he wants. He will make his move. You must be ready."

"I will be, Father."

"I know there's little that can be done while we live on water, but . . ." A wildness filled the king's eyes, driving out the steady somberness of the moments before. His hands began to tremble. He leaned close to Wilek and whispered, "We must keep a close eye on my mother. She and Brelenah have been plotting against me. If you see them together, inform me at once."

Wilek tried to keep his expression plain. He dared not remind his father that Gran had died in the Five Woes. "I promise to do so."

"Good," Father said, wheezing. "Now I must rest. Enjoy your new bride, my son."

"Thank you, Father."

As the king's attendants wheeled him away, Zeroah took hold of Wilek's hand and squeezed. He smiled at his bride and wondered how much longer the king would live and how Janek would take his being written out of the succession. Now that Wilek had married, he felt more vulnerable to attack. But as long as Janek had no access to evenroot, Wilek could handle him.

Trevn

In the recent upheavals and the panic of the serpent attack, a new order of command ruled the ship. Livina was now admiral, and with Quen arrested, Bussie had been made captain. This promoted Nietz and Shinn to first and second mate, respectively, which turned out to be no help to Trevn at all. Shinn now was at the whip more often. He knew full well that Trevn had no fear of heights, so rather than send him to work in the rigging, which was thought of as one of the worst jobs a sailor could draw, Shinn always made Trevn clean up messes and swab the decks.

For this evening one watch, he'd ordered Trevn to clean the railings on the stern deck. Thankfully this watch was only two hours long and Mielle would be waiting at the end of it, so Trevn didn't mind as much. He sat on the deck along the port rail and used his boot knife to pick grime off the posts, then rubbed them clean with a rag. As he worked, he pondered yesterday's council meeting in which Master Granlee had come to share his concerns about Nivanreh's Eye.

The farther north they traveled, the lower the southern pole star sat in the night sky. It was clear to the navigator that if they kept on, they would eventually lose sight of it completely. The terrifying concept of sailing without the guide star had sent the council into a commotion. Once Wilek had calmed them, Master Granlee shared his discovery of a new steady trio of bright stars that had been rising in the north. He had first seen them a month ago and, after careful study, believed them to be northern pole stars. Master Granlee suggested that once they lost sight of the Eye, they should sail on the trio instead.

The idea thrilled Trevn, but Canbek had been terrified. He felt they should keep Nivanreh's Eye in sight at all costs, even if that meant turning back. This was folly, of course—they must keep sailing to the northwest. Canbek's ignorance on the subject of astronomy made him irrational.

Wilek had granted Master Granlee permission to use the trio as a guide, but both he and Trevn knew that once Nivanreh's Eye no longer appeared in the night sky, people would panic—and not only on the *Seffynaw*.

Trevn sighed and turned his attention back to the task at hand. He had never realized how beautiful the *Seffynaw* was before he'd cleaned it himself. The posts along the inner rails of the stern deck, quarterdeck, and forecastle were each carved in a figure of one of the Rôb Five and intricately painted.

Cleaning a post that depicted the goddess Thalassa with fish leaping around her waist made Trevn think of the food shortage. Nearly eight weeks had passed since they'd left Bakurah Island. The entire fleet was running low on food, and the fish had not been biting in these rough seas. This did not bode well for those, like Rosârah Valena, who had fallen ill and needed nourishment. Dozens of people had already died from fever or other illnesses. With so much filth and little freshwater, it was impossible to fight off infections.

In addition, they'd had no more rain since the downpours and had started rationing the drinking water. Wilek was supposed to make a decision regarding the horses. The animals consumed far too much water and should be killed and eaten, but no one liked talking of such things.

Trevn stood and stretched, realizing his thoughts had turned bleak again. It was hard for them not to. For most, life on board was no better than a prison. Still, it was all they had, and if cleaning the ship improved things even the tiniest bit, then that's what he would do.

When the bells rang for the watch change, it was nearly sunset. The farther north they sailed, the shorter the days. Trevn told Ottee that he was going to meet with Wilek and wouldn't need him until after dinner. Then he set off for his cabin, where Mielle should be waiting. Cadoc had promised to fetch a dinner tray and bring it there, where Trevn and Mielle could share a private meal.

A week ago, life had changed after Wilek had received Father's blessing for Trevn to court Mielle. This had been exactly what Trevn had thought he'd wanted. But courting, it turned out, was painstakingly tedious. The king's blessing elevated Mielle's status to a place equal to any noblewoman. And apparently nothing was more important to a young noblewoman than her reputation. Trevn and Mielle were now permitted to keep company with one another as much as they pleased—but only when properly chaperoned.

No wonder Sir Kalenek and Wilek had insisted upon it.

This meant that Mielle was never to go anywhere alone with Trevn, and Trevn, in order to see Mielle on his off-hours, had to dress like a sâr and attend the "court of Rosâr Echad," suffering through simpering conversations with the most ignorant of people. How could these royals and nobles be so utterly clueless as to their fate? To actually waste time lecturing Trevn on courtly manners when they could all very well be dead in another month or two? It was madness.

Trevn knew exactly how much food and water was left in the hold and how long it would last. Unless it rained again, they had no way to replenish the drinking water. As to the food, all their hopes swam beneath the waves. Add the various fevers and illnesses . . .

All of it had Trevn concerned. He desperately wanted to live. He was doing all he could to make that happen, but if they were all going to die, he did not want to waste the few days he had left learning which tokens were acceptable gifts to give a lady. It mattered to him not at all.

So Trevn spent no more than one hour each day officially courting Mielle. The rest of the time, he'd found fun ways to slip her private, coded letters, proposing secret meetings in obscure locations. Rather than use her name, he called her *mouse*, and Mielle had started calling Trevn *jack*, short for jackrabbit. *"Because of the way your hair poofs out like a rabbit's tail when you tie it back,"* she had said. All of this was a risk, he knew. If Sir Kalenek discovered even one private meeting, they could lose his goodwill. But in light of the strict courting regimen and plain common sense, they both felt it a risk worth taking.

Trevn entered his cabin and found Mielle sitting on the floor inside, face streaked in tears.

"What's happened?" he asked, fearing the fever had taken Nurse Darlow.

"Your brother, Sâr Janek," she spat, looking up into Trevn's face. "He threatened to make Amala his mistress and tried to kiss me!"

Pressure filled Trevn's chest and he sank to his knees beside her. "Where did this happen? When?"

"Only just. On the foredeck. I went to visit Darlow in the infirmary, and Sâr Janek was there with his Order of the Sandvine. He said the infirmary was now under quarantine and that I was not permitted to go inside. As you can imagine, I was very upset. I started to cry, and he took my arm, told me that he understood, and said that if I insisted on visiting Darlow, he would sneak me inside, but only if I arranged a secret dinner between him and Amala!"

Typical Janek. Trevn took hold of Mielle's hand, annoyed that his brother was such a reprobate. "What did you say?"

"I told him I would not, and he said I must think on it and decide what was best. Then he tried to kiss my hand farewell, and when I told him not to touch me, he said I really should be nicer to him and help him convince Amala to become his mistress! When I tried to walk away, he grabbed my shoulder and tried to kiss me! So I punched his eye with my knuckles, like you taught me." She paused to gasp in a breath. "Then I ran down here and hid."

Trevn's anger instantly lifted. "You punched him?"

She met his gaze and brightened, laughed a little. "I didn't know how else to get away. He was determined to vex me."

Trevn brushed the tears from her cheek. "No, Mouse. He maltreated you. Did you tell Sir Kalenek?"

She shook her head. "His temper has been worse than ever. I'm afraid he might hurt Sâr Janek."

Good. "It would be no less than he deserves."

"But he is a sâr! Kal would be hung. Or at the very least face the pole."

That much was true.

"Do you think Darlow has the fever?" she asked.

"I know not."

"Is it as bad as people say?"

"Yes," he admitted. "I knew that Wilek might set up a quarantine area. But I didn't think he would put Janek in charge of it."

"The food is truly low?"

"It is. But the drinking water is the bigger concern." They had enough for another three weeks—if they got rid of the horses and rationed aggressively.

"Wilek and Zeroah's wedding was a good day, wasn't it?" Mielle asked.

"It was."

"It was the last good day I remember. We're going to die, aren't we?"

"Don't say that, Mielle. You must have hope."

"But you said the water is almost gone."

"We have time. We could find land any day."

"I don't think we will."

"Of course we will!" he said, wanting to stay positive. "I've studied the horizon, and the Northsea is so much bigger than most people think. There is lots more land out there, likely with other people already living on it."

"That's not very comforting," she said. "If people are already living there, they might not want to share with us."

"They will when they see what skills we bring. We have carpenters and laborers and weavers and artisans and women who are good with orphans." He tugged on her earlobe. "The Five Realms all traded with one another. It will be no different with new cultures."

"I'm trying to be hopeful, but it's just so hard."

It was hard, yet Trevn refused to waste time cowering in fear of what might be. "That's because you're putting your hope in you or me or Wilek or Admiral Livina. People are fallible, but Arman is not a man that he should stumble or fall into fear. He has promised us land. Will he not do as he said? Will his promise mean nothing? I don't think so."

Those dark brown eyes stared into his. "I want to believe. I'm just afraid."

"Afraid of what?"

She looked away, wincing. "That Arman is not all you believe him to be."

Trevn smiled, knowing exactly how she felt. "I thought that over and over as I was transcribing the book. Do you know what changed my mind? Besides the arrival of Miss Onika and her prophecies?"

She shook her head.

"That truth is truth. No matter what you believe. My father made laws to defend his lifestyle. Sacrificed people in the name of his truth. Until Wilek killed a cheyvah beast and proved that Barthos was nothing more than an animal."

"But what if Arman is nothing more than a sunbird?"

Trevn laughed, but her question had merit. "For years I have studied the prophecies of four different religions. Only in the Armanite faith did I find the hand of He Who Made the World. Prophecies that had been fulfilled and those that were fulfilling before my very eyes. He has shown himself to those willing to set down their pride and seek him. Will you look, Mielle?"

Her brief nod was enough. He kissed her, and for a few moments nothing else mattered in the Northsea but their two souls, entwined.

He finally forced himself to break away. "I must speak with Janek," he said, standing.

Mielle scrambled to her feet beside him. "Oh, Trevn, don't!"

"Do not dissuade me, Mielle. It is my duty to defend your honor. Besides, it is time someone put Janek in his place. Wilek is far too busy to be bothered, so I will do it. Go to dinner in the dining room. I'll meet you there."

✦ ✦ ✦

Trevn found Janek's cabin door unguarded, which likely meant he was elsewhere. He hoped he hadn't sent Mielle straight to him in the dining room. Entering, he discovered Lady Pia sitting in a chair by the window, watching the sea. She stood and curtsied. She appeared to be alone.

"Where is Janek?" Trevn asked, perusing the room for any clue.

"I know not, Your Highness. He was on the foredeck this midday with his Order."

"Yes, I heard." As Trevn walked toward her, his gaze fixed upon the sideboard under the window and the array of pots upon it. Only one held any sign of life. A small sandvine. He changed direction and picked it up. "This will do."

"You mustn't take that! He will blame me."

The look of horror on Lady Pia's face confirmed his assumption. Janek cared more for his plants than anything. Trevn shifted the pot into the crook of one arm. "You give him this message, lady. Tell him that I have his plant, and if he wants it, he can come and get it."

Trevn took the sandvine to his cabin and tucked it into his hanging cot, then made his way to the captain's dining room. There he found every member of the royal family except Rosârah Valena, who was ill, and Janek. Also present were Rystan, Miss Mielle, and her sister, Amala. Father was asleep in his rollchair.

"Good evening, Miss Mielle," Trevn said, taking his seat beside her.

"Any signs of land?" Wilek asked.

"None, I'm afraid, though Master Granlee believes that the lack of fish might be due to a change in the ocean's temperature. It has grown cooler. Much more so than the waters around Brixmead."

"Might we be headed toward a polar desert?" Wilek asked.

"That is Master Granlee's theory, yes. If we find land too cold to live on, we could still harvest ice and snow for water, then sail south along the coast until we reach a warmer climate."

Father grunted awake, his eyes sleepy and roving over those at the table. "Where is the prophet?" Father asked. "She must interpret a dream I had."

"She is not feeling well," Wilek said.

"I hope it's not the fever," Father said. "Are any of you ill?"

All shook their heads.

"If you are, I want to know at once. We must not let any affliction go untreated for even a day."

"Tell us of your dream, Father," Wilek said.

"Yes, well, I was a great fish, swimming in the sea. Above me a flock of birds circled. One at a time they dove down and pecked at my eyes. What do you think it means?"

Trevn frowned, thinking the dream rather ominous.

"Perhaps it means that land is near, since birds are a sign of land," Hrettah said.

"Have you seen any birds flying in the sky?" Zeroah's brother asked.

"I have not," Father said, "but perhaps I will soon."

The outer door burst in, and Janek tore into the dining room like a starving sand cat. His left eye was red and the cheek below it marred by a puffy red scratch that Trevn gave Mielle credit for. Janek surveyed those around the table until his enraged gaze fell upon Trevn. He stalked around the table, glaring. "Where is my sandvine?"

Trevn stood to meet him, took a deep breath. "Why should I tell you?"

"Because it's mine!"

"You think your claim is enough to keep me from taking whatever I want?"

"What's mine is mine," Janek said.

"Interesting," Trevn said. "But, brother, I am only doing what you've taught me by your own actions. You take from me without regard for my feelings. Why should I treat you any differently?"

"This is about her?" Janek gestured rudely to Mielle. "I didn't take her, you fool. I barely touched her. Do you even know the difference?"

"You have no right to touch the woman Father permitted me to court."

"*You* have no right to take my sandvine. Where is it?"

Trevn shook his head. "Not until you swear before our father never to touch Miss Mielle again. *Or* her sister."

Miss Amala gasped, a look of outrage on her face.

"Janek and Trevn," Wilek said. "This is not the time for such a discussion."

Janek's face broke into a smile and he chuckled. "He holds my sandvine hostage, Wil. Can you believe it?" Then to Trevn, "Will you charge a ransom?"

"I took it to get your attention," Trevn said. "Your selfish antics have gone too far. You nearly destroyed Sârah Zeroah's reputation and fully meant to. You have turned your Order of the Sandvine into a team of demoralizing brutes. Our people have been through enough. We all have. I await your oath."

Janek grabbed Trevn's throat and shoved him back against the bulkhead. "No one threatens me. Now, where is it?"

Trevn's head tingled as Janek cut off his air. Everyone stood, all talking at once, but Trevn focused his attention solely on Janek and recalled Nietz's fighting lessons. He wedged his fingers under one of Janek's and bent it back until it popped, ducking to the side as he did. Janek screamed, curled over his hand. Trevn stepped into an open space and crouched into position, ready for Janek's next attack.

"Enough!" Wilek yelled.

Janek rushed Trevn, fisted his hair, and knocked his head against the bulkhead. Pain spiked through Trevn's skull and blurred his vision. He flung an elbow at Janek's face and made contact, but Janek kept his grip on Trevn's hair, so Trevn kicked his brother's injured hand. Janek howled, swinging a left-handed punch at Trevn's face that missed completely. Trevn, invigorated by the idea that he might be winning, grabbed the neckline of Janek's tunic, pulled him close, and punched him.

His hand lit with fire, and Janek's tunic tore at the neckline. Trevn was about to hit him again when someone grabbed his arm. Novan Heln. Two more King's Guards descended upon Janek.

"This is shameful!" Father yelled. "Sârs fighting like combatants in a Rurekan arena."

"That sandvine is my only living plant from Armania," Janek said, gasping. "I must have it back."

"You will have it when I have your oath!" Trevn yelled.

"It seems a fair compromise to me, Janek," Wilek said.

Janek glared at Wilek, then licked his bloody lip and spat on the floor at Trevn's feet. "You have your oath. I won't touch your precious commoner again."

"Or her sister," Trevn amended.

"*Or her sister,*" Janek sneered.

"Your plant is in my cabin," Trevn said. "In my hanging cot."

Janek jerked away from the guards and made for the door. He pulled it open and scowled back at Trevn. "You and I are through being brothers." And he left.

Trevn glanced around the table at the many faces watching him in silent horror. His gaze stopped on Mielle's and he grinned. "Well, lady, I don't think Sâr Janek will bother you again."

WILEK

Wilek slept poorly that night, tossed along with the rest of the ship in a surprise gale. He met the morning groggy but at least comforted that they'd replenished a small amount of freshwater in the storm. The first news of the day, however, erased that bit of relief. Rosârah Valena had died of fever during the night. Wilek was still processing this when a sailor brought word that they'd come upon nine survivors of a pirated ship. Wilek ran out onto the quarterdeck, surprised to find the day sunny and bright after the previous evening's rain. He spotted Captain Bussie and Trevn talking to a shirtless, bearded man. Behind him eight other bedraggled men sat on the deck, drinking from stone mugs.

"Captain," Wilek said upon reaching their circle. "Is this one of the survivors?"

Captain Bussie bowed to Wilek. "Yes, Your Highness. This is Master Ardall. He was the second mate on the Armanian ship *Capaspie* out of Tal."

"The name of the ship that pirated you?" Wilek asked.

"*Malbraid*, Your Highness," Ardall said. "It was a small merchant cog. Came upon us during last night's rainstorm."

The name hit hard. Rand's ship. "How is that possible?" Wilek asked. "Can these pirates sail on a cloudy night as well?"

The old man shrugged.

"Tell the sâr-regent how your dinghy came to be in our path," Trevn said.

"They towed us here," the man said.

"Through the rainstorm," Trevn added.

Wilek drew Trevn by the arm away from the others. "What is Rand up to?" he asked.

"Clearly he wanted us to find these men," Trevn said. "But how he traveled through the rain while we waited out the storm . . . My only guess is a mantic. The pirates have at least a dozen ships now."

But Rand's mother was dead, and when Wilek had seen him at Bakurah Island, his son's face had been disfigured still. If Rand had a mantic at his disposal, wouldn't he have healed his son? Wilek rubbed his temples. His headache refused to leave. The physician said it was common when dehydrated. "We lost ten to fever yesterday," he told Trevn. "Another two this morning."

"Anyone we knew?" his brother asked.

"The fourth queen."

"No." Trevn looked away, exhaled a shaky breath. "The girls must be devastated."

"We all are. The *Seffynaw* left only fifty-two behind on Bakurah Island, but we've already lost one hundred thirty-nine to illness, infections, and fever."

"The quarantine should keep the fever from spreading," Trevn said.

"Uhley thinks he is infected. He has begun communicating to me by messenger for fear of contaminating me. I don't know what we'll do without a physician."

"He must have an assistant," Trevn said.

"Died last week."

"Oh."

"Trevn, question the survivors to see if you can learn anything about which direction the pirates came from. How they attacked. If there were signs of mantics aboard. Look for any clues we might use to capture them. Then see that these people find a quiet place to sleep. They have been through a harrowing ordeal, and I would feel better knowing they have a place to rest."

"Certainly, brother," Trevn said. "Consider it done."

Wilek started back to his cabin, accompanied by Novan and Rystan. *One step at a time,* he reminded himself, though he wished he could get one step ahead of his enemies. He'd kept an ever-present surveillance on the actions of the traitors who sought to sink the *Seffynaw,* but according to Lady Pia and Hinckdan, so far no plan had been hatched.

He reached his cabin and found Dendrick waiting outside his door with several guards and a woman. He ignored them and asked his onesent, "Do you have an answer from my mother as to the best time for Rosârah Valena's last rites and shipping?"

"She suggests two days from now," Dendrick said. "Also, Your Highness, Sârah Zeroah is waiting inside to see you."

Wilek stifled a sigh. He had no time for a pleasure visit but would not refuse his wife. He nodded to Novan, who entered the room first to ensure it was safe. Wilek followed with Rystan. Inside, Zeroah was sitting before Wilek's desk, her guardsmen standing by the window, talking softly to each other. She stood and curtsied. "Lord husband. And Rystan too. Hello."

"Good midday, sister," Rystan said.

"Give us a moment," Wilek said, and the guards, Novan, and Rystan left.

Wilek approached Zeroah and greeted her with a kiss. "How is my bride this day?"

"Grieved, I'm afraid," she said, taking his hands. "It's Sâr Janek."

Not again. "If this is about his behavior to Miss Mielle, we all saw that Trevn has dealt with it already." He shuddered at the memory of Janek's finger breaking. That horrible sound.

"This is a different matter altogether, lord. May I present the situation?"

Wilek released her hands and leaned against the front edge of his desk. "Please." *And get on with it, dearest.* His young wife had a tendency toward the dramatic at times, as if dragging out explanations would make them appear all the more severe.

Zeroah opened the cabin door and waved someone inside. "You may enter," she said.

In came the woman from the corridor. Now that Wilek got a good look at her, he found that he knew her. It was Shemme. Cook Hara's daughter. Very well into a pregnancy. When had *this* happened? Wilek could have sworn he'd seen the girl carrying a tray through a crossway a few weeks back with no sign of such distension. Why did Zeroah feel this required his attention? He hazarded a guess. "Sâr Janek is the father?"

Shemme's eyes flashed. "He is, lord."

"When Miss Shemme told him, he cast her out," Zeroah said.

That much, at least, was unsurprising. Wilek walked around to his chair and sat. "You cannot expect Janek to rejoice. He has several stray children already that he cares nothing for. That is the risk you take when agreeing to become the man's mistress."

This earned him a dirty look from his wife. He couldn't help that. She would learn the ways of Janek and his ilk soon enough.

"Miss Shemme, tell the sâr what your mother told you," Zeroah prompted. "Go on, now. Have courage. I will see you protected in all this."

Wilek's neck prickled. He wasn't certain he wanted to hear whatever this was.

"When Sâr Janek took an interest in me," Shemme said softly, agonizingly slow, "Mother urged me to try to conceive a child by taking evenroot."

The words chilled Wilek. Not evenroot again. "Where did Hara get the root?"

"She always keeps some in her pantry," Shemme said.

"Does Janek know this? Did you give him any?"

"No, of course not."

Wilek would have to destroy this evenroot supply at once. "Why would Hara do this?"

"Mother was born in Magonia. She believes evenroot has magical properties. She said if I took it before he summoned me, I was sure to conceive. She hoped that I might have a child as revered as Kamran DanSâr."

There were so many things wrong with all she said. That his father's cook was Magonian, that the woman had a store of evenroot when Wilek had thought it gone from the ship, that Kamran DanSâr was at all revered.

"Tell him the worst part," Zeroah said.

There was more? "Are you unwell?" If she had the fever, he wanted her away from Zeroah at once.

The girl looked at the floor. "I do not feel unwell, Your Highness. At least not any different than my mother tells me is normal for pregnancy, except that . . ." She shifted as if her skin were too tight and she wanted to shed it. "It's the time, Your Highness. Things are off. I . . ." Her eyes welled with tears as a flush spread over her cheeks. "What you see . . ." She set her hand on the shelf of her bulging belly. "This is but eight weeks' growth." She exhaled a pent-up breath.

"The midwives have examined Miss Shemme," Zeroah added. "They've determined that she is six months along. The child is growing alarmingly fast."

"It's not normal," Shemme said weepily. "I feel it moving always. It never rests. What if it's a demon?" She began to sob.

Wilek had no idea what to say. He needed to call upon someone who knew about such things. His first instinct was Harton, but even though he'd kept Harton close for his mantic expertise, he was hesitant to invite him into his confidence again. "Send Novan for Master Jhorn," he told Zeroah.

224

His wife ran to obey as if the room were on fire. Wilek felt awkward to be facing the wailing maid alone. "Do sit, Miss Shemme," he said, motioning to the chair before his desk.

She did, and thankfully Zeroah returned moments later. She poured Shemme a mug of water from the sideboard, hugged the girl with one arm, and helped her drink. To see her apply such ministrations to Shemme made Wilek smile. His wife was a woman of great compassion.

When Novan did not immediately return, Wilek made a suggestion. "My dear, take Miss Shemme to my mother. Make her comfortable there. I will speak with Master Jhorn when he arrives and call for you once I determine how to proceed."

Zeroah curtsied. "As you like, lord."

After the women left, Wilek immediately felt more at ease. For some reason, being in the presence of the pregnant woman unnerved him.

A short wait, and Novan brought Jhorn. Wilek repeated the entire conversation for both their benefits.

Jhorn frowned and tugged at his coiled beard. "This bodes ill, Your Highness," he said. "Though it does not seem that the cook has any concept of the dangers of conceiving a root child."

Wilek agreed. "That much is a relief. Can anything be done for Miss Shemme?"

"It partly depends on how much root she took during her pregnancy. If she is truly six months along at only eight weeks' time, she will likely die in childbirth. If the babe survives, it will be born with special abilities, like Grayson. You'd be wise to hide the child somewhere safe, where no one will find it and abuse its powers."

"What kind of powers will it have?" Wilek asked.

"It will age faster," Jhorn said. "It will be gifted in languages. Grayson has always known languages he's never learned. He can also make himself hidden and see into the Veil."

"The Veil between worlds? What good is that?" Wilek asked.

"It is good that he can see shadir when they are near him. Wouldn't you like to know if any are here now, spying for their masters?"

Panic shot through Wilek at the very idea. He had never considered such a thing possible. Did the traitors aboard the ship have shadir watching him? Did they know Lady Pia and Hinckdan were his spies?

He forced the worries aside for now.

"What do you suggest I do?"

"Make the mother comfortable," Jhorn said. "And keep a close eye on the child."

"I will do as you say," Wilek said. "Thank you for your advice."

"I am sorry it happened at all," Jhorn said. "From what I know of Grayson, being a root child isn't easy."

Wilek dismissed Jhorn and sat alone at his desk, thinking over the situation. He needed to find Hara's evenroot and destroy it. He needed to figure out if shadir were spying on him. And he needed to make sure the Magonians didn't find out about this root child or they might think it the child of their prophecy. Would he be forced to kill it someday? Perhaps he should kill it now before it killed its mother.

A chill of guilt raced through him at the mere thought. *Arman, forgive me.* How could he even contemplate such a thing?

Wilek thought of Charlon then. She had wanted to conceive a child by him. From the soul-binding they had shared, he recalled her daydreams of holding her child before her tribe as the all-revered Mother. She hadn't known she would have died bringing it into the world.

Sudden pity for Charlon made him wonder how much of Magonia's ultimate plan Chieftess Mreegan and her shadir were keeping to themselves.

KALENEK

The day following Rosârah Valena's death was Sârah Hrettah's thirteenth ageday, and Rosârah Brelenah threw a party on the stern deck in hopes of lifting the young princess's spirits. The loss of the fourth queen had fallen heavily over everyone, Kal included, but no one grieved more than sârahs Hrettah and Rashah.

Kal stood beside the king's table, where Inolah sat alone, watching the dancers. This was Kal's place now, to stand guard, in appearance only, over the prophetess Onika. But Onika was dancing with Oli Agoros. Again Kal found himself looking for them in the crowd. It annoyed him that he had not thought to ask Onika to dance first, though as her onesent and High Shield, it wouldn't have been appropriate.

The king was not present. A headache had kept him in his bed. Wilek, Novan, and Rystan had been here when the celebration began, but Dendrick had sought out the sâr-regent with some important matter of pirates, and the men ran off, leaving Kal behind. He caught sight of Sâr Janek dancing with Hrettah and knew the man would seek a dance with Amala before the festivities ended. Kal would need to find some legitimate way to interrupt them.

"Oh! This baby is coming soon," Inolah said, rubbing her own back and grimacing.

"Shall I call the midwives?" Kal asked.

"Thank you, no."

Kal went back to watching the dancers.

"I see how you look at the prophetess," Inolah said.

227

Fear spiked through Kal, and he tried to look indifferent as he turned his attention back to Inolah. "I don't know what you mean."

"Please. You looked at me that way once. Deny it if you must, but I know better."

Kal deliberately found a new focus for his eyes. Amala, who was dancing with Hinckdan Faluk. "Looking is not the same as acting, and the latter is not something I intend to do."

"Oh, Kal," Inolah said. "Stop punishing yourself. More are to blame for the war than you."

Mention of the war brought up his long list of regrets. "I should not have let my men linger in Magonia. Had we gone home on time, they all might have lived and I would have been home to stop the yeetta. In fact, I should not have insisted Livy stay home in the first place. She wanted to go to Everton, and I should have allowed it. The war never reached Everton."

"You couldn't have known that. She could have just as easily found trouble on the road."

"I dallied in Hebron with my squadron. We were on our way home and thought we were safe to linger for a few days." They had all died. All but Kal. Had he not given permission to stay, they all might have lived. Livy and their son too.

"Healing is a choice, Sir Kalenek. Why do you refuse it?" Onika's voice.

He pulled his gaze from Inolah and regarded Onika, standing at the table and holding on to Oli Agoros's good arm. The song had ended and a new one begun.

"Here is your chair, Miss Onika," Oli said, helping her sit.

Kal should have done that.

"Thank you, Your Grace. I greatly enjoyed the dance."

"You are most welcome, lady." The duke bowed, then paused awkwardly, as if he suddenly realized she could not see him, even after their spin around the stern deck.

Onika looked toward Kal, though not directly at him. She was facing where she had last heard his voice. "Have you no answer, Sir Kalenek?"

"I would gladly choose healing, Miss Onika, though I'm afraid there is no bandage large enough for the wound that ails me."

"Arman can heal all wounds," Onika said, "as I've been telling you since we met. The darkness is no place for you. Step out and find freedom."

"I want nothing to do with the darkness, Miss Onika," Kal said. "Nor am

I willing to stand in the light, for I am unworthy of it and all would see that plainly. There is no place for men like me but the shadows, where we can keep safely out of everyone's way."

"I too am a man like you, Sir Kalenek," Oli said, holding up his wooden arm.

"And I," said young Hinckdan. "We have all done things for which we are not proud. Some were our choices, and some were forced upon us. But they were our own actions, and the consequences often keep us apart from good company."

"What a mournful trio you three make," Inolah said. "I thought all men were meant to be brave and unselfish, yet you admit to intentionally cowering away."

"Only when life is quiet, Empress," Oli said. "When the battle comes our way or we see a need, we will pick up our swords and fight beside the bravest of men, even knowing we may fall. But once all is well again . . . that's when the darkness comes. Then we sit in the silence and struggle to grasp our peace as best we can."

The trueness of Oli's words surprised Kal.

"Yet Sir Kalenek has no peace," Onika said.

"My seclusion is my peace," Kal answered.

"Penance, you mean," Inolah said, "though none of you deserve it in the least!"

"I deserve death," Oli said.

"As do I," Kal echoed.

"Not me," Hinckdan countered. "I've acted the fool and have shamed myself, have killed to protect myself and my sâr, but I've done nothing quite so horrible as to qualify me for premature death."

"Now that is the first reasonable statement I've heard from a man today," Inolah said. "To reward you, Lord Dacre, I shall insist upon a dance." She lifted her hand toward him and waited for his response.

Hinckdan glanced at Janek's table, of all places, then took her hand and helped her stand. "I would be honored, Empress." They made an odd pair. The Earl of Dacre was not an overly tall man, and Inolah's great belly and lined forehead made her seem as if she must be carrying three children instead of one. As Hinckdan led the tottering empress away, a young King's Guard approached the table. "My pardon, Sir Kalenek, but the rosâr is asking to see you, sir."

The rosâr? This did not bode well. In the past few weeks, the king had summoned Kal several times. Delusional, and thinking Kal was still a royal assassin, he had ordered several kills of people long since dead.

"I will come at once." Distracted, Kal bowed to Onika before remembering she could not see, just as Oli had. "Miss Onika, I have been called away. I will return soon if I am able."

"You will be missed, Sir Kalenek," she said.

Kal wanted to believe it, but Miss Onika could find joy in most anyone's company. Proving his point, she went right back to speaking with Oli with so much ease that Kal was certain her words had been polite manners, nothing more.

"Keep a close eye on her," Kal told some guardsmen, "and Miss Amala too, if you can." His youngest ward was now dancing with Master Gelsly, the young backman who served Princess Hrettah. Kal glowered as he followed the King's Guard away.

They reached the king's cabin. Kal was ushered in and quickly found himself standing alone before Rosâr Echad, who demanded complete privacy. As Schwyl, the guards, and the king's attendants left, Kal studied the man. He looked worse than ever. Surely this would be more of his madness. When he spoke, Kal had to lean forward and strain to hear.

"Her name is Shemme," the king said. "The woman is spreading lies. Says she carries Janek's issue and that the child is a black spirit Janek made from dark magic. We are too small a kingdom upon this boat for such nonsense. End her life and throw her body overboard, where no one will find it."

✦   ✦   ✦

Kal could not carry out the command. Despite the risk of death should the king find out, he went to Wilek for help.

"Your Highness, I cannot do so horrible a thing. There is no Justness in it."

The Heir, his friend, did not seem surprised by the king's order. "I should have known news of the child would spread. You did right in coming to me."

"There must be another way to please the rosâr."

"No. The rosâr must believe you have obeyed his command." Wilek frowned and paced to the window and back. "If Inolah is willing, I will have her take Miss Shemme to the *Rafayah* right away."

Kal released a pent-up breath. "A wise idea, Your Highness." Doing so might solve the whole thing, for several years, at least. Mothers such as Shemme always came back, demanding aid in raising their stray children.

"Inolah and Miss Shemme could have their babies aboard the *Rafayah*, perhaps in some sort of isolation," Wilek said. "When each has delivered, Inolah can send word back here that she has birthed twins. That would explain away the second infant and give me a reason to keep the child close without drawing suspicion."

Take Shemme's child from her? Why? And how could such a plan be possible? "Inolah's child is expected any day," Kal said. "Won't the births be too far apart?"

"Miss Shemme's child is special, Kal," Wilek said. "It could come at any time."

Wilek's answer made no sense whatsoever. "But how can—?"

A knock on the door preceded Dendrick. "Forgive the interruption, Your Highness, but the empress, your sister, has gone into labor. She has been taken to her cabin, and the midwives are with her now."

Wilek growled out his frustration. "Thank you, Dendrick," he said. "Keep me informed." The man nodded and departed. Once the door closed, Wilek said, "What do I do now?"

"I can move Miss Shemme to the *Rafayah*," Kal said, "and take Mielle along to serve as her companion until you find a trustworthy replacement. I'll bring two of my guards."

"No guards from the *Seffynaw*," Wilek said. "Hire them from the *Rafayah*, and make sure they never learn Miss Shemme's true identity."

Was it so horrible that Kal rather enjoyed the thrill this small adventure promised? "I live to serve, Your Highness. I will do so immediately."

"Wait just a moment, Kal," Wilek said, waving him to sit. "First I must tell you what is so special about Miss Shemme's child."

✦　✦　✦

Kal rushed from Wilek's quarters, found Mielle, and set her packing, though the girl protested the entire time.

"I don't want to go to another ship," she said.

"You will do as you're told."

"But I must not abandon Sârah Zeroah. She has been feeling ill lately, and I worry it might be the fever. Also, Darlow is still so very sick."

"We are only going until a replacement can be found," Kal said. "A day. Two at most. This is the only way to keep Miss Shemme safe."

Mielle huffed and grabbed her cape. "If it is just a few days, I'll only need this."

"Put it on, then. Once we go above deck, we do not wish for anyone to know our identity as we are leaving."

"You are frightening me, Kal," she said.

There was every reason to be frightened. Kal held open the cabin door, and Mielle exited. They started down the corridor together.

"I must bid farewell to Sâr Trevn," Mielle said. "He is on watch."

"There isn't time," Kal said.

"Kal!" She stomped her foot. "I won't just abandon him! It isn't proper."

"Will you tell that to Miss Shemme as she lies dying or shall I?"

She wilted. "Surely you are overreacting."

"I have my orders, Mielle. I must obey them with haste." He drove Mielle up to Rosârah Brelenah's cabin and asked to see Amala. His younger ward came to the door wearing a slip, her face covered in a creamy white paste.

"Just look at me!" She ran her fingers along her cheek. "I have a terrible rash."

"It's from too much bathing in salt water," Kal said.

"It's tragic, is what it is. I am either filthy or covered in salt and a rash. I cannot stand this boat any longer."

"She can take my place," Mielle said.

"No," Kal said. "I want you with me." Then to Amala, "Mielle and I are going away for a day or two. Tell Sâr Trevn so that he won't worry."

Amala raised her eyebrows at Mielle. "He doesn't know you're going?"

"There isn't time to find him," Kal said. "We will be back soon enough. Behave yourself while we are gone. I have asked Sâr Wilek to keep a close eye on you."

"I don't need the sâr or anyone to act as my guardian." Amala flashed Kal a fake smile and closed the door in his face.

He stifled a groan and set off down the crossway. "That girl will be the death of me."

✦   ✦   ✦

Hooded and cloaked, Kal and Mielle walked to the boat fall on the foredeck. There they found Miss Shemme, also wearing a hooded cape, standing with Captain Veralla. Kal helped Mielle and Miss Shemme inside the dinghy while the captain sent word to the helmsman to heave to so the dinghy could be lowered. As Kal and the girls sat waiting for the boat to drop, he tried not to notice Miss Shemme's sniffling.

"What is wrong, Miss Shemme?" Mielle asked, setting her hand upon the girl's knee.

232

"My mother. I daresay she will be the only one to miss me."

"I'm sure there are others," Mielle said. "What about the baby's father?"

Kal kicked himself for not warning Mielle away from such topics in advance.

"He doesn't care," Shemme said. "People say a girl cannot resist him, but I could have. Sâr Janek has never been an impressive man in my eyes."

"Sâr Janek!" Mielle cried.

"Keep your voices down," Kal warned as the sailors began to lower the dinghy.

"I miss Kell," Shemme whispered. "Why did he have to die?" She shook from the tears that overcame her.

Mielle put her arm around the girl and held her close. Kal was glad of it. He certainly didn't know how to offer sympathy to a woman in such a state.

Once the dinghy reached the surging waves, Kal rowed them toward the *Rafayah* and explained the situation in a way both would understand. The goal was to keep Miss Shemme and her baby alive but to let everyone else believe them dead. From this moment forward she must choose a false name and never be Shemme again. He did not tell either of them that Miss Shemme would likely die birthing the child. He saw no need to do so.

"I will be called Kellah, after my Kell," Shemme said.

"That will do fine," Kal said.

At the *Rafayah* they were hoisted aloft and welcomed aboard by the first mate. Kal demanded a private cabin and two guardsmen assigned to him.

"I can get you the men, sir," the first mate said, "but there are no private cabins available."

"Find one," Kal said. "It need not be spacious or grand. This order comes from the sâr-regent."

The man bowed and set off. An hour later Kal stood in the doorway of a tiny cabin on the lower foredeck, watching Mielle get Miss Shemme situated.

"No one enters this cabin but me or these two women," Kal told his two new guardsmen.

The men nodded and took their place outside the door.

"Sh—Kellah will need a midwife," Mielle said.

"Not today, she won't."

Mielle collapsed beside Miss Shemme on the bed. "Are we to simply sit here like prisoners?"

Kal claimed the only chair in the room and settled down. "As we wait for our replacement, yes. Sâr Wilek promised to send someone who could stay permanently with . . . Miss Kellah."

But things did not progress as smoothly as Kal had hoped.

The first day passed, and as the second came to a close and no replacement had come, Kal began to worry. If by morning they were not relieved, he would give Mielle and Miss Kellah over to the care of the guards and take a dinghy back to the *Seffynaw* to see what had held up Wilek.

CHARLON ⊙

After weeks of silence Magon returned, true to her word. Charlon had been in the birthing tent mixing a tonic for a woman with intense morning sickness when the goddess spoke to her. She could not see Magon, but the goddess's voice rang clearly in Charlon's head.

Do you still serve me loyally, Charlon?

Charlon threw herself to the deck. "Yes, goddess. My allegiance is yours. I have done as you asked. I have served as a midwife. Will you take me back to the *Vespara*?"

Soon. But first I have two tasks for you.

"Anything, goddess."

The first is simple. I have learned that Sâr Trevn Hadar will soon be on his way to this ship. When he arrives, call on me. We must do whatever it takes to keep him preoccupied aboard the Rafayah.

Charlon bowed low. "It will be as you say, Great Goddess. And the second task?"

The woman Mielle Allard is on this ship. Have you seen her?

Charlon stiffened. "Yes." She had come with Prince Wilek's guardsman. The scarred one. Thankfully neither of them had ever seen Charlon's real face. "She does not know who I am."

She has a friend who is pregnant.

"Her name is Kellah. She will give birth any day now."

You must be there when the child is born. That child is the Deliverer.

235

The words stabbed deeply. "What?" Charlon couldn't believe it. Felt like she was falling. Hope destroyed. "I am not the Mother after all?"

Fear not. You will be Mother once you claim the child as your own.

"But I thought . . . You told me I would carry the child myself."

You failed, Charlon, but I have rewarded your faithfulness. You will soon see that as the Mother of the Deliverer, you will be blessed more than the child's birth mother.

Charlon did not understand. But she would not question. Not today. "Whatever you ask, Great Goddess, I will do."

Once the Deliverer is in your arms, use your magic to set sail for the Vespara, which will be nearby. Take the child before Mreegan, claim it as your own flesh, and stand before all of Magonia as Mother.

Hinck

When next Hinck's brand burned to signal a meeting of the La-havôtesh, his heart leapt with hope. Sâr Wilek had been anxious for news of the rebels. As Hinck made his way down into the hold of the *Seffynaw*, he hoped whatever was said today would be enough for Wilek to finally arrest everyone. When he reached the compartment, the guard there sent him back up to the Honored Lady Zenobia's cabin. When Hinck asked why, the man would only say, "Ask the mistress."

So Hinck climbed back up the four flights of stairs and made his way to the cabin of the king's oldest concubine, a room that turned out to be smaller than the compartment in the hold. Inside, he found everyone sitting along the walls or on the bed. All the usual faces were present except for Kamran and Janek.

Hinck took a seat beside his uncle Canbek. "Why are we meeting here?" he whispered.

"Because the mistress commanded it," Canbek said without looking Hinck's way. His uncle was wearing one of his old cat pelts, but it no longer gave him a rich and lustrous air. The fur had become as grimy as Canbek's hair, which had been slicked back over his scalp. Fashion and style, it seemed, had died with the Five Realms.

"Now that we are all present," Zenobia said, "I have—"

"No Kamran?" Lady Mattenelle asked.

"Not today," Zenobia said. "We have yet to make any progress on sinking the ship, but a new development has arisen. Madame Hara, the cook, came

237

to me with an offer. She has a bottle of evenroot juice and wants me to use it to kill the rosâr, who she believes had her daughter murdered."

Excited chatter broke out among the group.

Shemme was dead? Hinck had heard about the girl's pregnancy and that she'd named Janek as the father, but that she'd been killed for it . . . He felt sick.

"With root you can kill the Heir too," Fonu said. "Then Moon Fang can take the ship as his own, and we won't have to sink it."

"Sâr Wilek is looking for this root," Zenobia said. "The cook told him she had used it all. Their search turned up nothing. In truth, she had it hidden well."

"When do we get it?" Fonu asked.

"I overstepped in my eagerness and mentioned killing Sâr Wilek," Zenobia said. "This angered the cook. She insists Sâr Wilek not be harmed."

"So let her think you won't harm him, then kill her too," Fonu said. "So long as you get the root."

Zenobia sighed heavily. "Do stop interrupting me, Fonu."

He sat back on the bed and set one foot over his other knee. "Go on."

"I have consulted with Moon Fang," Zenobia said. "I will promise the cook that I will kill only the king. In the turmoil of his death, I will use the evenroot to take control of the *Seffynaw* and kill the sârs. Then Moon Fang will send a shadir to lead our ship to his."

"Kill all the sârs?" Fonu asked. "Janek too?"

"Janek is not to be touched," Zenobia said.

"Why not search the kitchen, take the root ourselves?" Canbek asked.

"Or have your shadir follow her and tell you where it is," Lady Mattenelle said.

"Even better," Fonu suggested, "get Janek to use the newt. It will find the root in no time."

"We are not going to do anything to jeopardize this opportunity," Zenobia said. "There is no point in stealing the juice. When Hara hears my vow, she will gladly give it over."

Not if Hinck could stop it.

They devised a plan for the mutiny. Once Lady Zenobia received the root juice from Hara, she would again summon a meeting. Everyone would get a sip, then all would set off to take the royals into captivity. They divided the list of targets between them. Lady Zenobia would poison the king. Sir Jayron would deal with Sâr Wilek. Canbek would distract his brother, Danek. Lady Mattenelle volunteered to subdue Sârah Zeroah. When Hinck volunteered

238

to capture Trevn, Fonu jumped in and said he had a plan to lure Sâr Trevn to another ship and keep Janek out of the way too. Lady Zenobia instead assigned Hinck the task of abducting Miss Onika. With the other royals confined, the guards would have no choice but to comply.

"The call could come at any moment," Lady Zenobia said. "You must be ready."

They left one at a time so as not to be seen together. When Hinck's turn came, he headed to his cabin. He wanted to go straight to Sâr Wilek, but Lady Pia's warning still rang in his mind and Lady Mattenelle's offhanded comment to have a shadir follow Cook Hara frightened him. It had never occurred to him that shadirs could do that. Had they been following him all this time? Did the entire Lahavôtesh know he was Sâr Wilek's man?

Surely he would be dead by now, if that were the case.

He entered his cabin and secured the door behind him, aware that doing so would not keep out a shadir. The waning moon outside sent pale light through his small window. Barely enough to see by. He sat on the bed he'd made on the floor under his hanging cot and sighed heavily. What was he to do now? Sâr Wilek had to be informed at once. But when? How?

"Was it that bad?"

Hinck pushed to his knees at the sound of the woman's voice and squinted in the dimness. Lady Pia, dressed all in black, sitting cross-legged on his desk.

"Lady Pia." He sank back to the floor.

She hopped down, and Hinck saw that she was wearing men's trousers. He had never seen a woman in trousers before.

"Come now, lord." She sank beside him and bumped her shoulder with his. "If they've sent you out, there isn't much time. What happened?"

Hinck relayed the main points of the meeting, feeling heavy. "I fear they still suspect me. I am sure to bungle this and end up dead along with everyone I am trying to protect. I found out tonight there are shadir everywhere. They could be watching me. I'm certain one of them will overhear a conversation between me and Sâr Wilek, or me and you, and they will kill us all."

"Worry not," she said. "Shadir cannot kill without a mantic to direct them. And the mantics do not have any evenroot. Yet."

"They will soon," Hinck said. "In the meantime Sir Jayron has a sword and a long reach."

"Chin up, poet. We are nearly there. I will tell Sâr Wilek what happened. In the morning he will advise you."

Hinck sighed. He'd grown weary of spying and longed for the days when his biggest concern was how Trevn had managed to lose him on the rooftops of Everton.

Lady Pia threaded her fingers with his. "I sense a connection between us, lord."

He looked into her eyes, and she surprised him with a kiss.

He went rigid. Or tried to, anyway. His lips trembled under her soft, sure ones. A beautiful, glorious woman liked him. Him! Hinckdan Faluk, who never, ever won the girl.

But this couldn't happen.

It took all his strength and willpower to turn his head and break the connection.

Her brow creased in confusion. "What's wrong?"

He chose his words carefully, not wanting her to misunderstand. "Forgive me, lady. You are not wrong about my feelings for you, but I . . . You are his."

Understanding softened her expression. "I belong to Sâr Janek, you mean."

He glanced down at their entwined fingers, suddenly embarrassed. "Yes."

She squeezed his hand and stood. "I must take your news to Sâr Wilek."

As Hinck watched her go, loneliness threatened to choke him. It didn't matter. One more night and all this madness would end. Sâr Wilek would arrest the traitors, and Hinck would be free to return to his life as Trevn's backman.

All he had to do was wait.

WILEK

Wilek had slept poorly yet again. Rough seas and Lady Pia's late-night message from Hinckdan about the rebels' latest plans had ruined any chance at rest. Wilek did not want to raise suspicion by calling a meeting in the middle of the night, especially with the growing concern that there might be shadir watching them all. At sunrise he bid Dendrick discreetly summon the few people he trusted on board the *Seffynaw*.

He surveyed the faces gathered in his cabin thus far. There were five besides himself: Rayim, Novan, Oli, Jhorn, and Miss Onika.

A knock at the door preceded Dendrick, who came to Wilek's side. "I was unable to locate Sâr Trevn, Your Highness. Captain Bussie says two of his men sent Sâr Trevn and Sir Cadoc down the boat fall just a bit ago."

Wilek sighed. Trevn must have found out that Miss Mielle had gone to the *Rafayah*. He cursed his own thoughtlessness at forgetting to tell his brother about Miss Mielle's temporary assignment.

"We will have to proceed without him." Wilek stood and waited for every face to focus on his. "I have gathered you here because I have discovered a plot against me and my father. There are some mantics on board in search of a bottle of evenroot juice. When they find it, they intend to use it to kill the king."

Gasps of surprise and shock passed between them.

"We must find the evenroot first," Rayim said.

Wilek nodded. "Our searches to this point have turned up empty."

"Seize Sâr Janek's newt, then," Novan suggested.

"Janek claims the creature has been stolen. I thought he must be lying, but my spies confirmed he is not. We must prepare for the worst. Should these traitors find the root before we do, what can be done to stop them?"

"Nothing outright," Jhorn said. "In the Great War a fresh mantic would destroy hundreds, until the moment she knelt to pray to her demons for healing. Then we'd cut her down."

"Was there no way to prevent the first attack?" Wilek asked.

Jhorn's brows pinched in thought. "Attacks depended on several criteria. The amount of evenroot taken, the skill of the mantic, the strength of the shadir. To take a life, a well-trained mantic needs a powerful shadir and a lot of root."

"At least a full vial," Oli said.

"These traitors must be arrested and executed at once," Rayim said. "It's the only way."

"But if they have taken evenroot, can't they do magic to avoid arrest?" Wilek asked.

"That or to escape," Jhorn said.

"We should move the king to a different ship," Rayim said.

"That might buy some time," Oli offered. "But . . . there is another way."

A hush fell as every eye focused on the duke.

"I have a bottle of evenroot juice in my cabin," Oli said.

Fire flowed through Wilek's veins. "You kept this from me?"

Oli held up his good hand. "I know, I know. You went on a crusade to purge root from the fleet. The truth is . . ." A breath quivered from his lips, and he lowered his gaze. "I've been suffering from the lack of root. When I heard about the mantic Charlon pretending to be Sârah Zeroah, I searched her cabin and found a canister of root powder."

"The stash Janek was looking for?" Wilek asked, stunned that so much root might be within reach of the people wanting to kill him.

"I stole it, that is the truth, but Empress Inolah discovered it and made me dump it into the sea." Oli glanced up at Wilek. "Except the empress didn't know that I had already made myself several bottles of juice from the powder. I kept it in wine bottles and have been taking it still, trying to wean myself slowly." He paused. "It's easier than going without."

No one spoke. Rayim and Jhorn were glaring at Oli as if they'd like to send him to the pole. The others watched in silence.

This was no time to deal with Oli's crime. Wilek needed to keep the discussion on topic. "You said there was another way?" he asked.

Oli took a deep breath and stroked the grain of wood on his fake hand. "I have bonded with a shadir to heal me from the root's poison. That means I can see into the Veil. If I am with you during the interrogations, I can—"

"One should not engage with a worshiper of demons," Jhorn said. "Arman forbids it. You've probably brought a host of them in here, listening to every word we say."

"I see none here now," Oli said, looking around. "Let me help."

"You cannot trust shadir," Wilek said. "I learned that the hard way."

"I know that," Oli said. "But shadir feed off their bonds with humans. Someone like me, rationing root, trying to wean myself . . . I give off so little power. Noadab won't share me with anyone. If he had told others, they would have come by now. And no others have."

"I can't deny that logic," Jhorn said. "Shadir have always been self-absorbed."

"I could also ask Noadab to make one of you a seer," Oli said. "I will tell him it's a grand joke I wish to play. He'll like that because shadir love tricks and they love humans who can see them."

"Who would you choose?" Wilek asked.

"That's your choice," Oli said. "But I must warn you. A seer is vulnerable to shadir if he makes himself known to them, so it would be best if the seer pretended he couldn't see the shadir. Like a spy." He gave Wilek a knowing look.

He meant Hinckdan. Wilek's heart sank for the young earl. House Hadar had asked too much of him already.

"Too dangerous," Jhorn said.

"But knowledge is power," Rayim said. "It would help to know where these creatures were and who they had bonded with."

It might be their only chance at an offensive. "Do you know the spell?" Wilek asked. "And the runes?"

"No," Oli said, "but Noadab has offered to do tricks for me, as pranks on my friends. He's eager to try to heal my arm, which has been difficult to resist, yet I know such a thing would require massive amounts of evenroot, increase my dependence, and give Noadab too much power over me. Not even the return of my arm is worth that."

"Now you're starting to grasp the meat of it," Jhorn said. "These are black spirits, yet you suggest we partner with one to help us, and the rest of you agree as if this is the best plan in the Northsea? It's daft, I tell you. Completely irresponsible and sacrilegious to boot."

Wilek paled at Jhorn's rebuke. His words mirrored those Trevn had once said to him, words Wilek had ignored. "Miss Onika?" he asked. "Are we wrong to consider asking the shadir to—"

"This is what the Sovereign Arman says: 'You did not destroy the evil as I commanded, but you mingled your nations and adopted the customs of your enemies.'" Her mesmerizing voice welled up from inside Wilek's head. "'You worshiped idols, which became a snare to you. You sacrificed your sons and daughters to black spirits, and the land was desecrated by their blood.'" She turned her glassy stare upon Wilek. "The sacrifices of pagans are offered to demons, not to Arman, and he does not wish us to be participants with black spirits. You cannot drink from the cup of Arman *and* the cup of Gâzar. Submit yourselves to Arman. Resist the temptations of Gâzar and his shadir, and they will flee from you."

Goose pimples had cropped up over Wilek's arms. "Thank you, Miss Onika. We seek to give honor to Arman and trust his guidance."

Still, he felt defeated. Here Oli had offered up what had seemed like the perfect solution, yet as it was against Arman's decrees, Wilek had no choice but to reject it.

"Duke Canden, I appreciate your offer to make a seer for House Hadar, and while I admit it might make everything easier, it is an order I cannot give. We will have to find another way, and you will surrender your bottles of evenroot juice to me at once."

"I understand perfectly, Your Highness," Oli said, looking shaken. "I cannot change the mistakes I've made, but the root I have ingested today will enable me to see until sometime tomorrow. If you do your interrogations now, you could at least make use of my eyes while I still have them."

"You can't trust a shadir, though," Jhorn said. "Never."

"I'm well aware of that," Oli said. "But my shadir would not be there. Only me. With eyes able to see any other shadir that enter."

Wilek wanted to accept, but he deferred to his expert. "Miss Onika? What say you? Am I wrong to suggest that using Duke Canden's eyes is not so different than using the eyes of a root child?"

Miss Onika closed her eyes and released a soft breath, as if she were going to take a nap right there at the table. Her body swayed with the rocking of the ship, and people began to fidget as time passed. A second exhale and her eyes opened, staring just past Wilek's right shoulder. "Arman gives me no immediate answer on this, Your Highness," she said. "I will pray about it, but in the meantime, it is my opinion that as long as the duke is not colluding with any shadir, I see no harm in him telling you what he sees."

It was all the answer Wilek needed. He picked up a scroll from his desk and held it out. "Rayim, arrest the people on this list and put them in the hold. Miss Onika and Master Jhorn, I thank you for your council. You are dismissed. Duke Canden, you will remain here."

It was time to put a stop to these traitors once and for all.

✦ ✦ ✦

Two guards led Hinckdan Faluk into the compartment in the hold and pushed him onto the seat across from where Wilek and Oli sat. The young earl's hands were bound before him. He glared at the guards, stood and bowed to Wilek, then took his seat again. Wilek nodded at Dendrick, who ushered the guards into the crossway and closed the door, leaving Wilek, Oli, and Hinckdan alone. The lantern hanging above the table swayed violently—the seas had been growing more turbulent as the day wore on.

"Your Highness, why have I been detained?" Hinckdan asked.

Wilek held up his hand to silence the man before he gave himself away.

"This conspiracy against your father is worse than the Five Woes," Oli said.

That was the code they had worked out in advance. Each time the guards left after delivering a prisoner, Oli was to say something that included the number of beings in the room—human and shadir combined. That the duke had said *five* meant that two shadir had entered with Hinckdan. Of the eight people Wilek had interviewed so far, seven rebels and the cook, each had been accompanied by at least one shadir. Three of the creatures had come in with Fonu Edekk.

Wilek wanted to warn Hinckdan that there might be shadir present so he wouldn't give himself away. All he could think to do was to say something so utterly false and ridiculous that the earl might catch the hint that something was amiss.

"Lord Dacre," he said, "I had been prepared to grant your request to marry Sârah Hrettah, despite it having been Rosârah Valena's wish that she marry Lord Barta and the fact that you do not match in fives."

Hinckdan's throat bobbed as he swallowed, eyes narrowed in thought. His gaze flicked toward Oli, then back to Wilek. He looked confused.

That's right, Wilek urged him. *Play along.*

"I am honored, Your Highness," Hinckdan said at last.

A polite and careful answer. Good. Wilek hated to put the young man through this, but he didn't want to lose Hinckdan's place amongst the traitors. Locking him up with the others was the best way to keep him safe.

"But that was before," Wilek said, continuing his fake interrogation. "I'm afraid Sârah Hrettah must be disappointed."

Hinckdan's brow wrinkled in confusion. "Must she?"

"Did the guards tell you why you're here?" Wilek asked.

"One of them said you think me a traitor."

"I had hoped it was not true," Wilek said. "You who have been a close friend to my brother Trevn. But I do not understand why you would attend a meeting with those plotting my father's murder."

Hinckdan frowned. "I don't know what you mean."

"When did you first join the Lahavôtesh?" Wilek asked.

Hinckdan thought about it a moment. "In Everton, shortly before the Woes came upon us."

Wilek had expected him to claim ignorance here as well. He hoped he would not answer the next question honestly. "Why did you join?"

He shrugged. "I was curious."

When in reality Trevn had made him join. "The Lahavôtesh is conspiring to murder my father. What is your role in the plot?"

"That's terrible! I don't know anything about that."

"Do you know that a bottle of evenroot juice is missing?"

A flicker of fear lit in his eyes. "No, Your Highness."

"Then you don't know who might have it?"

"I do not."

Wilek went on, asking Hinckdan all the same questions he had asked the others. Who were the other members in the cult? Were any of them on board the *Seffynaw*? Of those, were all of them mantics or only some? Who was their leader? Was Sâr Janek or Kamran DanSâr involved?

To all of these questions, Hinckdan claimed ignorance. Wilek ended his interrogation with the same words he'd said to all the traitors. "I'm disappointed in your disloyalty to House Hadar. You will remain in the hold until you are tried by the Wisean Council for treason."

"That is most unfair, Your Highness. On what evidence do you accuse me?"

"I will not reveal my sources until the trial," Wilek said. "Duke Canden, fetch the guards."

Oli stood and went to obey.

"Will you tell Sârah Hrettah about this?" Hinckdan asked.

Wilek almost smiled at the young man's brittle expression. No wonder the earl made such a good spy. He had a flair for acting. "No," Wilek said, "but she will likely hear about it once the trial has taken place."

Hinckdan nodded and said no more. The guards entered to take him back to his cell. Once they had gone, Oli returned with Rayim, Dendrick, and Novan.

Novan closed the door, and Wilek waited for Oli's signal. "Five," he said.

Wilek sighed, relieved that they were finally alone. "Tell us," he said to Oli.

"There were nine different shadir," Oli said. "Two were commons, which is the second strongest type of shadir. Kabada is one of them, and she is bonded to Lady Zenobia, who I'd guess is the most powerful mantic aboard the *Seffynaw*."

The king's oldest concubine. Interesting. "Which would explain Kamran's involvement."

"He has always fully supported his mother," Oli said.

Yet Kamran and Janek had not attended the last secret meeting and so Wilek had not arrested them, despite knowing they were allied with the traitors.

"What about Master Edekk?" Wilek asked. "He had three shadir with him."

"Fonu is the second most powerful mantic aboard," Oli said. "He has both his own shadir and a common that once served Beal."

"Trevn's former onesent?"

Oli nodded. "When Hinckdan killed Beal, the common took up with Fonu."

"And the third shadir?" Wilek asked.

"Kabada. She came inside for every interview. My guess is Kabada reports to Pontiff Rogedoth as well as her mistress."

"Shadir can go from boat to boat?" Wilek asked.

"Oh yes," Oli said. "Through the Veil."

"No one admitted taking the root," Wilek said.

"Of course they wouldn't," Rayim said. "The question is, could Hara be lying about having evenroot in the first place?"

"She had root at some point," Wilek said. "I know this for a fact." He had not told Dendrick or Rayim about Miss Shemme. "I can't imagine she'd be fool enough to offer root to a mantic if she had none. She either gave it to a mantic already or has hidden it somewhere."

"Or with someone she trusts," Novan suggested. "If she gave it to a mantic, the prisoners would have escaped by now."

"I will question her staff," Rayim said. "She might have given it to somone to hide."

"Could you make a list of all those on board who attended Sâr Janek's court?" Dendrick asked Oli.

"That wouldn't hurt," Wilek said, "but the Lahavôtesh has been around since before Janek was born. There could be someone on board who is loyal to Rogedoth but not Janek. Rayim, make a separate list of those who attended my father's court on a regular basis—their servants as well. There must be someone we're missing."

"Yes, Your Highness," Rayim said.

However, most of the nobles were aboard other ships. Wilek could not think of another noble on board to suspect. Danek Faluk would not have been involved. And surely Wilek's mother and the sârahs were innocent. Perhaps one of their maids or one of the guards? "Dendrick, work with Schwyl to make a plan for moving the king. I'd like to hear it tonight after dinner. Let's all meet then and see where we are. Rayim, we must find Teaka's newt. It's the best way to—"

"Seven," Oli said.

A fearful moment of silence passed. Wilek hoped the shadir had only just entered and had not overheard anything important.

"I'd say all nine are guilty," Dendrick said, covering for Oli's outburst.

All but Hinckdan. Wilek stood, wanting to be away from the creatures. "You have your orders. Dismissed."

TREVN

Approaching the *Rafayah* by dinghy, Trevn realized how much he'd learned about ships. He saw how she sat higher on the water than the *Seffynaw* and had high castles fore and aft with a low, open waist in the middle for the main deck. During the Centenary War the *Rafayah* had served as a flagship for Armania, and her visage was mighty indeed. The evergold hull was painted bright red and covered in carved multicolored motifs of grinning Rôb gods and goddesses slaughtering Magonian yeetta warriors.

"It would have been wise to tell Sâr Wilek where we have gone," Cadoc said.

"He would have made me stay," Trevn replied, annoyed that Wilek had kept secret the fact that he'd moved Mielle to a different ship. If what Kamran had said was true, and Janek was already aboard the *Rafayah* . . . If he harmed Mielle in any way . . . "No wonder I couldn't find her these past few days." He shook his head. "Why didn't Wilek tell me?"

"He must have had his reasons. I wonder why you didn't check with Sâr Wilek first. Are you sure Miss Mielle is really here? This might be a prank Kamran and Janek stirred up to—"

"No," Trevn said, staring at the red hull. "Miss Amala confirmed it. She was supposed to have told me days ago but forgot. Mielle is here." *She must be*. And if Janek broke his vow and dared lay one hand on her, Trevn would break more than his finger.

By the time Trevn and Cadoc climbed out of the dinghy, a crowd had formed on the *Rafayah*'s foredeck, including the captain and several of his crew.

249

Cadoc acted the part of herald and introduced Trevn. "His Royal Highness, Trevn-Sâr Hadar, the Third Arm, the Curious."

"I have come seeking Miss Mielle Allard, Captain . . . ?" Trevn paused.

"Stockton, Your Highness," the captain said. "And I thought as much. I have sent a man to inform Miss Mielle of your arrival. I welcome you aboard the *Rafayah* and hope your stay with us is a pleasant—"

"Trevn!"

With Mielle being so tall, Trevn caught sight of her head as she pushed through the crowd. When she finally reached him, she threw herself into his arms. He stumbled back a step and turned in a circle to keep from falling.

"You do know how to scare a fellow," Trevn said, gripping her arms. "Why didn't you say you were coming here?"

"Didn't Amala tell you?"

"Not until I asked her an hour ago."

Mielle growled and stamped her foot. "Tuhsh! She cares for no one but herself."

"What of Janek? Has he been bothering you?"

She frowned. "Janek is here? I haven't seen him."

"So there's the trick of it," Cadoc said, shaking his head.

"But why would Kamran say Janek was coming for Mielle if he wasn't?" Trevn asked. Kamran had found Trevn on the stern deck this morning and mocked his ignorance of knowing where Miss Mielle was—told him that Janek had come to the *Rafayah* at Fonu's dare that he could not steal Mielle from Trevn.

"The important question is: What would Sâr Janek gain from your coming here?" Cadoc asked.

Before Trevn could answer, a sudden devotion to Mielle seized him. "I will never allow us to be parted again." He pulled her close and kissed her.

A lone whoop brought forth scattered laughter from the crowd. Someone whistled.

Mielle turned her head, buried her face against his shoulder. "*Trevn* . . . people are watching."

Trevn made eye contact with an elderly woman who was grinning at him. Beyond the old woman many more faces stared: a man with rotten teeth, two little girls, a woman holding a child, and a young Magonian woman.

"Let them watch," he said. "I cannot go on like this another day."

Her dark eyes searched his. "What do you want?"

In a surge of recklessness, he fell to his knees, gripped her hands, and blurted out, "Marry me," shocking even himself.

Mielle stared at him as if he were mad. Well, he was mad. For her. He could not bear to be parted from her again. Not even for a moment. "I am tired of being away from you," he said.

"But your father will never approve."

"Then we will marry here, aboard the *Rafayah*. Father may rail at me afterward. Please, Mielle. Say you will." He would die if she refused him. Such a thought seemed melodramatic for someone as level-headed as himself, yet he could not deny the fear pulsing within his heart.

"But it isn't the proper way!" Mielle said. "Kal will be angry. Sâr Wilek too."

Trevn lifted her hand, folded it into a fist, and set her Renegade *R* against his. "I care not about the proper way or what anyone might say. I love you. And I want them all to know I mean it when I say so."

A slow smile. "I love you too."

He jumped back to his feet and looked into her eyes. "We will stay here on the *Rafayah*, where no one can order us about."

"Sâr Wilek will send for you eventually," Mielle said. "And the king will say our marriage isn't binding."

Trevn's mind raced to find a solution. "If we marry here on the main deck in front of all these people, then have them sign as witnesses, Father and Wilek cannot part us without upsetting the public. Say you will, Mielle. Please?"

She pulled his hand to her heart. "How could I refuse you?"

A thrill of contentment settled over Trevn. He lifted their joined hands above their heads and turned to face the crowd. "She said yes!"

The sea of strangers cheered wildly. Mielle laughed and threw her arms around his neck. He held her close, knowing that somehow, despite the nagging doubt in the back of his mind, this had been the right thing to do.

"Your Highness." Cadoc's voice interrupted Trevn's blissful reverie. The shield was standing beside them, grim. "I must caution you against this plan."

Trevn sighed. "Must you?"

"If you and Miss Mielle marry without the consent of your elders, I fear you will both regret it."

Cadoc's words troubled Trevn, but only for a moment. He led Mielle by the hand to Captain Stockton, who was still standing with his men, watching the goings-on. "Captain Stockton, will you marry us?"

The man cleared his throat. "May Athos deal with me, Your Highness, be it ever so severely, but I dare not anger my king in submitting to his son. If he gives his blessing, it would be my honor to hear your vows to one another."

"He will not give his permission," Trevn said, then raised his voice. "Is there a captain or priest aboard this ship who will hear our vows to marry?"

A remarkable silence ensued, and Trevn knew a moment of dread.

Why was he doing this? Wilek had gained them Father's permission to court. In time, surely he would also permit them to marry. Why rush things and risk angering the king?

At that thought he glanced at Mielle, and another deluge of affection for her drowned all doubt. No. Time was short. They might never find land. Trevn wanted to seize every happiness while he still could.

"Very well," he yelled to the crowd. "We must find a ship with someone who will hear our vows." He tugged Mielle toward the boat fall.

She stopped, pulled against him. "I can't leave," she whispered.

"Why not?"

"I can't say. Not here, anyway. There are too many people who—"

"I will hear your vows," a man said.

The crowd parted, revealing a bronze-skinned man wearing the cobalt robes of a Rôb priest, though he had a shaved head and the henna tracings of a Rurekan Igote soldier.

"And you are?" Trevn asked.

"Father Zeeshan, Your Highness." He bowed swiftly. "Unless you think the king might not honor vows heard by a Rurekan priest."

"Why wouldn't he?" Trevn asked. "Armania is allied with Rurekau. As long as these fine people will act as witnesses."

The crowd cheered.

"When would you like to marry?" Father Zeeshan asked.

"This very moment," Trevn said.

"Wait until tomorrow at least, Your Highness," Captain Stockton said. "Our cooks will need that much time to prepare a feast."

"We require no feast," Trevn said, not wanting to recklessly deplete the food stores. "No, Captain, I must insist we marry now. To tarry will only give room for opposition."

A young Magonian woman stepped forward. She stood a full head shorter than Trevn and Mielle and wore a blue-and-green kasah tied over one shoulder, leaving the other bare. Her reddish skin and gray eyes set him instantly on edge.

"This is Sonber," Mielle said, surprising Trevn. "She is one of the midwives aboard the ship. We are taking care of a mutual friend."

Trevn didn't like that Mielle had befriended a Magonian mantic.

Sonber curtsied. "Pleased to know you, Sâr Trevn. Might I offer a blessing as a wedding gift?"

"No," Trevn said. "No magic."

"Trevn, don't be rude," Mielle whispered, then to Sonber, "I'm sure it's not magic. Is it?"

"It is merely a prayer of blessing," Sonber said. "For my dear friend. On this special day."

Mielle squeezed his hand, eyes eager. "That's very kind, don't you think, Trevn?"

He supposed it was harmless, especially if Mielle trusted the woman. He lifted their entwined hands and kissed the back of hers. "As you like, my dear."

"During the ceremony," Sonber said, stepping back into the crowd.

The next hour became utter confusion. Trevn and Mielle were whisked to the main deck. Trevn caught glimpses of similarities to Wilek and Zeroah's ceremony—Father Zeeshan spoke familiar words and sacrificed a crow—but there were many differences as well. Sonber presented a seashell on a cord that she bid them clasp between their hands as she sang her blessing in what sounded like ancient Armanian. Her words made Trevn's chest ache with cold. When she finished, she put the shell necklace over Trevn's head. Father Zeeshan continued the ceremony with blessings and prayers of his own.

While Trevn meant every word of his oath to Mielle, he almost felt as if they were playing a game instead of truly becoming man and wife. Like the whole event might be a dream. Perhaps that was because they were surrounded by strangers.

Except for Cadoc. Trevn's shield had reunited with his parents and seemed pleased about that fact, but each time Trevn met the man's disapproving gaze, he wished he had listened, dreading that his shield had been right and this would only bring heartache when the king ripped Trevn and Mielle apart. But they'd gone too far now. To stop would hurt Mielle. So Trevn kept silent and refused to let his hesitation show.

With no wedding tent prepared, a group of sailors whisked Trevn and Mielle into the captain's cabin, shoved a white handkerchief into Trevn's hands, and firmly shut the door in his face. The men's laughter and teasing carried inside the room. Mielle sat down on the edge of the bed and burst into tears.

An overpowering sense of hopeless confusion rushed upon Trevn, pricking his eyes with moisture. He somehow knew with a shock that these were Mielle's feelings, not his.

"Please don't cry, Mouse." He sat beside her and took her hands, fighting the overwhelming pull of her mood. The imprint of a seashell on her palm surprised him, and he turned over his hand, wincing when he saw that the same symbol marked his own.

What did it mean?

"It all happened so quickly," Mielle said, her breaths coming short and fast as she searched for words. "It's not that I don't want to marry you—I do! It's only . . . I don't know those people out there. I'm just so . . . so . . ."

"It's my fault," he said, knowing it was true yet not understanding why he'd been so adamant to do this. "I guess I got carried away. If you want to go back to the *Seffynaw*, we can forget all this ever happened."

"You would erase our wedding?" Now her anger surged within him—all sorrow gone without a trace. "We are *married*, Trevn. You cannot pretend we aren't."

"I won't . . . We did . . . We are . . . You're right." Being unable to find his own mind apart from hers made him want to scream. "I only meant that I didn't mean to pressure you into this."

"I wouldn't have said yes if I didn't want to," she scolded. "I'm only embarrassed." She eyed the handkerchief with disgust. "I don't think I can . . . Not with those people out there."

"Then we won't."

"But we must! They are waiting."

Trevn pulled his boot knife and held it to his finger. "This will convince them, no?"

"Don't!" Mielle grabbed the wrist of his empty hand, turning it so that his palm faced upward. She stared at the red lines the shell had left on his skin, but instead of fear, her love flooded him, chasing away all negative thoughts.

Sands, women were seesaws of emotion.

Mielle turned her eyes to his. Her shy smile was all the invitation Trevn needed. He dropped the knife and kissed his bride.

To hear Hinck brag of his time with the temple prostitute had given Trevn the impression that such an act would happen almost by the magic of wanting it to. The folly of that thought quickly became clear as Trevn and Mielle's shared ignorance carried them from one awkward moment to the next with surprise, gentle floundering, and occasional laughter.

They had no expectations to disappoint, no memories to intrude. They gave themselves to each other with unfettered eagerness and somehow knew exactly what the other needed. It was over far sooner than Trevn had imagined it would be, which surprised and amused them both. They put themselves back together as best they could and left the room, handkerchief in hand and blushing deeply as they moved through the crowd of strangers to sign the contract Father Zeeshan had drafted.

As Trevn stood watching the line of witnesses sign their marks, Mielle fingered the seashell that hung around his throat. She wanted to wear it. But she also wanted him to be happy. As happy as she was. She couldn't believe he had married her! Had it been the right choice? She knew it had. But, oh, what would the king say when he found out? Would he—

"You wear this," Trevn said to Mielle, removing the necklace. Hearing her thoughts so vividly in his head jarred him, but he might as well put it to good use.

His wife beamed at him as he put the cord over her head. *Trevn, my husband. He is my husband, now and forever. No one will ever part us again. Not even Janek, let him try.*

"Janek had better not try," Trevn said.

She gasped. "How did you . . . ?"

"I can hear your thoughts. Can't you hear mine?"

She stilled. "I thought I imagined it. Do you think?" She took hold of the shell.

Trevn didn't want to even consider that he'd let a mantic put a spell on them, so he let his mind race with thoughts of how beautiful she was.

She beamed at him. "Do you really think so, Trevn?"

"I always have."

This earned him a lingering kiss, after which they followed the sailors to a place on the main deck where pipers and a harpist were waiting in a circle of onlookers. The people cheered, the music began, and Trevn led Mielle in their first dance as husband and wife. They passed by Cadoc, who stood beside his parents, arms crossed and looking morose. Trevn also noticed Sonber watching them with a wide smile on her face. Both made Trevn uneasy.

On their second time around the circle, Trevn slowed as they passed by his High Shield. "Do not we look happy, Cadoc?"

"You look happy *now*," he called after them. "But I do not believe you will look so when you stand before your family to explain yourselves."

The flitting thought that Cadoc was right filled Trevn with annoyance. Such negativity threatened to drown his hope, so he whisked his bride back into the crowd, fully intent on enjoying his wedding day to the fullest.

Aᴍᴀʟᴀ

Since the tragic death of Rosârah Valena, Rosârah Brelenah had poured much attention into helping sârahs Hrettah and Rashah. Proper dancing being the first queen's most favorite pastime, she had eagerly taken on the task of training the sârahs in the art of courtly quinate dancing. Since a proper quinate must have five couples, much to Amala's delight, she and two other honor maidens had been invited to learn along with five reluctant guardsmen.

Rosârah Brelenah had roped off a section on the foredeck for lessons with Master Hawley acting as dancing master.

"Let us first see the alloette, Master Hawley," Rosârah Brelenah said, sitting on her wicker throne with two greasy pups on her lap.

"Certainly, Your Highness." Hawley regarded the princesses. "Do you remember the starting position of the alloette?"

"A circle," Rashah said.

"Excellent," Hawley said. "Where do you stand in relation to your partner?"

"Across from him?" Sârah Hrettah guessed.

"Correct! Take your positions."

As usual Amala was partnered with Ulmer, since the rosârah paired by height. Amala had grown tired of the young backman's attentions. He was too afraid of Kal to fight to court her—to even kiss her! Just that morning she had decided to look elsewhere for love. The fever had taken Rosârah Valena, and now Darlow was ill. Death, it seemed, was coming swiftly for them all.

At the queen's command, the band—which was made up of three pipers, a lutist, and a man on tabor drum—began an upbeat tune. The dancers circled to the left.

"Posture straight, Rashah," Hawley called. "That's right. Two full rotations, then reverse." This they did as gracefully as possible with a rolling sea beneath their dance floor.

After the alloette they danced the rosegate, followed by the heart's bell. They had just begun the landrille when a shadow fell upon her.

"What lively fun goes on here?"

A quick glance showed the spectator to be none other than Sâr Janek, holding a potted plant in the crook of one arm, his half brother Sir Kamran DanSâr beside him. Amala's stomach tightened, and she focused on the last few steps, wanting to appear accomplished before such a man.

"We are learning to dance," Sârah Hrettah said once the song had ended. "Will you join us, brother?"

The way his eyes moved over Amala made her shiver. "I would love to, dear sister." He handed his plant to Kamran and bowed to Rosârah Brelenah. "Unless you object, Rosârah."

"It has been a long time since I've seen you dance, Sâr Janek," Rosârah Brelenah said. "Do you remember the tomandah?"

"I do, rosârah." He faced the dancers. "Whom shall I partner with? My youngest sister?" He grinned and stepped toward Sârah Rashah, who giggled.

"My, no," Rosârah Brelenah said. "You are far too tall to stand with Rashah. Take Master Gelsly's place beside Miss Amala. Do you know her?"

"I do," Sâr Janek said, "though if you recall, my brother Trevn made me vow never to touch her."

"Oh, pish," Rosârah Brelenah said. "Sâr Trevn is an accomplished dancer. I'm certain he understands the importance of pairing by height. Let us all agree that an exception should be made. Just this once, yes?"

Hrettah and Rashah curtsied to the queen, so Amala did too.

Janek bowed. "You honor me, rosârah." Then he turned and pushed Ulmer aside. "Off you go, man."

Amala curtsied deeply to show deference and appreciation, eager to dance with a prince.

The tomandah was a lively, longwise dance with steps made difficult by the rolling sea. Hrettah stumbled twice and Rashah nearly every step, but Amala did not falter.

"Do I frighten you, lady?" Sâr Janek asked when his turn came to circle Amala.

"No, my sâr," she replied confidently.

Once all had returned to their original positions, the pairs dance began. Hrettah and Master Rey went first, casting off from their positions and weaving their way around the dancers in their respective lines. They met at the end of the line, facing one another. There they took hands and advanced together down the middle, stopping every two steps so that Master Rey could twirl Hrettah under his arm. Next went Rashah and Sir Kenard, and once they had finished, Amala and Sâr Janek began.

Amala swished her skirt playfully as she danced around the other girls, wanting the sâr to see that she was not afraid of him in the least. She moved with as much grace and skill as she could, and when they took hands and advanced together down the middle, twirling as a couple, Amala felt that to dance with a prince in front of an audience was the most fun she had ever had in her life.

The song ended, and the audience applauded. Amala beamed, breathing hard from the exercise and excitement.

"Do you only teach group dances to the girls, rosârah?" Sâr Janek asked.

"For the most part," the queen said, "though we have introduced the corroet and somaro."

"That seems wise to start," Sâr Janek said. "I would imagine the rengia and nevett too fast for beginners, but the berga is nice and slow."

A guard pushed through the crowd and up to Hawley. They spoke quietly, then Hawley approached the queen and stood waiting to be addressed.

"Sâr Janek, the berga is hardly an appropriate suggestion for young girls." Rosârah Brelenah turned her reprimanding gaze on Hawley. "What is it?"

He stepped close and spoke so softly that Amala couldn't make out a single word.

The queen stood. "I am needed in the birthing tent. Sir Kenard, please see the girls safely back to my cabin."

Sir Kenard bowed. "Yes, Your Highness."

They all watched Hawley and the queen walk across the foredeck and descend the steps to the main. Once they were out of sight, Sâr Janek said, "Pipers, play me a berga." He stepped toward Amala, hand extended. "Well, Miss Amala? Will you dance?"

"I do not know the berga, Your Highness," she said, unnerved by the sound of her own voice. "The rosârah said we shouldn't."

"Worry not, lady. The queen is not here. As for the rest . . . I am a good teacher."

She set her hand in his, and when their fingers touched, a shiver ran up her arm to the back of her neck.

"The berga is a dance for lovers," Sâr Janek said softly. "It is forbidden in Sarikar, which, of course, is why Rosârah Brelenah dislikes it. The very idea of people embracing on a public dance floor—scandalous, don't you think?"

Amala's cheeks burned. She could think of nothing to say.

"We touch hands like this." Sâr Janek set his palm against hers, fingers splayed. "I place my other hand here." He circled Amala's waist with his other arm, his hand pressing against the small of her back. Amala's stomach tightened, but she held still and tried to remain calm.

"The man leads where he likes, but our hips and legs must stay together, as if we are attached at the navel. That's why the man must keep such a tight hold on his lady partner." He pulled Amala close against him, and she failed to stifle her gasp of surprise.

"The lady simply does the opposite of the man's lead. If I step forward with my right leg . . ." Sâr Janek did so, tapping the tip of his boot against the toe of her shoe. "Then you step back with your left leg."

Amala stepped back.

"That's right." He stepped forward with his left leg, and Amala stepped back with her right. "Whatever we do, our eyes must remain locked—never breaking the stare."

The music surged then, and Janek whirled with it. Amala found that as long as she concentrated fully on the sâr's lead, she made few mistakes. He walked her back and forth, from side to side, and even spun them in a circle, never once looking away from her eyes or letting go. He had brown eyes, lighter than Ulmer's. Like smoky quartz gemstones. Smoky eyes that seemed to smolder into hers.

A hand squeezed her upper arm and jerked her away. The air felt suddenly cold away from the warmth of the sâr's body. Alarmed, Amala stumbled and had to grab hold of her captor to keep from falling.

It was Kal.

"My pardon, Your Highness," Kal said, "but Miss Amala must go now."

"Must she?" Sâr Janek smirked, propped his hands on his hips. "I had heard you had gone to the *Rafayah*, Sir Kalenek. Did you just return? Where are Miss Mielle and my brother?"

Kal frowned, but he didn't answer. He simply tightened his grip on Amala's arm and dragged her away. With no control over her own speed, the waves seemed worse than ever. Her foot caught in her gown. She tripped and clutched the railing.

"Let go of me, Kal! You're going to make me fall."

Kal did not let go but slowed until they reached the main deck. "You will have *nothing* to do with Sâr Janek. Ever. Is that clear?"

"You cannot command such a thing of me," Amala said. "Rosârah Brelenah is teaching the sârahs quinate dancing and asked me to join them. Is obeying my queen a crime?"

"A berga is not quinate dancing," Kal said. "The suggestion was Sâr Janek's, wasn't it?"

Amala looked away.

"Deceiving impressionable young girls is a favorite pastime of Sâr Janek's. No matter how honored he might make you feel, his intentions are anything but."

"It was just a dance, Kal. It's so unfair how you treat me. That Sâr Wilek would plead to the king for permission for his brother to court Mielle when I cannot even speak to a young man without being scolded."

"Mielle is a woman. You are not. And what did Sâr Janek mean by his comment to me. Did Sâr Trevn leave the ship?"

"How should I know what Sâr Trevn does?" They reached the lengthway that led to Rosârah Brelenah's cabin, and Amala spoke her mind. "It shames me to have you always dragging me off. Have you no manners? Is it so difficult to bow and claim I am late for an engagement and escort me away like a lady?"

"You are a child, Amala. When I find you blatantly misbehaving, you will be punished as a child deserves!"

✦ ✦ ✦

Amala stepped into the room and slammed the door. She fell back against it, shaking. Just look what that man did to her! So unfair. Hang his interfering ways. Kalenek Veroth had raised her and been like a father to her, and she loved him dearly, but lately he did nothing but smother! It hadn't been so bad when Mielle had taken the brunt of his attention, but ever since Darlow had fallen ill and the king had granted Sâr Trevn permission to court Mielle, Kal had focused all his attention on Amala.

And this time she'd done nothing wrong.

The door opened and Hrettah and Rashah returned with Enetta, their bossy nurse, and all of the maids, everyone talking at once.

"Amala!" Hrettah said, grabbing hold of her hands. "Are you well?"

Amala tugged Hrettah across the cabin to the room they shared, wanting to put distance between them and Enetta. "I am mortified," she whispered.

Hrettah wrinkled her nose. "It was a horrible dance. I'm sorry Janek pressured you into it. Are you terribly embarrassed?"

"Only that Kal humiliated me in public. The berga I rather liked."

"It's not an appropriate dance for anyone," Enetta said, sweeping into the room with a tray of honey rolls and tea. "Really, Amala, whatever possessed you to accept?"

Hrettah shot Amala an apologetic smile and slipped over to where Enetta had set the tray on the sideboard.

"One does not refuse a sâr of Armania," Amala said. "Why is everyone making such a fuss? It was just a dance. If he asked me again, I would accept again."

Out in the main room a knock at the door was followed by a man's voice. "I have a message for Miss Amala."

Amala seized the opportunity to escape and hurried from the room. "I will take it myself," she said, joining the maid at the main entrance.

Sir Kamran DanSâr stood outside the door. A chill ran up Amala's arms. "Yes?"

Kamran handed her a scrap of parchment. "A private message for you, lady."

Amala took the paper, unrolled it, and read:

Lady Amala,

I greatly enjoyed the dances we shared this midday and request the pleasure of your company in my cabin this evening for a proper dancing lesson.

Yours,
Sâr Janek

Amala's heart fluttered. A private dancing lesson in the sâr's company! Wouldn't Kal love that.

"What does it say?" Hrettah asked, coming to stand beside her.

"Nothing." Amala stepped out into the corridor and pulled the door shut. "Tell him I accept," she told Kamran.

The king's stray son inclined his head. "I will pass on your message."

Amala watched him go, admiring his strong build. She tucked the letter into the neckline of her dress, where no one would find it, and went back inside.

Enetta was waiting, eyes narrowed. "Sâr Janek sent you a message?"

"He sent his thanks for the dances we shared this midday. Wasn't that kind?"

Enetta humphed. "*Forward* is more like it."

Amala returned to her room, trying not to smile and give away her secret. Sâr Janek wanted to spend time with her! It was terribly unfair that she had to sneak around behind everyone's backs when such an honor should be something she could share with her friends. Keeping it a secret meant that no one could help her dress for the special occasion.

But she didn't need any help. This was her chance, perhaps her only chance, to fall in love with a prince, just like Mielle had. Amala had heard what was being said about the lack of food and water and how many had already died from the fever. Her hope for survival dwindled day by day. How good of the gods to grant her this wish before she died. She walked to the wardrobe, wondering which of her gowns would most impress Sâr Janek.

KALENEK

After rescuing Amala from Sâr Janek, Kal had gone to see Wilek. The sâr had been too busy to receive him, but Dendrick had promised to summon Kal at the first opportunity. The day passed without a word, however, so after dinner Kal returned to the king's office to try again. He hoped Wilek had found a replacement to sit with Shemme. With Darlow sick, Kal needed Mielle back on the *Seffynaw*, where she could help keep an eye on her wayward sister.

He found Novan Heln outside the king's office door with a number of other guardsmen. Seemed excessive.

"I'm sorry, sir," Novan said to Kal. "The sâr-regent is not to be disturbed."

"Is there a problem?" Kal asked.

Novan grimaced. "I am not at liberty to—"

"No, no. Don't tell me. If he wishes me to know, he will tell me himself."

"I can say that Sir Jayron and Lady Mattenelle were among several arrested this morning, for Sâr Janek arrived in the sâr-regent's cabin shortly thereafter, raging about the injustice, as he called it. Captain Veralla figures the whole ship knows by now. But after Sâr Janek talked with the sâr-regent, he dropped the matter entirely."

"Most strange," Kal said, guessing that Janek's protests must have taken place long before Kal had returned to the *Seffynaw* and found him dancing with Amala. What had Sir Jayron and the concubine been involved in?

"Sir Kalenek, finally!" a woman called, running toward them. Enetta. The sârahs' nurse. She slowed to a stop. "I have been looking everywhere for you. Miss Amala is unaccounted for."

Again? She had likely run off with that Gelsly. "Where did you last see her?"

"At dinner with the royal family. Sârah Rashah was feeling ill, so I took her back to the cabin and left Miss Amala in the company of Sârah Hrettah. When the princess returned with her maids, she said Amala had refused to leave. So I went back for her and found her gone! Only the servants remained, cleaning up after the meal."

Though the news annoyed Kal, it did not surprise him as it once had. "This is nothing she hasn't done before, Miss Enetta. Do not worry. I will seek her out after I speak with Sâr Wilek. She is likely on the deck with Master Gelsly."

"I'm afraid not, Sir Kalenek," Enetta said, wincing. "The servants said she left the dining room in the company of Sâr Janek and Sir Kamran DanSâr."

The words were barely out and Kal was sprinting, Novan on his heels. He didn't stop until he reached Sâr Janek's cabin. Three guards were slouching against the wall outside the door. Kal's speed took them by surprise, and they were too slow to catch him as he burst inside without knocking.

The bed was empty. Relief staked its claim, but a female gasp turned his head to the longchair before the balcony. There Sâr Janek sat with Amala in his arms. The bodice of her gown had been unlaced, partly exposing one shoulder.

A monster reared up inside Kal. He reached for his sword but did not find it. Because he no longer wore one. For everyone's safety.

"What is the meaning of this interruption?" Sâr Janek asked, maintaining his compromised position. "You have no right to enter my cabin without permission." His tone was authoritative and crisp, but the corner of his mouth quirked into a smile.

Kal strode across the small room, grabbed Janek's warrior tails, and dragged him off the longchair.

"Kal, don't!" Amala yelled.

Kal punched him. Janek staggered back against wall, and when he got his balance, he grinned.

Before Kal could make sense of that smile, Janek's guards were wrestling him to the floor. Kal did not fight them. He cared only for Amala's safety.

"Take her back to the queen's cabin," he yelled to Novan. "Keep her away from Sâr Janek!"

The young man jumped to obey. He took hold of Amala's arm. When she resisted, he picked her up and tossed her over his shoulder. She screamed and kicked her heels and pounded her fists against Novan's back as he carried her out the door.

At least she was safe.

Kal, however, was not.

"We must teach this man a lesson," Janek told his guards, looking down on Kal as he circled him. "One does not barge into a sâr of Armania's cabin uninvited, strike him, and abduct his company."

"I have every right," Kal said. "She was unchaperoned. Not even of age! I will do what I must to safeguard the honor of my ward."

"That sounds like a threat, Sir Kalenek. You should really be more careful. Guards, show Sir Kalenek how I treat threats against me."

Two of the guards held Kal while the third used him as a pell. The violence took Kal back to the war, and he did all he could to escape. When he failed and understood that he had been beaten, he pretended to pass out, knowing it was not so easy to hold an unconscious man upright.

"Enough," Janek said. "I tire of watching this abuse. Take him to the hold to finish your work."

On that order the guards hauled Kal away.

✦　✦　✦

Kal slumped against the walls of his cell, eyes closed. Everything hurt, including a sharp pain in his nose. One of the guards had likely broken it on purpose. Normally such a disfigurement was a humiliation, but on a man whose face had been scarred long ago . . . effort wasted. No one would likely even notice a broken nose or a blackened eye on Kalenek Veroth.

"You attacked my brother?"

Wilek's voice startled him. Kal rose, and one short step brought him to the door. He looked through the fist-sized hole in the top and met Wilek's eye, seeing the disappointment there, the fatigue.

"Forgive me for causing you strife, Your Highness, but I did what I had to. If I am to be executed, please move Amala to the *Rafayah* with Mielle and don't tell Sâr Janek where they've gone."

"You are not going to die, Kal, but to ease your worry I will ask Rayim to assign both girls personal guards immediately."

Relief eased the throbbing in Kal's nose. "Thank you."

"Do not thank me yet. There are protocols to deal with when someone attacks a sâr, and I have not yet determined how to protect you."

"Had I waited on protocol, Amala would be ruined."

"I know my brother well enough to believe that. Your sacrifice will not be for nothing. I will make sure Janek stays far away from Miss Amala."

"She will hate me now more than ever," Kal said.

"If she hates anyone, let it be me. This is my order, not yours." Wilek stepped back from the window. "Open the door," he told a guard.

A key jangled and the door scraped open. Kal stepped carefully out into the corridor. The rocking of the ship knocked him off balance without the cell walls to lean against.

"Steady, Kal," Wilek said. "The sea has been growing ever more fierce." He frowned, his gaze flitting over Kal's face. "Oh, Kal."

Kal hated when men looked on him with pity. "It can't be worse than usual."

"I'm afraid it can, my friend. Let's get you cleaned up and into bed. Perhaps the swelling will lessen by morning, when I will have no choice but to call you before the Wisean Council."

Kal submitted to Wilek's demands that he wash, change, and allow Rayim to set his nose. Two guards then escorted Kal to his chamber with orders that he sleep. Kal obeyed without protest, though sleep eluded him as always. He thrashed about until a noise captured his attention. With the growing storm, the usual creaks and groans of the sea pushing against the wooden ship were louder and more frequent than normal.

But this was something else.

A shadow shifted near the door, the shape of an arm and dagger just visible from the darkness.

Come, then, if you must.

Kal made a show of groaning and shifting in his sheets so he could secretly retrieve the dagger from under his pillow and bring it down to his side, where he could better use it.

A creak of the floorboards as the assassin paused.

Kal quickly flexed his fingers to check their strength, then gripped his weapon.

Seconds passed. A full minute. Neither man moved. An unseasoned soldier might think the assassin had somehow slipped away. Kal knew better. An assassin had incredible patience.

But Kal was an assassin no longer. "The king wants me dead, does he?" he asked the shadow.

A stretch of silence passed, but the shadow finally answered. "The king isn't the only one to employ assassins," a man said, his voice disguised. "Sâr Janek thanks you for dying and bids you watch from the Lowerworld as he stakes his claim on both your wards and the prophetess."

The figure dove toward him. Kal rolled aside as a blade plunged into his mattress. He twisted around and stabbed his attacker in the back. A scream of pain carried Kal back to the war. His vision flashed bright with sunlight. Kal swung up on top and straddled the enemy. He lifted the man's head and slashed his blade across his neck.

The enemy made a funny noise in the back of his throat as the life and breath rattled out of his body. Kal's hand tingled and he lost his grip on the blade. It slipped from his hand and fell.

Kal wasn't certain how much time had passed before he returned to the present. He could smell death; too much blood had spilled. He was in his cabin, in the dark, on his bed, sitting on the back of a dead man. Janek's assassin. By their positions Kal surmised he had killed the man. He needed to move, to do something. He jerked off the man's hood, but in the darkness could not see who he was. He climbed off and lit a candle, held it close to his attacker's face.

Lebbe Alpress, captain of the King's Guard.

Unsurprising, really. Alpress had never been an honest man. His black-mailing Kal had long ago shown what kind of a man he was. That he would knife for Janek seemed to fit.

Kal had grown tired of Sâr Janek's games. He did no good in life and caused nothing but mischief and strife. If the sâr were dead, he could cause no more problems. Not for Wilek, not for innocent young women, not for the whole of Armania.

Kal had not started the Heir War. But he would end it. Now.

He knew what he had to do.

He dug into the bottom of his trunk and located his kit, set the dusty box on his bed, and opened it. It had been a decade since he'd looked inside. Gloves first, always. He pulled them on, then strapped his belt around his waist and buckled the various leg and arm harnesses, loading them with knifes. His short sword he strapped to his back. A jar of white powder contained a powerful soporific. He added a few drops of water, then loaded three quills into pinch holders and dipped the tips into the liquid.

He picked up the vial of ream snake poison, wondering how long the toxicity lasted. He couldn't rely on it, but it wouldn't hurt to be prepared. He poisoned the blade of his belt dagger and carefully sheathed it.

When the quills had dried, he slid them into the sheath on his belt, hooded himself, then set out.

By the time he reached the main deck of the ship and the chilled night air, the shock of having killed Alpress had lessened. Yet even in his calm, his agenda remained certain. There was only one way to stop Janek and only one man willing to do the job.

No moon hung in the sky tonight. No stars either. Thick clouds had blotted them out, and in the surrounding darkness, the waves roared and splashed, rocking the ship like a leaf riding the ream.

Kal made his way from the main deck toward the stern, stealing a length of rope as he slinked past a locker on the quarterdeck. A Knife did not simply barge in to an unknown situation. A kill was usually planned days ahead in meticulous detail. Kal had no time for that. He would stand before the Wisean Council in the morning, and while Wilek would plead for mercy, Kal knew better than to expect it. He had done nothing in his life that would cause the gods to step in and spare him. He was ready to die. He had been ready for a very long time.

Kal took a page from Sâr Trevn's book and used the rope to scale down the stern of the ship to the balcony of Janek's cabin. It had not occurred to any of Janek's guards to monitor that entrance.

A mistake they would never make again.

He crept into the cabin. A candle lantern swayed on a hook near the door, its wax nearly burned to nothing. It gave Kal enough light to see that Janek did not sleep alone. He crept slowly around the bed, dagger ready, and examined the occupants of the framed mattress. The prince and his concubine, Lady Pia. Because Lady Mattenelle had been arrested along with Sir Jayron.

Kal was glad Sir Jayron would not be an obstacle.

What to do? Kill the girl too?

Kal could not bring himself to slaughter a woman. He would drug her with the quill, wait for it to take effect, then kill the prince.

He removed a quill from the sheath on his belt, grasping the pinch holder between thumb and forefinger. He glanced toward Lady Pia and found her place in the bed empty. She was on her feet, a dagger in each hand, crouched into fighting position. The combination of her grip on the daggers and the twist of her foot gave her away.

Another assassin? Janek had likely surrounded himself with trained killers.

Thankful he'd worn his mask, Kal slipped the quill back into his belt, all the while keeping his eyes on the concubine.

"I can't let you do this," she said.

Kal lowered his voice to mask it. "You cannot stop me."

"Guards!" she yelled, then screamed, low and throaty as if she were in pain.

Janek groaned and opened his eyes. The door burst in, and three guards ran inside, the same three who had beat Kal hours ago.

Kal drew the short sword from his back sheath, knowing that he had made a mistake in letting the concubine live. His malady might allow him to kill one or two of the guards before he dropped his blade, but with the third guard, Lady Pia, and Janek, who had jumped from the bed and retrieved his own blade, Kal would never succeed. He would die for nothing, and Janek would live to wreak havoc on Kal's loved ones.

Arman, help me.

That he would release a desperate prayer to Onika's god surprised him. He doubted Arman would have mercy on an assassin.

The three guards swarmed, and it was all Kal could do to block their strikes. For a flashing moment he felt overwhelmed. The cabin's walls kept him in close quarters with his attackers. He caught a brief glimpse of Lady Pia standing beside Janek, the two of them watching. The smile on Janek's face ended Kal's fear. He steeled himself to finish the job he came to do. These guards were young, like Novan. And while they were good fighters, Kal was better—had fifteen years' experience over them.

Still, he did not want to kill these boys. He'd come for Janek alone. He kept back, teasing the guards with quick thrusts, judging their speed. The slowest of the three went down quickly with a deep cut across his thigh. With him on the floor, the other two closed in, working together. Their swords jabbed at Kal so fast that he parried constantly. He blocked a low cut to his stomach, spun away from the second sword coming at his left temple, and struck like a viper at the first, his blade snapping down over the boy's extended arm. Kal twisted away, picturing Onika's face to avoid the gory sight behind him that would rip his mind to dark places.

He found the third guard frozen, eyes glazed, the tip of a dagger protruding from his throat. Just over his shoulder, Kal could see Lady Pia's extended arm gripping the hilt and the snarl on her small mouth. Behind her, Janek leaned against the wall, staring at the handle of Lady Pia's second dagger, which stuck out from his chest, a fatal blow.

What in all the realms?

"Why?" Kal asked the concubine as the guard collapsed between them.

"He was about to kill you," she said.

Kal had meant Janek, but before he could clarify, the sâr, dagger still in his heart, pushed off the wall and raised his sword up to stab Lady Pia in the back. Facing Kal as she was, she did not see the attack coming.

Kal's world swam, and suddenly he was back there again, in the place from which he could never escape. The yeetta dared lift his sword to a defenseless woman? Kal sprang forward, pushed the woman to the floor where she would be safe, and drove his sword into the yeetta's chest. The man dropped his blade at the same time that Kal's clattered to the floor. With his left hand Kal drew a dagger from his belt and slashed again and again at the man's face, making scars worse than his own, scars that would follow this yeetta filth all the way to Gâzar's throne. There was no honor in such a thing, but Kal needed to make a statement. Evil men had butchered too many innocents. It would no longer be tolerated. With this kill Kal would send a message of Justness throughout the Five Realms. Sheep for sheep, hand for hand, life for life.

All would be even now.

WILEK

The scene in Janek's cabin was beyond anything Wilek could have ever imagined. Blood covered the floor in puddles, smears, and bootprints. One dead guard, another missing a hand, and a third with a leg wound that would likely leave him crippled. Lady Pia sat against the bulkhead, hugging her knees.

Janek was dead. His face bloodied to the point of hardly being recognizable.

When Dendrick had awakened Wilek with the news, his first fear was that Kal had taken vengeance. He certainly had motive. One look at the cuts on Janek's face seemed to confirm it. Who but Kal would inflict scars like his own?

Rayim approached Wilek, face pinched in thought. "Could the unknown rebel have done this?"

"Why would he? The rebels want the king dead. Maybe me. But not Janek. He is Rogedoth's heir." All yesterday they had searched the ship for the missing evenroot and Janek's newt. They'd found neither. None of the rebels had escaped. "I don't see how killing Janek would aid their cause."

Rayim sighed. "I must question Sir Kalenek. His attack on Janek last evening makes him suspect."

Wilek hesitated, worried that Rayim might find something to incriminate his friend, but he had no reason to refuse the request. "Of course you must speak with Kal."

"I can't imagine he had anything to do with this, Your Highness," Rayim said. "Lady Pia told me that the assassin remained professional until he killed

271

Sâr Janek. That the kill changed him somehow. He went mad, as if he were somewhere else. That doesn't much sound like Sir Kalenek."

Oh but it did. The man had confessed to hallucinating in moments of violence, and Wilek had kept it a secret. Had Kal, in his madness, killed Janek?

Arman, let it not be so!

✦　✦　✦

Wilek returned to his room and left Novan and two other guards standing watch outside. It was not yet dawn. The sea had been rocking the ship hard all night. Several items had fallen from Wilek's desk and onto the floor. He left them there and sat down.

Janek was dead. Forever. He was never coming back.

That Wilek had no tears for his brother made him feel callous. Had he truly hated the man so much?

"Your Highness."

Wilek jumped at the whisper and thought his startled heart might give up altogether.

Kal stood in the shadow of the office—had stepped out from the doorway that led to the king's royal cabin. He was dressed all in black with an assassin's belt around his waist. One of the daggers had a bloody tang. He sank to his knees at Wilek's feet, a black hood clutched in one fist.

"I've come to confess," he whispered.

"Oh, Kal." Wilek's eyes flooded with unshed tears. "Why?"

"Last night Janek sent Alpress to kill me," he whispered. "His body is in my cabin. He said Janek wanted me dead so he could have Amala and Mielle and Onika. He would have ruined them and a hundred others after that. I could not let it happen."

The reasons didn't matter. "What you have done I cannot undo."

Kal hung his head. "I know."

"You were more a brother to me than Janek ever was, but I . . . Kal, I . . ."

"Killing Alpress was self-defense. I didn't know it was him. But I went for Janek willingly. I—"

"I killed Janek." Lady Pia stepped out from the darkness. Appeared to have come from the same place Kal had.

Confusion knotted Wilek's thoughts. "Explain," was all he could muster.

"He was going to stab Sir Kalenek in the back. I felt Sir Kalenek too worthy a man to die in such a way."

"You knew it was me?" Kal asked.

"It was clear to me that one of them was going to die," Pia said. "I took a guess as to which you would have wanted to live. Did I choose wrong, Your Highness?"

Sands, what a mess. Wilek would have chosen Kal over Janek ten times out of ten, but he could not admit that to anyone.

"I want to hear what happened again. Kal first. Then Pia."

Kal told how he had snuck inside and planned to drug Lady Pia, but she was awake and called the guards. "I did not see what happened between Pia and Janek, but by the time I downed the second guard, one of Lady Pia's daggers was in Janek's heart." According to Kal she also fatally struck one of the guardsmen to save him. And when Janek had revived enough to attack Lady Pia, Kal had stepped in to save her, then lost himself.

"I remember nothing after that," he said.

"I had to call the guards lest I be implicated," Pia said. The rest of her story matched what had already been stated. "Had Sir Kalenek not quickened his death, Sâr Janek would have died from my blade alone."

Wilek rubbed his face, weary and angry that he must deal with this mess. If he had made time for Kal yesterday when he'd come seeking his replacement on the *Rafayah*, this might not have happened. Wilek would have told Kal he hadn't found a replacement—would have sent Kal back to watch over Miss Shemme. "The two surviving guards did not see Pia strike Janek," he said. "They both implicate you, Kal, as the murderer. What can I do?"

"I will confess," Pia said.

"That will only kill you both," Wilek said.

"Janek is dead because I sought to kill him," Kal said. "The blame is mine, and I will confess that before the council. There must be Justness. A life for a life as is law. Leave Lady Pia out of this."

"That you would take your punishment willingly is admirable, but as sâr-regent I must be the one to put steps in motion toward your execution. *I must sign your death warrant!*" Wilek sighed, and the breath hurt his lungs. *Arman, why?*

"More than anything, I regret causing you pain, Wil. I did not intend to."

Wilek choked back his emotions. "Justice always has repercussions, Kal." He tried to imagine what they might be. Kal hanging for Janek's death. Miss Mielle and Miss Amala hating Wilek for killing the man who'd raised them. Trevn siding with Miss Mielle, forcing the two remaining sârs to become estranged. Rogedoth and Rosârah Laviel waging war upon Armania to avenge Janek.

Worst of all was a world without Sir Kalenek Veroth. The man had been by Wilek's side nearly ten years. They had weathered many storms together, and Wilek had missed him these past few weeks. Rystan might be his new half brother, but he wasn't even a man yet. And Novan Heln, while smart and capable, was almost too good. Too polite, anyway, without a hint of Kal's sarcasm or bluntness.

What, if anything, could Wilek do for this man? His friend?

A thought came to him softly, like a breeze. Wilek focused on it, let it grow.

Yes, it very well might save Kal's life and at the same time protect Armania against her enemies.

"Lady Pia, you are free to go," Wilek said. "Speak to no one about this or the attack on Janek without first speaking to me."

"Yes, Your Highness." She curtsied and left.

Wilek waited until he was certain she had gone. "Before I call the guard to arrest you, I would have you do something for me."

Kal's pained gaze met his. "Anything."

"Go to the *Rafayah*. Move Miss Shemme to another boat—preferably a Rurekan one. I will write a missive to Emperor Ulrik asking him to accept you. Send a bird to me when the child is born and remain with it as its guardian. If the babe is indeed a root child as we fear, once we reach land, take a new name and raise the child in a place where it will be safe, as Jhorn did for Grayson. Any who discover this child might seek to use it to rule Armania. You must keep it hidden. Note any unnatural abilities. Any people who take an unhealthy interest in the child. Remain with the child as long as it lives, and keep me apprised of anything important. Should it become a problem . . . deal with it."

"Kill a child?"

Arman would not like that. "Only as a last resort."

"You're letting me go free?"

"Rayim is already looking for you. He will find Alpress in your cabin, and I will have no choice but to issue the warrant for your arrest. You must not be found aboard the *Seffynaw*. Likely someone will recall your leaving the ship, so move quickly and try not to be seen. You can never return to the *Seffynaw*. And once we land . . . if you are captured by Armanian soldiers, you will be tried and executed. I cannot imagine a future where I could pardon you for conspiring to kill a sâr of Armania."

"What will become of Mielle and Amala? My crime has forced them into a life of poverty."

"I will adopt them as my own wards, though I cannot help that their reputations might become tainted by association to your name."

Kal set his hand over his heart and then kissed his fingers. "Thank you, Wil."

"You must go with haste, my friend," Wilek said. "The longer you tarry, the greater the chance of your arrest." Wilek stood and held out his hand.

Kal removed his gloves and took hold, allowed Wilek to help him stand. "Forgive me, Your Highness, for my many failures and crimes and for abandoning you. I will miss our friendship."

Wilek held his sorrow in check and gave his friend a curt nod. "As will I, Kal."

He watched Kal retreat into the king's royal cabin. It occurred to him that he had forgotten to send guards to bring Trevn back from the *Rafayah* yesterday. He prayed that if Kal found Trevn there with Miss Mielle, he would stay in his right mind.

Surely Kal would not kill two princes of Armania.

KALEΠEK

Since Kal couldn't go to his own cabin, he went to Novan's and changed into a new set of plain clothes. He and Novan were close to the same size, though the shirt was snug across the shoulders. Kal took a few more essentials, wrote a letter to his girls, and set off to see Onika.

There was no way to sneak in. As High Shield of Arman, Kal had seen to that. So he took a risk and went to her cabin on the hunch that Nayman and Tanor wouldn't yet know of the recent happenings.

"Good dawning," Kal said as he walked up to the door and knocked.

"Sands! Look at you," Nayman said. "I heard you got a piece of Sâr Janek last night, but it sure looks like his dogs got you good."

Kal was suddenly aware of the ache in his nose. Rescuing Amala seemed to have happened days ago, not merely last evening. "I did what I had to."

"What most all of us have been wanting to do for years," Tanor said.

"Do you know what happened in Sâr Janek's cabin last night after they arrested you?" Nayman asked.

Kal feigned ignorance. "Something wilder than the High Shield of Arman attacking a sâr?"

"I'd say. Lady Pia came tearing out well after night bells. She brought back at least a dozen guards, and—"

Blessedly the door opened and Kempe, Onika's maid, looked out. When she saw Kal, her eyes widened and lingered on his bruised face. "Sir Kalenek, welcome back. Miss Onika will be pleased you are here." She opened the door wider.

Kal entered, dreading what he must say. Did Onika know what he'd done?

He found her sitting in a chair by the window, Rustian curled up by her feet. While he was still several steps away, she spoke.

"Sir Kalenek has returned, Rustian. No man walks with such purpose as he."

Kal stopped beside her chair and looked down on her face. The candlelight made her skin ghostly in the surrounding darkness of the cabin. It made him smile. Onika always brought light to the darkness.

"You are quiet this dawning, Sir Kalenek."

"I have come to say farewell."

Her brow pinched. "But you've only just returned."

"My work aboard the *Rafayah* is going to take longer than I had first thought. I . . . don't plan to return. Ever."

Her glassy eyes did not shift, but Kal caught the quiver of her chin. "So we are here. Who will Sâr Wilek put in charge of my guards now that you are going away?"

"Oli, I suppose. He will do a fine job."

"I prefer you to the Duke of Canden or anyone else."

"I am sorry, lady." He paused, digging deep for the courage to confess. "I have done something that even Sâr Wilek as my friend cannot forgive."

She reached for him, clutched his tunic near his hip. "Arman always forgives. Do not forget that."

"Not this, I'm afraid."

"Yes, Sir Kalenek! Even this, whatever it is."

"I—"

"Do not tell me! I am not a god to hear the confessions of men." She settled both hands in her lap, linking her fingers. "If you must leave, then promise me that should you see Grayson again, you will give him this message. Tell him: 'Hold tight to your secret until you come to those twice your size. Then embrace who you are and let all know what you can do.'"

Her words clogged Kal's thoughts. What was she talking about? When would he see Grayson? "That makes no sense."

"It will to Grayson when the time is right."

He repeated her message aloud, memorizing it, and said, "Should I find the boy, I promise to tell him." He crouched beside her chair, took hold of her hand, and gave her the letter he wrote to the girls. "Will you see that Mielle gets this letter when she returns?"

"Yes, of course. But why don't you give it to her yourself?"

"I have my reasons. Miss Onika, time and again you have spoken of a future that gives me reason to hope that all is not lost between our friendship. I beg you now to explain."

She fixed her glassy stare on his face, her lips frowning slightly. "I don't know for certain. You have always been Rescuer to me, a title given you by Arman. You found me in Magonia and led me safely here. And you will find me and rescue me again. This separation will be a difficult period for both of us. We will suffer greatly before Arman brings healing."

Always she came back to her god's healing. She needed to know the kind of man he was. She deserved so much better. "Suffering is all I deserve, Miss Onika. I've toyed with darkness my whole life. Now it has consumed me. Darkness wins, Miss Onika. Darkness always wins."

"You are wrong," she snapped. "Darkness only wins those who give themselves over to it."

"I have done just that."

"Then step back into the light! It is always one choice away."

She made everything sound so simple, but Kal knew better. Life was a tangled knot of pain that could never be straightened.

"You are not the only one who struggles with darkness, Sir Kalenek. Everyone does. It is coming to me as well."

"What do you mean?"

"Darkness will soon take me captive. If I can trust Arman in that place of horror, he will sustain me and help me keep sight of the light."

"Miss Onika, if you sense trouble, flee from it. Do not draw close to the darkness. Stay safe at all costs."

"Is that what you did on Bakurah Island when you stepped between Sâr Wilek and his assassin?"

Shame threatened to overwhelm Kal. She thought him a hero and knew nothing of the villain he really was.

"Some walk into the darkness eagerly," she said. "Some dread the duty. Yet others have darkness thrust upon them. But all who seek the light again will find it."

His words tightened in his throat. "I will miss your censure, Miss Onika. And your hope."

"And I your steady voice and hand in my own." She reached out, and he took hold of her hand. "Will you kiss me good-bye?"

She wanted his kiss? He glanced across the room at the maid and struggled to keep his voice calm. "That would not be appropriate."

"Propriety is the least of my worries. Besides, I will need the memory of your loving kiss when stolen kisses seek to rob me of my sanity."

After such an invitation Kal did not hesitate. He knelt before her chair and kissed her. Her lips were soft against his rough skin and tasted of salt water and mint. Her hands slipped up to his face, smooth thumbs caressing scarred cheeks. So long, it had been, since anyone had touched him this gently. That such a woman cared for him at all was miraculous indeed.

"I don't want you to go," she said.

Kal hugged her to him and kissed her hair, his chest and throat tight. How could he let her go, knowing something horrible loomed in her future? "When, Onika? How long must I wait until we meet again?"

"I know not."

Kal kissed her once more, which only placed a fierce longing in his heart to take Onika with him. He could not do that, however, and finally forced himself to walk away from a woman he had come to love deeply.

Outside her cabin door, he passed by the guards. "Keep her safe," Kal told them, walking away.

"Isn't the prophetess coming out for breakfast?" Tanor asked.

"You'll have to ask her." Kal continued on, making his way toward the forward boat fall and an uncertain future. Strangely the bittersweet longing of leaving Onika behind felt justified. He deserved no happiness.

+ + +

Kal reached the vice flagship just as the sun crested over the horizon. The waves had been raucous, and he was thankful to be on a ship again. He led himself to the door of the tiny cabin on the lower foredeck where he had left Mielle with Shemme—Kellah now, he reminded himself.

He nodded at the guards outside and knocked. "Are they here?"

"Uh . . ." The guard on the left side of the door looked across to the guard on the right. "I, uhh . . ."

"You don't know?" What kind of guards were these?

Kal pushed the door open and stepped inside. Someone lay in the bed, covered by a thin blanket. "Mielle?" Sorrow seized his heart. How could he leave Mielle and Amala? Yet how could he not? Watching him die as a murderer would be no better than abandonment.

He settled on a chair beside the bed, where he could sit and look upon her face.

But it was not her face he saw.

It was Sâr Trevn's face.

Kal drew back, despair seizing every inch of his body. Had he entered the wrong cabin? A quick glance revealed Mielle's cloak in the corner.

Despair quickly shifted to rage. One step and he had dragged the young man from the bed and onto the floor. Sâr Trevn wore only a pair of trousers. His chest and feet were bare. "Get up! Now!"

The young sâr sat on his heels and squinted up at Kal. His expression of confusion quickly faded, and he had the decency to look ashamed of himself. "Sir Kalenek, allow me to explain."

Kal fell upon him again, grabbed his arm, and yanked him to his feet. "You think me a fool? I know exactly what has happened here. A thief has committed a crime and he must be punished."

"We are married!" Trevn blurted out. "I beg forgiveness that I did not ask your permission first, but my father and brother would not have approved and we feared you would side with them."

Kal shook him by the arm. "You aren't the first sâr to stand through a false ceremony to convince a woman to lie with you."

An expression of horror crossed the young sâr's face. "I would never do that. I love Mielle. A Rurekan priest married us yesterday on the main deck. Ask anyone on board."

A Rurekan priest? "Where is she?"

"With Miss Shem—Kellah. The girl is having pains. Mielle feared the baby is coming and took her to the birthing tent."

"So soon?"

"Mielle believes the child is a black spirit. I think not. Miss Kellah confessed that her mother forced her to take evenroot when the child was conceived. I believe this early labor is an effect of the poison."

Sâr Trevn's logic was to be commended, but Kal had no desire to play friends at present. "Take me to them."

"I must dress first," Trevn said.

"Dress, then! I shall wait outside." Kal left the cabin and posted himself with the two now sheepish guards. "A little warning next time? And where is Sir Cadoc?"

"Sâr Trevn sent him to accompany Miss Mielle," one of the guards said.

At least the prince had some sense.

Married! It was too much. Yet his anger toward Sâr Trevn had already abated. How dare Kal wield judgement against Mielle and Trevn in light of his own crimes?

A short while later Sâr Trevn exited the cabin and frowned at the sky. "It's clouding over again," he said. "Swells are running deeper too. A storm is approaching."

Wonderful. Kal was not eager to row through waves worse than those he'd just experienced. "Lead the way to your *wife*, Your Highness."

Trevn's gaze latched briefly onto Kal's before he walked past him down the lengthway. He caught the arm of a middle-aged maid and bid her run ahead and tell Mielle they were coming to see her. "And tell the master's mate on duty to put out the water barrels. We must collect the rain."

The woman curtsied and ran off.

As they made their way up to the main deck, Kal shared his concern that the king would have Sâr Trevn's wedding annulled. "Did you not think of Mielle's reputation when you married so hastily?" he asked.

"Sir Kalenek." The prince stopped at the bottom of the galley steps and faced him. "I realize that words will not convince you of my honor and worth, especially when I have initiated this secret wedding without your permission. Let me ease your distress. I will never leave or forsake Mielle. Even if my family forces us apart, I will not give her up. I would renounce my heritage first, so great is my devotion to her."

Kal scoffed. "You think Sâr Wilek would allow that? I confess myself a fool, for I had conceded that you were well on your way to being the most intelligent of your brothers."

"I don't appreciate your tone. You may dislike me and what I've done, but I am still a sâr of Armania and should be treated with respect."

"Boy . . ." Kal gritted his teeth in an attempt to rein his temper. "I am no longer a citizen of Armania, so I owe you nothing. Sir Cadoc, good morning."

Trevn stopped outside a tent assembled on the main deck, where Sir Cadoc was standing guard. Sounds of crying infants were drowned out by the erratic screaming of a woman in pain.

Sir Cadoc nodded to Kal. "Glad to see you, sir."

"This is the birthing tent?" Kal asked.

Sir Cadoc nodded. "Men aren't allowed to go in without an invitation."

"What did you mean by that, Sir Kalenek?" Trevn asked. "No longer being a citizen of Armania?"

The door flap opened, and Mielle exited. "Kal!" She threw her arms around his neck.

Grief stabbed low and deep in light of Kal's newly bestowed exile. How could he leave this girl who had become like a daughter?

"How is Miss Kellah?" he managed to ask.

"Her labor has begun. The midwife says it won't be long." Mielle released him from her hug. "What happened to your face?"

Kal wouldn't confess his crimes to Mielle in front of Sâr Trevn. "I had an altercation," he said.

Mielle's jaw dropped. "Trevn!"

"Not me!" Trevn said. "But I did tell him about us."

Mielle turned pinched brows upon Kal and took hold of Trevn's hand. "Do not be angry, Kal. I swear to you that we love each other just as much as you loved my sister."

Kal doubted that very much. "I have orders from Sâr Wilek to check on Miss Kellah. He has given the guardianship of her and her child to me."

"Guardianship?" Mielle asked. "What does that mean?"

"It means I must speak with her immediately." Before she died in labor.

Mielle scowled at him as she slipped inside.

Perhaps Shemme wouldn't die. Perhaps Wilek had been mistaken and both she and her child would come through the labor healthy and strong. That would certainly make things easier all around.

"Something has happened," Trevn said, eyes narrowed at Kal. "My brother would not give you up so willingly to such a menial task. Not when he so recently assigned you to his most important prophetess."

The boy was a quicker study than even Novan. "You are too clever for your own good, Your Highness," Kal said. "Take care how freely you muse aloud, as it someday might provoke a villain to silence your wit."

"I've tried to warn him of that many times," Sir Cadoc said.

"Well, your life now belongs to another, Your Highness. If you will not take care for yourself, think of Mielle, would you?"

"I see your point," Trevn said. "But why would Wilek give you an infant child when it has a mother to care for it?"

"I do not believe it will have a mother for long."

The door flap opened, and Mielle waved them inside the tent. Sir Cadoc stayed behind. Sheets draped on lines partitioned one woman from the next. Mielle led them into a compartment along the left side. The space was twice as large as the narrow cot that Shemme was lying on. A Magonian woman sat on a stool beside the cot, holding Shemme's hand.

"She is nearly ready for the birthing stool," the woman said.

"This is Sir Kalenek Veroth, my guardian," Mielle said, settling on the edge of the cot. "Kal, this is Miss Kellah's midwife, Sonber."

Sonber. The name froze Kal. He searched for its meaning and quickly remembered. *Sonber* was Agmado Harton's true surname. Could this be his mantic sister? The one called Charlon?

The midwife regarded Kal, her eyes gray and suspicious. She was no bigger than Amala, had a small nose, downturned lips, and hair as curly and wild as a thornbush. She wore nothing but a blue-and-white kasah tied over one arm as a dress that left shoulders, arms, legs, and feet bare.

If this was the witch who had abducted Wilek and taken Sârah Zeroah's likeness for so long, what could Kal do? He pretended not to make any connection. "Who assigned a midwife?"

"When Kellah went into labor, I didn't know what to do," Mielle said. "I came looking for help and found Sonber. I just knew it was Arman's provision."

Kal nodded but doubted that very much.

"I have given custody of the baby to Sonber," Shemme said, panting, "in the event this child takes my life when it comes."

"Don't talk like that!" Mielle said. "You are going to be just fine."

The Magonian witch had already convinced Shemme to give over her child? Not if Kal could help it. "We will deal with that situation if it comes, Miss Kellah," Kal said.

"Which we pray it won't," Mielle added.

"I must remind you," Kal added, "that you do not have sole rights to this child. I have come to represent its father's interests."

"He wants nothing to do with me!" Shemme yelled.

"Perhaps not. But his family would not abandon the babe as you might have thought. I have been sent to act as the child's High Shield."

"What does a baby need with a High Shield?" Trevn asked.

Kal shot him a glare, hoping he'd take the hint.

"I can protect the child," Sonber said.

"No doubt you can, Miss Sonber," Kal said, "but I have my assignment and will not fail it. I have leave to act as the voice of the child's father in all matters concerning it and its mother's welfare."

"I can speak for myself a while longer," Shemme said.

"And I must protest," Sonber said. "In Magonia a father has no say in the upbringing of a child. That is for a woman to decide, and I insist that—"

Shemme's bloodcurdling scream ended all discussion on the matter.

"Out!" Sonber yelled. "We must move Miss Kellah to the birthing stool. Miss Mielle, fetch us water."

Mielle jumped to obey the midwife's orders and rushed Kal and Trevn out of the tent.

When they reached Sir Cadoc, Kal grabbed Mielle's arm and held tight until her eyes met his. "Take care with that midwife," he said. "She is a mantic and not to be trusted. I fear she may be the same one who took Sârah Zeroah's likeness."

Mielle went rigid, her expression one of shock. "How do you know?"

"Agmado Harton's real surname was Sonber. Charlon was his sister."

"What shall I do?"

"Pay attention," Kal said. "Stay with Miss Kellah at all times. We'll send a maid for the water."

Mielle nodded and slipped back inside the tent. Two maids eagerly went for water when the sâr asked.

"If that woman is dangerous, I don't want Mielle anywhere near her," Trevn said, his voice nearly a whisper.

"We need someone we can trust in there, Your Highness," Kal said.

"What is so special about this child?" Trevn asked. "Why does the mantic want it?"

"The Magonians seek to fulfil a prophecy." That much should not surprise this former priest-in-training. "It was why Charlon abducted your brother and later wore Sârah Zeroah's mask. Magonia seeks a child fathered by one of the princes of Armania. They care not which."

Trevn cleared his throat. "Because their prophecy states that Mother and Father will come together to produce their savior. The Deliverer."

"Your education does you credit, Your Highness," Kal said.

"So this child's father is . . ." Trevn's raised eyebrows awaited an answer. When Kal did not comply, the sâr made his guess. "Kamran's, perhaps, though likely Janek's."

Guilt overwhelmed Kal at the mention of the name that had caused his exile.

"How could the mantic know who fathered the child?" Trevn asked.

Kal shrugged. "Miss Kellah might have said. Or the mantic's shadir might know."

"A shadir!" Trevn cried. "Cadoc, we must arrest this woman immediately."

In Kal's turmoil, the thought had not occurred to him. "Certainly, Highness. You and Sir Cadoc fetch the guard, but promise me that you will return to the *Seffynaw* to inform your brother that I am with the child and will do all I can to protect it."

"I will go in the same boat with my captive," Trevn said, then set off with Sir Cadoc, leaving Kal alone outside the birthing tent. It wasn't long before one of the young maids came to fetch him.

"Is all well?"

"The babe is a healthy boy," she replied, her voice cracking, "but the mother . . . she did not survive."

Sorrow pinched Kal's heart. Lore come to life was difficult when there was little tradition to inform expectations. He steeled himself as he returned to Shemme's compartment. The air smelled horribly of blood, reminding Kal of the day he'd found Livy dead. He saw the body, lying on the bed, soaked in red. *Not Livy,* he reminded himself. Still, he backed out into the passageway, afraid to move closer until his heart calmed enough to look on the scene with indifference.

Someone was crying. A woman. She sniffled, spoke. "He's remembering the war. Kal?"

Her face appeared before his, streaked in tears. Mielle. His girl. She had grown so fast. He would miss her.

"Are you well, Kal?" she asked, her hand on his arm.

"I am." Though it was a lie.

"Miss Kellah died." Mielle's face crumpled, and she began to cry. Kal embraced her, held her tightly. "She lived long enough to hold the boy and kiss his swarthy head. She named him Shanek DanSâr, after herself and his father."

Kal winced at the name. He needed to get the babe off this ship before word of a child with Hadar blood began to circulate.

The mantic stood against one wall, a bundle in her arms, watching him warily. Mielle blocked his view of the dead mother, so Kal released his ward and walked inside, keeping his gaze on the child. "May I see the babe?"

"You won't harm him?" Sonber asked.

"No, I just . . . sometimes blood makes me remember things I'd rather forget. I did not mean to frighten you."

The woman handed Kal the bundle. The weight surprised him. The light inside the birthing tent was very dim, but Kal could see the child's skin was blotchy, like Grayson's. A carpet of mossy black hair covered his head, and he weighed as much as a whole ham. Hara must have given Shemme a lot of root while she was pregnant. The child's eyes fixed on his, clear like those of a mantic. Could this child someday be a threat to Armania? Might Kal have to take its life?

"He looks big, doesn't he?" Kal asked. "Compared to a normal infant?"

"I noticed that too," Mielle said, wiping her eyes. "Look at his hair. And he already has teeth." She put her finger in the child's mouth. "Two on the bottom and one coming in on the top. He is as big as a yearling. It's no wonder Miss Kellah did not survive."

The words made Kal cold inside. He focused on the warmth of the child, but strangely it offered little.

Shouts outside the compartment and the jangle of steel warned Kal that Sâr Trevn and Sir Cadoc had returned to arrest the mantic. The sâr stepped inside the compartment and pointed at the midwife. "Arrest that woman. She has committed crimes against the realm of Armania."

The mantic lunged at Kal, wrapped her arms around him and the babe, and yelled, "Magon, *shalosh soor!*"

Flashing light pinwheeled, blinding Kal. He felt weightless. His feet no longer found purchase beneath him. He landed hard on an unstable surface, and his legs crumpled. He clutched the baby close to protect it. Cool air, water lapping, the roll of waves. He blinked at the steady brightness and found himself in a longboat that was tethered to the stern of the *Rafayah*.

"Give me the child," a woman said.

Kal looked over his shoulder. The mantic was seated on the bench behind his. He turned to face her. "How did you do that?"

"I did not have enough strength. To carry us to the *Vespara*. Give me the child and row."

"Put us back on the ship."

"You will row us to the *Vespara*. And when we arrive, you will give witness to my people that I birthed this child from my own body."

"I will do no such thing," Kal said.

"You will, or I will end the life of your precious Mielle."

Kal stared into the mantic's pale eyes. "You bluff."

"Had I been holding the child when Sâr Trevn arrived, I would not have brought you along. But Magon sees value in your services to our realm. If you want to protect the child, you will do as I say. Now hand the babe to me and row."

Kal did not like this one bit, but he dared not risk Mielle to a mantic's wrath, and putting as much distance as he could between them seemed the best option. He gave over the child, unlatched the tether that held the longboat to the tow ropes, then took up the oars and began to row in the direction the mantic indicated.

Nothing to do now but bide his time, remain with the child, and, as Onika would say, hope for the best, though such optimism was against everything in Kal's nature.

CHARL⊙N

Triumph!

The Armanian High Shield rowed the wooden boat away from the *Rafayah*. Bound by his oath to obey Prince Wilek. And his fear that Charlon might harm Mielle.

Magon led the way out of the fleet. It did not take long. Many ships had put up their sails for the coming storm. Dark clouds filled the sky. Angry waves shoved the little boat up and down, no matter how hard the knighten pulled the oars. It began to rain. The baby fussed. Charlon looked down upon the child's face. Tried to cover it. But that only annoyed him further. Perhaps he was hungry. She hoped a milking animal still lived aboard the *Vespara*.

Shanek DanSâr. Round cheeks, pale eyes, and skin so strange. His size had shocked her, for he looked more like a sturdy youngster than a squirming infant. She had seen both in the brothel in Rurekau from time to time, and far too many newborns during her work as a midwife these past weeks. Only now did Charlon understand her debt of gratitude. The blessings Magon had heaped upon her. Had she conceived a child by Prince Janek, her body would have died when the child entered the world. So ignorant. All this time Charlon had been striving to secure her own death. Had Mreegan known? Had she wanted Charlon dead?

Magon had bestowed favor upon Charlon. She *was* the Mother! She would return to the *Vespara* a hero. The Magonian people would cheer and worship the goddess on her behalf. And Charlon would teach this child all things. He would become great because she would see to it.

And someday Charlon would rule them all.

This knighten from Armania would help her. Revered and valuable to Prince Wilek. He would remain her prisoner. An asset to Magonia. A witness to the child's heritage.

As the clouds dumped their water, Sir Kalenek rowed.

She focused on his long twists of black hair. The wounds and scars—old and new—on his face. The short beard he used to hide them. Charlon had always wondered who had cut him. The worst scar ran straight across his forehead. Turned and crossed over his eye, puckering his eyebrow strangely. It continued down his cheek and into his beard, making a hairless line. Other slashes marred his face. A thick white laceration trailed down the side of his neck and into his shirt. Pity welled. Evidence of so much physical pain likely meant heavier pain within. Did such scars cover the rest of his body too?

"What happened?" she asked, nodding to his face. "The scars, I mean."

His dark eyes glanced at hers. Shifted over her shoulder as his rowing quickened. Charlon quailed within. She had been wrong to ask. Something so deep. Her question must have dragged him away to a hellish past.

"In the war," he suddenly answered, pulling the oars. Once. Twice. "I was captured in Magonia and tortured."

Ah. She may as well tell him the truth of her own heritage. Perhaps it would make things easier. "I am not Magonian," she said. "I am from Rurekau."

"Because Harton was from Rurekau." He looked at her now, wounded eyes curious. Victims understood things others could not.

"My brother sold me to a brothel when I was thirteen," she said.

"I heard that," Kal said.

"It took years, but I finally escaped. Heard that women were treated better in Magonia. So I went there."

His only answer was to row and pant.

"Magonians don't treat men any better. Than Rurekans treat women," she said, choosing each word carefully. Wanting him to hear the threat. "You'll likely have a difficult time aboard our ship. I will do what I can. To safeguard you. That you are the child's protector is in your favor. Perhaps no one will harm you."

"Perhaps I should kill you and the child and be done with you both," he said.

Would he? His aggressive tone made her want to cower. But he did not understand her powers. He would not risk Mielle.

"If you talk that way aboard our ship, you will not live long."

He narrowed his eyes, then glanced over his shoulder. "That ship, there?"

She regarded the *Vespara* in the distance. "Yes." She was almost home. She would see Torol.

"That's the Sarikarian vessel you stole from King Jorger," Sir Kalenek said.

"A gift," Charlon said. "Before his heart gave out. You see it flies the Magonian flag now."

That silenced the man.

By the time they reached the hull beneath the pulley lines, a crowd had gathered at the rail above.

"Send down the lines!" Charlon yelled. "The Mother has returned with the Deliverer!"

Even with the growing wind and the three decks between her and the people above, the cheer that went up reached her ears. She smiled, elated to hear the Tennish language again after so many months of speaking Kinsman. Her gaze caught Sir Kalenek's stern one.

"If you look on me with such distaste, you will quickly earn yourself enemies. I decide your fate upon this ship. I will be your translator. Without me, you will be alone."

"I am used to being alone," he said.

Their boat was hoisted aloft and they boarded the *Vespara*.

A strong male voice cried out, "All hail the Mother!"

Her people cheered. So many familiar faces! Charlon held her head high as they lauded her return. She tucked the child into one arm and raised the other. "Silence!"

The people quieted. All eyes on her.

"This man is Sir Kalenek Veroth of Armania," she said. "He is my prisoner. No harm shall come to him. No compulsion set upon him. Unless ordered by me. Is that clear?"

Agreements rose up from the crowd.

"Where is the Chieftess?" Charlon asked.

"In her cabin." Torol's voice.

Charlon turned until she saw him step into the circle that had formed around her. The sight of his face filled her with longing.

"Two, find someone to bring milk and a gut sack to the Chieftess's cabin so the child can eat," Charlon said to Nuel. He scurried off to obey. Then she regarded Torol again. "Lead us to Chieftess Mreegan."

Torol bowed low, then set off. Charlon followed, admiring the bronze skin of his back and the broad reach of his shoulder blades. He was Four now. Had been promoted after the Omatta had killed Morten. When Charlon became Chieftess, she would make him One.

Torol led them across the deck to the captain's cabin, which Mreegan had transformed into her version of her red tent. The painted, black-and-white checkered floor had been covered in furs and mats. Her throne sat against the port wall, her bedding before the stern windows. Kateen stood on Mreegan's right. On her left, Gullik fanned the Chieftess with a yellowed palm leaf. Gullik had become Five after Torol's promotion.

Mreegan watched Charlon carefully, did not rise to greet her. "I thought you dead."

"With Magon's help I have succeeded." She knelt. For now she must. But in her heart, she knelt only to Magon. "I present to you Shanek DanSâr, a child born of Sâr Janek and myself."

"Impossible. I left you nearly three months ago. It takes far longer to bring forth a child."

"Not with Magon's help," Charlon said.

Mreegan studied the child. Magon appeared in the Veil and drew her attention. The goddess spoke to the Chieftess. Too low for Charlon to hear.

Please, Charlon's heart said. Surely Magon would not betray her.

The Chieftess laughed, delighted, it seemed. "I told you to try for Janek. If you would have listened to me from the start, you would have succeeded long before now."

Charlon bowed her head, as if penitent. "You were wise, Chieftess." But inside, she wondered. Had the Chieftess ordered her death by asking Charlon to conceive the Deliverer? Had she known mothers of root children died? Had she been using Charlon all along?

Charlon wished she knew for sure.

Mreegan jutted her chin toward Sir Kalenek. "And this?"

"He is Sir Kalenek Veroth of Armania," Charlon said. "Prince Wilek Hadar named him High Shield over Shanek DanSâr. I have taken him as my prisoner. He will prove useful as an instructor for Shanek on Armanian customs."

"Why would our Deliverer care about Armanian customs?" Mreegan asked.

"If he is to rule all nations," Charlon said, "he will need to be accepted by the Armanian nobility."

"He has magic," Mreegan said. "That is all he will ever need."

He is a witness to the child's royal blood, Magon said from the Veil. *Without him no one will believe he is Sâr Janek's heir.*

"Very well," Mreegan said. She switched to the Kinsman language. "Come, Sir Kalenek Veroth. Kneel before me."

Sir Kalenek stepped forward. "An emissary does not kneel before a foreign ruler, Chieftess," he said, surprising Charlon by speaking in rough Tennish. "But I am pleased to bow in deference." This he did. Gallantly.

Mreegan grunted her displeasure but let his actions pass. "You speak Tennish. How?"

"Armanian captains are taught Tennish."

"You were a soldier. I thought those scars looked like the work of Magonian yeetta warriors. That you survived is proof of your strength. Very well, Sir Kalenek Veroth, I accept you as Guard One to the Deliverer. As a sign of the coming peace between Mother and Father, I will not place you under a compulsion. But know this—you do not decide this child's future. Is that clear?"

"I live to serve." Sir Kalenek bowed his head. Was that his way of pretending? To comply without swearing to? The Chieftess seemed mollified. So Charlon thought on it no more.

"Four, find our noble prisoner suitable quarters," the Chieftess said to Torol. "He will need to be near the Mother's cabin. Sir Kalenek, do speak up if the arrangements bother you. The safety of the Deliverer is our top concern."

Sir Kalenek bowed again and followed Torol from the cabin. Charlon watched them go. Wished Mreegan would dismiss her so she could go with them. It was the first time in her life she preferred the company of men.

"My First," Mreegan said, "see that the Armanian is followed at all times. I want to know where he goes and who he talks to."

"Yes, Chieftess," Kateen said.

Charlon wondered how many shadir the First would set upon Sir Kalenek.

"Bring me the child," Mreegan said.

Charlon came forward and placed the bundle in her arms.

Mreegan grunted as she situated the child awkwardly on her lap. "He seems too large for one so new. When was he born?"

"Today," Charlon said.

"*Today?*" She looked Charlon over. "Yet you are walking around as if nothing pains you. How did you birth this child and live?"

"Magon healed me," Charlon said.

Mreegan turned to regard Magon in the Veil, but the goddess did not deny Charlon's claim. Mreegan's focus fixed back on the child. "Why does he look so strange?"

"The root makes him grow faster but does not poison him," Charlon said. "His dappled skin marks him as a root child."

Mreegan cackled. "Praise to you, Magon, for bringing this about. We shall all see prophecy fulfilled. To hold the Deliverer in my arms is a great honor."

"Excuse me, Chieftess," Gullik said, stepping forward and kneeling.

Mreegan did not take her eyes off Shanek. "What do you want?"

"The Mother mentioned the child's skin as a mark of a root child. I thought you should know that there is a young man aboard this ship with skin like that."

Mreegan's full attention fell upon Gullik. "How long have you known this?"

"Several weeks, Chieftess. He is one of the apprentices Nuel hired."

"Fool! Bring him to me at once."

Gullik stood, hesitating.

"Why are you still here?" Mreegan asked.

"The young man . . . He is a slippery one. I am not certain I can bring him here."

"You are clever, Gullik. Find a way."

"Yes, Chieftess."

As Gullik hurried from the cabin, Shanek began to cry. Mreegan held out the child to Charlon. "Take him."

Charlon rushed forward to claim the boy. "Could there be another root child?"

"They are rare," Mreegan said. "Most women know better than to take root while pregnant."

Mreegan *had* known!

Charlon settled onto Mreegan's bed of furs. Nuel had brought a bucket of milk and a gut sack, so Charlon set about feeding the child as she stewed over Mreegan's deception.

Eventually the door opened again, and Gullik's voice carried inside. "The feast is in here," he said.

A young man barely of age entered. He had brown skin, nothing like Shanek's. "Can't wait to eat. I'm starved," he said, slowing as his gaze took in the room. "Hey . . ."

Mreegan stood. "You!"

The young man vanished, bringing a gasp from those in the cabin. To escape in such a way . . . he must be a mantic!

A shimmer in the Veil caught her attention. Why, he had not vanished after all. He had only entered the Veil. Was creeping toward the exit. But where was his shadir? Charlon had never seen anyone move like that without a shadir present. How had he—?

"*Atsar!*" Mreegan yelled.

The young man stopped, arms and legs now stilled in full stride.

"*Ra'ah,*" Mreegan said.

The man cried out as he faded into view. His skin no longer looked brown but dappled gray.

Gullik was right! Here stood another root child—root man. Fully grown.

Mreegan crossed the room and circled to the front of her captive. "You are the mantic I saw on the deck the day the pirates attacked," she said. "What is your name?"

"Grayson."

"How came you to this boat?"

"Got hired in Odarka."

"How old are you, Grayson?" Mreegan asked.

He opened his mouth to answer, then sucked in a long breath and held it.

"You do not know?"

"I'm an orphan."

"You must have some idea of the years you've lived."

"Seventeen?"

"I think you to be closer to ten."

"Ten!" Grayson snorted. "I'm not ten, that's for sure."

Charlon agreed. This man could not be ten years old. Strange that Mreegan would suggest it.

"You *look* well past seventeen," Mreegan said, "but you behave much younger. I think you are of the same ilk as this infant boy." She gestured to the child in Charlon's lap.

"What's *ilk* mean?" Grayson asked.

"It means I think you are a root child," Mreegan said.

Grayson flinched at the title. "Never heard of roots having children."

Mreegan persisted. "Do you have magical abilities, Grayson?"

"If I did, why would I clean decks?"

But he had walked in the Veil without a shadir. Charlon had seen it.

"Where did you learn to speak Tennish?" Mreegan asked.

"My parents taught me."

"Before they died and orphaned you? Is that what you mean?"

"Right. Exactly."

"I think you're telling me falsehoods, Grayson. To prove what you are, you will be imprisoned. My shadir will watch over you. And when you walk through the Veil to escape my prison hold, the shadir will tell me that you have done so, proving my point." Mreegan walked back to her throne. "When you are willing to show me your magic, tell a guard and he will bring you to me." She sat down and crossed one leg over the other. "Until then, Grayson, enjoy the rats."

"This ship is full of rats," he said. "I'm not afraid of them."

"I'm sure you're very brave. Five, take him to the hold. *Carach*."

The spell holding Grayson in place lifted. He stumbled to catch his balance. Gullik grabbed his arm and hauled him toward the door.

"Does this mean I don't have to work?" Grayson asked as he was dragged out. "Is anyone going to bring me food? And what if I get seasick from . . ." His voice faded away.

"My First," Mreegan said, "douse his meal with ahvenrood. No more than one spoonful. I want to see if it affects his growth. My guess is not only will he grow, he will not be sick from the poison or require purging to any shadir. If I am proved correct in this, we will know how to proceed with our Deliverer."

How fortuitous. Better for Mreegan to test her theories on another than to risk Shanek. "If he can walk in the Veil, how can you be certain he will remain in his cell?" Charlon asked.

"I'm not certain at all," Mreegan said. "But he is a child, and I have frightened him. I think he will stay put to prove to me he has no magic. But he does. We all saw that much."

Shanek began to cry. Charlon tried to feed him, but he turned his head each time she placed the gut sack in his mouth.

"Can you not silence him?" Mreegan asked.

"He is not hungry," Charlon said. "What else could he want?"

"You are Mother. Take him away and figure it out."

Eager to leave, Charlon picked up the boy. Carried him from the Chieftess's cabin. The movement seemed to appease the boy, and he stopped crying. The seas were still rough. She took small steps to keep from falling. At her cabin she supervised the alterations. A carpenter had constructed a cradle from the bottom half of a wooden trunk. It was merely a hand's breath longer than Shanek. He would not fit in it for long.

When the child finally slept, Charlon sent all but Torol away. She had missed him. Showed her feelings the only way she knew how. The compulsion she had placed upon herself allowed her to touch and feel without fear or shame. It did not stop the insistent warnings in the back of her mind. But Charlon trusted Torol. He had always been kind. Kind even when the women abused him.

Home, her heart said as she and Torol reunited.

After a time, Charlon and Torol lay in each other's arms, feeling the ship roll as the sea continued to toss the *Vespara*.

Torol kissed her temple. "I revere you, Mother. You have done what no one thought possible. Even the Chieftess stands in awe of you. The child means so much to Magonia. And when he steps forward to claim the throne of Armania, there will be no end to your glory."

That much was true. Torol saw what Mreegan would not. Better even, he saw Charlon's potential. "Prince Wilek will rule Armania first," Charlon said. "Then Prince Janek."

"But if Prince Wilek could be killed," Torol said, "Prince Janek would take his place. That would put Shanek one step away from being Heir to the throne of Armania."

The idea both thrilled and horrified Charlon. That Shanek might rule had been prophesied. The fruition of all she had been working toward. Yet she had never considered that the child could grow quickly. That he might rule soon.

Her former bond with the eldest prince had allowed her to see. See into his heart. Prince Wilek had no evil within. No ambition other than to serve his people well. Such was the same reason Charlon wanted to be Chieftess. He did not deserve death for Magonia's gain.

Yet Torol's plan had merit.

"Whatever Magon deems prudent is what I must do."

"You are wise to ask the goddess," Torol said.

Charlon *was* wise. And in that moment she realized something awful. She loved this man. Loved him completely. It was Torol she dreamed about each night as she went to sleep, Torol she thought of when her imagination ran away, Torol's face she had pictured when she had gone to Prince Janek.

Tell no one, her heart said. And her heart was right.

Goddess help her. No one must know.

Trevn

Trevn, Cadoc, and two King's Guards took a dinghy through the rain to the *Seffynaw*. Trevn could no longer ignore the evidence in the sky. Even in late midday the dark clouds made it difficult to see. Thankfully they reached the *Seffynaw*, and as they were hoisted aloft, that alone seemed worthy of praise to Arman.

When Trevn stepped onto the foredeck, the slant of the wood under his feet from the steep roll of the waves proved the weather had worsened since he'd left Mielle. He wished more than ever that she had returned with him.

Through their magical bond, he felt her distant answer to his concern. She would be all right. She needed to take care of Shemme's body. Then she would come.

Interesting that the distance kept them from hearing each other as vividly as when they were close. Trevn liked being able to communicate with Mielle this way, but he hated knowing that the mantic had put some kind of spell upon them. Why had she done it? What could the woman possibly gain from such a thing?

This he must puzzle out later. Eager to relay all that had happened with Shemme, the mantic, and Sir Kalenek, Trevn ran all the way to the king's office. As he went, it pleased him to see the sailors setting up barrels on deck to catch the rainwater.

When he reached the king's cabin, the guards at the door bowed and let him in without delay. There Trevn found his brother, standing before the balcony, looking out to sea. Wilek turned at the sound of the door opening and closing and gave Trevn a relieved glare.

"You *are* alive. I was beginning to wonder. Where have you been?"

"I'm sorry," Trevn said. He slipped his marked hand behind his back, not ready to anger his brother further just yet. "I've been on the *Rafayah*. Miss Shemme gave birth, named the child Shanek DanSâr."

Wilek winced. "Unfortunate name. Born so soon?"

"Yes. The child was very large, and Miss Shemme died."

Wilek pulled out the chair at their father's desk and sat down. "Just as they said she would. Did Sir Kalenek arrive in time?"

"He did. But something else happened. A mantic has been serving Miss Shemme these past few days."

This brought Wilek back to his feet. "How?"

Trevn lifted his hands. "Miss Shemme needed a midwife. She called herself Sonber—"

"That is Charlon's surname."

"We didn't know, but Sir Kalenek recognized it right away," Trevn said, and he went on to tell Wilek the whole story. "The three of them vanished, but the lookout caught sight of them on the open sea."

"Did you have them followed?"

"By the time I was summoned to the main deck, they'd lost sight of the dinghy."

Wilek sat down again. "Will Kal kill the babe, I wonder? Or try to escape with it?"

"Why would he kill it?"

"Because I told him to—if he thought it necessary. Don't look at me like that. In Magonian hands that child is a weapon against us. There is nothing to be done now but await word from Kal."

Trevn stood in silence, staring at his brother, who was again looking out the balcony window. A surge of pity flashed over him. How thankful he was not to be the Heir and to have to make such decisions.

"There is more news," Wilek said, gesturing to a chair across from his. When Trevn sat, Wilek said, "Our brother Janek is dead. By Sir Kalenek's hand. He confessed it to me."

A sickly ache grew in Trevn's stomach. He recalled the shield's callous comments about no longer being Armanian. "Sir Kalenek killed Janek? Why?"

"He found Miss Amala in Janek's cabin in circumstances that were unrefined." Wilek went on to explain how Kal had first struck Janek, who had him arrested. How Janek in turn had sent Captain Alpress to kill Kal. And that Kal killed Alpress, then retaliated by killing Janek.

Trevn stared at Wilek, stunned that Janek was gone forever. Sir Kalenek's strange comments and bruised face all made sense now. "Sir Kalenek said you sent him to the *Rafayah*."

Wilek's eyes became hard and glassy. "That stays between us. I did what I had to."

"Sir Kalenek is your friend."

"The very best," Wilek said, voice wavering. "But he is ill. I did not understand just how deep his madness went. When I saw what he did to Janek . . . Master Jhorn tried to warn me. If only I had understood."

"What?"

"That Kal's pain unchecked could eventually hurt someone." Wilek sighed. He looked older to Trevn, and very tired. "Kal's life is now dedicated to keeping Janek's child from causing mischief. That I feel he can do well. You and I must prepare Janek for last rites and shipping. You are now the Second Arm of Armania. I need your help."

"But the child. What of Shanek DanSâr?"

"That child is a stray, who cannot inherit the throne. And rumor has spread that our father had Shemme killed. No one knows about the child but me, you, Mielle, Kal, Jhorn, and Zeroah."

"And all of Magonia in a very short time," Trevn said.

Wilek rubbed his hands over his face. "Leave Magonia to Kal." A pause. "Now, tell me what you've done, Trevn. I have seen the mark you've been hiding on your hand. Assure me it is not what I fear."

Trevn fingered the red impression on his palm. "I didn't know what it was at first. The midwife wanted to give us a blessing. In taking care of Miss Shemme, she and Mielle had become close. I saw no reason to refuse. I didn't find out until today that the midwife was Charlon Sonber."

"Did you learn nothing from my pain? And why would a near stranger have reason to give you a blessing? Did that not seem suspicious?"

Trevn's cheeks tingled as a horrifying realization settled into his mind. From the moment he had stepped foot on the *Rafayah*, Charlon had been there. Was that why he had been so adamant and eager to marry Mielle?

"Trevn? Answer me."

He lifted his head and met his brother's reprimanding gaze. "I think Charlon put a compulsion on me," he confessed, and the words brought heavy grief. "The moment I saw Miss Mielle, I knew I had to marry her without delay."

"Marry her!"

Trevn cringed. "Thinking back, that doesn't sound very much like me."

"Doesn't it? Eloping to marry someone without your father's blessing or approval? Sounds to me like something a Renegade would do."

"Well, yes, but that's not why I did it. I only knew that I must. There was no logic to it. Cadoc, Captain Stockton, even Miss Mielle tried to talk me out of it. But I would not be dissuaded. And when the midwife offered to say a blessing at our wedding, I figured it was a prayer from a friend. Why would the mantic have compelled me to marry Mielle?"

"Oli says that shadir love mischief. Perhaps Charlon's shadir wanted to play a trick."

"But we are happy."

"You and Miss Mielle are. The rest of us are not. You made a promise to me, Trevn, to put the realm before your own happiness. Do not think me callous. I understand how it feels to be compelled and soul-bound. It is terribly invasive. But who you marry was never for you to decide alone. We can try to hide this for now—"

"I do not wish to hide it!"

"Hear me out. Our brother is dead. Our father nearly so. If Father recovers, with you now the Second Arm, know that he will demand an annulment."

Trevn lifted his chin. "I love Mielle and will not cast her aside no matter what you or Father say. Whether or not a mantic tricked us, we were married by a Rurekan priest on the *Rafayah's* main deck in front of more than one hundred witnesses. Don't you care what I want?"

"Who spoke to Father on your behalf and garnered his permission for you to court Miss Mielle? I did. Yet you go behind my back and do this."

It did seem selfish when put like that. "Against my will! But what's done is done, and I will not abandon her."

The boat listed steeply to port. Wilek's inkwell and goblet slid off the desk and crashed to the floor. Trevn crouched and picked them up, grabbing hold of the desk to steady himself.

"The storm is getting worse," he said, knowing Mielle wouldn't be able to return tonight. He recoiled at the idea of being apart from her for so long.

A knock at the door preceded Dendrick. "Admiral Livina wishes to move the commoners below deck, Your Highness."

That bad? Trevn ran from the cabin, ignoring Wilek's call that he return. He sprinted onto the main deck, splashing through a hand's depth of water. Sheets of rain poured down like river holes in spring. Trevn caught sight of Rzasa and Nietz pulling on a cable and ran to help.

"I don't need any fair-weather sailors on my watch, thanks," Nietz said.

Trevn *had* abandoned his watch without a word. "*This* you call fair weather?" he asked.

Nietz didn't reply, nor did he insist Trevn leave. The crew worked hard and fast, jumping to the orders of the mates. The scupper holes could not drain the deck fast enough. Once they had taken in all the canvas, they set to work on the pumps for what felt like hours until the captain called all hands to the helm.

"We've got a hard squall ahead," Bussie said. "We've done all we can to prepare, so take heart, men, and have a bite and a nip while we can. I'm afraid it'll get worse before it gets better."

The cook from the sailors' galley had brought up a pot of fish stew and mugs. Each man took a cup. The hot stew seeped down Trevn's throat, warming him. When he emptied his cup, Nietz filled it with spirits, which warmed his belly more than the stew had and burned his throat and eyes as well. He'd never tasted anything quite so strong.

By the time they finished their meal and returned to the main deck, it had been totally cleared of commoners.

"Sands," Rzasa said. "Looks mighty strange empty like this."

It gave Trevn an ominous feeling, but he reminded himself that the people were safe below deck. "That was kind of the captain to feed us," he said.

Rzasa chuckled. "Captains often give their crew a nice meal before a bad storm in case we all drown."

"That's horrible."

"Why?" Rzasa asked. "If we're going to survive, we'll need the energy an extra meal provides. And if we're going down anyway, we might as well go down with a full belly and a smile."

They took another turn at the pumps, then kept out of the way to watch the storm and help where needed. The rain didn't let up. Screaming winds tore at the ship, ripping away anything that had not been tied down. All of the water barrels had tipped over, and Trevn and Rzasa set about lashing them to the rigging to keep them upright. Everywhere Trevn looked, a wall of sea spray obscured his view as the wind and water batted the *Seffynaw* like a cat toying with an injured moth.

It got so bad that Trevn gave up trying to stand and merely clung to the ratlines as the violent waves rocked him to and fro. He could not see the *Rafayah*. He could not see any of the rest of the fleet.

"Mielle!" Trevn yelled into the storm, barely hearing himself as the wind swallowed his words.

Someone tugged on his arm. Rzasa.

"Nietz says we're needed in the forward hold!" he hollered. "Cargo is loose!"

Trevn nodded, and he and Rzasa waded toward the companionway. They passed the commoners lining the stairs and descended into the depths of the ship. Beneath the deck the sounds changed. The cacophony of wind, rain, and splashing sea traded itself for the creaks, knocks, and rattles of a ship under stress.

The farther down they went, the louder the ship's groaning became. They reached a group of sailors at the compartment in the fore hold. Nietz stood in the entrance, holding a lantern aloft. In the dim light Trevn saw a knot of furniture. Thrones, beds, longchairs, tables, and sideboards had been lashed around an iron shrine to Barthos. Several smaller wicker or wood pieces had broken free and tumbled back and forth with the ship's motion. Each time the Barthos shrine slid across the full length of the compartment, it reduced some small wooden chair or table to kindling and sent tremors through the bulkhead.

"Can't we just leave it?" Rzasa asked.

"If it slides too fast, it might crack the hull," Nietz said.

So the crew did their best to lash the loose furniture back to the shrine, wedging pieces of broken lumber in as supports whenever they could. As soon as they secured one, a new tilt of the ship nearly broke apart their work.

They needed to get the shrine out of the way. If only they could lift it.

"Rzasa," Trevn said, seized with an idea. "Fetch me several hammocks. If we can lift the shrine into its own bed, then it will rock instead of crashing against the bulkheads."

"Put the shrine to bed?" Rzasa asked. "Are you crazy?"

"It might work," Nietz said. "Get the hammocks, Rzasa. At least three of them."

"Four," Trevn said. "One to hold each corner."

Rzasa was back in no time with the hammocks, and the group set to work. The shrine was too heavy to lift to get the hammocks underneath, so they looped ropes to the lashings and through the beams on the deck head to hoist it. The shrine continued to slide about, repeatedly destroying their efforts and forcing them to start again. Recognizing the importance of speed, Trevn laid out the hammocks on the floor with the rope eyes facing outward. Hopefully the moment the men raised the shrine, Trevn and Rzasa could slide the hammocks under in one unit.

"We're ready," Nietz yelled. "Once we get it up, you boys move the hammocks. You set?"

Trevn nodded at Rzasa, who said, "We're set."

"Heave!" Nietz yelled.

The men grunted, and the shrine lifted up off the floor.

"Go, go!" Nietz yelled.

Trevn and Rzasa each grabbed an end and slid the hammocks underneath the shrine.

When the web of ropes was in position, Trevn let go and yelled, "Done!" But one of his rope eyes flipped around and landed under the shrine.

"Lower it slowly," Nietz yelled.

"Wait!" Trevn fell to his stomach and reached for the eye, grabbing it.

Too late. The shrine fell on his hand and arm, shooting a spasm of agony through the limb. He screamed.

"Lift it up!" Rzasa yelled. "It's on Sâr Trevn's arm!"

"Heave!" Nietz yelled. "Back up!"

The shrine rose again. Trevn tried to move but could not. Bonds and Rzasa grabbed him. Dragged him back. Trevn ignored the throbbing pain and kept his eyes fixed on the tangle of hammocks.

"Get the eye!" he yelled, pointing at it with his other hand.

Rzasa lunged over Trevn's head and snagged the eye, held tight. "I've got it."

"Set it down," Nietz yelled.

Once the shrine sat on the hammocks, the men swarmed, making quick work of lashing the eyes of all four hammocks together and hoisting the bundle up.

A swell tipped the ship to starboard, sliding a pile of debris toward Trevn. Someone grabbed him and pulled him out into the lengthway just before the debris barreled past.

Nietz squatted before him. "How's that hand, Boots?"

Trevn glanced down and let out a pent-up breath he hadn't realized he'd been holding. His fingers looked like sausages, his hand like a blown-up pig's bladder. Just past his wrist the skin had ripped apart in a jagged line, leaving a gash where it had pulled away from itself and shifted, revealing tendons and pulsing veins along his wrist. He couldn't feel his hand. Just a cold burning. And lightheadedness.

"Sands, that's a nasty evil," Rzasa said.

Trevn looked up to Rzasa. He felt a single trickle of sweat run down his temple to his jaw. Then his world went black.

GRAYSON

Kateen shoved a bowl of fish and stale bread through the slot at the bottom of the cell door. "You cannot hide the truth from us, boy."

When he didn't answer, she stalked away, muttering about fools.

I see you. I see you. I seeeeee you, a shadir crooned as it drifted just far enough through the wooden door to show its three bulging eyes. The thick door presented no hindrance to a creature of the Veil.

Grayson pretended he could not hear or see the shadir. He was so hungry he scarfed down his meal, barely chewing before he swallowed. The shadir cackled and made slurping sounds. It soared in and out of Grayson's cell, a stroke of blurred yellow that almost looked like light in the darkness.

Come with me, boy, the shadir sang. *Come into the Veil, where you can be free. Come, come, come with me.*

Grayson ignored it, though he cringed each time it passed through his body. Once he'd licked the fishy juices from the bowl and his fingers, and there was nothing left to do but sit and feel the lump of food in his belly, he began to realize several things.

First, he was growing. It always happened slowly, like an ache in the back that needed a good stretch. They must have put evenroot in his food. He'd been so hungry he hadn't even tasted it.

Second, they meant to trick him. They'd sent the shadir to watch him. Grayson *could* push into the Veil and walk through the door, go hide. But the shadir would see. It would follow him. Call its companions to tell the Chieftess where he was, and she would use her magic to control him.

So Grayson pretended to be normal. A normal boy locked in a cell would call for help, so Grayson yelled and shook the door, pounded his fists on it, then got down on the floor and reached one arm out the food slot, feeling his way up the door as if he might find the latch. All the while he could tell that his hand was nowhere near the lock.

He didn't like his bigger body. Getting down on the floor was harder than it used to be. His arm was thicker, and the narrow slot pinched and scraped his skin. After a while he sat against the wall, listening for rats and brushing his fingers along the downy hair that had grown on his jaw. He fought back tears. Crying was something a boy would do, and he had told the Chieftess he was a man. If he cried, the shadir would see and tell. So he slammed his feet against the opposite wall, sending all his frustrations into each kick.

He shouldn't be here. Onika had never said he would be captured. Did that mean Onika was wrong about some things? Or . . . had she kept this a secret? It hurt his feelings that Onika might have thought Grayson was too little to understand important things.

He kicked harder.

In the distance bootsteps clumped along the walk. Someone was coming, though from the sounds, the person was still far off.

Time to flee, flea, the shadir said, spinning around Grayson's face, which made it very difficult to ignore. *Into the Veil and out the door, quickly, before your executioner arrives.*

That couldn't be. The Chieftess thought Grayson was valuable. She wouldn't kill him.

Something niggled in Grayson's brain, like he'd lived this moment before or was forgetting something important. As the steps neared, he scrunched up his brows and dug deep, trying to puzzle out the mystery. It came to him like a flash of light. The men on this ship went barefoot. So who was coming?

The bootsteps stopped outside. Grayson peered through the wall to get a good look at the boots, but even in the Veil the hold was too dark to see clearly.

"Grayson?" a man said.

Arman's blessing! "Sir Kalenek?" Grayson scrambled to his feet and peered out the tiny window at the top of the door. "Did you come to—?"

"Shh! You want out, you keep quiet, hear?" This Sir Kalenek whispered, staring so long and crossly that Grayson nodded. "Sands, you've grown fast. I heard talk that Chieftess Mreegan had found a grown root child who didn't know when to shut up. I knew it had to be you."

Grayson looked for the shadir, found it hovering behind Sir Kalenek's legs. The knighten had already said too much, but what could Grayson do? "Where did you get the key?"

"Is that how you keep quiet?"

Grayson looked down, shamed by Sir Kalenek's reprimanding tone, but his heart pounded in his chest, knowing the shadir would tell everything. He needed to warn Sir Kalenek but didn't know how.

"That's better," Sir Kalenek said. "Stay that way. Not a word." He lifted his hand to the lock and put a key into it.

Behind Sir Kalenek, the shadir's three eyes stared.

Sir Kalenek pulled open the door, the hinges squealed, and he glared at Grayson as if the noise had been his fault. At a jerk of Sir Kalenek's head, Grayson slipped out of the cell.

Sir Kalenek closed the door and locked it again. He started off down the corridor, and Grayson saw another shadir riding on Sir Kalenek's back. A blue one that looked like a jellyfish.

Grayson followed, wanting desperately to tell Sir Kalenek about the shadir, to turn around and see if the yellow one was following or if it had gone for help.

He kept quiet and followed. In a short while they turned. Another ten steps and they turned again. This corridor stretched out far into the distance. Every ten to fifteen steps they passed by another walkway or a storage room that held crates or barrels.

"So much wasted space," Sir Kalenek said. "Compared to the number of people on the *Seffynaw*, this ship is nearly empty."

Grayson wisely stayed silent. This made him feel proud. Sir Kalenek would see that Grayson could obey an order. He was nearly as tall as the knighten now, though his shoulders were much narrower and he still had skinny arms. They reached a stairwell. Sir Kalenek drew his sword, and up they went. Right before each landing, they paused so that the knighten could check the way. On one turn Grayson caught sight of the yellow shadir following behind and relaxed. It hadn't gone for help yet, but he doubted it would let them escape.

They met no one in the stairwell. Even when they stepped out into the cold, rainy night, Grayson saw no one. They were at the very nose of the ship, opposite the helm. The sea surged beneath them. Raindrops fell heavy and wet. The wind whipped, and Grayson pulled his tunic tight around his throat. Lightning flashed overhead, making him jump.

Sir Kalenek stopped at the rail, right under the hoist at the boat fall. They were going to escape! The two of them would row to the *Seffynaw*, and Grayson would see Onika and Jhorn again. He bit the tip of his tongue to keep from talking. Thunder rolled, a long while since the lightning flash. That much was good. Grayson bet the storm was almost over.

"Get in," Sir Kalenek said, extending a hand to help him over the rail.

A streak of yellow caught Grayson's gaze. The shadir had flown away! And he could no longer see the blue one.

"Sir Kalenek, two shadir! They followed us from the hold and just now flew away. I think they went for help."

"Why didn't you say something? Don't know if I can lower this fast enough on my own." Sir Kalenek grabbed Grayson and practically threw him over the rail, then started cranking the left pulley.

Grayson's heart fluttered inside. "You're not coming?"

"Can't. I have a mission to accomplish here."

Grayson was to go into the storm by himself? He couldn't! "I have to go alone?"

"It's the only way," Sir Kalenek said. "If I don't hurry, you won't make it."

Grayson slung back over the rail and onto the deck by the right pulley.

"What are you doing?" Sir Kalenek yelled. "Get in the boat now!"

"I can help you." Grayson reached for the pulley.

"A lot of good that'll do when the empty boat is on the water without you in it."

There was no time to argue. Grayson popped through the Veil and into the boat. Since he'd been in this boat lots of times, he landed perfectly, sitting on the center bench.

Sir Kalenek twisted in a circle looking for him.

"Down here." The moment Sir Kalenek's gaze found him, Grayson popped back to the right pulley and started to crank. "It's a trick I learned. I'll help you lower the boat, and then I can pop down into it."

Sir Kalenek blinked. "Good enough for me."

They worked the pulleys quickly and lowered the boat toward the dark waves.

"Do you know how to row?" Sir Kalenek asked.

"Yes, sir, but not where to go."

"See those lights?" Kal jutted his chin straight ahead. "There are three in a row on the right and one on the left."

As Grayson cranked the pulley, he squinted through the fat drops of rain until he saw the lights in the blackness. "I see them."

"That's the *Malbraid*. The ship Sâr Wilek gave to Randmuir Khal of the Omatta. Row right below the three lights. Catch yourself up against the side and start yelling. Someone will hear and hoist you up. Tell them you've escaped from the Magonian mantics. Join his crew and don't make any trouble. Then wait for your chance to get back to Jhorn and Miss Onika. Can you do that?"

"'Course I can."

"Good." The lines went slack. The boat had reached the sea. "I also bring you a message from Miss Onika."

Grayson held his breath.

"She said that when I saw you—which she somehow knew I would—to tell you to hold tight to your secret until you come to those twice your size."

"Twice my—?"

"Someone's coming. Don't worry about the lines. I'll cut them from here. Go!" Sir Kalenek pulled a knife and in three strokes had sawed the left pulley rope. "I said go!"

Grayson saw movement on the stairs from the main deck. He concentrated and popped down into the dinghy. He landed on the bench, but this time the boat was rocking wildly. Waves splashed over the end, cold on Grayson's back. He yelped, twisted down to the floor, and grappled for the oars.

That's when he noticed the red shadir. Not in the boat, really, but floating under the bench on the opposite end. It was red and wispy, like a horse's tail, and had one bulging eye.

Voices barked out above. A green glow lit the sky, then passed over the water. The dinghy bobbed wildly, just out of reach of the magical beam.

Grayson struggled up onto the bench and put the oars over the side. He tried to row, but the dinghy kept slamming into the ship. He was backward. That was the problem. He turned around on the bench and rowed again. This brought him out some, but the bobbing waves also carried him to the right.

Grayson fought the oars, the boat, and each rising wave. Bit by bit he pulled away from the *Vespara* and out into the deep. The green glow continued to drift over the waters. Any moment now they would see him. Surely the red shadir could tell them where he was.

Helplessness grabbed hold. How could he ever get away now that the shadir knew what he was? One of them would always follow him. Jhorn's greatest fears had happened. All he had warned Grayson about for years.

Don't think about it! Grayson pretended not to see the shadir and kept his aim on the three lights. He rowed until his arms burned. He took a break, but the wild waves scared him, and he picked up the oars again, eager to get onto a bigger, safer ship. His arms ached and he wanted to cry. Why was it so far? How was he ever going to get there?

The waves grew larger until one rolled beneath his little boat and stood it nearly on its nose. Grayson screamed and slid off his bench. The boat sailed back the other way, and he stored the oars under the seats and scrambled onto the floor, lying evenly under both benches. He tucked his toes up past the end of the back bench and clutched his fingers around the edge of the front bench, holding tight. He hummed Onika's song to try to stay calm.

The shadir was down by Grayson's feet, but he couldn't worry about the creature. The waves continued to pitch the little boat up and down. Lightning cracked overhead, and Grayson began to sing Onika's song aloud, screaming the words at the top of his lungs.

Something ran along the bottom of his boat, click, click, clicking. He opened his eyes, squinting into the stinging rain. Had he found land? Reached rocks or a reef?

He scooted up until he was sitting with his arms hugging the front bench. A glance over the side showed a pale beam of light cutting through the darkness. The moon had peeked through a break in the storm clouds, making them look purple and soft. The light shone on the crest of each wave, on the slashes of raindrops. For a moment Grayson feared he'd lost the three lights that marked the ship, but after much straining over the glistening waves, he located them again, as far away as ever. He checked for the shadir and saw it curled into a ball on the floor, looking bored.

In desperation Grayson went back to singing Onika's song, not wanting to think about where he was or how this night might end.

Again he felt the clicking under the hull, but this time the front end of the boat lifted up out of the water. A hiss sent a plume of rotten-smelling hot air against the back of Grayson's neck. He gripped the bench so tightly a sliver entered his wrist. He held his breath. Arman, help him not to die! Not like this.

A wet, throaty moan came from behind. Lightning flashed again, illuminating a glossy tentacle hovering in the air to his right.

The boat slapped against the water's surface, knocking Grayson's chin against the wooden bench. He bit his tongue and the tang of blood filled his mouth.

Something splashed outside the boat on his right. He peeked over the side and saw a giant black snake rolling through the waves. When next the creature came above water, its head loomed over the end of the boat.

In the pale moonlight the water beast was mostly dark shadow. Its eyes were three white gleams reflected on round circles of black. It was very much snakelike, with a flat head the size of the dinghy and a mouth bared with dozens of dagger-like teeth. Its skin glistened like wet, black fur.

It hissed again, sending a plume of steamy breath into the chilled night. It was looking right at Grayson. What did it want?

It slid forward and knocked its chin against the end of the boat. The dinghy sailed back over a wave and up and down another, moving faster than Grayson could ever row.

The creature followed, purring its throaty moan.

On a whim Grayson began humming Onika's song. The serpent lifted its head out of the sea until it towered above the boat, drizzling water over Grayson's head and arms. The beast's neck looked as high as the mainmast on the *Vespara*. The sight stifled Grayson's voice.

The serpent screeched, exposing a dark throat behind its slivered teeth. Grayson screamed and hunched down under the bench, shutting his eyes. The creature knocked against the boat again. The dinghy skimmed over the huge waves. His stomach roiled. Too much more of this and he'd be sick.

The boat struck something hard. Shouts above drew open Grayson's eyes, and he squinted up through the falling rain. He had reached a ship! Men looked over the rail, not at him. Farther past.

They must see the serpent.

Grayson's boat was already drifting away from the hull. "Hey!" he yelled. "Help me!" He climbed up onto the bench but could no longer see the serpent. "Help!"

"There's a boat down there!" he heard someone yell.

"Someone's in it!"

"Who goes there?" a man yelled.

Before Grayson could reply, a rope was thrown down. Grayson grabbed hold, and the men on the deck carried it around to the stern, towing the dinghy along the ship's hull until it was under the boat fall. From the lantern light on the deck, Grayson could see there was already a boat hanging above. It took moments for the sailors to unhook it and move it elsewhere. Then the pulley lines were lowered and Grayson attached them to his boat.

He did not see the serpent again, but as the men hoisted him up the side of the ship, he heard its groan from the blackness and thanked Arman that it had liked Onika's song.

WILEK

For three days the storm raged. The ship rocked from one steep angle to another, shuddering continually under the onslaught and shaking the contents of Wilek's office like dice in a cup.

Everyone stayed in their cabins, out of the way. Wilek could accomplish little. His mind was weary from the endless preoccupation of a hundred worries. Before the storm he had sent his father to the *Kaloday*, and he wondered how King Loran's ship fared. He thought of Trevn and his shattered hand. More died each day from the fever. And while the rain had blessedly replenished their drinking water, food was so low that if the fish didn't start biting again soon, Wilek would have to have another horse killed.

Then there were the rebels in the hold and the missing evenroot. Who had Hara given the root to? Or had there never been any evenroot to worry about in the first place? Wilek wanted to end the conspiracies once and for all, but he could not hold trials when more than half his council refused to leave their beds.

At least the storm should keep the pirates from taking more ships.

On the morning of the fourth day, the darkness retreated and overcast skies thinned to allow the glow of daylight. The sight eased some of the tension from Wilek's shoulders, yet he kept up his guard until the sun shone brighter and the clouds parted to show a blue sky beyond.

Captain Bussie reported minimal damage to the ship. As to the state of the passengers, Rayim had encountered lots of seasickness, several dozen minor injuries, one dead from a fall down the stairs, and a total of thirty-one lost to the fever. But it was Admiral Livina's words that made Wilek's chest tighten.

"At least twenty ships missing, that we can see from the lookout."

"What of the *Kaloday*?" Wilek asked of King Loran's ship.

"The *Kaloday* is within my sights, Your Highness," the admiral said.

Wilek breathed a sigh of relief that they had not lost his father, but he still struggled to keep his voice calm. "Did the missing ships go down?"

"Don't know, Your Highness. Could be they were only blown off course. Or maybe it's some of both. I've seen no sign of debris in the water thus far, but if they went down days ago, we likely left any wreckage behind."

"Is there any way to know how many ships were lost and which ones?"

"Once the fleet takes formation again, if a ship is missing, word will come through the flags. But unless we find evidence in the water, there's no way to know if a missing ship sank or was blown off course."

"Thank you, Admiral. Bring me a list of the missing ships as soon as you know."

"Yes, Your Highness." The admiral departed.

"How many people on twenty ships, Dendrick?" Wilek asked.

"Depends on the type of ship, Your Highness," Dendrick said. "Likely anywhere from one hundred to seven hundred people per ship."

Wilek did the math in his head but didn't want to say such numbers aloud. "Can we schedule a council meeting today?"

"We can try, Your Highness, but it might be best to have the shippings first."

"Right." Janek must be publicly mourned. Along with thirty-some others.

"There are only three death boats left," Dendrick said. "Might some share?"

Wouldn't Janek love that? The king would rage, were he here. But Wilek no longer saw any reason to fear tomorrow. With so much at stake, he could only live and rule one day—one moment—at a time. And this moment, he needed a break from disaster, if only for a short time. Zeroah had been asking to visit Inolah and her new baby. Wilek had put her off because of the storm, but he would do so no longer.

"A death boat is too small to share," Wilek said, standing. They were just big enough to hold a full-grown man lying down. "Find another way to ship the commoners, but Janek must have his own death boat." He headed toward the door. "Inform the council that we will meet this evening, during the dinner hour. If you need me, I'll be with my wife."

✦   ✦   ✦

Wilek and Zeroah wound through the crossways and lengthways until they reached Inolah's cabin.

The maid who answered the door yelped at the sight of them, curtsied, and ran back inside. A moment later she came back, curtsied again, and said, "My lady is not dressed, my sâr. She is not ready to receive visitors."

Inolah's voice carried over the woman's panic. "My brother has seen me covered in mud, Biinah. I am in a much better state today. Vallah, greet your uncle and let him in. I do hope he brought his wife."

Vallah came to the door and curtsied. "Good midday, uncle, aunt. Come to see the baby?"

"That we have, Vallah," Wilek said. "Can you take us to her?"

The girl whisked them inside the tiny cabin to a framed bed, where Inolah was sitting up, blankets tucked around her. Wilek's gaze locked on to the small bundle in her arms.

"Meet my daughter Tinyah, for though she did not feel tiny, you can see that she is."

The small, dark face was squished like one of Mother's dogs. Her eyes were open, alert, and looking around the room, fixed on nothing, despite the fact that Zeroah waved her finger before them.

"She is beautiful," Zeroah said.

"Just like her sister." Inolah smiled at Vallah. "I confess I am relieved she is female. Ulrik will not be so eager to make use of a girl."

Pain flashed across Inolah's face as she spoke of her son. Wilek wished he could fix all that was broken in her life. "Have you thought of marrying again?" he asked her.

Inolah stared at him silently.

"Of course I will provide for you. Do not doubt that," Wilek said. "I only wondered if you might be happier . . ." He cursed himself for bringing it up.

"I am not a project to be fixed, like the Duke of Canden, Wil." His sister lifted the baby to Zeroah, who took the girl into her arms with as much eagerness as if it had been her own.

"I should not have asked that," he said.

"No, you shouldn't have," Inolah said. "Tell me you seized Oli's bottles of evenroot juice, though. I am worried about him."

Wilek grabbed his head. "I forgot!" With interviewing the traitors, then the storm . . . "Have you seen him?"

"Not since I went into labor at Hrettah's ageday party. You must check on him, brother."

"I will do so the moment we leave you." Curse his overworked mind! How could he have forgotten so much evenroot juice? Was he a complete fool? He prayed that Oli had refrained from taking more and that no one else had discovered it.

They stayed only long enough for each to take a turn holding the newborn, then bade mother, sister, and infant farewell. Wilek didn't mean to hurry his wife back through the corridors to their cabin, but concern for Oli had very much distracted him. He thought of nothing but Oli until Zeroah took hold of his hand and squeezed.

"Did you like your niece Tinyah, Wilek?"

He smiled upon her. "Very much."

"I am glad, for I shall soon give you a babe of your own."

Wilek blinked, wondering what she meant. Was this a promise for the future? Or was she trying to tell him something? "Are you with child, lady?"

A shy smile. A nod.

Wilek whooped, grabbed his wife around the waist, and lifted her. A clunk brought forth a cry, and Zeroah clapped a hand to her head. "Oh! Forgive me, Zeroah." Wilek set her down again. "I forget how low these deck heads are."

But she was smiling wider than ever before. "I am not hurt."

He hugged her close and kissed the top of her head. On a day filled with death, missing ships, and trials of treason, news of this one new life filled him with a fresh purpose to forge on.

"You are pleased, then?" Zeroah asked.

"My dear, your gift has scattered a hundred burdens from my mind. I am overjoyed!"

Zeroah beamed.

✦　✦　✦

Janek's shipping took place that midday on the stern deck. Only royals and selected nobles had been invited, but commoners crowded the stairs and a few had climbed into the rigging to watch the sâr's last rites.

Two reamskiffs had been decorated for the commoner shipping earlier that day. With the benches removed, they had managed to fit sixteen bodies on each. Janek's death boat had been decorated with drapes of white and blue linen, curled ribbon, and an Armanian flag mounted on a pole at the bow. Dozens of silk flowers in a variety of styles had been stitched in bunches on the linen drape and, to Wilek's surprise, looked as nice as real ones. Janek had been dressed in his best, then wrapped in white linen and cloth of gold. His beloved sandvine had been tucked beside his body, along with a chest of gold coins, several sculptures of Janek's five gods, goblets, and a myriad of jewels. These were his grave offerings so that he would not appear before Athos empty-handed.

It all seemed a waste to Wilek, who no longer believed the dead would find Athos waiting. Where did these death boats end up, anyway? On the bottom of the sea? Looted by pirates? Drifting forever? He couldn't recall what the Book of Arman had to say on the subject. He would have to ask Miss Onika sometime.

Father Mathal conducted the ceremony, resplendent in white robes that reminded Wilek of Pontiff Rogedoth, the pretender.

"We gather here to pay tribute to the life of His Royal Highness, Janek-Sâr Hadar, the Second Arm, the Amiable. The death of a man is the order of things. It comes to all as surely as night follows day. Our ancient forefathers gave us life through the people tree, so we acknowledge the tree as a symbol. Each man sprouts as a bud, grows into a leaf that appears for a season, flourishes in the glory of summer, then dies with the coming of fall.

"For Sâr Janek, the journey on earth has ended and another begun, but for us, there is loss, sorrow, and pain. Iamos, deliver us from grief and despair. Give us the strength to accept what is past, peace to appreciate what is present, and good fortune as we look toward what is to come."

Wilek studied the faces of those in attendance. None appeared to have good fortune by standards of the past. Today good fortune meant having one's health, food, and water. What separated these men and women from the so-called commoners on the main deck? Birth? Blood? It seemed a fine line.

"Nivanreh, god of travel," Father Mathal went on, "we stand at the doorway between earth and Shamayim and pray for Sâr Janek's journey. Cethra, keep him safe as he sails. Be his eyes and protect him from any evil that comes his way. Mikreh, provide good fortune. Thalassa, give him calm waters. Iamos, heal his wounds. Avenis, restore his beauty. We ask all this for our sâr so that when he stands before Athos's bench, he will be judged fairly."

No mention of the evils Janek had done in his life. How would those be measured?

"Sâr Janek Hadar, the Second Arm, the Amiable, we thank the gods for your life, for being part of our lives, and we ask that they would bless your journey to Shamayim now that our time together has ended. May Yobatha grant you peace and joy in the hereafter. We will not forget you. Go well."

Two King's Guards worked the crank at the boat fall, and Wilek watched over the rail as his brother's death boat lowered to the water. The sea was calm today, after causing so much trouble and perhaps taking several ships into her depths. Wilek wondered where Janek was. If he could see them now. If he had met Arman, and if so, been pardoned or chained in the Lowerworld.

Wilek had never been close to Janek, but watching his death boat drift away, one thing became very clear. Death came to all. It could not be escaped. Wilek had lived most of his life in fear of his father—of death. Yet he had faced Barthos and lived; he had survived the Five Woes and seventy-three days at sea since Bakurah Island. He would no longer be afraid. He would live each day fully so that when his turn came to be shipped away, he would have no regrets.

A cry from the rigging caught his attention. A sailor pointed into the distance, where something bobbed on the water. Wilek left his place at the rail, found Captain Bussie, and urged him to investigate. A half hour later he stood again at the railing, looking down on the wreckage of an Armanian ship.

✦ ✦ ✦

This day would not end. Wilek sat at his desk, eager for the first sleep bells to ring so he could visit Zeroah. He'd barely found a free moment, whether it was investigating the wreckage or presiding over a search of Oli Agoros's cabin and watching the duke dump his evenroot contents into the sea.

Now Admiral Livina had come to deliver his account of the missing ships. There were twenty-two listed. Wilek sat at his desk, a square of parchment anchored on the wood before him. His eyes followed the strokes of the admiral's slanting penmanship, dazed by how the simple shape of a letter could convey such meaning. *Affrany, Colla, Dogstar, Eremon, Fairwing, Gallayah, Intrepid, Luvin, Nightflyer* . . . He read the names slowly, letting it sink in, asking Arman to protect the souls on each vessel. Halfway down he realized that the admiral had alphabetized the list. Such efficiency in a tragic situation felt wrong somehow. He continued reading the ship names until one caught his breath.

"*Rafayah*," Wilek said aloud.

Armania's vice flagship. The ship that Miss Mielle, Trevn, Miss Shemme, and Kal had been on. The ship Miss Mielle had remained on to prepare Miss Shemme's body for shipping.

Miss Mielle was lost.

How could this be? The *Rafayah* had sailed right behind the *Seffynaw* since the day they'd left Everton. How could it have gotten off course?

Arman, why?

Anger welled inside him. Anger at Arman. The Book of Arman said that He Who Made The World was good to those who followed him. "Well?" Wilek said aloud, then spouted off several verses Zeroah had encouraged him to commit to memory:

"Arman delivers his people through the power of his Hand."

"Arman is faithful and will keep his people from evil."

"A man who keeps Arman's decrees shall live."

"The beloved of Arman shall dwell in safety."

"Arman will guard the lives of his faithful servants."

He slapped the desktop, furious. Hadn't he obeyed Arman's prophetess and encouraged his people to flee their homeland, to leave everything behind and trust Arman to lead them to land? He recalled the words Miss Onika had prophesied to Kal.

"The remnant will set sail and begin anew. In northern lands they will give glory to Arman. In the lands beyond the sea they will praise his name."

The remnant had sailed north. So where was the land? "What did I do wrong?" Wilek asked. "Why would you punish me?"

Arman's ways are beyond understanding.

Zeroah's favorite verse came softly. Wilek could not recall the reference, but he pondered the words for a very long time.

In the end the words *did* placate him some. He could not wallow in despair over the lost ships nor could he rail in anger. His father was bedridden aboard the *Kaloday.* Janek was dead. And Wilek would meet with the Wisean Council in a few hours to combat a potential mutiny. He must remain strong. What was left of the fleet looked to him. He must lead well, with confidence and strength.

He would have to tell Miss Amala and Zeroah.

Worse, he would have to tell Trevn. Poor Trevn, his hand maimed, lying in a drugged stupor in his cabin. Wilek wondered if, in his sleep, his brother had felt his soul-bound bride's absence, and if he would wake, thinking it the worst of dreams, only to discover it to be all too real.

Amala

Amala stood with Sârah Hrettah on the main deck, just outside the makeshift ring. They had been watching a swordplay competition between several nobles and guards. The event had been Rosârah Brelenah's idea, intended to lift spirits after so many last rites shippings that morning.

It hadn't.

Who could forget the sight of thirty-two wrapped bodies crammed onto reamskiffs like sausages in a pan? And Sâr Janek—beautiful, agreeable, loveable Sâr Janek—killed by Amala's own guardian! Her eyes teared up just thinking of the injustice and how everyone blamed her.

Life had never been so hopeless, so grim. She desperately wanted to find someone who understood. Someone who didn't care about rules or rank or what anyone thought, the way Sâr Trevn loved her sister. He had married her in secret! So said Sârah Hrettah.

But now Mielle was gone too.

One potential option soothed Amala's despair. Agmado Harton. A week ago Ulmer had introduced them at a practice match on the main deck. Master Harton had won today's swordplay competition easily. He was handsome, spoke kindly to her, and the fact that he had been demoted for disobeying Sâr Wilek proved his independent spirit.

She watched him from across the ring as he spoke with several guards. "Walk with me, Hrettah?" Amala suggested. "I've been standing still too long."

Hrettah readily agreed, and Amala set off toward where Master Harton stood, intent on congratulating him for winning the match.

"I had no idea how talented Master Harton is with a sword," she said to the sârah.

"He'd have to be to have been Wilek's High Shield," Hrettah said. "I heard the maids say Lady Lilou is in love with him."

"I heard that too!" Amala said. "She was arrested, wasn't she?"

"Yes, my brother arrested several on suspicion of treason."

Good. Amala did not think she could compete with a woman as glorious as Lilou Caridod. She frowned, feeling altogether drab and hopeless in her black gown. "I hate wearing black."

"Wearing black to mourn is meant to be an outward display of one's inner feelings," Hrettah said. "I don't much like it either. It reminds me constantly that my mother is gone. But it also reminds others that I am grieving, and people have been very kind. Be thankful we are Armanite and only need wear it for five months. Sarikarians wear black for a full year when they mourn."

But Amala was not mourning. She was angry. Angry at Kal for killing Sâr Janek, angry at Sâr Wilek for ordering Kal's arrest, angry at Kal for running away like a coward, angry at everyone on board the ship for blaming her for Sâr Janek's death. Angry at Mielle, first for marrying Sâr Trevn without inviting her to witness, then for getting lost on the *Rafayah*! What color should one wear to display anger? Red? Amala would do it, if she owned a red gown. She could just imagine the gossip that would fly about the ship at *that* breech of etiquette.

"But there is no proof that the *Rafayah* sank," Amala said. "I am sure it has simply lost its way."

"I hope you are right," Hrettah said.

Of course she was right. Sâr Wilek could fix things if he wanted to. He could send a smaller ship to find the *Rafayah*. He could pronounce Sâr Trevn and Mielle's marriage legal. But he didn't care. And if he didn't care about his own brother . . . Amala did not like that as her warden he now held her future in his hands.

By the time Amala and Hrettah neared Master Harton, he was speaking privately with Kamran DanSâr.

"The cook must have given it to someone," she heard Kamran say. "But none of the guards have been able to find it."

"I would give anything to find it," Harton said.

Amala took Hrettah's arm and stepped up to the men. "Find what?" she asked.

321

The men stared at each other as if they'd been caught telling secrets. Oh, how vexing that they refused to answer.

"It's a bottle of evenroot, isn't it?" Hrettah asked. "I heard Rosârah Brelenah speaking to Wilek about it."

"The cook has given it to someone," Master Harton said, "but she won't say who."

"Cook Hara?" Amala asked.

"She was arrested with the rebels," Hrettah said.

"This is nothing you ladies should worry yourselves with," Kamran said.

But Amala wasn't worried. She believed she knew exactly what they were talking about! Enetta and Hara were old friends. A few weeks ago Amala had overheard the cook give Enetta something for safekeeping. Curious, she'd snooped into Enetta's room and saw that it had been a little vial of white powder. Unimpressed, she'd thought nothing more about it until now. "You're certain it was a bottle? Might it have been something smaller?"

Kamran narrowed his eyes. "Why do you ask?"

She didn't want to say. Not if she could tell Master Harton later in private. He might be rewarded for finding the evenroot, and Amala did not want Kamran taking that away. "I thought evenroot was kept in vials."

"It's kept in both," Kamran said.

"Congratulations on winning the match, Master Harton," Amala said, quickly changing the subject, and Hrettah added her compliments as well.

Many more came to offer Master Harton their praise on his heroic win. Kamran excused himself, but Amala and Hrettah remained on the deck until the crowd thinned. When finally Rosârah Brelenah said they must return to their cabin, Amala made sure to fall behind with the guards.

"Master Harton," she said. "Might I have a private word?"

"I suppose so."

The other guards went on ahead, and Master Harton followed at Amala's side.

Amala chose her words carefully, wanting to prove that she was a woman worth knowing better. "What you said about Cook Hara. I think I might know where the missing evenroot is, though it is a vial, not a bottle. Could that be possible?"

Harton's eyes grew eager. "Yes, where is it?"

She swallowed, hesitant to mention the full truth and be discovered as a snitch. "I don't know if I should say."

He took hold of her arm and pulled her close. He smelled of stale sweat, leather, and metal. "Miss Amala, please. This is very important."

His touch thrilled her yet warred with the fear that she might get caught. "I think I can get it for you. Would that help? Then I wouldn't have to say where I found it."

"That would be perfect. How soon can you get it?"

If she pretended to be ill at dinnertime, she would have the cabin to herself and could search Enetta's room. "Tonight. I think."

He squeezed her arm and his eyebrows sank. "Do your best, Miss Amala. And do not be afraid. I will be waiting right outside your door."

Hinck

Hinck jolted out from his slumber. He sat up, sleepily blinking and wondering what had awakened him when something fell down from the peephole above. Lightweight, the object bounced off his shoulder and landed in the squashed hay that lined the cell's floor. Hinck squinted, unable to see much at all, and felt the floor for the mystery item. His fingers found a scroll of parchment. He picked it up, stood, and looked out the peephole. The corridor was empty and dark but for the distant flicker and sway of a hanging lantern. Hinck unrolled the scroll and held it to the light, straining to read the messy handwriting.

> *You now can see shadir.*
> *Tell no one.*
> *O*

What in all the Eversea did that mean? *O* must mean Oli. Hinck had seen shadir the one time he'd tasted evenroot, and he had no desire to see them again. Before he had time to try to puzzle out what the duke was up to, Fonu called to him from his cell across the corridor.

"Hinck? You still there?"

"Where else would I be?" Hinck had spent four nights in this disgusting cell, which would have been unpleasant in calm seas, but the storm's first massive wave had upended Hinck's privy bucket, and each subsequent wave had tossed Hinck through the soiled hay, and eventually his own vomit as well. It

324

seemed that Sâr Wilek had deserted him as the traitor he'd commanded him to be. Surely the sâr would not let him die just to keep up the ruse?

"I heard a noise," Fonu said. "Thought the guards had come for you. Ragaz says they've been patrolling the corridors all day."

Ragaz. One of Fonu's shadir. Hinck shuddered at the thought of any human communicating with such beasts. "Does Sâr Wilek think we might suddenly find some way to escape?" Hinck asked, because he had examined his door fully and could see no way to gain freedom. It was a pocket door that, when opened, slid into the wall. There were no hinges to be tampered with. No latch or lock on the inside. And from what he could determine from staring out the peephole at Fonu's cell, the mortise lock was low enough that he could not reach it.

"Sâr Wilek thinks we're all mantics," Fonu said. "He knows about the cook's missing root. He'd be a fool to expect we'd sit in our cells and rot."

"But we have done exactly that. For four nights. If we had the root, we would have escaped."

"Ragaz knows who has it. The mystery mantic has bonded with Lilou's shadir."

"Someone had the root? "How is that possible? I thought shadir were loyal."

"Not at all. A shadir can abandon its master at any time, though Ragaz says the man knows Lilou intimately. I expect she must know about the bond."

Hinck tried to work out what that meant. "Are we going to escape?"

"Soon, I think. Ragaz went to talk to Zenobia. When I learn anything new, I'll let you know. Oh, and, Hinck. It's true about Janek. Haroan said they had his shipping today."

Haroan, Fonu's common shadir that looked like a wolf. "Sands," was all Hinck could think to say. Janek killed by Sir Kalenek. Hinck guessed the sâr had finally pushed the wrong man too far.

This also meant that Lady Pia was free.

It was a horrible, selfish thought, and Hinck pushed it aside as he knelt in the hay to destroy Oli's note lest it implicate him. Once he'd dropped the remains into the privy bucket, he had nothing to do but sit in the darkness and ponder his fate.

He must have dozed off because there was a sudden clamor of voices in the corridor. His cell door slid open and Fonu ducked his head inside.

"Get out here. We're going to attack."

Hinck never imagined he'd be reluctant to leave his cell. He pushed to his feet, stepped out into the corridor, and gasped. His memory flashed back to the night he was initiated into the Lahavôtesh.

The hazy forms of shadir drifted around the rebels from the prison cells, bathing the corridor in an eerie glow. A long green one curled like a snake around Lady Zenobia's waist and neck, its tongue flicking into the woman's ear. Lady Mattenelle was speaking with a blue-and-yellow cloud. A third shadir floated through Sir Garn's arm and into Uncle Canbek's back, its gray, catlike face exiting the man's chest just as Fonu said, "Gods, Hinck, you reek."

Trembling, Hinck remembered the note and pretended not to see the creatures, though when the gray drifted near him, he stepped aside to avoid letting it touch him.

The catlike shadir whipped around, coiled in the air, and fixed its beady eyes on Hinck.

"We all reek," Hinck told Fonu, well aware that the gray shadir was still watching him.

"Follow me," Lady Zenobia said. "Our rescuer awaits."

The traitors and their shadir went to the empty room in the hold where they had once met as the Lahavôtesh. Two people were waiting inside the compartment along with a pile of swords. Sârah Zeroah sat on the floor, hands and feet bound, a gag in her mouth. Beside her stood Agmado Harton.

"You?" Fonu asked.

"Mado!" Lilou ran into Harton's arms.

He caught her, pulled her into a kiss, then shoved her away, grimacing. "You're disgusting."

"Well, I like that." Lilou propped a hand on her hip and pouted. "Let's see how you'd smell after spending four nights in the hold."

"We all smell terrible," Lady Mattenelle said.

"Enough!" Zenobia said. "Where is the evenroot?"

"I took it," Harton said.

Zenobia stepped swiftly toward him. "All of it?"

"It was only a small vial," Harton said. "You wanted me to open the cell doors. I did what you asked."

"Surely that didn't require all of your powers," Zenobia said.

"No, but—"

"Then you must capture Sâr Wilek yourself."

"I look forward to it." Harton kicked Sârah Zeroah's leg. "She's expecting a child. Paliki heard her tell the sâr today."

"Are you!" Lilou crouched before Sârah Zeroah. "Congratulations, lady! Now you must listen to us and do everything we say if you want your baby to live." Zeroah nodded.

Hinck recoiled. Too much, too fast. That he could see the shadir, that Harton had joined the traitors and abducted Sârah Zeroah, who was with child! How was he to interfere?

Lady Mattenelle knelt beside Zeroah. "Ignore her," she whispered. "Lilou's just jealous because she can't have a child."

"Pick up a sword, everyone," Fonu said, giving one of the blades a practice thrust into the bulkhead.

Sir Garn handed Hinck and Uncle Canbek each a blade, then crossed swords with Fonu in a mock battle. Should Hinck take advantage of the rebels' relaxed state, try to grab Sârah Zeroah, and make an escape?

"What's the plan?" Sir Jayron asked.

"Sâr Wilek has moved the king to another ship," Zenobia said.

"Which ship?" Sir Garn asked.

"I don't know," Zenobia said. "We must use his wife to get the sâr to talk."

"I thought Isaro was watching him," Fonu said.

"He was, but he did not see Sâr Wilek move the king," Zenobia said.

"He knows we're watching?" Fonu asked.

"Not necessarily," Zenobia said. "He simply might have been exercising caution."

"Why would he hide the king unless he expects an attack?" Sir Jayron asked. "And if he does expect an attack, how could he surmise so much of our plans?"

"Oli is helping him," Fonu spat. "He was there for our interrogations, talking to Sâr Wilek in some kind of message, but the shadir could not puzzle it out."

"Oli is not a mantic," Zenobia said. "He would have no way to learn what we were planning."

"The prophetess," Uncle Canbek said. "The witch has a great shadir on her side."

"But the prophetess claims to serve Arman," Hinck said. "And Arman abhors shadir."

Fonu snorted. "Arman *is* a shadir, Hinck. A great, to be sure, and mighty clever to have set up an entire religion making himself the object of so much devotion. If the prophetess has truly bonded with Arman, we are in for an epic battle."

"It is impossible not to notice her power," Zenobia said, "but this is no time to discuss the prophetess. We will take Sârah Zeroah to the stern deck. That will lure Sâr Wilek to us. Master Harton, lead the way. Sir Jayron, bring up the rear. Lilou, untie Sârah Zeroah's feet so she can walk, then you and Lord Dacre keep hold of her. It's time to take this ship for Moon Fang and the King of Magic."

✦ ✦ ✦

It all seemed like a dream to Hinck, enhanced by the strange glow of what could only be the Veil between worlds. He followed the group, trying to ignore the shadir that flew among them like birds. He kept hold of Sârah Zeroah's right arm. Her skin felt silky under his grimy hand, and he regretted that he might leave his stench upon her. She glared at him several times, and he wished he might pull her aside and confess that he was her husband's spy. Instead he traipsed along the carpenter's walk to the stern with the other traitors, then up four flights of stairs until they exited on the quarterdeck.

Then it became real.

Ever since Trevn had sent Hinck to Janek, spying had terrified him. But he had done it, had learned to play a part in order to help his sârs Trevn and Wilek keep the realm safe. This time was different. When Hinck stepped out onto the quarterdeck, people saw him holding Sârah Zeroah's arm and walking with traitors, waving a sword for everyone to get out of his way. He moved in a haze of horror, knowing that he could never return to life as it had been. To the people of Armania—to Sârah Zeroah, the future queen—Hinckdan Faluk was a traitor.

They made their way up to the stern deck and claimed a section at the taffrail, waving nobles back with their swords. Men cursed them. Women screamed and ran away. A few guards tried to engage, but Harton used his magic and with a muttered word sent their blades flying over the rail.

Lady Zenobia demanded that Sâr Wilek come to the aid of his bride. Several guards scurried off with the message, and there they waited.

The crowd began to heckle them.

"Let the lady go!"

"Hasn't the sâr's wife been through enough?"

"What do you want with the sâr?"

"He's doing the best he can for all of us."

"Not for me!" Harton yelled. "I served him well. I saved his life time and again. I killed for him. I obeyed his every order. And I never questioned his reasoning. But I made one mistake and he cast me aside."

"You abandoned your post, Harton." This from Captain Veralla, who was standing at the top of the stairs to the quarterdeck. "Any soldier knows that is grounds for dismissal."

Harton pushed past Hinck and hooked his arm around Sârah Zeroah's neck, pinning her in the crook of his elbow. He held a dagger to her side. "Where is our sâr-regent?" he yelled. "Is he too cowardly to come forward and save his wife and unborn child?"

A new wave of murmurs passed through the crowd. People looked at each other and Sârah Zeroah, exclaiming in wonder.

"Release her." Sâr Wilek stepped out from the cluster of guards at the stairs, his expression fierce. Novan, Rystan, and Oli followed behind. "It's me you want, Hart. Let the lady go."

"On one condition," Harton said, jerking Zeroah close. "We settle this, the two of us. With swords."

"That's not the plan, Master Harton," Lady Zenobia said. "Immobilize him now. Use your magic."

"I will not use magic!" Harton yelled. "I want to fight him."

"You don't have the skill to defeat me with a sword," Wilek said.

Harton pushed Sârah Zeroah back to Hinck and lifted his blade. "Let's find out, shall we?"

Wilek wore no sword. He reached his arm toward Novan, who refused at first. Wilek motioned again, muttering something under his breath, and this time the shield drew his blade and tossed it to the sâr.

As the two men squared off, Sârah Zeroah began to mumble, eyes closed as if in prayer.

Wilek tried to circle, to get Harton to turn with him, but Harton was too clever to put his back to the sea of onlookers and guards. He maintained his position and lashed out to keep Wilek from advancing.

Wilek parried the blow calmly. "Arman has shown me favor, Hart," he said. "I am not afraid of you or your friends." He gestured to Hinck and the others.

"You should be," Harton said. He swung down on Wilek's head.

The sâr deflected the strike.

Harton twirled his sword up and slashed across Wilek's middle. Wilek blocked, spun, and crouched back into his ready stance.

It appeared that Sâr Wilek would not attack full on. He was keeping a hold on his temper, going carefully, one stroke at a time.

Hinck had watched Wilek and Harton spar before on the practice field in Everton. And while he had never seen Harton defeat the sâr, one never knew if a subordinate hadn't the skill to win or if he lost on purpose to gain favor with his master.

Beside Hinck, Sârah Zeroah continued to pray, now speaking with her full voice. "Be his shield, his refuge, his stronghold. Save him from violence that comes against him. Save him from his enemy."

Harton sliced downward. Wilek countered and darted aside.

Harton swung across the neck. This time Wilek knelt on one knee and cut for Harton's waist, his first offensive strike.

Harton jumped out of the way, but the tip of the sâr's blade whisked though his tunic, bringing a cheer from the crowd.

This only enraged Harton, who came after Wilek with fury in his gray eyes. He chopped his blade almost like an axe, growling as he did. Wilek staved off each attack, and while his crumpled brow glistened, he seemed to be exerting little effort in comparison.

Harton came at the sâr from the right, the left, above, below, straight on. Wilek repelled each blow. The clash of their swords and their lunging steps made a steady rhythm that appeared to have no end. Until Harton took several steps back. He swung his blade before him to keep Wilek away while he caught his breath.

"He will cover you with his feathers," Zeroah yelled, "armored and protected in the shelter of his wings. He is your hiding place. In his arms he protects you from the attacks of your enemy."

"Shut her up!" Harton yelled at Hinck, then screamed and ran at Wilek, sword raised.

Hinck pulled Zeroah back from the fray. "Lady, we should seize this moment to flee," he whispered.

She narrowed her eyes, keeping them focused on Wilek. "I will not abandon him."

Harton and Sâr Wilek fought hard, the sâr mostly defending. Harton attacked with a series of strokes Hinck had never seen before. Something about his footwork reminded Hinck of Sir Jayron and Rurekan Igote guards. He suspected Harton had decided to pull from his past in hopes of surprising the sâr with something he'd never seen before.

It made no difference. Wilek's blade made two more cuts on Harton, while Harton had yet to touch the sâr. Harton lunged. Wilek twirled his sword around Harton's blade and knocked it out of his hand. He pressed the point of his sword against Harton's chest. The crowd roared, lauding their sâr.

"Guards," Wilek said. "Arrest Master Harton and his associates and—"

"*Yaph!*" Harton yelled.

A pink shadir shot out from the cluster of traitors and knocked Wilek's sword from his grasp. To everyone else it would have looked like the blade had jumped out of Wilek's hand. It clattered on the deck by Sir Jayron's feet. The man picked it up.

Harton retrieved his own sword and pointed it at Wilek.

"You said no magic!" Novan yelled, stepping toward them.

The onlookers crowed and yelled their agreement.

Harton waved his free hand at Novan and again yelled, "*Yaph!*"

The pink shadir plowed into Novan, knocking the shield back into the crowd. Women screamed. People scattered. Two crouched to help Novan.

"Stop messing around, Hart," Fonu said. "Use your magic to make the sâr tell us where he took the king."

"He's stalling," Oli said, stepping out from the circle of onlookers. "He has little magic left."

"What do you know about it?" Harton asked.

"Go," Oli whispered.

A white shadir flew from behind Oli's arm and snatched Harton's sword.

The crowd gasped as the sword flew through the air and dropped into the sea.

Harton gaped after it. "How did you . . . ?"

Oli stepped closer. "Pick him up."

The white shadir zipped toward Harton and lifted him into the sky, above all their heads.

Harton screamed, limbs flailing. "Don't! Make it put me down!"

"Very well," Oli said. "Drop him."

The shadir released Harton, who fell and landed, back first, against the deck. Hinck cringed as Harton's head bounced off the deck and the man passed out.

Oli was a mantic? How?

The crowd cheered. Guards rushed in, swords drawn.

"Kill Sâr Wilek!" Lady Zenobia screamed.

The traitors lifted their swords, but only three advanced. Uncle Canbek and the women stayed put along the rail, while Fonu, Sir Jayron, and Sir Garn engaged the guards. Hinck wanted to get Sârah Zeroah away from the fighting and pulled her toward the stairs.

Something hard struck the back of his head and he staggered. Sârah Zeroah was taken from his hands. Another strike knocked him to the deck. A sword pricked his back.

"You will stay right there, Lord Dacre," Rystan said. "Or I will make you bleed."

Hinck's head throbbed, but he watched as the shadir swooped and shrieked. They seemed to be enjoying themselves in spite of their masters' impending failure. Uncle Canbek lay in a pool of blood. How he'd been struck while hiding with the women, Hinck couldn't guess. Novan stabbed Sir Garn, who tripped over Harton's feet when he collapsed. The guards swarmed, disarmed Sir Jayron, and seized the women.

"You will all serve my master when he defeats Sâr Wilek," Fonu yelled, then threw himself over the taffrail.

Several guards rushed to the rail, looking over. Hinck had no idea what they saw. He looked for Oli and found him lying on the deck, eyes locked with the white shadir, mumbling a petition of purging.

Rystan bound Hinck's hands and roused him to his feet. "Back to the hold with you," the young duke said.

Caught by a boy. Hinck should be humiliated, but compared to the entire realm thinking him a traitor, such a thing didn't really matter.

Until Hinck was marched past his father, who looked upon him as one whose heart has been ripped from his chest.

WILEK

I request we postpone any trial until we reach land," Kamran said.

"And give the mantic traitors time to find more evenroot so they can attack again?" Wilek asked. "Do you take me for a fool?"

In the aftermath of the skirmish, Wilek had gathered Rayim, Novan, Dendrick, and what remained of his Wisean Council in the captain's dining room for a quick vote to sentence the traitors, but it was already taking longer than necessary to reach a consensus. And Kamran's presence here, rather than in the hold where he belonged, annoyed Wilek deeply.

"Everyone knows there is no evenroot on board," Kamran said. "They can do no harm in the hold."

"Master Harton found evenroot," Danek said. "As did Duke Canden."

"Yes, *Oli*," Kamran said. "Where *did* you get your evenroot?"

"Kamran shouldn't be here," Oli said. "His mother's involvement in all this is a conflict of interest."

"Nor should I be here either, by that logic," Danek said. "My son is also involved with these traitors, though I cannot fathom why. I apologize again, Your Highness." He paused to compose himself, but when he spoke again, his voice trembled. "I don't know what has come over him."

"Oli has broken the law by his use of evenroot," Kamran said. "He should be in the hold with the other mantics."

"He saved the sâr's life!" Rayim said.

"Magic is still against the law, is it not, Sâr Wilek?" Kamran asked.

Wilek rubbed his face. "We will discuss Duke Canden's infractions another time. Right now I want to deal with the traitors in the hold. I intend to execute them first thing in the morning."

"A wise decision, Your Highness," Rayim said. "One should not harbor dissidents for long."

"I agree in theory, Your Highness," Danek said, "but wouldn't it be fairest to conduct individual trials?"

"Would that change the outcome?" Novan asked. "If all are guilty in any way of plotting a mutiny, shouldn't they all hang?"

"Indeed they should," Rayim said.

"But if some were coerced . . ." Danek said.

"Hinckdan is guilty, Highcliff," Kamran said. "He dragged Sârah Zeroah up onto the stern deck himself. I saw it with my own eyes."

Danek buried his head in his arms and began to sob.

Wilek took a steadying breath. The situation with Hinckdan had gotten out of control. Perhaps it was time to confess the young earl was his spy. He certainly wasn't going to let Hinckdan hang. "I blame myself for the earl's involvement. The truth is, I sent him to—"

"—to Sâr Janek as a backman, we know, Your Highness," Oli said, meeting his eyes. "But you could not have known what it was like to be part of Janek's crowd. If anyone is to blame, let it be me for not warning Hinckdan to take caution."

What was Oli playing at now? Why would he want Wilek to keep Hinckdan's status as a spy a secret? He supposed another few hours would make little difference. "Let's recess until dawn," Wilek said. "I will have Captain Rayim question everyone again tonight and inform them they are to be executed in the morning. Perhaps such an appointment will inspire any hidden truths to be revealed."

"Your merciful nature is a comfort, Your Highness," Danek said.

Being known for mercy would not make Wilek feared by his enemies. He only hoped he would not regret stalling a bit longer. "Dendrick and Rayim, remain behind with Duke Canden. We must discuss his crimes next. Novan, stand guard outside. The rest of you are dismissed. If I determine there is reason to conduct individual trials, I will inform you at dawn."

Everyone moved to obey. When Novan closed the door behind the last of them, Wilek folded his arms and regarded Oli Agoros, who sat at the end of the table on the right. "Why did you stop me from—"

"Six, Your Highness," Oli said. "There are six traitors in the hold who must be sentenced."

Wilek shivered, catching on to Oli's message. There were four men present, which meant two shadir had entered the room. They could not have a private conversation if the creatures were here listening. Or did it matter? If the mantics had no evenroot, what could the enemy gain by eavesdropping?

"Might you have some ink and parchment?" Oli asked.

Hope kindled in Wilek's chest. He waved at Dendrick, who brought forth both and set them on the table before Oli.

Wilek couldn't wait. He rose and went to watch over Oli's shoulder as he wrote.

If you reveal Hinck as a spy, he will be killed at some point by one of Rogedoth's people.

Oli glanced up, peering from Wilek to Rayim to Dendrick until all three men had read his words, then flipped over the parchment and continued writing.

My shadir made Hinck a seer. If he were to escape before his execution, he could go to Rogedoth and—

Wilek interrupted Oli's writing. "Now *that* would kill him," he said. "You can't be serious."

"I have to agree with the duke, Your Highness," Rayim said. "If he stays here, he's already dead. At least this way he has a chance."

Could that be true? Wilek had already asked too much of Hinckdan Faluk. Sending him to Rogedoth seemed downright cruel. "Why did you do this?" he asked Oli. "For that matter, you continued to take evenroot after I forbade it and used your shadir to do magic when you attacked Harton. How much root do you still have?"

"One flask."

"Give it to me now."

Oli reached for his belt, hesitated, then removed his hip flask and handed it over.

"Such carelessness risks Arman's wrath against our realm." Wilek walked to the window and dumped the contents. When he turned back, Oli was on his feet, staring longingly out the window.

"The evenroot is gone, Duke Canden," Wilek said. "Now why did you disobey me?"

Oli slowly took his seat again. "I thought it was what you wanted."

"I specifically said it was not!" Wilek said.

"Forgive me, Your Highness, but your exact words were, '*It is an order I cannot give.*'"

"Sounds clear to me," Wilek said.

"Yet a misunderstanding remains," Oli said. "My father has said as much to me or his men time and again. Those words meant that while he could not ask me aloud for the sake of his reputation or the law, he wanted me to act anyway. It is a common practice in the military when something of questionable morals needs to be done."

Wilek turned his attention on Rayim. "Is that true?"

"Not all officers make use of the practice, but it happens," Rayim said.

How did Wilek not know of this? Because he was the Dutiful. No one would have dared suggest such a thing to him. "It is now a forbidden practice," he said. "If something is of questionable morality, the Book of Arman will give us our answer. Is that understood, Captain?"

"Yes, Your Highness," Rayim said. "I will see that word is passed through the ranks."

Wilek would have to do so much more to retrain his people. He needed the nation to submit to Arman, to obey his decrees. But how?

He would have to think on it. There had to be a way.

In the meantime he would execute the traitors, then get his father back aboard the *Seffynaw*. But first he needed to get a message to Hinckdan Faluk, and if the shadir were watching, he must take care how he communicated the possibility of sending the earl into the enemy's lair. No matter what options were presented, he would let Hinckdan choose for himself how he would like to proceed.

Wilek would force him no longer.

HINCK

Hinck sat leaning against one corner of his new prison cell. Captain Veralla himself had brought him here, and without speaking a word, Hinck could tell from the gentle way the man had handled him that he knew Hinck was Wilek's spy.

Yet hours later, here he remained, haunted by the look on his father's face when he realized his only son was a traitor.

Hinck's new cell was no bigger than his last had been, but it had a clean privy bucket, fresh hay covered the floor, and a warm tub of seawater and a hard bar of soap had been waiting when he'd first arrived. He'd wasted no time dousing his head and scrubbing his face and hair. The salt water had made his skin tight and grimy, but he'd felt so refreshed that he'd tried to wash the rest of himself too. Sadly, Captain Veralla had not thought to bring Hinck fresh clothes, though he supposed that would have looked suspicious should he be questioned again.

They had separated the traitors this time. With two dead and Fonu overboard, there were only five left imprisoned—six counting Agmado Harton. Hinck bet they were none of them near each other.

To pass the time, he sang to himself and recited his favorite plays. Someone shoved a meal under the door. A tray of warm food as fresh as one could get aboard the *Seffynaw* these days. Again Hinck suspected Sâr Wilek was trying to make up for the unfortunate situation.

He was mumbling the words to *Magon's Betrayal* when the lock of his cell clicked and the door slid aside. He straightened, expecting to see Captain Veralla or Sâr Wilek, but the lithe, black-clad female who entered was far more welcome.

Lady Pia slid the door closed behind her and knelt at his side, facing him. "I am told you can see shadir."

"Oli put a spell on me, apparently. And here I thought he was my friend."

"He is a better friend than you think. Do you see any now?"

"No. I haven't seen any since Captain Veralla put me here. I think the guards spread us out so far apart that the shadir can't remember where we all are."

"Listen well, poet. You are in the fore of the ship. Here is a key to the cells." She placed a cold piece of metal against his palm. "Lady Mattenelle is in the first cell on the left, just before the stairs. You are to rescue her and take her to the boat fall where Sâr Wilek has arranged there to be no guards."

"Why her?"

"It was my idea. I thought people might think it sweet when they heard that the Earl of Dacre had run away with one of Sâr Janek's concubines."

Was she joking? "That's not very funny."

"You're so serious, Lord Dacre. The truth is, it would look suspicious if only you escaped. Sâr Wilek feels he can part with Nellie since she is useless to Rogedoth now that Sâr Janek is dead."

"What about the others?"

"Our Dutiful sâr wants to watch them hang before he eats his breakfast."

Hinck shivered as he pictured the scene in his mind. "And where am I going? Another ship?"

"Of course you must board any ship if you become desperate, but Sâr Wilek hopes that you might consider boarding the *Amarnath*."

Hinck sputtered. "Rogedoth's ship?"

"Oli thinks Nellie could ask her shadir to lead you there. If you can keep up the ruse long enough that you are one of them, you might yet be able to help stop Rogedoth."

"If . . . might . . . I don't know if I can act well enough to fool Rogedoth."

"Shh, I'm not finished. If you'd rather not do this, Sâr Wilek will admit to all that you are his spy. That would free you from your prison cell and give you back your life. But Kamran and the shadir would know the truth, and word would eventually get to Rogedoth."

"He'd kill me. Or send someone to."

"That is our fear as well. Sâr Wilek leaves the choice to you."

Hinck could only laugh at the ridiculousness of his *choice*. "Oh, how thoughtful."

"Isn't it? I rather like Sâr Wilek as a ruler."

"How would I get in contact with Sâr Wilek if I learn anything important?"

"I knew you would go." Her fingernails lightly scratched up the back of his neck and into his hair. Her touch soothed his frazzled nerves. "I have never met a braver man than you, Hinckdan Faluk."

He chuckled darkly. "Truth is, I'm terrified to do this."

"Yet you do it anyway. That's what makes you brave." She kissed the side of his neck, his ear. Her warm breath tickled and he shrugged away.

"Lady Pia, I'm fairly disgusting."

He heard a smile in her voice when she said, "Yes, you were always the fashionable one, weren't you? Which drives you madder—being locked up or covered in filth?"

He contemplated. "It's a draw."

"Janek is dead and still we cannot be together."

Hinck could not answer that. It was too horrible to think about. All of it.

"Everything about our circumstances has the stench of waste," Pia said, then kissed him full on the mouth. With lips still touching, she asked, "How was that for poetry?"

He smiled against her. "That's not poetry, really, though the double meaning is clever."

"Listen to me," she said, tone commanding while she splayed her hands on either side of his face. "If you must carry on a romance with Nellie to keep up your ruse, I will not hold it against you."

He shook his head. "No, I couldn't—"

She set her forehead against his. "Do not argue. I want you to live, and Rogedoth will test you. You must behave like them. There is no room for a kind, gentle poet in their society."

"I don't wish to go."

"This is the only way to keep you safe. Oli says not to take any evenroot and not to let them know you can see shadir. You can do this. I believe in you, Lord Dacre."

"Call me Hinck?"

"I believe in you, Hinck." And she kissed him for a very long time.

When she finally stood to leave, he grabbed her arm. "I want Sâr Wilek to tell my parents that I'm no traitor. Please?"

"If Sâr Wilek refuses, I will make sure they learn the truth somehow."

"Thank you, lady."

She kissed the top of his head. "Until next time, sweet poet."

She left the door cracked open behind her. Hinck glared at the dim stripe of light, tired of longing for things he could never have.

Fool! He had thought that in denying himself Lady Pia he would protect his heart from another disaster like Eudora. Yet here he sat, alone and without hope. No, not fully without hope. "*Until next time*," she had said.

Hinck doubted there would be one.

✦   ✦   ✦

Lady Mattenelle went eagerly with Hinck, clinging to his arm with every step.

"Is your shadir with you?" he asked, leading her up the fore companionway.

"No," she said. "Why?"

"I was hoping it could lead our boat to the *Amarnath*."

"We're leaving the ship?"

"I heard a guard say we're to be hanged in the morning."

"Oh!"

"Shh," he said.

"How did you get out?"

"The guard who put me in the cell didn't fully latch the door. A piece of wood was wedged in the crack. I didn't even notice it until my dinner came."

"You had dinner?"

Oops. "You didn't?"

"No. Where are the others?"

"I came around the corner just as you were being put into your cell. I don't know where anyone else is. If we go right now, I think we can escape. But you don't have to come with me if you don't want to."

She squeezed his arm tighter, eyes round and shadir-like. "I'm coming with you."

They continued on, slowing when they reached the foredeck. Hinck listened, heard no voices, peeked out, saw no one. He pulled Lady Mattenelle toward the boat fall, then helped her over the rail.

How was he supposed to lower the boat if they were inside it?

He was studying the crank when someone slid the flat of a sword along the side of his neck. He choked in a deep breath, then dodged to the left and over the rail.

Now standing in the boat, he looked on his attacker. Kamran DanSâr? And behind him his mother, Lady Zenobia, with Lilou Caridod, Agmado Harton, Sir Jayron, and . . .

"Miss Amala?" Hinck said.

"She is helping us," Kamran said.

"But why?" Hinck asked.

"Because she knows Sâr Wilek will ruin Armania," Kamran said, tweaking her chin. "What are you doing here, Hinck? How did you get out?"

"Got lucky," Hinck said. "Thanks for coming for us."

"We could say the same to you," Sir Jayron said.

They glared at each other until Miss Amala's voice broke the silence.

"Why did you bring *her*?" Amala asked Kamran, glaring at Lilou as Harton helped the king's young mistress into the boat.

"We couldn't leave anyone behind for the sâr to kill, could we?" Kamran said.

"Except for me and Lord Dacre, apparently," Lady Mattenelle said.

"We came for you, Nellie, but you were gone."

"And Lord Dacre?" she asked. "You came for him too?"

"No," Kamran said. "I do not trust Lord Dacre."

"Well I do!" She folded her arms and glared out at the dark sea.

"Nellie, don't be cross," Kamran said, but she did not respond to his plea.

"When will I see you all again?" Amala asked, glancing at Harton.

"I am not going anywhere," Kamran said. "We will see the others when we reach land."

"But . . ." Amala gave another longing look to Harton as he climbed into the dinghy. "Can't I go with you?"

"I need you here," Kamran said, putting his arm around her. "Get in the boat, Mother. Miss Amala and I will lower it."

Hinck watched Kamran and Amala work the cranks, nervous now that the other four had joined Mattenelle and him in the boat. When he finally lowered his gaze to those seated around him, he caught sight of the first shadir, a great golden bird hovering beside Lady Zenobia as it whispered into her ear. Hinck couldn't tell whether or not the woman heard, for she made no response.

The dinghy reached the water, splashing a few cold drops onto Hinck's arm.

"Unhook the other end," Sir Jayron said to Hinck.

He got up to obey, and soon the pulley lines sailed into the air. Hinck inched back to his seat beside Lady Mattenelle, but just as he settled down again, Lady Zenobia gave an order.

"Take up the oars, men. We have a long way to go."

341

WILEK

Wilek woke the next morning to news that—save Cook Hara—all of the prisoners had escaped. Livid, he summoned Lady Pia, who swore Hinckdan had understood his instructions perfectly. Wilek had no reason to doubt her. He hadn't told her where the others were being kept, nor could Hinckdan have known. Someone else must have helped them escape. Wilek had a guess who and hoped he might catch Kamran in some nefarious behavior very soon.

"Is that all, Your Highness?" Lady Pia asked.

"What happens to you now that Janek is gone?"

She curtsied. "My life is yours to command. Consider my training and your needs. How can I best serve you?"

She best served as a spy. Who did Wilek need to spy on now that Janek and all the traitors were gone?

Kamran DanSâr.

It felt wrong to ask such a thing of a woman not yet a full week free of Janek, but he took up a fresh sheet of parchment, in case any shadir were lurking about, and wrote:

I believe Kamran DanSâr is one of the traitors. I would like to catch him in his treachery. Could you become his concubine?

She nodded. "I know him well. He preferred Mattenelle, but with her gone, he will not refuse me." She left in a swirl of robes, and Wilek felt glad to have her on his side.

But as the day wore on, Wilek had doubts about his choice. What would

Zeroah have said if she knew what he'd done? There was likely another way to capture Kamran, though Wilek could not think of one.

Reluctantly, he ordered Cook Hara's execution. He hated to do it, knowing she had been defending her daughter's memory, but Wilek could not pardon a conspiracy to kill the king. Once that was done, he sent Rayim and a squadron of King's Guards to bring the king back to the *Seffynaw*, then ordered the signalmen to relay messages to the rest of the fleet about the prisoners' escape. Three squadrons of guards searched the *Seffynaw* for clues. None were found.

Waiting for morning to execute the traitors had been a risk. Wilek couldn't believe he'd cleared the deck for Hinckdan and made it easy for the others. Hinckdan's life was worth the lost prisoners, though, and they could not be so valuable to Rogedoth with Janek gone. He consoled himself that there should be no more shadir aboard the *Seffynaw*, save whatever creature Oli had secured. Though now that Oli's root juice had finally been disposed of, even that creature should move on eventually.

Wilek's father returned, nearly catatonic. By the time Wilek saw him resituated in the king's cabin, he caught himself wishing the man would die. Thoughts of mercy killings flitted through his head, but that would be too charitable for a man who had killed so many innocents. Wilek supposed the king should suffer as long as Arman willed it.

He left the king and found Dendrick waiting for him with Master Granlee, the navigator, who informed Wilek that they had finally lost sight of Nivanreh's Eye last night. While this seemed to upset the navigator, the news filled Wilek with hope. They could no longer be steered by the superstitions of the past. The future lay before them now, unhindered.

At lunch Zeroah mentioned that it might be time for Wilek to tell Trevn about the missing ship.

With the storm and the traitors, Wilek had ordered Rayim to keep Trevn sedated for his own safety. Twice now his brother had woken and stumbled from his bed, desperate to fetch Miss Mielle from the *Rafayah*. He must have sensed her absence. As Zeroah said, now was the time.

Wilek set out for his private cabin. He had insisted Trevn be kept there since the room had a framed bed, which was easier to get in and out of than Trevn's hanging cot. He found Sir Cadoc standing outside the door, eyes drooping. Wilek set his hand on Cadoc's shoulder, and the shield jumped to attention and grabbed the hilt of his sword.

"My pardon, Your Highness," Cadoc said, yawning. "Might you send a trusted guard or two to relieve me for a few hours?"

"After my visit," Wilek said. "How is he?"

"Awake but half dazed from so much soporific. He woke last night, tried to dress himself, ordered Captain Veralla to prepare the boat fall so he could look for Mielle. The captain got him sedated again, and I put him back to bed. He awoke again just a few minutes ago and tried to leave, so I've locked him in. He is not happy about it."

"He wanted to go to the boat fall again?"

"This time to the mainmast. Said if he could get to the crow's nest, he'd find the ship that everyone was too blind to see."

"He's heard the news, then?"

"Ottee told him a day or two ago when he was conscious," Cadoc said. "That boy has a bigger mouth on him than the Bay of Jeruka."

Immense relief filled Wilek at one nasty job he didn't have to do. "How did he take it?"

Cadoc snorted. "First he railed at Ottee for jokes of bad taste and dismissed him from his service as onesent. The boy ran off in tears and hasn't returned. Then the sâr kept trying to leave and see for himself. He demanded to speak with you a few times. I told him you'd be here when you could, and he didn't like that. Captain Veralla and I have done a fair job of keeping him sedated. The captain says his hand is healing well."

"Thank you, Sir Cadoc."

Wilek went inside. The sunlight coming in the curtained window cast a golden haze over the room. Trevn was sitting up in bed, propped against a half-dozen pillows, a tray of food balanced on his lap. His body was leaning drastically to the right, his head drooping so low it looked uncomfortable. Sleeping.

Wilek examined his brother's hand, which lay on top of the blanket at his side. The swelling had gone almost completely down. Captain Veralla had said that only two fingers had been broken, but all four fingers were splinted and had turned a deep purple shade that was quite ghastly.

"I must find the *Rafayah*."

Wilek lifted his gaze to Trevn's face. His brother's eyes were puffy and lidded. "You must stay in bed until you are well."

"Would you?"

Wilek glanced at the shell marking on Trevn's palm, remembering the pull

Charlon had on him when they'd been soul-bound. "Can you feel her? Hear her thoughts?" Wilek asked. "There were times when I could do that with Charlon."

With one purpled finger Trevn traced along the shell lines on his embossed hand. "We are too far apart to hear thoughts," he said. "When I came to the *Seffynaw* just before the storm, I noticed that distance changes the magic."

"Yes, I remember that," Wilek said. It had been both a blessing and a curse.

"My chest aches constantly, like it did when Father Tomek died. I cannot hear her, though I sense she is worried. No. She thinks *I* am worried."

"That's good, then," Wilek said. "I don't think you would feel like that if she were—" He stopped himself. "We're keeping a close watch on the seas. It's likely that the missing ships were merely blown off course. Perhaps they will soon find their way back to us."

A quiet knock and Rayim entered, tiny black box in hand.

Trevn's gaze fixed on the box and his face crumpled. "No," he pleaded. "I don't want to sleep anymore. Please don't make me."

But Rayim set about pricking Trevn in the neck. "Another day. Maybe two. It's for the best," he said.

Trevn moaned, shook his head as if trying to scare off a fly. "Mielle . . ."

Plagued by feelings of guilt, Wilek sat with Trevn until he fell asleep. He could not bring himself to mention any of the happenings of the past week with Janek's shipping and the traitors. And Hinckdan . . . Wilek would have to tell Trevn about that at some point.

"Under no circumstances should Sâr Trevn be left alone, Sir Cadoc," Wilek said. "Make sure that any guards who relieve you know that." His brother was probably a greater danger to himself at present than Kamran was to their father. "I'll ask my mother if she and the sârahs might take turns sitting with him until we convince Ottee he wasn't dismissed permanently."

"It will be done, Your Highness," Cadoc said.

Wilek departed for his mother's cabin. He left Novan with the honor maidens and the pack of tiny dogs and retreated with his mother into her bedchamber for a private talk.

"I am sorry that the prisoners got away," she said. "It is a frustrating defeat. But you must give yourself some grace. Both you and Sâr Trevn are grieving. You have lost people dear to you. Such an experience is not so easily overcome."

"Who have I lost? Surely you don't mean Janek?"

She frowned. "I mean Sir Kalenek."

The name tightened Wilek's chest. Kal had been slowly weaned away from

Wilek—first by his resignation—but now he was gone completely, and thinking of the man made it difficult to breathe. Perhaps his mother was right.

"I don't know how to grieve." When Lebetta had died, he'd kept busy, and with the Woes, before he'd realized it, months had passed and the pain no longer stabbed. "I wish he hadn't confessed. If I didn't know what he'd intended, it would have been easier."

"We all make choices," Mother said, "but they do not define us. Besides, he is not dead, so you don't have to let go completely. Think of him as being on a special mission for you, like when you sent him into Magonia. Ask Arman to watch over him. To help him in that dark place."

"That is a good idea." And not so far from the truth.

"You should also talk about him. Tell Zeroah stories about some of your exploits together. These things will help, little by little. Just remember, you never stop grieving death. You learn to live with it. Grief is not an illness; it's a transition."

Wilek thought of Chadek, his brother who had been sacrificed to Barthos at age ten. Though the memory of his brother on that platform still haunted him, the pain hadn't flared for years. Still, that experience had shaped everything about the rest of Wilek's life.

"I'm worried about Trevn. If we never recover Miss Mielle, with the soul-binding spell he might never learn to live with his grief. I've dealt with that magic. I know how it feels."

"Arman's ways are beyond understanding," Mother said, chilling Wilek with the same words Zeroah liked to say. "We might not understand now why these things happened, we might never understand, but we will survive."

Wilek hoped so. For all their sakes.

TREVN

Trevn awoke recalling a dream about riding the roof of a carriage with Mielle. The memory brought a smile to his face until the familiar ache reminded him that she was gone.

Every day since Ottee had told him the *Rafayah* was missing, it had been the same. For a few blissful seconds he would wake, not yet remembering, and for the space of a breath or two, life would seem normal.

But it wasn't.

Wilek had told him about Hinck and all that had happened while he slept, and there was still no sign of the *Rafayah*.

He felt Mielle's concern rise up in the back of his mind. *I'm fine.* He tried to think calming thoughts.

His distance from Mielle was slowly killing something inside him, and being confined to his room didn't help. Wilek had agreed to stop sedating him and let him out of the cabin if he promised not to leave the ship. So Trevn had promised, yet his oath plagued him. He daydreamed about commandeering a smaller ship from the fleet and taking it out to look for the *Rafayah*, certain the soul-binding would work like magnets and lead them to each other.

Trevn climbed from bed and didn't bother to wake Ottee as he dressed in his blacks. He forced himself from the room and met Cadoc outside. The man's eyes were red, and he looked exhausted.

"Is something wrong, Cadoc?" he asked.

"I was thinking of my parents, Your Highness."

Trevn felt ashamed. He had been so absorbed in his own grief that he had forgotten Cadoc's parents had been aboard the *Rafayah*. "The ship did not go down, my friend," he said. "If Mielle had died, I would have felt it. Trust the Magonian's magic in me as proof of that."

Cadoc merely nodded. Trevn set off for the king's galley. There he grabbed a handful of rolls, then made his way topside. The best thing he could do was to continue his apprenticeship and help Wilek find land. Once their people had a safe place to live, Trevn could focus on finding Mielle. And Cadoc's parents.

Captain Bussie sent Trevn to shadow the carpenter and caulker. These men he found on the carpenter's walk, patching up leaks gained after the storm. Trevn's hand kept him from helping, and he soon wandered topside again. Trevn hated the sympathetic looks people gave him. His blacks were for mourning Janek, not Mielle. People thought Mielle was dead, but she was not dead. He would know.

On the quarterdeck Bonds and Rzasa were splicing rope into pieces long enough to use for sheets and halyards.

"Boots!" Bonds hollered. "Come end an argument. Now that we no longer see Nivanreh's Eye, half the ship is certain we will sail off the edge of the sea."

"I never said the world was flat," Rzasa said. "Everyone knows it's a bowl."

Trevn sat cross-legged on the deck, happy to distract his mind with intellectual pursuits. He'd been intrigued by the new north-guiding stars. Rather than sitting at their backs as Nivanreh's Eye had, the trio rose before them like a beacon. To him this was proof that the world was spherical. But he must use a different type of logic with Rzasa. "The sun and moon and stars all appear to travel around us in circular fashion. It's the same every day."

"Which means the bowl's round," Rzasa said. "Doesn't mean it's a ball."

"When a ship is at the horizon, its hull is obscured due to the curvature of the earth," Trevn said. "That is all that has happened with Nivanreh's Eye."

Rzasa, who was also sitting cross-legged, smoothed out a wrinkle in his red socks. "If we've traveled over the side of the world, why haven't we fallen off?"

"Because we are on the surface of the sphere," Trevn said, "and the nature of most objects pulls them toward the Lowerworld, which exists in the sphere's center. Very few substances rise toward Shamayim. Smoke does. And steam."

"Cotton?" Bonds asked.

"No," Trevn said. "Cotton floats on the wind, but when there is no wind, it falls to the earth like any of us."

A shadow fell over Trevn. "Hey, Boots," Nietz said. "Cap'n wants you to go help Master Bylar in the forward hold."

"The world is a sphere," Trevn said, standing. "And it will soon carry us to land. I promise you."

✦ ✦ ✦

He found the steward in the forward hold working on an assessment of the cargo. The man had started in the aft and was nearly finished by the time Trevn arrived. This compartment was filled with barrels, which were topsy-turvy when they should have been stacked. Several were broken, and among the shards of wood were apples, some kind of dried meat, and swaths of crumpled fabric.

A squadron of ten soldiers worked hard to move the good barrels out into the corridors. Master Bylar stood on the left side of the entrance, wax tablet in hand as he carefully logged each food item. He wore on his belt the keys to the food compartments, never letting them leave his person. Such authority gave him nearly as much power as Wilek, when one considered the ship filled with slowly starving souls.

"I did not realize you kept such close tallies on the cargo," Trevn said.

"Oh yes, I must," Master Bylar said. "If I allow people to help themselves to an extra bite here and there, what will we eat next month? No, I must take care to pass out our provisions sparingly so that they last as long as possible. It does not make me popular. Many despise the jingle of my belt. But it has kept us fed so far."

Trevn caught the edge in the man's voice. "How much longer can we last on what's here?"

The man answered without hesitation. "Three weeks, unless we start catching fish again."

Trevn carried that cheery news back to the quarterdeck, wishing he could speak with Mielle about this. The morning fog had left everything wet, and the moisture still hadn't burned off. The farther north they sailed, the cooler the temperatures. Was Mielle cold? He spotted Admiral Livina at the rail, grow lens to his eye.

"He see something?" Trevn asked Captain Bussie, who was at the whip.

"Ahead on the water," Bussie said. "Looks like more wreckage."

Mielle. Trevn's heart leapt, and he joined Admiral Livina. The man passed Trevn the grow lens.

"Looks like it's been tied together," Trevn said. "I think I see movement."

They were too far out to recognize any of the people, but his bond with Mielle did not speak. "Pirates again?"

"Could be," the admiral said.

What would Randmuir of the Omatta need with so many ships?

But when the *Seffynaw* heaved alongside, it turned out not to be wreckage at all but three waterlogged dinghies lashed together. Inside, some twenty white-skinned passengers stared upon the great ship.

A chill ran over Trevn at the sight of them. And he'd been so certain that anyone but Mielle would have been a terrible disappointment. "They're pale, like Miss Onika."

"Which means they're not of our fleet," Admiral Livina said, excitement in his voice.

Trevn caught his meaning at once. These people had to have come from somewhere. Perhaps they would be able to lead the fleet to their homeland.

The pales, however, were in a dismal state. Their sallow, thin faces made it look as if they had been drifting for several weeks. They had lashed the dinghies with one in the lead and two behind and fashioned a mainmast of an oar. It carried no sail, however, merely a frayed and sun-bleached windsock made from a sleeve of what had once been a dark-colored tunic or jacket. The sleeve flipped about in the low wind.

Trevn gave a secondary count and determined that of the twenty-one bodies aboard the makeshift vessel, only seven were awake. By the look of the flies crawling over some of the faces, many of those sleeping might be dead.

"Should we lower a boat to bring aboard the survivors?" Trevn asked, eager to try to speak with them.

"Not yet," Livina said. "We've barely got a hold on the fever. We can't risk bringing ill people on ship."

"But they could lead us to land!" Trevn said.

"Not if we're all dead from disease." But the admiral did not abandon the pales. He threw out a line, which one of the survivors tied to their craft. This would tow them along behind the *Seffynaw* while the admiral went to speak with Wilek.

The sailors went about unsurprised by the admiral's actions, but the passengers stood along the rail, indignant at such barbarity, protesting that these people should be brought aboard at once. Trevn agreed with the passengers. These people might be able to lead them to land. Perhaps Mielle was there already.

In the end the hope of land outweighed the risk of disease, and Wilek ordered the nine surviving pales to be brought aboard and sequestered in the sickroom under Captain Veralla's care.

Trevn wanted desperately to visit them, but Admiral Livina had set guards outside the door to keep people away, leaving Trevn no excuse to skip his father's ageday dinner in the admiral's dining room, which Wilek had insisted he attend.

While Trevn had been sleeping away his life, Wilek had brought their father back to the *Seffynaw*. The man looked no worse than he had when he'd left, except now he rarely spoke. He just stared, his dark, glassy eyes fixed on nothing.

There were fifteen seated at dinner. In addition to the royal family, Miss Onika, and members of the Wisean Council, Mielle's little sister was in attendance. Amala looked so like Mielle that Trevn's heart ached. Why had she been invited? Could this be Wilek's way of easing his guilt over recent circumstances?

Then Wilek did something most intriguing. He introduced Amala to their father.

"May I present to you Miss Amala Allard. I have adopted her as my ward."

The rosâr, sickly as he was, perked up at this and reached out a shaky hand. Amala took hold of his hand and curtsied.

The king smiled.

This produced a round of applause as if the king were a babe taking his first steps.

"You approve of this, Sârah Zeroah?" Kamran asked her.

"Indeed I do. I loved Miss Mielle dearly. It is our duty to care for her sister now that she is gone."

Gone. The word rang in Trevn's head like a gong.

Somehow the moment passed without Trevn doing or saying anything unpardonable, and dinner was served. Conversation settled around the pales and finding out where they came from.

Miss Amala sat on Trevn's left, Oli on his right. The duke seemed withdrawn, and Trevn guessed he was still suffering from the lack of evenroot. Miss Amala, however, drove Trevn near insane with her endless chattering about the state of her overly dry skin. How could two sisters be so opposite in every way?

Trevn looked at the girl, really looked at her for the first time, and realized there was no warmth in her eyes. He might recognize their shape and color, but they carried an eager desperation that unsettled him.

"Your Highness," she whispered, leaning close. "I've been wanting to speak with you for some time. I am so desperately embarrassed that Sir Kalenek, my warden, killed Sâr Janek, your brother. I am mortified to be seen in good company. Do you think people judge me by association?"

"Yes," Trevn said, shocked the girl had broached the subject in this gathering. "But my guess is that your definition of *good company* and mine are very different. You should not care what people say, Miss Amala."

"It's just that everywhere I go, it seems as though people are talking about me. I hope that Sir Kalenek's crimes will not taint me forever."

Trevn held his tongue and imagined that Mielle would say *Tuhsh!* and scold her sister for such a remark. He decided to remain silent. This entire meal was a typical waste of time, and he'd just about convinced himself to beg leave when Miss Onika stood, clear eyes blazing in the direction of the king and Wilek.

"You must not follow the pales," she said. "Their way will lead you to destruction. A fatherless child is being trained to rise up against Armania. The land of shards is no place for his power. He must be lured north, where the magic of his people will diminish against the magic of Arman."

Trevn pressed his hand over his chest, which was thrumming at the prophetess's voice.

"I feel strange," Rashah said.

"Out," the king said. "Ooouuut!"

Wilek jumped up and motioned to Oli, who flew to Miss Onika's side and took hold of her arm.

"Miss Onika?" Oli said. "Will you come with me?"

"Dismissing me does not change the facts, Rosâr Echad. Continue on this course and you will all die."

Everyone stared in silence while Oli led her away and the king continued to moan.

Once the door closed on them, Kamran said, "I've always said she was a witch."

"She's no witch!" Brelenah said. "If you doubt her words, you are a fool."

"Silence," Wilek said. "This is the rosâr's ageday celebration. We will not discuss Miss Onika again today, is that understood?"

The remainder of the meal passed in awkward silence, and Trevn couldn't help but dwell on all that had gone wrong. Where was Mielle? Had poor Hinck made it to Rogedoth's ship? If so, what might the former Pontiff do to him?

While Trevn ate, he thought of all who were suffering and felt ashamed that he had been moping about the ship like some kind of victim. Yes, he missed Mielle, but he knew she still lived. He could not allow the spell the Magonian witch cast upon them make him useless and pathetic. The sooner they found land, the sooner he could find Mielle, rescue Hinck, and seek out a new normal for his life.

Trevn didn't finish his meal. He stood, bowed deeply, and excused himself. He set off for the sickroom, fully determined to use his position as the Second Arm to do all he could to find a way to communicate with the pale strangers.

Hinck

The men had taken turns rowing, directed by Lady Zenobia, who received her instructions from Kabada, the golden bird shadir. Kabada, Hinck had learned, was a common shadir, the most powerful of the five shadir that had come along.

Harton turned out to be the one who had stolen Errp the newt from Janek. He now kept the tiny creature in his shirt pocket, where it huddled in a ball to keep out of the chilly sea wind.

By the second day Hinck had lost count of how many times he had been at the oars and was completely out of strength. Still they saw no other boats, and each time he dozed off, Lady Zenobia prodded him in the back, nagging that his slowness was taking them off course. If she thought it was so easy, she should go ahead and row for a while.

Shortly after dawn the third day, a ship approached. It looked to Hinck as if it were being pulled by several hundred shadir attached to the bow with bands of color. An impressive and fairly terrifying sight.

"Moon Fang has come for us," Lady Zenobia said.

It appeared that he had.

Their dinghy was quickly attached to cables and hoisted aloft. Armed guards dressed in Sarikarian green escorted them to the stern, where they entered some kind of throne room. Three thrones sat in a row. The former Pontiff of the Rôb church, Barthel Rogedoth, also known as Prince Mergest III of Sarikar, sat in the largest, center throne. On his left sat his daughter, Rosârah Laviel, Sâr Janek's mother. No one occupied the third throne.

"Kneel before King Barthel of the Five Realms," a herald announced.

Surprised by that title, Hinck knelt with the others.

"You!" Rosârah Laviel pushed off her throne and stalked toward Sir Jayron. She raised her hand, yelled, "*Puroh!*" and a bolt of fire shot from her fingertips to Sir Jayron's face. He screamed, the flames circling his shaved head and catching fire to his tunic.

"You should have died!" she screamed. "It was your duty to protect him and you failed."

Again she launched a fireball at Sir Jayron. This one ignited his trousers. He fell thrashing to the floor.

Rosârah Laviel moseyed toward him, eyes gleaming as she watched him struggle. A wave of her hand doused the flames. "What say you, shield?"

Sir Jayron gasped from where he lay on the floor, his face blistered, his tunic burned to strips. "Had I been there, I would have gladly died for him. But we were arrested and put in the hold. Oli Agoros betrayed us."

They thought Oli had turned them in? Relief warred with fear for Oli's life.

"Do not speak that name. Guard!" Laviel waved over a guard, drew his sword, and raised the point above Sir Jayron's heart.

"Your Highness, please!" he cried. "Let me avenge him. I will go after the Duke of Canden and bring you his head."

"No," she said. "Your death will give me great pleasure." She stabbed down, but Sir Jayron twisted aside. The sword's point struck the floor. Sir Jayron scrambled back, got to his feet, and reached out to her with his hands spread wide. "Have mercy, lady. I can serve you better alive. Whatever you ask, I will do."

"I ask only that you die. *Natal.*" The sword floated out of her hand, pointed at Sir Jayron. She waved her arms forward, repeating that same magical word, and with each wave another sword slid out from the sheath of a guard and floated toward the first. Hinck watched in horror as two dozen blades spiraled through the air, slowly, heading straight for the first.

Sir Jayron turned and ran, but Rosârah Laviel cried out another command and the collection of blades shot forward, skewering the High Shield in unison from all sides before he could reach the door. The man grunted, choked out something indiscernible. Blood sprayed the floor around him and he toppled over.

Hinck looked away.

Rosârah Laviel clapped her hands a few times, laughing softly, and strutted back to her throne, the train of her light blue gown sliding across the floor behind her. "That felt good," she said, settling into her chair again.

"Have you had your fill of vengeance?" Rogedoth asked.

"We shall see," she said.

Hinck glanced at the others. Lady Zenobia stared straight ahead like a soldier. Harton and Lilou had both fixed their gazes on Sir Jayron's body. Lady Mattenelle had covered her face with her hands and was sobbing quietly.

"Speak, Zenobia," Rogedoth said to Rosâr Echad's concubine. "Give your report."

"We were to be executed two days ago by Sâr Wilek," she said, then went on to explain their plan to use Cook Hara's evenroot to kill Echad, how Sâr Wilek had found out and arrested them all, and the result of their attempted mutiny. "Canbek and Sir Garn were killed. Fonu jumped overboard and likely drowned."

"He did not drown. He is elsewhere," Rogedoth said. "Since when does Oli Agoros wield magic?"

"The shadir was Noadab," Zenobia said. "He did not even require the ancient words."

"Still loyal to Lebetta," Rogedoth said. "I will send some shadir to end its life."

"Just like Lebetta, Oli has deceived us all," Rosârah Laviel said. "Lady Mattenelle, stop crying and come here."

Lady Mattenelle ran to the queen and knelt at her feet.

Laviel stroked her hair. "My, you are filthy, all of you. Why do you cry, my dear?"

"My heart is broken. Sâr Janek . . ." She sobbed.

"I know," Laviel said, her voice cracking. "It is a tragedy beyond what I can bear."

Rogedoth questioned Agmado Harton next, asking about his sister, Charlon, why he'd wanted to serve in the King's Guard, and why he'd decided to betray Sâr Wilek. Then he questioned Lilou, who had little to say other than her stalwart support of his rule.

"My shadir have told me of a legless man who has befriended Sâr Wilek," Rogedoth said. "What do you know of him?"

"He is called Jhorn," Lilou said. "He boarded the ship after Bakurah Island. I believe he came from Emperor Ulrik's ship. He is close friends with the prophetess."

"Did he have a boy with him?"

"No, Your Highness. He came alone."

Rogedoth grimaced. He waved Lilou away, and his attention landed on Hinck. "You, Lord Dacre, are our connection to Sâr Trevn. What has he done with the Book of Arman?"

"Gave it over to Sâr Wilek, I believe," Hinck said.

Rogedoth grunted. "And how is your friendship with the youngest sâr these days?"

"Not strong," Hinck said. "Sâr Janek asked me to take the Duke of Canden's place as his backman. I agreed and have spent little time with Sâr Trevn ever since."

"Backman? You?" Rosârah Laviel pushed past Lady Mattenelle and approached Hinck.

Oh gods. She was going to kill him next.

She crouched before him, the fingers on her right hand bent like claws. One word, "*Puroh,*" and tiny streams of fire shot out of each fingertip.

Hinck held her gaze in his, trying to pretend he wasn't completely terrified.

Then, like an agitated fang cat, she scratched searing burn lines down Hinck's face, neck, and chest, leaving five long smoldering slashes in his tunic.

Hinck howled, gasping at the sting, but blessedly Rogedoth spoke.

"Enough! I let you have Sir Jayron, but we must not kill this one. He has royal blood and a childhood connection to Sâr Trevn that might be useful to us now that Trevn is the Second Arm."

"*My son* is the Second Arm!" Laviel screamed.

"We will avenge him, Laviel," Rogedoth said. "Soon our fleet will be bigger than Sâr Wilek's, and when we reach land before he does, he will have no choice but to bow to my will or sail on." He waved at the guards. "Take them away."

Two guards grabbed Hinck's arms and lifted him to his feet. His legs moved by instinct as the guards pulled him through a dark maze of corridors. They eventually entered a royal cabin and pushed him onto a soft bed. He lay there, his face burning and his mind a tumble with the sudden panic that he might die here alone on this ship, away from all those he loved.

Out of the darkness Lady Mattenelle appeared at his bedside. "Lord Dacre, I'm so sorry." She stroked his hair back from his face. "They've refused to let me heal you. Moon Fang—I mean, King Barthel—he says we all must bear the marks we take in war. But I have brought some ointment that will help."

Hinck tried to make sense of her words as she set about her ministrations. She cut off his ruined shirt and rubbed the cool ointment over the burns on his chest, neck, and face. Exhausted from rowing all night and from the pain, he dozed off until the sound of yelling women woke him.

"What are you doing here, anyway? You don't care about him."

"Don't start with me, Nellie. Like it or not, I'm queen here. Now leave us."

"I will not. I take my orders from Lord Dacre now."

"Get out or I'll have my guards drag you out!"

"Stop yelling." Hinck pushed up onto one elbow, wincing as the movement made his burns throb.

Standing with Lady Mattenelle at the foot of his bed was Lady Eudora. At first glance she hadn't changed, and it disgusted Hinck that he still thought her the most beautiful woman that ever existed. A deeper look revealed lines circling her eyes, a creased brow, and a rawboned face.

"Lord Dacre," Eudora said, softening. "I must speak with you in private. Tell your concubine to wait in the hall."

His concubine? It was on the tip of his tongue to deny her insinuation, but one look at Lady Mattenelle's steadfast posture changed his mind. "I have no secrets from Lady Mattenelle. Say what you must."

Eudora's lip curled as she skirted the bed. "You once swore you loved me," she whispered, as if that might keep the concubine from overhearing. "If that was ever true, you must help me escape."

Was she insane? "I have no intention of escaping."

"Kamran thinks you are Sâr Wilek's spy," Eudora said. "If you are, my husband will find out and kill you."

That Kamran had spoken against Hinck terrified him, but he could do nothing but continue to play his role. "I am sorry you wish to leave, lady, but I am here because Sâr Wilek ordered my death for taking part in a plot to kill Rosâr Echad. This is my only sanctuary."

Tears welled in her eyes, but she fixed a cold smile on her face. "See there? You have passed my little test. My husband the king will be relieved to know that Kamran was mistaken about your loyalties."

Hinck stared after her as she swept from the room, leaving him alone with Lady Mattenelle.

"I've brought you something to eat, lord." Lady Mattenelle hurried to the sideboard and carried a tray back to his bed. The smell of roasted meat made his stomach ache.

"Why are you doing this?" he asked.

Those huge amber eyes, glossy with tears, fixed on his. "You saved me," she said. "Kamran left me to hang." She began to cry, pursed her lips, and choked it back. "I don't care whether or not you are Sâr Wilek's spy. If you'll let me serve you, I will do all I can to help you survive."

Hinck didn't know what to say, so he gave her a small nod. Turned out he wasn't alone after all.

GRAYSON

When Sir Kalenek had told Grayson to row toward the *Malbraid*, he had neglected to mention that Randmuir Khal of the Omatta was a pirate.

The night Grayson arrived, the sailors had hoisted his dinghy up the side of the ship and dragged him to the captain's quarters where he'd met the grizzled man.

"What are you doing in a boat by yourself on a night like this?" Randmuir had asked. "Don't you know it's dangerous to go out in a storm?"

"Yes, sir," Grayson said, trying to be brave and speak like a man now that he had a man's body. "I was a prisoner aboard the *Vespara*. It's a ship Magonians stole from Sarikar. I had a chance to escape and took it. I'd like to join your crew and earn my keep."

"Would you now? Well, there ain't much to you but skin and bones," Randmuir said, "but I like that you escaped from those Magonian crows. Meelo, you've got yourself a new man. Get him a hammock. Now everyone out! I need my second sleep if I'm to maintain my charming disposition."

So Grayson had been passed to yet another master. Meelo turned out to be Randmuir's son. He was a wiry man with no lips—only teeth that looked to be bared in a constant snarl, no matter what his mood, which was almost always cross. He thrashed men who were slow to obey, and one such beating was all it took for Grayson to know he never wanted a second. The sound of the man's voice lit a fire under his feet that not even the Five Woes had done. In constant fear of Meelo's fists, Grayson worked harder than he had in his life.

The red shadir had stayed with him through the meeting with Randmuir, then vanished and never returned. Grayson figured it had reported back to the Magonian Chieftess. He didn't like that the woman knew what he was and where he was. If a chance came to leave this ship, he'd take it.

In the meantime he wondered daily over Sir Kalenek's message from Onika. *"Hold tight to your secret until you come to those twice your size."* Had Sir Kalenek gotten it wrong? Perhaps Onika had meant until Grayson had grown to twice his size. But . . . well . . . no man stood *that* tall.

Pirates made their living stealing from others, and Grayson had no choice but to join in. He learned some of sailing, which Randmuir's crew did much better than the Magonians, but more time was spent learning to fight from Meelo's second, a grisly man named Satu. The idea of learning to use a sword thrilled Grayson, but unfortunately, even though he was as tall as the other men, he was thin and couldn't make his long arms and legs move as quickly as he wanted to. After losing far too many matches, he was paired against Danno, a scrawny boy of twelve, who looked the age Grayson felt. The two sparred pathetically and were never allowed to join any of the raids, since Satu said they were more hindrance than help.

Grayson didn't mind that, and he and Danno formed a friendship. Days passed by and Grayson almost felt normal again. Randmuir attacked a ship every few days, always choosing smaller ships and always giving the crew the option to stay and sail the ship for him. Any who refused were set adrift in dinghies, tossed into the ocean to swim for it, or, if they put up a fight, killed. This had earned Randmuir a small fleet of about two dozen finships and fishing vessels. What he planned to do with his fleet, Grayson had yet to figure out.

One sunny midday when Grayson was on watch, the *Malbraid* came alongside a fancy ship bearing the name *Amarnath*. The ships were roped together peaceably, and the sailors lowered a gangplank between the two main decks. Curious, Grayson pushed into the Veil and went down to get a closer look.

Randmuir, Meelo, and six of their toughest men crossed over the gangplank to the *Amarnath*. Grayson followed, eager to find a better ship. If the ship wasn't better, at least he could continue his work as a spy for Sir Kalenek and the king of Armania.

A man in a blue-and-green uniform greeted the new arrivals. "Welcome to the *Amarnath*, Master Randmuir. If you'll follow me, I will lead you to the dining room, where a feast has been prepared in your honor."

"A real feast or rations dressed to look like one, Timmons?" Randmuir asked. "Because I've been pillaging for two months now, and most ships don't have any food left, let alone anything worthy of the word *feast*."

"King Barthel never goes hungry," Timmons said. "He is a king and sorcerer, and I would never presume to understand his powers."

"Oh, of course not," Randmuir said, rolling his eyes at Meelo.

Timmons led them to a dining room, where the table was set with fancy bowls brimming with food. A servant walked around the table, filling goblets with wine. Timmons seated the pirates and invited them to enjoy the wine and appetizers while he went to announce their arrival to the king.

Hungry as he was, Grayson couldn't risk stealing food, so he followed Timmons, curious about this mysterious king.

Timmons didn't go far before he knocked on a gilded door and pushed it open. "My pardon, Your Highnesses," he said, remaining on the threshold. "The guests have arrived. He will be expecting you."

Grayson slipped inside the room. A young woman in a fancy green dress stood before a full-length mirrorglass, three servants around her. One was lacing the back of her dress, another painting something on her face with a small brush, and the third kneeling and stitching the hem of her dress. The young woman was so beautiful, Grayson felt certain she must be a princess.

"Tell the king we are coming," said a woman, not among those Grayson could see.

"Yes, Your Highness." Timmons pulled the door closed.

Grayson shifted, looking for the person who had spoken. A chair came into view from behind the cluster of women. On it sat another woman, slightly older than the princess but dressed just as fine. A second princess, or perhaps a queen?

"I don't want to go," the young woman said. "I'm not hungry."

"You will go," said the woman in the chair. "And you will remain silent. I care not whether you eat."

The young woman sighed heavily. "What else would a prisoner do?"

"Oh, Eudora, really. I wish you would stop martyring yourself. Your life is not so bad."

"My life would end if you would let me take it."

"Killing oneself is not an acceptable death for royalty. I will hear no more talk of it. I would mute you, but Father doesn't want you to look like a prisoner to the pirates."

"He will have to compel me, then, for I will not lie or feign happiness or loyalty for anyone, least of all him. It is his fault Janek is dead."

The older woman shot to her feet, lifted her arm, and squeezed her hand into a fist. The princess gasped, grabbed her throat.

"We have been over this, Eudora. Sâr Wilek is responsible for my son's death. Is that clear?"

The princess nodded.

"Do not blame my father again." She lowered her arm.

The princess panted in several deep breaths.

"You will go to dinner and play your role," the older woman said. "The king must appear happily married and in control of his retinue. He must appear powerful enough to take the throne of the new Five Realms once land is found. And, Eudora, dearest, he must have an heir."

"Then he will fail," the princess Eudora whispered, rubbing her neck. "I have told you I do not want to have a child, especially not some beastly evenroot creature that will kill me when it claws its way into the world."

Grayson frowned. A root child had no claws. It simply grew too big for the mother to handle. At least that's what Jhorn had always said.

"Finished, Your Highness." The servant on her knees rose and tucked her needle into the apron she wore.

The older woman walked toward the door. "Come, Eudora, let us go and see how you will displease your husband the king today."

✦   ✦   ✦

Grayson followed the women back to the dining room. There a herald announced them as Queen Eudora of the Five Realms and Rosârah Laviel of Armania. Randmuir and his men stood, bowed, and the women took seats on either side of the empty throne at the table's head. Rosârah Laviel picked up her wine goblet. Queen Eudora merely stared off into nothing.

"Fancy me having dinner with you, Rosârah, after all this time," Randmuir said. "How is that son of yours, anyway?"

Rosârah Laviel flinched, eyes glittering as if Randmuir had taken something precious and destroyed it. She did not answer, but sipped her wine.

"That well, huh?" Randmuir said. "Then I'm glad to hear it."

Grayson, who was standing near the door and the end of the table, heard Meelo whisper to his father, "Ask them how much longer."

"You were told to remain silent," Randmuir said.

The rosârah drained her goblet of wine, and a servant rushed forward to fill it. The door opened and the herald announced, "His Royal Highness, King Barthel Rogedoth of the Five Realms, the Powerful, the Sorcerer."

Everyone stood as a man dressed all in red entered, accompanied by a swarm of shadir.

Seeing so many shadir at once surprised Grayson, and even though the Veil hid him from human eyes, he slid back against the wall beside a guard, trying to look as though he belonged. The shadir paid him no attention, and likely wouldn't, so long as he didn't make eye contact with any of them.

Then he saw the great. It stood no taller than the king as it glided along beside him. It had skin of brown mud and clothing of moss and leaves. Its fingers were thin sticks, eyes gray stones, and its hair . . . it looked like a gentle waterfall that cascaded down its back, disappearing into mist before it reached the floor.

Grayson could not look away. He had seen this creature before but could not remember when. The great turned his way, and Grayson averted his eyes, staring through the shadir's waist and focusing on a tray of honey tarts.

Onika had warned of a future where shadir tried to rule kings. She had always said that Grayson might somehow prevent such a thing from taking place. He couldn't imagine how. He had no desire to bring attention to himself. Besides, Onika had warned him not to reveal himself until he met those twice his size. While he still didn't understand what that meant, no one here could be described that way.

The king took his seat at the head of the table, and everyone else sat down. Servants swarmed the room, carrying platters of steaming fish and bowls of some kind of pudding.

Grayson's mouth watered.

"I hope my wife and daughter have been hospitable," the king said.

"They spoke not a word," Randmuir said.

The king glared at Rosârah Laviel and then returned his attention to his guests. "Have you at least enjoyed the wine while you waited?"

"I always enjoy wine," Randmuir said, "but let's not waste time with polite drivel. You want us to take the *Baretam* and bring you the emperor and his brother. Then you'll fix my son's face. Do I have that right?"

"Once I have the emperor and his brother alive and unharmed, yes, I will do this," the king said. "Keep in mind, Master Randmuir, creating a permanent change to someone's appearance takes a great deal of evenroot and strength. That I've agreed to do this at all is a rare favor I bestow upon you."

"Have you learned anything from our prisoner?" Randmuir asked. "He say anything about his homeland?"

"He says plenty," the king said, "but I understand none of it. Not even with the aid of my shadir."

But couldn't shadir speak every language? Grayson fought the urge to look at the great, wondering why the king would lie. Unless the shadir had lied to the king.

"Have you tried drawing? A sketch of a boat and land might speak better than foreign words."

"We are not incompetent, Master Randmuir," the king said. "We've drawn, even taken charts down to him. He simply stares like he cannot make sense of anything. Perhaps his vision is impaired or he cannot read. Or maybe he's not the captain, and they tricked us into putting the real captain out to die with his crew."

"Couldn't blame them for pulling a trick like that." Randmuir stood. "Take me to him. I'd like to give it a go."

"Surely that can wait until after dinner," the king said.

"Look, Rogedoth, or whatever name you're going by these days, you and me, we have a business arrangement. We're not friends and never will be. I answer to no king, and I've got plenty to eat on my own boat. So don't bother buttering me up with your fancy meal. I want three things in life. My son's face put back to normal, land where the Omatta can live, and Sâr Wilek's head on a pike. That's it. Your prisoner can get me one of those things, so don't take it personally if I'd rather spend my time with him."

"Very well," the king said. "Timmons, escort these pirates to the hold, where they can speak with the prisoner. Will you be returning to dinner once you fail, Master Randmuir?"

"I'll let your man know," Randmuir said, striding from the room.

✦ ✦ ✦

Grayson followed the pirates to the hold, where they stopped before a tiny door. As Timmons set about opening it, Randmuir muttered to Meelo.

"Don't know why that pompous windbag thinks he should rule the Five Realms."

"Because he is the only one left with a supply of evenroot," Meelo said.

"He's not," Randmuir said. "The Magonians have root too. Rogedoth is as bad as those crows, using dark magic to control everyone. My mother would have hated that I'm helping him, but the alternative is far worse."

Timmons opened the door, and they crowded around the entrance and looked inside. The cell was half the size of a horse's stall and had a low ceiling. A man sat in the corner, knees pulled up to his chest. His eyes and hair were brown, but his skin was pale like Onika's.

"Will you look at that," Meelo said. "Never saw skin like that before."

The sight thrilled Grayson. Another prophet?

"What's your name?" Randmuir asked him.

The man flinched and ducked his head.

"Nice job, Father," Meelo said. "You scared him."

"It's your face he's scared of," Randmuir said, crouching before the pale-skinned man. He reached out, and the man scrambled across the hay-lined stall to the other corner, raised his fists, and started to talk. Randmuir and his men stared, clueless, but Grayson understood him perfectly.

"Don't come any closer," he'd said. "You attacked my ship, killed my crew, and locked me in this animal pen. What do you want from me?"

"Well, he's not mute," Randmuir said. "But by that tone and the angry look on his face, I don't think he was wishing us a happy day."

"What did they do to him, I wonder?" Meelo asked.

"Who knows?" Randmuir said. "My mother could cast a spell to understand any language. Rogedoth is lying to us about not being able to communicate."

"Unless the man is pretending not to understand him," Meelo said.

"Why would he?" Randmuir asked. "He can't enjoy being locked up." He patted his chest. "Rand. I'm Rand." He pointed at his son. "Meelo." Then tapped his chest again. "Rand." Back and forth he went. "Meelo. Rand. Meelo. Rand." Then he pointed at the prisoner and raised his eyebrows in question.

The man snarled.

This went on for quite some time. Randmuir tried dozens of ways to talk and gesture to the prisoner. He withdrew a shard of charcoal from his pocket and drew pictures on the wall. This seemed to amuse the man, but when Randmuir handed him the charcoal, he dropped it in the privy bucket and laughed.

Randmuir finally gave up and stormed back toward the stairs, his pirates following closely behind. Timmons closed and locked the door and set off after them.

Grayson remained outside the cell until he could no longer hear the men. Then he walked through the wood door and made himself visible.

The man jumped and yelled, "Away, you mage-gifted! Do not touch me with your magic."

"My magic cannot harm you," Grayson said.

"You walk through walls. That is great magic. Plus you speak Gallimayan yet have dark skin like the others. Go away!"

"My magic is different than theirs," Grayson said. "If the king knew about me, he would force me to help him. But I want to help you."

The man narrowed his eyes. "Then tell me what the king wants with me."

"He wants to know where your homeland is. The sea swallowed our land. We have no homes but these boats, and we are quickly running out of food and drinking water."

"They stole my ship, killed my crew, and want me to help them? Why should I?"

Though Grayson hated to say it, he had to be honest. "You shouldn't. You can't trust these men. Their king is a fake. He is trying to steal the throne from the real king. The one called Randmuir is a pirate."

"Jah, we have pirates in Gallimau. Can you let me out?"

"The door is locked, and I don't have the key. I'll try to find a way, but I have to return to my ship soon or I'll be stuck here."

"You don't want to be here?" the pale man asked.

Not with so many shadir on board, especially that great. "This ship is dangerous. My name is Grayson. What's yours?"

"Bahlay Nesos, captain of the *Weema-ell*. I named her after my wife. Was teaching our son to sail her." He cleared his throat, which looked to Grayson like he was trying not to cry. "Are there any other prisoners like me?"

"Not aboard this ship. The pirates sometimes leave people in the water. It could be that your son was picked up by another ship."

"How many ships do your people have?" Bahlay asked.

"Hundreds, but they're not all my people. There are five nations in the fleet. Some of them are good people. What is your home like?"

"Gallimau is a chain of islands, much smaller than the others. They run the full length of the Land of Shards, from the northernmost tip of Lantvegard around the southern tip of the Conch."

More islands.

"Is there room in the Land of Shards for more people?"

"There are many uninhabited islands, but they are not very large. The biggest islands might welcome workers for their fields, flocks, or forests, but none will welcome a king."

"Several kings," Grayson said.

Bahlay shook his head. "They would not be welcomed."

"It would be a war?" Grayson asked.

"Perhaps. I do not know the numbers of your soldiers. The mage-gifted are trained to end wars swiftly. How many mage-gifted are among your people?"

"We don't have any mage-gifted," Grayson said, wondering what might happen when so many ships landed in such a place and tried to claim land for themselves.

He feared it would not be good at all.

✦ ✦ ✦

"Ready a boarding party," Randmuir told his son.

Three days had passed since Grayson's visit to King Barthel's ship, where he had spoken with Bahlay the Gallimayan from the Land of Shards. Ultimately he'd been unable to free the man.

As Randmuir had promised King Barthel, he sailed the *Malbraid* up near Emperor Ulrik's *Baretam* in the dead of night with plans to attack at dawn. Grayson wished he might warn the emperor that the pirate was coming, but he was still too afraid to pop between ships, worried he'd end up in the ocean and drown. He did not want to be part of the boarding party, but when Meelo grabbed him by the scruff of the neck and shoved him out into the open, and Satu handed him a tarnished bronze sword, he didn't know how to argue.

The sword felt heavy and long in his hand, despite all his practice. He found Danno in the crowd, and the two compared weapons and found them nearly identical.

In the increasing light of dawn, he saw the *Baretam* for the first time in months. The sight of the gilded trim and red paint brought back happy memories of having survived the Five Woes with Jhorn, Onika, and Sir Kalenek. A morning fog hid parts of the ship from view. Its sails had been furled for the night, and her naked shrouds looked like scaffolds rising out of The Gray. Lights shone brightly from the windows and lanterns on deck.

By this time nearly the entire crew of the *Malbraid* had gathered on the main deck, dressed and armed for battle. Grayson stood at the back of the mob between Satu and Danno with the rest of Meelo's watch. At least they weren't leading the raid.

"Once you board her, work your way toward the stern and the imperial cabin," Meelo told his men. "Let the others worry about taking the ship. Our goal is to find the emperor and his brother. We want them alive."

The *Malbraid* came apace with the *Baretam*'s port side. At the front of the line, grapples were thrown. Hooks dragged across the deck of the emperor's ship, caught on the railing. The *Malbraid* pulled in tight and jolted as she ground against the freeboard of the *Baretam*. Randmuir's pirates swarmed over the sides. Someone lowered a gangplank, and more pirates flooded across.

"Close quarters, men!" Randmuir yelled as he charged along the deck, sword raised. Shouts of surprise gave way to screams and yells as he and his men slashed and stabbed their blades at anything that moved.

Grayson had almost reached the gangplank.

"Here we go," Meelo yelled. "Look alive!"

Scrambling forward and yelling like madpersons, the mob swarmed from one ship to the other, a solid mass of bodies. As Grayson put both feet aboard the *Baretam*, a voice yelled in alarm from the quarterdeck. A bell began to clang. Up ahead the clash of bronze and cries of pain rose above the trampling bootsteps.

"At arms!" came a cry from an Igote captain.

As the two groups clashed, Grayson hoped Emperor Ulrik and his family had found some place to hide.

GOZAN

Gozan heard commotion from above, but by the time he made it up to the main deck to investigate, the fighting was over. Dead Igote guards lay in bloody puddles on the deck beside the occasional man clad in black.

Pirates.

An authoritative voice barked orders at the raiders, who scrambled up the masts or began picking up dead Igote. Bodies splashed overboard. Sails were quickly set.

All this would have been an intriguing turn of events if not for the number of shadir present. The Veil swarmed with color, though Gozan recognized not one creature. A slight slipped past him, and he snagged hold of it with his claws. It squealed like a pup whose tail had been trod upon.

"Who is your master?" Gozan demanded.

"Dendron," he said.

Gozan released him, tingling with dread. Dendron's swarm? Here? This did not bode well. Especially if Dendron's humans had evenroot.

He flashed instantly to Jazlyn's quarters. All was calm inside. They had no idea the ship had been attacked.

The ship has been attacked by pirates, Great Lady, he told Jazlyn. *We must hide.*

Jazlyn stood slowly, ear cocked toward the ceiling, but the sounds of battle had ended.

The door burst open. Jazlyn's maidens screamed. Yet it was not pirates who entered unbidden, but Emperor Ulrik with one of his personal guards.

"Forgive me, lady. Pirates have taken the ship. I have a boat ready to launch from one of the master's cabins in the lower deck. It's not far from here, but we must hurry."

"You destroyed all that I hold sacred when you cast the evenroot into the sea. I'd rather take my chances with the pirates," Jazlyn said.

That is unwise, Great Lady, Gozan said at the same time as the emperor yelled, "They're pirates!"

Rosârah Thallah pushed past the emperor and into the room. "Whoever trusts in her own mind is a fool, Your Highness. I suggest you come with us and quickly."

Jazlyn raised her hand to the emperor. "A moment while I speak with my shadir."

Ulrik rolled his eyes, rocking from foot to foot, eager, it seemed, to be on his way.

"With patience a ruler may be persuaded," Thallah murmured to him.

Jazlyn walked deeper into the cabin. "What say you, Gozan?" she asked.

These pirates are escorted by an unfamiliar swarm. I asked one of the slights who his master was, and he said Dendron.

"Did you see Dendron?" Jazlyn asked.

I did not. But we are without enough evenroot. He could destroy us both.

"Your Eminence, we must go," the guard said to Ulrik.

"What say you, lady? Are you coming or staying?"

"Where are you going, Emperor?" she asked.

"To the *Gillsmore*, my vice flagship."

She nodded at Qoatch, and the eunuch fetched a satchel holding her last vial of evenroot from the cupboard.

"First sense I've seen out of her in a long while," Rosârah Thallah said.

Ulrik and his great-aunt took off with the guard, moving aft down the lengthway. At the stairs they descended two levels, then followed a crossway until it ended at a door. The guard opened it, and Gozan saw the sea where the wall should be. There was no furniture inside. Only a small dinghy attached to lines that were threaded through a set of davits. The outer wall of the cabin consisted of two plank doors that had already been opened outward. Two men wound cranks that extended the davits out over the sea. Once the men had cranked them to their full extent, the Igote pushed the boat to the opening.

"It is ready, Your Eminence," a soldier said.

"Rosârah Thallah, Ferro, and Queen Jazlyn first, if you please," the young man said.

The Igote obeyed, seating the passengers per the emperor's instructions. Soon the dinghy was filled with Jazlyn and her ladies, Qoatch, Rosârah Thallah, the emperor, his young brother, and a dozen staff and Igote. Two men remained behind to work the boat fall.

"Lower us," the emperor told them, and the men set to work.

"What about the rest of my people?" Jazlyn asked.

"There are eight of you here," Ulrik said. "I have saved forty percent of your people and left ninety-eight percent of mine behind. I have done the best I could for you, lady."

Jazlyn turned her attention to Gozan. "Go back and see what these pirates do. And keep them from noticing our getaway."

Gozan was not eager to return to Dendron's swarm, but his curiosity got the best of him. As long as he took the appearance of a slight, no one should pay him much attention. He let his form disintegrate to vapor and swept back toward the *Baretam.* The pirates had led the passengers to the main deck, sorting the able-bodied men from the elderly, women, and children. Igote who continued to fight were being killed and thrown overboard. Gozan saw the boy Burk, who had traveled with them through Rurekau. He lay down his Igote blade and joined the pirates.

The boat fall at the stern was heavily guarded, but no one had thought to stand watch over the rails themselves. A second boat of Igote had been launched from the bow. Gozan saw no sign of Dendron or any mantics issuing orders to the swarms of shadir.

The leader of these raiders would likely be in the imperial cabin, so he passed through the wall and found he was right. A crowd of terrified servants huddled behind a grand dining table. Before it, a man with no lips held a sword to the throat of a servant. Three other servants lay dead at the man's feet.

"Tell me where he is!" the lipless man yelled.

"The emperor has an escape plan for when his ship is attacked," the servant said. "Only his private security guards know what it is. You may kill us all and still learn nothing."

At this the lipless man snarled and sliced the man's throat. Several women screamed.

"Bring me another," the lipless man said.

"Enough!" An older man entered the imperial quarters. "He has either fled the ship or hidden himself somewhere. Meelo, take some others and man the crow's nest. Look for longboats that might have recently launched. Joben, take a squad to look over the railings for anyone lowering themselves into the water. Satu, organize a full search of the ship. Check the lady's hole in the stern, inside every mattress and trunk, and under every bed. If he has escaped, I will be very upset. Go!"

The men scattered.

Gozan followed the lipless Meelo to the lookout, doing what he could to slow the man by whispering taunts into his ear, telling him he should go back and argue with the leader, speak his mind.

Meelo growled, annoyed by Gozan's influence, yet he kept his pace all the way to the mainmast.

"Get up there," he said to a boy. "Be quick about it."

The boy obeyed and turned out to be a swift climber. Gozan shot ahead of him and, from the crow's nest, took note of the emperor's dinghy. It had reached the *Gillsmore* and was circling around the stern. Good. By the time the crew set about hoisting the boat, it would be hidden from the pirate's view.

The second dinghy that the Igote had launched from the bow was headed in the same direction as the *Gillsmore* but was much farther behind. Gozan drifted alongside the climber, whispering into his ear.

Go carefully, he said. *The fog has left the rigging slick. Don't want to fall. Hold tight!*

The boy's grip on the futtock shroud slipped, and he gasped, holding tight and cursing Randmuir of the Omatta and his son, whoever they were.

By the time the boy reached the top and got a good look at the surrounding waters, the emperor's boat had long since rounded the side of the nearest ship. The Igote boat had covered half the distance, and the climber yelled down the location of the craft.

Gozan considered his job complete and returned to the main deck to see what the pirates would do with this information. There he found a common shadir mustering a swarm for a non-magical attack.

"Hwuum, lead your swarm to the boat and do what you can to slow it."

"Yes, Mikray," the blue-and-yellow slight said. The group of shadir shot away toward the dinghy.

Gozan studied the common giving orders. He'd heard much of Mikray, who presented himself to humans as the god of fate and fortune. What human had he bound?

"Shama," Mikray said, "return to the *Amarnath* and ask the mantics to wield a wind to stop the boat."

Gozan followed Shama, curious about the number of mantics this *Amarnath* carried, employing so many shadir. Perhaps Gozan should join them. He longed for a human with evenroot who craved power and destruction, yet he didn't want to be subservient to any shadir. Gozan had loved the freedom and power he wielded over Jazlyn once she left Tenma and journeyed to Lâhaten. Destroying that ancient city had been one of his grandest moments. Gozan liked his freedom and wanted to keep it if he could.

The swarm approached a ship of average size, though considerably higher quality than the pirate ship. It flew through the ship's walls and stopped in a luxurious cabin.

It had been over a century since Gozan had seen Dendron. He stood beside a throne on which sat an elderly human male. The man appeared strong, fierce, and exuded a level of self-absorption that Gozan hadn't felt since being in the presence of High Queen Tahmina. He was talking with a middle-aged woman. Both wore crowns. More kings and queens, Gozan supposed. Beside the queen hovered the common shadir known as Iamos, who currently held the form of an elderly healing woman.

Three famed shadir in one swarm? Gozan could not help but be impressed.

Both humans glanced at the swarm. Mantic rulers? Interesting. The one Mikray had called Shama approached the throne.

"What is it?" the human king asked.

"The emperor escaped on a dinghy," Shama said. "Mikray requests the mantics wield a wind to hinder its progress."

"Mantics are needed," the king said to a tiny yellow slight. "Fetch Yohtheh-reth and Lau. Tell Lau to bring a bottle of root juice."

"Yes, Your Highness." The slight sank through the floor.

Gozan followed it, keeping as far back as he could, not wanting to be seen. The slight moved down one floor and through several rooms before stopping in a small cabin that was ornately decorated. Only one man occupied the cabin. Gozan saw no shadir.

"King Barthel requests your immediate presence in the throne room," the slight said. "Yohthehreth as well. He also asks that you bring a bottle of evenroot juice."

The man jumped to his feet, grinning. He was short and bald but for a thin priest's braid that curled down the middle of his back. "Tell the king we're on our way."

The slight flitted up through the ceiling. Gozan let it go and instead followed the man, who exited the cabin and let himself into a room across the corridor. "Rogedoth wants us to do magic. I sensed from the messenger this is urgent."

An older man sat at a desk, dressed in white robes. His ashy gray hair had been bound in a bun at the nape of his neck, and a short beard hung from his chin. He stood and pulled a chain from the neckline of his robe. "Since when is anything Rogedoth wants not urgent?" He walked to a cabinet that lined the wall and used the key to open the door. Inside, bottles wrapped in packing cloth stood side by side. There were at least thirty behind this door alone.

Evenroot juice.

The man in white removed one bottle and closed the cabinet, relocking it and tucking the key back into his robes. "Best be off, then. He's in the throne room, I assume?"

"So said the shadir."

The older man opened the door for the younger. "After you, Lau."

Out they went.

Gozan remained for a time, staring at the cabinet, longing for just one bottle of root juice to carry back to Jazlyn. If they were on land, he might find a way to entice a new mantic to his service and convince him to steal one and take it to Jazlyn. But the distance was too great, and the mantics on board this ship seemed too powerful to be tricked.

It was hopeless.

He might as well present himself at the *Gillsmore* and report to Jazlyn what he had learned about this King Barthel and his—

"Who are you?"

Gozan spun around. Leaning against the wall opposite the cabinet stood Dendron, the great shadir.

Gozan still held the form of a slight. He bowed deeply. "I am Chelo, great one."

Dendron laughed, a moist sound that raised Gozan's hackles. "Chelo died in the Great War. I killed him myself when I discovered he was a spy for the High Queen of Tenma. There is no need to hide your true self from me. I sense your power is great. To whom are you bonded? Or are you without a host?"

"I am Zitheos," Gozan said, shifting into the black fang cat form that Zitheos preferred. Priestess Omarietta had been in Tenma when the Five Woes had struck, so choosing the form of Zitheos seemed a safe choice. "My human is dead."

"One of the Tennish priestesses? Did she die in the Five Woes?"

Gozan saw no reason to keep the facts secret. "Priestess Omarietta died by the hand of rebels. The humans called it the Eunuch Rebellion. The eunuchs called themselves Kushaw. In the confusion of the Five Woes, they killed many of the Great Ladies of Tenma."

"What became of the other Tennish shadir?" Dendron asked.

"I am uncertain. The carnage of the Five Woes absorbed me for many days. When the rapture faded, I found myself alone. I bound a novice mantic and made my way north with him and a group of Tennish refugees. We ended up in Larsa and bought passage aboard a Rurekan vessel. Pirates just now over-took it. When I saw the number of shadir, I grew curious as to who controlled such a swarm and came to see for myself. My mantic has little evenroot left. I have been growing restless."

"Evenroot is rare in these times," Dendron said. "It was fortuitous that my human had been hoarding it in secret long before the Five Woes became reality. I suspect that once land is found, by that fact alone he shall become ruler over this rabble." Dendron narrowed his eyes. "What ship did you say you came from again?"

Gozan knew he could risk no more. "I didn't," he said and vanished.

✦ ✦ ✦

It had been a risky move, facing Dendron in such a way. Gozan shouldn't have done it, but the temptation had been too great. For too long he had been idle. By the time Gozan passed the dinghy of Igote that had been blown off course, two more dinghies had reached them and taken the soldiers captive. Gozan slowed to study the soldiers, pleased to see that three of them were young enough to at least be mistaken for Emperor Ulrik. It should give the *Gillsmore* enough time to move on. Or if they were followed, to prepare for an attack.

On the *Gillsmore* Gozan found Jazlyn installed in a cabin no bigger than she'd had aboard the *Baretam*. He was about to share an adapted version of his exploits and discoveries in regards to Dendron and King Barthel when Masi and a swarm of his own shadir appeared before him.

"Where have you been?" he roared, relieved to finally see them.

"We have found land, master!" Masi said, bowing low. "Magon's shadir have gone to report to her."

"How far? Is it big enough for all?"

"With a strong wind it's as many as two weeks' sailing to the west," Masi said. "They are islands, but some are as big as Tenma once was. A local shadir knew nothing of our ways—nothing of evenroot and bonding with humans. His land has a magic of its own, vastly different from ours. I do not think we would be welcomed there."

"I do not care," Gozan said. Once the fleet landed, King Barthel's evenroot would be unloaded and Gozan could find a way to steal some for Jazlyn. "Tell me everything in detail. Go slowly, Masi, and leave nothing out."

KALENEK

K al sat alone on the stern deck, watching Shanek toddle across the smooth wood. Every few steps the boy would pause to look behind him, then shriek and run as if being chased, giggling madly. Occasionally he'd turn around and become the chaser. Kal marveled at how well Jhorn had taught Grayson to ignore the shadir.

Had Grayson made it to the *Malbraid*? Was he still growing from the root the Magonians had given him? Would Kal recognize him if he saw him again?

Shanek lost his balance and fell to his backside, which was padded in thick cotton wraps. Though it had happened dozens of times this morning alone, each instance made the boy's eyes pop in surprise. His bottom lip poked out and trembled, and he twisted his head around to find where Kal sat on a bench beside the stern rail.

"You're fine," Kal told him. "Get up and try again."

Such encouragement produced a toothy smile. The child pushed himself to standing, caught sight of something Kal could not see, and his legs took off again.

Kal already loved the boy, though he tried to distance his affection with logic. The women were raising Shanek DanSâr to usurp the Armanian throne. Kal must keep that from happening. As a trained assassin he should have killed the boy and ended the impending disaster Shanek-the-man was certain to become. Yet each time he looked into those wide gray eyes, he found he could not harm one hair on the child's head.

Shanek had been alive but two weeks and looked to be two years old.

Mreegan had commanded he be fed evenroot with every meal, and it was working. Shanek's body was growing faster than his mind could be trained. If he kept up this rate, Kal worried he'd be a man before he could even speak clearly.

Kal wanted to ask Chieftess Mreegan to lessen the boy's evenroot, but he doubted she'd believe his concerns had merit.

He had lost his freedom when he'd helped Grayson escape. At the Chieftess's command and Kal's shame, Charlon and the other maidens had tattooed a slav rune onto the back of his neck to punish him, though they had thankfully left his hair and clothes alone. While only Charlon was permitted to command him and she had not yet taken undue advantage of that power, Kal knew he must tread carefully. He could not risk being parted from Shanek.

The boy fell, and this time he began to cry. Kal reached out to him, "You're all right, Shan. Get up. Come to Kal."

The boy crawled the rest of the way. Chubby hands clutched Kal's feet and moved up his legs until Shanek was standing and holding on to Kal's knees. He buried his face in Kal's lap, looked up and flashed that toothy grin, then hid his face again.

"I see you," Kal said. "You can never hide from me, Shanek DanSâr. I'll always find you."

Shanek continued his game, oblivious that his life was not his own to live. Poor lamb. Kal's heart twisted, and he pulled the child onto his lap and hugged him. Shanek giggled and hid his face in Kal's tunic.

Footsteps padded up the stairs from the quarterdeck. Charlon's head appeared above the coaming, and each step revealed more of her as she ascended. She looked haggard and thin, nothing like the shrewd woman who had managed to steal Shemme's child.

"Did you do this, Shan?" Kal asked. "Did you keep Mother up all night?"

Kal's use of *Mother* caught the boy's attention, and he whipped his head around. "Mahn!" He grabbed Kal's beard and ear and pulled himself to standing on Kal's thighs.

"Ow!" Kal turned the boy so he stood facing out.

Shanek, completely confident in Kal's grip, leaned dangerously far, reaching for the only mother he knew.

Charlon ignored the child's eagerness and sank to the bench beside Kal. Shanek climbed into her lap, and she habitually tucked him into the crook of her arm without a glance or word of greeting. Shanek found each of her hands and turned them over, demanding, "Mohk," each time.

"Are you ill?" Kal asked.

"I fear I might be."

Shanek climbed to standing on Charlon's lap and took her face in between his chubby hands, looking intently into her eyes. "Mohk, Mahn. Mohk."

"It's not time for your feeding," she said, resituating the child back on her lap.

Shanek arched his back and screeched.

"Ugh. I have no patience for fits today." Charlon pushed Shanek off her knees until he stood on the deck, hands clutching the foxtails of her skirt. "Deal with him, Sir Kalenek."

Though she likely hadn't meant to command him, Kal felt the compulsion tug at his gut. He scooped up the bawling child, drew a biscuit from his shirt pocket, and offered it with one word. "Bite?"

Shanek instantly quieted and grabbed the little snack with both hands, shoving it whole into his mouth as if he'd been starved for a week.

"You're so good with him," Charlon said.

"I think he's ready for adult food," Kal said. "He's growing so fast; he needs the energy."

"I'll tell the cook to feed him. Whatever we eat tonight."

"Sit him in the circle with the rest of us," Kal said. "He will need to learn manners if you expect him to someday make an impression on the Armanian court."

Charlon sighed. "Whatever you think best is—oh!" She clapped her hand over her mouth.

"Miss Charlon, are you well?"

She ran to the railing, bent over it, and heaved.

A prickle of remembrance swept over Kal. He set Shanek on the deck, gave the boy another biscuit, and went to Charlon at the rail. "You are with child."

She swiped the back of her hand over her mouth. "Don't be ridiculous." But this she said in a weeping whisper as tears filled her eyes.

She had been gone from the *Seffynaw* too long for it to be Janek's. They'd only been here two weeks, but considering the amount of evenroot she took, Kal made a guess. "Torol is the father?"

"Do not speak of it! You mustn't."

"I would imagine the news would please him."

"I haven't told Torol yet. Haven't decided. What to do."

"What is there to decide?"

She flung out her hand toward Shanek. "Look there and know my answer."

Understanding settled in Kal's mind. "You will die. Because you take evenroot."

"And I would leave Mreegan with two children. To study and use to her liking. My child would not be Deliverer. It would be expendable. Like your friend Grayson. Nothing but a tool. A tool for Mreegan to use how she sees fit."

"Could you avoid evenroot from now on?" Kal asked. "A normal child wouldn't be so easily used."

Charlon's brows sank as she considered this. "Mreegan would know."

"Would she? You move in separate circles. She has asked little of you but to raise Shanek. As long as we're at sea, I can't imagine she would need much else from you in the way of mantics."

"I could not hide the child for long. Not dressed like—" She focused suddenly on something Kal could not see. A shadir, likely. He'd grown used to the way the mantics interacted with the invisible creatures.

"We will come right away," she said. Her attention shifted back to Kal. "The Chieftess likely knows the truth already. Pick up Shanek and come. She has summoned us."

✦ ✦ ✦

"Make the boy kneel," Charlon said as she sank to her knees on the straw mat.

Though the compulsion forced Kal to obey, last week he'd found a way around this particular command. He had no intention of making the boy kneel before the Chieftess and had instead been teaching him to bow respectfully. Shanek thought the words *kneel* and *bow* meant the same thing, so when Kal set the boy on his feet and whispered, "Kneel to the Chieftess," Shanek bent over until his hands and head touched the floor.

The boy turned his head, grinning at Charlon as if enjoying a splendid game. The servants in the cabin chuckled, endeared as they believed this the best little Shanek could do. Kal stood at attention beside Charlon and Shanek.

"Magon tells me many interesting things," Chieftess Mreegan said. "Her swarm has discovered land to the west. I have informed the captain, who has altered our course."

Land. Kal's chest swelled with hope. Perhaps this would be where Kal and Shanek could escape and make their way to a place where he and Onika might be reunited.

"She also tells me that Sâr Janek is dead," Mreegan said, staring at him. "Why did you not share this information when you first came to us, Sir Kalenek?"

Kal's daydream shattered. "It was not your concern."

"Should not the Mother know that the Father is dead?" Mreegan asked, gesturing to Charlon.

Kal had nothing to apologize for, not in this court. "Had any of you asked, I would have told you. I am not ashamed of my actions."

"*Your* actions?" Charlon asked.

"Oh yes, Mother. Our dear ambassador killed the sâr himself," Mreegan said. "Why was it, Sir Kalenek? To avenge your child?"

"Something like that."

"What you have done is a boon to Magonia," Mreegan said. "Sâr Janek's death puts Shanek next in line for the throne of Armania."

"Shanek is illegitimate," Kal said. "Strays cannot rule Armania."

Mreegan waved her hand. "A technicality that can be easily explained away when the time comes." She stood and sauntered toward him. The newt on her shoulder shifted to get a better foothold, curling its tail around her throat. "I reward those who serve Magonia, Sir Kalenek." She stopped before him and looked down on Charlon. "Take the child and leave us. All of you go. Now."

Charlon rose slowly, scooped Shanek into her arms. She glanced at Kal as she departed, gaze curious, on edge.

Nothing had been said of her unborn child. She should be thankful for that.

When all had gone and Kal was alone with the Chieftess, she pointed to the floor between them. "Kneel before me, Sir Kalenek. I would bestow upon you a great honor."

"I have already been knightened by Rosâr Echad for my service in the Great War," he said.

"You have not been knightened by me."

Kal supposed he could play along—having a rank here could only help his position—though he did not recall that Magonia knightened their soldiers. He lowered himself to his knees, apprehensive.

"*Qadosh Magon âthâh. Bâqa ze mishchâth. Châdâsh hay ânaph ba Kalenek. Te lo châlaph.*"

A chill clamped down upon Kal's face. His skin grew cold and tight. He lifted his hand to his cheek and wiped away blood.

"What are you doing?" His breath hissed out in a vaporous cloud. His lips grew dry and stiff; the curly hairs of his beard turned white with frost. His eyelashes clung together with each blink. He shivered, watching the frost creep across the floor from his knees, painting the mats, fur rugs, and the checkered floor in swaths of ice crystals.

The Chieftess's dark hair turned white. Beads of sweat on her brow froze into pearls of ice. The newt became a statue. Kal closed his eyes for the last time and felt himself falling.

He stood on top of the ocean, the waves barely lapping the sides of his boots. An illusion of some kind. Why?

Mreegan appeared before him, ocean breeze blowing her gown against her body, her hair waving about her face like eggs dropped in boiling water.

"Give yourself to me, Kalenek Veroth, and you will find the peace you seek. I can heal all your wounds, inside and out." She reached toward him, and the moment her dark fingertips touched his face, he woke, back on his knees in the Chieftess's cabin.

The hair on his arms danced as he tried to understand what her spell had done. He looked up into her eyes and found her staring at him with a hunger that made him instantly uncomfortable.

"You are a handsome man, Sir Kalenek," she said, extending her hand to him. "But I left the scars on your body. I rather like them."

Kal reached up, touched his face. The smoothness he felt churned his stomach. He jumped to his feet and pushed past the Chieftess to a mirrorglass bolted to the wall. He stared, both astounded and repelled by what he saw.

Dark brown skin, smooth and perfect. Unmarred eyebrows, dark and thick. The line of his beard full and trim.

She had healed his face. Removed his scars.

He wheeled around and roared, "What have you done?"

She frowned as if surprised by his reaction. "This does not please you?"

"I deserve those scars. Earned them with my own blood. They are all I have of my men. Of Liviana and our son."

Mreegan bristled and crossed her arms. "I make you beautiful and you rail at me about the past?" She strode back to her throne. "I meant to make you my favorite, but now I've changed my mind."

"I have no desire to be anyone's favorite," Kal said. "I am here only to protect Shanek."

"You are here because you have nowhere else to go," Mreegan said. "Return to the *Seffynaw* and you will be executed for murdering Sâr Janek. You are mine now, Sir Kalenek, and I do what I like with my people. They serve me alone. Your rudeness has put me off from you today, but you will not evade me forever. Get out and send Torol in your stead. I will tell Charlon it was your idea that I take him as my new favorite."

Her words churned in Kal's mind as her command compelled him toward the exit. When the door closed behind him, he stopped and leaned against the bulkhead to feel his face again. She had assaulted him in the worst way. Had taken the curse he deserved.

Perhaps Onika would like him better now?

Truth instantly replaced that vain thought. Onika had seen his scars and accepted him, felt each track and pockmark, traced the trails in his beard and eyebrow where hair refused to grow.

Onika would not recognize him now.

WILEK

Wilek stood on the main deck with his wife watching the shipping ceremony. Today they were sending only six dead to Shamayim. One was a sailor who had died in a brawl, and the other five were commoners, dead of the fever. One was Darlow, Mielle and Amala's nurse, and two were children under ten. Wilek's gaze continually roved to the small bodies wrapped in strips of shredded clothing. He felt responsible.

It didn't help that so many glared at him.

It was not only deaths that angered his people but his refusal to allow any more traditional shippings. There were no more death boats to spare for the dead, no more old sails to be used as shrouds. Mourners were left with no choice but to ship their loved ones without a boat.

Despite all this, Wilek felt hopeful.

Not one new case of fever had been reported in the past fourteen days. The quarantine seemed to have accomplished its purpose. And while two hundred and twenty-seven had died thus far, fewer died each day. Wilek believed they were on the other side of the crisis. Not only that, but his wife was expecting a child, and encountering the pales had given them all hope that land would be discovered soon.

When the shipping was over, Wilek left his wife with her guards and set off to meet with the Wisean Council. He had invited Admiral Livina, Captain Bussie, and Rayim to report.

The admiral went first. "The pirates have taken out both warships on our western flank and three merchant ships."

"So many?" Wilek asked.

"They are working as a team now. Two or three ships circle one. Pirates come aboard. Some survivors say that there is fighting. Others say people throw themselves into the sea willingly, though they cannot recall why."

"Stinks like magic," Oli said.

"Perhaps he has allied with Magonia."

"Rand wouldn't work with Magonians," Wilek said, though maybe Teaka hadn't been the only mantic among Rand's people.

"How do they move so fast?" Inolah asked. "I thought the *Seffynaw* led the fleet."

"That she does," Admiral Livina said, "but with so many ships staying together as a group, we move mighty slowly. Plus it's been too long since any of us beached to clean our hulls. I've a feeling we're all carrying a lot of barnacles beneath us."

"What have we done to reinforce our western flank?" Wilek asked.

"I brought around one of our eastern warships to fill in for the time being," Admiral Livina said. "I'm currently in the process of commandeering two new vessels, but it's taking time to relocate the passengers. There is little room on any ship to take on so many newcomers."

"Thank you, Admiral. Captain Bussie? Tell me you have spotted land on the horizon and end all our misery."

"I wish I could, Your Highness," Captain Bussie said. "We are maintaining a heading of north-northwest. My lookouts have seen no change in the water, no debris, no birds, and very few clouds. No change in the wave pattern either."

"What about the pales?" Admiral Livina asked.

Wilek sighed. "We've yet to find a way to communicate with them. Sâr Trevn has given himself fully to the task, and I've no doubt he will succeed, in time."

"We have little time left, Your Highness," the admiral said.

Wilek nodded. "I'm well aware of how much time we have, Admiral." He glanced at Rayim. "Captain Veralla? How are the people?"

"Going mad, I'm afraid. Though disease has tapered off, the people are still afraid. They've lost friends and family. Food is low, and we're not catching enough fish to keep up. A rumor has begun that the only healthy people on board are mantics."

"That's nonsense," Oli said.

"Fear brings out the worst in people, I'm afraid," Wilek said.

"Crime is also at a high," Rayim said. "When we first set sail, violent crimes were a weekly event. They happen several times a day now. There is no room for another soul in the hold, so I have been flogging offenders on the pole. But as the closest thing this ship has to a physician, I can tell you that a flogging is a death sentence with such malnourished people and the ease of infections."

Wilek looked around him, really looked at the faces around the table. They were all of them gaunt and greasy-haired. Everyone's eyes seemed to have dug deeper into their skulls. Clothing hung on bony frames. Wilek had sores on his arms and what looked like bruises, though he couldn't recall having been hit by anything. And he was royalty, ate better than most.

"How many horses are left, Rayim?" Wilek asked.

"Six, Your Highness."

"Kill another." A horse would feed the entire ship one meal for four days. "Hunger, dehydration, and confinement will continue to turn the best man, or woman," he added with a look to Inolah, "into animals. We have no choice but to continue using the pole as a way to keep people in line. We can't afford not to."

✦ ✦ ✦

Wilek entered the cabin where they had housed the pales. Trevn sat on a crate across from the youngest pale man, who was sitting on the narrow bed built into the bulkhead. Behind him two other pales lay head to toe, asleep.

"Wil!" Trevn stood, smiling from ear to ear, a sheet of parchment in each hand. "I've made an important discovery."

His brother's unbridled joy surprised Wilek. He looked truly happy. No moping or pining for Miss Mielle, for the moment, anyway. The sight brought Wilek great relief.

"Tell me," he said.

"It *was* Randmuir Khal of the Omatta who attacked Maleen's ship, as you suspected, but there was another ship there. Rogedoth's. He and Randmuir are working together."

"Impossible."

"See for yourself." Trevn thrust the sheets of parchment at Wilek. "I asked Maleen to draw the ship that attacked his. He drew two."

Wilek accepted the pages from his brother and smoothed them out in his hands. "Maleen?" he asked.

The pale man tapped his chest. "*Ingohah* Maleen." He pointed at Trevn. "*Ingohah* Trevten."

"Tre*vn*," his brother corrected.

His brother had learned the pale's name. This was excellent. "Well done, Trevn," Wilek said, hoping to bolster his brother's sense of accomplishment.

He examined the sketches. They were indeed drawings of two ships. Similar in size, both were three-masted, though one was wider than the other, and the jagged letters on the hull of each gave them away. The first said "Malbrid." The *Malbraid* was the ship Wilek had given to Rand to help his tribe escape the Five Woes. The second ship had higher castles in the bow and stern, and the name scratched onto the stern hull was also misspelled yet unmistakable: "Armanah" could only be *Amarnath*. The flag drawn from the mainmast confirmed it, bearing the unmistakable rune that Lebetta had drawn in her dying moments.

"Rogedoth has declared himself king of the Five Realms," Trevn said, "married Eudora. It's clear he seeks to take the fleet right out from under us. Maleen says the pirates kept his father aboard the *Amarnath*. I bet Rogedoth is trying to get him to lead them to land. If he gets there before we do . . ." Trevn winced. "It would be bad, don't you think?"

If Rogedoth landed first, he could spin whatever tale he liked to any natives who lived there. He would have first say. And Wilek, coming after that, might have a great deal of trouble earning the trust of the people he hoped would share their homeland with the passengers of six hundred ships. "I want the *Seffynaw* to land first and greet the native inhabitants peaceably. Can your friend direct us to land?"

"I think so. But you'll have to let him come up to the quarterdeck and advise the helmsman which way to sail. Plus, look at this. Maleen?" He gestured to Wilek. "*Powhatu koi.*"

The pale held up some kind of square locket on the palm of his hand. The lid was open, hinged on one side.

"This is the best discovery yet," Trevn said, grinning wider than he had in weeks. "He calls it *powhatu koi*. See the markings? I believe they signify north, south, east, and west."

Wilek stepped close to the pale man and looked down on the locket. Inside, a sliver of black stone—pointed on one end, forked on the other—hovered above markings Wilek did not recognize. "Is it magic?"

Trevn shook his head. "The spinner is made of lodestone. No matter which way you turn the device, the arrow points south. Can I take Maleen to Admiral Livina right away? I want to show him the locket and see if Maleen can point us in the direction of his homeland."

"Absolutely," Wilek said. "I insist you go at once."

"Excellent. Thank you, brother." Trevn opened the door and waved the pale to follow. "Come on, Maleen. We're going to see the admiral."

✦ ✦ ✦

Maleen's locket fascinated Admiral Livina, who summoned Master Granlee, the navigator. Wilek stood by, watching as Trevn and the two old men showed their navigational tools to the pale. There was more demonstrating going on than talking, since the pale could barely understand the Kinsman language. The foursome went out onto the admiral's balcony with their tools, looking through them, taking down measurements. Wilek paced inside, anxious to have an answer—to have good news to share with everyone.

A shout on the balcony drew his attention. Trevn and the admiral ran inside, Trevn in the lead.

"His home is to the southwest!" he exclaimed, passing Wilek by at a jog.

"He seems quite certain," the admiral said, following Trevn.

"Sâr Trevn does?" Wilek asked.

The admiral glanced over his shoulder. "No, the pale."

Wilek gave chase, leaving the pale and the navigator on the admiral's balcony. They found Master Shinn at the whip, sitting on a stool, hat tipped down over his face, arms folded across his chest.

"Why aren't we moving?" Admiral Livina roared.

Shinn jolted awake and to standing in one great leap. "Sorry, sir," he said. "We've got no wind. I was waiting for a breeze to pick up."

"If there is no wind, row," Wilek said. "Is that not the saying?"

"Any fool can man the whip in a breeze," the admiral said, "but it takes skill to move a great ship in light air. Even if Thalassa is sleeping and we've got nothing but three knots of her breath to harness, we can put that to good use. Move the crew to lee and loosen everything off so that the mainsail and jib hang like bedsheets in a laundry basket. Let's get the passengers over on the leeward side, closer to the bow, and ease some halyard tension."

Master Shinn barked the orders to his crew. "Let's go, men. Hoist every rag you can until we get some motion."

Before long they began drifting.

"See now?" Livina said, clapping Master Shinn on the shoulder as he chuckled. "We're moving forward at a blistering two knots! Now set a course southwest."

Indeed, the *Seffynaw* had begun to crawl along. Wilek wondered where Rogedoth was, if he had yet to discover the location of the land, and if so, whether he had wind enough to get there first.

✦   ✦   ✦

While there had been no wind at midday, by evening the gales were so strong that the admiral ordered all passengers below deck. Wilek had called a council meeting during the dinner hour, ecstatic to have news to share.

"We are close to land," he said. "The pale tells us that he is from an island chain southwest of here. We have changed course and are headed in that direction now. He believes he is but two weeks from home."

"That's excellent!" Danek said.

"Wonderful," Rystan said.

"I'm not so certain," Inolah said.

Wilek's joy sputtered. "What do you mean?"

"Miss Onika has consistently said we should travel to the northwest and that we were not to follow the pales."

Wilek's stomach tightened at the mention of the prophetess. His sister was right. But surely Arman would not ask them to bypass land! He needed Miss Onika here to speak for herself. "Novan, send for Miss Onika at once."

Novan ran off to fetch the prophetess, and the discussion continued. No one seemed to care that Arman might be displeased. Oli, Danek, and Rystan began talking about what they would do first. Doubt kept Wilek silent. Surely Arman would not tease them so cruelly. They had little time left, were nearly out of food and water. Miss Onika must be mistaken. Or perhaps Inolah had misunderstood. The pale man had to be a sign of which direction to sail. Why else would they have found him?

Onika had barely stepped into the room when Wilek questioned her. "You disagree with the direction we've taken?"

Her head turned slightly toward Wilek's voice as Rustian led her along the end of the table after Novan. Only after the shield had helped her find her chair did she answer. "The fleet is no longer moving to the northwest. You have changed course."

"Because we found a man who can lead us to his homeland."

"It is the wrong land."

"Wrong? Who cares?" Oli said.

"We are nearly starved. Dying!" Danek added.

Wilek tried to be kind, though he felt as frustrated by her comments as the others. "Even if this is the wrong land, even if we cannot stay there forever, can we not at least replenish our supplies?"

"Arman does not wish for the fleet to reach these islands."

Hot anger filled Wilek's veins. "That is not a good enough answer! It is too much to tempt us when we are so broken. I cannot endure it. We will continue forth as the pale has directed us. That is all."

He strode toward the exit, adrenaline pulsing in his head.

"The God struck you," Onika said, her voice mesmerizing, "but you felt no pain. He crushed you, but you refused correction. If you continue on this path, a fang cat will attack, drice will ravage you, a serpent will tear to pieces any ship that ventures near forbidden lands to punish the rebellious and set the nations to right."

The words gripped Wilek's heart, pained him. "I have given my order. See that it is done." He continued through the doorway, overwhelmed by the power of that voice and the way her words cut through his resolve more deeply than a sword on the battlefield. Out in the corridor he stopped and leaned a hand against the bulkhead, choked in an emotional breath.

"Are you well, Your Highness?" Novan asked from behind him.

Wilek didn't answer. He continued on to his cabin, shut himself inside alone, and began to rail at Arman.

"I have done all you asked! But this is too much. I cannot turn this fleet from land! How dare you even suggest such a thing? So many have died, and they look to me. To turn back is folly. They will think me as mad as my father."

Wilek fell to his knees, unhindered in this place, where no man or woman could see his distress, his anguish.

"Why did I not die with Chadek that day at The Gray? Why did you not feed me to Barthos then? I could be at peace now, rather than in this horrible place. Why this choice, Arman? Why now? Would you have my people hate me? How then could I lead them to you? You have bound me. Again and again you target me. Can I have no peace in this life? Is death to be my only resting place?"

Someone touched him. Wilek jumped and lifted his head. Zeroah had entered and knelt beside him. She took his hands in hers and squeezed.

"He will cover you with his feathers, armored and protected in the shelter of his wings."

Wilek shook his head. "He does not cover me."

"You have faced death time and again and won. The Gray, the Magonians, the cheyvah, the Pontiff, the mutiny with Master Harton . . . But you must remember that your life—all our lives—belong to him. As our creator, he decides when we enter into his presence. Until then we live here, and we must not give up."

Wilek blinked, not wanting to lose this time. "I'm not giving up, I'm just . . . I'm tired. I want this to be over. I want us to be safe."

"You can never ensure that. Arman will lead us step by step. The future belongs to him, and it is his task to define it. We must relax and let him lead the way. All he asks is our trust."

It made sense. Could Wilek control the wind or rain? A good crop? These things were beyond his control. So why rage about them? "Trust is obedience," he said.

"Yes."

"Why is it so desperately hard?"

"Because we are used to being in charge of our lives. But if we learn to rest and trust, if we can be still, the God will fight for us."

Such a notion seemed foreign to Wilek. No one in authority had ever fought for him. He'd had to hire people to do that. Even then, Kal, Harton . . . they failed him. Zeroah's faith was so bold. So certain. He wished he could be as strong.

"I will tell Captain Bussie to put us back on a northwestern heading." He took a deep breath, reluctant to move. "Will you help me?" he asked Zeroah. "Remind me to trust Arman when I go off on my own?"

She smiled and squeezed his hands. "Always."

CHARL⦿N

Shanek wailed. Wouldn't stop. The rocking of the ship was too wild. Not at all comforting.

Charlon glared into the child's bed. "Calm down," she told him.

But the child continued to cry, face crimson, tongue curled in fury, arms waving, legs kicking.

"I do not like the storm either," she said.

The door opened. Sir Kalenek entered. Thank Magon!

"What are you doing to this boy?" He picked up Shanek. The child instantly calmed. Looked at Charlon.

See? Shanek seemed to say. *The knighten knows what I need.*

Charlon sighed, irritated. "He hates me. Hates his own mother."

"He wants to be held," Sir Kalenek said. "Why won't you hold him?"

"I do," she said. "Sometimes."

"You will never improve if you do not practice."

Chieftess Mreegan wants to see you on the quarterdeck immediately. The voice belonged to Hali, one of Mreegan's common shadir. But Charlon could not see it.

She had stopped taking ahvenrood. Could no longer see into the Veil. But the shadir could still speak to her. This surprised her. Would she eventually lose the ability to hear them? How long would it take?

"The Chieftess needs me," she said, leaving Sir Kalenek and Shanek alone.

She made her way to the quarterdeck. Held on to the walls. The ocean had grown fierce. She exited into icy rain. Strong wind whipped her kasah about.

393

She shuffled toward the helm. Found Mreegan standing beside Captain Krola. The Chieftess was dry. Had likely cast a spell. To keep the elements away.

"Is something wrong?" Charlon yelled over the pounding rain.

"Magon has cautioned us against following the ships," Mreegan said. "They're headed toward the land—at least where the shadir have said the land is—but Magon says we should wait out the storm. I've never seen the goddess more uncertain, but I trust her judgment."

Charlon wiped the water off her face. "Then why call me?"

"Because the Armanians are headed into the storm. If something should happen to them, Shanek will inherit their realm. I want you to send one of your slights to spy on the *Seffynaw*, see what Prince Wilek is doing."

"You could have done this yourself. In the time it took to summon me."

"Do you refuse my command?" Mreegan asked.

Charlon glanced at Krola. She did not want him listening. "Of course not, Chieftess. I will do this at once." She turned to walk away. Wondering. How would she find an answer? To satisfy the Chieftess? Without speaking to a shadir?

"Call the shadir from here," Mreegan yelled. "I wish you to stay close so that I might have your answer right away."

Charlon froze, turned back. Mreegan suspected. It was the only explanation. The Chieftess knew Charlon had stopped taking ahvenrood.

"The storm has made me queasy," she yelled, again wiping the rain from her face. "I have been fasting to clear my stomach. I will need to take more ahvenrood."

Mreegan removed her hip flask and held it out. "Take some of mine."

Fear welled within. To take root juice was to risk her child. Yet Mreegan's wrath was a greater risk. Charlon took the flask. Drank. Handed it back.

Fool! her heart said. *What have you done?*

Charlon maintained eye contact with the Chieftess. Staring her down. Having been dry for so long, the effects rushed upon her. The juice pooled in her belly like ice. Nerves burned with cold. Coupled with the rain, Charlon shivered. The Veil flickered into view, bright and colorful.

"Nwari," she called, her eyes still locked with Mreegan's.

The wispy orange slight appeared beside her. *Yes, lady?*

"The Chieftess wishes to know what Prince Wilek is doing aboard the *Seffynaw*. Go now and bring back a report."

Yes, lady. Nwari vanished.

"Anything else, Chieftess?" Charlon asked.

"Report to me when you hear back from Nwari."

"Certainly."

Charlon left. Quickly. Went to Torol's cabin. There she purged to the nearest slight. It was too late. She felt her belly. It had grown since she'd ingested the root. Not much. A tiny paunch. But the baby had clearly been affected.

What could she do to protect the child now? All seemed hopeless.

GOZAN

Gozan flew away from the lush archipelago. His swarm had shown him their discovery, and he felt certain that between all the islands, there would be room enough for what remained of the fleet. Though he had the ability to return to the *Gillsmore* instantly, he took his time coming back, curious at the distance the ships would have to cross to reach the islands. Some of his shadir followed, cackling over the prospect of reuniting the humans with a harvest of evenroot. So content was Gozan in light of the discovery of land that he ignored their clamor.

Dark, ominous clouds filled the horizon. Gozan didn't like the look of them and transported himself underneath. He could barely see from the storm's eye. Twists of water spun down from the clouds around a massive whirlpool. Interesting. It had been centuries since Gozan had seen one of those. He went a bit farther, stopping only when he had reached calmer weather. There he found the fleet on the edge of disaster.

His first thoughts were delight at the waves of fear exuding from the humans. He'd always enjoyed watching them suffer in severe weather while he, safe in the Veil, felt none of it. But his own interests quickly pushed aside his joy. If the ships lost direction in the storm, how much longer until they found land? And if they sank . . . who would Gozan bond with?

Human screams captured his attention. He followed the sound and saw that a ship had been caught in the whirlpool's current. He instantly put himself down on the main deck, eager to watch the disaster unfold. He found this ship surprisingly familiar. It was the *Baretam*, the ship the pirates had taken from

396

Emperor Ulrik. Fortuitous, then, that Jazlyn had accompanied the emperor to his vice flagship *Gillsmore*.

The ship sailed quickly around and around the maelstrom. It appeared the captain had given up, as a handful of sailors knelt at the port rail. Some prayed, some stared over the railing at their impending death, and all clutched the rail as if doing so might spare them. Gozan put himself in their midst and fed off their fear, immensely gratified.

The ship tipped slowly, and the sailors slid toward the foredeck, screaming and clutching for handholds.

You're going to die, he said into one man's ear and relished the way the man's face contorted.

The *Baretam* jerked nearly upright, its bow caught in the downdraft. The sailors shot along the main deck and piled up against the forward bulkhead.

Gozan flew into the sky to get a better look. Stern in the air, the ship spun on its nose, whipping around the center of the maelstrom. The foremast dipped into the opposite side of the whirlpool and ripped clear off, causing its sails and rigging to bounce and tangle as the current dragged them along.

More shadir arrived as the humans began to die. The presence of so many of his kind dampened Gozan's thrill, and he left, drifting back toward the rest of the fleet.

Several more ships were headed right for the maelstrom. If Gozan waited, he might witness a crash when another ship got caught in the vortex and ran into the *Baretam*.

First he must ensure the safety of his future.

He took a wide look at the fleet, surprised to see it had started to split into two groups. On one side Dendron and his mantic king were headed right for the storm and the islands beyond. A collection of pirated ships followed. Then came a gap where a second group of pirates lagged.

On the other side the Armanians had steered away from the storm and resumed their northern course, leading the majority of the fleet away from land.

In the very back, as usual, the Magonian ship lingered out of sight.

Gozan found the *Gillsmore* far enough back in the fleet that he need not hurry to alert Jazlyn of the situation. He would rather know what these captains had in mind before advising her.

First he went to the *Amarnath*, where Dendron sailed with the mantic king. A series of waterspouts twirled down from black clouds like a wall. The ship bucked on the turbulent sea like a horse looking to unseat its rider. Six mantics stood along the quarterdeck rail. A group of people sat on the deck behind them, tied to the rail with ropes. Malleants. Jealousy surged through Gozan. Dendron was rich indeed.

The mantics drew strength from the malleants and cast their spells. A protective cylinder formed around the ship. Overhead, the sky opened up in a patch of clear blue. The storm and rain curled around the outside of the void the magic had created. Dozens of shadir flew about, feeding off the humans' loyalty and the malleants' fear.

The *Amarnath* passed through one of the waterspouts. The funnel twisted against the outside of the protective barrier, pelting it with water. The intensity of the spray produced a well of fear from the malleants, and Gozan reveled in it.

The whirlwind passed over to the other side of the ship, and everything seemed to calm, though rain still beat against the sides of the magical barrier around the ship, making rivulets run down what looked like glass.

Gozan lingered while the ship passed through two more waterspouts, then went to the *Vespara* at the very back of the fleet. He found Magon hovering beside her human twin.

"How have you advised your human?" Gozan asked her.

"I told her to stay back from the storm. I cannot risk losing them to the sea."

"Dendron sails into the eye of it," Gozan said.

"He is a fool," she spat. "But I should like to see that for myself."

And she vanished.

Gozan passed through the Veil to the first of the pirate ships lagging behind. At the helm he found the pair who had led the raid to take the *Baretam* from Emperor Ulrik. A common shadir that had taken the form of a brown wolf stood between them, gleaming teeth bared as it watched their argument.

"Why have we slowed down?" the lipless man yelled through the pounding rain.

"King Barthel has sailed into the storm," the captain said. "He's madder than a Magonian crow if he thinks we can sail through that without the help of his mantics."

"We're just going to wait?" the lipless man asked.

"We're going to change course," the captain said.

"What about my face?" the lipless man asked. "A mantic is the only one who can fix what that crow did to me."

"I'm all sympathy, son," the captain said. "I did my best. Truly I did. But the gods are against me. About time you learned to live with it. Look at the bright side. You're terrifying to look at. That face makes people instantly fear you. We'll call you Growler or Fangs or something delightfully horrible. We're better off on our own without the mantics trying to control us."

A strange comment coming from a man who kept a common shadir. Gozan could not tell which human the common was bonded to, so he took the form of a common of equal strength and struck up a conversation. A few questions and praises and he had the common, whose name was Haroan, bragging all about its exploits.

"My master is in his cabin. We snuck aboard when Randmuir the pirate met with King Barthel. We've put the pirate under our control, so we rule this ship now."

"How clever," Gozan said, noting the tattoo on the back of the captain's neck. "So you'll compel him to follow the *Amarnath*?"

"No," Haroan said. "Our orders are to follow the pirate and report back. The compulsion will only be used when it best serves the king."

Interesting. Dendron's reach was far. Gozan bid the common good luck and set off to see why the Armanians were leading the majority of the fleet away from land.

He arrived on the *Seffynaw* and found the Armanian princes with the captain on the quarterdeck.

"I am certain I can steer us around the storm and back toward land, Your Highness," the helmsman said.

"I have no doubt of that, Master Shinn," Prince Wilek said. "But I was wrong to counter an order from Arman. We will sail north until the prophetess tells us we have reached our original course. I will issue new instructions then."

"Yes, sir," Shinn, the helmsman, said, and Gozan reveled in the man's anger.

Prince Wilek walked away, and the younger prince chased after him. Gozan followed.

"But, Wil. Maleen says land is southwest."

"I know it. But Arman does not wish us to go that way."

"But . . . why?"

Prince Wilek set his hand on the younger prince's shoulder. "Miss Onika says *that* land in particular is not for us. Obeying her caution was not easy for me, brother. I need your support in this."

"Of course," the young man said, though frustration rose up inside him.

Gozan soaked it in as he considered their words. Miss Onika? The pale blind woman Sir Kalenek had been leading through Rurekau? That she had been advising the Armanians annoyed Gozan. The prophetess swore allegiance to Arman, enemy of Lord Gâzar. Gozan could not allow her to have influence over Jazlyn. He set off to convince Jazlyn to urge Emperor Ulrik to stay away from the Armanians at all costs.

Trevn

The next morning when Trevn was on watch, he stood at the top of the mainmast, gazing out at the horizon and the distant crest of land. Devastated by the sight, knowing they were not to go there, Trevn did not call down what he saw. No matter. The lookouts on other ships did, and signal flags had shot up all over. The flagmen on the *Seffynaw* were doing their best to communicate Wilek's wishes.

That land was not for them. They would continue north.

It likely sounded insane.

Trevn watched ships ignore the flagship's orders, peel away from the fleet, and sail toward the land. By the end of his watch, at least three dozen had done so, but by then another storm had risen up in the distance, hiding the land from view.

A large portion of the fleet had stayed with them, including the Sarikarians, which did not surprise Trevn considering they had wanted to travel northwest from the start.

Trevn reached for Mielle. At first he felt nothing but the hollow pit where her presence should abide. This brought on a panic that she might have died. Without wanting it to happen, tears sprung to his eyes.

A familiar concern pressed upon his heart, and he knew that it was Mielle, worrying about the worry she felt from him.

"Where are you?" he asked, wishing she might hear and answer.

He stared at the blackish skyline that now completely hid the pale's land from view. Surely Arman wouldn't allow Mielle's ship to reach the pale's islands if that wasn't where he wanted them to go. The *Rafayah* must be in the fleet, somewhere behind them, perhaps. Once they found land, Trevn would know for sure.

The question was, how much longer would they have to wait?

WİLEK

Going north was easy sailing. Not only that, but fishing improved, and calm rains were frequent enough to keep the water barrels filled.

This did not appease the passengers. As rumor spread of land passed by, they began to rebel. Crime increased, and as a result, so did floggings. Wilek hated it, but he didn't know what else could be done. One week passed, then a second. And while the fish and water kept everyone well nourished, morale bordered on rebellion.

Until one late midday nearly three weeks after they'd changed course. Oli Agoros barged in to Wilek's office, followed by Novan.

"It's land, Your Highness," Oli said.

Wilek shot out of his chair and ran.

As he made his way to the quarterdeck, he could feel the ship listing to port. He sprinted outside, greeted by a blast of frigid air. The deck was nearly clear, as everyone had crowded the port side. Hope clawed its way up Wilek's throat, making it difficult to breathe as he pushed through the crowd toward the rail.

"Make way for the sâr-regent!" Novan yelled.

A cheer rose up. The people parted, and Wilek stepped into the opening. A sheen of sunlight painted the water in brightness. Wilek squinted and held his hand above his eyes. There on the horizon was something solid. Something brown and gray. And white.

Land. It stretched out to both sides as far as he could see. Surely this was large enough for their remnant. He spotted a distant white mountain peak and grinned. This place would have to be vast to host such a monument.

403

"Fetch Miss Onika," he told Novan.

Novan echoed his order to a soldier as Wilek devoured the sight with his eyes. He saw no grass, though there were spindly gray trees with branches that stretched toward the white ground. Was that sand? He had never seen white sand before. This place looked nothing like Bakurah Island, Armania, or any place Wilek had seen in the Five Realms.

"How long . . . ?" He twisted about, suddenly uncertain where the captain or admiral might be. "Novan, I must speak with the admiral."

"He's at the whip with the captain, Your Highness."

Wilek made his way through the crowd toward the men. "How long until we reach it, Admiral?"

"Distances from land can be deceiving, Your Highness," Admiral Livina said.

"Hazard a guess."

"It's nearly sunset. We'll get as close as we can, then drop anchor for the night. We'll take the longboats out at first light. I'd like to sail around it, look for a sloping beach where the surf is gentle before making landfall."

"No. I must land today," Wilek said.

"One should never land in a foreign port at night, Your Highness."

Wilek put a grow lens to his eye, studied the rocky beach with tufts of yellow plants sprouting up here and there. "It looks gentle enough, don't you think?" He passed the lens to Admiral Livina.

The man looked through it and sighed. "Very inviting, I'd say."

"We're on the leeward side," Captain Bussie added, "so that's a boon."

"There could be coral reefs in our way," the admiral said. "I'd much rather wait until morning."

"I cannot wait, Admiral," Wilek said. "To wait is to give our enemies first pick of the land." He gestured behind them. "Even my own people won't wait, I assure you. I must be first."

The admiral sighed. "The land is likely occupied already."

"Then I will be the first from the Five Realms to know it. Captain Bussie, monitor the depths and get us as close as you feel comfortable before setting anchor. Rayim, prepare four longboats and three dozen men. Dendrick, pack enough tents and whatever supplies you deem necessary. We will see the Armanian flag flying on that shore by nightfall."

"I'm coming with you," Trevn said.

Wilek met his brother's eyes. It wasn't a good idea for them both to leave the ship, but he had no right to deny Trevn this moment. His brother had worked harder than most to get them here. "Captain Bussie, I'm removing Sâr Trevn from your crew."

"Yes, sir," the captain said.

Trevn grinned. "Thanks, Wil! I'll get my things." He sprinted away.

As the longboats were made ready, Wilek sought out Miss Onika. He found her with Inolah and Oli, who were standing on the stern deck at the taffrail.

"Miss Onika," Wilek said. "Please tell me this land is acceptable to Arman."

Her joyful expression answered before she spoke. "I have no objection to it, Your Highness. It will not be long until Arman confirms it himself."

Cryptic but enough of a yes for him. "Thank you, lady."

Zeroah found him then and slipped her arm around his waist. "Another island?" she asked, resting her head on his shoulder.

"I don't think so," Wilek said, pointing to the mountain. "See that peak? No tiny island could hold something that big."

He kissed his wife's hair and left her with Inolah and Oli, then walked to his cabin to gather his things. When he returned to the boat fall, Trevn was helping the sailors load the longboats. Time seemed to crawl. The sun had already begun to set. Lately it had been doing so much earlier than it ever had back in Everton.

Soon they were on their way. The longboat jerked across the inshore currents, the men rowing hard. Wilek stood with one knee on the forward-most bench that was nestled in the bow, eagerly looking ahead. Trevn stood beside him, leaning forward with both hands gripping the boat's edge. Seagulls swarmed the rocky beach like gnats, and higher up, raven-like birds circled. The wildlife gave him hope that this was land to be lived on.

Let it be so, Arman. Let this be home.

The beach was smaller than that of Bakurah Island. To the east a forest of droopy charcoal trees met the sea. The air held a combination of salt and the strong, bitter scent of earth.

By the time Wilek's boat first scraped over the rocky sand, dusk had fallen. The oarsmen jumped out into the water and ran the boat up onto the beach. Trevn didn't wait for them to finish. He leapt over the side and into the shallow surf, gasped.

"Sands! That's cold," Trevn said. Breath fogged from his lips as he swung his arms and pulled his legs along. "Good thing I wore my boots."

Wilek followed him into the frigid water. It came up to his knees, quickly filling his boots and making his trousers cling to his legs. "Mine don't seem to be helping," Wilek said.

They slogged up onto the white sand. Wilek took two steps, and the sound and feel of the ground under his boots made him realize that this was not sand at all. He picked up a handful of icy wetness and it melted in his palm.

"It's snow!" Trevn yelled, tossing a handful at Wilek.

Snow. Wilek had heard talk of snow from those who'd visited the Polar Desert, but he'd never had reason to make the journey himself. It was said nothing could live there. Sarikarians knew more of it. He kicked some dead stalks of golden grass that poked up from the ground. He would have to consult with King Loran right away as to how to live in such an environment.

"Do trees grow in the Polar Desert?" he asked Trevn.

"I don't think so. The Polar Desert is nothing but plains of ice and snow. Look at this." Trevn crouched beside a twiggy bush. "See these knobs along the branch? That's a sign of leaves. There are seasons here, Wil, like in Sarikar and Magonia. This must be winter."

"But it's summer," Wilek said.

"By the Five Realms calendar, yes, but we've traveled a long way. It's winter here."

They had landed on a point where both sides of the coast seemed to run northbound. Their breath puffed out in clouds. Trevn's lips were turning blue, and Wilek's feet already felt numb. Would it be too cold to live here?

They were out of food. Out of water. Out of time. This place was their last chance. And Onika had concurred. This was home. They would have to find a way to make it work.

Wilek sank to his knees, grabbed two handfuls of snow, and lifted them up before his eyes. He squeezed and let the icy water drip from his fists. Glorious land. They should build an altar, sacrifice a burnt offering, but there were no animals left to sacrifice but three horses and some hens. Wilek would not sacrifice a human.

A vow offering would have to do until he could bring the horses ashore or hunt something better.

"To you, Arman!" he yelled at the top of his lungs. "I know now that you can do all things. No plan of yours can be thwarted. That I doubted you . . . I despise myself. I repent!" He looked up to Trevn, grabbed his brother's wrist. "Kneel in worship before He Who Made the World, Trevn. The God led us here, and we must thank him."

Trevn knelt beside Wilek and grabbed his own handful of snow.

"We thank you, Arman, for this land," Wilek said, "and dedicate it to you. Our people will honor you here." He glanced at Trevn. "We vow to you they will, as long as it is in our power to lead them. Vow it, Trevn."

"I vow it," Trevn said.

Wilek bowed down and kissed the cold, gritty rocks. Trevn mirrored him. Heat grew within Wilek's chest, and words came from inside his head.

"WELCOME, LITTLE KINGS. WITH YOU BOTH I AM WELL PLEASED. TAKE THIS LAND AS YOUR OWN AND MAKE A PLACE FOR MY PEOPLE. FOLLOW MY COMMANDS AND YOU WILL PROSPER. DO NOT HARDEN YOUR HEARTS AS YOUR FOREFATHERS DID IN THE DESERT OF ARMANIA, WHERE THEY TESTED AND TRIED ME. THEIR HEARTS WENT ASTRAY FROM MY WAYS, AND THEY SHALL NEVER ENTER MY REST."

Wilek gasped, overcome by warmth and love. He glanced at Trevn and found his brother's face amazed and streaked in tears.

"We will not harden our hearts, Arman," Wilek said. "We will follow your commands as they are written in your book."

"I HAVE SET ASIDE FOR MY CHOSEN PEOPLE A GIFT," the God said. "FOR THOSE IN WHICH THE BLOOD OF KINGS RUNS TRUE, IF USED WELL, THIS GIFT WILL SAVE YOU FROM THE EVIL YOU BROUGHT TO THIS LAND. USE IT NOW. SPEAK TO YOUR BROTHER IN SILENCE, WITH YOUR MIND. THINK AND HE WILL HEAR YOU."

Wilek glanced at Trevn, who shrugged. *What did the God mean?*

Trevn grabbed his arm. "He means think to me and I will hear you. I just did! You thought, 'What did the God mean?'"

"You heard that?"

"Yes." Trevn's voice in his mind. *"Do you hear me?"*

"Yes!"

"It's like the soul-binding," Wilek said, wary.

Trevn nodded. "But no mantic cast a spell. Arman spoke to us, Wil."

Wilek could not deny that the voice was unlike anything he'd ever experienced.

"Is it just for us?" Trevn asked.

"He said it was for his chosen people. For those in which the blood of kings runs true."

"So . . . royalty?" Trevn asked. "See if you can talk to Sârah Zeroah."

"Zeroah?" Wilek thought.

He heard no answer.

Perhaps he needed to concentrate or be closer. "I don't want to frighten her," Wilek said. "Let's move ahead cautiously. Tell no one of this for now, at least until we understand it better."

"A solid plan," Trevn said. "Let's post the flag and get a fire built. I can't feel my feet. It would be a shame to freeze to death after coming so far."

"A person can freeze to death?" Wilek asked.

Trevn pushed off Wilek's shoulder and stood. "You really should read more, brother."

"Wait!" Wilek pulled Trevn back down beside him. "We must thank Arman for this gift."

✦ ✦ ✦

The first night came with no sign of pirates, Rogedoth, Magonians, or natives, or dangerous beasts. Wilek and Trevn shared a tent and built up a strong fire in their brazier, but it remained so cold in their beds that they dragged their mattresses over by the fire. Despite being warmer, Wilek couldn't sleep. Everything felt too still without the constant rocking of the ship. The waves crashing on the shore and strange birdcalls kept him alert. From the sounds of Trevn's thrashing about, it was the same for him.

In the morning, once Wilek realized they were still alone, he sent messages to the *Seffynaw*, *Kaloday*, and *Gillsmore* to announce his plans to stay. King Loran came ashore at once and set up his own camp, but Emperor Ulrik sent back a message that he wanted to settle his own land apart from Armania and would take the remainder of his ships up the western coast.

Wilek and King Loran met, and several plans were put in motion. Three groups of explorers set out to survey the land. Wilek sent Rost Keppel and his team up the eastern coast. King Loran sent his explorers to the west. And Wilek allowed Trevn to take a group of soldiers inland to search the immediate area for signs of life and to determine the best means for building shelters.

"Do not go far," Wilek reminded his brother. "I need you to bring me answers with haste. We have to accommodate a hundred thousand people coming ashore."

Trevn looked out to sea and the ships that had anchored along the coastline. "I don't think we have near that many left, brother. I doubt we have half what we came with."

Surely not.

"It will take time to gain an accurate count," Wilek admitted. "But we can't have lost that many. Now, I want you back before midday. No drawing maps today. We must organize or we'll have a disaster on our hands. Plus I need some time with you to figure out how this blood gift works."

"I need to find Mielle."

Wilek sighed. "Please don't do that until we can practice. It unnerves me."

"I didn't mean to do it that time," Trevn said, grinning. "But it *is* rather easy." And he started to sing a song in his head about the first king of Armania.

Wilek scowled at his little brother. "There must be some way I can block your thoughts if I don't want to hear them."

Trevn shrugged. *"Concentration, perhaps?"*

"I don't have time for this. Prepare your team. And find someone else who can mind-speak and practice with them."

"Can I try Hinck?"

"Excellent idea," Wilek said. "I would like to know where he is. If he made it to Rogedoth's ship."

"If he's alive?" Trevn added.

"That too. Investigate this mind-speaking quietly, please. I want to know who has this ability, and I want them to keep it private for now. It might frighten people."

"Did you talk to your wife?" Trevn asked.

"I have yet to see her today," Wilek said. "I will ask her tonight. Right now we have a settlement to build."

✦ ✦ ✦

By the end of the first full day, the new settlement consisted of nothing more than several dozen military tents. Wilek wanted to build a watchtower fortress, but Trevn pointed out that Armanian builders were mostly masons, so they would need to apprentice with some of King Loran's carpenters if they were to build anything worthwhile out of wood.

Just after dinner Wilek met with the Wisean Council, King Loran and his advisors, and another two dozen staff from both realms. For now, Rosâr Echad remained bedridden on the *Seffynaw*, in no condition to be moved in this cold until they had a safe place to put him.

Initial reports from all the explorers confirmed that the land was vast. They had encountered no natives on their brief tour but had found signs of life in several abandoned settlements, some with brush shelters, others with pit houses. Master Keppel believed the natives to be nomads who likely followed a herd of animals.

This worried King Loran that the winter would be hard if large game was scarce, but Rayim was optimistic over rabbit tracks he'd seen. He felt that smaller animals were usually more prevalent than big game. This started a long discussion over food. Trevn volunteered to take Maleen, the pale, exploring to see if the young man knew anything of this land.

The topic shifted to housing. Wilek didn't want to see tens of thousands of commoners homeless and wandering the frozen land. The brush shelters and pit houses could be used, temporarily, at least. The ships could continue to be lived in as well, though each needed to be beached for repairs and for cleaning the hulls.

King Loran volunteered his carpenters to train the Armanian masons to log trees, mill the wood into lumber, and assemble simple wooden structures. It was also decided that they would build a fortress that both Armanian and Sarikarian royalty would share for the time being. Once warmer temperatures came, King Loran wanted to explore farther west.

The discussion ended on the topic of how to let people off the ships. Each captain would be responsible for communicating with his passengers and crew to determine who would continue to live on board and who would move ashore. Once all the captains' reports came in, Wilek and King Loran would have some idea of how many people would need shelter and could be put to work building or hunting.

✦ ✦ ✦

When Wilek lay in bed that night in his tent with Zeroah beside him, he told her about hearing Arman's voice and the mind-speaking gift the God had given to him and Trevn.

"He said the gift was for his people, for those with the blood of kings. I wondered if you might have it too."

"How would I know?" she asked.

"Send me a thought."

"You sound crazy."

"I'm not crazy, my dear."

She gasped and touched her temples. "I heard your voice in my mind."

"Strange, isn't it?"

"What does it mean?"

"Arman said it would save us from the evil we brought to this land."

"What evil?" Zeroah asked

Wilek took a deep breath. "I wish I knew."

"What do we call this place?" she asked. "The *New* Five Realms?"

"Tenma is practically extinct. The Five Realms are no more." A word came to Wilek then. It was the ancient word for land and seemed somehow appropriate. "Others may choose whatever name they please, but I will call this new land Er'Rets."

Hınck

Rogedoth had demanded Hinck, Lady Lilou, and several others serve as malleants while the mantics wielded magic to survive the storm. Hinck had tried to fake a drink from the evenroot bottle that Timmons had forced on him, but a tiny swallow had seeped in and made him sick enough to fall into a delusion. When he'd finally awakened, he found himself in bed in his cabin. He'd refused the shadir that came to him, which had made Lady Mattenelle so nervous she'd cast a spell to heal him herself.

"You must be more careful," she'd said. "If the king finds out you refuse the milk of Gâzar and the healing of shadir, he will be very upset."

Hinck had seen what Rosârah Laviel did when she was angry. He had no desire to find out what her father might do.

The *Amarnath* had continued on for three more weeks in search of an island chain that Rogedoth's shadir was supposedly leading them to. But when they finally reached land one rainy morning, it turned out to be no more than three islands.

The *Amarnath* dropped anchor, as did the twenty-some other ships Rogedoth had pirated in the past few months. An army of dinghies carrying Rogedoth and his mantics stormed the beach. Despite the pouring rain they attacked a village of pales, subdued the leaders, and enslaved them all. By the time Hinck came to shore with Lady Eudora and her retinue of maidens, the worst of the evils had ended.

The island was covered in woodlands, though barren trees and bushes and yellow grass spoke of a winter season. The place reminded Hinck of the

412

forest east of Faynor back in Sarikar, where the trees met the fog of The Gray. Though it had stopped raining by the time Hinck stepped ashore, the air itself seemed heavy with cool moisture. On the horizon forested hills rolled into the distance. The village itself consisted of several dozen stilted, reed-walled houses with steep, thickly pitched grass roofs. Mosquitoes were everywhere, and their bites itched madly.

In all there were eight mantics: Lady Zenobia, Zithel Lau, Filkin Yohtheh-reth, Sârah Jemesha, Rosârah Laviel, Rogedoth himself, Harton Sonber, and Lady Mattenelle, who, at her request, Hinck now called Nellie. Each mantic commandeered a stilted house. Hinck was to live in Nellie's, Eudora told him as they made their way from the beach to the largest house in the village—the one Rogedoth had claimed for himself.

"Nellie gets a house but I don't?" Hinck asked. "How does a concubine rank higher than an earl?"

"Your status in this kingdom has nothing to do with your birth or rank," Eudora said. "It's about loyalty. Lady Mattenelle is to keep an eye on you, because your loyalty remains in question to the king."

Wonderful. "How can I prove my loyalty?" he asked.

"Stay out of the way for now. And if you are called upon, obey and be polite."

Hinck was always polite. "So I'm to be a slave like the pales?"

"We all must obey our king," she said, sneering.

But Rogedoth was not Hinck's king. He met Eudora's dark eyes, wondering how he would ever find his way back to the Armanians.

They reached the biggest house and climbed a short ladder to enter. The place seemed to be built of sticks, though inside, the floor was sturdy. Thin rods lashed together created walls that let the moist, cool air flow through the room. The inside was one large, rectangular space with several glassless windows on every wall. Grass mats covered the floor and some of the windows. Ladders on each end of the room led up to separate lofts.

Already Rogedoth had set up the thrones. He and his daughter were seated. Eudora left Hinck at the door and claimed her spot beside the king.

"I sense a new magic here, my queen," Rogedoth said. "I first believed it to be an enhancement of our mantic abilities, but now I think it is something different."

"What kind of magic?" Eudora asked.

"A form of mind-speak," he said. "I am able to do it, as are Sârah Jemesha and Rosârah Laviel. But none of the others. I think it shall prove most useful to my plans."

"It sounds awful," Eudora said.

Rogedoth frowned at his bride, then looked away, his shrewd gaze scanning the room. He spotted Hinck and seemed to snarl like a fang cat about to pounce. "I see you brought Lord Dacre."

"As you commanded," Eudora said.

"Come forward, Lord Dacre," Rogedoth said.

Hinck made his way to the front of the room. He glanced from Eudora to Rogedoth to Rosârah Laviel. He was still looking at Sâr Janek's mother when he heard Rogedoth's voice in his head.

"Do you hear me, Lord Dacre? I think you a traitor."

Panic seized Hinck's nerves. He kept his gaze steady, his thoughts blank, then slowly looked to Rogedoth, determined not to let the man know he could hear this new magic.

"I would have you swear fealty to me, Lord Dacre, and serve House Rogedoth as I see fit," he said, then added silently, *"Or you can die."*

Hinck bowed his head, trying to look honored and not completely terrified, though his hands were trembling. The words of such a vow meant nothing to Hinck, but to swear fealty meant that he would be Rogedoth's man. He would have to take evenroot and worship the King of Magic and obey whatever insane command the man gave him.

Or die, apparently.

"I . . . am honored to swear loyalty to my king, Your Highness," he said, thinking of Rosâr Echad and Sâr Wilek as he dropped to his knees.

Hinck had gone from being a pawn of princes to being the slave of a tyrant who wanted to kill him.

"Very good," Rogedoth said, though Hinck could hear the mistrust in the man's voice. "You, Lord Dacre, will join me as we begin our preparations. Already evenroot is being sowed in the ground, and soon we will have power enough to claim all the kingdoms as our own. Sarikar will fall. Armania will fall. And we shall rule."

Hinck forced himself to keep from trembling, from picturing the terrible future the man claimed. He knew only two things: First, he would do all he could to stop Rogedoth's plans.

Second, freedom was a long way off.

PART SIX

VOICES
OF BLOOD

CHARLON

The *Vespara* sailed behind the Rurekan fleet. Following a coast of ice and snow. No sign of the tropical islands Magon had spoken of. The Armanians had passed those by. And Magon had willed the *Vespara* to follow.

But when the Armanians found the icy land and stopped to stay, the Chieftess said Magon wanted the *Vespara* to sail on farther. So they trailed the Rurekans along the western coast. Keeping their distance. Two days of sailing and the Rurekans anchored at the mouth of a vast river.

Charlon had never seen anything like it. Water wide enough for five ships to sail abreast. It ran above ground and emptied into the sea. Charlon stood along the rail with Mreegan and Captain Krola, watching through grow lenses as the Rurekan ships launched dinghies to go ashore.

"That waterway leads to our new home," Mreegan said.

"Shall we make landfall, then?" the captain asked.

"We will wait," Mreegan said, "and see what the Rurekans do."

And so the *Vespara* waited. Three days passed by as the Rurekans explored. Charlon suffered.

Abstaining from ahvenrood brought pain. Intense headaches and shaking. Weakness in her bones. Heat like a fever, though Sir Kalenek told her she had none. She longed for a taste of root. For the cold. For the magic to fill her veins with power. To be strong again.

She fought the desire. Pretended to be healthy and strong. To protect the baby. The baby Torol had given her. The baby she would keep when the Chieftess took Shanek away to rule Armania.

417

On the fourth morning the Rurekans returned to their ships and sailed past the river. Up the coast to the west.

"It is as Magon decreed," Mreegan said. "We will follow the river inland to our new homeland."

"What about the *Vespara*?" Krola asked.

"Magonians are land dwellers," Mreegan said. "The ship is unimportant."

Charlon did not like putting her trust in the Chieftess. She missed not being able to speak with Magon. Could no longer see the goddess since she'd stopped taking ahvenrood. Charlon ached for the goddess's attention. For the confidence that came from knowing her. For the fulfillment of the promise that she would one day make Charlon Chieftess.

"We must not stray too far from the Armanians," Charlon said to Mreegan. "For Shanek's sake."

"No," Mreegan said. "We need distance, for now. And time. Shanek is growing quickly, but it might take several years for him to reach manhood."

"Surely not." Charlon glanced at the boy. He now looked five or six years of age. He was climbing the lower part of the rigging like a ladder. Sir Kalenek stood by, one hand grazing the boy's back.

"No me do it." Shanek pushed Kal's hand away. "Shanek do it myself."

Charlon winced. "His speech may take longer to mature."

"I am glad you can see that much," Mreegan said. "His mind is not developing as quickly as his body."

Sir Kalenek had warned the Chieftess that Shanek was growing too quickly. "Give him less ahvenrood," Charlon said.

"Sir Kalenek would have him remain a boy for too long," Mreegan said. "We must rush his body to manhood, then train his mind. Magon assures me this is best."

"Her wisdom is all surpassing," Charlon admitted.

"While we wait, we will plant and harvest ahvenrood," Mreegan said. "Then, when Shanek is ready, we will have the power we need to assist in his takeover of the father realms."

Charlon studied the icy landscape. "It seems too cold to grow anything now."

"Magon assures me that spring will come soon."

Charlon wanted to believe it. Growing up in Rurekau, she had never known seasons beyond dry, cool, and stormmer, when the rains flooded the desert for a solid month. But Magonia, being farther south, had a more temperate climate. Even had snow in the forests bordering the Polar Desert. Evidence of so many plants and trees on this frozen land gave good reason to hope that root might grow eventually.

Shanek screamed.

Charlon's heart leapt within. She sprinted toward Sir Kalenek, who was now on his knees, holding the boy in his arms.

"What happened?" Charlon asked. "Did he fall?"

Sir Kalenek shook his head and tapped his temple.

Charlon studied Shanek's small face, scrunched and streaked in tears, mouth muttering, "Be quiet, you. Right now. Be quiet, be quiet."

Her heart sank. Since they'd reached this new land, Shanek had begun to hear voices. She suspected a shadir might be toying with him. All his short life, the creatures had been his playmates. But they were also tricksters. Tricksters who might torment him just for amusement. Unfortunately, she could no longer see into the Veil. And she dared not ask for help. That would only cast suspicion.

"Keep him away from people when he gets like this," Charlon told Sir Kalenek. "Take him to his cabin."

Sir Kalenek scooped Shanek into one arm and carried him away. The boy curled his body around the knighten, eyes screwed shut, still mumbling, "You don't talk to Shanek. You stop it."

Charlon watched them go as Krola ordered the anchor dropped into the sea. Roya and the other maidens oversaw the unloading of the ship.

This did not happen quickly. Two days later, by the time the sun had reached its pinnacle, their tribe was trekking inland along the river through ankle-deep snow. Weak horses moved slowly, pulling heavily laden wagons. Looked as weary as Charlon felt. Tufts of yellow grass sprouted from the whiteness of the barren flatland. Dead. Mreegan continued to assert that spring would bring everything to life. They would plant ahvenrood. It would grow.

Charlon wanted to believe. But everything looked dead. The only life she saw were black birds with red eyes. They flew overhead in groups. Followed the tribe, circled. Roosted nearby and screeched. Always watching. Mreegan ordered the men to kill some for dinner, and arrows flew.

Though Charlon's head ached, her body shook, and her bare feet were numb, she liked the snow. It reminded her of shadir magic. But when they stopped for the night and set up their tents, she found her toes were red and raw. Torol heated water. Helped Charlon soak her feet. She needed healing but didn't dare risk taking ahvenrood.

KING'S BLOOD

The next day Torol wrapped Charlon's feet in strips of leather. It helped. But pain still ached with every step. Feet went numb. In late midday Charlon staggered. Tripped and fell.

"What is wrong with you?" Mreegan asked, standing over where Charlon had fallen.

"My feet hurt," she said.

"Call on Magon to heal them."

Torol crouched at Charlon's side and helped her sit.

Mreegan stared at Charlon, eyes boring within. Her smile ended the confrontation. "You cannot. You stopped taking ahvenrood, didn't you? To protect your child?" She glanced at Sir Kalenek, who held Shanek's hand. "Not that child." She turned her gaze on Torol. "Another."

She knows. "I want it to be normal," Charlon said.

Mreegan sneered down on her. "You dislike what Shanek is?"

"The root burdens him. I want this child to be free of root. At least until it is born. Then I can teach it to wield the magic like the rest of us."

"Lies!" Mreegan yelled. "Magon tells me you want a family, like those who live in the father realms. After what you suffered in Rurekau, you would give a man control of your life?"

Charlon sputtered. Met Torol's gaze. Kind eyes. No words came forth to explain.

"You are not fit to be Mother," Mreegan said.

"Can't you see?" Charlon said. "The goddess has made me Mother twice now."

"You fool. Magon did not do this. There is nothing special about the child you carry." Mreegan raised her hand. "I have wasted too much time on you."

Charlon braced herself for pain.

But Mreegan lifted her hand. Toward Torol. "*Âtsar hebel.*"

Torol fell. Into the snow beside Charlon. Silent. Unmoving.

"No!" Charlon screamed. Lifted Torol's limp hand. Clutched his bearded cheek. "Bring him back. Magon!"

"You abandoned the goddess," Mreegan said.

Charlon shook her head. Everything blurred. Tears blinding. She wiped them away, desperate. Desperate to look clearly upon Torol's face. While she still could. "Magon can revive him." She dug through the snow. Grabbed fistfuls of icy dirt. Rubbed it on her face. "Goddess, please. Have mercy on your servant."

420

"She will not." Mreegan stood tall and fierce, glaring down. "This man divided your loyalties, caused you to keep secrets from Magon, from me. He made you forsake us both by ceasing to take ahvenrood."

Sobs shook Charlon. Stabbed shards of pain within. "My idea." She heaved a breath of air. "Not his." Another breath. "And only for a time." Only so she could live through the child's birth.

"Magon is a jealous goddess," the Chieftess said. "She shares her people with no one."

Charlon wept. Choked as the tears clogged her throat. So unfair. So cruel. "Torol was loyal. To you. To us all."

"No, Charlon. He was loyal to you."

He was! Torol had always been loyal to Charlon. He had been her One. And Mreegan had killed him.

Fury welled up from within. Brought inexplicable strength. *Take revenge*, her heart said.

Charlon sprang to her feet. Tackled Mreegan. They fell into the snow. Charlon punched the Chieftess. Pulled a handful of hair. Clawed her face.

A single word from Mreegan sent Charlon flying through the air. She hit the ground on her back. Felt something break inside. The strength from anger wilted. Without ahvenrood, she could not. Could not stand against Mreegan's power.

"Put her in the wagon," she heard Mreegan say. "I will deal with her later. For now, let her suffer."

Rone appeared above. Crouched and picked up Charlon. Movement sent shocking pain. Pain that pulled Charlon into darkness.

✦ ✦ ✦

Charlon woke. Lying in her tent on a bed of furs. A fire crackled in the brazier. Beside it Sir Kalenek sat with elbows on knees, staring into the flames.

Her head ached. Her limbs trembled. But other than feeling the loss of ahvenrood, Charlon felt no pain.

"Sir Kalenek?" Her voice sounded small. Broken.

The knighten looked toward her. Got up and approached. "How do you feel?"

"Fine. Mreegan healed me?"

"Roya."

Fear spiked through Charlon. "The child?" She pressed her hand against her stomach.

Sir Kalenek's lips drew into a straight line. Since Mreegan had healed his scars, his expressions were far easier to read. "Roya said it died when you fell."

When Mreegan had thrown her.

Anger stretched deep. Anchored roots within. *Fight back,* her heart said.

Charlon would fight. And Mreegan would pay. For everything.

"Roya also said you're no longer the Mother," Sir Kalenek added.

Panic pushed anger aside. "Where is Shanek?"

"The Chieftess is keeping him in her tent. She says . . ." His voice grew hoarse. "We cannot be trusted."

A mournful cry came from Charlon. Like the drone of One's lure.

Mreegan had taken everything.

Too much pain, her heart said. *We must fight.*

But Charlon could only weep.

She remembered little after that. Deep sobbing. Ceaseless tears. An endless ache. Life without hope.

And arms that picked her up and held her.

If not for Sir Kalenek's merciful arms, Charlon would have died from sorrow. She had no doubt.

TREVΠ

Seated on a longchair in his tent, Trevn stared at Oli Agoros, concentrating with every ounce of strength and focusing on the man's mind. A week ago, almost accidentally, he'd overheard his sister Hrettah's thoughts, and since then it was almost the only thing he could think about. He'd had no trouble listening in on Wilek's or Hrettah's thoughts, but he hadn't been able to hear anything from Rashah, Vallah, or Inolah. Now Oli's mind was proving difficult as well.

"Are you thinking at all?" Trevn asked.

"Yes, Your Highness, about the fire." Oli grinned from where he sat beside the brazier and stretched his hands toward the flames. "Having trouble?"

Trevn squinted, focusing more and more, hoping for even a single thought to emerge. Oli sat back and tucked his hands behind his head.

Nothing. This new gift was tricky.

"Sâr Trevn Hadar," a voice whispered in Trevn's mind. *"This is Hinckdan Faluk. If you can hear me, answer."*

Trevn answered right away. *"These are thoughts, Hinck,"* he said. *"What are you whispering about?"*

"I don't want to be overheard."

"You don't have to talk out loud to use the voices, you fool. Why must you make everything harder than it need be?"

"I'm not speaking out loud, Your Bossiness. I just don't want Rogedoth to know I can do whatever this is. He spoke to my mind a few times this morning. I ignored him, but I'm worried he knows I'm ignoring him."

"Rogedoth can mind-speak?" Trevn asked, dismayed.

"He has royal blood," Hinck said. *"Apparently Arman doesn't discriminate."*

Arman had given them this magic as a way to guard against the evil they'd brought to this land. If Rogedoth wasn't evil, Trevn didn't know who was.

"Oli," Trevn said, "Hinck has contacted me. You and I will continue this experiment later."

"Very well." Oli pushed to his feet and left the tent.

"Did you figure out where you are?" Trevn asked.

"We're on some islands. Not the islands Rogedoth was trying to reach. At least that's what Nellie's shadir said. They're off the coast of your continent, not terribly far from where Emperor Ulrik is building New Rurekau. About twenty leagues, I heard Timmons say."

"A rider could make twenty leagues in a day," Trevn said. *"Three days for an army."* He'd have to tell Wilek to send a warning to Ulrik that Rogedoth was closest to him.

"But there's three leagues of water between the islands and the shore," Hinck said. *"So that would add some time to the journey."*

"Any ideas as to Rogedoth's plans?" Trevn asked.

"He hasn't said outright. I eavesdropped on his mind, as you suggested."

"It worked?"

"Yes. At first all I heard was him thinking about root, root, and more root. He's got a ton of the stuff hoarded up in his fortress of reeds, but he wants to grow more. He has compelled a bunch of native pales and has them plowing. He's paranoid he'll run out and be powerless."

A powerless Rogedoth. Ideal. *"We need to sabotage that field,"* Trevn said. *"I'll ask Captain Veralla for ideas. What else has been happening?"*

"He's thought a lot about building an army. He thinks Sarikar is rightfully his—married Eudora to satisfy the Sarikarian law that a king must be married—but he wants Armania too. Thinks Wilek stole the Heir ring from Janek unfairly."

"What does that matter now? Janek is dead."

"That's just it. Laviel is crazy mad about Janek's death. She wants to kill lots of people to make them pay for it. Wilek is one of them. I told you what she did to Sir Jayron, and it looks like a fang cat scratched my face. But no one will heal me because Rogedoth says our scars are badges of honor or some such nonsense."

"Yes, yes, I'm sure you're hideous. Stay on topic. Rogedoth wants Armania . . . ?"

424

"*Right. He wants to conquer Armania to avenge Janek, though he isn't sure how to go about it. Randmuir Khal helped him steal a lot of ships, but the pirate abandoned Rogedoth and kept half the fleet for himself. Plus now that both Sarikar and Armania are planning to move north, Rogedoth no longer thinks it best to attack from the sea. He's made Agmado Harton his general, and they've had a few meetings on the subject. Harton has been telling him all Armania's war tactics.*"

"*Harton has never fought in a war for Armania,*" Trevn said.

"*No, but he trained in our military. He knows plenty, Trev. Trust me. I've listened in on his thoughts too. He has some ambitious ideas for attacking just about everyone, Magonia included.*"

"*You listened in on Harton's thoughts? How? He shouldn't have the mind-speak ability.*"

"*Oh, he doesn't,*" Hinck said. "*But I can hear him just the same. Nellie too. And Timmons and Lady Zenobia and Lilou.*"

"*That's fascinating,*" Trevn said, slightly jealous of his friend's effortless mastery. "*I haven't yet succeeded with eavesdropping on non-gifted.*" On all the gifted either.

"*Is Lady Pia well?*" Hinck asked. "*She helped me escape my cell on the* Seffynaw. *I've been, um . . . curious if she survived.*"

"*She's around. Wilek gave her to Kamran, I believe.*"

"*To Kamran?!*"

The connection between them vanished.

"*Hinck?*" Trevn called out, concentrated, tried again. "*Hinck?*"

"*I'm here.*" He seemed to be whispering again.

"*You closed me out of your mind. How did you do that?*"

"*You think you have a right to hear all my thoughts? You're unbelievable. Anything else I can do for you, Your Royal Nosiness?*"

Trevn didn't know what had upset Hinck, but when he tried to read his thoughts, he found them blocked off, as if Hinck had hidden them somehow—while he was voicing. This was new. Another twist in the gift Arman had provided them. He wondered how many more twists they would find.

"*Keep pretending you can't speak with the voices,*" Trevn said, "*and keep eavesdropping on everyone. In the meantime you and I will practice blocking our thoughts and closing our minds to each other like you just did to me. Because if you can listen in on Rogedoth's thoughts, we need to make sure he can never get into any of ours.*"

"Can't argue with you there," Hinck said. *"He's the last man I want reading my mind."*

✦ ✦ ✦

The moment Trevn severed his connection to Hinck, the soul-binding he shared with Mielle settled upon him, a dull ache that had no remedy. It had remained steady ever since they'd landed a few weeks ago, but the distance between them must have been too great to sense emotions because Trevn had not felt any distinct thoughts or feelings from her since he'd been at sea.

"Are you ready to go, Your Highness?" Cadoc asked.

"In a moment." Trevn sent thoughts to Wilek, filling him in on all Hinck had shared. News that Hinck could listen in on any mind sent Wilek into a panic, terrified that someone might spy on him. Trevn did his best to calm his brother, promising that he would continue to study the gifts and find a way to protect them all. Now he and Hinck only needed to work out how Hinck had closed his thoughts.

Since landing, Trevn had spent nearly all his hours helping Wilek deal with thousands of refugees and establish their new home. They weren't nearly close to done yet, but being trapped in one place when there was a whole new world to be explored was driving him mad. Trevn had convinced Wilek to let him go hunting and scavenging today with Captain Veralla, Maleen, and Cadoc. Hunting had never been one of Trevn's interests, but he was anxious for any reason to see the new country and possibly draw closer to Mielle.

"I am ready now," Trevn said, standing up from his chair.

"Can I come?" Ottee asked.

"Not today," Trevn said. "See that my fire is kept up. I will likely be frozen when we return. Now help me with my cloak."

Ottee sighed but said, "Yes, Your Highness."

The boy brought forth Trevn's heaviest cloak and a pair of leather gloves. When Trevn was dressed, he and Cadoc left the tent to meet up with Captain Veralla and Maleen. The young pale man did not recognize this land as his own, but Trevn hoped he might at least have some ideas of what might be edible here in winter.

The horses that had survived the voyage were still too malnourished to ride, so they set out on foot, walking north through a village cobbled together from freshly constructed log cabins and formerly abandoned brush shelters, now covered in leather and furs. It wasn't long before the slushy pathways gave way to a snow-covered prairie. Trevn sank up to his shins with each step, and the snow quickly soaked his pantlegs.

As they hiked, Trevn tried to listen in on the thoughts of those around him, again practicing. If Hinck could master the skill, he could as well. He focused on Captain Veralla's mind and instantly heard the man reminding himself what he knew of rabbits as he sought out prints in the snow.

Amazing.

When it worked, eavesdropping simply required him to concentrate on someone's mind, as he did when voicing, and he could hear the person's thoughts until he pulled away.

Trevn next fixed on Maleen, and the pale man's thoughts came in a language he couldn't understand. He focused on Cadoc and heard the man thinking about his parents, hoping they were somewhere on this land, perhaps to the north. They might even stumble upon them today.

Trevn doubted that. Cadoc's parents had been on the *Rafayah* with Mielle, and Mielle felt far from their current location.

At the thought of his wife, the soul-binding magic panged. The idea of trying to hear what Mielle was thinking came upon him suddenly, and while it seemed too far-fetched an idea, he focused on his wife as he had with the others, but this time he spoke as well. *"Mielle?"*

The soul-binding surged upon him like an anchor pressing on his chest. It was so powerful that he slowed, his boots shuffling in the snow. He pictured her in his mind: big brown eyes, wide smile, finely braided hair. *"Mielle, can you hear me?"*

"Trevn? Is that you?"

Trevn slipped. He caught his balance on his hands, crouching in the cold wetness, and yelled after the others, "Wait!"

The men stopped and looked back.

"She's alive!"

As he had the night of their wedding, he could sense everything about her. She was tired and a little hungry. Her heart pounded at the excitement of hearing his voice. He smelled smoke and the tang of the sea. All of these things had wrapped around him instantly, as if he were sitting beside her—no, as if he *was* her. Yet her voice had come into his mind, the same way Wilek's had with Arman's new magic.

"Yes, it's me, Mouse," he said. *"Where are you?"*

He felt tears well in Mielle's eyes. *"I'm aboard the* Rafayah. *We can see land but are caught up in ice not far off the coast. We hunkered down to wait it out, cleared space in the ship's hold, and converted it into living quarters. We have a good stove but are running out of fuel. Captain Stockton sent men down onto the ice to try to chop a path for the ship, but it hasn't worked. We also met some natives who were walking on the ice."*

Natives. *"Are these pales?"*

"Yes. They traded us furs, which has greatly helped us stay warm."

Were there pale-skinned natives here in Er'Rets? Or had the *Rafayah* found Maleen's homeland?

Captain Veralla, Cadoc, and Maleen returned to Trevn and circled around.

"Who is alive?" the captain asked.

"Mielle. A moment please, Captain, while I determine her whereabouts." Then to Mielle he thought, *"We've made landfall on a snowy plain, though there are trees and a mountain range in the distance. One mountain looms higher than the rest and is covered in snow. What does your land look like?"*

"I looked through Captain Stockton's grow lens only once. We are surrounded by a snowy flatland. I do see snow-topped mountains in the distance to the south, but I cannot see that one is higher than the rest."

"Which side of the ship is land on?"

"The starboard side."

"You were traveling along a western coast. We made landfall on the southern tip of a great land mass. You might be on the other side of the continent from us. Or it could be that you are in a different place altogether. Is the Rafayah *alone?"*

"There were eight ships with us, all Armanian. Four managed to escape the ice when we turned south. The other three are stuck with us. I don't know their names from memory, but I can ask the captain."

"Please do. Wilek will want to know."

"Trevn, how are we talking? Is it the soul-binding?"

"Partially, perhaps. But there is a new magic here. I will explain later. First let me tell all this to Captain Veralla. We are out hunting, and he's looking at me as if I am mad."

Trevn told Captain Veralla, Cadoc, and Maleen all that Mielle had said, somehow remaining connected to Mielle and hearing in his mind her additions to his version of the story.

"My parents?" Cadoc asked, and Trevn put the question to Mielle.

"Yes, they are here," she replied.

Trevn passed on the news, and Cadoc whooped for joy.

"What a happy turn of events," Captain Veralla said. "I am pleased for you both, and for everyone else who feared having lost loved ones aboard those missing ships."

"Only eight of the twenty-two missing ships," Trevn said, "but it is still a blessing."

They continued walking, and Trevn filled Mielle in on all that had taken place since the *Rafayah* had vanished. He told her that her sister, Amala, had taken on the role of honor maiden to Lady Zeroah and seemed to be doing well, and that Wilek and Zeroah planned to name their child Avenelle if it was a girl, after Gran, and Chadek if it was a boy, after Wilek's elder brother, who had been sacrificed to Barthos. All this news pleased Mielle, who had been passing the time by helping the captain's wife and Cadoc's mother care for the orphans aboard the *Rafayah*.

Trevn would have to attempt mind-speaking with Captain Stockton soon. Perhaps he could use navigation to determine the whereabouts of his ship.

Trevn followed Captain Veralla and Maleen across the snowy flatlands, paying little attention as he conversed with Mielle. At one point the captain found tracks of some kind and must have set several snares, which Trevn discovered the hard way when he set one off; he had been too distracted speaking to Mielle to pay much attention. As Cadoc helped him up, Captain Veralla said, "Your Highness, I am thrilled that Miss Mielle is well, but would you mind continuing your conversation when we are finished?"

Ashamed, Trevn readily agreed. He told Mielle he would speak with her later that day, bid her farewell, and broke their connection. Doing so left a void that filled him with panic and a dull ache. He reminded himself that it was only the soul-binding magic, but his thoughts continued to plague him with fear.

As he learned to set snares, he ignored the throbbing and fought the temptation to reach out to Mielle again. It was enough to know she was alive and well. Soon enough he would make plans to find her and bring her home.

After setting several dozen snares, they came upon an icy creek running alongside a marsh. Maleen stopped and hacked through the ice with an axe, then pulled up cattail roots. He also cut the tops off a leafy green plant that had been floating on the surface of the water. Trevn put the cattail roots and greens into fresh muslin sacks. Maleen then foraged several tiny brown lobsters and mussels from the icy water. Trevn, Cadoc, and Captain Veralla removed their gloves to help, and before long they had enough for several pots of chowder.

The fingers on Trevn's right hand had never healed fully after the shrine fell on them. The skin had turned permanently black—black like coal compared to his brown skin. At the moment, the rest of his fingers were bright pink and stinging from the frigid water.

Trevn pulled his gloves back on, and they followed the stream south. Halfway back something else caught Maleen's eye. He waded into the creek toward a cliff of dirt and what seemed to be piles of bark clinging to the soil.

Trevn followed and ripped away a piece of bark. It felt like dried paper pulp—like a beehive—though it was massive. A cocoon big enough to hold a grown man.

"What do you think lives in that?" Cadoc asked.

"Not sure I want to know," Trevn said, slogging to the shore, suddenly eager to get out of the water.

Once they had returned to camp, Captain Veralla took Maleen and the foraged food to the kitchen tent while Trevn changed into dry clothes and went to see Wilek. His brother was delighted to hear the news of Mielle and the missing ships, and even more intrigued by what Trevn had learned about their new magic.

"I could set out tomorrow to look for Mielle."

"No," Wilek said. "You must wait. At least until the snow melts."

Rage flashed over Trevn that his brother would deny him this. "But the snow may never melt. And what about the ice around their ships? They could die stranded out there."

"King Loran assures me the snow is melting already. He believes we are about to enter the season of spring. I'm sure the ice will release them soon enough."

"I need my wife, Wil. The soul-binding . . . Please."

Wilek gave Trevn that look—the one that meant he felt sorry for him. "I can't, brother. Not now."

"But—"

Wilek held up a hand. "Continue to speak with her. Gather clues to her whereabouts. Speak to Captain Stockton if you are able. Once you can give me something definite as to their location, I will consider letting you put together a rescue party. But if she is on another continent . . . Well, if that is the case, we will deal with that then."

✦ ✦ ✦

That night, after eating Maleen's mussel stew and bread made from cattail flour, Trevn lay in his tent and talked to Mielle for several hours, gathering clues to her location. She'd yet to give him much of anything he could use to find her, which frustrated him greatly. He told her what he'd learned about the new mind-speak magic and asked her to prepare Captain Stockton to hear his voice tomorrow. She agreed, then began to talk about the clothing she and Cadoc's mother were sewing for orphans.

The weight of the day settled on Trevn, and his eyes grew heavy. He found himself lulled by Mielle's voice, and suddenly, as if dreaming, he *was* her. She got up from her bedroll and lifted a lantern from a hook on the wall. She set it on a desk and admired an array of children's clothing. She ran her hand over the items, then sat in a chair at the desk, took up a half-sewn garment and a needle, and began stitching, humming softly.

As she set about fitting the sleeve, she pushed the needle too far. Pain shot through her index finger and she jumped.

Trevn jolted awake, his own finger pulsing with pain. *"Mielle!"* He sat up and found himself still looking out from her eyes.

"Trevn?" she answered. *"Is everything okay?"*

"I dreamt I was you," he said. *"You were sewing, and when you stabbed yourself with a needle, I felt it. Even now I can see through your eyes."*

"How is that possible?"

"Another trick of this new magic, I suppose." An idea came to him. *"Go topside,"* he said. *"Go and look at the stars so I can see them for myself."*

He felt the hope surge within her chest as she ran from the cabin and up the stairs. When she stepped out onto the main deck, the night air was cool and she shivered. Bare feet took three steps over icy wood to the railing. Though it was dark, Trevn could make out what looked like a barren plain of ice.

"Look up, Mouse," he said. *"Let me see the stars."*

She tipped her head back, blinked. Breath clouded from her lips.

The stars were bright in the black sky, the moon a mere sliver. He instantly recognized the trio of pole stars and the constellation that Master Granlee had named Athos's Scales.

Trevn needed to look at his own sky.

He leapt from his bed and ran into the tent wall, shaking the entire structure. His connection with Mielle broke, and he found his eyes focusing on the interior of his own tent.

Perhaps it was not wise to try to walk whilst he was looking out someone else's eyes.

He carefully exited his tent and nearly ran into Cadoc, who had drawn his sword.

"I heard a noise inside, Your Highness. Are you well?"

"Perfectly." Staring up into the cloudy night sky, Trevn asked his shield, "Where is the moon?"

"I last saw it over there." Cadoc pointed.

Trevn recalled Mielle's view of the night sky and tried to position himself in a similar fashion. Though it was cloudy, he was able to locate part of the Scales and the lowest two stars in the trio. His view looked nearly the same as Mielle's, which didn't mean a whole lot. She could still be leagues away, but it gave him hope.

"Mielle, when you prepare Captain Stockton for my communication tomorrow, tell him I will also need his assistance in taking some sightings with his cross-staff."

"A what?"

"It is a tool used in celestial navigation. If Captain Stockton can determine your latitude, then I will have an idea of where you are in comparison to me."

He felt her heart leap with joy. *"You could learn that by looking at the stars?"*

"It works on sea. It should do the same on land."

"Your Highness." Cadoc's voice pulled Trevn away from the stars. His shield was staring at him, brows heavy with concern. He nodded slightly beyond Trevn, who followed the motion and took note of the audience that had gathered outside several tents. Hrettah and Rashah, their ladies and maids, a dozen or so guards, and much of the kitchen staff.

"Tomorrow night I will pinpoint Miss Mielle's location," he told them, smiling.

No one smiled in return.

✦　✦　✦

Encouraged by his new mind-speaking discoveries, Trevn continued experimenting the next morning as they set out on a longer hunting expedition. While listening in on Maleen's thoughts told him nothing, he did get a sense of the man's mood, which was weary and sad. Curious, Trevn attempted to sense the mood of each man around him and became thrilled when he found he could sense distinct emotions from each. Cadoc felt apprehensive. Ottee joyful.

Captain Veralla thankful. One of the soldier's straps broke on the pack he was carrying, and Trevn was quick to sense the man's frustration. And once Ottee began hinting that he was hungry, his mood became wistful and dissatisfied.

They checked the snares they had set the previous day and found they had caught several rabbits, which were as big as cats. They reset the snares and continued on, following the creek north.

"Trevn? My son? Can you hear me?"

Mother. Trevn hadn't seen the woman since her trial on Bakurah Island.

"Sâr Wilek tells me you have the voices," Mother said. *"I've heard rumor that you married Miss Mielle in secret. If you can hear me, answer."*

He did not want his mother to have the ability to speak to him at any time of any day. He had always been able to hide from her before, but if he answered, he was nearly certain she would never leave him alone. And he certainly didn't want to hear her opinion about his marrying Mielle.

So he ignored her. For now. Once he learned more about how this magic worked, perhaps he would speak to her. Just . . . not yet.

As the morning passed by, Trevn continued experimenting. With a quick warning to Cadoc, he tried speaking to the man's mind and was shocked when Cadoc answered. His shield had no royal blood and no soul-binding connection, so how could he use the voices?

Trevn and Cadoc had several voiced conversations, and it wasn't long before Trevn realized the power was all his own. He could listen to Cadoc's mind, speak to him, and Cadoc could think answers, but his shield had no ability to initiate conversations.

Arman's voicing magic held so many more possibilities than Trevn had originally thought. What else might he discover?

When Mielle told Trevn that Captain Stockton was prepared to hear from him, no matter how hard Trevn attempted to voice with the man, he could not hear the captain's thoughts and received no answer. When Trevn asked Mielle about it, she said that the captain had heard nothing.

How vexing. There must be some limitation to this magic that Trevn did not understand. To be fair, he did not know Captain Stockton well—could barely recall what the man looked like. Perhaps familiarity had something to do with the ability to communicate.

Following this hunch, Trevn spent the rest of the morning trying to hear the thoughts of those he barely knew. He succeeded with the soldiers around him, but when he focused on some of the servants back at camp, he failed.

An unfortunate discovery, but understanding the magic better pleased him nonetheless.

When they stopped for lunch, Trevn talked again with Mielle, whose distress filled him with foreboding.

"What is wrong?" he asked.

"Captain Stockton asked me to give you a message. He says that the creaking and groaning of the ship is because the ice floes are breaking it up. Apparently there have been some leaks in the hold. He has kept this from the passengers so as not to alarm us, but now he says the end of the ship is at hand and we must take our chances walking over the ice to shore. We leave at dawn."

Trevn knew little to nothing about ice, but such a thing seemed impossible. *"Is the captain too busy to attempt a conversation? Perhaps you could mediate?"*

Mielle agreed, and Trevn learned all he could about the impending disaster. Three of the four ships caught in ice were starting to break up, and the captains had decided to move the crew and passengers to land while they still had opportunity.

Captain Stockton promised to take sightings so that Trevn could try to ascertain their position compared to his. Then he helped Trevn with another idea. With Mielle acting as translator, they walked each other through the process of making a sun clock, each building one as they talked. When both were complete, Trevn measured the angle of the sun's elevation and wrote down Captain Stockton's figure. These two measurements gave him enough information that, combined with Pollon's calculation of the earth's circumference, he was able to figure the distance between himself and the *Rafayah*.

The result so thrilled him that he did his math one more time, and only when he confirmed that his number matched Captain Stockton's calculation did he give Mielle the news. *"You are just over sixty leagues away."*

"That's all?" Mielle asked.

"Unless Pollon's teachings are terribly skewed, which I don't believe them to be. If I left now on horseback and there were no obstacles between us, I could reach you in six or seven days. Except I don't know which direction to go. You're west of here, that much is clear from your description of the coast, but I'll need Captain Stockton's sightings to figure your latitude. Tell him I want them the moment he wakes tomorrow. Still . . . Arman be praised, we will be together soon, Mouse."

✦　✦　✦

Trevn woke the next morning and instantly reached out for Mielle, eager for news from his wife.

"Mielle, did you reach land?"

"We did. And the ice did not crack even once. Captain Stockton says the ice here is as thick as a child is tall. We have set up camp on the shore. It is still very cold."

"I am relieved to know you are safe," Trevn said. *"Did Captain Stockton give you his sightings?"*

"He did two, just as you asked," she said. *"One of the sun at midday yesterday and the other of the top star of the trio last midnight."* She gave him the information, and he passed along his sightings from last night for her to give Captain Stockton. Then he compared the measurements. It took Trevn a while to work through the numbers, but he finally decreed that Mielle's latitude was above theirs, to the north northwest.

Still about sixty leagues away. Praise Arman!

They packed up camp and continued on. That midday they came upon a great lake surrounded by snow-covered trees. The water was a crystalline blue, the color of Miss Onika's eyes. A large island sat near the shore on the northern end of the lake. Almost without thinking, Trevn could envision the island as a keep and hold for their new home.

"We should build there," he whispered, almost to himself, though Captain Veralla nodded. "A new Castle Everton."

"A fine idea, Your Highness. The water would make a nice barrier against enemies."

They had no boats to reach the island, so they continued around the northern edge of the lake, camped on the shore, and the next morning turned south along a worn trail. It made Trevn nervous, using these trails. Where were the natives? And how would they respond when they finally came face-to-face with a new people?

"Trevn," Wilek said to his mind. *"Do you hear me?"*

"Good morning, brother," Trevn said. *"I have thought more on my plan to rescue Mielle and believe a sea voyage might be—"*

"Our father is dead."

A pang of hair-raising terror shot through Trevn, and he stopped on the trail. "A moment!" he yelled, and Ottee ran up the line to make sure those in front had heard the halt.

"What happened?" Trevn asked Wilek.

"Schwyl found him just after dawn," Wilek said, sounding weary. *"He died in his sleep. A peaceful death the man did not deserve, in my opinion, but Arman's mercy is his own business."*

Trevn reached out for his father's mind and found nothing. *"What shall I do?"*

"Come back. We must have the shipping ceremony as soon as possible."

"I will return at once," Trevn said, *"and do whatever I can to ease the burden."* Then he added, *"Wil, I'm sorry."*

Wilek laughed wryly. *"I've been doing the job for months now, brother. Nothing much will change."*

But it would. Everything would be different. Second Arm would become the first, which meant even more responsibility than ever for Trevn. And Wilek would be king.

Trevn ended the conversation and refocused on his surroundings. The procession had scattered somewhat. Some soldiers explored the woods just off the path, while others stood in groups, talking and laughing.

"What is it?" Cadoc asked. Captain Veralla and Ottee also stood by, waiting to hear.

"The king is dead," Trevn said softly.

Three sets of eyes went very wide.

Before another word was said, a commotion at the front of the line caught Trevn's attention. He pushed through the crowd to see what was happening. A group of soldiers had circled the remains of a campfire. Bones littered the snowy ground around it. Deer bones, it looked like.

"They're fake," one of the soldiers said.

"Why would someone make fake footprints?" another replied.

"What's fake?" Trevn asked.

The soldiers stopped arguing and bowed.

Their manners annoyed Trevn, who only wanted to see what had them so rattled so he could call everyone to attention and announce his father's death. "Show me," he said.

"There." The first soldier pointed to the ground on the other side of the stone circle. Trevn crouched in the snow and examined what appeared to be human footprints. The problem was, they were twice as long as any grown man's foot.

"They look real to me," Captain Veralla said from Trevn's side.

Trevn glanced up. "It appears that the natives are big men, Captain."

"Very big, Your Highness," Captain Veralla replied. "I hope they are peaceful."

GRAYSON

*D*on't tell anyone I told you," a girl said, "but he said he talks to her. Says she's alive."

"That's so sad," a second girl said.

From some other place a gruff voice demanded, "Bring me another platter of sausage rolls."

A moment of silence teased Grayson that the voices might go quiet, and then: "You can scarcely expect me to pay attention to every word you say," a different man said. "You prattle on endlessly. No man could do better than I do."

From farther away a woman said, "He could have saved him and didn't. For that I can never forgive him, but undermining him will not be easy."

And then from much closer: "You don't talk to me," a boy said. "Be quiet, be quiet."

Grayson agreed with the boy. The voices had started the night before Randmuir's men had sighted land. He had no way of silencing them and ignored them as best he could. Was he going crazy? Did that happen to people as young as him?

He trudged along through the snow beside Danno, the two of them bringing up the rear of the line. Randmuir had anchored the *Malbraid* in a cove and led an exploring party inland. The pirate wanted to take shelter until winter ended and wanted a place that was far enough away from the Armanians that they might not know where he was, but close enough that he could reach them if he wanted to. He had sailed up the coast for three days, and when a forest of

437

massive trees had come into view, he had anchored, formed a landing party, and come ashore.

It had to be time to stop walking soon. The snow came up to Grayson's knees, and his toes had long ago gone numb. Probably because Satu had sawed off the front ends of Grayson's boots when he'd caught him limping around the ship. Grayson's feet had grown as fast as his body, and the boots had become far too small. They fit much better now that his toes had room to stretch. He had wrapped his feet in rags before putting on his boots this morning, but the rags were stiff with ice now. A few leagues back he'd played around with his magic and found that he was able to let only his feet walk in the Veil. There was no hot or cold there, and his toes felt better. Doing this made his feet invisible, but the fact that he was tramping through deep snow at the back of the line made him fairly sure no one would notice. Besides, everyone—including him—was looking at the trees.

Never could he have imagined such trees existed. They were twenty times as tall as any tree Grayson had ever seen. They had long reddish-brown trunks that stretched toward the sky. The branches didn't even begin until the upper part of the trees—far too high to climb—and they were covered in thick layers of snow, like icing on a cake. If Grayson looked long enough, a black bird would fly between branches and knock down a clump of snow.

The line of men curved up ahead and Grayson spotted Burk. The bully still hadn't recognized Grayson. Probably never would, since Grayson now looked older than Burk. The thief turned soldier had quickly abandoned the Igote and become a pirate when held at swords' points in Randmuir's attack on Emperor Ulrik's *Baretam*. Burk was now walking with the mantic named Fonu, who was one of King Barthel's men. Grayson didn't know when Fonu had come aboard the *Malbraid*, but he'd brought with him two shadir. Grayson had never seen him perform any magic, but he wore a hip flask that reminded him of the kind yeetta warriors wore to hold their root juice. Grayson didn't like to see Burk making friends with anyone so powerful. And he didn't like the sight of the two shadir—Ragaz and Haroan, Fonu called them. Ragaz the slight was as red as cranberries and looked like a horse's tail, all wisps of long hair. Haroan was a common shadir and took a more dignified form of a brown wolf. He walked alongside Fonu the way Rustian walked with Onika. Neither of the creatures had learned that Grayson could see them, and Grayson hoped to keep it that way.

"I've got some kind of road here!" Satu yelled from the front of the line.

Randmuir and several others crouched with Satu to examine the snowy ground. Grayson kept back out of sight but strained to hear what was said.

"Looks like wagon tracks," Satu said. "Pulled by a horse, maybe?"

"Big hooves for a horse," Randmuir said.

Beyond the cluster of men, something moved, gray and black.

"Danno," Grayson hissed. "Did you see that?"

"See what?" Danno asked, not even trying to be quiet.

Now two things moved: the gray-and-black thing, still dead ahead, and a brown mass off to Grayson's right.

"Something is out there," Grayson said, backing toward one of the massive tree trunks.

A trilling chorus rang out, loud and fierce. It seemed to come from all around them simultaneously. Grayson didn't wait around to see what it was. He dove behind the tree and pushed into the Veil, instantly feeling safer, but the yells, grunts, boots trampling over the snow, and more of the high-pitched trilling kept his fear running high.

Danno! He suddenly remembered poor, tiny Danno.

Still in the Veil, Grayson crawled through the gigantic tree trunk and peeked out the other side. Randmuir's black-clad pirates lay in the snow. He saw Burk and Fonu's bodies and wondered if they were dead. A few other pirates had cowered behind trees like Grayson. Satu and Randmuir had hidden behind a burly bush. Danno was lying on his stomach in the snow, hands wrapped over his head. Haroan crouched over Danno, a satisfied leer on his wolfish face. Ragaz cackled as he swooped over the frightened men.

Grayson saw no one else.

"We could take Eudora away," a woman said. *"There are others in the royal line she could marry."*

"Give it back!" a girl yelled.

"I told you I don't have it," said a second girl.

The voices in Grayson's head seemed louder now in the surrounding silence. He concentrated hard to push them down, straining to hear any sounds over those in his mind.

A rock flew through the air and smacked Randmuir in the head. The pirate captain slumped over. Satu just managed to catch him.

Another rock struck Satu. The man roared, dropped Randmuir, and drew his sword. He marched out to the clearing. "Show yourselves, you cowards!" he screamed.

A rock shot out of the forest and hit Satu square in the forehead.

He collapsed in the snow.

Not a soul moved but Ragaz the shadir, who flitted from man to man, crowing. Danno opened one eye and peeked at the scene. Relief rushed over Grayson. His friend was all right. Just pretending to be hurt. Grayson wanted to call out, wave him over behind the tree, but the silence of the forest smothered his courage. Someone was out there, watching.

"*Wee datla wa ahkeeah.*"

Though the voice had spoken in a foreign tongue, Grayson's magic allowed him to understand the meaning: "Load the prisoners."

Warriors stepped out of the forest. All of them were huge. Beyond huge. They were—for lack of a better word—giants.

Grayson caught his breath. They were twice his size!

Well, not quite. They were about three or four heads taller, but Grayson was certain this was who Onika had meant.

He counted four. All were male. All wore patchwork leather that was criss-cross stitched with leather cord and trimmed in white—colors that blended in with the trees and snow. They had pale skin like Onika, and one had braided yellow hair and wore a brown animal skin as a cape. Grayson scrambled to remember the exact words of Onika's message from Sir Kalenek.

"Hold tight to your secret until you come to those twice your size."

What did it mean? Should he reveal his magic? Now?

The giants pulled a flat-bed cart into the clearing and began to pile the pirates' bodies onto it.

"Skin is strange," one giant said.

"Looks like dirt," said another.

Randmuir roused, but a giant punched him in the head and he slumped over again. As the giant bent to grasp Randmuir's ankles, Satu jumped to his feet and stabbed the giant in the lower back with a knife.

The giant screamed in fury and dropped Randmuir. He spun around to meet his attacker, but Satu was ready. He'd retrieved his sword from the snow and drove it into the giant's stomach.

Another giant bounded forward and bashed his fist against Satu's face. The pirate collapsed, his face cracked like a coconut.

"No killing!" the yellow-haired giant yelled. "Dead slaves are useless."

But the giants weren't looking at Satu. They stood in silent awe, staring at their slain comrade who was still bleeding in the snow.

The yellow-haired giant approached, took hold of the sword's hilt, and pulled it out. From the back, Grayson saw that the animal-skin cape the giant wore had a hood that was partly the skin version of the animal's face.

"What is it?" a giant asked.

"Like a stick," said the yellow-haired. He whacked the flat of the sword against a tree, then tried and failed to break it over his knee, his braids and cape swinging with the effort. "Sharp like black rock. Others carry these weapons?"

"Yes, Toqto." A giant near the cart pulled the sword from Randmuir's scabbard and lifted it up to the yellow-haired giant.

"Collect them," Toqto said. "To study. Don't like a weapon that can kill the Yeke. Now finish loading the cart."

The other giants each ran to the body of a pirate. A fifth giant that Grayson hadn't seen before stepped out from behind a tree and stalked toward Danno. He was by far the shortest of the giants, though he was still two heads taller than any pirate. His leather was black, stitched with zigzags rather than crisscrosses. He wore a wolf-skin cape with the hood up, which made it look like he had the face of a wolf. He crouched in front of Danno, side by side with Haroan, though he couldn't see the wolf-like shadir. He reached out.

"Stop!" Grayson pushed through the tree and out of the Veil. "Don't touch him," he said, standing. "He's my friend."

The giant turned, and Grayson could see the face under the hood. Huge brown eyes fixed on his, so intense it felt like such a look might cause pain if Grayson let it go on too long. A beard the color of fire clung to the giant's cheeks and chin. He pushed off the wolf's-head hood, which showed that his hair was bright orange as well.

"Speak Yeke, dirtman?" he asked.

Grayson crouched beside Danno, tapping his shoulder. "Get up, Dan. Hurry."

Danno jumped to his feet at Grayson's side. The orange-haired giant reached for Grayson, so he stepped into the Veil, ran to the giant's other side, then pushed back out.

"Over here," he said.

The giant turned, grunted in surprise. "Dirtman moves fast, Toqto," he said over his shoulder. "Magic is here."

The other giants had loaded the pirates onto the cart and stood guarding them with obsidian-tipped spears.

"Always you are last, Ulagan," Toqto said. "Be quick about your task or your uncle will beat you again."

Ulagan scowled, then lunged at Grayson, who again pushed through the Veil, this time exiting beside Toqto.

"Ulagan speaks the truth," Grayson said. "Don't doubt him again." Then, just to be safe, he popped to the middle of the clearing, well out of anyone's reach.

Ulagan dropped to his knees in the snow. "A god-man! Ah-oom."

Toqto and the other giants knelt as well, some calling out, "Ah-oom, ah-oom."

Shocked by their behavior, Grayson thanked Arman that he had listened to Onika's message. But now what?

"What word carry you from the godhead?" Toqto the yellow-haired asked Grayson.

A word from God? Grayson scrambled for something true. "Listen well to me." Onika had often started that way. But what did Arman want to tell these giants? "The God, um, the godhead is named Arman. I am his servant. He has brought his chosen people to this land. Many enemies followed, but all who come in the name of Arman should be given aid."

For a long second there was silence. Grayson waited, unsure if he'd said the right thing or not. Just as he opened his mouth to try something else, one of the giants nodded.

"As you say, god-man, it will be done." Ulagan the wolf stood and walked toward Grayson, who had to remind himself not to be afraid of the orange-haired mountain of a man. "If it pleases you, I will walk as your protector."

Grayson fought the urge to smile. "A god-man needs no protector, but I would not deny anyone the pleasure of serving me."

From the cart, Fonu snorted. He and his two shadir were staring. Several of the pirates were awake now and looked on Grayson as well, some with wonder, some with fear. Grayson had shocked them all, no doubt.

Ulagan bowed. "As you say, god-man. What of the little one?"

Danno stood shivering in the snow, eyes full and frightened. "Danno stays with me."

"We go," Toqto said.

He set off through the trees. The giants pulled the cart after him. Ulagan followed with Grayson and Danno.

Grayson didn't like having brought himself to the attention of Fonu the mantic and his shadir, but he had likely saved the pirates from whatever horrible fate the giants had originally planned. Was that why Arman had wanted Grayson to show his powers to these people? To protect them? What was he supposed to do now? He wished he could ask Onika, but he had no idea where she was or if he'd ever see her again. He was on his own now, alone with his powers and the permission to use them.

Arman, keep him from doing something foolish.

✦ ✦ ✦

As they trekked through the snowy wood, Grayson asked Ulagan many questions. They were headed to the village of Zuzaan, which was the home of the Ahj-Yeke, which translated as forest giants. These giants were ruled by a headman named Bolad mi Aru.

"He is my uncle," Ulagan said. "I am from the Uul-Yeke." This translated as mountain giants. "We follow the wolf and keep no slaves. When my father died, I came to live here."

"Sorry about your father," Grayson said. "Why do the Ahj-Yeke take slaves?"

"To hunt the tsok."

The translated word seemed wrong. "They hunt *beetles*?"

"Oom. The tsok live in the narrow caves beneath the mountains. Yeke are too big to gather them. Many Yeke believe the tsok give strength, but Uul-Yeke are strong without them."

"What is he saying?" Danno whispered to Grayson.

"He's talking about his village. I'm trying to learn more about them."

"They killed Satu," Danno said.

"Because he killed first. Don't worry. I don't think they mean to hurt us." Though Grayson wasn't sure about that.

He tried to keep Ulagan talking just to drown out the continual voices in his head. The two girls were still fighting. He'd heard no more about the woman named Eudora, but now a man was arguing with his wife about a tear in his shirt, and two other men were discussing ships that had been destroyed by ice.

Several hours later the group entered a village of stone houses, each domed with snow-covered thatched roofs. The snow on the ground had been cleared to form a ridged pathway that wound around the houses. They met only two giants out in the cold, and both stepped off the path to let the cart go by. Grayson caught sight of several pale humans, clad in furs and raking paths in the snow. Two more pales were struggling to pull a cart loaded with a stack of longboats made from some kind of animal skin. After the fifth or sixth turn, the giants passed into a clearing and approached a whole-stone fortress built into the side of a mountain. An aboveground river in a deep crack ran along the front of the fortress, and they could not enter until some giants inside lowered a walkway over the crack.

Toqto entered first, followed by the cart, the wooden wheels of which clattered over the walkway. Ulagan, Grayson, and Danno brought up the rear. The winter chill lessened inside, but it was difficult to see. Grayson kept close to Ulagan as the giant walked through a spacious and empty chamber. In the center of the room, a half wall bordered a stairwell that zigzagged several levels up and down.

Toqto left the others behind and climbed the stairs. He was holding Satu's bronze sword. "Bring those two along, Ulagan."

Ulagan led Grayson and Danno up the stairs behind the golden-haired giant and his strange brown animal cape. Ragaz the shadir followed, trailing alongside Grayson's feet. The rest of the pirates remained on the entry level.

Though Grayson was as big as a grown man now, the height of each step felt awkward to climb and quickly made his legs sore.

"Where are we going?" he asked Ulagan.

"Toqto must report to the headman. We captured you and your friends as slaves, but if the headman sees your magic, he might change his mind and let you go."

That did not comfort Grayson in the least. "They mean to enslave us," Grayson murmured to Danno. "Ulagan thinks I should try to convince the headman not to."

"Can you do that?" Danno asked.

"I don't know."

They ascended two full flights of stone steps and entered a warm and bright room. Grayson's cheeks tingled at the change in temperature. In the center of a torch-lined wall, a large pile of sticks and bark covered with blankets of fur and leather created a sort of nest. Atop it sat a giant, cross-legged and cross-armed. He had pale skin like Onika, but his hair was black and done up in four fat, looped braids that hung with their ends tied back at the top, where they were lashed in tubes of hemp and red yarn. Like Toqto this headman also wore the hide of a brown animal over his shoulders like a cape, though his seemed to have been taken from a much larger beast. He wore a crown of animal claws, which looked like twigs on such a large head. He had a square, scowling face and dark, suspicious eyes. His massive shoulders and arms were twice as wide as Ulagan's.

Toqto the yellow-haired bent to lay Satu's sword on the floor by the nest, then went down on both knees. Ulagan knelt beside him, looking nearly two full heads shorter.

"Sixteen slaves captured, Headman," Toqto said. "Dirtmen from another land with skin like soil and weapons that do not break. Among them this god-man, who can do magic. He chose Ulagan as his protector."

The headman picked up the bronze sword and inspected it. "Show him to me." His voice was low, like a growl.

"Move forward, god-man," Ulagan the wolf whispered.

Grayson slipped around the giants and came to stand at Ulagan's side. With the giant kneeling, they were nearly the same height.

"Why come you to us, god-man?" the headman asked in his low voice.

"Arman, God of all gods, sent me to you," Grayson said, slightly terrified, but he believed Onika's word, so he felt justified in making the claim. "He has brought his chosen people to this land and asks that you give aid to all who come in his name."

The headman grunted. "Not know this god you speak of. Why should I release slaves?"

Grayson scrambled for an answer. "Myself and this youth Danno are the only servants of Arman here. Release us, keep the others, and you will have earned the favor of Arman."

"Magic he wields is impressive, Uncle," Ulagan said.

"Show me this magic."

Grayson considered popping over to the headman to put up his animal hood, then popping back, but that seemed a childish prank. "My magic has many abilities," Grayson said. "The first is to speak any language. I can also travel at a thought." He jumped through the Veil, appearing on Toqto's left, moved to the doorway, then popped back where he had been standing.

A smile stretched across Bolad's hardened face, revealing several rotten teeth. "Very well, god-man. You and your friend will go free. But first you must share story tonight at feast where you are honored guest."

✦　✦　✦

After leaving Bolad mi Aru's chamber, Ulagan took Grayson and Danno to the bowels of the fortress and into a steamy stone chamber. The air smelled sour, and at first Grayson couldn't see. Slowly he made out that the steam was rising from a reamway that ran past the far end of the chamber. The sight of an underground river in this new land filled him with memories of home. Several pale men were cleaning the floor. Another sat cross-legged next to a stack of animal-skin longboats.

Ulagan left them to bathe. In spite of a few mosquitoes, the bath was the most comfort Grayson had experienced in months. Somehow the water managed to warm his very bones, which had been frozen for weeks. He might have stayed in that reamway for the rest of his days had the voices not seemed so much louder in that place and had Ulagan not come back to fetch them. The giant brought clean clothing: scratchy hemp shirts, some leather breeches, and two pair of soft fur boots, which shockingly fit.

"Things little brother outgrew," Ulagan told them. "You are hungry, oom?"

"Oom," Grayson said.

✦　✦　✦

The giants feasted in an open chamber on the ground floor of the fortress. A fire pit in the center cast golden light over the room, making the pale faces glow. Bolad had a second nest throne situated on the wall opposite the entrance. Though currently empty, it was the first thing Grayson saw upon entering the room with Ulagan. Larger groups of giants sat on swaths of fur or leather with a collection of stubby candles between them. There were no tables. Pale slaves carried around paper-like bowls filled with greasy meat, some kind of flatbread, and what first looked like rounds of wet charcoal.

Ulagan approached one such slave. He took a piece of flatbread and used it to pick up a chunk of meat. "Eat bread and meat." He gestured toward the tray. "I avoid tsok."

Danno and Grayson exchanged glances of disgust, then examined the pile of beetles. They were black and slimy—covered in some kind of sauce. They each grabbed some bread and meat. Ulagan began a conversation with another giant, so Grayson spoke to the slave. The man looked to be in his twenties, but the rings around his eyes made him seem much older. "You're human."

"I am Conaw, taken from my village in a raid. Who are you to be treated with such courtesy?"

"I am Grayson. And this is Danno. I can, uh . . . I can do magic."

Conaw's eyes widened and he lowered his voice. "If that is true, you must free us. For too long the Puru have had no champion."

Free the slaves? Could that be Grayson's purpose here? "I will think on it," he said.

Conaw smiled and bowed his head. "Enjoy your dinner, Son of Gray."

"Oh, I'm not . . ." But Conaw was already walking away.

A cheer rose up, drowning out all other voices. Bolad mi Aru entered the room with two giants, followed by Randmuir and his men, whose hands were bound behind their backs. Four more giant guards ended the line.

Ragaz the shadir flitted over to Grayson, circled his waist, and soared back to Fonu, who stood behind Randmuir. The creature whispered in his master's ear. Fonu's gaze settled on Grayson, and the look in the man's dark eyes made him shiver.

Bolad's men had the pirates sit in a row along the wall adjacent from Bolad's nest, where the headman had already taken his seat. Grayson and Danno remained with Ulagan, standing against the wall opposite the pirates.

The headman helped himself to some bread and meat and a handful of beetles from a slave's tray, then uttered a strange trilling cry, "Ah-loo ah-loo ah-loo ah-loo ah-loooooo . . ."

The room fell silent, all eyes fixed on the headman.

"The forces of winter have brought to us a god-man and his tribe of dirt-men. Come, god-man, and tell us the tale of your people, your god, and your magic." Bolad motioned Grayson forward.

All eyes fixed upon Grayson. He glanced at Randmuir and the other pirates, noting their mixed expressions of curiosity, frustration, or annoyance. Grayson must be careful. More than anything, he wanted to return to the Armanian king, where he would find Jhorn, Onika, and Sir Kalenek. He recalled what Onika liked to say when she caught him in a lie. "*Truth brings freedom.*"

So Grayson told about growing up in Magonia with Jhorn and Onika. He told about Onika's prophecies of the Five Woes and the Rescuer who would lead them to safety and how Sir Kalenek had done just that, taking them on a journey across the Painted Dune Sea. He told about the destruction of Lâhaten, the sinkhole after the flood, and traveling underground to the Port of Jeruka. Then of sailing on the *Baretam* all the way to Armania, getting lost when he'd tried to board the *Seffynaw*, and how thieves had stolen the dinghy. He shared how the Five Realms had died before his eyes and sank into the sea like a castle made of sand when the tide comes in. How he had ended up with the Magonian witches. How he'd used his magic to hide. And when he came to this part of the story, he pushed into the Veil, drawing a gasp from the crowd. He exited the Veil beside Bolad's nest, which brought forth a second gasp, this time with applause and cheers. He went on to share how the great Rescuer Sir Kalenek had saved him again. How Grayson had rowed through the dark sea and sung to the serpent. How he had come aboard the pirate ship and joined their crew.

He rather enjoyed the way the audience hung on his every word, and he realized then that his story was truly remarkable.

He ended with how Ulagan and his group had brought them here, and the giants cheered.

Bolad cut through the din with a request. "Show more magic!"

Grayson relented and made a show of popping around the room, swiping paper bowls of food and delivering them to others, snuffing out candles, and tugging on fur rugs or leather mats. It was far too long before he finally got to sit and eat his fill. He was well into his third piece of meat when he heard a voice in his head that was different from the others.

"I know what you are." The voice belonged to Master Fonu, who was seated across the room.

Grayson met the man's gaze, fighting back the urge to shiver.

"A root child is the proper term," Fonu said in Grayson's mind. *"Master Jhorn shouldn't have taken you from your mother."*

The air tickled Grayson's eyes. Jhorn hadn't taken him from anyone. Grayson's mother had died in childbirth.

Fonu chuckled, and the nearby candlelight reflected in his dark eyes. *"Your thoughts betray you, boy. I wasn't certain you were that specific root child, but that you know Master Jhorn is all the answer I need. Your grandfather and aunt will be happy to know you are alive and well. Ragaz, tell them."*

The red shadir vanished. Grayson's mouth went dry as he realized he'd fallen for Fonu's trap. But how could the man hear his thoughts? Mantics couldn't do that.

"It is a new magic," Fonu said. *"Help me and I will teach you to use it."*

Grayson shook his head, trying not to think about anything.

"No? Then I will kill your friend."

Beside Grayson, Danno started to cough. The boy grasped his throat and wheezed.

Magic! Fonu still must have access to evenroot. Fear burned in Grayson's stomach. "Don't hurt him."

"Agree to translate for me, and I'll stop," Fonu said.

Translate? That's all he wanted? "I agree."

Danno stopped coughing. Grayson fetched him a cup of water, and the boy guzzled it down.

Gasps across the room pulled Grayson's attention to Fonu, who stood with his hands unbound and lifted like some kind of jester about to perform. A wave of one hand and a food tray rose from a slave's grasp and floated in the air.

"Behold, I am Fonu, great sorcerer of Haroan the wolf god."

Reluctantly, Grayson translated.

Fonu waved his other hand and Bolad mi Aru floated into the air, nest and all. Around the room, giants responded with shouts, gasps, and whispers.

"Down!" the headman yelled. "Put me down."

"Free my companions and give us your best rooms," Fonu said. "We will be staying awhile."

Grayson translated this, to which the headman replied, "Oom, free the dirtmen."

Fonu returned the nest to its position at the front of the room. Some of the giants clapped. The guards set about untying the pirates. Ulagan leaned close to Grayson, his brows knit tightly.

"He blasphemes the wolf. Is he a servant of your Arman?"

"No," Grayson said. "He is not."

WILEK

The royal family had barely launched the king's death boat when Schwyl and the king's advisors had descended upon Wilek with talk of a coronation.

Wilek had more pressing things to worry about. Reports from scouts came in almost daily of giant sightings in the north, near the mountains and forests, but there had yet to be any interaction with these natives. They did not seem to come down onto the plains and hadn't approached any of the settlements.

It seemed strange to Wilek that no one currently inhabited this section of land. With all the pit houses and brush shelters, it was obvious that someone had once lived here—and that they weren't giants—yet there was no indication that the land had ever been cultivated. Perhaps these nomadic people were strictly hunters who followed a herd, like those Miss Mielle had met in the north. If so, what would happen when the herd brought them south again and they found that several nations had made a home of their land?

With the need to build hundreds of shelters for commoners, King Loran had commissioned the Bikoor Watchtower in Er'Rets Point much smaller than Wilek would have liked. It would be more of an outpost really, with a single tower that would provide an excellent view of the ocean and surrounding land. So far only one wing had been completed—enough to house the royal families Hadar and Pitney, temporarily anyway.

Such small quarters were not big enough for two regimes. King Loran was anxious to move the kingdom of Sarikar north to a castle his carpenters were staking out in the forested foothills of the mountains. The king was in the north now, inspecting the progress.

Wilek would need a stronghold as well—something more defendable than this outpost by the sea. The island Trevn described sounded like an ideal option, and if all went well, Wilek hoped to begin as soon as the ground thawed. It felt strange to build on this land without permission, but Arman continued to voice his approval through Onika, and with the land seemingly empty and Wilek's people in need, he had no other choice.

Dendrick opened the door and peeked inside. "Your Highness? Prince Rosbert has arrived to collect his son."

"Send him in," Wilek said.

The mind-speaking magic was another problem that continued to grow more complex by the day. Wilek was not eager to see Prince Rosbert and discuss his son's indiscretions.

So far as Trevn had been able to determine, the primary function of the mind-speak ability was communication. The magic enabled the gifted to speak to any mind—gifted or not. Wilek had been thrilled to discover he could speak with Kal, learn what the Magonians were up to, and what had become of Janek's child.

When word of the magic had leaked out to the general population, panic ensued. Athosian priests said the gift was evil and advocated that any who could use the voices be put to death, and it wasn't only the Athosian priests who felt that way. The population was divided. Some sided with the Athosians, but others believed the voices were a gift to Arman's chosen.

In an attempt to assuage fear, Wilek had imposed the first law of voicing: Use it well. This had come directly from the words Arman had spoken when Wilek and Trevn first knelt on the soil of this land. The ability was not a plaything to toy with non-gifted as a prank or for nefarious means. It was not to be used to eavesdrop on others without reason, nor should anyone use a man's thoughts against him.

As Trevn practiced and refined the different ways to use the ability, Wilek instituted training, usage guidelines, and punishments for lawbreakers. Trevn had discovered a polite way to "knock," as he called it, when one wanted to communicate. He had also, with Hinck's help, learned to shield his mind from eavesdroppers, which was the newest ability the duo had discovered. All this was excellent training for the gifted, but Wilek's concern was the commoners. Trevn had taught the royal guards and high-ranking staff to shield their minds at all times, since all were pathways of information that Rogedoth might seek to infiltrate, but training the entire population was not feasible. And now several young maids had come forward, claiming that Lord Kanzer—Prince Rosbert's son and King Loran's nephew—had been speaking lewdly to their minds and would not stop. Bound by his own laws, Wilek had arrested the boy, which had upset Rosbert, who had been in the north with Loran.

Now he was here to retrieve his son.

There was simply no way to monitor the use of this magic. At last count, between the three father realms, nearly thirty people had some form of the voicing gift. All were third-generation royalty or better with the exception of two: Miss Onika the prophetess and her elderly maid Kempe. Wilek could guess why Arman might bestow the magic on his prophetess, but the maid had puzzled him until a short line of questioning induced Kempe to admit that she was the illegitimate daughter of Prince Wodek, Wilek's great-uncle on his father's side, a man who had died over thirty years ago and had never had children, or so everyone had thought.

Considering royal blood, Wilek and Trevn believed there to be another five people capable of the magic—those in Rogedoth's camp: Barthel Rogedoth, Rosârah Laviel, Sârah Jemesha, Lady Eudora, and Hinckdan Faluk.

A knock at the door preceded Dendrick, Prince Rosbert, and a Sarikarian guardsman. Novan brought up the rear. Wilek inclined his head to Prince Rosbert, who curtly responded in the same manner.

"Where is my son?" Rosbert asked.

"Confined to his room," Wilek said. "Dendrick can take you to him."

The man narrowed his eyes at Wilek. "Kanzer is innocent. Did he not tell you as much?"

"He did," Wilek said, "but after hearing both stories, King Loran and I both chose to believe the maids."

"Ridiculous. Commoners lie, Your Highness."

"Liars are found in all classes of men," Wilek said.

Rosbert sputtered. "Those maids conspired against my boy. I will not forget this, Sâr Wilek." And he pushed his way past the guards and back out into the corridor. "Take me to my son. Now."

Dendrick hurried out the door after him. "His room is this way, Prince Rosbert."

The footsteps faded and Novan closed the door. "That went well," he said.

Wilek sighed. "Inappropriate use of the voicing magic is a new type of wrongdoing, Novan. A young maid who fears her master could take precautions to keep out of his path, but what is to stop a magic that can enter any head at any time, without notice or invitation?"

"Nothing," Novan said, "except learning to shield the mind."

"And for the moment I cannot teach every man, woman, and child to do that."

"No, but you could offer lessons to anyone who wished to learn," Novan said.

Wilek imagined throngs of commoners flooding the keep, desperate to learn ways to guard against the frightening new voicing magic.

"On the other hand, if you could train a spy to eavesdrop on any mind, it might be useful in stopping treason before it happens," Novan added.

He meant to listen in on the thoughts of Kamran DanSâr, Wilek's half brother and the only traitor who had not been outed. The idea was a good one. Lady Pia had been keeping a close watch on the man, but she could not read his thoughts. Wilek had seen Kamran in Trevn's training class on the voicing ability. If he hadn't yet mastered the ability to shield, he had at least heard about it. "I will think on that."

He dismissed Novan to his place outside the door and sat down at his desk to use the method called "knocking" that Trevn had devised. Concentrating on King Loran was more challenging now that he had traveled north, but it did not take long to find him. A thick fog seemed to separate their thoughts, part of the shields King Loran had erected around his mind. Wilek sent Loran his name, *"Wilek Hadar."*

The barrier between their minds dissolved, and King Loran spoke, *"Has my brother arrived?"*

"Come and gone in less than five minutes' time," Wilek said.

"I am sorry. Rosbert is set on defending his son."

"It is understandable, coming from a father. Yet Lord Kanzer refused to admit any wrongdoing. Until he does and issues a formal apology to all three maids, I will not accept him in court. I hope that you will demand the same. We should strive to keep the voicing rules equal for all nations."

A moment of silence passed, and Wilek wondered if he had offended King Loran.

"I understand your intent," Loran finally said. *"And while I acknowledge that the boy crossed a line, I'm not so certain his behavior warrants such a harsh penalty."*

"He purposely invaded the minds of three women to antagonize them."

"He is a boy. A royal. Had he tumbled one of the maids, it would have gone unmentioned. I agree that it was a misuse of his power, but enforcing too strict of laws will incite revolt in our people, and in this uncertain time we must keep them united."

Was Wilek overreacting? No. He was decided on this. *"I have seen the opposite happen in Armania. My father extended too much freedom to his people, which only invited Arman's wrath. We must have discipline. We must have morality."*

"Somewhere in the middle, then, is what we must strive for," Loran said, *"though only time will show what that looks like."*

Wilek supposed that was true. *"Are we at peace, you and I?"* he asked.

"I have no plans to wage war." The man chuckled. *"Actually, there is a matter I would like to discuss that would strengthen our alliance. It involves my daughter Saria and your brother Trevn."*

Wilek took a deep breath, knowing Trevn would not like where this conversation might lead. *"What do you have in mind?"*

✦ ✦ ✦

"Loran has proposed an alliance," Wilek told Trevn that night at dinner in the great hall.

"We are allied with Sarikar already," Trevn said. "Plus you are married to Lady Zeroah, and her brother is your backman. How can we possibly make it stronger?"

Wilek chose his words carefully, though he doubted any phrasing would change his brother's reaction to the proposal. "Soon Loran and his people will move and we will no longer be part of the same community. In order to keep our mutual interests strong . . . he wishes for you to marry Princess Saria."

Trevn began to laugh, loud enough to turn several heads. "Well, that's a surprising offer, coming from a monogamous Sarikarian. He knows I'm already married."

Trevn's unsanctioned marriage to Miss Mielle remained a sore spot with Wilek. "Many do not believe it, brother. Loran included."

"But I have said so, and Cadoc has given his witness. Once I bring Mielle here, she will present our wedding contract and the list of one hundred witnesses."

"I don't doubt the ceremony took place," Wilek said carefully. "But Loran thinks she died."

Trevn's easy smile vanished. "He thinks I would invent having spoken with her? Is that supposed to make me eager to join his family with mine?"

"It's just that no one but you has been able to mind-speak with Miss Mielle—not even Zeroah."

"No offense, Wil, but Zeroah is afraid of the new magic. She hasn't come to any of my trainings to learn to shield. I don't think she's putting forth much effort."

"She has been ill of late and overly tired from the pregnancy," Wilek said.

"Even if Mielle and I did not speak for hours every day, our soul-binding is all the truth I need. If she had died, I would have felt it. If you would permit me to go rescue her, this conversation wouldn't be necessary."

Wilek could not let Trevn go traipsing about this land when there were giants out there. "I want you to at least consider a temporary betrothal to Princess Saria."

Trevn stood, knocking over his chair. "Absolutely not!"

Wilek noted the faces that had turned their way at Trevn's outburst. "Sit down and hear me out," he whispered. "Please."

Trevn folded his arms and remained standing.

"The betrothal would be acted upon only if Miss Mielle were not found by your twentieth year or—"

"I would certainly hope I find her before then," Trevn spat.

"*Or* if I were to die and you became king," Wilek finished.

"Is someone planning to kill you?"

Wilek shrugged. "One never knows. It hasn't been an easy year. You accept, then?"

Trevn's face flushed. "No, I don't accept."

"You won't have to follow through if you find Miss Mielle before you are twenty or if I live a long and healthy life. We must keep peace with Sarikar, Trevn. Should Rogedoth attack . . . we would not survive against his magic without their numbers."

"Hinck says Rogedoth won't attack with magic. Not yet, anyway. And if they do attack, Rurekau or Sarikar will be their first target, not Armania."

"Regardless, we must be ready to defend ourselves and our neighbors."

Trevn righted his chair and sat down again. "Why would Loran agree to such vague terms?"

"Because I fought for them. And because his son is sickly. There is no one else for him to marry Saria to. I want you to agree to this, brother. It will help mend the rift I started by arresting Lord Kanzer."

"You make a mistake and I must pay for it? Mielle is out there," Trevn said, pointing at the wall as if the girl were in the next room. "Let me go find her and prove it to you."

He would have to give something to convince Trevn to agree. "I will let you go look. *If* you agree to the betrothal."

Trevn rubbed his face and growled.

Had that been acquiescence? "You agree, then?"

"Draw up the contract," Trevn said, his voice hoarse, "but know that I will read every word to make sure the two of you aren't trying to trick me. In the meantime I will pack for my trip so that I can find my wife and void this contract as soon as possible."

"I can't do without you at present, Trevn. You must stay with me at least until Zeroah gives birth."

"You have kept me prisoner here long enough. And now I have agreed to your ludicrous betrothal. Let me go as you promised not one minute ago."

"You have never been a prisoner," Wilek said. "I've needed your help to understand the mind-speak magic. And you've done very well. But we never heard from the four ships that turned back from the ice. I don't feel it's safe to let you wander out there on your own."

"I am not completely incompetent, you know."

"I never said you were."

"I might be able to reach them by land if you'd let me go through the mountains."

"Where the giants roam? Absolutely not. If something happens to me, you are all that is left for Armania."

"I'll stay until your coronation. It's my final offer, or you can forget the whole thing."

Wilek could not recall anyone being so stubborn in negotiations with their father. "You're going to tell me how things are now? Is that how this is going to work?"

"If I must," Trevn said, standing again. "I no longer trust your word. First you said I had to wait to explore until I learned to forage food. Then until we found housing for everyone. After that you put me in charge of learning to mind-speak, then training others how. And now I must wait for your child to be born? Wil, I cannot stay here while Mielle and the passengers of those ships are lost. I must find them. And if it means defying your order, then I will do it. Lock me up, if you must, because that is the only way you will stop me."

Wilek had pushed too hard; he saw that now. There was no fair way he could think of to disagree. "Very well. Put together your contingent for my approval. After the coronation you may sail north, but you will travel the eastern coast. You also must voice with me daily, make maps as you travel, and should an emergency arise, you must return at once, whether or not you've found Miss Mielle. Is that clear?"

"Yes, Wil. Thank you!" And the Second Arm of Armania took off in a sprint.

GOZAN

I have taken my last taste of ahvenrood," Jazlyn told Gozan while Qoatch looked on.

I know, Gozan replied.

The three of them stood in the tent that Emperor Ulrik had given to Jazlyn for her own private use. Since they landed, Gozan had bided his time, knowing that his human would soon realize she was out of options.

"Did your slights find the other mantics?" she asked.

The Magonian camp is about twelve leagues to the southeast, Gozan said. *King Barthel is on a trio of islands nearly that far west of here, building an army.*

Emperor Ulrik, on the other hand, had led his people to an expanse of rolling hills. He had ordered his fortress built atop the tallest hill around, which afforded a pleasant view—strategic too, should anyone wish to attack. Unfortunately, the Rurekan masons had little skill with wood, and the building had yet to break ground, despite them having been here nearly two months already.

The young ruler might be able to see an attack coming, but he would have no way to stop anyone once they arrived.

It seemed the wrong season for sieges, though, and the emperor and his Igote had grown lax as the task of learning to build consumed their days. If only Jazlyn had a supply of ahvenrood, it would have been the perfect time to conquer this nation, but she had no more. She had sent Gozan on countless errands to locate more root, and while Gozan had found the camps, he

458

had no way to steal root from such distances—especially not when Magon watched over the Magonians and Dendron guarded King Barthel's hoard.

"I should have gone to them," she said. "I still could."

Even if you survived the long journey, Gozan said, *there is little reason to believe you would be well received. King Barthel might be willing to make use of you as one of his sworn servants, but the Magonians would not trust a Tennish priestess anywhere near their ahvenrood stores.*

"I am unwilling to give up so much power," Jazlyn said. "I must consider my choices carefully."

Gozan barked out a laugh. *You have no choices, Great Lady. No good ones, anyway.*

"I could leave. Build a home of my own. Live peacefully."

How? You know less of building than the emperor's masons and nothing of survival without ahvenrood to assist you.

"There are plenty of brush shelters and pit houses around," Jazlyn said. "I could live in one of those. And Qoatch would not abandon me."

I am sure that no matter what, Qoatch will remain loyal. But didn't you just say you were unwilling to give up your power?

"There is power in freedom."

You would be old.

"I will be old no matter what," she snapped.

There is a better way, Gozan said. *Why do you continue to deny it?*

"I will not speak to you of Dominion. I will never be that desperate."

If I know you, and I do, Great Lady, you will do what gives you the most power, which means you must choose between Dominion to me or marriage to Emperor Ulrik. I promise you, I am the lesser of two evils.

She stared at him, a vein pulsing over her left eye. "Qoatch," she said, still glaring at Gozan. "I require your assistance in drafting a marriage agreement."

"Yes, Great Lady." The eunuch immediately went to the priestess's trunk.

Fool, Gozan said. *Such an action goes against everything Tenma stands for.*

"I am well aware of the cost," she said.

If you choose this path, I cannot promise to answer your call should you find ahvenrood again.

"I understand," she said, nose in the air. "You have served me well, Gozan. May you find a mantic worthy of you."

He bowed to maintain respect in hopes that once she married the emperor and hated it, she would call out to him and beg for Dominion.

Gozan made a show of leaving but instead lingered out of sight. He would not pass up the chance to witness such a deception against the emperor.

+ + +

Emperor Ulrik Orsona and Priestess Jazlyn of Tenma were wed in a tent surrounded by the highest-ranked Rurekan and Tennish people to have survived the trek across the sea. They were one nation now. Tenma had been absorbed into New Rurekau by a marriage of desperation. Gozan fed off Jazlyn's horror, eager to see her reap the consequences of her choice in denying a more permanent bond with him. The woman had negotiated hard with the emperor to protect her interests—Gozan had to give her that much. The marriage agreement was so specific, it even included a clause that would allow a female ruler should the couple's firstborn child be a girl.

And Jazlyn would need a child if she were to keep her hold on the emperor for long. Without the asset of a child, once the vain young man saw Jazlyn's true self, he would discard her, maybe even have her killed for deceiving him.

Gozan stretched the last of Jazlyn's magic as far as he could, delighted to aggravate the coming catastrophe. He was able to maintain her appearance long enough for her to conceive, though he wasn't about to tell her that she had succeeded. He reveled in the degradation she felt in submitting to this man, her husband, time and again. That she felt like a weak female brought Gozan joy. As he fed off her misery, he plotted his final plan, intent on finding as many witnesses as possible; otherwise people might think her an impostor.

Gozan chose Queen Thallah's ageday celebration to end her charade. While the emperor did not particularly enjoy the company of his great-aunt, he was bored living in such a spare camp, and the idea of a party intrigued him. Gozan enjoyed watching the emperor make plans, and when the special day came and the festivities began, he took on a gaseous form and swam through the crowds of people, blissful in his anticipation. He watched the feasting, the dancing, and the performers who did all they could to entertain the imperial family. When the time came for the emperor to make a speech to honor his great, toad-like aunt, Gozan waited for the perfect moment to end the spell.

"I did not grow up knowing my great-aunt Thallah, Rosârah of Armania," Ulrik began, standing at the high table, goblet in hand, "but since she came aboard my ship at Bakurah Island, we have spent much time together. She is a wise woman. No matter the stakes that came against us, she remained positive and hopeful for the future. After my mother left me, I was glad to have someone wise to confide in. The rosârah knew of my ardent affection for my now bride, and I credit her for helping our marriage come about. It is partly due to her wisdom and advice that New Rurekau has a queen."

Applause and cheers rang out, and Jazlyn waved to her people like the good little empress she was now, despite being a traitor to the ideals of the Tennish nation.

Ulrik went on. "I admire and respect my great-aunt for her endless energy and commitment to me and my realm. And so it is with immense honor that I announce to you, Aunt Thallah, that my beautiful bride, Empress Jazlyn, is with child."

Gasps of delight swept through the crowd. People began to cheer and applaud. Thallah waddled over to embrace the emperor in her stubby arms.

Gozan reeled at the perfection of such timing. Eager to seize the moment, he withdrew every drop of magic left in Jazlyn's body, absorbing it into himself.

Jazlyn coughed.

No one noticed, as all were still cheering.

She convulsed and clutched her throat, which caught the concerned eyes of some.

Ulrik waved his hands to calm the crowd. "Such an announcement is more of a gift to all of us than to my great-aunt, so to honor her specifically on her ageday, I name her the third guardian over our child."

Queen Thallah hugged her nephew again, cooing over the very idea.

Someone in the audience screamed, "The empress!"

Murmurs and gasps tore through the crowd as every eye focused on where Jazlyn sat. Her skin bubbled, as if it were boiling. She waved her hands as if trying to catch her balance. She had no control at the moment. The magic was putting everything back where it belonged, and there was much to do on that account.

Ulrik knelt at her side, grabbed her arm. "Jazlyn, beloved, what is happening?"

"My magic," she croaked. "It is finally gone."

"But I thought . . ."

Oh, the turmoil on the cocky young emperor's face as her words sank in. Gozan breathed in the man's trepidation. Glorious as it was, he knew it was the last he would consume for some time, so he and his swarm languished, not only in the emperor's emotions, but in the fear, the horror, and the dread of everyone present.

Jet-black hair turned gray. Smooth brown skin wrinkled and sagged. Eyes sank into deep sockets. Lips thinned. Teeth browned. Fingers twisted.

When the transformation finally ended, Jazlyn sat at the high table, looking her true age for the first time in decades.

"What is this?" Ulrik cried. When no answer came from his bride, he stood and repeated his question to Qoatch.

"This is the Great Lady's true physical form," the eunuch said. "She has used the last of her ahvenrood."

The young emperor could not hide his mortification. The bellowing scream that came from his lips filled Gozan with more pleasure than watching the *Baretam* break apart in the whirlpool.

Thus the bond was severed between High Queen Jazlyn, Empress of Rurekau, and Gozan the Great. He lingered until the horrified crowd calmed and there was little left to feed off of, then left Masi to spy on Jazlyn and set off with his swarm to the southeast.

If Gozan did not find a new human soon, his swarm would abandon him. He faced two options. The choice, while unpleasant, was not difficult. Gozan had no desire to lose his freedom. He would never humble himself beneath another shadir, and if he must attempt a coup, taking over Magon's domain should be far easier than taking on Dendron. After all, she did say she had a plan to protect herself from Dendron. If Gozan chose the right human, he might be able to steal everything from Magon without her even knowing.

Surely among the Magonians he would find a human to bond with—one who was ambitious, hungry, and unscrupulous. He would start by looking at the two humans who shared Magon. No human would prefer sharing power when they could wield it alone.

Gozan reached into the past and shifted his form to one he had used long ago—one that Magon, when he finally made himself known to her, would recognize and understand what it represented. Gone was the ghoulish form of Gozan. In his place came the likeness of a man, a hulking giant shrouded in armor and weaponry.

Rurek, god of war, had returned.

WILEK

Wilek stood in his new chamber in Castle Armanguard, arms held out to his sides while the tailor marked the hem on the sleeves of his coronation robes. He perused the trunks stacked around him that had yet to be unloaded. Much had happened in the past few months. King Loran had established and fortified his new castle in the forested foothills of the mountains. Wilek had gone north as well and commissioned Castle Armanguard to be built upon the island Trevn had discovered on the northwestern end of Lake Arman. A simple stone keep stood complete at present, surrounded by a wooden bailey. And finally, in three days' time, Wilek would be crowned King of Armania.

Many had pushed for his coronation sooner, but he'd insisted the more important job of protecting his people must come first. With that mostly taken care of, he no longer had excuses. And yet he wasn't ready to be king. Not here.

Had they still lived in the Five Realms, Wilek would feel better equipped for what lay ahead. While trusted friends surrounded him, already he could see that the public did not understand his faith in Arman. According to his staff most people believed Arman the favorite of Wilek's Rôb Five. He needed to find a way to communicate his newfound faith in the One God to others.

Now that most people had learned to shield their minds against mind-speaking, things had quieted down a great deal within the castle walls. Everyone was guarding against being spied upon. Wilek had taken Kempe, the illegitimate maid, away from Miss Onika and put her on the task of shadowing

Kamran's thoughts, but the man never dropped his shields long enough for the woman to hear a single one.

According to Hinckdan Faluk, Rogedoth had learned to shield from an outside source. Wilek believed Kamran responsible, though he had no proof. Because of this, Wilek decided to keep Trevn's other voicing discoveries private to keep Kamran from spreading more information to Rogedoth. So far Lady Pia hadn't noticed any unlawful behavior from Kamran, but she had promised to keep Wilek informed of his every move.

Spring had blossomed in full. Wells had been dug, making drinking water easily accessible. Occasional herds of deer had been spotted with fawns among them. Life was vibrant and plentiful in this new land. Among the remnant as well. The thirty-some horses that had survived between the remaining ships had been bred. Pregnant women abounded too. Having lost nearly half the population of Armania in the exodus across the sea, Wilek considered it a blessing. The first generation of Armanians was about to be born in this new land, his own heir among them. It was an exciting time in the history of his people.

Yet their troubles were not over. Both Emperor Ulrik and King Loran had reported that small groups of giants had raided smaller settlements, stealing tools, weapons, and, in some cases, entire families. While no one in Armania had yet come face-to-face with giants, they had been seen, watching the construction of Armanguard from a distance.

Then there was Rogedoth, the self-titled King Barthel. According to Hinckdan's reports, he had not only waylaid the four Armanian ships that had escaped Captain Stockton's ice field, he had enslaved their crews and passengers and was hard at work building an army that would someday march upon Sarikar and Armania. The man intended to claim rule of the entire remnant from the Five Realms—felt it was not only his birthright, but that he had earned the position with years of service to Armania. Wilek had always hoped that if he would ever rule, he would rule a realm of peace. That, it seemed, was not to be.

The door opened and Trevn came inside. He dropped onto a longchair and helped himself to a tart from a tray Dendrick had brought in earlier, then looked at Wilek and smiled.

"You look . . . pompous," Trevn said over a full mouth.

"I made several modifications to tone down the overall gaudiness," Wilek said. "Are you telling me it didn't work?"

"Not in the least."

Wilek sighed. "It doesn't matter. I'm only wearing it once." He shrugged

out of the coronation robe and handed it to the tailor, who bowed and quitted the room.

"I like the new insignia."

Wilek's new royal blue tabard had five sunbird heads embroidered in gold
thread to represent Nesher, Arman's spirit form. "I hope it will unify our realm
and show my allegiance to Arman."

"It's a good idea," Trevn said. "Is Lady Zeroah feeling any better?"

"Not really," Wilek said. "The midwives assure me it is only a reaction to
the child within her."

"Little Chadek making her ill, is he?"

"So they say. You got my message about adding Kempe to your expedition?"
Wilek asked, sitting at his desk.

"She's an old woman, Wil. I'm not sure she'll be able to keep up with us."

"She doesn't have to. Leave her on the ship. With her ability to mind-speak,
she will be an extra means of communication should you need her."

Trevn sighed. "If you insist."

"I do. And, Trevn, be careful. I remain concerned about these giants. We
still don't understand why some attack and some don't."

"There are scoundrels in any people group. I'll be careful."

"And if you get a chance to trade with them—"

"Don't trade weapons, I know."

"And don't forget that Rand is out there somewhere."

"Yes, yes. I remember."

Wilek regarded his brother and sighed deeply. "I feel like I'm sending you
to your death."

"I'll be on the *Seffynaw*. It's like a fortress."

"So long as you remain on board."

"I can't do that and map the coast."

"Just . . . promise me you'll be careful."

Trevn reached for the tray of tarts and grabbed a second. "Wil, it's me. I'm
always careful."

"You're always curious," Wilek said. And that worried him more than any
tribe of mysterious giants.

✦ ✦ ✦

Wilek stood in an anteroom off the front of the great hall, which had
been built on the second floor and doubled as the throne room at Castle

Armanguard. He wore his blue tabard bearing his new insignia over his blacks. He also wore his white velvet coronation robe and one of his father's brown velvet capes, edged in black fur.

A servant entered the room and informed Dendrick that the time had come. Wilek exited the anteroom. Novan and Rystan moved along behind him, helping to transition his cape. He stopped in the open doorway of the great hall. Somewhere inside, a lone piper played the king's song. From Wilek's position, he could see straight down the short walkway to the throne. The stone walls of the hall had been covered in blue silk. Golden drapes ran along the molding, met in the center back wall, and cascaded behind the bronze throne. The four legs that ran up the corners of the chair in pillars to support a pointed canopy roof had always appeared more like a shrine to Wilek, so he had requested some alterations. Gone were the bronze busts of his father's five gods. They had been melted down and recast into four roundels for each of the corner posts to symbolize Justness, Virtue, Wisdom, and Prosperity. And on the pinnacle of the canopy, a bronzed Nesher head signified Wilek's allegiance to Arman. He had also added a shelf underneath the seat to hold Arman's holy book.

There were no tables in the great hall today. People stood on both sides of the aisle, crammed shoulder to shoulder, all looking toward Wilek at the entrance. He could sense their collective mood as excited and hopeful, which bolstered his courage. The piper ended the song, and the herald played Wilek's tune on his trumpet—one short note and four long ones.

"His Royal Highness, Wilek-Sâr Hadar, the First Arm, the Dutiful, the God-slayer, Heir to Armania."

A cheer rose up from the crowd as Wilek started down the aisle. The freshly sanded wooden planks felt rough under his bare feet. Wilek crossed the room quickly. No dais had yet been built, so the throne sat at floor level. He stopped just before reaching the footstone. The ancient relic had been fitted into the floorboards a few paces in front of the throne. It held the very footprints of Sarik, Arman's son and the first king of Armania. For centuries tradition decreed that when a new king took his vows, he must stand in the steps of King Sarik himself and all who had come after him.

The priest, Father Burl Mathal, wore white robes and stood to the left of the throne. Novan and Rystan joined Trevn, Rayim, and Dendrick at the front, and the five men each lifted a pole from the canopy until the cloth of gold and blue silk stretched above Wilek's head.

Mathal broke the silence with a question. "Who comes to lay claim to this throne and realm?"

"I am Wilek-Sâr Hadar, son of Echad Hadar."

"Stand, then, in the footsteps of your forebears, then come kneel before the throne."

Wilek stepped onto the footstone. A quick shift of his feet and they fit mostly into the impression Sarik had left centuries ago, though Wilek's feet were a few hairs longer. He took a long breath, then stepped out on the other side and sank to his knees before the throne.

"I hold in my hands the Book of Arman that you carried across the sea," Mathal said. "You have expressed your desire to rule by Arman's will over your own. Is this true?"

"It is," Wilek said, and his heart swelled with hope that he might put an end to the evil practices of his father and lead his people into a new era of peace and safety.

"Then I bestow upon you the wisdom and mouthpiece of the God, the most valuable thing this world has to offer."

Wilek accepted the book from the priest and slid it onto the shelf under his throne. "Upon Arman's word I vow to rule this land. Arman's word is the only foundation that is unshakable."

He felt a shift in the mood of the crowd. Very few of these people had been alive for King Echad's coronation, so most didn't know what to expect here today. Still, the words of his vow had confused some. How would the people react when they all finally understood he had converted to the Armanite faith?

"Stand and face your people," Mathal said.

Wilek did so, and the hem of his cape twisted around his feet. He caught sight of Zeroah, sitting in his father's old rollchair, and beside her his sisters and Miss Onika, whose pale eyes gleamed in the low light.

"I hereby present unto the people of this new land, His Royal Highness, Wilek-Rosâr Hadar, the Head, the Dutiful, the Godslayer, King of Armania, and Servant of Arman. Arman save the king."

The crowd solemnly uttered a mixture of "Arman save the king" and "Gods save the king."

Father Mathal then poured oil over Wilek's head and anointed him king, then turned to lift the crown from a pillar behind him. Wilek had seen it hundreds of times in his life, mostly atop his father's head. It was made of gold and blue velvet and encrusted with hundreds of jewels.

Mathal held the crown above Wilek's head. "Arman, we offer up this crown. May it be a reamway that carries your abundant wisdom to your chosen servant's mind."

As the inner cap settled on Wilek's head, a chill ran over him at its weight—heavier than he'd imagined. It was meant to be a burden, he reminded himself. Ruling a nation was no simple task.

Mathal then presented a wooden staff. This Wilek had also commissioned, wanting to replace the scepter of the five gods that had been used in Armania for over five hundred years. The staff had been carved from a tree that had grown on the Er'Retian shore where Wilek had first stepped foot. It was taller than he was and topped with an ivory carving of a two-headed Nesher sunbird, looking behind and ahead—an heirloom from his mother's collection. Two golden rings had been banded under the ivory carving. The first was engraved with the name Echad Hadar, the second Wilek Hadar. Someday the staff would hold a ring for every king who ruled Armanguard.

Mathal held the new scepter before Wilek. "Arman, we offer up this scepter. May it be an extension of your Justness from your chosen servant's hand." He passed the staff to Wilek. "Sit then, chosen king, and accept this throne as yours."

"Before I do so, Father, I wish to address you all. People of Armania, here we stand together after surviving a harrowing journey across the Northsea. And yet our trials are not over. A group of mighty foes seeks our ruin. This nation was founded upon worship of Arman, and it is to Arman alone that I pledge loyalty. His prophet warned of the destruction of the Five Realms and led us here, and the God's magic will protect us from the evil we brought to this place. I hope you will all join me in worshiping Arman. Only then can we stand against what would surely be an onslaught of tyranny."

Wilek sat down, surprised to find the ancient cushion soft. A cheer rose up. Father Mathal knelt before the throne.

"I, Burl Mathal, priest of Arman, swear to serve faithfully and honestly, my Sovereign King of the Realm and his god Arman."

The canopy was put away, and Trevn, Rayim, Dendrick, Novan, and Rystan each knelt in turn before Wilek, swearing their own oaths of fealty. Beyond, the audience surged forward and formed a line to do the same. Not everyone who knelt and swore allegiance harbored emotions that matched their words. When Wilek sensed hatred or animosity, he mind-spoke the names of each to Dendrick and asked the man to write them down for further study. The worst of the loathing came from Sir Kamran DanSâr, his half brother. Wilek had yet to discover any way to break through the man's shields and hear his thoughts.

Wilek remained seated until everyone present had taken their chance to kneel—even Zeroah, who had determinedly risen from her chair to complete the task. Afterward Wilek, his guards, and a vast majority of people from the coronation paraded through the bailey to the cheers of those who hadn't been invited inside.

When Wilek returned to the great hall, it had been transformed for a banquet. He ate heartily, seated between his wife and brother, content and hopeful for the future.

Not halfway through the feast, he received a knock from King Loran.

"What news?" Wilek asked.

"Yet another group of giants has attacked a Sarikarian settlement, this time taking more than three dozen of my people captive, including my daughter, Saria."

"That's terrible!"

"As we speak I am preparing a squadron to get her back, but there is more. Two witnesses reported seeing runes tattooed on the backs of the giants' necks."

The horror of such a thing stunned Wilek. *"Could the giants have partnered with the Magonians?"*

"I care less about that than I do about rescuing my daughter. How can I get her back when there is magic at play?"

Wilek sat back in his throne and took a deep breath. He looked around at the joy of his subjects, his beautiful wife. He could not let anyone destroy what they had worked so hard to build. If mantics had taken control of the giants, what could stop them? First they would conquer New Sarikar; then Armanguard would be next.

"I don't know," Wilek said. *"But we cannot allow this to continue. Whatever you need, you have my support."*

TREVN

The day after Wilek's coronation, Sâr Trevn's expedition left Armanguard. It was the first day of the first month of what would have been the season of stormmer back home in Armania. In Er'Rets it was the height of spring. Tiny leaves had budded and bloomed on once-barren trees and bushes. Flowers blossomed. Grass sprouted, bright and thick. This new world was an uprising of color. For Trevn it was yet another reminder of how much time had passed since he'd last seen Mielle.

Left to himself he would have marched across mountain and valley to find her, but so far he'd followed his brother's leadings, and Wilek was cautious. Short explorations hadn't been enough, and even now Wilek had pushed back against Trevn's desire to travel west, where he knew Mielle was. Wilek feared his eventually meeting up with the Magonians or Rogedoth's army, so Trevn had agreed to sail the *Seffynaw* up the eastern coast. He would either circle the continent and come upon her from the north or cut across the interior of the land at some point.

Trevn did not sail as captain or crew member but as a sâr of Armania heading up an official expedition. He had wanted to take a smaller ship, but Wilek had insisted upon the *Seffynaw*, convinced that a bigger ship would give the small party an illusion of strength. The expedition consisted of Trevn and his staff; Kempe; Maleen; Captain Bussie and a smaller crew of sailors, including Nietz, Bonds, Shinn, and Rzasa; explorer Rost Keppel and his team of scholars and assistants; and a squadron of fifty soldiers—all outfitted in

470

uniforms that had been modified to display the circle of five Nesher heads, Armania's new insignia.

Though Trevn was eager to find Mielle, Wilek had also entrusted him with the arduous task of mapping the coastline—a sly decision. Trevn's love of maps might be the only thing able to distract his mind from his true objective. He instructed Captain Bussie to sail the *Seffynaw* slowly up the coast, stopping once a day so that the explorers might gather samples or make illustrations of plant and animal life. Trevn went along on these excursions, eager to look around, though he kept in constant communication with Mielle, telling her about everything he saw. Besides his own sketches of maps, trees, and animals, Trevn's journal was filled with facts and stories about the pale nomads Mielle was getting to know.

Three days into the journey Captain Bussie anchored the ship in a cove, and Trevn ordered a team to go ashore and explore. While the men prepared the boats for launch, Trevn saw Kempe on the main deck and decided to have a word. The elderly maid was no taller than his half sister Hrettah, was small boned, and had more wrinkles than a prune. Her teeth were white, and she was nearly always smiling, which made her eyes seem to glitter.

"Sâr Trevn, good morning," she said in her silvery voice. "The waves are raucous today. Tell your men to use a sea anchor to keep the dinghies from capsizing."

The woman mothered everyone, but she did so with such kindness and a smile that Trevn never minded. "You are wise, madam. Please keep me posted should anything go wrong on board."

"Certainly, Your Highness. Rest well in Captain Bussie's competence. He will take good care of your ship."

Trevn left her and, by late midday, set out with the explorers. The men did indeed use sea anchors as they made their landfall. Trevn spent some time exploring the coast, but a forest of ridiculously tall trees beckoned him farther inland. He had never seen anything like them. The sun cut through the long trunks like spears of light, and he felt like an ant in a patch of dandelions. Trevn and Ottee had been attempting to climb the trees, with Cadoc keeping watch, when one of the soldiers brought the message that Master Keppel had made a discovery.

They found the elderly explorer's team at the top of a rocky incline, standing in the narrow end of a conical hole in the ground that appeared to be the entrance to a steep cave. Trevn wasted no time climbing down the large boulders at the cave's mouth. When he reached the explorers at the bottom, he found them in the midst of a heated debate.

"We will never learn where it goes unless we go in!" Master Keppel yelled, his face flushed. The head explorer's round face and belly and stumpy arms and legs gave him the appearance of a quill pig, and he had a temper to match.

"Go in if you like, master, but I will not." This from Lanton Jahday, Keppel's assistant. The young man had golden eyes, a flat nose, and shoulder-length braids.

"You dare defy my command?" his master said.

"It is too risky," Jahday replied. "With the hour so late in the day, the tide could come in and trap us."

"You know as well as I do that the tide will not again reach its height for another two to three hours. You see clearly a worn path that leads down," Keppel snapped, pointing inside the cave. "That is a sign of life. Someone or something has traveled this way many times to create such a trail. You will be perfectly safe. Bring back your report in an hour or two."

"Are you unwilling to go yourself, Master Keppel?" Trevn asked.

The man's eye twitched. "I am in the middle of documenting some coral, Your Highness. This is why I have assistants, so that we can cover more ground in less time than one man could manage alone."

"I will accompany you, Master Jahday," Trevn said, intrigued by the cave.

"I don't think that's a good idea," Master Keppel said.

A surprising contradiction. "It's safe for your man but not for me?" Trevn asked.

The head explorer pursed his lips. His eye twitched again.

"You have no objection, then?" Trevn asked.

Keppel shook his head and shockingly said nothing.

"I have an objection, Your Highness," Jahday said. "The tide—"

"Has a good two hours before it comes in," Trevn said. "Your concern is noted." He walked into the dark mouth of the cave. "Ottee, fetch me a lantern."

"Your Highness, wait," Jahday said. "Let us do this properly."

And so Trevn, Cadoc, Maleen, Ottee, and four soldiers accompanied Master Jahday and three other explorers into the dark cave. The path was mostly smooth, but every so often they had to climb over a series of rocks that had fallen from above. Jahday and one of his men held lanterns aloft, but once the cave turned a corner and cut off the light from the entrance, the lanterns did not shine far in such blackness. From that point on, they moved very slowly.

"Mielle," Trevn called out. *"I am in a cave."*

"Whatever for?"

"We are exploring. The last time I was in a cave, it was with you."

Fond memories washed over her, and he sensed her smile. *"Where we found the orphans in the evenroot mine,"* she said. *"Would you believe that the natives have an unusual amount of orphans?"*

"How unusual?"

"Based on those we share camp with, there are twenty-three children to every adult."

"That is high. What do you think happened?"

"A war perhaps? Or maybe they fell victim to some catastrophe. Madame Wyser, Madame Stockton, and I are sewing extra clothing to share with the native children. They are ever so excited to wear anything made of a bright color. Who knew that orange and blue linen could bring such joy? But they don't really have fabric here, only leather and furs and the occasional piece woven from dried grass or—"

A scream pulled Trevn's attention back to the cave. *"I will speak with you later, Mielle. I am needed."*

Up ahead the men held the lanterns out in front as they peered down at their feet. Trevn pushed between them. "What happened?"

"It was the boy," Jahday said. "He slid down there."

Ottee. Trevn took Jahday's lantern and crouched, setting the light in the dirt at the top of a steep incline. "Ottee?"

A faint reply came, but Trevn couldn't make out the words. He reached for the boy's mind. *"Are you hurt?"*

"No, Your Highness. It's just . . . dark."

"Stay put. We are coming." To the men he said, "Let us slide down, gentlemen. The boy requires our assistance."

"I would caution against it," Jahday said. "At least not without pounding a safety line first. We have no idea how steep this becomes. It would not do if you were injured or trapped at the bottom of a pit when the tide comes in."

Trevn saw the sense of that. "Pound your safety line quickly, Master Jahday. My onesent awaits."

The moment the line was secured, Trevn took the rope in one hand, a lantern in his other, and started down the steep trail. His boots slipped so often that he began to walk sideways, right foot first, which provided some traction.

Down, down, he went, calling for the boy but never seeming to get any closer. Jahday's concern about the tide gnawed at the back of his mind. This exploration was taking much longer than he had originally predicted. "There must be a drain below," he said, "otherwise with such a steep incline, this entire cave would be filled with water."

"An astute observation, Your Highness," Jahday called from behind.

Trevn's legs grew stiff from the tenseness of his muscles and the repeated motion. He turned around, switched the lantern to his other hand, and took a turn with his left foot first to ease the strain.

When he came to the end of the rope and called for Ottee, the boy sounded so near that Trevn let go and continued without the safety line.

A few steps later Cadoc called after him. "You left the rope, Your Highness?"

"We are close, Cadoc. Tell the others to stay on the line so we can find our way back to their lanterns."

Cadoc growled but passed the message back up the line as Trevn continued on. A musty smell wafted on a warm breeze. It reminded him of a wet horse. Was there animal life down here? And how could the wind blow through a dead-end cave? Not a dead end, he reminded himself. There must be an outlet for the water or he'd be swimming right now.

Cadoc left the line, caught up to him, and took the lantern, which enabled Trevn to move more quickly. Just as he began to despair that this incline stretched into the Lowerworld itself, the ground leveled out and someone grabbed him.

"You came!" Ottee nearly climbed on Trevn, hugging him tightly around the waist.

"Calm, boy. We've brought the light."

"Don't much care for the dark, do you?" Cadoc asked.

"It's not even this dark in a ship's hold," Ottee said.

A shout back up the tunnel caught Trevn's attention. Above them lantern lights swayed from side to side.

"We should go back, Your Highness," Cadoc said.

"Agreed." Trevn started toward the incline, but a wailing howl stopped him cold. He held his breath, listening. Where had that come from? Behind them? Off to the side?

The sound of trickling water met his ears. He took the lantern back from Cadoc and lowered it to the ground, which was now wet. A sudden gush flowed past and slowly seeped into the dirt.

The tide was coming down.

"Hurry," Trevn said, starting up the hill. He slipped and took his next step sideways. A glance back to Cadoc and Ottee sent a jolt of fear through him.

A field of dark movement swayed behind Cadoc and the boy, sending a gust of animal smell over them. Hundreds of eyes reflected the lantern light. Bodies as big as his own squirmed and rippled. A howl rang out, accompanied by a second of a higher pitch, then a third.

Another gush of water ran past Trevn's feet, this time deeper and stronger.

The animals, which did not seem to have arms or legs but rather some kind of fins, surged toward the water in jerkish, waddling motions, grunting and yipping. Ottee screamed. Cadoc picked up the boy just as one of the beasts shuffled past. There must have been thirty of them, and they advanced in a mob up toward the water. Trevn, Cadoc, and Ottee got out of the way and watched the strange animals struggle to climb the hill.

"What do we do?" Trevn asked Cadoc.

His shield didn't answer, but his eyes darted around the dark cavern as if he might suddenly see something that hadn't been there before.

"We follow the creatures," he said finally. "To stay here is to die."

"You have a way with words, Cadoc," Trevn said, inching his way toward the herd.

"*Ohloo.*"

Trevn stopped and scanned the darkness. That voice had been human.

"Look!" Ottee pointed up behind them, where a figure stood holding a torch. A man.

"*Wee sapla wa sen. Niseh.*"

"Let's go." Trevn headed toward the man, eager to avoid the creatures.

They descended a bit deeper into the cave. The ground had become slick beneath his boots. He stepped as carefully as he could through the muck, slowly making his way toward the light on the opposite side of the cavern.

"Do you think this wise, Your Highness?" Cadoc asked.

"Does it matter?" Trevn kept going, running two or three steps whenever the ground looked dry. Several more surges of sea water rolled into the cave, and soon the water reached his ankles.

Trevn reached an incline of rocks and boulders and began to climb, relieved to get out of the water's path. He slipped on something like sawdust and had to slow down. It would not do to fall and break his leg.

He sent a thought to the explorer's assistant. *Master Jahday, speak if you can hear me.*

475

The man's distress nearly overwhelmed Trevn. *"I hear you, Your Highness."*

"We have met a native who we believe is leading us to an alternate route from the cave. Tell the others not to fear for our safety."

"I will do so at once."

The climb seemed to take an eternity. Every few steps Trevn turned back to hold the light for Ottee and Cadoc. He peered into the darkness. The rush of the tide was strong now. Full waves ran down the incline and crashed against the rocks below. The strange animals were gone, as was the lantern light from the explorers. Trevn hoped they had gotten out of the path of the creatures.

As he continued to climb, his free hand found more of the sawdust, which turned out to be the same dried paper pulp that had formed the cocoon Maleen had found by the creek near Armanguard. Could the substance be connected to those strange animals?

Trevn reached a smooth rock ledge, straightened to his full height, and came face-to-chest with the biggest man he had ever seen in his life.

A giant.

Though it was dark, the man appeared to have pale skin and hair that looked golden in the torch and lantern light. He waved Trevn to follow and took off along the ledge, ducking occasionally beneath overhead rock formations that were too high to obstruct Trevn's path.

Trevn reached for the giant's mind, could not understand his language, but sensed no deception or ulterior motives. He seemed curious and amused.

A glance behind confirmed that Cadoc and Ottee had reached the top. Trevn set off after the giant, whose torch revealed much. He wore clothing of pieced leather with decorative stitching. His boots were fur, and looked soft, like slippers. A leather strap ran over one shoulder and across his back to his opposite hip. It held a collection of spears and knives, all crude with rock or bone blades or tips. No sword. No metal that Trevn could see.

The giant hunched over and led them through a narrow rock tunnel that, in fewer than ten steps, exited into a wash of pale light. Trevn's eyes adjusted. They stood high up on the inner wall of a rock ledge, looking down on a cavern that opened up to the sea. Jagged dripstones that resembled hardened honey covered the ceiling, which was high enough that the *Seffynaw* could anchor inside.

The animal smell was overwhelming, as were the grunts and howls of the creatures. Hundreds of the strange animals covered the banks along the sides of the cavern and the massive rock formations in the middle of the water. With the light streaming in through the mouth of the cave, Trevn could now see that the beasts were covered in thin fur. Some were swimming in the water, but most were sitting in a lazy heap atop the rocks or on the banks. They were very fat with faces like dune cats and stubby, flipper-like feet with long claws.

"What are they?" Trevn asked.

"*Sey badla wa reekat,*" the giant said. "*Tee badla wa sahjen.*"

Trevn looked up at him for the first time since entering the lit cavern. Trevn was known as tall, but the top of his head didn't even reach the giant's shoulder. The man was golden, like Miss Onika, with hair and beard to match, both twisted and looped into a tangle of knots, braids, and bits of bone. His pieced leather garment was open at the front, revealing a muscular chest and a collection of claws and beetle carapaces on a leather cord.

Trevn shook his head, tapped his lips, then his ear. "I don't understand."

"I am name Toqto," the giant said, in halting Kinsman. "You to wear colors and bird of god-man." He pointed at the insignia on Trevn's tunic.

The giant spoke Kinsman? How? And what was he talking about? "Arman?"

"*Arman,* oom." The giant nodded.

"Where did you learn my language?" Trevn asked, thinking that someone from Mielle's group might be nearby.

"God-man teach. Many to learn from Gray son of Jhorn."

Trevn perked up at that name. Could he mean the youth that Sir Kalenek had lost? Wilek believed that the boy might have ended up on a Magonian vessel.

"Was Grayson with others?" Trevn asked.

"Others, oom. Came to here with tribe of Rand Moor."

A chill ran over Trevn. Randmuir Khal of the Omatta had made peace with the giants? Could he have pirated the Magonian ship? "Where are they now?"

"Zuzaan," Toqto said, pounding a fist against his chest. "My home."

Wilek would want him to find Grayson, but he would also worry about Trevn joining the company of a giant. Still, he should try to make peace, and perhaps learn why so many giants had abducted Kinsman people. He might even find Princess Saria.

But that would mean delaying his search for Mielle, at least for a time. Trevn reached for her, not to speak, but to sense her nearness. The soul-binding swelled in his chest, a familiar ache that would only be satisfied when he held her in his arms.

Though he hated it, she would have to wait a few more days.

The giant led the way out of the cavern to the beach, where the other explorers were waiting a good ten paces from three other giants—each as tall and intimidating as Toqto, though they were all dark-haired. Trevn offered the giants a tour of the *Seffynaw*, but they were too frightened by his dinghy, which, to be fair, looked like it might capsize if all four giants climbed in. Instead they each took a turn looking at the ship through Trevn's grow lens, which seemed to delight them all, while Master Keppel inquired about their weapons.

Toqto removed the leather strap he wore over one shoulder and slid off the loops that held his weapons. He demonstrated how to use the strap to climb the branchless trees by wrapping it around the trunk and using it for leverage. Toqto was halfway up the tree when another giant removed his strap and offered it to Trevn. Eager to try, Trevn accepted. Cadoc, as always, raised caution, but Trevn waved him off. His boots proved a hindrance, so he kicked them off and quickly made progress.

He used the strap to pull himself all the way to where the branches began, and from that point on climbed as he would any other tree. When his head finally popped above the prickly needles that adorned the ends of the branches, Trevn could see for miles over treetops. As it turned out, they were on the southeast side of a peninsula that stretched north and then wrapped back around into an inlet. To the west, where Mielle should be, he caught sight of an expanse of water—a channel, he hoped, that he could sail through.

"Dirtman!"

Slightly offended at the title, Trevn sought out the faint voice and spotted Toqto's pale head above the branches of a tree just behind his.

"*Zuzaan, badla wa men.* My home. Is there." Toqto pointed to the southwest. "You to come."

Trevn wasn't sure if he should accept, but by the time the two of them shimmied back to the ground, he had a plan.

He made a quick trip back to the *Seffynaw* to gather supplies and divide his team. Captain Bussie would sail the ship around the peninsula and continue the exploration with Master Keppel. Kempe would remain on board so that the ship would have a way to communicate with Trevn, who would go on foot with Toqto to the giant village, find Grayson, and attempt to learn more about the giants and where Princess Saria and the other Kinsman captives might have been taken. In a week's time Trevn would meet the *Seffynaw* at the southernmost cove of the inlet, then continue his search for Mielle.

The sun hung low in the sky by the time Trevn and his men had returned to shore and set out with the giants. He waited until they'd gotten a good start on their trip before voicing Wilek an update on the situation. The new king did not take the news well.

"You left the ship? Trevn, you put yourself in danger traipsing off into the woods with giants."

"I kept nearly half the soldiers with me, plus some of the explorers and my entire staff."

"You still must take care, brother," Wilek said.

"I see no runes tattooed upon them, and I sense nothing but amusement and curiosity in them at the moment," Trevn said. *"I don't think they mean us harm. Besides, Toqto speaks Kinsman because Grayson taught him. He calls the boy god-man, says he can do magic."*

"I'm sure he can. He is a root child."

"Well, isn't it important to find the boy? He might be able to help us locate Princess Saria and the others."

"That would be good, yes. See if you can communicate with Saria. Her father tells me she has been taken to a mine of sorts and made to work. Perhaps you could learn something from her directly. And if what Jhorn said is true and Rogedoth is Grayson's grandfather, then the boy has royal blood. Why don't you try to voice him as well? Perhaps you could find your answers now."

"I will try, but as I've never met him, I can't imagine I will succeed."

✦　　✦　　✦

They moved slowly through the forest, and several times Trevn spotted the strange rat birds watching them. As they traveled, Maleen picked greens along the road and the men hunted the birds. By the time the sun had set the group had reached a road. They lit torches and lanterns and walked for several more hours, the giants' long legs setting a pace that was faster than Trevn's men were used to.

Trevn spoke to Saria, who confirmed all that Wilek had said. She and her people had been taken underground to a mine, where they had been forced to gather beetles.

"I don't know what they want with them," she said. *"There are pale natives here as well, and they have given me the impression that the giants eat these beetles."*

A bizarre practice. Trevn recalled the carapaces Toqto wore yet assured

Saria that the giants he'd met were friendly and spoke some Kinsman. *"I hope to discover where they mine these beetles and come to set you all free."*

"I pray Arman grants you success," Saria said.

After that, Trevn played with his mind-speaking ability, alternating between trying to voice the boy Grayson, talking with Mielle, and monitoring the giants' emotions. He had no success in reaching Grayson, and the only emotions he could sense from the giants were hunger, contentedness, and an eagerness to please. Trevn saw nothing sinister in such feelings, so he went back to talking with Mielle.

"I am disappointed that our reunion will be delayed yet again," she said, *"but I am proud of you for doing the right thing. Princess Saria is surely terrified, and I am sure Grayson will be thrilled to get back to Master Jhorn and Miss Onika."*

Trevn tried to imagine how frightening it must have been for a young boy to have gotten lost for so long. *"Wilek says he is quite resourceful. Sir Kalenek told several stories about—"*

"Trevn? This is your mother. Answer me at once. I have important news."

Trevn grimaced. Important news to his mother could mean she'd had a new gown commissioned. He had no desire to be lectured over his marriage to Mielle. However, it had been several months since they'd spoken, and a sense of guilt twisted his heart. He should at least attempt a conversation, shouldn't he? With a heavy sigh he bid farewell to Mielle and let his mother in.

"Hello, Mother."

"My son! Oh, how you try my patience. I thought you had made yourself dead to me. Sorrow had swept out the joy from my heart, but your answer brings a dawn of hope. Did you hear that Ulrik has wed the Queen of Tenma?"

Ah, so she wanted to gossip. Trevn could indulge her for a time. *"I did. I admit it surprised me. Doesn't she hate him?"*

"She is a great deceiver, who used your nephew cruelly. She married him for the power he offered her. And then on my ageday, mind—which you neglected to remember to my own bitter heartache—on that very day the empress's magic ran out. I tell you, she wilted before my very eyes, aged some thirty years in the space of ten seconds. I have never been so horrified in all my days."

This story Trevn had not heard. *"Sands alive. What did Ulrik do?"*

"How quickly the boy's love faded, let me tell you. But as this happened at my ageday celebration in front of the entire population and Ulrik had just announced that she carries his heir, what is he to do but await the birth of his child?"

"Will he arrest her?"

"He wants to kill her, but he has no valid reason but his own pride. I hope you will heed the misfortune of your nephew and find Princess Saria."

"I have already spoken with Saria, Mother. I do hope to find and help her escape her captors."

"What a blessing to hear, my son. She will be good for you and all Armania. She was bred to be a queen."

Trevn would not have this conversation again. *"Armania already has a queen, and I a wife. Farewell, Mother."* And he ended their connection.

"Trevn! I'm not finished speaking with you about Princess Saria. You are legally betrothed now. Give up this foolish crusade to keep your common bride, and do your duty. Think of the tales the minstrels will write after you rescue Saria from giants and then make her your wife. Trevn? Do you hear me?"

Trevn sighed and stared at his boots as he walked the ruts in the dirt road. Would his mother never learn that bullying him didn't work?

"A stiff-necked man will be destroyed, Trevn, and I cannot help the dead. Do you hear me? If you do not marry Saria, you will forever regret it."

She continued to rail, but Trevn found that by reopening a conversation with Mielle, he could muffle his mother entirely.

They finally stopped and made camp just off the road. The giants ate dried meat and squares of flatbread. Trevn's soldiers roasted the game they'd killed, and Maleen created a salad of the greens. The fowl tasted good but could have used salt and spices. The greens were horribly bitter, though Trevn ate them to be polite.

After the late dinner Trevn draped his cape over a thick carpet of moss and lay down, staring past the distant treetops at the stars. He checked in with Wilek and told him about his conversations with Saria and his mother.

"Ulrik informed Inolah of Jazlyn's deception a few days ago," Wilek said. *"Telling you slipped my mind."*

"He was a fool to wed a mantic in the first place," Trevn said.

"Yes, and while I pity Ulrik, I cannot worry about him at present. Not with my brother traipsing through strange forests with giants. I am glad you were able to speak with Saria. Any luck contacting Grayson?"

"None. I tried on and off all afternoon."

"Well, keep trying. The closer you get, perhaps. It's worked before. Didn't you—"

"Wil?" Trevn sat up, searching for a connection to his brother. He could find none.

How odd.

"Wilek?"

Only the crickets answered.

Panicked, Trevn reached for Rystan, worried something had happened to his brother. Rystan did not answer.

He tried Oli, Miss Onika, Inolah, his sisters, and even Lady Zeroah, who never answered.

"Mielle, can you hear me?"

She did not reply, which planted a seed of fear within his heart.

"Kempe?"

"Cadoc?"

"Hinck?"

Again and again Trevn tried to speak with Mielle and Wilek. Then finally, in total desperation, *"Mother?"*

No reply, even from her.

Arman, he prayed. *Did I do something wrong that you would remove your gift?*

Arman did not answer.

No one did.

"My pardon, Your Highness," Cadoc said from his left. "Rosâr Wilek is speaking to my thoughts. He is concerned that you do not answer. What shall I tell him?"

Trevn sat up and stared at Cadoc in the darkness. Wilek still had his gift? "Tell him I cannot hear him. I cannot hear anyone."

A moment of silence passed, then, "He asks if you have been drinking."

"You both know me better than that."

Cadoc paused a moment, then said, "He would like to know if you ate anything strange."

Now there was an idea. "Let me think." Trevn ran over his meals in his mind. He'd eaten some dried reekat meat Toqto had given him. The soldiers had hunted the rat birds. And Maleen had picked those bitter greens. All three were new to Trevn. Perhaps one had somehow stifled the voices. "Tell Wilek I tried three new foods today. I will investigate the matter fully. Ask him to check in with you tomorrow morning to see what I have discovered."

CHARLON

Charlon had no strength. No ahvenrood. Magon had abandoned her. Everyone had. So she waited. Plotted her revenge. Let her body heal. But no amount of time could mend her wounded heart. So Charlon shut away the pain.

Months ago Mreegan had declared war. Murdered Torol and Charlon's unborn child. The wait had been long and difficult, but Mreegan had given Shanek back. The child was too much of a burden for the spoiled and lazy Chieftess. Though she remained firm in her order. Her order that he take ahvenrood each day. The boy looked ten years old now. Sir Kalenek worried about Shanek's mental development. The knighten had somehow managed to end the boy's torment. From the voices he had been hearing. Sir Kalenek gave credit to a trick he had learned during the war. Some kind of meditation. This brought immense relief. When the boy had stopped screaming and muttering to himself.

The Chieftess had finally permitted Charlon to taste small rations of ahvenrood again. Put her in charge of planting a new crop. This gave Charlon a greater purpose and hope.

Hope that she might find the strength to take on Mreegan and win.

Ahvenrood did not grow overnight. Without magic it took months to ripen. So Charlon used the small amounts of root Mreegan permitted. To hurry along one of the crops. She dared not risk them all to experiments.

Now, a cool spring morning, on her knees in the field. Pulling up flowering ahvenrood plants. Removing scrawny tubers. Placing them in a basket.

A basket Shanek held in his lap. From the opposite end of the field, Sir Kalenek worked twice as fast. Without magic. Charlon appreciated his speed. She planned to uproot this entire row. To test it. So far none of the new root she'd quickened in growth had been magical. Worried that she had harvested prematurely before, this time she had waited. Until the plants had flowered. Still, the roots were disappointingly small.

Had her magic interfered? Would she have to wait until fall to reap the naturally grown field? Or could the rat birds be the problem? Too often she sent Shanek to chase away the strange creatures. They liked to nibble at the ahvenrood greens. Eventually pulled the entire plant to gnaw at the roots. She had tried. Tried to place a protective spell over the crop. She no longer had the power. The slights Mreegan had permitted to serve her were not capable of such a complex spell. Charlon missed Magon's power.

Shanek screamed, nearly stopping her heart. Surely it wasn't the voices again. "Practice your quiet, Shan," she said. Spun around on her knees in the dirt. Faced the boy. She found him looking up at a warrior surrounded by an army of shadir.

"What happened?" Sir Kalenek's muted voice came from the end of the row. He started toward them. Walking. That he did not see the warrior told Charlon what it was.

The great shadir appeared as a demigod. Tall, barrel-chested, robust. Black tunic, breeches, boots, cape. Lined in pale gold silk. Gold thread embroidered a fang cat on his chest. Bronze longsword at his waist. Face and head were clean-shaven. Covered in black henna tracings resembling lace. Handsome, perfectly balanced face. Eyes, dark and probing. Mouth, thin and grim. He looked Rurekan.

"He king?" Shanek asked, gazing up at the great.

"No, Shan. He is a shadir." Charlon stood, not liking the way the great towered above. "What do you want?" she asked.

The time has come for you to rule as Chieftess, he said, his voice low and rich, pleasant. *Magon will never allow this, but I can help you.*

"Magon promised me," Charlon said.

She lied.

Charlon's throat tightened to hear such words. She *had* wondered. Wondered if Magon had changed her mind about making her Chieftess. The goddess had refused all Charlon's attempts to reconcile. And Mreegan had made her an outcast.

Sir Kalenek arrived then. Ruffled Shanek's hair. "You all right, Shan?"

"A shadir king is here. He show Shanek how be king?"

"Not a king," Charlon said. "A great and his swarm. Take Shanek for a walk, Sir Kalenek."

The knighten quickly scooped up the boy and carried him off.

"No!" Shanek cried. "Me stay. Shanek stay with king."

The shadir chuckled. *Giving root to a child? I did not realize Magonians were so generous.*

"Why would you help me?"

My human ran out of ahvenrood and has no access to more. She was unwilling to have a relationship apart from it.

Why would a human turn away a great? "Who was your human?"

Jazlyn, Queen of Tenma and Empress of Rurekau.

Charlon shivered at the mention of that name. "We heard she lost her beauty."

Some spells are permanent; others are temporary. Her beauty, alas, was maintained by me. It humiliated her to lose it, but I was able to maintain it long past the wedding, which secured her a future as Empress of Rurekau.

"Is it true she is with child?"

Yes, it is.

"She will die in childbirth," Charlon said, remembering Shanek's birth mother.

Possibly, he said. *Jazlyn is old for childbearing, but I would not be surprised if she lives. She is the most tenacious woman I have ever known—throughout all time.*

Such a comment prickled. "You have not yet known me," Charlon said.

The great shadir chuckled. *I would like to.*

"Why?"

You are wasted here, he said. *A great does not bond lightly. I need someone gifted, someone open and willing. I am a warrior general, and as you see, I come with my own army of shadir who would serve us faithfully. You will not become Chieftess by accident or chance, Charlon Sonber. You must fight for the position. You must reach out and take it. You must kill Chieftess Mreegan and her great shadir.*

Charlon drew back in surprise. "That is possible? To kill a shadir?"

Oh yes. When a shadir manifests itself in the human realm, it can die like a human.

"I have never seen Magon appear in the human realm," Charlon said.

She has never transported you? A shadir cannot carry a human through the Veil.

Charlon recalled her escape from the Armanian ship *Seffynaw* when Magon had carried her over the ocean. "She carried me once."

Magon is no fool, he said. *That is why we must trick her. I have been watching, waiting, planning. If you are willing to learn, I am willing to teach. Though you must take care that Magon does not hear my name, or she will grow suspicious.*

"Must we kill Magon? Can't we just kill Mreegan?"

If you killed only Mreegan, Magon would choose a new human, and it would not be you. No, we must kill Magon first. Once Mreegan has lost her shadir, she will die from old age, and you can easily take her place. Will you join me?

Charlon knew her answer. Magon had shunned her. Mreegan treated her like a slav. Bonding with this great warrior might be Charlon's only chance. To become Chieftess. "I am willing," she said.

Sir Kalenek approached. In the distance behind him, Shanek sat playing in the dirt. "What is happening?" he asked.

Charlon smiled at the great shadir. "The time has come for Mreegan to die."

Rurek, god of war.

He knew pain.

He knew victory.

His words were a balm. His plans, genius.

Charlon had once sworn never to submit to any male. Human or god.

Now to make an exception. Only Rurek was strong enough. To stand against Mreegan. Only Rurek was wise enough. To defeat Magon.

He promised to make her Chieftess. Soon.

But first she must obey his every word. And so, starting that day, she had.

No one knew Charlon had a new shadir. At Rurek's insistence she kept him—and his entire swarm—a secret.

Her last harvest of ahvenrood tubers again held no magic. Still too early? Rurek thought otherwise. Had lived many years in Tenma. There, he said, even the first root string held enough power for a day's worth of spells.

Was it a problem with the soil? Too much rain? Too cool? Had the magic she used to quicken the growth counteracted the new magic? Or something else, entirely?

Rurek was not overly concerned. At his urging Charlon stole extra root from Mreegan's stores. Only enough to help her remain in power. Once she had killed Magon and Mreegan. Rurek also suggested she process the non-magical ahvenrood. Mix it with Mreegan's supply to weaken it.

Rurek was not only wise. He was devious. His ideas gave Charlon hope.

The next night Charlon, Sir Kalenek, and Shanek sat around the fire in her tent. Mashing failed root into pulp. A mountain of greens between Charlon and Shanek nearly hid the boy from view. In between herself and Sir Kalenek lay a wire screen. A screen covered in thick, starchy pulp.

"I don't trust this new shadir," Sir Kalenek said.

Charlon glanced at Rurek. He stood sentry at the entrance of her tent. Like a guard.

"Do not put your trust in such creatures," Sir Kalenek continued. "Miss Onika warned about them. They are deceitful above all things."

Fool humans, Rurek muttered.

"Fooolll!" Shanek echoed, then shoved a handful of mashed root into his mouth.

Sir Kalenek couldn't hear Rurek like Charlon and Shanek could. He narrowed his eyes at the boy. "Don't eat that, Shan. It might make you sick."

Shanek spat out the root. It slid down his chin and plopped into his lap. Sir Kalenek removed a handkerchief from his pocket and wiped the boy's face clean.

"Miss Onika tires me," Charlon snapped. "She is all you talk about. Her beauty, her skin, her wisdom, her purity. No woman is so perfect. Especially a blind one."

"Her blindness makes her see people more deeply," Sir Kalenek said. "She is goodness and light and joy and absolute perfection."

"Then I hate her," Charlon said. "I forbid you to speak of her."

Sir Kalenek's smooth face, which had once been a tapestry of scars, crumpled at her words. The compulsion Mreegan had set upon him forced obedience. Sorrow and fury poured from his eyes. "You can order my silence, but you cannot control my thoughts."

"Care to tempt me?" she asked. "I compelled my own thoughts. I assure you, I can do the same to you."

That silenced him. He took to beating his pot of root as if it had been the one to punish him.

Regret surged through Charlon. Besides Shanek, and now Rurek, Sir Kalenek was her only friend. His kindness had saved her life more than once. She should not treat him cruelly. She owed him much. He had raised Shanek. Taught the boy when Charlon had been unwilling. But to rescind a command would make her look weak. She would not do it. Surely he would stop pining over the blind woman someday. Charlon had gotten over Torol.

Nearly so, anyway.

"Bird." Shanek's voice pulled her gaze up. One of the rat birds had gotten inside. It hopped up the pile of ahvenrood tubers. Bit into one.

"Shoo!" Charlon waved her arm at the creature. It flew to her bed, carrying its snack with it. "Are you unable to kill these pests, Sir Kalenek?"

As that hadn't been a command, he did not jump to obey. "Birds must eat too."

It's looking at me, Rurek said.

"Looking, looking," Shanek crooned.

The great shadir walked to the bed. Reached for the bird. It hopped back a few steps.

"How can it see you?" Charlon asked.

"See who?" Sir Kalenek asked.

Charlon shushed the knighten.

I know not, Rurek said, *but I sense power in it.*

How could a bird have magic? "Because it ate the ahvenrood?"

Rurek met her gaze. His dark eyes held her question between them. *Give it an order. Use the old language. I will try to harness the power.*

Charlon didn't move for fear she might scare the bird away. "*Rurek âthâh. Tsamad ani. Ten shel—*"

I am already here, woman! Rurek yelled. *Cast the spell. The spell!*

Flustered, Charlon blurted out the first thought that came to mind. "*Bara* bird *tselem ba* Onika."

She felt Sir Kalenek's gaze burn into her. She winced inside, wishing she had not cast that particular spell.

Nothing happened.

Rurek hummed. *I have an idea.* He disintegrated into shimmering yellow light. Poured himself into the bird. It screeched and flapped its wings as if pained. Did not fly away.

The temperature dropped. The bird's red eyes brightened. Gold, like the sun. It squawked. A layer of white frost coated its feathers. Then it grew. Swelled. Silky feathers melted into watery black mud. Mud that stretched into the shape of a leg. A hand. The substance shifted. Slowly solidified into the shape of a woman. A woman lying curled on the bed. Sculpted from a glob of black clay.

The woman took color. Skin pale. Hair like wheat. Eyes glassy. She sat up on the bed and blinked.

"It works!" Charlon cried out, triumphant.

Shanek squealed in delight and clapped his hands. "Pretty lady."

"Ahhh . . ." Sir Kalenek stared. Charlon's compulsion forbade him to speak Onika's name.

The manifestation of Onika opened her mouth and emitted a long squawk.

Shanek began to cry. He pushed to his feet and ran to Kal, who picked him up.

"What is the matter with you?" Kal snapped at Charlon, and he carried Shanek out of the tent.

"*Âtsar*," Charlon said.

The creature squawked, as if someone had severed its foot. The form of Onika collapsed into a pool of black mud on the bed. Something rose from the goo. A rat's face, then a trembling black wing.

A blur of yellow light and Rurek appeared beside her. *Do you know what this means?*

"There is magic in this land," Charlon said. "Different. But magic just the same."

We can use it, he said. *We'll tell Mreegan that magic can only be done when a shadir takes Dominion over one of the birds. If we can convince her to try it and Magon is with her, Magon might wish to enter one of the creatures . . .*

Charlon understood. "And I can kill it while she is inside."

+   +   +

Perfecting the plan took hours of practice. When they were ready, Charlon told Sir Kalenek to build a cage. Capture two rat birds. Gowzals, she had named them. The ancient name for bird. Charlon took the likeness of Roya, and when Mreegan had gone to the altar to worship, Charlon entered the red tent. Tampered with Mreegan's ahvenrood. Mixed in new powder to dilute it.

When the time came to lure Mreegan into the trap, Charlon sent Sir Kalenek and Shanek away from her own tent. Fed each bird a tuber. Rurek entered one of the gowzals. Then Charlon compelled the birds to speak.

Roya was the first to complain of the noise. Kateen next. Then Astaa.

489

Charlon mustered as much rudeness as possible, knowing the maidens would lose their tempers. Ask Mreegan to intervene. They finally left to do just that. By the time Mreegan arrived, the noise had given Charlon a headache.

The Chieftess barged into the tent. "What are you doing?"

"I have made a discovery," Charlon said. "These birds are the key to doing magic in this land."

"A bird?"

"They are similar to malleants," Charlon said. "When a bird is fed ahvenrood, a shadir can claim Dominion over it. Then the mantic can speak a spell to power the magic."

"Show me."

Charlon tried not to smile. She removed the gowzal from the cage. The one Rurek had entered. "I have sent a shadir into this one already," she said, then cast her spell. "*Bara* gowzal *tselem ba* Shanek."

A chill fell upon the tent. The gowzal screeched. And just like before, its feathers grew frosty. Then it changed. Bubbled and morphed into the form of little Shanek.

"Fascinating," Mreegan said, walking toward the fake boy. "Did it eat the new root? That you planted here?"

"Yes," Charlon said. "The birds have been eating the crops. I grew frustrated. Sent a shadir into one of the birds by mistake. The shadir felt magic in the creature. I tried a mask spell and it worked."

Magon appeared in the Veil beside Mreegan. The two looked identical. *Is there any pain, slight?* Magon asked the impostor.

The boy's mouth opened and he crowed. Blinked, then shook his head.

"I haven't yet discovered. The voice." Charlon sighed, pretending to be a failure. A novice with no hope. "I still have much to learn. I had wanted to perfect this. Before showing you. I'm sure you will have many ideas. How to improve the process."

"No doubt," Mreegan said.

I will try this, Magon said.

Charlon kept her expression plain. She opened the cage. Removed the second gowzal. "I fed it root already. Let me give it a bit more so it will hold still." She picked a tiny tuber from the bucket beside the cage. Set it on the ground. Released the bird. The creature wasted no time. Snapped up the tuber in its beak.

Magon floated toward it, shrinking as she did into a wisp of white smoke. Smoke that absorbed into the gowzal. Red eyes turned glassy gray.

Charlon fought to contain her excitement. This was going to work!

"What kind of spell should I cast?" Mreegan asked.

"Illusions seem to work best," Charlon said. "I've been casting masks." She made a show of backing out of the way. Of giving Mreegan room to work. Stopped beside the wooden cage. The cage where she had hidden a shard club.

"*Bara* bird *tselem ba* Torol," Mreegan said.

Charlon cringed. Mreegan had done the same to her that Charlon had accidentally done to Sir Kalenek. But Mreegan meant to hurt Charlon. Wanted Torol's likeness to bring Charlon pain.

Cruel woman, your end is near.

The gowzal melted into black mud. Began to change. Formed the shape of a human male. A man curled on his side.

Rurek, still in the form of Shanek, watched, eyes golden and bright.

Charlon must act now. Before the gowzal made the transition. She would not otherwise be able to cut it down. Not if it looked like Torol.

She drew the shard club out from hiding. Chopped over the muddy neck. Winced as obsidian shards sliced easily through moist clay. The featureless head jumped apart from the body. A body that sank into a muddy puddle.

A blast forced Charlon off her feet. She crashed backward. Shook the tent. Landed on her side.

Mreegan lowered her hand, glaring down, eyes fierce. Betrayed. "What have you done?"

Charlon glanced past the Chieftess to the puddle. Beneath it a hole had opened up in the Veil. Wide at the top, it grew narrow the deeper it went. Like the inside of Rone's lure. A creature struggled inside. Hands clutching the outer rim. Fighting to hold on as an unseen force pulled. It was the color of a newborn pig. Had spindly arms, black eyes and lips. Three stubby black horns protruded from its forehead like a crown. A gash in its waist bled black liquid into the deep.

Could it be? "Magon?" Charlon whispered.

Chieftess Mreegan gasped at the creature. "No! I don't belieeeee . . ."

She trailed off in a gargling croak. Hair turned white. Skin slowly shriveled. Eyes burrowed deep into sockets. Hands reached toward her face. Fingertips touched cheeks while disintegrating into bones. Flesh, hair, and bone crumbled. Dry dirt in a giant fist. The vortex swallowed everything. What had once been Mreegan flew past where the pig-like shadir held tightly.

Rurek left the gowzal and materialized in his warrior form. Stepped toward the vortex. He smiled down on what once had been Magon. *I told you I was stronger,* he said.

The creature snarled. Spoke in a language Charlon had never heard.

Rurek chuckled, then uttered a single word in that same, guttural tongue. *Nadach.*

Magon's hands lost purchase. She fell.

The hole closed up. Lifeless on the ground, the gowzal's head and body looked small. No sign of Mreegan or Magon. Both were gone.

Rurek's gaze rested on Charlon. *You did it.* He sounded surprised, if not slightly mortified.

"*We* did it." Charlon turned to leave and found Roya, Astaa, and Vald standing in the doorway, eyes gleaming in horror.

"Come, Rurek," Charlon said as she marched past them and out of the tent. "Send one of your swarm. Fetch Sir Kalenek and Shanek to the red tent." She walked the path between the two rows of white tents. Head held high. A victor. In the distance the red tent gleamed in the morning sun.

She had done it! The rule of Magonia. The title of Chieftess. Both were hers. Won fairly. Taken because she was superior to Mreegan and even Magon.

She approached the red tent. Rone stood sentry outside, lure around his neck. He stepped in front of the entrance. "You may not enter, Mother. The Chieftess is not here."

"She is Chieftess now." A woman's voice. From behind. A glance over Charlon's shoulder revealed Roya. Behind her Astaa, Nuel, Vald, and Kateen.

"Mreegan is dead," Charlon said, "as is Magon. I killed them."

Rone's eyes swelled slightly, and he knelt at her feet.

Charlon fought back a smile, wanting to look strong and regal.

Shanek ran forward. Reached for her and jumped as if she might lift him. "Shadir said come. We mash root?"

"No, my son," Charlon said, taking hold of his hand. "The red tent is my home now. I am Chieftess of Magonia."

Are you certain you want your realm to be called Magonia? Rurek asked.

Charlon had not considered that. No reason to honor Magon the betrayer. "You are wise to suggest a new name, Rurek. I owe much of my accession to you. There is, unfortunately, a realm that already bears your name."

How about Magos, Chieftess? Rurek suggested. *For it was by magic that you claimed rule over this people.*

"Magos," she said, liking the sound of it. "So be it. Send your swarm to call everyone here. It is time they bow before their new Chieftess."

Rurek mumbled something to a fat shadir, who flitted away.

"Rone, pass the lure to Sir Kalenek," Charlon said. "He will serve as my One."

Rone stood and looped the cord that held the lure over Sir Kalenek's head.

"Kneel before me, Sir Kalenek," Charlon said.

Because of the compulsion upon him, Charlon had no idea if the knighten would have knelt of his own volition. But kneel he did.

Gullik and Eedee approached then, the young Zweena close behind.

Charlon paused, waited for them reach her. "Sir Kalenek Veroth, do you accept your position to serve me and my son Shanek as One?"

Though he did not look pleased, he answered, "I live to serve, Chieftess."

Yes, he did. And she would see to it that he would serve her well. They all would. She was Chieftess Charlon of Magos. There was no one higher in all the land.

GRAYSON

The snow had long since melted, and while Grayson had come to know the giants well, his time in Zuzaan had made him ever more suspicious of Master Fonu and his mysterious hold over Randmuir the pirate and now Bolad mi Aru as well. One night some ten days ago as they'd been eating in the hall, he'd overheard a conversation that changed everything.

"Tomorrow you will gather your men and leave," a man had said.

"Tomorrow we must leave."

Grayson immediately had recognized the second voice as belonging to Randmuir. He'd located the man across the room, sitting in a dark corner with Fonu Edekk.

"Tell the headman that we will sail south to the Armanians," Fonu had said.

"I will tell the headman we will sail south," Randmuir had echoed.

Dread had filled Grayson's chest as he recognized the signs of a man under compulsion. How long had Fonu held such power over Randmuir? He tried to think back, to remember if there had been other times when the pirate had made strange decisions, but could think of none.

"The giants will not wish to part with Grayson," Master Fonu had said, "but he must come with us."

"Grayson must come with us," Randmuir had echoed.

Terrified, it had been all Grayson could do to keep silent and creep away. He'd told Danno everything, and the two of them asked the help of Ulagan the wolf in leaving the place.

An hour later, Ulagan and the slave Conaw had met Grayson and Danno in the chambers the boys shared in the giant's fortress. The giant and the pale human each carried bulging sacks. Conaw set his down by his feet.

"Is safe?" Ulagan had asked.

Grayson saw no shadir in the Veil, but Ragaz was never far. "Yes."

"You to go now," Ulagan said. "Fone Ool to leave tomorrow. Want to take you."

"I'm not sure Master Fonu could take Grayson anywhere," Danno said. "He moves too fast."

Grayson wasn't so sure about that. "The Magonian Chieftess was quick enough to catch me with one of her spells. I bet Fonu could do the same. We must leave, but what about the slaves?"

Grayson had learned much about the Ahj-Yeke in his time here, including the horrible slavery that happened underground, all for the magic the Ahj-Yeke believed came from eating the black beetles. Ulagan, being Uul-Yeke, held different beliefs on the matter. He disdained slavery yet felt helpless to stop it.

"Giants oppress the Puru too long," Ulagan said in his native tongue. "Now not time to free them. Your magic can bring you again where you to speak to slaves and plan escape."

"What about Danno and Conaw?" Grayson asked. He could pop away at any time, but the others could not.

"River tunnel," Ulagan said. "You to take *bohaj* to ocean. To find Puru people. We to make supplies to nourish you." He tapped the leather sack.

"What about you?" Grayson asked.

"Someone to stay. To help the slaves when time comes to run."

So Ulagan had led Grayson, Danno, and Conaw down to the steamy reamway where they had once bathed. He moved one of the bohaj, which were animal-skin longboats, into the water. He looped a twine cord over a stone spike to hold it and loaded the two packs. The boat bobbed in the rippling current, tugging at the cord, eager to sail away. Ulagan held it steady as the three humans climbed inside.

The boat had seemed overly large to Grayson, built as it was for giants. He settled cross-legged onto the ribbed interior and could barely see above the gunwale. He wrinkled his nose at a stale, sour scent. "What's that smell?"

"Reekat fat," Ulagan said. "To make bohaj waterproof."

He then retrieved a small ceramic bowl from a shelf and used one of the wall torches to light a small flame inside.

"This to help see. To keep light out of wind." He'd handed it to Grayson, who set it on the floor between him and Danno. "Current to carry you. To paddle and keep bohaj from rock. Three days to reach ocean. You to see reekat, stay away."

So they had set off. During that long, dark journey, Grayson had heard the voices, as always. Sometimes they were longer conversations, but most often they were random, unrelated statements.

"*We might ask the queen to help,*" a woman said.

"*Eudora would never support us,*" said another woman. "*The only side she takes is her own.*"

"*Why are you like that?*" a man yelled. "*Why do you always accuse me of wrongdoing?*"

"*I'll have to climb down inside it,*" a girl said. "*Do you think I'll get stuck?*"

"*Rystan,*" a man said. "*Come to the throne room.*"

"*Yes, Your Highness,*" a young man answered.

"*Fonu, have you found Grayson yet?*" a gruff voice asked.

Hearing his name—and Fonu's—had changed the voices for Grayson. He'd begun listening intently to the things that were said, realizing that all along he'd been hearing bits of conversations from real people.

Someone had sent Fonu after him.

Grayson lost track of time in the reamway, but finally, days later, the boat had exited the underground river and drifted into the sea on a bright, sunny morning. Conaw rowed to a nearby cave and tied the boat with several others. The pale then led them north on foot along the shore. The threesome had eventually met up with Conaw's people, the Puru.

The tribal, human-sized pales reminded Grayson of Magonians in the way they wore scraps of animal skins and furs. They lived in pit houses, which were marked above ground only by a rectangular opening with a ladder sticking out adjacent from a round hole made for smoke from the campfire below. Underground, each circular room had been built of mudbricks. No furniture filled the space but furs or mats made of leather or grass.

Conaw's grandmother, Muna, was the matriarch of the tribe and had welcomed her grandson and his new friends warmly. The woman was short and very old. Her skin was tanned and wrinkly. She had blue eyes and silvery hair braided in a circle around her head.

She called Grayson "Massi" and Danno "Komo," for the gray and brown of their skin, and told them many stories about the people who lived in the great homeland. Grayson translated for Danno some of the time, but Muna talked so fast he could barely keep up.

That night, as they sat around the fire, she talked about all the people who lived in this land. "Some tribes have moved over the years, and some have combined. Two peoples remain: Yeke and Puru. There are three Yeke tribes. The Ahj-Yeke are the forest-dwelling giants. They are the strongest of the Yeke tribes, which they credit to their consumption of the tsok."

"The beetles?" Grayson asked.

"*Owi*, Massi. All the Yeke once ate the tsok," Muna said. "The Jiir-Yeke stopped eating the tsok when they created the karah."

"Bird giants?" Grayson asked.

"They are the bird makers," she said. "The Uul-Yeke live in the mountains of the wolf. They feel shame for what the Yeke did to our people and do what they can to protect our tribes. We Puru follow the herd along the eastern coastal plains, moving south in the summer and wintering in the north. The Puru way is the way of peace, but we are often forced to contend for our survival when the Yeke attack, though we lack the desire or skill to fight back."

"Why do the Yeke eat the beetles?" Grayson asked.

"They believe the beetles give strength," Muna said, "without which they would be small, like us."

"What is she saying?" Danno asked, and Grayson translated.

"I wish I could help you free the slaves in Zuzaan," Grayson said.

"That's kind of you, Massi," Muna said, "but how? The Yeke are too powerful."

"I could go back and forth," Grayson said. "And Ulagan is there. He is Uul-Yeke and might be willing to help. Maybe we could sneak out one boatload at a time, down the river, the way we came. There are so many slaves. Maybe the giants wouldn't notice a few people missing."

Muna's eyes glistened. "Do you think it would work, Conaw?"

"It might, with Ulagan's help." Conaw turned to Grayson. "You could start with the older people and perhaps some of the younger children. You would have to find Honaqa. She is the eldest slave, and she could organize from within so that everything is kept quiet."

"How will I find her?" Grayson asked.

"You would have to go into the tunnels and seek her out."

"Down into the tunnels," Grayson said, thinking it over.

"What?" Danno cried. "You could get killed down there."

Grayson continually forgot that unless Conaw attempted the Kinsman tongue, Danno could only understand what Grayson said and the parts of the conversation that he translated.

"I must have this magic for a reason, Danno," Grayson said. "What could be a better reason than rescuing slaves?"

"Staying here where it's perfectly safe," Danno said.

Grayson did not think he could do that. Not after what he had seen exploring the tunnels under the Zuzaan fortress. Some of the narrow passages were unsafe and sometimes collapsed on people, the beetles blistered the skin, and the giants fed their slaves poorly. Many people were sick from lack of food and sunlight.

"I will help you free your people," he said to Muna. "Tell me what Honaqa looks like."

TREVN

The greens had been responsible for stifling Trevn's ability to mind-speak. It had taken two days to figure it out and another for his own voicing ability to return, but the discovery had thrilled Trevn. He asked Lanton Jahday to fully document the plant, which he named âleh, an ancient Kinsman word for leafage, then ordered his men to pick as much as possible.

Near sundown on the third day of their journey to Zuzaan, Kempe sent a knock.

"What is it?" Trevn asked.

"It is Master Shinn, Your Highness," Kempe said, her voice soothing even in Trevn's mind. *"I passed by him on the quarterdeck, and his thoughts bled into my mind. He had started a mind-speak conversation with Master Fonu Edekk. Your Highness, Master Shinn has the voices."*

Trevn was so shocked that he nearly walked over Ottee. Neither Fonu nor Shinn descended from royal blood. *"What was said?"*

"Master Fonu asked many questions about you and many more about Miss Mielle. When you find her, Master Shinn is to tell Master Fonu where she is. He told Master Fonu about some measurements you took of the stars but was unable to find the figures in your cabin."

Because Trevn had taken them back in Armanguard and given them to Captain Veralla. *"What else?"*

"Master Shinn is to eavesdrop on you and, when he is able, Miss Mielle, so that he can give her location to Master Fonu before you are able to reach her. Master Fonu wants to capture her and use her against you somehow."

Rage coursed through Trevn. *"Anything about Fonu communicating with Rogedoth?"*

"Nothing like that, Your Highness. But Master Fonu told Master Shinn that he instructed a shadir to follow you everywhere. Said it would keep him informed of your movements. That was all."

A shadir! Following him even now? *"Thank you, Kempe. You've done very well. Continue to monitor Shinn's thoughts when you can."* He closed her out of his mind, barely managing to restrain himself from reaching for Shinn.

The man was a traitor. That he had kept his mind-speak ability a secret when Wilek had demanded all come forward . . . And telling Fonu their plans? The latter was enough to have him hanged. That he would conspire to abduct Mielle so that the enemy could control Trevn? Utterly despicable.

And Fonu. Trevn had heard rumors. About an old love affair between Fonu's father and Princess Jemesha, years before the princess had married. Could Fonu be Oli and Eudora's half brother? And what of the shadir? Was the creature following Trevn even now? What should he do? His first thought was to voice Captain Bussie and have him arrest Shinn, but that might alert Fonu that Trevn knew his plans. Better to give Kempe time and see if she could learn—

"Trevn? What is wrong?"

Mielle's voice startled him and pulled him back from his spinning thoughts. He must have reached for her without thinking. He told her everything Kempe had said, and her despair flooded his mind.

"What purpose would Master Fonu have in taking me captive? I don't know anything important about the ruling of Armania."

Naïve, sweet girl. *"This is war, Mielle. And our enemy is ruthless. Rogedoth is the man who continually encouraged my father to sacrifice to Barthos. He would do anything to get what he wants. It is me he seeks to control in this. Not only do you have my heart, we are soul-bound. Hurting you would hurt me. It would certainly render me useless to help Wilek with the rule of Armania."*

"What can I do?"

"I will teach you to shield your mind. It will take time for you to get good at it, so we must practice every day. It is all I can think of that might protect you at the moment, except . . . Mielle, should anyone arrive in your settlement—other citizens of the Five Realms—you must hide. Ask Captain Stockton or Cadoc's parents for help, but trust no one else until I say otherwise. Is that understood?"

"I am not one to hole up under a rock like a worm, Trevn."

"I know that, Mouse, but I need you to promise me you will protect yourself. For my sake?"

He felt Mielle surrender to his will. *"Very well,"* she said. *"Now teach me how to shield."*

✦   ✦   ✦

Late the next morning, just before midday, Trevn's party reached Zuzaan. Two of the four giants in their party ran ahead to announce their arrival. The village was made of several dozen domed houses of simple drystone. It surprised Trevn that with so many trees around, these people used no wood in their construction. Trevn saw several dogs the size of ponies and two horses with backs as high as Trevn was tall. Could there be something in the land or water that had caused these people and their animals to grow overly tall? He pondered that theory as they crossed a drawbridge and entered a fortress of drystack boulders—each rock as big as a grown man. Just inside the entrance they met a wall of giants armed with battle-axes.

A flurry of confusion followed. The Armanian soldiers drew their swords, and Cadoc whisked Trevn within the circle their bodies made.

"Wait!" Trevn yelled, struggling to see. "Do not be the first to strike."

"You to put down weapon," Toqto said.

The eagerness Trevn had sensed in the giant suddenly made sense in light of their current circumstances. Toqto hadn't been eager to return home or to introduce newcomers to his people. He had been eager to lead them all into a trap.

"What do you want with us?" Trevn asked.

"You to hunt tsok," Toqto said.

Arman, what should I do? Should he refuse? Fight? He couldn't imagine that his men, however well trained, could stand against these giants. There was no time to ask Wilek for advice; his soldiers looked ready to spring.

"We do not want to fight you," Trevn said. "We came in peace. To know you better and to see our friend Grayson."

"God-man special," Toqto said. "Bring many dirtmen to hunt the tsok."

This time the epithet stung. Trevn could order his men to fight, but they were inside the stronghold. Even if they somehow managed to kill every giant here, there was an entire village to get through on the way out—a village with giant dogs and horses to aid their captors in the chase that would undoubtedly follow.

"We will not fight you today," Trevn said, "but know that detaining us is an act of war against my realm. I'm certain Grayson the god-man would agree."

"Small men not harm the Yeke," Toqto said, squeezing his fist. "You to be like tsok. Obey without fight or we to crush you like tsok."

✦   ✦   ✦

Trevn told his men to lay down their swords.

The soldiers obeyed but averted their gazes. Did they think he'd chosen wrong? "We must choose our battles wisely," he said, firm in his resolve. "This battle we cannot win."

The giants prodded them down an oversized set of stone steps that zig-zagged deep into the bowels of the fortress. As they descended, Trevn used his magic to talk with Wilek and Captain Bussie, admitting the disaster he'd walked into. Bussie was sympathetic and promised to remain nearby in hopes that Trevn would find a way out. Wilek, on the other hand, lost his temper.

"Gone but one week and captured by giants? How am I supposed to get you out of this?"

"You're not," Trevn said. *"I'll get myself out of it."*

"And how will you do that?"

"I have no idea. But at least give me a chance. And maybe pray."

The stairs ended in an underground cavern filled with scores of pale humans with filthy skin and blistery warts. Men, women, children even. All carried baskets woven of straw or the paper substance that had formed the pulpy cocoons.

A giant shoved an empty basket and a lit torch into Trevn's hands, then pushed him down a path that led deeper underground. Trevn stumbled along with his men, suspecting they were meant to fill their baskets with some kind of beetle. Was Saria down here? He thought to call out to her, but decided to wait and keep his wits about him for the moment. Deeper and deeper they went. Tunnels branched off like the hairs on a root, and Trevn realized he had the freedom to choose which path to take. He led his men down one of the offshoots. The tunnel became very narrow, almost too small for Trevn to navigate. He forged on anyway, curiosity growing with each step.

A sound grew, something like the warbling song of a flock of birds. Trevn slowed, tense and suddenly reluctant to see what lay ahead.

A sharp turn brought him into a subterranean cavern that ended the mystery. The walls were indeed coated in a horde of crawling, shiny black beetles.

✦   ✦   ✦

Days passed by as Trevn and his men gathered beetles into baskets with the rest of the slaves. If they were not careful, the pests bit, which resulted in bulbous blisters tight with yellow fluid that usually popped within two days, leaving behind flaccid itchy skin. What the giants wanted with so many of the bugs, Trevn couldn't imagine. Some of the pales implied they were food, so Jahday, ever the explorer, smashed one with a rock and ate it raw. His report was not favorable.

The slaves slept wherever they could find a clear bit of ground. Most crammed inside the open cavern at the foot of the stairs since it was the same place that, three times a day, the giants delivered trays of flatbread and water in exchange for a full bucket of beetles. Anyone who missed coming at the right time or didn't have enough beetles went hungry. And for reasons unclear to Trevn, some of the giants made anyone with dark skin find twice as many beetles to exchange for food.

Trevn talked with Saria, who, after hearing his description of the place, did not think they were in the same mine. She believed the underground tunnels were all connected, if one could find the right path. They made tentative plans to try to find each other, though the idea of searching the hundreds of possible tunnels branching off the main caverns overwhelmed Trevn.

One day as he and Cadoc were exiting a dead-end tunnel, Trevn met several men with brown skin. "Are you from the Five Realms?" he asked.

"We are Sarikarian," said one of the men, staring at Trevn and Cadoc. "Name's Matto. Three families from my village were taken from our settlement a month ago. Who are you?"

"I'm Trevn, and this is Cadoc."

One glance at Trevn's clothing, filthy as it was, and the Sarikarian's eyes popped like a bullfrog as he put the puzzle together. "Sâr Trevn of Armania?"

It wasn't long before word spread and enslaved Kinsman people were flocking to Trevn to beg for help.

"The giants make us get more beetles than the pales."

"A tunnel caved in and broke my son's arm, but the giants won't help him."

"You can use the mind-speak magic, Your Highness, can't you?"

"Call for help."

"Confuse their minds so we can escape."

"Compel them."

"Put a spell on them."

Trevn answered as best he could. Cadoc was able to help the boy with the broken arm, but Trevn felt like no one truly listened or tried to understand how his magic worked. They just wanted someone to complain to.

One morning as he was eating his share of flatbread, four Kinsman men approached. The smallest stepped forward and slouched against the wall, folding his arms in front.

"Well, there you are, Sâr Trevn. You could have put a little more effort into rescuing your betrothed."

The familiar voice had been female, and upon closer inspection Trevn recognized the young woman before him, though he could barely believe it.

"Princess Saria?"

She was wearing men's clothing—part of a soldier's uniform. Her fine black hair had been bound back in a warrior's tail with several prize braids of varying shades threaded into it, giving the appearance of stripes. One golden twist looked to be a lock of giant's hair. She bore two blisters on her right cheek and a third on her forehead.

Saria barked a mannish laugh. "He thinks I'm Princess Saria? Now there's a long tale for the minstrels to sing about. I don't know whether to be insulted or flattered." Then to his mind, she said, *"None but these three know it's me, and I'd like to keep it that way."*

"But why would anyone—"

"My decision, not yours," she snapped. "Any ideas on how to get out of here?"

"Not yet. You?"

"The tunnels go on forever in places, but we found no exits beyond this one here and the cave we were first brought into. Exploring is dangerous because some of the tunnels are unstable. There have been some cave-ins. I've lost six men since my arrival. How many do you have down here?"

"Twenty-six."

"Any children? Some of the tunnels are very small."

Trevn nodded to Ottee, who was sitting on the floor beside Cadoc, munching on a piece of flatbread. "Just my onesent."

Saria pushed off the wall and all but swaggered around Trevn to get a good look at Ottee. "He'll do." She kicked Ottee's boot. "You afraid of the dark, boy?"

"No, sir," Ottee lied. "I'm a ship's boy. There ain't nothing I can't do."

Saria fought back a smile. "A ship's boy turned onesent. Now there's an interesting twist, but unsurprising for a *Renegade*." Saria's gaze fixed beyond him. She inched backward, then swung around and walked away. Curious, Trevn turned to see what had scared her off.

Four giants, walking toward them.

Toward him.

Toqto in the lead.

"Trevn?" Mielle asked.

"I'm fine," he said, annoyed that he kept reaching for her unintentionally. Perhaps it was becoming habit.

Cadoc jumped up and put himself between Trevn and the threat. Toqto grabbed Cadoc's tunic in his fist, lifted him, and passed him to his comrade as if he were a cushion.

"You to come with Toqto," the golden-haired giant said.

"Not without me." Cadoc elbowed his captor and twisted away. Two steps and he had again positioned himself in front of Trevn.

"Finla wa bey," Toqto told his men.

The three giants advanced. A short struggle sent Cadoc sprawling into a group of pales who were eating.

Toqto clamped his massive hand onto Trevn's arm and pulled him toward the stairs.

"I'll be fine, Cadoc," Trevn voiced. *"I'll tell you everything that happens. Take care of Ottee."*

"Don't tell them anything, Your Highness," Cadoc said.

"I'll be careful. I promise."

Toqto dragged Trevn up at least four flights of stairs and into a brightly lit chamber. There he met a giant with orange hair, who, in broken Kinsman, introduced Trevn to Headman Bolad mi Aru, ruler of Zuzaan. The headman oozed eager ambition. He asked Trevn something in his own language, and the orange-haired giant translated.

"You to have value to your tribe? You to be headman?"

Did the giants think they could trade him for a greater number of Kinsman commoners? Trevn wasn't about to be the cause of enslaving more people.

"Trey van had dar?" the orange-haired giant asked. "You to be named this?"

"Have no fear, Cadoc," Trevn said to his shield. *"They are only questioning me to see if I am someone important."*

"You are someone important, Your Highness," was Cadoc's frustrated reply. *"Don't tell them anything."*

Trevn decided to ask his own questions. "Grayson taught you our language? Where is he?"

Irritation spiked through Bolad mi Aru at the name Grayson, yet Trevn felt anxious fear well up within the orange-haired giant.

"What have you done with Grayson?" Trevn asked.

"Gray son of Jhorn is not in Zuzaan," the orange-haired giant said.

"*Wee badla wa pûm det!*" the headman yelled at his translator. He picked up a bronze sword, which Trevn recognized as his own. "*Etla way wee. Mah?*"

"You to make. How?"

Trevn waved his hands in a slow arc, wiggling his fingers. "Magic."

This started a long discussion between the two giants, and even Toqto chimed in. Trevn understood nothing, so he gave Cadoc an update.

"They wanted to know how we make swords. I told them magic."

The two giants continued to pelt Trevn with questions, but he answered nothing truthfully and continued to shoot his own questions back.

Why eat beetles? Why enslave Puru? Where was Grayson? Had they always been so ugly?

He received no answer but a glare to that last question. Finally he was dismissed, and Toqto led him to a chamber a few doors down. The golden-haired giant lifted a torch off a scone in the corridor, carried it inside, and lit a torch on the wall. Then he left, shutting Trevn inside.

Trevn voiced Cadoc to assure him he was fine, then voiced Mielle, Wilek, and Saria to update each.

"Don't tell them about me," Saria said.

"I'm not going to tell them anything," Trevn said.

He examined the chamber. It was completely empty but for two overly long beds of furs in adjacent corners. Until his eyes caught sight of a worn leather satchel that Trevn knew in a glance had come from the Five Realms.

He dumped its contents on the floor and surveyed the meager items. A ratty wool blanket, a threadbare tunic, a rusty knife, and a pair of boots with the toes cut off.

Curious, Trevn reached out to Cadoc. *"Why would anyone cut off the ends off their boots?"* he asked.

"Feet grow too fast," Cadoc said. *"Makes the boots last longer."*

Pity welled in Trevn's stomach. He thought of the orphans Mielle cared so deeply for. The months he'd spent on the ship had given him some idea of what it meant to be hungry, but he had eaten far better than most. He had no comprehension of what it meant to be so poor.

He bent down and picked up the boot, turned it over, and examined the sole, where he found two holes worn through—one in the heel, a second in the middle of the pad. He wondered over the owner. Was this young man in the tunnels beneath the fortress this moment, gathering beetles?

Where are you, boy? he wondered.

His vision blurred and he found himself transported to a dark, smoky room, surrounded by pales. Shocked, he sat down on one of the beds, wondering if he might be looking out through the eyes of the satchel's owner.

An elderly pale woman handed a platter toward him. A man's arm reached out to accept the food, and Trevn saw his dappled skin.

"Grayson, son of Jhorn?" he asked and felt the man jump—the boy. *"This is Sâr Trevn Hadar. You have the gift of mind-speak that Arman bestowed upon those with royal blood in their veins. Can you hear me?"*

The pale woman frowned and said something that Trevn didn't understand.

"Yes," came a tentative reply. *"I hear you, sir."*

Trevn smiled. Finally something had gone right. *"Excellent. I am pleased to know you, Grayson. We have much to discuss."*

"Like what?"

Where to even start? *"You escaped somehow from the giants? My men and I are captives here, made to hunt beetles in underground tunnels."*

"Are you in the tunnels now?"

"No, actually. They brought me to a chamber upstairs where I found your satchel and old boots."

Trevn felt a thrill course through Grayson and lost the connection with his mind. His eyes had just refocused on the room around him when a person materialized not three steps from where Trevn sat—a bedraggled young man with dappled skin who was dressed in the leather and furs of the giants.

Trevn yelped and clapped a hand over his heart. "How in sand's sake did you do that?"

"Sorry," the young man said, fidgeting. "My magic is getting to be a habit. This was my room when I was here, so it's easy to come back. I can't believe a sâr found me. I should probably bow, yeah?" He bowed deeply, sweeping his arm across his waist.

He was rail thin and had skin the color of ashes, mottled in at least three shades of gray. His hair was black and bound in a puffy tail at the back of his neck, similar to the way Trevn wore his own. His cheeks were coated in a downy layer of facial hair that had never seen a blade. The look on his face was joyful and childlike.

"So you are Grayson, son of Jhorn?"

"That's right," the young man said, sinking to sit cross-legged on the floor. "Though Jhorn is not my real father."

"Oh." That was not what Wilek had told Trevn, but it was also not his business to refute. "You are truly eight years old?"

"Uhh, never knew my day of birth. I'm nearly ten now, I think."

He looked closer to twenty. *"I should inform you,"* Trevn said to the boy's mind, *"a shadir is likely following me."*

"Yes, he's here," Grayson said aloud, glancing over Trevn's head. "A green slight. Looks a bit like a frog. I've never seen him before."

Trevn looked above him. Saw nothing. "You can see shadir?"

"Oh yes. Ragaz isn't here right now, so that's good. He serves Master Fonu and has been following me for weeks."

Trevn was thankful for that much. "The giants wouldn't tell me where you were."

"They didn't know. When I heard Master Fonu wanted to capture me, I left."

"What role does Fonu Edekk play here? Tell me everything."

Grayson shared his story, which was like something from mythology. Secret magic, prophecies, kidnappings, a sea serpent, pirates, giants, pale slaves he called Puru. With all the boy had been through, it was a miracle he was still alive. Arman had truly been watching out for him.

Fonu had not only compelled Randmuir Khal of the Omatta and Bolad mi Aru, he had compelled an army of twenty giants, which he'd taken south through the mountains for some mysterious purpose.

"No ideas why?" Trevn asked.

Grayson shook his head. "All I know is he compelled Randmuir the pirate captain to catch me and bring me to him."

"How did you teach the giants to speak Kinsman?"

"It's part of my magic. I can understand any language, which sort of made me a tutor."

"I would like to learn more about your magic," Trevn said.

"I'll tell you all I know." Grayson winced. "If you'll teach me more about this magic in my head."

"We call it voicing or mind-speaking," Trevn said. "Those with royal blood have the ability."

"But I don't have royal blood." He squirmed, uncertain. "Do I?"

"Through your mother, yes."

His eyes popped. "You know my mother?"

Trevn realized he might have overstepped. "Hold on to that question." He reached for Wilek. *I have found Grayson—or he found me—and I let slip that his mother had royal blood. What can I tell him?*

I have no idea. I will summon Jhorn at once and find out.

Trevn distracted the boy with a lecture on the mind-speak ability, telling him about the different tricks he had discovered.

"Will the shielding quiet the voices? There are always so many. I thought I might have broken my mind somehow by popping around too much."

The question puzzled Trevn. "I've never heard anyone's voice without either trying to or when someone gifted speaks to me." Though Kempe had overheard Shinn. Perhaps the traitor hadn't shielded himself properly. Or maybe Kempe and Grayson were somehow more perceptive.

Grayson's brows pinched. "But none of the voices I heard were talking to me. I'm not surprised to be different. I've always been."

Trevn squeezed the young man's shoulder. "Don't take it that way. Different is special. And being special is a blessing. I will teach you to shield your mind. Perhaps that will help with the voices you hear."

The young man lit up, smiling wide. "That would be great. Thanks."

"So, any ideas how someone without your special magic can get out of this place?"

"Ulagan and me, we've been helping Puru slaves escape. Three boats so far, one each night, through an underground river. It goes all the way to the ocean. The boats hold about thirty Puru."

Hope swelled inside Trevn. "That's wonderful. Do you think you could help me and my soldiers get out of here?"

"Sure," Grayson said. "I'll just go ask Ulagan."

And he vanished.

Hinck

What the natives called the Shelosh Islands, King Barthel had re-named Islah after his first wife. It had been a beautiful jungle when the *Amarnath* and its pirated fleet had landed several months ago. It now resembled a military training camp. Hinck stood at the back of the practice field, watching his archers miss their targets. Adjacent to him Harton Sonber was running native slavs through a sword-training exercise.

Rogedoth was building an army.

He had originally planned to take New Sarikar from his nephew with mantics alone, but once he learned that the evenroot grown here produced no magic, he sought a secondary plan. Despite the vast stores of the magical substance he had brought across the Northsea, it would not last forever, and he was unwilling to waste it all defeating New Sarikar, then have nothing left for Armania.

But building an army was not without problems. He had no soldiers besides a handful of personal guards. His lone military asset, Harton Sonber, Rosâr Wilek's ex-shield, had been made general. While Harton had no combat experience beyond small skirmishes to protect his charge, his training in Armanian camps made up for his lack of experience. He knew everything there was to know about Armanian military practices—in theory. But theory was enough to set Rogedoth's plan in motion. At Harton's urging he built an infantry of enslaved natives, compelling all to obey. This infantry would be used to weaken the armies of New Sarikar and Armania so that Rogedoth would not have to exhaust his evenroot stores once he joined the battle.

Harton also convinced Rogedoth to abandon plans to mine for metal to forge swords and instead produce enormous quantities of bows and arrows. Harton believed that focusing on ranged weapons was the only way to pit such weak and untrained infantry against seasoned soldiers.

Hinck, who had never been good with a bow, had, insanely, been put in charge of training the native slavs to shoot. As he had been known as one of the worst archers to grace the Five Realms in the past decade, his charges were not exactly advancing in skill at the rate Rogedoth demanded—not that he was trying very hard. Poor archers would only help Armania's chances, but the dismal results often left Hinck feeling the false king's wrath. So when the summons from Rogedoth boomed in Hinck's head—*"Come to the throne house"*—he was unsurprised, expecting yet another lecture.

Hinck's fear over Rogedoth learning he had the ability to use the mind-speak magic had subsided when Rogedoth discovered that a gifted man could speak to the non-gifted. He now ordered everyone around without audibly speaking a word, so Hinck conveniently managed to start hearing the man along with everyone else.

He had also been able to eavesdrop, for a little while anyway, which had been terribly convenient. Eventually, Rogedoth discovered the concept of shielding, which Hinck believed he'd learned from Sir Kamran DanSâr, though he had no proof. Interestingly enough, Rogedoth kept this new skill to himself, which amused Hinck. So both Rogedoth and Hinck had the ability to listen in on the minds of those around them. Better yet, Rogedoth wasn't very proficient at shielding, especially when he was speaking to another, and Hinck was often able to pick up entire conversations to pass along to Wilek and Trevn.

Curious if Rogedoth meant to lecture him for his incompetent archers again, Hinck concentrated on the man's thoughts and found his shields down.

"Mattenelle is too much a fool to betray me. Zenobia might, if she wished to make her son Kamran king. It wouldn't be Laviel or Jemesha. Eudora's compulsion wouldn't allow it. Then who?"

Hinck leaned against the bow rack, set his feet well, and risked a quick glimpse through Rogedoth's eyes—another trick Trevn had taught him.

The self-made king was pacing between his throne and his mantics, who were lined up before him. Rogedoth suspected one of his most trusted adherents of treason? The options were plentiful. The man could have a mutiny on his hands any day, yet Hinck's stomach clenched at the idea that he might be the one to be found out.

He left the practice field and walked through the camp to Rogedoth's fortress of reeds, dwelling on his most recent list of transgressions. Trevn had asked for information on Fonu and his army of giants, so Hinck had been eavesdropping on everyone—he was a spy, after all. Likely the best spy in the history of mankind. What spy had ever been able to gather so much intelligence without even leaving his bed? Hinck could flit from Rogedoth's thoughts to Rosârah Laviel to Eudora to the servant who came in each morning to tend his fire. Anyone. It was an incredible magic, though he found it could be just as tedious. He quickly became sickened by the lewd things that occupied the minds of certain individuals and wearied by the tedium of minds that were nearly empty of thought altogether or that flitted from one idea to another like a bee in a garden of flowers.

Lady Eudora, for example, whose every movement and word had once captivated Hinck. Beyond the horror of her compulsion to obey Rogedoth, all she thought about was herself. Her own beauty. What she would wear. She must always be the most beautiful person present, hated any woman who drew attention away from her, and actively sought reasons to malign such competition with real or invented gossip or simply send them elsewhere.

One constant victim of Eudora's libel was Lady Mattenelle, who had become Hinck's only real friend in this place. Hinck had been shocked to find the mind of this gorgeous creature nearly vacant. He had lost count of how many times he'd listened in on Nellie's thoughts to find her thinking nonsense words. Sometimes humming a tune. Beauty distracted her, be it nature, gowns or jewels, architecture, an impressive horse, a man she found attractive, or a hot meal when she was hungry. When her eyes locked on such things, they ensnared her thoughts, rendering her quite useless.

The practice of eavesdropping had not been an entire waste of time, however. He had once caught Rogedoth voicing with Fonu about his compulsion on giants. Rogedoth wanted Fonu to encourage the giants to raid the smaller settlements on the outskirts of New Sarikar, and Trevn verified that very thing had been taking place for months.

Hinck had also discovered that Rosârah Laviel and Princess Jemesha were plotting against Rogedoth. Hinck hadn't believed it at first. Why would the man's own daughter work against him? But Rogedoth had made a mistake in handling Janek's situation. Rosârah Laviel had been pleading with the man ever since they'd left Everton to bring her son aboard the *Amarnath*. He had not prioritized this, and deep down she blamed him, both for Janek's death and for not destroying Armania the moment they'd learned her son had been killed.

Princess Jemesha and her husband, Zeteo, had always wanted their daughter to marry Janek, and when Rogedoth had claimed Eudora as his own bride, Jemesha had been horrified. She had kept all this inside, of course, until Laviel confessed her lack of confidence in the man. After that the two women had started stealing away evenroot for their eventual escape or attack—they still hadn't decided which they would choose.

Then there were the shadir. While Hinck couldn't listen to their thoughts, because of Oli's spell he could still see and hear them when they were nearby. This had taught Hinck much about the nature of these creatures. They did not like humans. They used them—fed off them in many ways.

Being able to see shadir when they thought no one was looking . . . it gave Hinck a chance to study them, and doing so stripped away all their mystery. They were demons, nothing more.

Hinck reached the throne house. He had barely stepped foot inside when Rogedoth was in his head.

"Come and join the ranks, Lord Dacre."

The line of mantics and malleants arced out from each side of the throne like a claw about to draw Hinck into its grasp. His gaze locked with Nellie's, and her bloodshot eyes about made his knees buckle.

Looked like trouble.

Somehow Hinck managed to cross the room and take position at the end of the row beside Lilou Caridod.

"Someone is betraying me," Rogedoth said. "Confess now, and I will let you live."

No one answered. Hinck adopted the posture of Harton, staring straight ahead like a soldier. He sensed a presence in his head and checked the shields around his mind. They were solid, as always.

"If you know anything," Rogedoth said, "tell me and you will be rewarded."

Hinck knew plenty, but he wasn't about to say anything. He was tempted to listen in on Laviel or Jemesha's minds to see if they were worried they'd been caught, but it seemed too risky at present.

"Lord Dacre sees the shadir yet takes no evenroot," Rosârah Laviel said.

Hinck jerked his head toward the former queen.

"He somehow blocks off his thoughts as well," she added. "He is the only person on the island I cannot listen in on, and I also heard him ask Lady Mattenelle about Master Fonu and the giants."

She would betray *him*? Hinck couldn't let her get away with that.

"Rosârah Laviel steals your evenroot," he said.

She gasped. "Liar!"

Hinck looked to Rogedoth, expecting an expression of shock and betrayal. Instead, he found only sternness in the man, directed toward himself.

"We will deal with Laviel's accusation first, Lord Dacre," Rogedoth said. "I too have noticed the fortress of your mind. Step forward and defend yourself."

Alarmed, Hinck walked to the center of the half circle and faced Rogedoth. "I don't know why you cannot hear my thoughts, Your Highness. I take evenroot when it is asked of me, but I am no mantic and hate to waste such a precious resource for the rush it gives."

"A reasonable answer," Rogedoth said. "Some of you are gluttons with my root."

"But, Father, no one has seen the young lord take root except Lady Mattenelle," Laviel said, "and concubines always lie for the man who tumbles them."

Her words made Hinck's cheeks hot. "I have not seen any of your mantics take evenroot except for Lady Mattenelle, Your Highness," Hinck said. "I am not in the habit of watching others eat or drink."

"I might accept that response if not for the reports from my shadir," Rogedoth said. "They've been watching you for months, Lord Dacre. Not one of them has bonded with you for healing after I have used you as a malleant. So if you are taking root, who is healing you?"

"Hwuum," Hinck said, using the name of Nellie's blue-and-yellow shadir that looked like wisps of curly hair. Though he didn't see it in the room. Oddly enough, he didn't see any shadir in the room.

"Hwuum swears he has never once healed you," Rogedoth said. "All of Dendron's shadir say the same."

Nellie sniffed and wiped tears from her cheek. Hinck knew then that he had walked into an ambush. This was the trial before his execution, yet it seemed he'd already been found guilty. His mind spun for any logical answer. "That's strange, for I thought he had." What else could he say? "I admit, it is difficult to remember what happens when I'm in a haze. If not Hwuum, it must have been Noadab." Hinck purposely used the name of Oli's shadir, hoping the creature had not returned to Rogedoth's service once Oli had run out of evenroot.

Rogedoth narrowed his eyes. "When did Noadab come to you?"

"When you fought in the eye of the storm," Hinck said.

"More lies, Your Highness," Lady Zenobia said. "Noadab had bonded with Oli Agoros when he fought against us in our final attempt to take the *Seffynaw*."

"What does that matter?" Hinck asked. "Shadir are fickle creatures, as are we malleants when the poison begins to take our breath. We will beg mercy from whichever shadir is closest, whether they be the shadir of our enemy or Dendron the Great." Hinck kept his expression fierce, hoping—begging and pleading, really—that the gods would have mercy on his traitorous, lying soul a wee bit longer.

Rogedoth sighed and turned to Timmons, who stood behind him to the left of the throne. "A simple test will prove all." He reached out his hand, and Timmons handed his king a dark bottle.

Oh, gods.

Rogedoth pulled the cork and walked slowly toward Hinck, passed him on the right, circled behind. Hinck felt the weight of everyone's stares upon him. This faithful remnant of the Lahavôtesh believed him a traitor, and they were right. Now they sought to prove it.

Oh, gods, why?

Rogedoth finished his loop and stopped before Hinck, then held out the bottle. "Drink."

Hinck did not hesitate—any hesitation would look like fear, and he must not appear afraid to do something that a loyal adherent would be eager to do. The moist condensation on the outside of the bottle surprised him. He took a small sip of the icy drink, knowing he had twice survived that much evenroot. He would likely be able to again.

Rogedoth's smile widened until it bared his unnaturally white teeth. "Drink it all. The whole bottle."

Hinck balked. The silence in the room made everything worse, until Nellie choked back a sob. Sands, could she be any more obvious?

"I've never taken so much at once," Hinck said.

"You have been accused of treason," Rogedoth said. "Of stealing from me, lying to me, and sharing my secrets with the enemy. This is your chance to prove yourself. Or die."

Nellie fainted. Harton just managed to catch her as she went down, then held her as she came to, panicked.

"Must I compel you to drink, Lord Dacre?" Rogedoth asked.

The brief thought to run flitted through his mind, but any attempt to leave would prompt one of these mantics—Rosârah Laviel, likely—to attack. Hinck recalled how Sir Jayron had died and made his decision.

"If you insist, Your Highness." And Hinck drank.

Dismay churned inside him as he chugged the icy juice. This would surely kill him. Painfully. Yet he had no choice but to obey.

The sweet, gritty liquid coated his mouth and throat in frost. He could feel it slowly making its way through his veins, down his arms, past his stomach and into his legs. Everything burned and throbbed with the cold, as if the substance were eating his flesh from the inside out.

He heard himself gasp and began to lose the feeling in his limbs. He dropped to his knees and found them numb, fell forward and caught himself on deadened hands. His teeth chattered as shivers combed his body. Nellie screamed his name over and over, but she did not come to him. He collapsed on the polished wood floor and fought to bring in one small breath at a time.

Still no shadir filled the Veil.

Rogedoth must have told them to stay away, no matter the pull of the evenroot available for purging. No matter that Hinck might give in and trade his soul to extend his life.

Rogedoth wanted him dead.

Hinck's only defense was to tell Trevn what had happened. *"Trevn, I am dying. Rogedoth made me drink a whole bottle of evenroot and ordered the shadir to stay away. He knows I am against him."*

Trevn's compassion blasted Hinck with such force he felt warm for a moment. *"What can I do?"*

"There's nothing to do. Tell Sâr Wilek—I mean, the king. Tell him I'm sorry. Tell my parents—"

"I'll voice for help." And Trevn severed their connection.

Typical. Even when he was dying Hinck couldn't hold Trevn's attention for more than a few breaths.

A woman called out to him. Nellie, probably. Or perhaps it was Iamos, goddess of healing, standing at the Lowerworld gates. She would receive his dead body and rejuvenate it for eternity. Then he would stand before Athos's Bench to be judged.

"Answer me," the woman said.

"Iamos," Hinck said. *"I hear you."*

"This is not Iamos. I am Onika, prophetess of Arman. And you must call on him if you wish to live without giving in to your enemy."

Hinck's thoughts knotted. *"Miss Onika?"*

"If you pledge your life to Arman, he will bring you into his presence. He will vouch for your life on earth. He might even heal you."

It could help to have a god vouch for him as he stood before Athos's Bench. Hinck had not always made the best choices.

"Call on Arman, Hinckdan," Miss Onika said. *"Only he can save you."*

Arman.

Hinck's throat had swelled so much that he could barely pull in a hitch of air. He could see his body twitching, though it was too numb with cold to feel the movement. A sudden panic shot through him. He didn't want to die. Not without seeing his parents and apologizing for leaving them. Not without trying to help Sarikar and Armania stand against Rogedoth. Not without seeing Lady Pia again.

Arman? Hinck tried. *Miss Onika says you can help me. Would you?* He sucked in a desperate breath. *Please?* he added as an afterthought.

"I AM HE, AND THERE IS NO GOD BESIDE ME. I GIVE AND TAKE LIFE. I WOUND AND HEAL. THERE IS NO OTHER WHO CAN DELIVER YOU FROM MY HAND."

At the sound of that voice, heat pulsed through Hinck as if someone had opened a door to the deserts of Dacre. Hinck knew then, without a doubt, that Miss Onika had been right. This was *the* God.

Have mercy on me, Arman! he cried out. *I have wasted my life on empty pleasures. My bloodguilt is so deep I am drowning. Forgive my feebleness. I am nothing. You are everything. I will praise you with my last breath.*

"BECAUSE YOU HAVE HUMBLED YOURSELF AND ASKED IN FAITH, I WILL RESTORE HEALTH TO YOU AND HEAL YOUR WOUNDS. I AM ARMAN."

Hinck reveled in the warmth and love of that supernatural voice. As it faded, he heard himself moan. His throat cleared and the chill left his body. He made a fist and wiggled his toes.

His body had been healed.

He opened his eyes and rolled onto his back, breathing easily now. Rogedoth stood over him, face slack, ridged brow pinched.

"Have I appeased my accusers, Your Highness?" Hinck rasped.

Rogedoth walked back to his throne. "You have appeased me, Hinckdan Faluk, and that is all that matters. Now all of you, get out. We march on Sarikar on my command."

Hinck sat up. The adherents rushed to the door, averting their gazes as they passed. All but Nellie, who fell to her knees beside him, sobbing, and grabbed him in a suffocating embrace.

"Help me stand," Hinck said, wanting to leave the throne house and never come back.

Nellie obeyed and the two left together, Hinck's legs still shaky.

"How did you do it?" she asked when they were outside.

"I didn't," Hinck said, awed by the sight of the wide blue sky overhead, thankful to be alive. "Arman did."

Now he needed to warn Wilek and King Loran that Rogedoth was coming soon.

WILEK

It was early summer, and Wilek had finally found time to visit New Sarikar. He sat at the table in his guest chamber, head in his hands as he voiced with Trevn. His brother had found Grayson, son of Jhorn, and they were beginning to fashion plans to help the Armanians and Sarikarians escape from the giants. Giants that Rogedoth had somehow brought under his thumb.

"*I still don't understand how Fonu Edekk ended up with Randmuir,*" Wilek said.

"*Grayson doesn't know,*" Trevn said, "*but I think Fonu must have swum to the* Malbraid *after jumping overboard and escaping arrest during the rebellion on our ship.*"

"*It seems like the only way.*"

"*Regardless, Fonu has put Rand under a compulsion and ordered him to find Grayson. Do you think Rogedoth knows that Grayson is his grandson?*"

"*I suspect he does now. Is the boy upset that Jhorn wishes to tell him about his parentage himself?*"

"*He's curious, but it takes a lot to upset Grayson. He's quite upbeat. Like me.*"

A knock on the door startled Wilek. He glanced up and saw Dendrick enter.

"*Focus on getting yourself and your men to safety, brother,*" Wilek said. "*Princess Saria as well. Then do what you can to protect Grayson. I want you both back here as soon as possible.*"

"*And Mielle too.*"

"*Yes, Mielle too.*" Wilek severed the connection, exhausted by the mounting frustrations. "What is it?" he asked Dendrick.

"At Lady Amala's recommendation, Sârah Hrettah voiced a message of concern to the Duke of Tal on behalf of his sister, Lady Zeroah," Dendrick said.

Wilek smirked. "Are you certain you got that message correct, Dendrick?" he asked.

"Quite, Your Highness. Young Rystan repeated it twice. He too is concerned for his sister."

"Rayim saw Zeroah only yesterday. He believes this illness is related to the pregnancy, and my mother and her midwives agree." He said a quick prayer for his wife, knowing it must be difficult to carry a child and be so very ill. "Please tell Rystan to fear not and to pass on the message to Lady Amala that her concern for my bride's welfare is appreciated."

"I will do so," Dendrick said.

Not ten minutes later Dendrick returned. "Your Highness, King Loran and his staff await you in the throne room."

"Excellent." It was time to make plans to deal with their common enemy before it was too late.

Wilek followed his onesent out the door, where Novan, Rystan, and two other guards were waiting to accompany him. The Sarikarian castle was quite ornate. The four-level keep comprised the kitchens, cellars, storerooms, and granaries—empty thus far—on the ground floor; the great hall and privy chambers on the second floor; royal apartments on the third level; and small chambers for staff and servants on the fourth.

The skill of King Loran's carpenters never ceased to impress. Yet Loran had always intended that this should be a temporary structure until he could find stone, since wood rotted and could easily be destroyed by fire. Wilek couldn't imagine tearing down something so fine.

The room was full and awaiting Wilek, as Dendrick had said. A table had been brought into the throne room and set lengthwise from where King Loran sat his throne. His brother Rosbert sat on his right, then Rosbert's son, Kanzer. Across from them sat Prince Thorvald. Also present were several lords, a half dozen white-robed prophets, and three priests dressed in blue.

Blue didn't seem the right color for Sarikar. Armanite priests wore brown. Perhaps Loran was making some changes of his own.

Everyone stood to greet Wilek, who took his place at the foot of the table. The room felt strange, cold and heavy, like the walls might fall in at any moment. Wilek brushed aside the strange observation.

"Thank you, King Loran, for welcoming me to New Sarikar," Wilek said.

"It was the least I could do," Loran said. "Knowing that your brother will rescue Saria from those giants . . . It is an answer to all our prayers."

"All credit goes to Grayson, son of Jhorn," Wilek said. "He is the true hero."

"Then he shall be knightened for his service to House Pitney," Loran said.

"I imagine that will please him and his father," Wilek said. "I must congratulate you on this magnificent structure. It is glorious."

King Loran nodded his thanks. "My carpenters are unsurpassed in skill. Do call upon them whenever you have need."

"Thank you," Wilek said. "I will waste no more of your time. I have come here for one purpose. Will you go to war with me against your uncle?"

"We will join any war that comes," Loran said, "yet I am uncertain it's wise to strike first."

"We must," Wilek said. "If we wait, he will continue to pick us off until we are small enough to defeat with magic. Already I fear we have waited too long."

"Sarikar can stand against his magic," Loran said.

"How? Have you mantics of your own?"

"Of course not," Loran said. "But do not take my word alone." He gestured to the men seated on Wilek's end of the table. "Here you see my prophets. What say you, men? Shall we go to war against Prince Mergest the betrayer, or shall we wait for him to attack us?"

"Wait," said one.

"If you attack now, he will certainly destroy you before winter comes again."

"Bide your time and be victorious."

"The gods will give it into your hands if you are patient."

At the word *gods*, Wilek grew curious. "Do you no longer have a prophet of Arman here of whom we can inquire?"

"There is one," King Loran said. "Wolbair, brother of Queen Daria, my mother. But he is arrogant and completely biased. His advice to my father always made the nobles rise up in protest."

"I would like to hear his opinion," Wilek said.

King Loran said nothing for a long moment before motioning to his onesent. "Bring Wolbair here at once."

The men at the table began to grumble, and Wilek felt dismayed that this once pious nation had drifted away from Arman's teachings just as he had begun to embrace them.

"Which gods have told you to wait?" he asked the prophets.

"With Emperor Ulrik, your nephew, on the throne of Rurekau, surely Rurek god of war is on your side," said the priest on Wilek's left. "A cunning warrior knows when to wait."

"Zitheos as well," said another. "With the horns of Zitheos you will gore any Barthians who come to your door until all are destroyed. Defending from a fortress is safer than being vulnerable on the battlefield."

"Athos gives Justness to his adherents," said a third. "King Loran has been loyal, and Athos will repay that loyalty with safety."

The prophets were still touting their false gods when Loran's onesent returned with an old man. He was short, slight, had black skin and golden eyes. His hair and beard were long and white, and he wore a plain brown robe.

"Wolbair," King Loran said. "My prophets all agree that we should not attack my uncle at this time. Let your word match theirs and speak favorably about this action."

Wolbair looked around the table from face to face. He paused at Loran, then spoke, "Is there no god in New Sarikar that you would consult with the gods of Rôb? When did you forsake the One God?" His piercing eyes shifted to focus on Wilek. "King of Armania, do not let these prophets deceive you. Inaction will not deliver you from your enemies. Do not let them persuade you to trust in their false gods. Act now and Arman will deliver you."

"Do not listen to Wolbair," Loran said. "Has Arman ever delivered us from the hand of our enemy? Never. Not when our enemy was Prince Mergest, not when he was your Pontiff Rogedoth, and not when he is now King Barthel. Arman has done our nation no favors. We would be wise to make offerings to more than one deity."

This coming from King Loran stunned Wilek. King Jorger had always been extremely pious in his beliefs, but Wilek had spent little time talking faith with Loran. He hadn't realized the man's beliefs were so far from his father's.

"What say you, prophet?" Wilek asked Wolbair.

"Since I do not commune with the black spirits of Gâzar, I can tell you only what the God says," came Wolbair's answer. "I saw New Sarikar scattered on the plains like sheep without a shepherd. Arman said, 'These people have no master. I will put deceiving spirits in the mouths of their prophets and decree for them disaster since they have turned away from me.'"

"You dare curse us?" King Loran said, his expression fierce. "Guards! Take Wolbair back to his chambers."

Two guards rushed forward and seized the old prophet. As they dragged he out the doorway, he yelled, "If you remain safe by hiding in your fortress, Arman has not spoken through me!"

Loran sighed. "I apologize, King Wilek. His intolerance is very off-putting."

The entire exchange had left Wilek in shock. "You believe him wrong?"

"He speaks nonsense," Loran said. "I ask, 'Should we remain here?' I expect a simple yes or no. Not to be berated as if he is an angry woman seeking to wound with words."

"Was not he the prophet who bid you sail northwest when we crossed the Northsea?" Wilek asked.

"He was one of many, yes. All agreed on that matter."

"Did all worship Arman then?" Wilek asked.

"We all worship Arman now, King Wilek," Loran said. "I am surprised that you would think otherwise."

Wilek did not know what to think. It seemed to him that something had changed in Sarikar. Had Rogedoth somehow affected them? Wilek longed to remain on good terms with King Loran, but he could not take so lightly the scene he had witnessed here today.

Sarikar had turned their backs on Arman. Wilek would return home to Armanguard and inquire of Miss Onika. She would know what to do.

✦ ✦ ✦

On Wilek's journey home, he sat in his carriage, speaking with Hinckdan Faluk.

"*Rogedoth plans to attack Sarikar with his army of native slavs.*"

"*When?*" Wilek asked.

"*'On his command' is all he will ever say, but as it will take five or six days to reach New Sarikar, I can give plenty of warning. His army consists of mostly archers—and not very good ones. I, as their marshal, should know. Still, you might focus on making armor and shields. Bows are inadequate to pierce such defenses at any significant range, and keep in mind, Rogedoth's slavs have no armor at all, so your archers should be able to take them out easily.*"

"*That is helpful, Hinckdan. I shall let Captain Veralla know at once. Do keep me informed should you learn anything—*"

Zeroah's voice burst into his mind with force. "*Wilek? The baby is coming. It is early, the midwife says. I am frightened.*"

"*Hinckdan, I will speak with you later. Good midday.*" Wilek closed off the connection and grabbed the wrist of Dendrick, who was sitting beside him on the bench.

"Is something wrong, Your Highness?" Dendrick asked.

"Zeroah's labor has begun. Ask the driver to hurry."

"If you like, Your Highness, but rest assured that she does not need your assistance. Women have been having babies for centuries without the aid of men."

"I would like to be there just the same."

Dendrick gave the word, and the carriage surged ahead. Wilek kept his mind connected to Zeroah's, which increasingly began to terrify him. For the first few hours she was able to talk clearly about where she was and what she was doing. The midwives had joined her in her bedchamber along with her honor maidens and several noblewomen who would act as witnesses to the child's validity. Zeroah reported much chatter from the women about names for boys and girls and stories of each other's childbearing ordeals.

Wilek tried desperately to look through Zeroah's eyes the way Trevn had learned to do, but he found no success. Nor could he feel her pain or sense her emotions—more abilities Trevn had discovered. His brother had more time to waste practicing, while Wilek had been running the kingdom. Still, his failure shamed him.

Zeroah grew more agitated as the pain quickened. Wilek understood why midwives insisted men keep away. Had he been there, he would want to help, but there would be nothing he could do.

The labor escalated quickly, and each time the pain struck, Zeroah screamed. Wilek recalled how she always prayed for him when trouble came, and so he prayed. It was all he could think to do as she fought to bring their child into the world.

In the middle of his prayer, his wife went completely quiet.

"Zeroah?" he asked. *"Are you well?"*

"Yes," she breathed. *"It is over. They say it's a boy. Our Chadek is here."*

"A boy!" Wilek whooped, nudging Dendrick beside him. On the opposite bench Novan and Rystan both offered congratulations.

"How does he look, my dear?" Wilek asked. *"Describe our son to me."*

"I have not seen him yet," Zeroah said. *"The midwives are bundling him."*

"You are a father," Novan said, grinning.

"You will be a fine one," Dendrick said.

"Oh! Wilek, he is ill. Our baby is not well, they say."

Zeroah's words nearly stopped his heart.

Wilek shushed the men in the carriage. *"Ill? How?"* He strained to hear her answer, but she was no longer speaking to him.

"What is wrong?" Zeroah yelled. *"Tell me at once. I demand to see my baby."*

"Zeroah?" Wilek asked.

"Do not say such things. My only comfort is to hold my son."

Wilek reached for his mother instead. *"What is happening, Mother? Tell me at once."*

"I don't know, Wilek. The midwife says he is small. He is struggling to breathe."

A chill clapped onto Wilek and would not leave.

"Wilek?" Zeroah again. *"Your mother says he is very small."*

"My dear, tell me everything."

But there was nothing more to tell. Zeroah's demands for more information went unanswered by the midwives. The physician came and declared the same. He was small. Likely came too early. Time would tell.

Finally Wilek's mother gave Zeroah the boy to hold, and Wilek heard his wife weep.

"Is it so bad?" he asked.

"I have never seen a baby so new. He looks beautiful to me."

"We will pray for Arman to strengthen him."

"I am afraid."

"'He will cover you with his feathers, armored and protected in the shelter of his wings,'" Wilek said. *"'He is your hiding place. In his arms he protects you from the attacks of the enemy.'"*

Zeroah broke down, so Wilek repeated her favorite verses again and again until she said, *"I love you, Wilek. When will you be home?"*

"Tomorrow at dawn. We will ride through the night."

✦ ✦ ✦

The next morning Wilek sat on the edge of Zeroah's bed, looking down on his son as he cradled him in one arm. Chadek had a flat little nose, thick black hair, and Zeroah's golden eyes, which were watery as if the babe was on the verge of tears. Zeroah's eyes were watery too, though when a tear seeped out it was thick, more like custard than water. Each gentle, wheezing breath from the babe took effort. Wilek reached for his son's mind but heard no thoughts. How foolish. What could he possibly hear? He did sense an overwhelming weariness, but that might be coming from him or Zeroah. None of them had been sleeping well.

Wilek thought of his older brother and their father. Rosâr Echad had sacrificed Chadek I to Barthos—to a cheyvah beast. It had always haunted Wilek, but as he held Chadek II in his arms, he was ever so much more shocked at the depravity of such a choice. How could any man have his own son killed?

A great terror welled up in Wilek's chest. What if his son someday felt the same way toward Wilek as he had felt toward his father? Wilek had despised nearly everything about the man. The mere idea of little Chadek hating him seemed to suffocate him, and tears welled in his eyes.

No. Wilek was not his father.

Rosâr Echad had always prioritized his own pleasures and vices. Nothing had ever mattered but that which he had deemed important. Wilek sought peace and to help the people in his realm thrive. And he had been trying to bring his people to worship Arman alone, but now that Sarikar seemed to be straying away from the monotheism King Jorger had worked so hard to maintain, Wilek felt alone in his endeavors.

Sarikar was becoming what Armania had once been.

In his weariness Wilek longed for a friend who understood his frustration. Using his voicing magic, he reached out to Kal.

"Your Highness," Kal said. *"I have been hoping you would check in with me."* And he went on to tell Wilek much about what had been happening in the realm now called Magos.

Wilek listened, shocked by Kal's report. Charlon had killed a shadir to become Chieftess, and Shanek was already nearing the throes of adolescence. Such news only strengthened Wilek's resolve to deal with Rogedoth before Charlon unleashed her plans for Shanek.

"Will the boy cause trouble?" Wilek asked.

"He certainly could," Kal said. *"He is eager to please Charlon and myself. When he discovers we are divided, I don't know what he'll do. Though I've known him only a short time, he sees me as a father. I am . . . uncertain I could take his life."*

Wilek studied Chadek's peaceful face. *"I would not ask that of you unless there was no other choice."*

Kal talked until he had said all he must, and only then did Wilek share his own news of the meeting in Sarikar, Zeroah and Chadek's ill health, and their son's small size.

Kal listened well before answering. *"Something seems amiss. Could someone have poisoned the queen?"*

The question startled Wilek. *"I think not,"* he said. *"Zeroah has been sickly since we reached land. In fact, she has always been somewhat frail, but surely I would have seen the effects of poison."*

"There are many poisons," Kal said. *"Some are slow-acting and difficult to detect. Find an expert to look into the matter. Increase security and make sure that no one has a chance to tamper with your food. Perhaps even appoint a taster."*

Wilek had no argument, so overwhelmed was he at the mere thought that someone might have purposely harmed Zeroah and their child. *"You are wise, Kal,"* he said finally. *"I will do as you suggest."*

Wilek felt better after talking with his friend and promised to voice him more often for updates. Wilek set Chadek in the cradle, then went to his office. He paced about, eager to investigate Kal's hunch. He would have Dendrick speak to the kitchen staff immediately about security, have Rayim find an authority on poisons, and then he would summon Miss Onika and tell her all that had happened in New Sarikar and Magonia—now Magos.

His enemies were working hard against him, and Wilek would not remain idle. He must do whatever possible to protect his family and his realm.

Amala

Amala left Rosâr Wilek's office and retreated to the castle roof, where Sir Kamran DanSâr was waiting. She crossed to the parapet and stopped beside him, leaning on the crenellation and gazing out over the clear water of Lake Arman.

"Well?" Kamran asked. "Did he speak with you?"

"The rosâr treats me like a ward, not a princess. He is bossier than Kal ever was and always refuses to see me. If I want to speak to him, I must send messages through his sisters, guards, or staff. His wife is desperately sick, yet he has no time for her either. He cares about nothing but his own agenda. It rules his life."

"Master Harton would never have treated you so ill."

Her heart pinged at the mention of that name. She loved Harton Sonber, so help her. "But he left me. He is gone and cannot return. So I am trapped here, ruled by a man who wants nothing to do with me."

"You are too impatient, lady. I told you that if you helped me, Harton would be able to return."

She shook her head and dabbed a tear before it fell. "He has Lilou Caridod now. I saw the way she looked at him the night they escaped. He wouldn't remember me."

Kamran put his hand on her shoulder and squeezed. "Harton misses you, my dear."

"How would you know?"

"Because I talk to him. With the voices. And he tells me things."

She perked up. "But Harton is not royalty. I thought only royals could—"

"I am royalty, lady. And just as I can talk to you, I can talk to him."

Her pulse quickened as it always did when Sir Kamran spoke to her mind. "Master Harton mentioned me? Truly?"

Kamran sighed as if speaking of such things pained him. "Being parted from you torments him, lady. He feels responsible for your welfare, having deserted you to save his own neck."

Does he really? "But he had no choice. Had he stayed, he would have been hanged for attacking the sâr."

Kamran looked out at the horizon. "He sometimes tells me he wished he had stayed and died honorably rather than to have deserted you like a scoundrel."

Oh, Harton! "No, he was right to flee. I wanted him to live."

Kamran took her hand in his. "If you wish to see him again, you must help me, good lady. Rosâr Wilek is destroying New Armania and must be stopped. Once a man of sense takes the throne, Harton can return."

"Then Sâr Trevn could rule. Everyone says he is very clever, and if he brings home my sister as his bride, then I would be sister to the queen."

"Now there is an idea. With your sister as queen, you would surely be heard. Do you think *Rosâr Trevn* would pardon Master Harton?"

She considered it. "I'm not sure. If Mielle asked him to, he might. So I would have to convince Mielle to help me."

"I am sure your sister would do anything to see you happy."

Amala frowned, no longer certain. "She never has before. She scolded me as much as Kal. Who else could rule Armania if not Sâr Trevn?"

"Well, let me think." Sir Kamran tapped his chin. "What of this idea? Harton serves King Barthel, who has made a claim to Sarikar. He might be persuaded to bring Sarikar and Armania under one nation. Greater numbers would protect us against the giants. And King Barthel would bring Armania back to the Rôb faith."

Amala knew nothing of King Barthel. "What would become of Rosâr Wilek and Sâr Trevn? And the sârahs and Rosârah Brelenah? King Barthel wouldn't do anything dreadful, would he?"

"Royals have immunity in such situations," Kamran said. "They would be given a new role in the realm—at worst be stripped of their titles and made lords and ladies. But King Barthel would need a reason to challenge Rosâr Wilek. Harton asked me to help, but I can't do it alone."

Amala wrung her hands. "What do you want me to do?"

"It's very simple. I need to look around the royal chambers every now and then to see what I can learn. As one of Queen Zeroah's honor maidens, you have access. When the rooms are empty, unlock the servants' door. That way I can go inside and have a look."

"But how will you know to come?"

"I have my ways. Now, you must not wait for me. Unlock the door and go elsewhere. Can you do that, lady? Will you?"

Amala heaved a deep sigh, reluctant to give any man access to a woman's bedchamber. "I don't see why I can't search for whatever it is you are looking for. I am competent, you know."

"I dare not risk your safety, lady. If something were to happen, Harton would never forgive me. I don't mind risking myself. Even as the stray son of a dead king, I can still get away with much that you could not."

"I'm *supposed* to be royalty." Adopted royalty. But royalty all the same.

"You see why we cannot trust Rosâr Wilek as king, don't you?" Kamran said. "He does not keep his word."

No, he did not. "Very well," Amala said. "I will help you."

So from that day on Amala began unlocking the servants' door to the royal apartment in Castle Armanguard whenever it was empty, hoping that when King Barthel took over and Harton returned, they might finally be together.

KALENEK

K al made his way through the dark tent toward the sound of Shanek's screams. The boy looked to be about fifteen now, practically a man. Once Charlon had become Chieftess, Kal had convinced her to stop giving Shanek evenroot, and his growth had slowed some. This did not stop the voices from sometimes waking him in the night.

Kal crouched beside the boy's bed of furs and rubbed his back. "Wake up, Shan. You're safe. I'm here."

Shanek's eyes opened and he stopped squirming. "He want kill Rosâr Wilek."

The words struck Kal deep. "Who?"

"Barthel."

Rogedoth. "It's just a dream," Kal said, though he knew that it wasn't. It had only been a few days since he had spoken with Wilek. They likely wouldn't speak again for another week. "Do you still hear them?"

Shanek shook his head. "Shut them out."

"Good," Kal said, thankful that Wilek had known what to do with this new magic. "That's good." He hoped Rogedoth had only been venting his desire to kill Wilek and not planning anything concrete.

Kal stayed with Shanek until he fell asleep, then returned to his own tent, his mind a conflicted tangle of thoughts. The boy might look fifteen and the root might have helped his mind develop faster, but as he had been alive less than a year, he had not the benefit of life experience to teach him judgment and common sense. Each day he got into more mischief. There were no children in the Magosian camp, so Shanek had no one to play with but shadir. Kal had tried to fill that role, but Charlon kept him busy hunting, plowing fields, and planting root. And while Kal was busy elsewhere, Shanek ran free with the shadir.

Shanek was known by all to be a pest, always sneaking into places he didn't belong. Far too many times Kal had punished the boy for stealing or playing pranks or watching the women bathe or dress. The sound of a scream delighted him, whether it be in anger, surprise, or frustration. Once Shanek had learned to move like Grayson, there was no catching him. He appeared and disappeared all over camp, frightening people to the point of madness. Roya, Kateen, and Astaa had all demanded he stay away from their tents.

As unabashed as these women tended to be, Kal didn't know why they cared what the boy saw. Regardless, most saw the ever-growing Shanek as a nuisance. Only Charlon treated him like the king she hoped he'd someday turn out to be.

In the past week his actions had gotten bolder. Not only did he spy on the women or play pranks, he grabbed them. Kal had sat him down, man to man, and explained about how a man must respect a woman's privacy. None of it mattered. Shanek might have the body of a young man, but his mind was that of a spoiled child. He saw himself as superior to everyone else, an opinion bolstered by Charlon's near worship of the boy, and he did not understand why he couldn't do whatever he wanted.

"You cannot expect him to live like an Armanian," Charlon said when Kal complained.

"You brought me here to train him to behave like one," Kal said. "I warn you, if you take him to Armania and try to claim the throne and he pops in and out of women's private chambers like a deviant, don't be surprised when no one wishes to make him their king."

"I don't like it. Any better than you," Charlon said, "but what can we do?"

"He needs discipline," Kal said. "He needs to learn right from wrong."

"But he doesn't listen," Charlon said.

"Punish him. Put a compulsion on him to keep him from leaving his tent. After a few days you can remove it and give him another chance. If he disobeys again, put the compulsion back on him. He must learn about consequences."

"A prince is above punishment," Charlon said. "I will give him servants. Servants of his own. Any other prince would have them."

"That will only fuel the fire," Kal said.

"You have tried and failed, Sir Kalenek," Charlon said. "Now it's my turn."

So Charlon gave Shanek two male servants to attend him, and Zweena, the youngest of her five maidens, to teach him the ways of romance. It sickened Kal, but it was not all that different from when Wilek had been given Lady Lebetta on his fifteenth ageday. The difference was that Wilek had been raised with some concept of morality and self-control and Shanek had neither.

That did not keep Kal from trying to teach him. Though such things had never been Kal's strength, he gave daily lessons in etiquette, speech, manners, and even dance. Zweena's patience surpassed his own, and he admired the girl for it, though as the days passed, Kal could sense her frustration deepen.

One midday in Shanek's tent, Kal had seated Shanek and Zweena across from each other at a table and chairs he had built. He had also carved trenchers and bowls from trees and was attempting to teach Shanek table manners.

"Why we can't sit on the mat?" Shanek asked.

"Because that is not how it is done in Armania."

"I'm gone be king; I change it."

"But you will never be king if you cannot impress the people of Armania, and sitting on the floor and eating with your hands will not impress them."

"Don't glare," Shanek said to Zweena.

"I am not glaring," she replied.

"Smile," Shanek said. "I want you smile."

Zweena faked a smile.

"No! Real smile. Smile real smile right now."

"There is nothing to smile about," Zweena said. "I hate you. I only spend time with you because the Chieftess makes me."

Kal took a deep breath. "Zweena, that was uncalled for."

"Why?" Shanek asked. "Why everyone hate Shanek?"

"Because you're strange and scary and I don't like the way you look at me," Zweena said. "You aren't normal."

"Am too!" Shanek yelled.

"Normal people care about other people's feelings. You only care about yourself."

"Stop talking!"

"Don't yell at me, you disgusting lecher!"

Shanek stood up, breathing hard and fast through his nose like a bull about to charge. He reached across the table. Kal darted forward but stopped when Shanek's hands started to glow with green light. The boy's eyes widened and he stared at his hands—they all stared.

As suddenly as the light had come, it vanished.

"What was that?" Kal asked, wary.

Shanek choked back a sob, his eyes fixed on Zweena. "I didn't mean it."

Kal turned his head, and what he saw stole his breath.

Zweena still sat in her chair, clearly dead, face ashen, glassy eyes open and staring at nothing. How she'd died, Kal couldn't guess. He saw no marks on her.

Dread coiled in Kal's gut. "Has that happened before, Shan?"

The boy was visibly shaking. "Not a girl. A gowzal bit me, and I kill it."

"How did you do it?" Kal asked. "What went through your mind?"

Tears pooled in Shanek's eyes. He seemed shocked and hurt. Zweena had hurt his feelings and died because of it. "She made Shanek mad." He panted, losing control of his emotions. When he spoke again, his voice came out whiny and slurred. "Grabbed her thoughts. Gone make her say nice words. Felt . . . strong. Hands burned. Then light went out."

Leery, Kal studied the boy. What *was* he?

When Kal got angry, he was a danger because his mind flashed back to the war and he sometimes hurt people without meaning to. While that was clearly terrible, this was far worse.

"Said Shanek not normal. Disgusting. Only care for Shanek." His voice trailed off.

"Do you?"

A tear dripped down his cheek as he looked up from Zweena and met Kal's eyes. "What you think?"

"Maybe sometimes," Kal said, hoping to speak the truth and still keep the boy calm.

Shanek's eyebrows sank low, and he looked so much like Janek at that moment that Kal shuddered. "How Shanek learn?"

So help him, Kal loved the boy. What Mreegan had done in making him grow so fast wasn't fair. Nor was Charlon's decree that everyone treat him like a king. Shanek wasn't evil. He was a babe in a man's body with far too much freedom and zero consequences apart from Kal's censure. "We can talk about that later, Shan. I will teach you what you want to know, but you'll have to listen to me. You'll have to try to change, do you hear me?"

Shanek sniffled, nodded, and ran the back of his hand over his nose.

"Good," Kal said. "We must teach you to handle your anger." He nearly laughed. People had been trying to teach Kal to handle his anger for years.

He recalled some of the things Jhorn had suggested and supposed it couldn't hurt to try.

He would have to warn Wilek the next time he checked in, though he worried his king would demand Kal kill the boy. Shanek hadn't meant to hurt Zweena. Perhaps once he understood his power better, he would be able to control it. If Kal could work on Shanek's conscience, he might someday refuse Charlon's demand that he attempt to usurp the Armanian throne.

It was worth a try, wasn't it? Kal had put in too much time and hard work to give up on the boy now.

Trevn

In the dead of night, Ulagan—who turned out to be the headman's orange-haired translator—led Trevn, Saria, and fifty-two of their people from the slave tunnels along a wide corridor in the lowest level of the fortress. There were still over two hundred Sarikarians left behind, but Grayson said they shouldn't take more than two boats at once, and so they'd brought as many as they could fit.

They entered a steaming chamber that housed an underground reamway hot spring. Where the stone floor ended and the river passed by, two animal-skin longboats were tied to the landing with twine ropes. Above the water, on the topside of the reamway, dripstones hung thick, sprinkling drops every now and then.

Mosquitoes swarmed. Trevn must have slapped several dozen away as he waited for the people to climb into the boats. Ulagan gave instructions about the bowl lamps, reekats, and using the paddles to keep the crafts from crashing into the stone walls. There would be no place to stop, so they'd have to take shifts.

"Tell me when you reach the ocean," Grayson said, "and I'll come meet you."

"How long will it take?" Trevn asked.

"Two and a half days," Grayson said. "Since it's night, you'll probably get there around dawn three days from now. I'll meet you there and help you find your ship."

Trevn bid farewell to Ulagan and Grayson, and climbed into the first boat. Ulagan untied the rope, and the current sucked the craft down the reamway, blowing a soft, humid breeze back in Trevn's face. The low bowl light cast a faint gleam over the rock walls, which were slimy, brown, and had formed dripstone-like textures down the surface. Overall it was very dark. Waterdrops fell from the dripstones like a light sprinkling of rain. The river was mostly straight, and the paddles were rarely needed.

Trevn sat in the bow a long while, but he finally realized that there was nothing to see and settled down to voice Captain Bussie, Mielle, Wilek, and Hinck in that order.

Trevn told Captain Bussie he was on the way and to remain anchored in the inlet until he arrived.

Mielle was thrilled to hear Trevn had escaped without trouble. *"I hope it won't be long now before we see each other."*

Trevn's escape pleased Wilek too. *"One burden lifted,"* he said. *"Now if only I could get Sarikar to join me against Rogedoth, defeat him, and my wife and son's health would improve."*

"They are still unwell?" Trevn asked.

"Their eyes no longer water, and Chadek has gained a little weight. Kal thinks they might have been poisoned. Rayim suggested I ask King Loran for help, and he is sending his personal physician, who should arrive soon."

"Surely he will know what to do," Trevn said, sensing the worry in his brother.

Hinck had been spying more carefully ever since Rogedoth had tried to kill him. Arman's healing had cleared his name, as far as he could tell. Even Rosârah Laviel had been kind of late. Rogedoth had focused on New Sarikar and continued to direct Fonu and his squadron of compelled giants to wreak havoc on the outer settlements. He also wanted to capture Grayson. He had sacrificed his daughter Darlis to create the root child and felt the boy belonged to him. Trevn promised Hinck he would do everything he could to keep Grayson far from Rogedoth's grasp.

Trevn grew restless trapped in the longboat, but as predicted, on the third day the reamway emptied into the inlet. The morning was bright and sunny. A cool breeze gave welcome relief after days of stifling, humid air. As the movement of the boat slowed against the gentle rocking waves, the motion filled Trevn with a longing remembrance of the months he had spent at sea.

"Grayson," Trevn voiced. *"We've reached the inlet."*

The boy appeared suddenly in their boat, landing atop Maleen, who howled in surprise.

Grayson laughed it off. "Sorry about that. Knowing where I'll pop out is always tricky."

The boy directed the soldiers to paddle the boats to a nearby cave, where they tied them up with several others.

Grayson led the way on foot along a reddish-brown, clay-like dirt road that wound north along the coast. A narrow expanse of giant trees separated them from the beach, the ground underneath covered with spongy green moss and stiff ferns big enough to sit under.

Trevn walked in the middle of the procession near Princess Saria, who looked a little more like herself in the light of day. He voiced updates on their location to Wilek, Bussie, and Mielle, who felt closer than ever before.

"I feel it too," Mielle said. *"It won't be long until we are together again."*

The force of their combined joy caused Trevn to stumble into Princess Saria.

"Sorry." He loosened his hold on the connection to Mielle, fighting for a semblance of calm so that he could keep his balance.

"You're talking to someone, aren't you?" Saria asked. "I can hear it, muffled like a conversation someone is having behind a very thick door."

Surprised, Trevn asked, "Can you tell what was said?"

"Not at all. It's low, whispered nonsense. Who are you speaking to?"

"My wife," Trevn said.

Saria frowned, suddenly looking fragile. "Miss Mielle is truly alive, then?"

"Oh yes," Trevn said. "Captain Stockton and I estimate that she is but forty leagues—"

The soldier in front of Trevn and Saria grunted and fell. Up ahead two more went down. Men shouted as they whipped around or dove into the ferns, weaponless.

Trevn felt Mielle's fear spike as she reacted to the excitement within him. *"Trevn, what's wrong?"* she asked.

"We are under attack. Pray."

Cadoc pulled Trevn under some leathery ferns. Saria's guards had done the same, and she was crouched but an arm's length from him. The foliage hid them from sight, but it also obstructed their view of their attackers.

From what Trevn could see, the road was deserted now but for the body of the soldier who had been walking before them.

Grayson appeared under the bush, and Trevn barely managed to block Cadoc's arm as he instinctively moved to strike the newcomer.

If Grayson had noticed Cadoc, he didn't let on. "Giants attacking," he said. "There are eight. You've got four men down."

"We have no weapons," Cadoc said. "What can we do?"

Trevn despaired at the idea of being taken back to the beetle caves. On his left he could see the open water, a pale backdrop against a couple dozen tree trunks. "To the ocean?" he suggested.

"It'll put us out in the open," Cadoc said.

"*Wee nopla way. Suu!*"

Trevn peeked over the fern. A giant stood above them, hand raised and clutching a rock the size of a melon. As the giant glared down, an arrow pierced his cheek. He howled, dropped his rock, and doubled over.

"Go!" Cadoc yelled.

Trevn ran. Grayson quickly took the lead, disappearing and reappearing at intervals only a few steps ahead of each previous location. Cadoc clenched Trevn's arm and propelled him after the boy. The spongy moss underfoot made running awkward. Around them arrows and rocks flew as the giants and their mysterious attackers engaged in battle. A rock grazed Cadoc's shoulder, struck Trevn's wrist, and tumbled into the moss. Trevn lurched, but only slowed a moment before Cadoc yanked him onward.

The forest ended on a ledge, dropping sharply to where the sand of the beach began. With no time to stop, Cadoc yelled, "Jump!"

Trevn leapt down the incline. His feet sank into deep sand that shifted under his weight. Beside him Cadoc slipped and dragged Trevn down with him.

Trevn hit the ground on his side and rolled, ripping out of Cadoc's hold. When he stopped, he looked back up the hill. Saria and her men were running toward them. A few paces to the right, Maleen and Ottee were crawling down the slope. Ten total, Cadoc and himself included. They were missing four-fifths of their party. And where had Grayson gone? On the plus side he saw no giants, even though he could still hear the occasional scream within the forest.

"Your Highness," Cadoc said, nodding out to sea.

Trevn pushed himself up and followed Cadoc's gaze. A ship was anchored in the small cove. Hope soared at the idea of boarding the *Seffynaw*, but this ship was much smaller, a two-masted, lateen-rigged cog. Trevn quickly sought out the name on the side.

Taradok.

He knew that name but couldn't place it.

Grayson appeared between Trevn and Cadoc. "Zahara rescued us," he said.

"Will you stop doing that?" Cadoc asked.

Grayson frowned. "Should I, Your Highness?"

"It's all right, Grayson. It will just take some getting used to. Now, who is Zahara?"

"She wants to talk to you. See? She's coming now." Grayson pointed up to where some bedraggled pirates were easing their way down the incline. Behind them groups of Trevn's and Saria's men emerged from the forest.

Trevn suddenly remembered where he'd heard the name *Taradok*. "She's Randmuir Khal's daughter. Grayson, you should hide yourself."

"She's on our side," Grayson said.

"Pirates are only ever on their own side," Cadoc said.

The woman arrived then, dressed in a black tunic and breeches like the rest of the pirates. She was short and stocky; the sleeves of her tunic clung to muscled arms. She smirked as she appraised Cadoc. "Who's the smart one, Grayson? He knows a lot about pirates."

"That's Cadoc. He's Sâr Trevn's shield."

Zahara turned her dark gaze on Trevn. "And you're the highborn royal."

Trevn's cheeks burned, and he did his best to return her smoldering stare. "You wish to talk to me?"

"Not me," she said. "My father does."

Cadoc stepped between Trevn and Zahara. "That's not going to happen."

"My but you're a loyal man." Zahara winked at Cadoc. "Your concern is unnecessary. My father needs your royal's help. None of us mean him any harm."

"Why would I help the man who wants to kill my brother?" Trevn asked.

"Because if you help him, he'll declare a truce with all you royals."

A simple conversation was a fair price to pay for a potential truce with the pirates. "Where is he?"

Zahara walked away and motioned him to follow. "I'll take you to him."

✦ ✦ ✦

A short hike through the forest brought them to a clearing filled with the one-sided cape tents of the Omatta nomads. The tops of the canvas clung to a single pole while the wide ends were pegged into the ground, forming an army of half-circle cones. Trevn selected ten soldiers to follow him into Randmuir's camp. He made Grayson stay behind with Princess Saria.

Cadoc and three soldiers entered the tent with Zahara to make sure it was safe before allowing Trevn inside. When Cadoc declared all was well, he and

Trevn stepped inside alone, leaving the others to guard the entrance. What Trevn found inside rendered him speechless.

Randmuir Khal had been tied up like some kind of captive. Thick braided hemp circled his torso at least twenty times, pinning his arms to his sides. Not only that, his legs were bound as well, trussed from ankle to knee. Additional ropes had been lashed to those bindings and staked into the ground like guy lines.

"You found the mantic boy?" Randmuir asked Zahara, eager.

"He's obsessed with catching Grayson," Zahara told Trevn. "It got so bad I had to tie him up. He's forgotten who he is. What matters to him."

"Who is this?" Randmuir asked, eyes narrowed at Trevn.

"This is Sâr Trevn Hadar," Zahara said.

Randmuir's eyes lit up. "Royal spawn. Tell me how your brother broke the soul-binding between him and the mantic witch."

Pity for the man gave Trevn pause, but he could only answer truthfully. "He got lucky. His backman at the time turned out to be a mantic. He was able to undo the spell."

Randmuir grunted. "I doubt his mantic would be willing to help a pirate."

"He's no longer Wilek's mantic. He turned traitor and is in Rogedoth's camp now, serving as the man's general."

Laughing, Randmuir tipped back his head, which was the only part of him that wasn't tied in place. "See now? You royal spawn use people enough, they'll pay you back."

Trevn hadn't come here to be insulted. "Is there anything else I can do for you, Master Randmuir?"

His face twisted in sorrow. "Help me break this compulsion. I can't go on like this."

"I'm sorry," Trevn said. "I don't know how."

Randmuir's face darkened with rage and he screamed, straining against the ropes that bound him.

Zahara raised her voice over her father's fit and asked, "Why did Sâr Wilek kill my grandmother?"

That quieted Randmuir.

"He didn't," Trevn said. "Charlon Sonber killed her."

"That crow who soul-bound your brother?" Randmuir asked.

"The same. She has also killed the Magonian Chieftess and taken the role as her own. Last I heard, she has settled midway up the Great River. We suspect she means to attack us at some point, so Wilek is doing all he can to ensure peace between the realms."

"See now? That's exactly why I hate royalty. Who do they think they are to tell the rest of us what to do? I'm done with it. Because of your brother king, my mother is dead and my son is still deformed. We'll all be better off when Wilek Hadar becomes worm food."

Trevn didn't care for the pirate's threats or caustic tone. "I understand your anger, but your blame is misplaced. All of our troubles have been caused by mantics and their shadir, looking to further their own agendas. If you want to blame someone, look there."

"You think I don't know that?" Randmuir snapped. "But what else can I do? My daughter has had to bind me so I won't lead my tribe into madness."

"Trust Arman," Trevn said, thinking of how the God had saved Hinck. "Only the Father God can set you free."

Randmuir chuckled at this, so Trevn went on.

"My friend Hinck was dying when he called out to Arman. The God answered his faith by healing him. I ask only that you consider the possibility. Understanding takes time."

"Crazy royal spawn," Randmuir mumbled. "You have no idea how powerful shadir are, do you? They are always watching. You might think you can hide things from them, but you can't. They see everything."

"Without Arman, the only way to remove the spell is to find a mantic," Trevn said. "There are no mantics in Armania anymore. If you want one, you have to go to Rogedoth or Charlon. Otherwise, the compulsion will stay with you your whole life."

Randmuir's eyes widened. "Finally an option that makes sense. Dying is the way to free the Omatta tribe from my compulsion. Zahara, bring me a knife."

"No one is dying," Zahara said. "I thank you for coming, Sâr Trevn. I'll walk you out."

✦ ✦ ✦

Trevn voiced Captain Bussie as they left the Omatta camp, and with Grayson's help, by dusk, they had reached the ship. Trevn stepped out of the dinghy and onto the quarterdeck, where Captain Bussie, Nietz, and Rzasa were waiting.

"Shinn is in the hold?" Trevn asked.

"Yes, Your Highness. Still doesn't know why, though."

Trevn had no time to talk with Shinn now. "He'll have to go on wondering. We'll stay here for the night and leave at dawn to find Mielle and the others."

"How will we find them?" Cadoc asked.

"With Grayson's help."

Trevn sent Ottee to fetch Mielle's cloak from the cabin. The moment he returned and placed it in Trevn's hands, Mielle felt closer.

"The mind-speak magic doesn't work well between strangers," Trevn said, handing Grayson the cloak, "but as I learned with your boots, if you hold a personal belonging, it can create a link. Use this and see if you can travel to Mielle. I've already told her to expect you and what you look like. If you can find her, maybe you can figure out the best route to reach her."

"I'll do it right now," Grayson said, and he disappeared.

"Can he not give a warning?" Cadoc asked. "Say farewell before he pops away?"

"He is eager to please, Cadoc. I like that about him."

"I don't see her," Grayson voiced.

"Don't give up so soon," Trevn said.

"I'll find her, Your Highness. I promise."

Trevn hoped so.

✦ ✦ ✦

It took a lot of willpower not to voice Grayson and Mielle constantly to ask whether or not they were together. Trevn stood on the main deck with a grow lens and surveyed the surrounding land. From this vantage point the great forest ran for leagues to the south. The mountain range filled the distant southwest, with that one massive peak towering above the others. Directly west were flatlands and forest. And in the distant north another mountain chain stretched out of sight. Mielle was somewhere between the two mountain ranges, that much Trevn knew.

"Are you going to leave me behind?"

Trevn lowered the grow lens and regarded Princess Saria. She had cleaned herself up but still wore the uniform of a Sarikarian soldier. "I claim no authority over you, Princess," he said. "Whatever I have is at your disposal. If you want to leave, feel free. Or you are welcome to remain on the *Seffynaw*."

"Being here makes me nervous," she said. "I had no desire to step foot on a sailing ship ever again. Might we go with you? My men would double your numbers."

"I would welcome the help." Trevn had no idea what they would do if they met giants; he also doubted Mielle would be pleased to see Princess Saria in his company. He would have to warn her ahead of time.

"Your Highness!"

Trevn had barely spotted Grayson waving at him from the quarterdeck when the boy vanished and, in a blink, appeared at Trevn's side. Saria yelped and clapped a hand over her heart.

"You scared me!" she said.

"I found her, Your Highness," Grayson said. "There's a—" His eyes lost focus as he stared just above Trevn's head. *"Ragaz is here. We should talk in our heads. There's a great lake not too far that way."* He pointed west. *"It stretches for leagues and leagues. We are at one end of the lake, and Miss Mielle is at the other."*

✦　✦　✦

Because of the presence of Fonu's shadir, Trevn wrote out his orders to Captain Bussie. Trevn would take a party west on foot, heading toward the great lake. The *Seffynaw* would remain anchored until receiving further instructions.

"We will await your orders, Your Highness," Captain Bussie said. "It sounds like a fair distance to travel on foot. How will you find her?"

Trevn tapped his temple. "We will find each other, Captain. Communication is the most powerful tool Arman has given us. If we use it well, we cannot fail."

QⓄATCH

Months had passed since Empress Jazlyn's magic had run out. A small wooden castle had been built in New Rurekau, and still Qoatch wasn't used to his Great Lady's true visage, especially now that she was pregnant.

The child was growing far too fast. It must have somehow kept a portion of its mother's magic, even though she could no longer wield any power. In late summer the labor pains began.

Emperor Ulrik and his great-aunt sent in their midwives, but Jazlyn cast them out and called her own women to attend her. Qoatch was commanded to stay. He was a eunuch, after all, and the empress's most loyal servant.

Qoatch did not recall seeing Masi the slight leave, but as the Tennish midwives coached Jazlyn through one of her greater pains, Gozan arrived in all his intimidating hideousness. Qoatch hadn't seen the great shadir since he had deserted them months ago and left Masi behind to spy.

"What are you doing here?" Qoatch hissed. "Leave us be."

Gozan swelled in size until his head brushed the ceiling. *Do not worry, eunuch. I'll not interfere.*

"You'd better not," Qoatch said, as if there was something he could do about it. "Did you find a new host?"

That is none of your concern.

"Neither is our life any longer your concern, yet you leave Masi to spy on us and report back to you. Now you come here where you are not welcome. What do you want from us?"

545

I have invested many more years with this woman than you have. I've earned the right to witness this moment.

Qoatch doubted Jazlyn would agree. "Stay then, but once the baby arrives, take your slight and be gone."

Gozan chuckled. *So fierce for a eunuch.*

Qoatch fought the urge to continue arguing with the creature. The labor did not seem to progress, and he worried for his Great Lady. Tenma had laws against women taking root when they meant to conceive, and for good reason. Everyone knew that a woman who conceived while taking ahvenrood would surely die. Qoatch hoped that the little root Jazlyn had taken to maintain her beauty hadn't been enough to matter.

Day passed into night, and still the baby did not arrive. Qoatch mopped Jazlyn's brow with a wet cloth. He fanned her. He sang when she asked and ceased when she lost her patience. He prayed continually to Tenma for mercy and even made offerings to the bronze figurine of Tenma in Jazlyn's chambers.

Just before dawn, nearly two full days after Jazlyn's pains had begun, she delivered a boy with dark brown skin and eyes like coal.

The women cooed and cheered and exclaimed over the child. He did not seem overly large. Had Jazlyn somehow managed to hoard the last of her magic to speed up the pregnancy but keep it from affecting her child? That didn't seem possible, yet here was a healthy baby boy, squealing and delighting all the women. At fifty-four years of age, his Great Lady had given the young Emperor Ulrik a son and lived. Praise to the great goddess Tenma for her generous mercy.

A scream from Jazlyn silenced the revelry. The baby was handed to Qoatch as the women rushed to the empress's side.

"There is a second child!" one of the midwives exclaimed.

A second.

Things happened quickly this time around. Qoatch barely had a chance to comprehend the idea when a girl was lifted into the air to a round of exultation.

Two children?

The girl was slightly larger than her brother, had gray eyes, and skin like a dapple gray. Qoatch instantly thought of the boy Grayson, who had traveled with them through Rurekau and had left the ship with Sir Kalenek. What did it mean?

Gozan's laughter caught Qoatch's attention.

"Why do you laugh, dark one?" Qoatch asked.

She does beat every expectation, does she not?

"I am proud of her," Qoatch said.

Two children. And one a root child. My, won't Chieftess Charlon be jealous?

"Root children are myth," Qoatch said.

I assure you they are not, Gozan said. *If not for the boy, the female would have grown overly large and Jazlyn would have died.*

"Then I am grateful for Tenma's provision," Qoatch said. "I shall go now to make an offering of thanksgiving. When I return, I hope you will be gone."

✦ ✦ ✦

Jazlyn named her children without input from her husband. The girl she called Jahleeah, the boy Jael. She sent Qoatch to make the announcement to the people waiting outside the castle walls. A great cheer rose up, and a soldier demanded that Qoatch bring the children to the emperor's chambers so he could meet them. Jazlyn allowed only one child to leave at a time, worried that Ulrik might try to keep them from her. When the midwife brought Jael to trade for Jahleeah, she informed Jazlyn that the emperor had renamed the children Adir and Noyah.

"He is impossible," Jazlyn said. "I am hungry. Bring me some food."

Worried that someone might try to poison her now that the children had been born, Qoatch went to the kitchen, prepared her food, and served her himself. Once she was calmly eating, he told her about Gozan's visit and what the great shadir had said about Jahleeah being a root child.

"He is right, you know," she said. "I can feel the magic in her. If only there was some way to harness it."

"Gozan said that Chieftess Charlon of Magos would be jealous of you. She might have access to ahvenrood, but you have a treasure she would covet."

"Is that so? I must travel to Magos and meet this new Chieftess. As soon as I have recovered, I will take Jahleeah, and together we will form an alliance. The mother countries must help each other in this time of transition. While I am gone, you must—"

"A thousand pardons for interrupting, Great Lady," Qoatch said, bowing, "but Gozan has again sent Masi to spy on you. He is here now. Know that whatever you say, the slight will repeat to his master."

Masi hissed at Qoatch.

Jazlyn's face darkened into a mask of rage. "After all our years together Gozan would betray me? Fetch me parchment and quill."

Qoatch did, and his Great Lady wrote:

Jahleeah and I will travel to Magos and meet the new Chieftess. While I am gone you must kill Ulrik and his brother Ferro. Do it discreetly so that you are not caught or suspected. And keep my son safe. My goal is to barter enough ahvenrood from the Magosians to take control of New Rurekau in the aftermath of the emperor's death. If the Chieftess refuses my offers of riches, I am prepared to offer her Jael. He is male, but his being a prince should more than make up for his gender.

"Do you understand me?" she asked when he finished reading.

Qoatch nodded. As a trained assassin it would not be difficult to follow through on the order. His concern was that Jazlyn had overestimated her chances of success, and he didn't like being parted from her. He flipped over the parchment and wrote on the back.

The risk is too high. Gozan could have been lying about the Magosian Chieftess's interest in the child. If she were to refuse all your offers and you came home without ahvenrood to find the emperor and his brother dead, the emperor's officials would take the boy from you and put men in place to rule until Jael comes of age.

The Magosian Chieftess might simply kill you and keep Jahleeah for herself, then attack Rurekau and take Jael as well. You are too vulnerable without ahvenrood of your own.

"Which is why I must get some," Jazlyn said, crumpling the parchment. "I am just as vulnerable now, so I might as well try. You worry too much, Qoatch. The mother countries have always worked together. My plans remain unchanged. You have your orders." She handed him the parchment. "Burn this."

✦ ✦ ✦

Jazlyn's impending trip to Magos would be the first time Qoatch had been parted from his Great Lady since he had been given to her as a child. He helped her prepare for the trip in secret while pondering the orders she had given him. He was torn. The odds that the Magosian Chieftess would give up even a single vial of precious ahvenrood were absurd. And since the Chieftess was Rurekan born, he doubted she would care about the history between the mother and father realms. Qoatch feared she would kill Jazlyn, conquer New Rurekau, and take both children as her own. If that happened and Qoatch killed the emperor and his brother, he would only be making a takeover easier for the Magosian Chieftess.

Yet he could not deny his Great Lady.

The killing, however, would be difficult. As a Kushaw assassin trained in countless ways to kill, his current circumstances made most of them impossible. Qoatch did not dare risk a physical attack, and he no longer had access to the poisons or venoms found in plants and animals from the Five Realms. Poison existed in all things. The danger was in the dosage. Anything could be toxic if one ingested enough, but Qoatch did not have time to test local plants. He needed something trustworthy. He opened his kit and found it poorly stocked. Most of his herbs were so dry they likely had no toxicity left, and his powders were quite low.

He picked up a vial of ground torterus fangs, and an idea seized him. When burned, the powder produced noxious fumes that, when inhaled in large quantities, put one into a dead sleep. Rurekans were obsessed with incense and burned it while sleeping. If Qoatch were to coat an incense stick with a liquid version of the powder, he would accomplish his task without leaving any kind of trail. After inhaling the poison, Ulrik and Ferro would die in three to four weeks without an antidote, and the dead sleep would give Qoatch ample time to prepare for Jazlyn's success or failure. Unless she was killed in Magos, he would be able to ensure her survival and position of power in Rurekau whether or not she succeeded in her own plans.

That decided, Qoatch created the incense sticks and ran through several test runs as to how he would deliver the poison, preparing for every eventuality. He did not want to get caught.

✦   ✦   ✦

One day when Emperor Ulrik, Prince Ferro, and their men had ridden into the mountains to hunt, Jazlyn took her daughter and her Tennish retinue and set off for Magos under the guise of taking a picnic. Masi went with her. Qoatch did not.

Qoatch's duty was to distract Queen Thallah from Jazlyn's departure, so he took Prince Jael to the woman and asked if she might be willing to keep watch over the boy for a few hours, claiming that Jazlyn was sometimes overwhelmed by having two infants. The only stipulation was that Qoatch remain as the child's bodyguard.

Queen Thallah was delighted to spend time with the babe, annoyed that the empress felt Qoatch superior to her own guards, and filled with criticism and advice for Jazlyn's care and rearing of the princeling. Qoatch bore it as well as he could. The longer he remained with Queen Thallah, the farther Jazlyn's party would get before anyone noticed they had not returned.

The day passed. Queen Thallah left for dinner, so Qoatch took Jael back to Jazlyn's chambers. Still, no one had noticed the empress was missing.

To be fair, Jazlyn had not been the most popular woman, even before her deceit had uncovered her true age. Despite her not having cast a spell in months, many still feared her. They had accepted her as empress only because Ulrik had chosen her, and once her true age had been revealed, she became hated. Giving birth to the twins had lifted some of the animosity against her, but Qoatch knew she was still thought of as rude, condescending, and unyielding.

Qoatch left Jael in the care of his nurse, and while the royal family was at dinner, he gathered his poisoned incense sticks and set out. He made an easy task of slipping into the emperor's bedchamber unnoticed. There were five incense holders in the room: three positioned near the bed and two on the opposite wall. Qoatch removed the incense sticks in each holder and replaced them with his own.

He went to Ferro's bedchamber next and met a maid there. He tucked his hands behind his back, hiding the incense sticks, and greeted her warmly, quickly spitting out the first excuse that came to mind.

"Might you help me? One of the midwives hinted that Prince Ferro had a box of toys from his younger days that he no longer plays with. She thought there might be something in there to please the twins."

The maid's face lit up. "Yes, I imagine there would, but I'm not certain where that box might be. So many things are in the wrong place after moving from the ships to the tents and then into the castle. Oh, perhaps in the wardrobe. Let me just take a look."

When the woman entered the wardrobe, Qoatch switched out the incense in the holders. Here there were only two, mounted on the walls on either side of the bed. Prince Ferro was much smaller than his brother. Qoatch hoped that two would produce enough smoke to affect the boy.

He folded the remaining incense sticks into his gathered waistband and awaited the maid. She returned shortly with a small box, which she set on the bed and opened. Qoatch moved to her side and inspected the contents as she lifted out a coconut rattle and shook it.

"They should like that, don't you think?" she asked.

"So much that they might fight over it."

The maid pulled more toys from the box, cooing over each: a carved wooden bear, a ceramic spinning top, a wooden ox on wheels, and a striped ball made of linen. The sight of these worn things birthed a terrible chill in Qoatch's heart. Ferro had always been a nice child. Qoatch didn't like the idea of killing him.

"I should get back," he said, closing the lid on the box. "Thank you for these."

"I'm just glad I found them," she said. "Every child should have a toy."

Qoatch had never had a toy. He tucked the box under his arm and returned to Jazlyn's apartment. He found Jael awake and tried to give him the rattle.

"He's too little to hold that now," the maid said. "Another six months, perhaps?"

Qoatch realized he knew nothing at all about children beyond guessing their weight to figure the proper dosage of poison. Ferro's face flashed in his mind again, and relief at having completed his assignment warred with regret.

Qoatch would remain here in Jazlyn's apartment until he heard news. Had he any peers, the action might be considered cowardly, but he felt it better not to risk a chance at meeting the eyes of the child he had murdered.

CHARL⊙N

C harlon had achieved all she'd desired. She was now Chieftess. Both Mother and ruler. Ultimate power. It didn't matter that some of Magon's shadir had fled. Refused to serve Rurek. Charlon had plenty of loyal supporters.

As summer neared its end, Charlon ordered the harvest—of the natural crop, grown without spells to quicken growth. Tested it. The root remained plain. No magic through human ingestion.

No matter. She was learning to make magic here. Using the gowzals. The abilities were different than what she could power with magical ahvenrood. Gowzals could be used to create masks and illusions. The creatures could even be turned into weapons like balls of green flame, arrows, or swords. But Charlon could not use them to cast compulsions. She could not inflict pain. And she could not control the forces of nature.

Still, in light of her dwindling ahvenrood stores, she was thankful to be able to perform some magic. She had told no one about her discovery. So while her ahvenrood stores from the Five Realms decreased and her mantics despaired, Charlon remained powerful. Respected by her people. Safe.

No one could hurt her again.

So why did she feel so unsettled?

The prophecy Mreegan had lived by promised renewal. Promised that the Deliverer would restore the mother countries to power. Maybe then Charlon would find peace. For now, Shanek wasn't ready.

Rurek appeared at her side. *Empress Jazlyn of Rurekau comes with a con-*

tingent of thirty guards and twenty more servants. My slights say she will arrive before nightfall.

A tinge of fear. "Comes here? Why?"

I did not ask her.

"How many shadir accompany her?"

None, Chieftess. My guess is that she comes seeking ahvenrood.

Amusing. The empress had once been a Great Lady, Priestess of Tenma. A highly revered mantic. But the woman had run out of ahvenrood. Had married the young emperor to retain some level of power. Charlon pitied her. Saw again how her new magic set her apart. Gave hope for the future.

An hour later Gullik escorted a messenger to the red tent. Charlon sat the ironthorn throne. Received them.

"You bring word of Empress Jazlyn, I presume?" Charlon said to the messenger. "She will be here before nightfall."

The young man's eyes swelled. "Yes, Chieftess. How did you know?"

"I know many things," Charlon said. "Your empress is welcome. Will she require lodging?"

"No," the messenger said. "We have brought tents. I will tell her she is expected."

A nod of dismissal and the messenger scurried away.

"What do you think?" she asked Rurek.

My opinion has not changed. She comes to beg ahvenrood.

"Shall I give her some?"

That would be foolish. She is cunning and not to be trusted.

"Yet she would make a powerful ally."

To what end? Magos has no threats at the moment.

"But we might someday," Charlon said. "Best to have friends in place. Before trouble comes."

✦ ✦ ✦

Magos prepared for visitors. Prepared a feast. Planned a celebration. Charlon received Empress Jazlyn in the red tent. Shanek and her Five Men were all present. Sir Kalenek permitted only four of Jazlyn's guards to enter.

Charlon had heard rumors. The old mantic priestess had fooled the young emperor into marriage. She now had long gray hair and a slight frame. Regal posture. Fierce brown eyes. She honored Charlon with a deep curtsy.

"Welcome to Magos, Empress," Charlon said, nodding.

"I am pleased to make your acquaintance," Jazlyn said, straightening back to her full height, which wasn't much taller than Charlon. Her dark gaze flitted between Sir Kalenek and Shanek, brow creased. Something about the men bothered her. "Thank you for receiving us so warmly. Your predecessor did not approve of Tennish mantics."

"We are the realm of Magos now," Charlon said. "Everything is new. The one called Mreegan is dead. Along with the great shadir Magon."

Jazlyn's eyes widened. "How was this done?"

Charlon smiled, amused. Did the empress think her foolish? Foolish enough to share such information? "That is my secret to keep."

She will ask about me next, Rurek said in Charlon's ear. *Tell her I am Mitsar.*

As if Rurek had read Jazlyn's mind, she asked, "What shadir powered such magic?"

"She is called Mitsar," Charlon said.

Shanek laughed. Sir Kalenek scowled, shushed the boy.

Charlon's answer seemed to pacify the empress. "I am surprised to see Sir Kalenek of Armania here," she said. "Is he your prisoner?"

She knew Sir Kalenek? Charlon tried not to let surprise show. "He is the first of my Five Men. Shield to my son Shanek." Charlon nodded to Shanek, who dutifully dipped his head to the empress. Behaving again, thankfully.

Jazlyn fixed all her attention on Sir Kalenek. "His scars are gone. He looks different."

"Magic can change appearances. As you well know," Charlon said.

Jazlyn sighed. "But the shadir decide when to make it permanent or temporary. My beauty required a continual spell. After I ran out of ahvenrood, my true age was revealed."

"Yet you married," Charlon said. "Married the man who destroyed your root."

Annoyance flashed in Jazlyn's eyes. "I did what I had to do to maintain some level of power. Otherwise my people would have been forced to live in Rurekau as foreigners with no rights. You have a vast settlement here. Is that field I passed all ahvenrood?"

How quickly she steered the conversation. In the direction she wanted it to go. "It is."

She is desperate now that she has no root, Rurek said.

"No root, no root," Shanek said.

Irritation flared. Could Sir Kalenek not keep the boy silent?

Jazlyn peered at Shanek, but she spoke just as Rurek had predicted. "How I would love a taste of Er'Retian root," she said.

"I fear it would disappoint you," Charlon said. "It does not grow the same here as it did in the Five Realms."

Concern wrinkled Jazlyn's brow. "I would like some just the same."

"Why would I give ahvenrood to my enemy?" Charlon asked.

"We are not enemies," Jazlyn said. "Tenma and Magonia are allies."

"They *were* allies. But this is no longer Magonia. This is Magos. And you are no longer from Tenma. You are from Rurekau. And Magos and Rurekau are not allied."

"Perhaps we should make a new allegiance," Jazlyn said.

"I am willing. To discuss the possibility," Charlon said. "But the emperor rules Rurekau. Not you."

"He will not rule for long," Jazlyn said. "There are many who hate him. I should not be surprised to find him dead when I return."

Interesting. Had she plotted to kill her husband? "That matters not," Charlon said. "Ahvenrood grows here. But it has no magic."

Jazlyn's eager expression folded. "That . . . that cannot be."

"It is," Charlon said. "See for yourself. Vald, bring the empress an ahvenrood plant. Wrap roots and soil in a moist cloth."

"Yes, Chieftess." He departed.

"You would give me a plant?" Jazlyn asked. "For nothing?"

Charlon waved away the woman's surprise. "It is no great gift. My ahvenrood from the Five Realms is all but gone. I planted most of it. Hoping to reap a great harvest. Alas, the roots have no magic. The soil is missing something. Or perhaps the overabundance of rain swamps it. Whatever the reason, the root has no magic."

Wild eyes. Fidgeting fingers. Charlon had crushed the empress's hope. "I don't believe it."

"This is a new land, Empress," Charlon said. "It will take time. Time to understand it fully."

An awkward moment of silence filled the tent. Jazlyn's dark gaze shifted from Charlon to Shanek and back.

"I don't know whether or not you've heard, but I recently gave birth to twins. A female and a male. I have brought my daughter Princess Jahleeah with me. Might I present her to you?"

"If you like," Charlon said.

A whisper from Jazlyn. One of her ladies scurried away. Returned shortly with a babe. A babe dressed in white linen like her mother.

Rurek had told Charlon about the root child. Dappled skin did not surprise Charlon. This child was much smaller. Smaller than Shanek had ever been. Yet the sight startled Charlon. Something foreign tightened inside. Brought back memories.

Shanek had grown far too fast.

"I cannot help but notice that my child and yours share the same skin and eyes," Jazlyn said, glancing again at Shanek. "Such attributes are rare, yet Sir Kalenek and I knew another young man like this. I did not know what he was at the time or I would not have parted with him."

More secrets? Charlon met Sir Kalenek's eyes. "Who was this root child?"

"His name is Grayson," Sir Kalenek said. "He traveled with us out of Rurekau during the Five Woes."

Grayson. The boy Sir Kalenek had helped escape the *Vespara*.

"What mantic birthed Grayson, Sir Kalenek?" Jazlyn asked.

"I know not," he said.

He is lying, Rurek said.

Charlon would make Sir Kalenek talk later. Once the empress had gone.

"Darlis," Shanek said, drawing everyone's attention. "Sister to queen, Kal says. Rogedoth Mergest's daughters. He a prince, like me."

"Shanek, hold your tongue," Kal said.

Rogedoth, the man who had betrayed Armania? Grayson's grandfather? No wonder Sir Kalenek had helped. Helped him escape. But why had Kal told Shanek this?

"You help him?" Shanek asked Sir Kalenek, eyes wide with surprise. "Mother said it."

Mother *thought* it. "What magic is this? Not even a root child can read minds."

"It appears to be the new magic they call voices of blood," Jazlyn said. "According to my husband, the god Arman bestowed the mind-speak magic upon the royal lines of the father realms. This Rogedoth has royal blood in the line of Sarikar."

Charlon recalled the voices that had driven Shanek mad. When they'd first arrived in this new land. Voices she had thought came from deviant shadir. Voices Sir Kalenek had taught the boy to silence. "You knew Shanek could do this?" she asked Sir Kalenek.

"Yes," he said.

"How? And when did you discover it?"

Sir Kalenek stiffened. The compulsion made it impossible. He could not lie to Charlon. "Rosâr Wilek told me about it."

More betrayal? Rage welled within. "You speak to the rosâr? About us? Tell him where we live? What we are doing?"

Sir Kalenek grimaced. "Yes."

"I forbid you to speak to Rosâr Wilek again."

Sir Kalenek took a step back. Face contorted. Bringing to mind the scars he once had. "Take back that command."

"I will not."

"Please." His voice was choked. "He is my friend."

"You have compelled Sir Kalenek?" Jazlyn asked, thin lips twisted. A faint smile.

"Mreegan did it," Shanek said. "She punish him 'cause he help Grayson get away. Mother no stop it 'cause she like controlling him."

"Stop doing that!" Charlon yelled. "Sir Kalenek, make him stop speaking my thoughts."

"Come, Shanek," Sir Kalenek said. "Let us see how the preparations for dinner are coming along."

Charlon watched them go. Furious and embarrassed. To have been kept in the dark. About this new magic. About so many things.

Sir Kalenek would pay for that.

"Would you like to hold Princess Jahleeah?" Jazlyn asked.

No, Charlon would not. Sir Kalenek's betrayal had soured her mood. But she said, "Yes." Took the babe in her arms. Looked down on Princess Jahleeah's face. So much smaller than Shanek had been. A great ache welled within. To look upon this child hurt her heart. Why?

You should have this, Rurek said. *Use your magic. Keep her child as your own.*

Charlon met the shadir's cold eyes. Typical of a man. To suggest such a thing. *I will not take a child from its mother.*

But I can see that you want it, Rurek said.

I want Torol's child. My child.

Ahh, a child of your own flesh would surely heal the wound inside you.

Yes. Charlon remembered. So much hope. And joy. Talking with Torol about their child. Making plans. Guessing what the babe would look like. Wondering whether it was male or female. Arguing over what they might name it. Had

Charlon's child lived, would it have had dappled skin? Would it have been a root child? Would it have been a girl or a boy? Would she have survived the birth? Would its existence have kept her from becoming Chieftess?

Charlon finally returned the child to the empress's servant. Her guests departed to rest until the feast. Charlon watched them go.

Rurek had seen her pain. Spoken truth. Charlon now understood what she was missing. Surely having a child of her own—a normal child—would appease the ache within. And now that she no longer needed to consume ahvenrood constantly to do magic, such a thing was a real possibility. She would have to plan carefully. To go without ahvenrood would make her vulnerable. Even with the new magic. She would have to hide the old root from her maidens. She could not let them do to her what she had done to Mreegan.

Sir Kalenek was the only logical choice for the child's father. She had watched him raise Shanek. He was firm yet patient and kind. Shanek loved him. Besides, the other men had been compelled for so long, they had no minds of their own. Charlon needed someone who understood what was at stake.

Sir Kalenek owed it to her, after his treachery.

He would refuse. He loved his blind woman too much to betray her. Charlon would have to compel him. Yet compulsions rarely masked all thoughts. If he discovered what she was doing, he would grow to hate her.

It might help to trick him with kindness. Give back his freedom from the other maidens. Allow him to talk with Sâr Wilek. As long as he could not speak of Magos or Charlon or Shanek.

That just might work.

Charlon liked this plan. She was Chieftess of Magos. Shanek would someday rule Armania, but Magos needed its own heir.

Sour mood lifted. Charlon feasted with Empress Jazlyn. Talked of alliances. A future of peace.

A treaty was drafted. A celebration followed. A celebration of peace and mutual support. And plans. Many plans for the future.

TREVN

Trevn, Saria, and their men traveled west, following Grayson's lead. The boy flashed from location to location—popping, he called it. Back and forth he went, trying to find the best route. He led them due west, and finally, near sunset one evening, they came to the shore of a great lake.

"Keep back from the water," Trevn called to his men. "At least until Master Jahday can test it for poison."

The young explorer set out at once for the water's edge.

"It's not nearly as wide as it is long," Grayson said.

Trevn couldn't see any distant shore. "Which way does it stretch?"

"Uh . . ." Grayson turned around, squinting up the shore. "That's the long way," he said, pointing to the northwest.

"And that's the way we must go?" Trevn asked.

"Yes, or we can go around the end and walk up the southern side. Miss Mielle is on the south shore, but she's also on the end of the lake. We can get to her both ways, and I think the northern route is faster."

"I trust you to lead us, Grayson," Trevn said. "Let us camp here for the night and set out early tomorrow."

Too unsettled to remain idle, Trevn pitched in to help the men erect his tent. Three more days, Grayson had said. Only three days until he might be reunited with his bride. He could hardly believe it.

Once Trevn had eaten, he settled down to voice Mielle and give her an update on their location. They were so close now that each time their minds connected, the force of the soul-binding knocked him flat. This was why he no longer forged a connection between their minds unless he was seated or lying down.

As soon as he reached for her, a sense of horror washed over him. *"Mielle? What is wrong?"*

"Trevn! I have been praying you would speak to me. Giants came to the village. They were awful, half-naked beasts, and the Puru people gave their children away! Some of us women, we tried to protest, but the Puru men carried us off to one of the tents and held us captive until the whole thing was over. Captain Stockton tried talking with the Puru chief, but they cannot understand each other. And now the Puru are packing up as if they are going to leave. Can you send Grayson to translate? Please? We are desperate to understand what is happening."

Trevn steeled himself against the onslaught of Mielle's emotions. "Fetch Grayson," he yelled to Ottee, who was attempting to build a fire.

The boy jumped up and scurried away.

Grayson came, and Trevn sent him straight to Mielle. Trevn tried to console her, but she would hear nothing until she got the truth from the Puru people. When Grayson reached her, she closed her mind against Trevn so she could figure it all out.

Trevn waited, curious what Grayson would discover and fairly relieved to be released from Mielle's passions. When Grayson returned asking Trevn to contact Mielle at once, Trevn braced himself and reached for her.

She had calmed down a great deal, yet overwhelming hopelessness bled through their connection. *"What happened?"* he asked.

"They would say only that the children belonged to the giants. But, Trevn, the children didn't want to go. Most of them were crying. And some of the Puru women were crying too. It was very dubious. And now the Puru are leaving."

"Going where?"

"Migrating south along the lake. They've invited us to join them—said it's too dangerous to stay when the Jiir-Yeke come—that is what they call the giants they gave the children to. It is incomprehensible. Captain Stockton wants to go with the Puru. He knows you are coming and thinks it will save time. But most of the people want to stay with their crops."

"Let's ask Wilek."

So eager was Trevn to see Mielle *and* please Wilek, he had to force himself to remain neutral. Over the next hour he and Mielle passed messages back and forth between Wilek and Captain Stockton until a plan was agreed upon. Captain Stockton would head south with a group that included Mielle and

Cadoc's parents. Captain Gior Neuma, who had captained the *Luvin*, would stay and take leadership of the Armanian settlement. This gave the people a choice whether to stay or go.

"There are only about seventy coming with us," Mielle told Trevn late that night, *"and mostly because they had family on other ships. The rest want to stay."*

Since Captain Stockton's people would be taking the southern route, Trevn informed his men that they would circle the end of the lake the next morning and take that same path. If all went well, they should meet up in less than two days' time.

The next morning Grayson led Trevn's group from one location to another around the southeastern end of the lake and up the southern shore. This continued the rest of the day and into the next. When they stopped for a midday meal, Trevn's soul-binding cut his emotions to shreds. He could hardly sit still, knowing Mielle was so near. He forced himself to try, desperate to focus his mind. He removed a nub of charcoal and a fold of parchment from his pack and set about sketching the coastline. This land was lush and beautiful, and a rush of thankfulness overcame his emotions.

"Your Highness." Three soldiers approached, and Cadoc stood to meet them. "There are pales camped just north on our side of the lake."

"Show me," Trevn said.

The soldiers led Trevn and Cadoc past a copse of trees and pointed down a slight incline into a valley. A peek through his grow lens confirmed they were pales, but he saw no buildings or tents of any kind. A native man climbed into a hole in the ground, and it occurred to Trevn that there were pit houses ahead.

He reached for Grayson with his mind. *"There is a pale camp just up the shore from here. Go and ask them if they've been there long."*

"Yes, Your Highness."

Grayson was gone less than five minutes. He appeared beside Trevn without warning, startling him so badly that he yelped.

"It's Conaw," Grayson said. "He's a friend of mine. Sort of. We met in Zuzaan."

"Good," Trevn said. "Let us go and meet your friends. Then you must find Mielle and lead her to us."

✦ ✦ ✦

Grayson popped ahead to the Puru camp while Trevn and his men trudged behind, one step at a time. The pales watched warily as they approached.

Before they reached the camp, a man with golden hair and pale, freckled skin walked out to meet them.

Trevn spoke the names Grayson had mentioned. "Muna? Conaw?"

The pale man nodded. "*Conaw maqto. Muna kiva-peq.*"

Trevn patted his chest, then waved to his men. "Take us to Conaw? Or Muna?"

"*Owi. Nu maawi uma. Pewi.*" The man turned around and walked toward the camp.

Hopeful, Trevn followed. *"Grayson, where are you?"*

"With Miss Mielle. We are very close."

Those words put a bounce in Trevn's step. Mielle was close.

As Trevn's procession reached the middle of the settlement, the pale people stopped to stare. Children hid behind the legs of adults, who stood in groups, scrutinizing the Armanians' clothing, dark skin, and swords.

The freckled man yelled to a group of boys. "*Uma! Aqni Muna-ti.*"

One of the boys sprinted away.

The man continued to lead them in the direction the boy had gone. Trevn saw the boy crouch at a hole in the ground. By the time they reached it, an elderly woman was coming up.

The Armanians circled around the pit house's entrance. Cadoc gave orders to the soldiers to remain on guard. The elderly woman came to stand before Trevn. Portly and strong for her age, her pale skin was tanned and wrinkled as much as Kempe's. She had bright blue eyes and wore her long, gray hair in a crown of braids.

"*Uma* cross ocean, *owi*? Come far?" she said.

"Yes," Trevn said, shocked to hear his own tongue. "You speak Kinsman?"

"Masaoo teach. Uma Masaoo friend?"

"Who is Masaoo?"

"Masaoo Massi. Massi gray." She stroked her fingers down one pale cheek.

"Grayson, yes. He is my friend. He is coming soon."

"Uma stay? Visit Conaw?"

"Yes," Trevn said, remembering that Conaw was Grayson's friend. "We will stay." He turned to his men. "Set up camp to the south of this settlement. We will stay here tonight."

Trevn wanted to talk more with the pales, but he guessed it would be best to wait for Grayson. Besides, the soul-binding was grating so strongly he didn't wish to be around people at the moment for fear he might behave strangely. The soldiers hefted their packs, and the procession set off to the southern end of the native settlement. They had made it nearly halfway when a voice called out behind them.

"Sâr Trevn?"

He turned at the sound of his name. Grayson stood with Muna, back at the entrance to her pit house. Behind them, a crowd of Kinsman people had congregated.

Mielle.

Trevn jogged toward the group. He dared not open his mind to Mielle or he would surely fall flat on his face. As he got closer, he decided to use his actual voice. "Mielle?"

"Trevn!"

He did not see her, but the sound of her voice made his heart race faster. "Mielle!"

Movement in the crowd. People ducking aside, making way. A woman stepped out from the pack and stopped.

Trevn's breath caught. *Mielle.*

So many emotions struck him at once. He found himself struggling to breathe, trying to keep from being overwhelmed. Elation, affection, happiness, weariness, joy . . .

Mielle started running, so Trevn did too.

They collided. Mielle wrapped her arms around Trevn's neck, and he grabbed hold of her waist and spun her around, squeezing her tightly.

He set her down and kissed her full on the mouth. The soul-binding made everything blur. He not only felt her weight in his arms, he felt the strength of his arms around her. While she smelled like honey, mint, and some kind of flower, he was also inhaling his scent of leather, campfires, and sweat. The fervent intensity of their affection weakened their legs, and they sank to their knees, still clinging to one another, completely engrossed in their love.

When finally they broke apart, Trevn studied her face, the flecks of gold in her brown eyes, her full lips, her narrow nose, and found himself struggling to separate what he saw from what she was seeing and thinking about him. She looked different. Her hair had changed. The braids were thicker. Shorter too.

"Trevn? Did you hear me?"

"No," he said, still staring at his glorious wife. She was his. Reunited. Together again. "You are so beautiful."

She chuckled. "Tuhsh, Trevn. You are sweet."

"And you are mine. I will never lose you again."

WILEK

W ilek sat in his council chambers with the Wisean Five, discussing the options for an offensive attack against Rogedoth. He could barely keep his eyes open. He inhaled a slow, deep breath. Why did that seem so difficult?

"Attacking the island won't work," Oli said. "He would simply use his malleants to create a magical shield over his land. His archers could shoot out of it, but our soldiers would not be able to penetrate."

"Could we get him to come to us?" Danek asked.

"Waiting is King Loran's strategy," Wilek said, his voice raspy.

"I didn't mean wait, Your Highness," Danek said. "I meant to purposely lure him into a trap of some kind."

"Grayson might be able to," Inolah said. "Rogedoth wants the boy, and if he truly can move as Sâr Trevn says he can, he could surely escape before being captured—maybe even after capture."

"He is just a boy." Wilek picked up his glass of water. "I hesitate to risk him." He took a sip, but the water didn't help.

"We simply need to weaken him," Barek said. "Destroying his evenroot would do the trick."

"Will root burn?" Inolah asked. "It would be too risky to try to transport it."

"Most of it is root juice," Oli said. "We only need dump it out. Any idea how much he still has?"

"We don't have access to the room in which it's kept," Wilek said. "I can ask. Maybe there's a way to get inside."

564

"Perhaps a small team could sneak onto the island and target his evenroot stores," Barek said.

"If we're sending a team, why not kill him?" Inolah asked. "An assassination would end all this. He has committed treason against Armania. Had he not escaped, he would have hanged months ago."

"A mantic is not easy to kill," Oli said. "The assassin would have to catch him completely off guard, which would be nearly impossible considering all the shadir he has employed."

"What about defensive strategies?" Wilek asked. "Harton has likely told him everything he learned of Armanian military plans. Rayim, think back. Are there older strategies that he might not have learned? I don't want them anticipating every move our men might take."

"Certainly," Rayim said, "but there are reasons why such strategies would have been discarded. They might not be the most efficient maneuvers."

"I just need to know that we can fight without the enemy knowing our every move," Wilek all but whispered. He was losing his voice. He should probably be in bed, resting.

"The problem is, you are talking about battlefield strategies," Rayim said. "If we attack the island, we won't be fighting on a battlefield. We'll be fighting in a village or inside structures we know little about."

A knock at the door preceded Dendrick and Master Vento. The two men entered, with the latter wringing a handkerchief in his fists. Since Master Uhley had died at sea and Rayim knew little of poisons, King Loran had sent his personal physician to examine Zeroah and Chadek.

"Master Vento, you have news of my wife and son?" Wilek asked.

"Your suspicion that they have been poisoned is correct. I found traces of rôsh powder in both their beds and yours as well."

"What is that?" Wilek asked.

"It comes from a deadly type of coral found in deep reefs," Oli said, brows furrowed in concern.

"His Grace is correct. It is deadly when ingested in large doses, but exposure to the skin can also kill over time."

Wilek shifted in his seat. "Kill?"

"I'm afraid so, Your Highness," Vento said. "After a thorough examination of both, I believe the queen ingested the powder at some point—likely for several weeks before the babe was born. Rôsh powder is particularly danger-ous because it is initially painless, so people can become exposed without realizing it, and visible damage may not appear for weeks. Rôsh powder seeps through the skin and into the blood, initially causing fatigue and watery eyes, appearing as nothing more serious than a common cold. Over time it damages the lungs and eventually causes drowning."

A hush fell over the room, and Wilek felt the weight of every stare.

"Survivors may suffer lingering breathing problems," Master Vento said. "Now that I know what we're dealing with, I can see at a glance that you've been exposed."

Wilek recoiled, struggling to form words over the rising panic in his chest. "My wife and son?" he managed.

"Yes, well, while the queen is stronger and I do believe she will improve in time, your son, I fear, has reached the end of his short time in this world. There is nothing I can do."

The words had been softly spoken, but they ripped violently at Wilek's chest. "Surely not." He stood, his legs shaky. "I will remove Prince Chadek at once. Fresh air will help him improve, will it not?" He circled the table and headed toward the door. "Continue the meeting without me."

Novan Heln was waiting out in the corridor and walked with Wilek as he headed up the stairwell.

"Your Highness?" Master Vento said, following him from the council chambers.

"Tell him I'll return in a moment," Wilek said to Novan. His shield dropped back briefly, and Wilek took the stairs two at a time up to the fifth floor and the apartment he shared with Zeroah. He bade the guards at the door let him in, then fought for breath. He'd gone too fast, perhaps. He couldn't breathe.

Because he'd been poisoned.

Someone inside the room screamed. The guard wrenched open the door, and Wilek and Novan followed him inside.

In the drawing room that separated Wilek and Zeroah's bedchambers, a man was bent over a woman, his hands squeezing her throat. At first Wilek thought the woman might be Zeroah, and he leapt at the man. His guards were quicker, though, and pulled the man and woman apart. Wilek got a good look at both. A chambermaid and Kamran DanSâr.

How had he gotten inside the apartment?

"Novan, see to the queen and prince," Wilek said, glaring down on his half brother.

"They have already been moved, Your Highness," a man said from the doorway. Master Vento. "I saw to it the moment I realized what we were dealing with."

"Your Highness." Novan picked up a bottle from the floor and held it up. It was filled with white powder. Kamran was wearing gloves.

"You would poison my wife and child?" Wilek roared.

Something flickered in Kamran's eyes. "You are not fit to rule," he spat. "King Barthel will destroy you and return Armania to its former glory."

Wilek snapped. He shoved Kamran against the wall and swung, striking this traitor with all the force he could muster. Rage consumed him. He couldn't stop swinging, each punch fueled by the full force of his anger, hatred, determination, revenge. This ruttish, hedgeborn miscreant had tried to kill his wife and child!

Suddenly he couldn't breathe. He took a step back. Staggered. Kamran sank to the floor, bleary-eyed, face bloody and swollen, mouth open and drooling.

Wilek's head spun, vision blurred. He swayed. Fell.

Novan caught him under the arms and lowered him to the floor. Wilek choked, gasping in hitches of air. Something was blocking his throat. He sputtered, as if a good cough might clear it. His eyes watered. Despair swarmed like a fierce wind, mocking him.

"Take him . . ." He wheezed. "Dungeon."

Two guards hauled Kamran away. Wilek sat on the floor until he got his wind, and he realized that he hadn't seen Lady Pia for some time. "I want to talk with Lady Pia right away." His voice came dry and grating.

Novan motioned to another guard, who ran from the room.

Wilek caught sight of the chambermaid, cowering in the corner.

"Question the maid."

Master Vento crouched beside Wilek. "Let me get something to wrap your hand, Your Highness."

Wilek glanced at his bloodied knuckles, shook his head, and sucked in as much air as he could. "Zeroah and Chadek." He reached for Novan, who hoisted him to his feet.

Novan helped him down the stairs. His breath improved with each step. He had just reached the ground floor when Zeroah came running toward him, followed by her guards and honor maidens.

"Wilek!" Her voice cracked, and her face was pale and tear-streaked. "Our son is dead!"

Wilek caught her in a tight embrace, and as she collapsed upon him, he sank to the floor, the two of them giving in to their grief.

Amala

Lying in bed in the new honor maiden's chamber, Amala couldn't sleep. She had listened to the queen weeping through the wall for several hours before she finally fell silent. Amala felt responsible. Sir Kamran DanSâr had been arrested for poisoning the royal family, and she had let him in! It was her fault the queen was ill. Her fault the prince had died.

"Amala? Do you hear me?"

Amala froze, terrified by Kamran's voice in her head. Should she try to make shields around her thoughts? She had taken the training with Hrettah and Rashah, but had paid little attention and never practiced. *"Do not speak to me,"* she thought. *"What you did was horrible. You are an evil man, and I am glad you are going to die at first light."*

He chuckled. *"If I am going to die, so are you."*

Terror ran up from the pit of her stomach and clogged her throat. *"What do you mean?"*

"You helped me, Amala. You let me into the royal chambers. And if you don't help me escape, I will tell everyone that you were my accomplice."

"I can't!"

"It's very simple. There are only three guards at night, and they take turns patrolling the corridors while the other two play dice down the hall where the torches are brightest. If you enter when I tell you and go where I say, my shadir will be your eyes and help you avoid them."

Shadir? He was a mantic? She should have guessed as much. Harton was a mantic. The man they wanted as king was too.

Amala gritted her teeth, disgusted that she could find no way to refuse. *"When am I to come?"*

"I hang at dawn. If you are to help me, you must come now."

Amala climbed out of bed. *"I am on my way."*

"Thank you, Amala dear. Oh, and do be quiet."

✦ ✦ ✦

Amala crept through the dark castle and down the stairs into the dungeon, hating herself with every step. She could not go on living here, knowing that she had helped a man kill the baby prince. The guilt grew heavier each second. She was a traitor. A horrible person. She wanted to die.

She had put on two dresses and packed a bag of things. Left it just inside the stairwell. She would run away with Kamran. Agree to serve King Barthel. It was her only chance at any sort of life. And Master Harton would be there.

"Stop," Kamran said, making her jump. *"Go back to the turn in the steps. Hurry!"*

Amala spun around and ran silently on her tiptoes, back up the second flight of steps to the landing. She paused. *"Is this good?"*

"Yes, wait there for just a moment."

Her breath sounded very loud, and she tried to quiet it. Something clanked in the distance. Chains, perhaps.

"Now. Go! Run right down the stairs and across the lengthwise corridor."

Amala was already halfway there. She passed by the lit corridor and into a dark one. She slowed and reached her hands out to the walls, scared she might run into something or someone.

"There is an empty cell on your left just up ahead. Go inside it and wait for my instructions."

Amala couldn't see anything. She ran her fingertips along the cold stone walls, and when her hand fell away on the left, she felt around until she found the door jamb, then crept slowly inside. *"I'm in the cell. Kamran?"*

No answer came.

She waited, nervous about the loudness of her breathing. Footsteps paced in the distance and slowly grew nearer. Amala held her breath, not trusting herself to be silent enough otherwise.

Light suddenly illuminated the space around her, spilling in through the open doorway. It revealed a heavy wooden door with empty brackets. Sharp angled shadows painted the floor and shifted slowly as the light came nearer and the footsteps grew heavier.

Movement in the corridor. She drew back, her body stiff with fright. It had been a man's sleeve and his hand, holding a torch. He passed by, his steps like rocks scraping over stone. She cringed and closed her eyes, praying he would continue on without seeing her.

"It's safe to continue. You will come to a T. Turn right, and I am at the door at the very end. Hurry now."

Moving as fast as she could in the darkness, Amala rushed down the corridor until her hands fell away from the walls on both sides. Figuring she had reached the T, she turned right and crept along.

"A few more steps . . . And stop."

Amala stopped.

"Remove the beam from the door."

Amala reached out. The side of her fist struck a wooden door. She patted the door with both hands until she found the beam. She heaved it off the brackets, surprised by how heavy it was. She set it behind her, and it made a dreadful sound against the stone floor. She cringed, then shrank back at the sound of the door scraping open.

He was coming out.

Oh, gods, why had she helped him? Why had she ever thought him to be honorable and kind? A friend?

She couldn't go with him. She would stay here and say nothing.

But what if someone found out what she'd done? Going with Kamran was her only chance. She would never make it if she ran away on her own.

She couldn't see him, but she felt his presence brush up beside her, crouch. She tensed, waiting for the noise as he picked up the beam, but it barely made a sound this time.

Kamran quickly replaced the beam, then took Amala's hand and dragged her along.

Light appeared at the opposite end of the corridor. Amala could see where the stem of the T veered off to the left. The light grew brighter. She heard the guard's footsteps coming.

Kamran jerked her into the stem of the T. A few rushed steps, and they were in the empty cell. He grabbed her waist and swung her to his other side, holding her there. She wanted to squirm away—didn't like the way his hands controlled her. Light filtered into the cell. Again she held her breath and waited for the loud footsteps to fade. Before she was ready, Kamran pulled her onward. The next thing she knew they were ascending the steps.

At the top, when he paused at the doorway to peek out and check the way, she reached down and grabbed her bag.

"What is that?" he asked.

"I'm coming with you. I packed some things."

"You're not *coming with me."* He darted out the door and raced down the corridor that passed by the kitchens.

Amala gave chase. *"You owe me,"* she thought, but he had disconnected his mind from hers.

Movement at the end of the hall sent him ducking inside the kitchens. Amala followed. Just inside the door he grabbed her arm, yanking her beside him.

A serving man was filling a kettle with hot water from the cauldron in one of the hearths. Once he'd carried it out of the room, Kamran pulled Amala past the brick hearth ovens and to a door on the outer wall.

Then they were outside the keep, in the cool night. The sky was cloudless and filled with bright stars. She felt as if they were watching her and would tell the gods all she had done. How could she go with this man? This murderer?

How could she not?

He paused behind a butcher's cart and released her hand. The smell of blood turned her stomach.

"This is where I leave you."

"No!" She grabbed his arm with both hands and held tight. *"I am going with you."*

"You are going back to bed."

"I can't stay here, listening to the queen sob over the baby I helped kill."

"It's a very long way, Miss Amala. You'll only slow me down."

"I'll scream if you don't take me with you."

"You scream and we both die."

"I'll follow you, then. But without your help, I might accidentally make too much noise or bring attention to the direction you went."

He groaned. *"Mikreh's teeth, woman."*

"Please, Sir Kamran." She wanted to say again that he owed her. That he had tricked her into murdering a baby, ruined her life. But she was hesitant to make him angry.

"You must do exactly what I say. And if you don't like what happens to you, blame yourself." Kamran took her hand and led her around the circular keep toward the boat gate.

WILEK

On and off Wilek slept, catching a few minutes here, waking in a rush of sorrow, then dozing off again. Beside him, Zeroah slept soundly, and for that he was thankful.

He prayed that Arman would strengthen his wife, for though she had claimed to feel better, she did not look it. The poison had deteriorated her body so much it reminded him of how she'd looked after coming out of Charlon's trunk. She was thin and pale and weak, struggled to breathe, and now was broken by grief as well.

Please help her, Arman. Spare her life. I cannot bear to lose another.

The more he thought and prayed and fumed and spun, the more he knew he must act swiftly. The enemy would not stop with Prince Chadek's death. They would come after Zeroah and Trevn and the sârahs and himself. And if Rogedoth succeeded in his attempts to take the throne of Armania, even more innocents would die. He would bring back human sacrifice, legalize magic and the owning of slavs.

Rogedoth could not be allowed to prosper. He must be destroyed, and soon.

A knock. Dendrick entered and strode to the bedside. "Forgive me for waking you so early, Your Highness."

"I was already awake. What is it?"

"Kamran DanSâr has escaped."

No! Wilek leapt from the bed. "How did this happen?"

"The guards are still questioning witnesses, but it appears that Lady Amala assisted. She has fled with the prisoner."

Amala? Confusion clouded Wilek's mind. He hurried into his wardrobe, and Dendrick instantly set about dressing him. Wilek struggled to make sense of the news. When he could not, he released a scream of frustrated rage. "I wanted him dead!"

"He tricked her; I'm certain." Zeroah's soft voice startled him. She stood in the wardrobe's doorway in her long nightdress, her minibraids loose and hanging in long coils down to her waist. The tears that welled in her eyes softened Wilek's anger. "Sir Kamran was always well liked by the ladies. Clever with words and compliments. Maids often went out of their way to do him favors."

"She will discover his true nature soon enough," Wilek said, motioning for Dendrick to continue dressing him.

✦ ✦ ✦

An hour later Wilek rode Foxaro west with Rayim and a group of guards, using Barek Hadar's hounds to track Kamran's trail. His half brother had taken a longboat from the castle to shore, then stolen two horses from the guardhouse stables and rode west-southwest. At first Wilek had assumed he was heading across the land toward Rogedoth's islands, but when he did not adjust his course, Rayim stopped and circled the horses.

"He is riding toward Magos," he said.

Wilek growled, frustrated. They couldn't go to Magos. Not with Charlon and her great shadir. "How far ahead is he?"

"Several hours," Rayim said. "We won't catch him, and I doubt the Magosian Chieftess would hand him over."

"She would not," Wilek said. Nor could he send his men to Magos, where they might discover Kal and attempt to bring Sâr Janek's killer to justice. "I will deal with this another way."

Wilek turned his horse and started back. Before he had worked up the courage to voice this news to Kal and tell him of Lady Amala's betrayal, King Loran spoke to his mind.

"My uncle has sent an army of pales to the continent. They are camped outside New Sarikar. A herald arrived this morning with a missive demanding that I surrender the throne to its rightful king. A negative answer will be considered a declaration of war."

Rogedoth was here? Hinckdan had not told Wilek he'd left. *"I will speak with Hinckdan to see what I can learn."*

"I need more than clues from your spy, Rosâr Wilek. I need your help to stand against him. Can I count on you?"

"Absolutely," Wilek said. *"We can reach you in three days, though we will try for two."*

"I shall do all I can to hold out until then."

The time had come to protect the innocent from the threat of evil. "Sir Kamran will have to wait," he told Rayim. "King Loran is under attack."

✦ ✦ ✦

"None of the island armies have left," Hinckdan said. *"Could it be Fonu's squadron of giants?"*

"King Loran said nothing of giants. He specifically said a pale army."

"I will see if I can learn anything, Your Highness."

"Thank you, Hinckdan."

Wilek stood with Rayim and Dendrick on the edge of a field near the castle, observing the ranks as they assembled to march. "Hinckdan knows nothing," he said.

"That is unfortunate," Rayim said.

"Rogedoth must still suspect he is a spy, though I don't see how." Wilek feared for the young man's safety. "I wish we could call him back."

"He might still learn something valuable by eavesdropping," Rayim said.

Hinckdan had almost been killed once. After what Kamran had done to Lady Pia . . . "Have you any update on Lady Pia, Dendrick?" Wilek asked.

"Master Vento said she will recover. Sir Kamran meant to punish her, not kill her."

Lady Pia had been found in Kamran's chambers, bound and gagged. She had been assaulted and disfigured, yet her first words when freed were to warn that Kamran planned to poison the royal family.

If Wilek had only remembered he hadn't heard from the woman, there might have been time to save Chadek.

"Look who comes, Your Highness." Rayim nodded toward the castle bridge.

Oli Agoros, escorting Miss Onika, her dune cat, and her honor maidens toward where Wilek stood.

Wilek had been too busy to consult Miss Onika about his plans. He sent a brief prayer to Arman to give him wisdom and patience.

"My pardons, Your Highness," Oli said when they reached them. "But Miss Onika insisted on speaking with you at once."

The sun shining on Onika's hair made it seem white. Wilek took in the blind woman's crumpled brow and winced, dreading what censure she had come to deliver. "Speak, Miss Onika. You have found me."

"You aligned yourself with Sarikar without asking of Arman? Without consulting me?"

Wilek's face heated at the boldness of her public attack. "Armania has a treaty with Sarikar. When either are in need, the other must offer aid."

"You told me you did not trust King Loran's prophets," Onika said. "That only Wolbair spoke truth. What says Wolbair of this attack?"

"I have not heard from Wolbair. I know only what Loran has told me. He is under attack. He has asked for help. We will set out at once to keep our word."

Her glassy eyes seemed to look right through him. "The death of your son and the escape of his killer is not the real reason you go to war?"

That made him angry, and he fought to keep his voice calm. "Rogedoth is a traitor to Armania, sentenced to death by my father. I have been seeking a way to attack him for months. Arman has finally provided one."

"You think Arman made Rogedoth's army attack Sarikar? Arman does not move his people around like clay figurines."

No, that wasn't what he'd meant. "Miss Onika, I must keep my word to King Loran. To accept evil without protest is to cooperate with it, and to stand by and do nothing is cowardly."

"Your fight is not against Pontiff Rogedoth and his army of mantics," she said, "nor is it against the Magosians or the Tennish. Your fight is against the forces of evil that followed us to this land."

"Those *forces* are allied with Rogedoth. Do you have a prophecy for me, Miss Onika?"

A deep breath. "I do not." She swallowed, and tears welled in her eyes. "This frightens me. I am not often frightened by Arman's silence."

Never had he seen the woman so vulnerable, and it terrified him. He did his best to ease her fear. "I will not act rashly. I promise you that. Duke Canden, prepare the prophetess to join me on this campaign. I will need her wisdom."

"Shall I come along as the head of her guard?" Oli asked.

"No. Her guard will do fine without you. I need you here to help my wife. She must be trained to shield her mind. She has put it off for far too long."

"Yes, Your Highness," Oli said. He returned to Onika's side, took hold of her arm, and led her back toward the keep.

Wilek watched them go, feeling uneasy. "Am I making a mistake, Rayim?"

"The only mistake I see you making is constantly fearing you will make one. Trust your instincts, Your Highness. You are not a fool."

Wilek nodded and again took note of the ranks. He wished he could readily accept Rayim's advice and carry on, but the death of his son, Kamran's escape, Amala's betrayal, and Miss Onika's fear drowned out what little confidence he had.

That midday Wilek penned a proclamation, a physical copy of which Dendrick sent to all of Armanguard, Er'Rets point, and each of the smaller Armanian settlements. Oli Agoros voiced the words to Trevn, King Loran, and Emperor Ulrik, who did not respond. Oli instead voiced the proclamation to Rosârah Thallah, who said that Ulrik had fallen ill, and she would inform him the moment he recovered.

For months the threat of impending conflict between this nation and its former Pontiff has been ever present. In his lust for conquest and domination of all, Barthel Rogedoth has persisted in his attempt to take control over peoples and nations to which he has no legal claim. He has loosed the forces of evil upon us all with no regard for the sanctity of free will. He would take freedom from every man, woman, and child, be they from the Five Realms or natives of this new land.

The realm of Armania will not allow this aggression to continue. War against the perfidious Barthel Rogedoth and his rebellious allies will commence three days hence.

KALENEK

Kal wasn't himself. He knew that much. Charlon had altered the compulsions against him. He could now speak with Wilek when he voiced, but he could say nothing of Magos or the actions of any who lived here, including himself. When he tried, his thoughts froze. So when Wilek voiced him for an update on Kamran DanSâr and Amala, Kal had to get creative in his answer.

"The last time I saw your half brother or my ward was aboard the Seffynaw. *"*

Wilek sighed. *"I had estimated their arrival in Magos by last night. Perhaps they will reach you today."*

"I have always believed it my duty to enact Justness upon traitors."

"Upon Kamran, Kal, please do. But I would never ask you to harm Amala. Zeroah believes Kamran tricked her."

The words eased the growing pressure in Kal's chest. *"Thank you, Wil."*

"You should know, I ride to Sarikar at present to wage war. Rogedoth's compelled native army has taken Sarikar, and we attack in two days' time to defend King Loran. Any words of advice for me?"

Though war's effects had plagued Kal for years, he longed to be at Wilek's side, where he might do some good. *"Always appear cheerful and undaunted. If you look otherwise, your men's spirits will fall with yours in the belief that disaster is impending. Overall, trust your instincts, Your Highness. You are a well-trained warrior. I wish I could fight beside you."*

"Thank you, Kal. You have bolstered my courage."

"May your victory be swift as your enemy falls at your feet," Kal said, quoting a phrase from his army days.

"Farewell, my friend," Wilek said. *"I will voice you after the battle."*

The connection vanished, and Kal found himself standing in the middle of the evenroot field, far from where he had been when Wilek had first spoken. A coldness swept over him, though the day was hot. He felt confused and overwhelmed by a deep loneliness.

Wilek was going into battle, and Kal could not fight alongside him. That must be it. Kal longed to see his friend.

Again he pondered the changes he felt in himself and the magic upon him. He no longer had to obey any mantic but Charlon. Gone was the original compulsion Roya had placed upon him in exchange for something Charlon had cast anew.

For a time Kal believed Charlon had been rewarding him for his loyalty to Shanek—she had said as much. But then he began to look at her differently. He admired her ambition, her wit, her beauty, despite never having found her beautiful before. His thoughts drifted often to dwell on Charlon, and he found himself staring at the strangest moments. Worse, when she paid special attention to any other man, a jealous rage overcame him, the likes of which he had not experienced since Rosâr Echad had married Inolah to Emperor Nazer back when Kal was barely of age.

The logical conclusion was that Kal loved the woman, though some small part of him knew better. He loved someone else, he was certain, but could not recall who. Straining to remember drove him nearly mad, and he resolved to ask someone. Surely Wilek would know, yet again the opportunity had come and gone and Kal had forgotten to ask.

When giants had been sighted near the evenroot fields over a week ago, Charlon had asked Kal to stay in her tent, claiming that his presence gave her comfort. He hadn't minded. He'd felt peace in the red tent, for some reason, and when one night he'd found himself sharing Charlon's bed, it had also seemed to fit.

Afterward, however, Kal had felt an overwhelming sense of shame and revulsion over what they had done and could not look the woman in the eye. That had been the first of many such interludes that always ended in remorse. Occasionally there were instances, brief flashes of clarity, in which he knew for certain it was all a trick of magic, yet those thoughts vanished as quickly as they came.

Kal existed to do anything the woman asked.

✦ ✦ ✦

"Are you sure you don't want to be healed?" she asked the next morning, tracing the ridged, pink scar under his arm.

They lay together in her bed in the red tent. Gullik had brought breakfast, then Charlon had sent him away. Demanded they not be disturbed. Kal disliked how empty he felt with this woman in his arms. Twice he had tried to leave, and twice he had changed his mind.

"I never wanted healing," Kal said. "Mreegan took away my scars without permission."

"That was her way." Charlon's slender finger trailed over his chest to another scar. "How did this one happen? The yeetta?"

"They're nearly all the yeetta. They held me captive for thirteen weeks." His scars covered his chest, arms, and legs. Lacerations, slashes, and punctures had healed in puckers of pink skin.

"So much physical pain means heavier pain within," Charlon said. "I hope you do not suffer."

Charlon's empathy continued to surprise him. She understood things most did not, likely due to her own tortured past. "There is much I can't remember, yet I can still see my men being killed. And I will never forget finding Livy and our child dead."

"If you wish to forget, I can compel you."

Fear for his sanity chilled him. "No," he said carefully, not wanting her to know how desperate he was to keep her from further altering his mind. "The memories are my punishment for failure. I deserve far worse."

"Do not blame yourself, Sir Kalenek. You are a brave man. A hero to your realm."

He snorted. "I don't feel like a man. Certainly not a hero."

She looked stunned by his words, and he couldn't believe he had admitted something so vulnerable aloud. He did not feel comfortable with Charlon, so why did he continue to behave in opposition to his instincts?

"You are *my* hero," she said, kissing him softly, and the desire in her eyes swept him along.

Kal had always felt like he walked a thin line between light and darkness—that he was constantly fighting to stay in any part of the golden glow—but Charlon continually pulled him into a blackness so deep that despair threatened to drown him. All he could do to hold it back was to submit to her and hold on, hoping she would keep him afloat.

Charlon suddenly pushed him away. "I told you not to disturb me when Sir Kalenek is here."

Shaken by the sudden change in her passion, Kal searched the room, listened. No one was there.

"What does he want?" Charlon's gray eyes had fixed on something only she could see. His arms pimpled. She was talking with her shadir.

"I will prepare to receive him." She threw off the furs and began to dress. "Sir Kamran DanSâr is approaching our camp."

Rage welled up in Kal's gut. He could not fathom why Amala would have helped such a man. Why leave a life as a princess to become a fugitive?

Regardless, Kamran would die. Kal would see to it. When next Wilek voiced, Kal would be able to report the traitor's execution.

Kal scrambled out of bed, pulled on his tunic, and stepped into the chill morning, suffocated by shame that he had yet again submitted to this woman.

The Magosian camp consisted of two parallel lines of white tents with a grassy path between them. The red tent had been erected on a small hillock at one end of the path. At the opposite end stood an altar that had once been built to honor Magon. The Magon pole had come down upon her death, however, and in place of the bronze of Magon, Charlon had mounted a bronze of Rurek, the very name she called her new shadir.

Two riders had already bypassed the altar and were steering their mounts up the grassy path toward the red tent. They were still a ways off, and Kal could not make them out.

Movement behind Kal turned his head. Charlon stepped out of the tent and stopped beside him.

"Rurek says the woman is named Amala. Do you think it your ward?"

"Yes," Kal said, heart sinking.

"Inside the tent, Sir Kalenek," Charlon said, "where you won't be a distraction."

Kal's body moved at Charlon's command, which brought a flash of anger at his lack of freedom. Just beyond the curtain the compulsion ended, so he positioned himself at the door flap where he could see and hear everything that happened.

Several more minutes passed as Charlon gathered her retinue to receive the illegitimate prince of Armania. Four of Charlon's men and Shanek stood on her right. All five maidens lined up on her left.

Kamran and Amala reached the top of the hillock. Both were filthy: clothes soiled and torn, hair knotted and frizzy, faces haggard and thin. Kal studied his girl, noting the changes in her over the past year. She was a woman now, despite not yet being fifteen. Her eyes were cold and bloodshot, her posture somewhat wilted, and she jumped three times when others motioned harmlessly toward her.

Kal had seen this before. Someone had hurt her, and if Kal's guess was right, that man would die slowly, screaming for mercy that would not come.

"Weary travelers," Charlon said. "What brings you to Magos?"

Kamran bowed low, extending full courtesy to the Chieftess. "I come representing my king, Barthel Rogedoth," he said. "As mantic nations, King Barthel believes we have a mutual enemy in the father realms. I extend to you, Chieftess Charlon, an invitation to Islah, my king's island city, where he wishes to make an alliance with you."

"King Barthel . . ." Charlon said. "This man puzzles me. I have also heard him called Pontiff Rogedoth and Prince Mergest. Which is he?"

"He is all three," Kamran said, "though he only goes by King Barthel Rogedoth now."

"I see," Charlon said. "Miss Amala, we have met. You do not likely realize it."

"You're the mantic witch who pretended to be Lady Zeroah and seduced Sâr Janek," she said, her voice fiery despite her haggard appearance.

Shanek perked up. "My father?"

Kamran frowned at Shanek. "Who is this?"

"Meet Shanek DanSâr, son of Janek Hadar," Charlon said.

Kamran barked a laugh. "Good joke, lady. He looks enough like Janek to be convincing, but I'd go with Janek's twin, if I were you, seeing as they're practically of age. Or would've been, anyway. Where did you find him?"

"You Father's friend," Shanek said. "You jealous. Want his Lady Mattenelle."

Kamran folded his arms and inched back from Shanek. His evident fear made Kal smile.

"Silence, Shanek," Charlon said.

"Sâr Janek was my half brother, you fool," Kamran said to Shanek, then asked Charlon, "What's wrong with him?"

"Shanek is a root child, born of mother, father, and ahvenrood on the voyage across the Northsea," Charlon said. "With the help of ahvenrood, he grew very fast. He also has the mind-speak magic that runs in the blood of kings and a rude habit of speaking others' thoughts aloud." This last statement she said with a glare at Shanek, who hung his head.

Kal expected Kamran to laugh again, but instead he looked at Shanek in horror. "I have heard Rosârah Laviel speak of root children, but I believed them myth."

"He is no myth," Charlon said. "Sâr Janek was rightful heir. To the Armanian throne. Shanek will therefore rule."

A slow grin spread over Kamran's face. "Now that's a good plan. Even with all his mantics and evenroot, King Barthel has nothing so creative as this to help him take power. You two should talk—work together. If this root child is Janek's son, he is Barthel's heir as well."

Whether Charlon agreed or disagreed with Kamran, she did not reveal. "I would like to meet this King Barthel. We will make plans tomorrow."

"He will be pleased to hear that," Kamran said.

Kal did not like this development. If Charlon and Rogedoth worked together, Wilek wouldn't stand a chance against their magic.

"My men will show you to your tent, where you can bathe," Charlon said. "We have no clothing in your style, but you may wear ours while yours is washed."

"I want my own tent," Amala said, shrinking when Kamran's dark eyes seared her with a glare.

Charlon had compelled Kal to go inside the tent, but not to remain there. He seized this moment to push past the curtain and into the group of people. "I will show you to my tent, Amala."

"Kal!" Amala threw herself into his arms. He held her close, and her body shook from the force of her tears.

"Sir Kalenek Veroth," Kal heard Kamran say. "So this is where you've been hiding yourself."

"Sir Kalenek is Shanek's high shield," Charlon said. "If you'll excuse me, Sir Kamran." She shot Kal a dirty look and entered her tent.

"Show Sir Kamran to his tent," Kal told Gullik. "Miss Amala will stay with me."

Kamran started down the hill before Gullik even moved. Kal wasn't surprised. The man would be wise to flee while he still had the chance.

✦ ✦ ✦

Kal took Amala to his tent and fed her. While she ate, her story spilled forth. She had been angry with the rosâr for so many things: demoting Master Harton, not trying harder to find Mielle, not supporting Mielle's marriage to Sâr Trevn, banishing Kal. "When Kamran asked for my help, I felt certain he would find some evidence of the rosâr's wrongdoing. It never occurred to me he would try to kill Prince Chadek and the queen."

Kamran had then used his mind-speak abilities to blackmail Amala into helping him escape. "I fled with him because I thought they'd hang me otherwise," Amala said. "I didn't know what else to—"

Shanek appeared in the room then, sitting cross-legged between them as if he had been there all along.

Amala screamed.

"Shan, go back to your tent," Kal said. "It's rude to enter someone's space without being invited."

"He hurt her," Shanek said. "I saw. They got different memories. He was happy. She was scared."

Amala stared at Shanek, her face a mask of shock. "He ate all the food I had brought along. His shadir helped him find more, but he wouldn't share. I was hungry. I didn't know what else to do."

She burst into tears and collapsed on her side, curled into a ball. Kal went to her, rubbed her back, and pondered the best way to kill Kamran.

"He hurt her," Shanek whispered, then vanished.

Amala choked in a sniffling breath. "Where did he go?"

"Who knows with Shanek." Kal hoped he behaved himself.

"He is really Sar Janek's son?" Amala asked.

"Yes, Sar Janek and Miss Shemme." And magic.

Amala gasped. "The kitchen maid? Is she here?"

"She died giving birth," Kal said.

A man's scream caught their attention.

Kal jumped to his feet and tore out of his tent. "What happened?" he asked Gullik.

"Don't know. Sounded like it came from the guest's tent."

Gods, no. Kal sprinted to Kamran's tent, which was five away from his own. A crowd had formed outside. Kal pushed his way toward the entrance.

"Let me by. Move!"

They parted and he ducked inside.

Sir Kamran lay crumpled on the floor, clean, half dressed, and two steps from a tub of dirty bathwater, head twisted at an odd angle. A trickle of blood ran from one nostril and down his cheek.

Kal stood over him, looking down on glassy eyes that stared, horrified, at nothing.

A deep breath brought no pity for Kamran DanSâr. The man had always been a reprobate, and after what he had done to Amala and Wilek and Wilek's wife and child, Kal only wished his death had been more painful.

Still, the way it had happened was a problem.

Feeling helpless, he walked to Shanek's tent and let himself in. He found the young man in bed, huddled under a heap of furs.

"Shanek," Kal began, but what could he say? Kal had fully intended to kill the man once he had assured himself that Amala was safe and cared for. Shanek had likely heard Kal's thoughts about killing the man. Considering that the boy had also listened in on Kamran's vulgar memories, could Kal blame him for taking action?

Of course he could. Killing was wrong.

So said the trained assassin responsible for the deaths of his own wife and child and Shanek's father.

"I did it," Shanek said, peeking out from under the furs. "All gone bad man."

Kal sighed heavily. "He *was* a bad man, Shan, you are right about that. But it was not your job to punish him."

"Girl is happy now?" Shanek asked, rising to his knees. "She happy?"

Kal blew out a sigh. "I don't know, Shan."

How could any of them find happiness when magic continued to destroy lives? The unwelcome pull of Charlon's compulsion forced Kal to stand. He growled deep in his throat and spat out a curse as his legs propelled him toward the exit. "Mother calls, Shanek. We'll talk later."

Shanek scrambled from his bed and chased after Kal. "You hate Mother."

"No," Kal said, far too quickly. "She uses too much magic on me. That's all. Magic hurts people sometimes, Shan."

"Mother hurts you?"

"When she takes my freedom, it hurts my pride, yes."

Shanek fell behind then, and when Kal looked back, the boy was gone.

Kal wondered if Shanek might kill Charlon to avenge him. The thought brought immense sorrow, which maddened him. Why should he care? He wished he knew what that witch wanted from him. He needed his mind back—his whole mind—not just the parts she permitted, but he could see no way to break free from her spell.

As he entered the red tent and found Charlon waiting, a great emptiness opened up inside him, pulling him into a darkness from which he could not escape.

WILEK

The day of battle had come. At dawn Wilek bid a formal farewell to Zeroah in his mind, and she promised to pray all day and keep her mind open to him for updates. Miss Onika still had no word from Arman, but she prayed over Wilek and his men that Arman would bless their endeavors.

Wilek's veteran army of two thousand set out from camp and marched toward the fortress at New Sarikar. He had brought only half his fighting forces, not willing to leave Armanguard completely vulnerable. Since horses were still rare, the only men riding were Wilek, Rayim, Novan, and Rystan. Everyone else was on foot. The two front infantry squadrons carried two ladders each for breaching the fortress walls.

Wilek wore the king's bronze armor, the helmet of which had a thin fillet of gold that circled the crown. The armor hadn't been worn in over forty years, and Wilek hoped it would bring him victory as it had for his grandfather King Chorek.

Hinckdan had not been able to learn anything as to the numbers of compelled natives within the Sarikarian fortress. All he knew for certain was that Rogedoth was pleased with what was taking place there and was preparing a trip to claim the throne of Sarikar. King Loran believed there to be as many as one thousand pales within his fortress, and so Wilek relied on those numbers when planning his assault.

The enemy would have the advantage, defending from a fortress while the Armanians attacked from the plain, but Wilek felt his seasoned force would quickly subdue the untrained natives, compelled or not.

Wilek had five squadrons of four hundred men each. Sixteen hundred were divided into infantry units. The final four hundred were archers, who had been divided and positioned on each flank.

By the time they reached the outskirts of New Sarikar, the midday sun hung high overhead. Not a cloud graced the bright blue sky, and the heat of the day combined with the bronze armor Wilek wore had him in a sweat before he had even unsheathed his sword.

The impressive fortress sat at the top of a large hill. Made of squared, hand-hewn beams, the castle keep was a four-level timber towerhouse surrounded by a palisade of thick hewn logs, sharpened to points on top and anchored at intervals by watchtowers.

They would use the ladders to scale the palisade and open the doors from the inside. Then they would pour into the fortress like ants and liberate King Loran and his family.

An envoy rode up to the fortress, carrying a missive demanding the pales surrender. It would likely be ignored, but Wilek preferred to always offer negotiations of peace before engaging in war.

The envoy had nearly reached the wood plank doors when two pales appeared at the top of the wall and threw down several objects.

Wilek's heart sank. "You don't think . . ."

"Looked like heads to me," Rayim said.

One of the pales raised a bow and fired an arrow at the envoy. He missed completely, but the Armanian soldiers cried out, indignant. Wilek was just about to ask Rayim his opinion when the front squadron of the left wing attacked prematurely.

"Call them back!" Rayim yelled.

But it was too late. The palisade doors yawned open, and clusters of pale warriors charged out, screaming and brandishing spears.

"Go, go!" came Rayim's order, and the entire Armanian first line rushed forward to meet the enemy.

Wilek had never experienced a battle like this, watching from a distance. He didn't like the way it made him feel incompetent. The men had their orders, but clearly men would sometimes do as they pleased.

The infantry's bronze blades cut easily through the pales wielding spears. The bowmen were the real danger, though as Hinckdan had said, they were not the best shots. The Armanian army advanced. On the right a ladder went up. Men began to climb.

The smell of smoke caught Wilek's attention. "Is something on fire?" he yelled to Rayim.

"There." Rayim pointed to a plume of gray smoke rising up on the front right. "The pales are setting the grass on fire. All across the front line."

The fire grew swiftly, separating the infantry from the officers and reserves and forcing the latter half back a short distance. The flames devoured the dry grass and left a choking cloud of smoke hanging over the battlefield. This greatly impeded the infantry efforts to enter the fortress. Not only that, it blocked Wilek's view of his men.

Rayim growled. "I don't like this."

"I cannot see the head of my own horse," Wilek said.

"The men won't be able to fight in that heat, heavily armored as they are," Rayim said. "I'm tempted to call a retreat until this smoke dies down."

The fire greatly increased the already hot temperature. Wilek was tempted to remove his helmet just to get a clear breath. His health had improved since discovering the poison, but too much physical activity sometimes made breathing difficult.

"Behind us!" Novan yelled.

Wilek turned Foxaro to face the distant forest, but Novan's warning had come too late. An army of giants had hemmed them in from behind and set upon their reserves, the two groups already in combat.

"Arman, no." Hinckdan had said only a few giants had been compelled by Fonu, and King Loran had not mentioned giants at all. They must have snuck out of the fortress when the smoke was thickest and launched their counterattack from the rear. "We must retreat," Wilek said.

"Retreat!" Rayim screamed.

Those in between the two battles scattered, but by now the giants had launched a full assault around the perimeter, engaging the Armanian forces in a fierce fight. As the giants surged forward, Kinsman soldiers crumpled like sheep against a herd of fang cats.

These were the first giants Wilek had seen. Unlike the pales, the giants wielded stone axes that could cut down a Kinsman soldier in one swing.

"We must go, Your Highness," Rayim yelled, gesturing for Wilek to ride before him.

Novan led the way, and Wilek followed. They rode through the calm eye of the storm as two battles raged around them. Giants were pouring out of the fortress now, decimating the infantry on the front lines. Men fled for the trees, but the giants had formed a ring around the battlefield. The Kinsman soldiers were surrounded on all sides, and none of them knew enough about this enemy to fight well.

They were trapped.

Rogedoth had tricked them. And now they would all of them die.

Novan bellowed a war cry and urged his mount into a sprint. Wilek kept on his tail. The giants did not carry shields but stood shoulder to shoulder, swinging their axes like scythes.

Novan's horse broke between two giants. He cut his sword into the neck of the giant on his right, holding his shield tight against his left side. The giant on his left hacked his axe into the flank of Novan's horse, and it fell.

Foxaro reared up. Wilek held tight to the horse's mane, but a force struck his left side and knocked him off the animal. He hit the ground hard, losing his breath and his shield. He scrambled to his feet and drew his blade.

"Go for the legs!" Rayim yelled from somewhere nearby.

Wilek ducked as an axe whirled overhead. He slashed his sword across a giant's thick calves. A blade clipped his shoulder from behind, the sharp pain making Wilek stumble. He landed in a crouch and scrambled behind the giant, who wore thick fur boots that protected his ankles. Wilek cut the backs of the giant's knees, then drew a knife from his belt and stabbed another giant in the lower back, losing the knife as the giant wheeled around.

Wilek darted out of his attacker's path but felt pain in his shin as the axe's blade nicked him. They were so tightly surrounded that there was no room to safely step back. Wilek had three more knives on him, though, and put them to good use as he cut down the enemy with slashes and stabs. All around him men grunted and cursed, swiping and lancing as they were able. The strange rat birds Trevn had told him about soared over the battle like a swarm of gnats, occasionally diving in to nip at the entrails of the dead.

Only when enough bodies lay motionless on the bloodstained grass did the Kinsman soldiers have a chance to fight back with any effectiveness. Wilek found an abandoned shield and went after the giants with all his skill as a swordsman. His shoulder and shin stung and were bleeding badly, but he ignored them. Over and over his blade pierced through leather and into flesh until the bronze had bent so baldly he discarded the blade and claimed a straighter one from the ground. Hemmed in on all sides, Wilek's men perished, often in agony. The giants killed the Kinsman soldiers five to one. What a disaster. Heat, fire, dust, and an unknown enemy were too much of an obstacle to surmount.

The giants were far more brutal and aggressive than the Kinsman soldiers. It reminded Wilek of the stories of troops fighting yeetta warriors during the Centenary War. The only wisdom he could recall in defeating such foes were the sword drills to sever shard clubs in two. The handles on the giant's axes were twice as thick, however, and would not break under such tactics. The giant's size, weapons, and numbers were sickeningly effective. Wilek wished for help. Rain. Mercy. A chance to retreat. A moment to catch his breath. But wishing for miracles would do no good.

Or maybe it would.

Arman, have mercy on us. Spare Armania. Let my men escape to defend your people another day.

Wilek crouched as an axe slashed toward his chest. He stabbed the giant in the side, losing his sword. Beyond the collapsing giant, he saw another giant backhand Rayim and send the man sprawling. Wilek retrieved yet another sword from the trampled grass and lunged toward his friend, intent on offering a hand up, when a trilling cry tore through the battle. In the distance another army of giants sprinted toward them.

Horror washed over Wilek. What remained of his army would be slaughtered now.

But these new giants did not attack the Kinsman fighters. Instead, they engaged the giants. They were somewhat shorter than the original giants and wore red paint smeared over their faces.

Rayim was back on his feet, sword in hand. "Get the king out of here!" he bellowed.

Novan ran up to Wilek from the left, grabbed his arm, and dragged him away. They raced toward the tree line, leaving the bodies of their comrades on the battlefield. How many had died? Wilek's gaze swept the field ahead, trying to quickly count the number of men fleeing the battle. Seven, twelve, fifteen, twenty-two . . . Far too few.

Novan somehow found Foxaro. Wilek sheathed his new sword, and Novan hoisted Wilek up into the saddle, then climbed on behind. Foxaro sped away, carrying them over the field and toward the forest.

It had all gone so very wrong. Rogedoth had tricked them, had likely sent shadir to deceive Loran's prophets. And this second group of giants fighting alongside Wilek's men. What did it mean?

Wilek reached the forest and slowed the animal, weaving around trees and back toward their camp. He caught sight of their blue military tents to his right and steered the horse that way.

A woman screamed. Wilek slowed the horse to listen. Men laughing, sounds of struggle, the occasional outburst of a tortured woman or a man in pain.

He stopped Foxaro behind a thick patch of bushes. He and Novan dismounted, and Novan tied the horse to a tree.

"Anyone who would attack defenseless women and servants deserves to die," Novan said.

"We shall take care of that," Wilek said.

"You should remain here, Your Highness."

"For what purpose?"

"Your safety, of course."

"What if someone should come upon me here? No, Novan. We go together."

Novan nodded once and crept around the bushes. Wilek went behind, his gaze roving over Novan's shoulder.

Their camp was under siege. Giants, pales, and Kinsman pirates were carrying furniture and supplies from the tents and loading it all into massive carts. Wilek caught sight of several dead men upon the ground. By their attire, all were servants. A group of ten or so maids were huddled together, half of them sobbing, nearly all of them wounded. Swollen eyes, cheeks, and lips. He recognized Tulay and Yoana, Miss Onika's honor maidens. Clearly Wilek and Novan had missed the worst of what had happened here, but where was the prophetess?

"Get going!" a man screamed.

There came a clank of metal against wood. A hiss of an animal.

"Kill the foul critter," a man yelled.

"It's too quick," said a second.

"Look there," Novan whispered, pointing at one of the carts.

Inside, Miss Onika and Dendrick sat bound and gagged. A pirate stomped around the end, sword swinging wildly after an animal. Rustian, Miss Onika's dune cat. He sank to his belly and slithered under the cart.

"Aw, he's under the cart again," said the second man.

"Leave him be and help me with this trunk," said the first.

The second pirate kicked the side of the cart. "I hope we run you over, you crazy cat." He spat on the ground, then circled the cart to join his comrade.

"I'll distract the pirates," Wilek said. "You rescue Miss Onika and Dendrick."

"Absolutely not," Novan said.

"We can't leave them."

"I don't intend to. But *I* will distract the pirates, Your Highness. You get the prisoners back here. If I am killed, ride for Armanguard."

"It would be better if we attacked them together," Wilek said.

"That will take too long. We have only a moment of surprise. You need to free Miss Onika and Dendrick before reinforcements come."

Wilek didn't like it, but Novan's plan was the best to ensure that the prisoners would be freed. They waited until the pirates were lugging the trunk toward the cart, then sprinted upon them.

Novan killed one of the men easily. Wilek rushed past him and leapt into the back of the cart. Dendrick's eyes widened, and he struggled to his feet as Wilek drew his sword and sliced through the ropes binding Miss Onika's wrists.

"Come quietly, Miss Onika," he said. "Your rescue has arrived."

"Rosâr Wilek?" She frowned, as if she'd been expecting someone else.

Shouts and the clash of weapons behind him increased his speed. He cut Dendrick's bonds next, then both men helped Miss Onika to her feet and out of the cart. Novan was fighting two other pirates now. The first lay on the ground near the cart.

"Take her to the other side of those bushes," Wilek told Dendrick, pointing. "Foxaro is tied there. The two of you ride for Armanguard."

"You know I cannot leave you, Your Highness," Dendrick said.

"Novan will protect me, Dendrick. You must save Arman's prophet. We will be right behind you. Now go."

Dendrick squeezed Wilek's shoulder. "Arman be with you." And he led Miss Onika away.

Wilek went to help his shield. He and Novan quickly defeated the two pirates, but when they started toward the forest, they ran right into a line of giants, standing shoulder to shoulder, blocking the way. There were six. All held obsidian axes in their fists and looked eager to fight.

A man pushed out between the middle two giants and set his hands on his hips. Fonu Edekk.

"You," Wilek said.

"You were expecting someone else?" Fonu asked.

"I would *expect* a soldier like yourself to be on the battlefield, not stealing spoils of war."

"I came for the prophetess," Fonu said. "What have you done with her?"

"She is not your business," Wilek said.

"No matter. We don't need her to win. We are smarter than you. I compelled King Loran, and when he called for help, you came running, just as I knew you would. Now he is dead and Sarikar belongs to its rightful heir. We crippled your army today. Enough that when my king attacks Armanguard, your brother will have no one left to fight us."

"Leave my brother out of this."

Fonu laughed. "But Trevn will be king now, don't you see? You will die here."

"Not if I can help it," Novan said.

"Oh, you can't." Fonu waved the giants forward. "Kill them."

The giants advanced, swinging their axes. Wilek set his feet and braced himself. He gave all he had, holding nothing in reserve. He did not fight carefully or courteously. He moved as quickly as he could, ignoring his weariness and aching wounds. As he had on the battlefield, he aimed for the legs, slashing wherever he could make purchase.

The enemy was mercilessly strong but not as fast, so their best strategy was to dodge and outrun them. This left little time to think and no chance to catch their breath. Wilek dodged, ducked, and even rolled a couple times. He cut and sliced any place he could manage to reach. Despite his and Novan's combined skill, the giants were bigger, stronger, and fresh, while Novan and Wilek had been wearied and bloodied by the first battle.

Novan slashed across the backs of a giant's knees. The giant stumbled, and Wilek hacked his blade down over the giant's neck to end him while Novan deflected an attack on Wilek's back.

"This one next!" Wilek yelled, voice growing hoarse. He nodded to a giant who was cradling one arm.

Pairing up in this manner, they managed to kill a second giant, but the giants were smarter than they were fast and used Wilek and Novan's strategy against them. The remaining four cornered Novan easily. As his shield screamed in agony, Wilek stabbed one of the four through the back. The giant swung around, ripping Wilek's sword from his grasp.

Weaponless, he jumped back as an axe arced down toward his head. Another giant stepped into Wilek's path, axe aimed for Wilek's chest.

He lurched to the side, but the sharp stone blade moved with him, cleaved into his bronze breastplate, and cracked it. Sharp pain brought a gasp from his lips. He screamed, soundless, breathless. Heat wrapped his whole body, throbbed. He fell. His eyes rolled back.

A giant leaned over him and jerked the axe free. The wound in Wilek's chest pulsed. He made the mistake of glancing at it, saw the blood pooling in the crack that split his breastplate.

"Zeroah!" Oh, his bride. He had forgotten to send her any update all morning. She would be brokenhearted and lost after all that had—

"What has happened?" she asked. *"Wilek, is something wrong?"*

Her voice in his head shocked him. *"Zeroah, my love. The battle. It was a trick. Rogedoth had allied with the giants. We got away, but Fonu had taken over our camp and I think . . . I think I'm dying."*

"No!"

"Find the woman, quickly!" Fonu yelled to his giants.

Two stepped over Wilek's body on their way toward the woods.

"Leave her be," Wilek rasped.

Fonu leaned over Wilek, eyebrows pinched. "You know I cannot do that. But you might do me a favor, my king. I killed a woman in cold blood. Will you take my confession before Athos's Bench? Her name was Lebetta." A slow smile stretched across his face.

The confession took Wilek off guard. Lebetta's death seemed so long ago. "Why?" he managed to ask.

"Because my master bade me. She refused to harm you. She had to die."

A year ago Wilek might have raged to defend his concubine, but there was no point now. Not that he had the strength, anyway. The wound was too great. And he could barely breathe.

Behind Fonu something moved. A man on his feet. Bloodied face, bloodied arm.

Novan Heln.

In one smooth movement he shoved a sword up into Fonu's lower back and, with his other hand, brought a knife's blade across his throat. The sword exited bloody out the front of Fonu's chest.

Both men fell. Novan pushed Fonu off and crawled to Wilek's side.

"Think you got him?" Wilek chuckled, but it hurt and he had to stop.

"Didn't want him to make any noise. Let's go, Your Highness."

Novan lifted Wilek over his shoulder and staggered into the woods. Wilek lulled in and out of consciousness, held hostage by excruciating pain and thoughts of failure.

Why hadn't he suspected a trap? Had there truly been no signs? And now Trevn was left to pay for his mistakes. His brother would inherit a fractured kingdom with half an army and no allies. Rogedoth would devour his untrained little brother.

"I'm sorry, Trevn."

"Wil?"

He ignored Trevn's voice, in no hurry to ruin the young man's life. Let him have a few more hours. Wilek instead thought of Zeroah, her golden eyes, her long coils of hair. He wished he could see her one last time. Apologize for being such a fool.

Instead he found himself standing in a vast meadow before a gleaming white gate, intricately carved with scrolls and flowers. It was not silver, not ivory . . . It seemed to be made of light. Behind him a thick, leafy forest, greener even than the trees on Bakurah Island, hedged the meadow. The sky was a glorious blue—and red and purple and orange all at the same time. The colors seemed to move as if someone were painting them this very moment. He could hear music, completely transcendent, like nothing he had ever heard before. And the smell . . . Wilek inhaled something like honey and pine and fresh bread and the sea. It smelled like everything he loved, and his heart swelled at the idea that he might go inside this place.

He was not alone. Others had crowded outside the gate. Some of his own men. Rystan and Dendrick among them.

Though Dendrick's presence struck Wilek as odd, he felt no fear. No concern for anything. Peace radiated within him. Aches and pains gone. No gash in his chest, no cuts on his shoulder or leg. Amazingly, he could see through his body to the fresh blades of grass beneath his feet. He was transparent, which seemed perfectly normal.

From a distance he heard someone call his name. He looked through the gate, finding that he could see ever so far. A group of people stood on the other side, waving. He knew them at once. His brother Chadek. And Gran, holding an infant. Holding Chadek II, Wilek's son.

Suddenly he stood at the gate and reached between the bars. He kissed his family and felt the force of their love.

"We've been waiting for you," Gran said.

The gate opened, casting a beam of light that radiated glorious warmth. The light beckoned. Wilek heard another voice call his name, and he walked inside.

TREVn

I tell you he is dead."

"*That cannot be, Mother.*" Trevn set his jaw and started up the ladder out of the pit house he was sharing with Mielle. It was far too hot and stuffy underground. His mother's news had so upset him that he needed to go up for some fresh air to pace and think.

"*One of Rosbert's daughters voiced Hrettah and said her maid saw all the Sarikarian royal men beheaded.*"

How awful. "*What does that have to do with Wilek?*"

"*The battle was a trap and a slaughter, Trevn. I have voiced with Zeroah, and she confirms it. Wilek is dead. Thank Mikreh you weren't there. Now, you must return to Armanguard at once and—*"

Trevn pushed her out of his head. He climbed the rest of the way up and sat on the ground beside the entrance to the pit house. Took a deep breath. "*Wilek?*"

He had been calling to his brother ever since Wilek had voiced the words "*I'm sorry, Trevn.*" There was still no answer.

Cadoc climbed out of the house and stood a few steps away. Reluctantly, Trevn tried a different tactic. "*Zeroah?*"

She answered almost instantly. "*Trevn? Is that you?*"

He would get the truth now. He took another breath. "*Have you spoken to Wilek?*"

"*I have, Sâr Trevn.*" There was no doubting the shaky timbre of her voice. "*I think he has died.*"

Emotion choked Trevn's throat and knotted his stomach. *"You think? Do you know it for a fact?"*

"He told me he thought he was dying. And that was the last I heard from him." She began to cry.

Trevn shook his head, closed out Zeroah, and reached again for Wilek. *"Where are you, brother? Tell me you are alive."*

No answer came.

A great weight pressed in on Trevn's chest. What did this mean? *Arman? Help me.*

"Trevn, there you are." Mielle jogged toward him, flanked by the two soldiers he had assigned to guard her. Her anger washed over him, mixing with his shock over Wilek and completely disorienting him. She had been angry ever since hearing about her sister's involvement in poisoning the queen and prince, but he sensed this was something new. "I have been speaking with Grayson and Conaw and have learned the most alarming thing. The Jiir-Yeke are sorcerers. Conaw believes they practice human sacrifice. That's why they took the orphans, and the Puru gave up the children because they're afraid. Isn't that despicable?"

He watched his wife. She was beautiful when she was upset. So determined to right the wrongs in the world.

Some things couldn't be fixed.

"Trevn, what's wrong? You are frightened. I'm sorry I only just felt it." She knelt beside him and took hold of his hand. "Trevn? What is it?"

"I . . ." What could he say? He knew nothing, really. Only guesses and rumors.

"They're all dead," a woman said.

Trevn glanced over his shoulder. Princess Saria and five of her guards marched up behind him. Her eyes were raw, her cheeks streaked with smudged tears.

Mielle's alarm mingled with his, strengthening the negative emotion. "Who is dead?" she asked.

"Everyone!" Saria said. "My father, my brother, my uncle, my cousins, and Rosâr Wilek too."

Mielle's eyes bulged. "Surely not."

"You are king of Armania now, Trevn," Saria said, "and I am—"

"No," Trevn said. Such a thing could not be possible.

"—queen of Sarikar."

"Trevn." Mielle tugged his arm. "What have you heard?"

"My mother . . . Zeroah . . . they think it is true," Trevn said, his voice sounding hoarse in his ears. "Who else could I ask?"

"You ask Novan Heln," Mielle said. "You ask Captain Veralla. You ask Dendrick. They are always with him."

"I tried. They did not answer." Trevn found himself breathing rapidly, his eyes blurring with unshed tears.

"Sâr Trevn, this is Barek Hadar."

Trevn inhaled sharply at the knock. There was no reason that Barek should be contacting him. None at all. "The Duke of Odarka is voicing me," he told Mielle. *"I hear you, Duke."*

"I am at Castle Armanguard," Barek said. *"I have just received news of the battle of New Sarikar. It was a trap. Master Fonu Edekk had infiltrated the fortress a few weeks ago. He had compelled King Loran and the other royals to obey him and lure Rosâr Wilek and his army into a rescue. When the rosâr attacked, Master Fonu's compelled army of giants ambushed them from behind. And while there were many casualties, the army did manage to take and hold the fortress."*

Hope kindled within Trevn's chest. *"They did?"*

"We owe the success to two things. First, a tribe of giants joined us in battle against their comrades and saved us from complete slaughter. We have had little success communicating with them. They claim to come from the mountains, though I thought all the giants came from there."

"The Uul-Yeke come from the mountains," Trevn said. *"I'm told they are a peaceful tribe, and one of them helped us escape from the mines. Fonu compelled giants from the Ahj-Yeke forest tribe. They are the ones who made slaves of me and my men."*

"Ah, well, that is helpful to know."

"What was the second success?" Trevn asked.

"Novan Heln killed Fonu Edekk. He was the only mantic stationed in New Sarikar, and upon his death, the giants and pales he had enslaved fled. What was left of our army entered the fortress and claimed it."

Good. That was good news. He swallowed. *"And Wilek?"*

"I'm afraid Rosâr Wilek fell."

Trevn's throat tightened. A tear fell down his cheek, and he quickly wiped it away. His breath quickened, and he breathed in long and deep to try to control it.

Mielle wrapped her arms around his waist and held tight.

"*How soon can you return, Your Highness?*" Barek asked.

Trevn shook his head. "*I am not strong like he was. Not as wise about politics. I'm no warrior. There must be someone else who can rule.*"

"*There will be claimants, for sure. Rogedoth will act swiftly. And I'm told there is a potential threat to the throne in Magos. You can help us stop them, but only if you are here.*"

Trevn choked out a sob. "*Will you advise me?*"

"*Of course I will—you will have the whole council. But do not treat yourself as incompetent, Sâr Trevn. You can do this.*"

Trevn wasn't so sure. "*How can we stop Rogedoth? His magic is so powerful.*"

"*Worry about that later. For now, get home. You must be crowned king before Rogedoth or anyone else tries to claim the throne.*"

"*But I don't want to be king, Your Grace.*"

"*I know, but you must, my boy. This is your role to play.*"

Not the End.

A Note
From the Author

Thanks for reading *King's Blood*, the second book in THE KINSMAN CHRONICLES, which includes the parts *Kingdom at Sea*, *Maelstrom*, and *Voices of Blood*. Continue the adventure in *King's War*, which opens with *The Reluctant King*.

King's Blood was challenging in a very different way from *King's Folly*. Part of it was in the details. I had to learn about ships, seafaring, and navigation—topics of which I had no prior knowledge. The real struggle, however, in writing this book was how the themes mirrored my life. Circumstances always influence in some way the projects I write, but the season in which I wrote *King's Blood* was one of the most difficult of my life. I dealt specifically with loss, betrayal, heartbreak, and suffering, so to be writing characters who were living through similar grief was a blessing and a curse. Any emotion that bled onto the page came directly from my wounded heart. While I learned much during that season and grew closer to God, my husband, and our children, I still have many questions, the biggest of which is *Why?* We may never know why God allows troubles to derail our lives, but I also learned that God does not want us to cling to that question with all that we have. It is not a question that matters. I think God would rather we ask *What?*

What now?

What does it mean to have reached the other side of this valley?

What shall I do with myself now that I'm here?

What does life look like in this new place?

What can I do to love others?

What can I say to people who are suffering as I did?

What have I learned?

What will I do differently now that I've learned it?

If you've been caught in one of life's storms, know this: God sees you. He knows the way out, even if you don't. And if you will trust him, he will bring calm in the midst of the storm (Mark 6:45–52). Thank him for the blessings, because a thankful heart cannot so easily become bitter.

I'd love to hear from you. You can email me through my website and sign up for my Sanctum newsletter to get updates on upcoming books and events. If you'd like to help make this book a success, tell people about it, loan your copy to a friend, or ask your library or bookstore to order it. Writing a book review for online stores is also very helpful.

✦   ✦   ✦

Discussion questions for THE KINSMAN CHRONICLES series can be found online at www.jillwilliamson.com/discuss.

If you'd like to see a larger version of the *Seffynaw* cross-section map, check out the book's Pinterest inspiration page, or discover a lot of fun extras, visit my website at www.jillwilliamson.com/books/kinsman-chronicles.

Acknowledgments

First I want to thank my husband, Brad, for all his help. I also want to thank my loyal readers on the Readers of Jill Williamson Facebook page, who helped with brainstorming here and there whenever I asked. As always, I would be lost without my writing world friends: John Otte, Dana Black, Amanda Luedeke, Stephanie Morrill, Shannon Dittemore, and Melanie Dickerson. A special thank you to Tom Luque for his help with sailing and to Peter Glöege for designing such gorgeous book covers. And I am indebted to the amazing team at Bethany House Publishers, including editors Dave Long and Elisa Tally, who helped make the book so much stronger, and marketing geniuses Noelle Chew and Amy Green, who continue to amaze me with everything they do. I am thankful to be working with such talented people.

About the Author

Jill Williamson writes fantasy and science fiction for teens and adults. She grew up in Alaska, staying up and reading by the summer daylight that wouldn't go away. This led to a love of books and writing, and her debut novel, *By Darkness Hid*, won several awards and was named a Best Science Fiction, Fantasy, and Horror novel of 2009 by *VOYA* magazine. She loves giving writing workshops and blogs for teen writers at www.GoTeenWriters.com. She now lives in the Pacific Northwest with her husband, two children, and a whole lot of deer. Visit her online at www.jillwilliamson.com.

Sign up for Jill's Newsletter!

Keep up to date with Jill's news on book releases, signings, and other events by signing up for her email list at jillwilliamson.com.

Don't Miss Book One in This Series!

Prince Wilek's father believes the disasters plaguing their land signal impending doom, but he thinks this is superstitious nonsense—until he is sent to investigate a fresh calamity. What he discovers is more cataclysmic than he could've imagined. Wilek sets out on a desperate quest to save his people, but can he succeed before the entire land crumbles?

King's Folly
THE KINSMAN CHRONICLES #1

You May Also Enjoy . . .

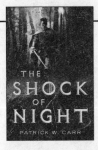

Reeve Willet Dura is called to investigate when a brutal attack leaves one man dead and a priest mortally wounded. As he begins questioning the priest, the man pulls him close, cries out in a foreign tongue—and dies. This strange encounter sets off a series of events that pull Willet into an epic conflict that threatens his entire world.

THE DARKWATER SAGA: *The Shock of Night, The Shattered Vigil*
by Patrick W. Carr
patrickwcarr.com

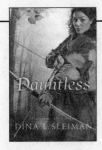

History and legend collide in this medieval series packed with adventure and romance! Inspired by the legend of Robin Hood, the heroine of *Dauntless* protects a band of orphans who must steal to survive. In a land like Camelot, Lady Gwendolyn dreams of being a knight, not a marriage pawn in *Chivalrous*. And in *Courageous*, Maid Rosalind embarks on a crusade to the Holy Land, seeking redemption.

VALIANT HEARTS: *Dauntless, Chivalrous, Courageous*
by Dina L. Sleiman
dinasleiman.com